The Pilot;
A Tale of the Sea

The Writings of
James Fenimore Cooper

The Pilot;

A Tale of the Sea

James Fenimore Cooper

Edited with an Historical Introduction
and Explanatory Notes
by Kay Seymour House

"List! ye Landsmen, all to me."
  G. A. Stevens, "The Storm," 1. 2.

State University of New York Press   Albany

The preparation of this volume was made possible (in part) by a grant from the Program for Editions of the National Endowment for the Humanities, an independent Federal agency.

CENTER FOR
SCHOLARLY EDITIONS
AN APPROVED EDITION
MODERN LANGUAGE
ASSOCIATION OF AMERICA

The Center emblem means that one of a panel of textual experts serving the Center has reviewed the text and textual apparatus of the printer's copy by thorough and scrupulous sampling, and has approved them for sound and consistent editorial principles employed and maximum accuracy attained. The accuracy of the text has been guarded by careful and repeated proofreading according to standards set by the Center.

Published by
State University of New York Press, Albany

© *1986 State University of New York*

*For information, address State University of New York
Press, State University Plaza, Albany, N.Y., 12246*

Library of Congress Cataloging in Publication Data

Cooper, James Fenimore, 1789-1851
  The pilot: a tale of the sea

  (The Writings of James Fenimore Cooper)
  I. House, Kay Seymour. II. Title III. Series:
Cooper, James Fenimore 1789-1851. Works. 1980.
PS1412.A1 1986   813'.2   184-8765
ISBN 0-87395-415-7
ISBN 0-87395-791-1

Contents

Acknowledgments

For institutional support in the preparation of this volume, I wish to thank James Thorpe, Director of the Huntington Library, for a research fellowship and Marcus McCorison, Director and Librarian of the American Antiquarian Society, for a Fred Daniels fellowship. Small grants from San Francisco State University and the National Endowment for the Humanities partly repaid costs for student assistance and photocopying.

In addition to members of the Cooper family, the following persons, collections, and institutions have generously given permission for the use and publication of manuscript and illustrative materials: the American Antiquarian Society; the Clifton Waller Barrett Collection, University of Virginia; the British Library; the Henry E. Huntington Library; the Massachusetts Historical Society; the U. S. Naval Academy Museum, and Victor D. Spark of the Spark Gallery in New York City.

Among the many librarians and curators who have helped in the preparation of this book, I wish particularly to thank Frederick E. Bauer, Jr., Mary E. Brown, Georgia B. Bumgardner, and Joyce Ann Tracy of the American Antiquarian Society; Cynthia English of the Boston Athenaeum; Mr. Hardy of the British Library; Carey S. Bliss, Susan Naulty, Elizabeth Orr, Barbara Quinn, Virginia Renner, Elsa Lee Sink, and Mary Wright of the Huntington Library; John D. Cushing of the Massachusetts Historical Society; D. J. Orton of the University of Hull; Jean St. C. Crane of the University of Virginia, and Gerald Morris of the G. W. Blunt White Library of Mystic Seaport.

For research and editorial assistance I am indebted to Genevieve Belfiglio, Barr McReynolds, Erika Nielsen, and Katherine Scott. Colleagues who have come to my aid in various ways include: Don Brown, Department of Geography, San Francisco State University; Don L. Cook, Department of English, Indiana University; Robin Craig, Department of History, University College, London; Jack Eliason, Harris Corporation; Dick Kalkman, Department of Classics, San Francisco State University; R. D. Madison, Department of English, U. S. Naval Academy; Yvonne Noble, Department of English, William and Mary, and Paul Zall, California State University at Los Angeles. I am also grateful to Mrs. Ella Conger for preparing part of the typescript.

K.S.H.

San Francisco State University

Illustrations

The illustrations for this book attempt to connect the book with history and indicate some contemporary artists' responses to the novel. The three portraits of John Paul Jones, of which the one by Moreau le Jeune is generally considered the best, represent Jones as the hero he was, in contrast to the picture showing him as the piratical and murderous monster wartime propaganda had said he was.

The Johannot illustrations for the two-volume edition of *The Pilot* in the *Oeuvres Complètes de J. Fenimore Cooper* show what scenes the Johannot brothers thought were most worthy of illustration. The map, drawn for the same edition, makes it clear that Cooper's action was set in a partly imaginary part of England conveniently furnished with Abbeys and anchorages that suit the action of the novel rather than vice-versa.

The wreck of the *Ariel* was an artistic challenge few illustrators could resist, and Long Tom Coffin proved more popular than the titular hero as an engraver's subject. Darley's engraving of Long Tom straddling the bowsprit of the wreck best represents Tom's domination of at least that portion of the tale.

The two heroines predictably attracted the attention of painters and engravers in all the illustrated editions. It is interesting, however, that none of the many critics who admired the "Pyramids of fog!" scene (Plate XV) saw fit to mention the fact that the acute observer who first noticed the "pyramids" was a woman.

Following page 60

PLATE I.   This frontispiece for *The Interesting Life, Travels, and Daring Engagements, of that Celebrated and Justly Notorious Pirate, Paul Jones; Containing Numerous Anecdotes of Undaunted Courage, in the Prosecution of His Nefarious Undertakings* (London, 1803) shows Jones as he was popularly depicted, even in the United States, prior to *The Pilot*. The scene is based on a garbled version of an occurrence on the *Bon Homme Richard*. Reproduced by permission of The Huntington Library, San Marino, California.

PLATE II.   Notte's portrait of Jones, engraved in Paris by Carl Guttenberg, was also printed in London where a C. G. Notte exhibited his art between 1779 and 1795. Reproduced by permission of The Huntington Library, San Marino, California. The portrait of Jones by J. Chapman, dated 1796 and used as the frontispiece for Nathaniel Fanning's *Narrative* (1806) shows the same head without a hat.

PLATE III.   The 1906 catalogue of James T. Mitchell's collection of engraved portraits of Army and Navy officers lists this portrait as "done from original designed at Amsterdam" and printed in January 1780. Reproduced by permission of The Huntington Library, San Marino, California.

PLATE IV.   John Paul Jones "Dessiné d'après nature ai mois de May, 1780 par J. M. Moreau le Jeune" is reproduced by courtesy of the U. S. Naval Academy Museum.

Following page 208

PLATE V.   Cooper may have helped construct this map for readers of Gosselin's illustrated edition of *Le Pilote* (Volume IX of *Oeuvres Complètes de J. Fenimore Cooper* [Paris: Charles Gosselin, 1827]); in a letter to Gosselin [1–7? April 1827], he said he wanted Gosselin to "retain" the translations even though he had heard that an Admiral was translating *The Pilot* (*Letters and Journals*, I, 211).

Historical Introduction

Historical Introduction

The preface James Fenimore Cooper wrote for his revision of *The Pilot* in 1849 candidly described as "accidents" and "impulses" the circumstances behind the creation of the first sea-novel in literature. "The author of *Waverley*" had published *The Pirate*, a book with some nautical scenes, late in 1821. The following year, both the book and the identity of its author were discussed at some length by Cooper and Charles Wilkes, the "Englishman" Cooper mentioned in the preface.[1] A letter Wilkes wrote to Cooper in 1827 suggests that Scott's novel prompted Cooper's impulse to act on an idea he had been incubating for some time.

> I have not seen your Red Rover, but I hear it is to be published very shortly. You are quite mistaken in thinking its being a nautical story will lessen my inclination to see it. On the contrary, my decided opinion is that "your home is on the deep." I remember very well many years ago long before you published the Pilot or had even composed it, as it now is, but when [you] had conceived it, you told me that you would write on a nautical subject & [make] the principal scenes on the ocean.[2]

Having drawn on local knowledge and private information for *The Spy* and on his own boyhood experiences for *The Pioneers*, it was inevitable that Cooper would seek a way to convert yet another area of his special knowledge into art. His first choice of career had been the U. S. Navy, in which he served as a midshipman from 1 January 1808 until he obtained a furlough (to get married and settle some private affairs) 12 May 1810. These years were important for the friendships Cooper made in the Navy and for initiating a dedication to that service that he never relinquished. Equally important to his career as a writer, however, was a voyage he made, when he was just seventeen, on the merchant ship *Stirling*. After being expelled from Yale, Cooper had gone to sea as a sailor before the mast and his eleven months as a sailor in 1806—07 were rich in experiences that the writer would exploit. Cooper later found that he could count on his prodigious memory to furnish the details necessary for *vraisemblance*. Writing to the former captain of the *Stirling* in 1843, Cooper boasted of being able to give to a former shipmate "many little particulars of our voyage that he seemed to have forgotten."[3] While the most direct use of his adventures on the *Stirling* went into *Ned Myers* (1843), all Cooper's sea tales seem indebted to his teenage impressions; and he recalled, just months before his death, the taste of some delicious Spanish grapes he first discovered on that voyage.[4] It is probably because the *Stirling* sailed through the English channel and docked at London, thus acquainting Cooper with the channel and the eastern coast of England, that the naval actions of *The Pilot* take place off that coast.

Hoping to write a book that seamen would appreciate for its fidelity and yet one that landsmen could understand, Cooper realized that he had set himself a complicated task: "It had been my aim to avoid technicalities, in order to be poetic, although the subject imperiously required a minuteness of detail to render it intelligible."[5] In order to test the intelligibility of part of the first volume on a seaman, he chose Benjamin Cooper, a distant relative and the seaman alluded to in the 1849 preface.

> My listener betrayed interest, as we proceeded, until he could no longer keep his seat. He paced the room furiously until I got through, and just as I laid down the paper he exclaimed, "It is all very well, but you have let your jib stand too long, my fine fellow!" I blew it out of the bolt-rope, in pure spite.[7]

When the seaman Ben Cooper and the skeptical landsman Charles Wilkes both approved parts of the first volume of *The Pilot*, Cooper must have felt, in spite of lingering doubts about the book's general success, that he had managed to combine poetry with intelligibility.

This first volume was composed during the spring of 1823. Cooper seems to have been in fine fettle at the time: he toasted La Fayette at a celebration at the fortress President Monroe had ordered named for the Marquis (8 April);[7] he escorted the comedian Charles Mathews on a trip up the Hudson (19–24 April);[8] and he described "the most interesting [horse] race ever run in the United States" for the *New-York Patriot* (28 May 1823).[9] With the summer months, however, a series of disasters befell the Coopers. Their stone house at Fenimore burned in July, and their infant son, Fenimore, died 5 August "after a protracted sickness."[10] Cooper himself had been ill most of the summer and suffered a sunstroke in late August or early September; he wrote his friend Captain Shubrick (7 September) that he had "not look'd at" *The Pilot* in "near two months" but that he intended to get back to it the following day and publish in October.[11] Cooper seems to have been unduly optimistic about his health, for we find the *New-York Statesman* of 17 November explaining the book's delay:

> The inquiry is often made why Mr. Cooper's fourth novel, the *Pilot*, which was announced many months since, has been so long delayed, and when it will appear? We regret to state, that the author has been so seriously ill for the greater part of the last season, as to compel him to suspend his literary labours. The public will be gratified to learn that he is now convalescent, and enabled to resume his unfinished work. We understand the Pilot is now in a state of forwardness and will appear in a few weeks.[12]

Yet all was not well with the Coopers as the year neared its end. Their household goods were inventoried for debt in October or November, and Mrs. Cooper, having lost one son in August, was pregnant with another who would be born at the beginning of February 1824. A time-consuming nuisance was the Navy's belated demand that Cooper account for or repay money advanced to him for recruiting in New York City in 1810.

Even though he was no longer in the Navy, Cooper felt himself very much associated with it and he may have been collecting material for a naval history even as early as 1823.

The original preface to *The Pilot* asserts the historical purpose of rescuing former naval heroes from "obscurity" and conveys Cooper's anxiety about the disappearance of both men and the facts about them that a historian would need to know. One source of information that he could use for *The Pilot* was the *Narrative of the Adventures of an American Navy Officer, who served during part of the American Revolution under the command of Com. John Paul Jones, Esq.*[13] First published anonymously in New York City in 1806, the *Narrative* was identified as the work of Nathaniel Fanning and reissued in 1808, the year Cooper became a midshipman. As the prominence of Jones's name in the title and the use of Jones's portrait as the frontispiece of the 1806 edition indicated, Fanning (or the publisher) was counting on public interest in John Paul Jones to sell the book. Cooper, as his preface makes clear, also felt that Jones was a remarkable man and mariner. Yet no biography of Jones existed when Cooper began to compose *The Pilot*. Certain documents (such as Jones's letter to Lady Selkirk) were in print, as were many chapbooks portraying Jones as a pirate and repeating stories — none to his credit — that were clearly English propaganda.[14] The nearest thing to a trustworthy account of Jones's services in behalf of the French and Americans during the Revolution was a report Jones had written for presentation to Louis XVI. Translated into French and published in Paris in 1798, the *Mémoire* had been reprinted, in English, in the Baltimore *Weekly Register* starting 6 June 1812. It begins,

> At the commencement of the American war (during the year 1775), I was employed to fit out the little squadron, which the congress had placed under commodore Hopkins, who was appointed to the command of all the armed vessels appertaining to America; and I hoisted with my own hands the American flag, on board the Alfred, which was then displayed for the first time.[15]

This dry account of his professional activities during a portion of his life gave few clues about what kind of a person Jones had been.

Ironically, publication of *The Pilot* hastened the discovery of the very details Cooper lacked when he wrote the book. As *The Albion* pointed out six months after the novel's publication:

> We may safely conclude that no one will read "The Pilot," without feeling some interest and curiosity respecting the mysterious character who forms the prominent feature in the tale; . . . for, although his name is cautiously withheld, there are allusions to acts and circumstances which can apply to none but the once celebrated Paul Jones.[16]

The Pilot reawakened an interest in Jones as a naval hero, brought to light documents Jones had left in the United States, and resulted in the first attempt at a biography a year later. By the time he wrote the sketch of Jones for *Lives of Distinguished American Naval Officers* (1846), Cooper possessed much information about Jones's character that had not been available in 1823.[17]

Forced to rely on Fanning's *Narrative* for suggestions about Jones, Cooper turned some of Fanning's allegations into a shadowy history that lies behind some of the novel's allusions. For example, on p. 120, Alice says,

> "The wars, and the uncertainties of the times, together with man's own wicked passions, have made great havoc with those who knew well the windings of the channels among the 'Ripples.' Some there were who could pass, as I have often heard, within a fearful distance of the 'Devil's-Grip,' the darkest night that ever shadowed England; but all are now gone, of that daring set, either by the hand of death, or, what is even as mournful, by unnatural banishment from the land of their fathers."

This speech could be based on a number of passages from Fanning's *Narrative*. Fanning reported that the defeated captain of the *Serapis* told Jones, " 'It is with the greatest reluctance that I am now obliged to resign you this [sword], for it is painful to me . . . to deliver up my sword to a man, who may be said to fight *with a halter around his neck*.' " Making it clear that treason was not the only charge, Fanning explained, "The English were in the habit of saying that captain Jones fought with a halter round his neck, in allusion to his having been imprisoned for murder." Fanning said that Jones had been arrested at Hull and jailed "as the murderer of his carpenter,"[18] but that he escaped and fled to the colonies. Yet Fanning's version of the "murder" is not credible and Cooper converted such charges into Alice's more general references to "wicked passions" and "unnatural banishment."

Fanning seemed more trustworthy when he reported that Jones sent to the governor of Leith

> *fictitious names* for his ships and the commanders, corresponding with the names of ships in the British navy, of the size and number of guns as those of his squadron, the captains whereof had already English names assigned them, and by which they were then called.[19]

In the novel, Alice tells the Pilot that Dillon has gone to send ships to intercept the Americans, and he asks,

> "But, Alice, heard ye the force of the ships, or their names? Give me their names, and the first lord of your British admiralty shall not give so true an account of their force, as I will furnish from this list of my own." (p. 367)

Cooper's Pilot thirsts for glory, and Fanning's portrayal includes a speech that Jones made to his officers:

> "Gentlemen, you cannot conceive what an additional honour it will be to us all, if in cruising a few days we should have the good luck to fall in with an English frigate of our force, and carry her in with us; . . . this would crown our former victories, and our names, in consequence thereof would be handed down to the latest posterity, by some faithful historian of our country."

An asterisk follows this passage and Fanning added in a footnote, "Jones had a wonderful notion of his name being handed down to posterity."[20]

The Pilot's attempt to be friendly and informal when he boards the *Ariel* (p. 90) as well as the relationship of Barnstable and Mr. Merry may be the result of a hint in Fanning. Jones. he said, "almost always conversed with his midshipmen as freely as he did with his lieutenants, sailing-master or purser; but he made us do our duty."[21]

Some of the "Byronic" traits critics have found — and mostly objected to — in the characterization of the Pilot also come from Fanning. We learn that Jones was "passionate to the highest degree one minute, and the next, ready to make a reconciliation."[22] When the motley crew at one time turned mutinous and refused to fight an English frigate, Jones "appeared much agitated, and bit his lips often, and walked the quarter-deck muttering something to himself."[23] When political intrigues at Paris robbed Jones of his ship, "His passion knew no bounds; and in the first paroxism of his rage he acted more like a mad man than a conqueror."[24] Yet, for all of Fanning's personal dislike of Jones (or any authority for that matter), Fanning's Jones is always calm in battle or when the ship is in danger, always leads his men brilliantly in action, and never makes an error in seamanship.

Fanning concluded the John Paul Jones section of his *Narrative* with a cluster of defamatory anecdotes that reveal as much about Fanning as they do about Jones. For an entertainment aboard the *Ariel*, a kind of pavilion on the quarter deck was

> hung with a great variety of French pictures and looking glasses; some of the first had been drawn by one of the most finished artists in France, and many of which were quite indecent, especially to meet the eyes of a virtuous woman. . . . French cooks, and waiters or servants, were brought from the shore to assist in this business and for nearly twenty hours preceding the serving up of dinner, we were almost suffocated with garlic and onions, besides a great many other stinking vegetables. A French lady . . . was gallanted on board by captain Jones the evening before the day on which the company were to dine, and was by him directed to take upon herself the superintendance of the approaching feast . . . . we were directed by captain Jones to conduct ourselves with propriety and to pay implicit obedience to my *lady superintendant* of the ceremonies.[25]

Cooper would have seen through the provincialism and sexism

of these remarks, but he could not have known that the log of the *Ariel* shows this "Grand Entertainment" as taking place 2 September and that the entry for that day ends: "the Capt. Kicked Mr. Fanning, Midshipman, and Ordered him below,—"[26] Fanning moved this entertainment to "about the tenth of December" and made it part of a smokescreen of libelous tales about Jones thrown up to obscure Fanning's own departure from both the *Ariel* and the American service—in order to become a privateer.

Fanning's charges that Jones patronized whorehouses ashore and seduced married women may have something to do with those discussions between Alice and the Pilot that reveal the difficulties, for a man in Jones's situation and profession, standing in the way of marriage. Fanning also depicted Jones as a coward when in port because Jones had refused to duel with various challengers. Cooper, who thoroughly approved Ben Cooper's refusal to duel with a man "not worthy of his notice,"[27] has the Pilot ignore Burroughcliffe's challenge.

Fanning's ambivalence toward Jones produced an ambiguous portrayal which Cooper adapted temporally to his plot. The reader first sees the mysterious yet nondescript Mr. Gray largely through the distrustful eyes of Barnstable and Griffith. As the action progresses, the Pilot increases in solidity and stature only to fade from the sight of the anxiously watching Griffith at the end. Becoming a "dark speck . . . lost in the strong glare that fell, obliquely across the water, from the setting sun," the Pilot disappears just as the real John Paul Jones had been all but lost in incomplete or untrue versions of history.

The *Narrative* also contained suggestions about some of Jones's subordinates aboard the *Bon Homme Richard*. The sailing-master, "a *true blooded yankee*" named Stacy, was one of Fanning's heroes. Cooper's concern about his own New England characters appears in one of the earliest allusions to *The Pilot*—in a letter Cooper wrote to Richard H. Dana:

> I percieve by the concluding paragraph of your letter, that those worthies, "Hiram Doolittle" and "Dr. Todd" are not favorites in your section of the Country—I regret it the more, because I deprecate the reason; but the hour is

not far distant when "Dick Barnstable" will remove the impression—[28]

Cooper's letter, written 14 April 1823, suggests that he had not written very far into the first volume since Long Tom Coffin and Boltrope,the sailing-master whose importance Cooper enlarged near the end of the work to compensate for the loss of Long Tom, are both better examples of New England character than Barnstable. Given Long Tom's popularity with the public, Susan Cooper's remarks deserve consideration:

> With Long Tom Coffin . . . he was, in his own last years, less satisfied than many of his readers. As he looked back at the character, in the maturity of long experience, he saw it with a clearer view, a greater fulness of conception, a more complete finish of detail—he considered it as a sketch only, and would gladly have wrought up the sketch of the old salt, a man after his own heart, to a finished picture, as he has done with Natty Bumppo. Of the two characters he considered that of Boltrope better, perhaps, as a piece of workmanship than that of the old Nantucket hero.[29]

One piece of action in *The Pilot* links Boltrope with Fanning's Yankee Stacy. Fanning said that during the famous battle Jones "assisted Mr. Stacy in making fast the end of the enemies' jib-stay, to our mizzen-mast." But Stacy was irreverent and Jones "checked" him for swearing, saying " 'Mr. Stacy, it is no time for swearing now, you may in the next moment be in eternity; but let us do our duty.' "[30] In *The Pilot*, Boltrope and the Pilot have been "among the foremost" in lashing the bowsprit of the enemy ship to their own mizzen-mast when Boltrope swears, " 'for by the eternal—' " and is interrupted: " 'Peace, rude man,' said the Pilot, in a voice of solemn remonstrance; 'at the next instant you may face your God; mock not his awful name!' " (pp. 399–400)

Since Cooper freely acknowledged that Scott's *The Pirate* first challenged him to write an authentic sea novel, we can expect some awareness of the British book to appear in the American competitor. The most notable, and detachable, example of Cooper's good-humored response to Scott is the whale-taking scene, an episode that is otherwise difficult to justify. In Scott's novel, a mob swarms down to the seashore to butcher a whale which has been trapped in shallow water at low tide. Scott's description of their weapons anticipates the messy and dangerous outcome of the whole fracas. "Harpoons, swords, pikes, and halberts, fell to the lot of some; others contented themselves with hay-forks, spits, and whatever else could be found, that was at once long and sharp."[31] The whale, mortally wounded, gets away. Cooper's own answering scene shows the New World whalers as properly equipped, skillful, and successful.

A number of names and incidents from *The Pirate* may have remained in Cooper's memory to reappear in *The Pilot*. Scott referred to the original rulers of the West Indies as "Caciques" and mentioned a haunted islet named "Coffin-key."[32] *The Pirate* opens with a storm which wrecks a ship that later breaks up near shore. Ruins are conveniently found near the scene of the action at one point, and the pirates drink punch "without producing any visible effect upon their reason"[33] just as Long Tom and Manual drink Madeira without losing their ability to act. In *The Pirate*, Brenda, the heroine, defies her family's ban as well as propriety to gain a stolen interview with her lover[34] just as Kate sneaks out of the Abbey to meet Barnstable. A small but striking parallel is the pirate's rage at the light mention of his beloved's name: " 'Bring not *her* into your buffoonery, sirrah,' said Cleveland . . . 'for if you name her with less than reverence, I will crop the ears out of your head, and make you swallow them on the spot!' "[35] When Colonel Howard makes a bitter remark about Alice being at the " 'disposal' " of their captors, the Pilot interrupts, saying: " 'Breathe not that name in levity again, thou scoffer, or even your years may prove a feeble protection!' " (p. 338)

The similarities and differences between the characters and actions of the two books make an interesting study, but all such comparisons finally seem minor as compared with the one great difference. Scott's sea is like a stage; it is a scenic backdrop for some actions and the wings from which characters emerge for others. Even in those rare moments when the characters are found on board a ship, the cabin might just as well be on shore. Ships have no identities, navigation no problems, and winds and waves are but part of the machinery that moves the plot.

In *The Pilot*, Cooper reversed the emphasis and it is the scenes set on land that would be suitable for the stage; many of them, with their sudden reversals of fortune, verge on melodrama. Cooper's poetic power is reserved for the sea, which is no backdrop but a separate world with forces and laws of its own. The individuation of the ships, particularly the personification of the *Ariel*, contributes to the magic, but the exhilaration of the book comes from the triumph of human skill and intelligence over the uncertainties and downright hostilities of a world of waves, winds, and hidden reefs. The land offers neither a comparable challenge nor so heady a victory.

II

Only seventeen days after publishing *The Pioneers*, Charles Wiley announced

> as being in preparation for the press, another work of the same author, to be entitled "THE PILOT—A Tale of the Sea." It is in such a state of forwardness, as to authorize the expectation of its appearance in March or April.[36]

Actually, Wiley did not file the first volume for copyright until 1 August, and on 7 September Cooper wrote to Shubrick that only the first volume and part of the second were in print.[37] The second volume was copyrighted 29 December 1823, and *The Pilot* was published 7 January 1824.[38] Meanwhile, the *Cincinnati Literary Gazette* had conjectured on New Year's Day that the work "was to have been published on Christmas day. Its publication has probably been delayed by the arrangement, to have it published in this country, and in England simultaneously."[39]

Besides trying to protect the copyright in England, Cooper was in the process of changing publishers in London. John Murray, who had published *The Pioneers*, had not been answering Cooper's letters, and on 20 May 1823 Cooper had written to John Miller about *The Pilot*. Miller, pleading lack of "security for the Copy right," proposed sharing the profits, with Miller standing all expenses.[40] On 26 August, Miller wrote Cooper again, saying that he had announced *The Pilot* and was hoping for an answer to his June letter.[41] In the meantime, Cooper had entrusted his reply to Miller and the first volume of *The Pilot* to James D. P. Ogden, who became involved with Murray and complications more fully described in the Textual Commentary. Ogden finally advised Cooper to write to Miller saying that he, Ogden, had misunderstood Cooper's instructions.[42] Cooper apparently took Ogden's advice and furnished Miller with such a letter as well as any other documents Miller might need to convince Murray that Cooper intended for Miller to become his English publisher. John Miller accordingly published 1,000 copies of *The Pilot* shortly before 30 January 1824.[43]

Cooper seems to have left New York immediately after the American publication of *The Pilot* to make a long-promised visit to Shubrick in Boston. The *Boston Commercial Gazette* of 12 January reported: "Mr. Cooper, the author of the '*Spy*,' '*Pioneers*,' &c. is now on a visit to this city. His last work, the '*Pilot*,' is announced for sale by the booksellers."[44] On Wednesday, 14 January, the *Independent Chronical and Boston Patriot* announced on page 1:

> *Mr. Cooper, the American Novelist.* — We are happy to inform our readers, that the new production of our fellow citizen, Mr. Cooper, the Pilot, has been received in this city and is now on sale. The genius of Mr. Cooper has no longer left it in the power of foreign journalists tauntingly to inquire, who has ever read an American Book?

The writer of this brief notice went on to say that Cooper was "now in our city" and hinted that one purpose of Cooper's visit was to collect materials for *Lionel Lincoln*. Cooper also had a chance to discuss *The Pilot* with Shubrick and later, writing about the Wiley second edition, added ". . . so much for our *joint* efforts."[45]

Niles Register of 7 February reported that "the first edition of 3,000 copies was disposed of in a few days,"[46] but Wiley had already announced, on 26 January, a second edition and managed to publish the revised edition 11 February 1824.[47] Eight days later, the *New-York Statesman* reported that *The Pilot* "has already run almost through the second edition."

Wiley died in January 1826 and Cooper, preparing to leave for Europe, sold Carey & Lea the right to reprint *The Pilot* to the end of its copyright period.[48] In 1827, Carey and Lea published a stereotyped edition (the third) from the Wiley second edition without authorial correction or supervision. The Carey plates, with an occasional correction of spelling and frequent repairs, were still in use as late as 1870. The Carey & Lea text is in the main line of transmission since it was used by Colburn and Bentley for their own edition in 1831. *The Pilot* was the first of Bentley's Standard Novels, but Cooper never had a chance to revise it for Bentley.[49] He did, however, use Bentley's one-volume edition as printer's copy for his final revision of the work—for Putnam—in 1849. In preparing for Putnam's "fine edition" 5 March 1849, Cooper asked his stereotyper, John Fagan, to borrow the English copy of *The Pilot* from Lea, who had some of the Bentley editions in his office, and send it to him.[50] Cooper wrote a new preface and made some revisions for the Putnam edition, and the Putnam text—as well as the old Carey and Lea text—was reissued for many years after Cooper's death in 1851. By 1854 the firm of Stringer and Townsend of New York was selling both the old Carey text and the revised Putnam text, and it was the 1849 Putnam text that W. A. Townsend, successor to Stringer and Townsend, reissued in 1859 with illustrations by F. O. C. Darley and a curious antiquing of the dedication by attempting to reproduce the old long *s*.

III

Badly as he needed money in 1823, Cooper was chiefly anxious about the critical reception of his experiment in a new genre of fiction. He wrote Shubrick,

> Pilot is decidedly successful—The sale is the best criterion in such matters, and that is very great—It is very little if any short of Spy in popularity, though opinions are as various as men's minds— . . . If it has not been as much commended it has certainly been less assailed than any book I have ever written—[51]

Cooper's hint here that American critics were neglecting *The Pilot* is consistent with his later memory: "Pilot hung a month

in suspense in New York."⁵² In the 1840's Cooper contrasted
American and European critics of *The Pilot.*

> This book was on a plan so novel, that the critics, if there
> are any in this country, did not know how to recieve it.
> For several weeks its fate was doubtful. Its American
> reputation certainly came from the East, though the
> North American "damned it with faint praise" as it had
> previously done the Spy. In Europe, its success was quick
> and decided.⁵³

> Until we heard from England, Wiley and I fancied it a
> failure; though Wiley certainly maintained it ought not to
> be one.⁵⁴

The perplexity of even the friendliest American critics is evident in the early reviews. Robert Walsh, editor of the
Philadelphia *National Gazette* and apparently an acquaintance
of Cooper, declared that the "author is evidently at home on
ship board" and predicted popularity "with the American
Navy."⁵⁵ A review by "Quintus" in the *New-York Spectator* chiefly
praised the author for giving "*nationality* to his sketches" and for
paying tribute "to the memory of a man whose patriotism and
courage have yet found no historian." J. G. B.,⁵⁶ writing in
The Minerva, absolved *The Pilot* of "the sin of monotony," even
though the two volumes were filled with a "Tale of the Sea,"
but expended most of his energy in drawing an elaborate
parallel between modern seamen and the knights of more
chivalric ages. The *New-York Commercial Advertiser* declared "the
most signal success" of the author was the "faithful representation of the duties, feelings, habits and manners of seamen and
naval characters, without any coarseness in tho't or language;
and in inculcating morality and magnanimity, and correct notions of duty, honor, and patriotism." Only the *Cincinnati
Literary Gazette* avoided nationalism and praised the work for its
faithful representation of seamen and its scenes at sea that
display "the hand of a master."

The February issue of *The Port Folio* carried a fifteen-page
review in which four pages summarized the plot and nine gave
quotations from scenes that take place on land. In his two
pages of commentary, the critic vented his irritation at an

author who invites landsmen to listen, on the title page, and then waves off "lubber" critics in the preface. Approving of the scenes on land, the writer declared that all Cooper's "nautical operations, we fear, will be thrown away upon many of those whose attention he has invoked." The reviewer regretted

> the undue admixture of maritime occurrences, detailed in the peculiar jargon of seamen. To such persons, all the circumstances to which we allude and the language in which they are described, present nothing new. They are, moreover, not precisely that description of readers, whose approbation, a man of letters should be ambitious to obtain.[57]

Considering the hostility of *The Port Folio*, the "faint praise" of Wendell Phillips in the April *North American Review* seems relatively innocuous. He compared Cooper's Pilot with similar figures in epic poetry and seemed close to grasping what Cooper was trying to do:

> From the first appearance of the vessels in the evening, until their escape from the impending perils the next morning, the dangerous situations, the combinations of incidents, the pictures of the heavens and the ocean, and the management of the vessels, inspire the reader with intense interest and anxiety; while, at the same time, his imagination is filled with a succession of grand and vividly drawn images.

But Phillips ended with praising the work as a patriotic celebration of "our naval skill and prowess." Then he added, "This is a string to which the national feeling vibrates certainly and deeply; and this string the author has touched with effect." By implication, any success the book was having was due to its subject and a ready market among patriots. Cooper's reaction to this review might have been, as Clavel suggested, "exaggerated"[58] but Richard Henry Dana was also offended. He wrote William Cullen Bryant 4 July 1824:

> I was sorry on Phillips's account to see such a review of "The Pilot." It can do no harm to Cooper; he is to the windward of the American reviewers, at least. It seemed

to me altogether unworthy of Phillips in point of ability. I am afraid he meant to steer a middle course between Cooper's petty enemies and those who have the good sense and the fairness to relish him and speak well of him.[59]

Some praise "from the East" appeared in the *United States Literary Gazette* of 1 April 1824, but the compliments were largely directed toward Cooper's increasing ability in drawing character "to the life," in "natural eloquence," in "graphic pictures" and in observing the unities of time and space. A brief review in the *New-York Mirror, and Ladies' Literary Gazette* of 17 April mentioned the sea as Cooper's "own element" and praised the "succession of beautiful sea pictures, that would do honor to any pen" but lost this point in complaints about obscure passages and the lack of classical allusions. The reviewer regretted that the Pilot had not "announced his name to the terror of his enemies."

A review from the *Edinburgh Scotsman*, reprinted in this country in December 1824, finally pointed American critics in the direction Cooper had indicated in his preface. Not Scott, but such writers as Smollett and Defoe were to be the standards of comparison, and the *Scotsman* judged Defoe "in some respects, thrown at a distance" by Cooper. As for Smollett, he "had been at sea; but Cooper is body and spirit a sailor. The ocean is truly his element, — the deck his home." Discussing *The Pilot* as a sea-novel, the *Scotsman*, along with other British reviews reprinted in the United States, helped Ameican critics gain their sea legs. From 1825 on, *The Pilot* was treated as a sea story and by 1827 the *New-York Mirror* had reversed *The Port Folio's* earlier judgment and declared that "the interest flags the moment we leave the company of sailors."

Criticism of *The Pilot* from Great Britain was not only welcome but prompt. In a letter of 5 February 1824, John Miller wrote, "one favorable notice has already appeared in a weekly publication which I enclose to you."[60] Miller may have sent the first of a two-part review in the London *Museum*, which said

The work, though blending history and fiction together is drawn with so vivid a pen, as to approach nearer the former than the latter; . . . . There appears to be a freshness in Mr. Cooper's writing which we seldom meet with (nor can scarcely expect) in the present day, when the fields of literature rarely present an uncultivated spot.

The reviewer went on to say that Cooper approached "our favourite Smollett" more nearly than "any author of the day" and proclaimed Tom Coffin the best of the nautical characters, "which are sketched with great vigour." While the second part of the review on 7 February, complained of a "want of relief from nautical affairs" it declared the book the "work of a powerful pen." On the same day, the *Literary Gazette* ran a lengthy review singling out as the novel's "great merit" the "group of sea characters which its action displays." After giving extracts of action at sea and praising the scene of Boltrope's death, the review concluded: "there is so much force and originality in these volumes, that we dare say they will float for some time on the tide of public favour before they sink into Davy's locker." A third review, also printed 7 February and continued the following week in the *Somerset House Gazette and Literary Museum*, showed another critic playing with nautical lingo as he declared the author/captain and critic/customs-officer "joint proprietors in the freight." After pronouncing the "description of this short coasting voyage" both "picturesque and highly amusing," the critic reprinted the whale-taking scene and regretted the lack of space to include "the author's animated and original picture of a sea fight."

The British reviewers' stress on originality must have been balm to Cooper's spirit for, as he was to write Griswold in 1843, "It has been said there is no original literature in America. I confess an inability to find the model for all the sea tales, that now so much abound, if it be not the Pilot."[61] In *Gleanings in Europe: England*, he referred to *The Pilot* as "an essay in nautical description, a species of writing that was then absolutely new."[62] Cooper's phrasing in a letter to Samuel F. B. Morse made clear his belief that *The Pilot* began a new genre; speaking of *The Heidenmauer*, he insisted that it was "a good book and better than two thirds of Scott's. They may say it is like his if they please; they have said so of every book I have written, even the 'Pilot'!"[63]

British critics supported Cooper. Having designated Smollett as the only thinkable competitor, one of them said Cooper's *Pilot* was "as superior to Smollett, as the navy of the present day . . . is superior . . . to the navy of George the 2nd."[64] A thoughtful essay, "Naval Novels," in 1831 pointed out that Smollett's "sea-scenes are only incidental to his stories," and concluded that "the praise due of having written the first genuine and thorough naval romance" belonged to ". . . an American. Cooper's *Pilot*, though full of national prejudices, has unquestionably led the way in this species of literature."[65] *The Pilot* became the standard of comparison not only for Cooper's own later sea-novels, but for works by Marryat, Michael Scott ("Tom Cringle"), R. H. Dana, Jr., and Herman Melville.[66]

Meanwhile, Edward Fitzball turned *The Pilot* into a "nautical burletta in three acts" which played at the Adelphi Theatre in 1825 and made the reputation of T. P. Cooke, who selected the role of Long Tom Coffin for his debut at the Adelphi in October. The introductory remarks to the printed play commend the "spirit" and "energy" of Cooper's "well-known tale" which has the "boldness of character and colouring, that mark an original genius."[67] On 14 January 1828, D. Straker published *The Pilot*, complete with stage-sets and cut-outs of characters, as part of his Juvenile Dramatic Repository of plays for production at home. A bizarre addition to *The Pilot*'s history, about this same time, was the publication of yet another chapbook *Life of Paul Jones, the Pirate* who is described on the title-page as "one of the principal characters in the celebrated novel, 'The Pilot,' by Sir Walter Scott, Bart."[68]

The number of British piracies are further evidence of *The Pilot*'s fame and popular appeal. Writing to Cooper late in 1824, John Miller explained his earlier worry about "security for the Copy right."[69]

The thing most of all to be feared here, is the reprinting by some one without authority—it is not long since [Legg?] threatened Mr. Murray with a reprint of the Pioneers—if he did not relinquish his intention of printing a book which interfered with Legg's [?] interests. Another large dealer in Novels told me when I took Pilot round, that had it been in any other hands he would have reprinted it. . . . There are two or three persons on the alert in New York, who send off Copies of all popular works the instant they are published, & by great exertions here one of your novels might be printed, by a rival house in four days; this will shew how much care is necessary in despatching the sheets.

Early in February of 1826, Cooper wrote to Miller, "I see by our papers, that 'Pilot' has been printed by some adventurer or other—Is there no way of stopping this?"[70] Apparently John Miller was not powerful enough to stop the thefts, for not only was a piracy by G. Cowie & Co. printed in 1826 from Miller's own text, but another printing (by Spence, Coull and G. Cowie & Co.) appeared in 1827 and a third, also based on Miller's text, was printed in England by Thomas Mason in 1829. Once *The Pilot* became the property of Colburn and Bentley, pirates used the Carey and Lea text, but piracies continued into the 1830's.

Baudry published an English-language edition of *The Pilot*, using Miller's text, in Paris in 1825, but even before this A. J. B. Defauconpret had translated Miller's text into French so rapidly that Gosselin could publish it in four volumes 10 April 1824. It was reprinted (as four volumes in two) in 1825 and again in 1826, and in 1827-29 the Defauconpret translation became volumes 7-9 in the *Oeuvres* of Cooper with illustrations by Alfred and Tony Johannot.[71] Reissues of the Gosselin edition continued through 1862-66, while a translation by Laroche was printed in Paris in 1836 and one by Bédollière in 1850.

French criticism of *The Pilot* had been favorable from the beginning and in 1827 one perceptive critic called attention to strengths that English and American critics had missed:

> Il y a une magie étonnante dans l'intérêt répandu par l'auteur sur les deux bâtiments qui sont pour lui comme deux de ses principaux personnages, dans cette sorte de vie, d'existence individuelle, de personnification qu'il leur prête; et l'on concoit, après cette lecture, l'idée d'animation attachée en anglais par le genre féminin à tout nom de navire.[72]

Possibly even more flattering than the French critics were such imitators as Eugene Sue and Corbiere, or the "continuation" of *The Pilot* by Dumas the elder (*Le Capitaine Paul,* 1838).

Der Lootse was printed in Leipzig in 1824, in Frankfurt-am-Main in 1827 and 1839, and in Stuttgart in 1842, 1844, and 1851. *Der Lootse* also appeared as part of sets of Cooper's work in Stuttgart in 1853–54 and in Berlin in 1858–60.[73]

The first Italian translation, *Il pilota*, was published at Livorno in 1828–29 and at Naples in 1829. The translation is based on the Miller text with some help from the French translation of Defauconpret. Another edition was printed in Milan in 1831, and the book was again printed in Milan in 1868.[74]

A Swedish edition of *Lotsen* was published in Stockholm in 1831 and a Dutch translation in Amsterdam in 1835. Two Spanish translations were printed in 1832 (Madrid) and 1836 (Paris), and a Portuguese translation was published in Paris in 1838.[75]

IV

There is no doubt that *The Pilot* helped to establish Cooper's reputation in Europe and to call his work to the attention of other writers. Sir Walter Scott saw the play of *The Pilot* in London about a year after it opened,[76] but he had read the book shortly after its publication and had written to Miss Edgeworth that "the novel is a very clever one, and the sea-scenes and characters in particular are admirably drawn; and I advise you to read it as soon as possible."[77] Dining with Scott a few months later, Samuel Griswold Goodrich heard Scott say *The Pilot* "'is very clever, and I think it will turn out that his strength lies in depicting sea life and adventure. We really have no good sea-tales, and here is a wide field, open to a man of true genius'." When Scott's daughter objected that nautical jargon and unfamiliarity with the sea would keep the "'mass of readers'" from appreciating sea life and manners, Scott replied, "'It is no doubt a task of some difficulty to bring these home to the hearts of the reading million; nevertheless, to a man of genius for it, the materials are ample and interesting . . . . And besides, this book to which I refer — the Pilot — connects its story with the land.'"[78]

Another early English admirer of *The Pilot* was Mary Russell Mitford, who wrote to Sir William Elford 5 March 1824,

> Pray have you read the American novels? I mean the series by Mr. Cooper—"The Spy," &c. If you have not, send for them and let me hear the result. In my mind they are as good as anything Sir Walter Scott ever wrote. He has opened fresh ground, too (if one may say so of the sea). No one but Smollett has ever attempted to delineate the naval character; and then he is so coarse and hard. Now this has the same truth and power, with a deep, grand feeling. I must not overpraise it, for fear of producing the reaction which such injudicious enthusiasm is calculated to induce, but I must request you to read it. Only read it. Imagine the author's boldness in taking Paul Jones for a hero, and his power in making one care for him! I envy the Americans their Mr. Cooper. Tell me how you like "The Pilot." There is a certain Long Tom who appears to me the finest thing since Parson Adams.[79]

Washington Irving, traveling in Spain in 1827, wrote that he was sorry to have left Paris before Cooper arrived. "I have a great desire to make his acquaintance, for I am delighted with his novels. . . . His naval scenes and characters in the Pilot are admirable."[80] Unbeknownst to Irving, he was about that time considered a possible author of *The Pilot* by William Hazlitt's James Northcote:

> I asked if he had seen the American novels, in one of which (the *Pilot*) there was an excellent description of an American privateer expecting the approach of an English man-of-war in a thick fog, when some one saw what appeared to be a bright cloud rising over the fog, but it proved to be the topsail of a seventy-four. N[orthcote] thought this was striking, but had not seen the book. "Was it one of I[rving]'s?" Oh! no, he is a mere trifler—a *filligree* man—an English *littérateur* at second-hand; but the *Pilot* gave a true and unvarnished picture of American character and manners. The storm, the fight, the whole

account of the ship's crew, and in particular of an old boatswain, were done to the life—every thing

Suffered a sea-change
Into something new and strange.[81]

Reviewing *The Wept of Wish-ton-Wish* in 1830, John Greenleaf Whittier complained, "It has not the originality of his ocean narratives. In the 'Pilot' and 'Red Rover,' the hand of a master is visible."[82] R. H. Dana, Jr. noted that the proliferation of sea-stories following *The Pilot* made his own bid for attention risky, but was glad to cite Cooper's example as sufficient precedent for using seamen's terms:

Thousands read the escape of the American frigate through the British channel, and . . . follow the minute nautical manoeuvres with breathless interest, who do not know the name of a rope in the ship; and perhaps with none the less admiration and enthusiasm for their want of acquaintance with the professional detail.[83]

Another contemporary, William Gilmore Simms, used the publication of *The Two Admirals* (1842) as justification for a long review of Cooper's work, with his discussion of *The Pilot* focusing on the Pilot himself as an example of "moral manhood."

In his hands the ship becomes a being, instinct with life, beauty, sentiment—in danger, and to be saved; —and our interest in her fate, grows from our anxiety to behold the issue, in which human skill, courage and ingenuity, are to contend with storm and sea, rocks and tempest—as it were, man against omnipotence.[84]

The republication of *The Pilot* in the Putnam edition elicited from W. C. Bryant a commentary that should be added to his later remarks in the Putnam *Memorial*.

. . . it was Cooper who first gave us the poetry of a seaman's life, extracted a dramatic interest from the log book, and suspended the hopes and fears of his plot upon the maneuvering of a vessel. He showed us also what rich materials for the lineation of character . . . are to be found in naval life, and in this novel of the Pilot, created a character which will live as long . . . as any of those of Shakspeare. He became the master and founder of a numerous school of writers of sea romances, who learned their art from reading the Pilot and his other tales of the sea . . . .[85]

After Cooper's death, Parkman wrote that *The Pilot* "is usually considered the best of Cooper's sea tales. It is in truth a masterpiece of his genius . . . ."[86] Also writing after Cooper's death, H. T. Tuckerman had high praise for *The Pilot* and claimed for it — and Cooper — a permanent place in world literature.[87]

Many years later, Susan Cooper wrote that her father had been "dissatisfied" with his characterization of Jones who "was represented as a man of higher views and aims, in a moral sense, than the facts of the life of Paul Jones would justify."[88] Ironically, Susan was here perpetuating the very injustice to which her father had tried to draw attention elsewhere. In *Lives of Distinguished American Naval Offices*, for instance, Cooper had written of Jones:

> . . . it is not to be concealed that a species of indefinite distrust clouded his reputation even in America, until the industry of his biographers, by means of indisputable documents and his own voluminous correspondence, succeeded in placing him before the public in a light too unequivocally respectable to leave any reasonable doubts that public sentiment had silently done him injustice.[89]

Cooper did, however, express his lack of satisfaction with *The Pilot* as a sea-novel; writing to Henry Colburn, 17 October 1826, he announced, "I intend the next book to be nautical, for I never was satisfied with the Pilot — myself — "[90] His conscious attempt to develop sea fiction as a genre continued throughout his career. Between the romantic *Red Rover* (1827) and the satiric *Jack Tier* (1848), Cooper explored the possibilities of nautical fiction in a number of different ways, and *The Sea Lions*, the next-to-last published work before his death, was still another metaphysical extension of the genre.

In 1838, a British critic had started a review by musing, "It is singular that maritime novels should be of foreign origin when the sea itself had been so long the favorite and boasted possession of Great Britain . . . . "[91] In pre-empting the sea for fiction, Cooper had in one sense carried the American Revolution beyond the limits of the continent, and in 1849, when he published his last maritime novel, he was still master of the realm he had conquered.

NOTES

1. Born and bred in England, Charles Wilkes became one of New York's most prominent citizens, but never relinquished his business and social ties with London. *The Letters and Journals of James Fenimore Cooper*, (cited hereafter as *Letters and Journals*) ed., James Franklin Beard (Cambridge, Mass.: Belknap Press of Harvard University Press, 1960–1968), I, 247 and IV, 343. Susan Fenimore Cooper elaborated on the conversation with Wilkes in "Small Family Memories," (1883) in *Correspondence of James Fenimore Cooper* (cited hereafter as *Correspondence*), ed., James Fenimore Cooper (grandson of the novelist) (New Haven: Yale University Press, 1922) I, 52–53.

2. Wilkes's letter of 29 December 1827 is in the Collection of American Literature, Beinecke Rare Book and Manuscript Library, Yale University (cited hereafter as YCAL). Cooper answered from Paris the following month. *Letters and Journals*, I, 240, 247 n.2. (The date 1829 in the note is a misprint.)

3. *Letters and Journals*, IV, 374.

4. *Letters and Journals*, VI, 141.

5. *Gleanings in Europe: England* (Albany: State University of New York Press, 1981), p. 10.

6. Ibid.

7. *New-York Statesman* 8 April 1823.

8. *Letters and Journals*, I, 95–97.

9. Ibid, p. 102.

10. Ibid, p. 103.

11. Ibid, p. 104.

12. Monday, 17 November 1823, p. 2.

13. The book was printed in New York by an unnamed printer. In 1808, the title was changed to *Memoirs of the Life of Captain Nathaniel Fanning, an American Navy Officer, who served during Part of the American Revolution under the command of Commodore John Paul Jones, Esq.* Internal evidence indicates that Fanning pulled his narrative together about 1801 when he was trying to get a regular commission in the United States Navy. Never a Captain, in spite of the 1808 title, Fanning was commissioned Lieutenant on 4 December 1804 only to die of yellow fever at Charlestown, S. C. on 30 September 1805. (*The Magazine of History*, New York, 1913, p. xiv.)

14. Susan Cooper wrote in an introduction to *The Pilot* that an "allusion in the letter to Lady Selkirk, declaring that he had 'sacrificed the softer affections of the heart and prospects of domestic happiness,' led to the introduction of . . . Alice Dunscombe." (New York and Cambridge: Houghton, Mifflin and Co., 1884, p. xx.) Besides the letter to Lady Selkirk, chapbooks usually included such well-publicized events as the cruise of the *Ranger*, Jones's descent on Whitehaven, the plot to kidnap Lord Selkirk, and the battle off Flamborough Head; they filled out the "life" with incidents (mostly rape, mayhem and murder) that would explain why a British citizen would act as Jones had. Fanning's own "Biographical Sketch" of Jones (pp. 105-119) is a compound of chapbook material and scuttlebutt.

15. The French title was *Memoires de Paul Jones, ecrits par lui-meme en Anglais et traduits sous ses yeux par le citoyen Andre*. An English translation in the *Weekly Register*, Vol. II, No. 40 beginning on page 230 had been used by Thomas Clark for his *Sketches of the Naval History of the United States* which was reviewed by Cooper in *The Literary and Scientific Repository, and Critical Review*, II (January 1821), 20-37. Reprinted in facsimile with Introduction and Headnotes by James F. Beard in *Early Critical Essays (1820-1822) by James Fenimore Cooper* (Delmar, New York: Scholars' Facsimiles & Reprints, 1977 [1955]).

16. The notices in *The Albion* of 17 July 1824 and in *Atheneum* of 1 July 1824 are identical except that the *Atheneum* article is labeled a reprint "From London Magazine."

17. When Jones was last in the United States in 1787, he stayed in New York with Robert Hyslop, a Scottish attorney who was a friend of the family and who became Jones's American executor. Hyslop died of yellow fever in 1797 and his property passed to his cousin John, a baker, whose shop was later sold to a man named Harding. After the publication of *The Pilot*, George Ward spotted Jones's signature on some papers in the bakery window and obtained them from Harding. We do not know when Ward first saw Cooper, but a letter from him to Cooper (dated 28 July 1824 and now in YCAL) begins, "Since I had the pleasure of seeing you I have traced the correspondence to the family of J. Paul Jones." Ward continued:

> I have upwards of seven hundred letters and documents from which I have selected (and you will please receive herewith) *all* that are in the *hand writing* of the hero and many official and private letters to him from which I hope may be deducted finer principles of action than he has hitherto been allowed to have possessed and such as would entitle him to a higher cast of character than even the Pilot has asserted: —

The London *New Monthly Magazine* printed news of the discovery on 1 November 1824 and speculated that Cooper might persuade Wiley to publish the letters. Ward, probably on Cooper's advice, turned the papers over to John Henry Sherburne, Register of the Navy, who published a *Life of Paul Jones* in 1825. Sherburne did little more than arrange and annotate the papers, but he enlarged and improved the work for a second edition in 1851.

After Cooper's brief biography of Jones appeared in *Graham's Magazine* in July and August of 1843, Jones's niece, Janette Taylor, sent Cooper a twenty-page letter (28 October 1843) to correct errors "of minor importance, it is true, but still they are errors" and to furnish information Cooper had lacked. She said she was aware that "the sketch will be introduced in another work" and Cooper made the appropriate changes in *Lives of Distinguished American Naval Officers* (Philadelphia: Carey and Hart, 1846). Miss Taylor's letter is in YCAL and was published in *Proceedings of the U. S. Naval Institute* June, 1907, pp. 683–709.

18. Fanning, *Narrative*, pp. 54, 106, 114.

19. Ibid, p. 40.

20. Ibid, pp. 81–82.

21. Ibid, p. 74.

22. Ibid, p. 37.

23. Ibid, pp. 82–83.

24. Ibid, p. 85.

25. Ibid, pp. 99–100.

26. *The Logs of the Serapis — Alliance — Ariel*, ed. John S. Barnes, (New York: Naval History Society, 1911), p. 109.

27. *Letters and Journals*, I, 110.

28. Cooper to Dana, 14 April 1823, *Letters and Journals*, I, 94.

29. *The Cooper Gallery* (Philadelphia: Lippincott & Co., 1865), p. 77.

30. Fanning, *Narrative,* p. 48.

31. [Sir Walter Scott], *The Pirate* (Edinburgh: Archibald Constable, 1822), II, 71.

32. Ibid, p. 222. As Long Tom says, however, the name of Coffin is common; anyone would connect it with American whaling.

33. Ibid, III, 199.

34. Ibid, II, 49ff.

35. Ibid, III, 113.

36. *The Pioneers* was published 1 February 1823; this announcement appeared in the *New-York Statesman* 18 February 1823, p. 2.

37. *Letters and Journals*, I, 104.

38. Wiley advertised *The Pilot* as available "in a few days" at the end of December. (*New-York Statesman*, 30 December 1823, p. 3.) The same notice ran through Tuesday, 6 January 1824. Publication was announced 7 January in an advertisement on page 3 stressing Cooper's epigraph for the book: *List, ye landsmen, all to me.*

39. 1 January 1824, p. 7. The same day the New Haven *Christian Spectator* mistakenly announced, on page 53, that *The Pilot* had been published in Philadelphia in December. *The Albion* and *The Minerva*, both of New York, announced publication 10 January 1824, and the Boston *New-England Galaxy* reported the book on sale in Boston 28 January.

40. Cooper's letter has apparently been lost, but John Miller's reply of 28 June 1823 says, "I am favoured with your letter of the 20th May, by my friend Mr. Mathews." Miller's letter is in YCAL and most of this letter was reprinted in *Correspondence*, I, 95.

41. MS: Cooper Family Papers.

42. The Ogden letter of 13 September 1823 is in YCAL.

43. The size of the first English edition is given in letters from Miller to Cooper 5 February 1824 and 4 December 1824 (YCAL). A notice in the weekly London *Literary Gazette* for Saturday, 31 January 1824 establishes the approximate date of publication by saying that *The Pilot* "has appeared too late in the week for our Review. We have glanced over it, however, and form a favourable opinion of its merits." "About 150 copies" of a second edition of 750 had been sold by 14 April 1825 according to Miller's letter to Cooper on that date. (MS: YCAL)

44. On Wednesday, 14 January, the *Massachusetts Spy — Worcester Advertiser* also reported that Cooper was visiting Boston and that *The Pilot* was for sale.

45. *Letters and Journals*, I, 110.

46. p. 357. The Harpers Ferry, Va. *Ladies' Garland* of 14 February gave the same sales figures and announced that a second edition was in the press. Boston's *The Christian Register* of 20 February reported the first edition as sold and "a second edition still larger, is in the press, the greater part of which is already ordered." (p. 111)

47. *New-York Statesman*, 26 January 1824, p. 3 and an announcement dated 11 February in the 12 February issue of the *Statesman*.

48. David Kaser, *Messrs. Carey & Lea of Philadelphia* (Philadelphia: University of Pennsylvania Press, 1957), p. 80. For the third edition see Kaser, *The Cost Book of Carey and Lea 1825-1838* (Philadelphia: University of Pennsylvania Press, 1963), p. 246. The "fifth edition" of 1829 is from the same plates as the "third edition" of 1827 and so is the "new edition" of 1835 published by Carey, Lea and Blanchard.

49. *Letters and Journals*, II, 130.

50. Ibid, VI, 11.

51. Cooper to Shubrick [25-30? January — 5 February 1824], *Letters and Journals*, I, 110.

52. Cooper to Carey, Lea and Carey, 13 October 1827. This letter is bound into the second volume of Charles Haven Hunt's *The Life of Edward Livingston* (Huntington Rare Book 39009) in The Huntington Library, San Marino, California and is quoted by permission.

53. Cooper to Rufus Griswold [10-18 January 1843?], *Letters and Journals*, IV, 343.

54. Cooper to Griswold [27 May-June ? 1844], Ibid, IV, 460.

55 This review was reprinted in the *American & Commercial Daily Advertiser of Baltimore* 16 January 1824, p. 2 under the heading: "LITERARY — The new novel of "*The Pilot*" which has just been published in Philadelphia, is thus spoken of by the editor of the National Gazette: — " The same review was reprinted in *New England Galaxy*, Boston, 28 January.

The following citations locate other contemporary American reviews or critical comments about *The Pilot: The American Monthly Magazine*, 1 (March 1824), 193-203; *The American Quarterly Review*, 17 (June 1835), 414-19; *American Whig Review*, 11 (April 1850), 408-10; *Cincinnati Literary Gazette*, 1 (14 February

1824), 49–50; (19 June 1824), 198; *Cyclopaedia of American Literature* (1856) II, 108–13; *Democratic Review* (November 1849), 476; *Graham's Magazine,* 36 (February 1850), 168; Griswold, *The Prose Writers of America* (1847), 264; *Holden's Dollar Mazagine,* 4 (December 1849), 764; *Hunt's Merchant's Magazine and Commercial Review,* 21 (November 1849), 588; 22 (February 1850), 251; *The Literary Gazette,* #394 (7 August 1824), 502; *The Minerva,* 2 (24 January 1824), 334–5; *National Quarterly Review,* (September 1860), 301–14; New Haven *Christian Spectator,* (February 1825), 80–90; *New-York Commercial Advertiser,* (21 January 1824), reprinted *New-York Spectator* (10 February 1824); *New York Evening Post,* ([15–30] September 1851), reprinted *Littell's Living Age* (October 1851), 87; *The New-York Mirror,* 1 (31 January 1824), 210–11; (17 April 1824), 301; (11 August 1827), 39; (16 February 1833), 262; *New York Quarterly,* 1 (June 1852), 215–28; *New York Spectator,* 27 (23 January 1824), 2; *The New Yorker,* 1 (23 April 1836), 65–6; *Niles Weekly Register,* 30 (June 1826), 265; *The North American Review,* 18 (April 1824), 314–29; 23 (July 1826), 155, 179; (April 1831), 16; 46 (January 1838), 12–13; 74 (January 1852), 158; 89 (October 1859), 290–314; *The Port Folio,* 17 (February 1824), 132–46; *Sartain's Union Magazine,* 6 (February 1850), 174; *The Saturday Evening Post,* 6 (19 February 1825), 2; *The Southern Literary Messenger,* 3 (April 1837), 254–55; 4 (June 1838), 375, reprinted *The New Yorker* (23 June 1838), 211–12; 15 (December 1849), 763; *United States Literary Gazette,* 1 (1 April 1824), 6; (1 March 1825), 340; *The United States Magazine and Democratic Review,* 25 (November 1849), 476.

56. Probably James G. Brooks, one of the editors.

57. A similar reaction was expressed by someone (probably Mrs. Henry D. Sedgwick) who wrote to Catherine M. Sedgwick 22 February [1824].

> The Pilot is all in vogue, even those who never liked Cooper before like him now — except me — but I smell the tar & the air of the Cabin in every line so that he makes me sea-sick — I have not the least doubt of his genius, but what sailors write sailors should read. — This book just suits Mrs. Rogers who is never well but in Sea air & even Mrs. Coles was delighted with some of it.

MS: Sedgwick Papers, Massachusetts Historical Society.

58. Marcel Clavel, *Fenimore Cooper and His Critics* (cited hereafter as *Critics*) (Aix-en-Provence: Imprimerie Universitaire de Provence, 1938), p. 183.

59. Parke Godwin, *A Biography of William Cullen Bryant* (New York: Russell & Russell, 1883), I, 194.

60. MS: YCAL.

The following citations locate contemporary British reviews or critical comments about *The Pilot: The Athenaeum,* 3 (1830), 658–9; #1249 (4 October 1851), 1047–8; *Atlas,* 6 (20 March 1831), 188; *Bentley's Miscellany,* 33 (1853), 428; *Blackwood's,* 16 (October 1824), 426–8; 19 (March 1826), 353–74; *British Critic,* 2 (July 1826), 432–4; *Colburn's New Monthly Mazazine,* 12 (1 March 1824), 123–4; reprinted (U.S.) *New York Patriot* (5 May 1824) and *Museum of Foreign Literature* (May 1824) and (London) *The Ladies Magazine* (August 1824); 20 (July 1827), 80; 35 (April 1831) 360–1, reprinted (U.S.) *Museum of Foreign*

Literature (June 1831); *Dublin University Magazine*, 47 (January 1856), 47–51 and
(March 1856), 294–308; *Eclectic Review*, #96 (1852), 414, partly reprinted in
Eclectic Magazine (June 1852), 209; *Edinburgh Literary Journal* (29 August 1829),
172; *Edinburgh Review*, 50 (October 1829), 128–9, reprinted (U.S.) *Museum of
Foreign Literature* (30 March 1830); (April 1835), 23–4; *Edinburgh Scotsman* [Oc-
tober? November? 1824] reprinted *The New-York Mirror* (4 December 1824)
and the *Cincinnati Literary Gazette* (11 December 1824); *Family Magazine*, 2
(1830), 282; *Foreign and Colonial Quarterly Review*, 2 (October 1843), 474–5;
Foreign Quarterly Review, 21 (July 1838), 422–3, 429; *Fraser's Magazine for Town
and Country*, 4 (December 1831) 662–9; *Gentleman's Magazine*, 101 (1831), 609;
The Hive, 3 (1824), 324; *La Belle Assemblée*, (March 1824), 123–4; *Ladies' Monthly
Museum*, (March 1824), 158–9; *Literary Gazette*, 8 (31 January 1824), 77; (7
February 1824), 83–4 partly reprinted in the Philadelphia *The Saturday Even-
ing Post* (20 March 1824); (August 1824), 502; (December 1827), 787; *Literary
Museum*, (31 January 1824), 61; *Marryatt's Metropolitan Magazine*, (August 1831),
370–6; *Monthly Magazine* (May 1830), 562; *Monthly Review*, (March 1824),
330–1; (June 1826), 123; (May 1831), 145–6; *The Museum*, (31 January 1824),
61–2; (7 February 1824), 84–6; *Newcastle Magazine*, 4 (February 1825), 68–71; 6
(August 1827), 358–9; *New London Literary Gazette*, (8 December 1827), 80;
Somerset House Gazette and Literary Museum, 1 (7 February 1824), 283–5; (14
February 1824), 293–5; *Spirit of Literature* (30 October 1830), 426; *Tait's Edinburgh Magazine*, (September 1832), 661; *The Tatler*, (7 April 1831), 737; *Universal Review*, (May 1824), 382; *Westminster Review*, (January 1832), 180–1;
(January, 1852), 289.

61. *Letters and Journals*, IV, 343.

62. *England*, p. 10.

63. *Letters and Journals*, II, 310.

64. *Newcastle Magazine*, February 1825, p. 69.

65. W.N.G. in *Marryatt's Metropolitan Magazine*, August 1831, p. 376.

66. The critical neglect of Cooper, Dana, and Melville at home in the
latter half of the nineteenth century contrasts with the admiration of "A
Trio of American Sailor-Authors" (*Dublin University Magazine*, January 1856,
pp. 47–54), the running comparison (to Cooper's advantage) that concludes
"Marryat's Sea Stories" (*Dublin University Magazine*, March 1846, pp.
294–308), or the use of Cooper and Melville as standards of comparison in
James Hannay's "Sea Novels—Captain Marryatt" (*Cornhill Magazine*,
February 1873, pp. 170–190.)

67. *Cumberland's Minor Theatre* (London: John Cumberland, 1828), I, 5.

68 This *Life of Paul Jones* is in the Huntington Library Rare Book collection. "About 1826" is penciled in on the title page and also written, in blue
ink, on the last page.

69. Letters of 28 June 1823 and 4 December 1824 cited earlier.

70. *Letters and Journals*, I, 128. The earliest known piracy of *The Pilot* may
be in the Brynmor Jones Library at the University of Hull. It is a three-
volume edition using the Wiley text and identified on the title page as being
"By the author of 'Lionel Lincoln,' 'Spy,' &c." which suggests 1825 as the
year of printing.

71. Clavel, *Critics,* p. 246. Robert E. Spiller and Philip C. Blackburn, *A Descriptive Bibliography of the Writings of James Fenimore Cooper* (New York: Burt Franklin, 1968), pp. 36, 180-181.

72. F.A.S. in the *Globe,* 2 July 1827, p. 205 as quoted by Clavel, *Critics,* p. 250.

73. Spiller and Blackburn, *Bibliography,* pp. 37, 189-93.

74. The Livorno copy is at Yale University, the 1829 Naples at the American Antiquarian Society, and the 1868 Milan at the Vieusseux in Florence. The 1831 Milan edition, still listed in the catalogue at the Vieusseux, seems to have been lost in the last flood of the Arno.

75. Spiller and Blackburn, Ibid, pp. 37-8. John de Lancey Ferguson's *American Literature in Spain* (New York: Columbia University Press, 1916) lists two additional Spanish editions, one in 1857 and another undated but existing in 1915, and shows that the first Spanish edition was translated from the French (p. 208).

76. Scott wrote in his journal 21 October 1826,

. . . we saw the Pilot, from an American novel of that name. It is extremely popular, the dramatist having seized on the whole story, and turned the odious and ridiculous parts, assigned by the original author to the British, against the Yankees themselves.

John Gibson Lockhart, *Memoirs of the Life of Sir Walter Scott, Bart.* (Edinburgh: Robert Cadell, 1837), VI, 361-362.

Samuel French made *The Pilot* No. XLI in *French's American Drama* (New York: Samuel French, n.d.), returned the action from the coast of America to the coast of England, and restored the characters to their original nationalities.

77. Lockhart. *Memoirs of . . . Scott,* V, 342.

78. *Recollections of a Lifetime* (New York, 1857), I. 202.

79. A.G.K. L'Estrange, *The Life of Mary Russell Mitford* (New York: Harper & Brothers, 1870), II, 23-24.

80. Irving's letter is dated from Madrid, 4 April 1827. Pierre M. Irving, *The Life and Letters of Washington Irving* (New York: G. P. Putnam, 1864), II, 260-261.

81. *Conversations of James Northcote, Esq., R. A.* (London: Frederick Muller, Ltd., 1949), p. 87. (Originally published in 1830)

82. Review of 2 January 1830 for the Haverhill, Mass. *Essex Gazette. Whittier on Writers and Writing,* ed., E. H. Cady and H. H. Clark (Syracuse, N. Y.: Syracuse University Press, 1950), p. 26. When Whittier edited *The Literary Remains of John G. C. Brainard* (Hartford: P. B. Goodsell, 1832) he included "Mr. Merry's Lament for 'Long Tom'" pp. 152-53.

83. Dana's preface was dated July 1840. *Two Years Before the Mast,* ed., John H. Kemble (Los Angeles: Ward Ritchie Press, 1964), I, xxii. Persons who did understand the professional details, however, valued Cooper's sea-novels for their accuracy. *The Pilot* was one of Cooper's works that James Kirke Paulding, then Secretary of the Navy, ordered "added to the Libraries of the Public Ships, for I know not where our young officers may

find better practical illustrations of seamanship than they contain." *Letters and Journals*, III, 381.

84. Simms's essay, "Cooper, His Genius and Writings," was originally published in *Magnolia*, September 1842, pp. 129–139. *Views and Reviews*, ed., C. Hugh Holman (Cambridge, Mass.: Belknap Press of Harvard University Press, 1962), p. 271. A similar response appeared in a review of *Der Lootse* in the *Blätter*, 5 January 1825, when a despondent man, failing "to derive comfort from Marcus Aurelius and Sophocles," reveals that he "has been lifted out of his melancholy by Cooper's story." Harvey Hewett-Thayer, *American Literature as Viewed in Germany, 1818–1861.* (Chapel Hill, N.C., 1958), p. 25.

85. Bryant was quoted in *Hunt's Merchant's Magazine and Commercial Review*, February 1850, p. 251.

86. *North American Review*, January 1852, p. 158.

87. *North American Review*, October 1859, p. 294. Saying that *The Pilot* wrung "from the reluctant justice of British critics an acknowledgement that his 'was the empire of the sea'" Tuckerman may have had in mind the end of an article in *Dublin University Magazine*, March 1856, p. 308:

Such were Marryat and Cooper. If the former was the *King* of the naval novelists of Great Britain, Cooper was the EMPEROR of the naval novelists of *all* countries; and there is this enormous difference between the King and the Emperor—the former was an estimable writer of versatile talent, and the latter a glorious prose-poet of the very loftiest genius. The gulf between the two is, and ever will be, impassable.

88. *The Cooper Gallery*, p. 77.

89. (Philadelphia: Carey and Hart, 1846), II, iii.

90. *Letters and Journals*, I, 167.

91. *Foreign Quarterly Review* (July 1838), p. 422.

TO

WILLIAM BRANFORD SHUBRICK,

ESQ.,

U.S. NAVY

MY DEAR SHUBRICK,

Each year brings some new and melancholy chasm in what is now the brief list of my naval friends and former associates. War, disease, and the casualties of a hazardous profession, have made fearful inroads in the limited number; while the places of the dead are supplied by names that to me are those of strangers. With the consequences of these sad changes before me, I cherish the recollection of those with whom I once lived in close familiarity with peculiar interest, and feel a triumph in their growing reputations, that is but little short of their own honest pride.

But neither time nor separation has shaken our intimacy: and I know that in dedicating to you this volume, I tell you nothing new, when I add, that it is a tribute paid to an enduring friendship, by

Your old messmate,

THE AUTHOR

Preface.
[1823]

THE PRIVILEGES of the Historian and of the writer of Romances are very different, and it behooves them equally to respect each other's rights. The latter is permitted to garnish a probable fiction, while he is sternly prohibited from dwelling on improbable truths; but it is the duty of the former to record facts as they have occurred, without a reference to consequences, resting his reputation on a firm foundation of realities, and vindicating his integrity by his authorities. How far and how well the Author has adhered to this distinction between the prerogatives of truth and fiction, his readers must decide; but he cannot forbear desiring the curious inquirers into our annals to persevere, until they shall find good poetical authority for every material incident in this veritable legend.

As to the Critics, he has the advantage of including them all in that extensive class, which is known by the sweeping appellation of "Lubbers." If they have common discretion, they will beware of exposing their ignorance.

If, however, some old seaman should happen to detect any trifling anachronisms in marine usages, or mechanical improvements, the Author begs leave to say to him, with a proper deference for his experience, that it was not so much his intention to describe the customs of a particular age, as to paint those scenes which belong only to the ocean, and to exhibit, in his imperfect manner, a few traits of a people who, from the nature of things, can never be much known.

He will probably be told, that Smollett has done all this, before him, and in a much better manner. It will be seen, however, that though he has navigated the same sea as Smollett, he has steered a different course; or, in other words, that he has considered what Smollett has painted as a picture which is finished, and which is not to be daubed over by every one who may choose to handle a pencil on marine subjects.

The Author wishes to express his regret, that the daring and useful services of a great portion of our marine in the old war should be suffered to remain in the obscurity under which it is now buried. Every one has heard of the victory of the Bon-Homme Richard, but how little is known of the rest of the life, and of the important services of the remarkable man who commanded, in our behalf, in that memorable combat. How little is known of his actions with the Milford, and the Solebay; of his captures of the Drake and Triumph; and of his repeated and desperate projects to carry the war into the 'island home' of our powerful enemy. Very many of the officers who served in that contest were to be found, afterwards, in the navy of the confederation; and it is fair to presume that it owes no small part of its present character to the spirit that descended from the heroes of the revolution.

One of the last officers reared in that school died, not long since, at the head of his profession; and now, that nothing but the recollection of their deeds remains, we should become more tenacious of their glory.

If his book has the least tendency to excite some attention to this interesting portion of our history, one of the objects of the writer will be accomplished.

The Author now takes his leave of his readers, wishing them all happiness.

Preface.
[1849]

I T is probable a true history of human events would show that a far larger proportion of our acts are the results of sudden impulses and accidents, than of that reason of which we so much boast. However true, or false, this opinion may be in more important matters, it is certainly and strictly correct as relates to the conception and execution of this book.

The Pilot was published in 1823. This was not long after the appearance of "The Pirate," a work which it is hardly necessary to remind the reader, has a direct connection with the sea. In a conversation with a friend, a man of polished taste and extensive reading, the authorship of the Scottish novels came under discussion. The claims of Sir Walter were a little distrusted, on account of the peculiar and minute information that the romances were then very generally thought to display. The Pirate was cited as a very marked instance of this universal knowledge, and it was wondered where a man of Scott's habits and associations could have become so familiar with the sea. The writer had frequently observed that there was much looseness in this universal knowledge, and that the secret of its success was to be traced to the power of creating that *vraisemblance*, which is so remarkably exhibited in those world-renowned fictions, rather than to any very accurate information on the part of their author. It would have been hypercritical to object to the Pirate, that it was not strictly nautical, or true in its details; but, when the reverse was urged as a proof of what, considering the character of other portions of the work, would have been most extraordinary attainments, it was a sort of provocation to dispute the seamanship of the Pirate, a quality to which the book has certainly very little just pretension. The result of this conversation was a sudden determination to produce a work which, if it had no other merit, might present truer pictures of the ocean and ships than any that are to be found in the Pirate. To this unpremeditated decision, purely an impulse, is not only the Pilot due, but a tolerably numerous school of nautical romances that have succeeded it.

The author had many misgivings concerning the success of the undertaking, after he had made some progress in the work; the opinions of his different friends being anything but encouraging. One would declare that the sea could not be made interesting; that it was tame, monotonous, and without any other movement than unpleasant storms, and that, for his part, the less he got of it the better. The women very generally protested that such a book would have the odour of bilge-water, and that it would give them the *maladie de mer*. Not a single individual among all those who discussed the merits of the project, within the range of the author's knowledge, either spoke, or looked, encouragingly. It is probable that all these persons anticipated a signal failure.

So very discouraging did these ominous opinions get to be, that the writer was, once or twice, tempted to throw his manuscript aside, and turn to something new. A favourable opinion, however, coming from a very unexpected quarter, put a new face on the matter, and raised new hopes. Among the intimate friends of the writer, was an Englishman, who possessed most of the peculiar qualities of the educated of his country. He was learned even, had a taste that was so just as always to command respect, but was prejudiced, and particularly so in all that related to this country and its literature. He could never be persuaded to admire Bryant's Water-Fowl, and this mainly because if it were accepted as good poetry, it must be placed at once amongst the finest fugitive pieces of the language. Of the Thanatopsis he thought better, though inclined to suspect it of being a plagiarism. To the tender mercies of this one-sided critic, who had never affected to compliment the previous works of the author, the sheets of a volume of The Pilot were committed, with scarce an expectation of his liking them. The reverse proved to be the case; — he expressed himself highly gratified, and predicted a success for the book which it probably never attained.

Thus encouraged, one more experiment was made, a seaman being selected for the critic. A kinsman, a namesake, and an old messmate of the author, one now in command on a foreign station, was chosen, and a considerable portion of the first volume was read to him. There is no wish to conceal the satisfaction with which the effect on this listener was observed. He treated the whole matter as fact, and his criticisms were strictly professional, and perfectly just. But the interest he betrayed could not be mistaken. It gave a perfect and most gratifying assurance that the work would be more likely to find favour with nautical men, than with any other class of readers.

The Pilot could scarcely be a favourite with females. The story has little interest for them, nor was it much heeded by the author of the book, in the progress of his labours. His aim was to illustrate vessels and the ocean, rather than to draw any pictures of sentiment and love. In this last respect, the book has small claims on the reader's attention, though it is hoped that the story has sufficient interest to relieve the more strictly nautical features of the work.

It would be affectation to deny that the Pilot met with a most unlooked-for success. The novelty of the design probably contributed a large share of this result. Sea-tales came into vogue, as a consequence; and, as every practical part of knowledge has its uses, something has been gained by letting the landsman into the secrets of the seaman's manner of life. Perhaps, in some small degree, an interest has been awakened in behalf of a very numerous, and what has hitherto been a sort of proscribed class of men, that may directly tend to a melioration of their condition.

It is not easy to make the public comprehend all the necessities of a service afloat. With several hundred rude beings confined within the narrow limits of a vessel, men of all nations and of the lowest habits, it would be to the last degree indiscreet, to commence their reformation by relaxing the bonds of discipline, under the mistaken impulses of a false philanthropy. It has a lofty sound, to be sure, to talk about American citizens being too good to be brought under the lash, upon the high seas; but he must have a very mistaken notion who does not see that tens of thousands of these pretend-

ing persons on shore, even, would be greatly benefited by a
little judicious flogging. It is the judgment in administering,
and not the mode of punishment, that requires to be looked into; and, in this respect, there has certainly been a great improvement of late years. It is seldom, indeed, that any institu-
tion, practice, or system, is improved by the blind interference
of those who know nothing about it. Better would it be to trust
to the experience of those who have long governed turbulent
men, than to the impulsive experiments of those who rarely
regard more than one side of a question, and that the most
showy and glittering; having, quite half of the time, some
selfish personal end to answer.

There is an uneasy desire among a vast many well-disposed
persons to get the fruits of the Christian Faith, without troubling themselves about the Faith itself. This is done under the
sanction of Peace Societies, Temperance and Moral Reform
Societies, in which the end is too often mistaken for the means.
When the Almighty sent his Son on earth, it was to point out
the way in which all this was to be brought about, by means of
the Church; but men have so frittered away that body of
divine organisation, through their divisions and subdivisions,
all arising from human conceit, that it is no longer regarded
as the agency it was obviously intended to be, and various con-
trivances are to be employed as substitutes for that which proceeded directly from the Son of God!

Among the efforts of the day, however, there is one connected with the moral improvement of the sailor that commands our profound respect. Cut off from most of the charities
of life, for so large a portion of his time, deprived altogether of
association with the gentler and better portions of the other
sex, and living a man in a degree proscribed, amid the many
signs of advancement that distinguish the age, it was time that
he should be remembered and singled out, and become the
subject of combined and Christian philanthropy. There is
much reason to believe that the effort, now making in the right
direction and under proper auspices, will be successful; and
that it will cause the lash to be laid aside in the best and most
rational manner, — by rendering its use unnecessary.

Cooperstown, August 10, 1849.

The Pilot

Chapter I.

"Sullen waves, incessant rolling,
  Rudely dash against her sides."
    "Fresh and Strong," *Dibdin's Charms of Melody,* ll. 3-4.

A SINGLE glance at the map will make the reader acquainted with the position of the eastern coast of the island of Great Britain, as connected with the shores of the opposite continent. Together they form the boundaries of the small sea, that has for ages been known to the world as the scene of maritime exploits, and as the great avenue through which commerce and war have conducted the fleets of the northern nations of Europe. Over this sea the islanders long asserted a jurisdiction, exceeding that which reason concedes to any power on the highway of nations, and which frequently led to conflicts that caused an expenditure of blood and treasure, utterly disproportioned to the advantages that can ever arise from the maintenance of a useless and abstract right. It is across the waters of this disputed ocean that we shall attempt to conduct our readers, selecting a period for our incidents that has a peculiar interest for every American, not only because it was the birth-day of his nation, but because it was also the era when reason and common sense began to take the place of custom and feudal practices in the management of the affairs of nations.

Soon after the events of the revolution had involved the kingdoms of France and Spain, and the republics of Holland, in our quarrel, a group of labourers was collected in a field that lay exposed to the winds of the ocean, on the north-eastern coast of England. These men were lightening their toil, and cheering the gloom of a day in December, by uttering their crude opinions on the political aspects of the times. The fact that England was engaged in a war with some of her dependencies on the other side of the Atlantic, had long been known to them, after the manner that faint rumours of distant and uninteresting events gain on the ear; but now that nations, with whom she had been used to battle, were armed against her in the quarrel, the din of war had disturbed the quiet even of these secluded and illiterate rustics. The principal speakers, on the occasion, were a Scotch drover, who was waiting the leisure of the occupant of the fields, and an Irish labourer, who had found his way across the channel, and thus far over the island, in quest of employment.

"The Nagurs wouldn't have been a job at all for ould England, letting alone Ireland," said the latter, "if these French and Spanishers hadn't been troubling themselves in the matter. I'm sure it's but little rason I have for thanking them, if a man is to kape as sober as a praist at mass, for fear he should find himself a souldier, and he knowing nothing about the same."

"Hoot! mon! ye ken but little of raising an airmy in Ireland, if ye mak' a drum o' a whiskey keg," said the drover, winking to the listeners. "Noo, in the north, they ca' a gathering of the folk, and follow the pipes as graciously as ye wad journey kirkward o' a Sabbeth morn. I've seen a' the names o' a Heeland raj'ment on a sma' bit paper, that ye might cover wi' a leddy's hand. They war' a' Camerons and M'Donalds, though they paraded sax hundred men! But what ha' ye gotten here! That chield has an ow'r liking to the land for a seafaring body; an' if the bottom o' the sea be ony thing like the top o't, he's in gr'at danger o' a shipwrack!"

This unexpected change in the discourse, drew all eyes on the object towards which the staff of the observant drover was pointed. To the utter amazement of every individual present, a small vessel was seen moving slowly round a point of land that formed one of the sides of the little bay, to which the field the labourers were in composed the other. There was something very peculiar in the externals of this unusual visiter, which added in no small degree to the surprise created by her appearance in that retired place. None but the smallest vessels, and those rarely, or, at long intervals, a desperate smuggler, were ever known to venture so close to the land, amid the sand-bars and sunken rocks with which that immediate coast abounded. The adventurous mariners who now attempted this dangerous navigation in so wanton, and, apparently, so heedless a manner, were in a low, black schooner, whose hull seemed utterly disproportioned to the raking masts it upheld, which, in their turn, supported a lighter set of spars, that tapered away until their upper extremities appeared no larger than the lazy pennant, that in vain endeavoured to display its length in the light breeze.

The short day of that high northern latitude was already drawing to a close, and the sun was throwing his parting rays obliquely across the waters, touching the gloomy waves here and there with streaks of pale light. The stormy winds of the German ocean were apparently lulled to rest; and, though the incessant rolling of the surge on the shore, heightened the gloomy character of the hour and the view, the light ripple that ruffled the sleeping billows was produced by a gentle air, that blew directly from the land. Notwithstanding this favourable circumstance, there was something threatening in the aspect of the ocean, which was speaking in hollow, but deep murmurs, like a volcano on the eve of an eruption, that greatly heightened the feelings of amazement and dread with which the peasants beheld this extraordinary interruption to the quiet of their little bay. With no other sails spread to the action of the air, than her heavy mainsail, and one of those light jibs that projected far beyond her bows, the vessel glided over the water with a grace and facility that seemed magical to the beholders, who turned their wondering looks from the schooner to each other, in silent amazement. At length the drover spoke in a low, solemn voice —

"He's a bold chield that steers her! and if that bit craft has wood in her bottom, like the brigantines that ply between Lon'on and the Frith at Leith, he's in mair danger than a prudent mon could wish. Ay! he's by the big rock that shows his head when the tide runs low, but it's no mortal man who can steer long in the road he's journeying, and not speedily find land wi' water a top o't."

The little schooner, however, still held her way among the rocks and sand-spits, making such slight deviations in her course, as proved her to be under the direction of one who knew his danger, until she had entered as far into the bay as prudence could at all justify, when her canvass was gathered into folds, seemingly without the agency of hands, and the vessel, after rolling for a few minutes on the long billows that hove in from the ocean, swung round in the currents of the tide, and was held by her anchor.

The peasants, now, began to make their conjectures more freely, concerning the character and object of their visiter; some intimating that she was engaged in contraband trade, and others that her views were hostile, and her business war. A few dark hints were hazarded on the materiality of her construction, for nothing of artificial formation, it was urged, would be ventured by men in such a dangerous place, at a time when even the most inexperienced landsman was enabled to foretell the certain gale. The Scotchman, who, to all the sagacity of his countrymen, added no small portion of their superstition, leaned greatly to the latter conclusion, and had begun to express this sentiment warily and with reverence, when the child of Erin, who appeared not to possess any very definite ideas on the subject, interrupted him, by exclaiming—

"Faith! there's two of them! a big and a little! sure the bogles of the saa likes good company the same as any other christians!"

"Twa!" echoed the drover; "twa! ill luck bides o' some o' ye. Twa craft a sailing without hand to guide them, in sic a place as this, whar' eyesight is na guid enough to show the dangers, bodes evil to a' that luik thereon. Hoot! she's na yearling the tither! Luik, mon! luik! she's a gallant boat, and a gr'at;" he paused, raised his pack from the ground, and first giving one searching look at the objects of his suspicions, he nodded with great sagacity to the listeners, and continued, as he moved slowly towards the interior of the country, "I should na wonder if she carried King George's commission aboot her; 'weel 'weel, I wull journey upward to the town, and ha' a crack wi' the guid mon, for they craft have a suspeecious aspect, and the sma' bit thing wu'ld nab a mon quite easy and the big ane wu'ld hold us a' and no feel we war' in her."

This sagacious warning caused a general movement in the party, for the intelligence of a hot press was among the rumours of the times. The husbandmen collected their implements of labour, and retired homewards; and though many a curious eye was bent on the movements of the vessels from the distant hills, but very few of those not immediately interested in the mysterious visiters, ventured to approach the little rocky cliffs that lined the bay.

The vessel that occasioned these cautious movements, was a gallant ship, whose huge hull, lofty masts, and square yards, loomed in the evening's haze, above the sea, like a distant mountain rising from the deep. She carried but little sail, and though she warily avoided the near approach to the land that the schooner had attempted, the similarity of their movements was sufficiently apparent to warrant the conjecture that they were employed on the same duty. The frigate, for the ship belonged to this class of vessels, floated across the entrance of the little bay, majestically in the tide, with barely enough motion through the water to govern her movements, until she arrived opposite to the place where her consort lay, when she hove up heavily into the wind, squared the enormous yards on her mainmast, and attempted, in counteracting the power of her sails by each other, to remain stationary; but the light air that had at no time swelled her heavy canvass to the utmost, began to fail, and the long waves that rolled in from the ocean, ceased to be ruffled with the breeze from the land. The currents, and the billows, were fast sweeping the frigate towards one of the points of the estuary, where the black heads of the rocks could be seen running far into the sea, and, in their turn, the mariners of the ship dropped an anchor to the bottom, and drew her sails in festoons to the yards. As the vessel swung round to the tide, a heavy ensign was raised to her peak, and a current of air opening, for a moment, its folds, the white field, and red cross, that distinguish the flag of England, were displayed to view. So much, even the wary drover had loitered at a distance to behold; but when a boat was launched from either vessel, he quickened his steps, observing to his wondering and amused companions, that "they craft were a' thegither, mair bonny to luik on than to abide wi'."

A numerous crew manned the barge that was lowered from the frigate, which, after receiving an officer, with an attendant youth, left the ship, and moved with a measured stroke of its oars, directly towards the head of the bay. As it passed at a short distance from the schooner, a light whale-boat, pulled by four athletic men, shot from her side, and rather dancing over, than cutting through the waves, crossed her course with a wonderful velocity. As the boats approached each other, the men, in obedience to signals from their officers, suspended their efforts, and for a few minutes they floated at rest, during which time, there was the following dialogue:

"Is the old man mad!" exclaimed the young officer in the whale-boat, when his men had ceased rowing; "does he think that the bottom of the Ariel is made of iron, and that a rock can't knock a hole in it! or does he think she is mann'd with alligators, who can't be drown'd!"

A languid smile played for a moment round the handsome features of the young man, who was rather reclining than sitting in the stern-sheets of the barge, as he replied,

"He knows your prudence too well, Captain Barnstable, to fear either the wreck of your vessel, or the drowning of her crew. How near the bottom does your keel lie?"

"I am afraid to sound," returned Barnstable. "I have never the heart to touch a lead-line when I see the rocks coming up to breathe like so many porpoises."

"You are afloat!" exclaimed the other, with a vehemence that denoted an abundance of latent fire.

"Afloat!" echoed his friend; "ay! the little Ariel would float in air!" As he spoke, he rose in the boat, and lifting his leathern sea-cap from his head, stroked back the thick clusters of black locks which shadowed his sun-burnt countenance, while he viewed his little vessel with the complacency of a seaman who was proud of her qualities. "But it's close work, Mr. Griffith, when a man rides to a single anchor in a place like this, and at such a nightfall. What are the orders?"

"I shall pull into the surf and let go a grapnel; you will take Mr. Merry into your whale-boat, and try to drive her through the breakers on the beach."

"Beach!" retorted Barnstable; "do you call a perpendicular rock of a hundred feet in height, a beach!"

"We shall not dispute about terms," said Griffith, smiling; "but you must manage to get on the shore; we have seen the signal from the land, and know that the pilot, whom we have so long expected, is ready to come off."

Barnstable shook his head with a grave air, as he muttered to himself, "this is droll navigation; first we run into an unfrequented bay that is full of rocks, and sand-spits, and shoals, and then we get off our pilot. But how am I to know him?"

"Merry will give you the pass-word, and tell you where to look for him. I would land myself, but my orders forbid it. If you meet with difficulties, show three oar-blades in a row, and I will pull in to your assistance. Three oars on end, and a pistol, will bring the fire of my muskets, and the signal repeated from the barge will draw a shot from the ship."

"I thank you, I thank you," said Barnstable, carelessly; "I believe I can fight my own battles against all the enemies we are likely to fall in with on this coast. But the old man is surely mad. I would—"

"You would obey his orders if he were here, and you will now please to obey mine," said Griffith, in a tone that the friendly expression of his eye contradicted. "Pull in, and keep a look out for a small man in a drab pea-jacket; Merry will give you the word; if he answer it bring him off to the barge."

The young men now nodded familiarly and kindly to each other, and the boy, who was called Mr. Merry, having changed his place from the barge to the whale-boat, Barnstable threw himself into his seat, and making a signal with his hand, his men again bent to their oars. The light vessel shot away from her companion, and dashed in boldly towards the rocks; after skirting the shore for some distance in quest of a favourable place, she was suddenly turned, and, dashing over the broken waves, was run upon a spot where a landing could be effected in safety.

In the mean time the barge followed these movements, at some distance, with a more measured progress, and when the whale-boat was observed to be drawn up along side of a rock, the promised grapnel was cast into the water, and her crew deliberately proceeded to get their firearms in a state for immediate service. Every thing appeared to be done in obedience to strict orders that must have been previously communicated; for the young man, who has been introduced to the reader by the name of Griffith, seldom spoke, and then only in the pithy expressions that are apt to fall from those who are sure of obedience. When the boat had brought up to her grapnel, he sunk back at his length on the cushioned seats of the barge, and drawing his hat over his eyes in a listless manner, he continued for many minutes apparently absorbed in thoughts altogether foreign to his present situation. Occasionally he rose, and would first bend his looks in quest of his companions on the shore, and then, turning his expressive eyes towards the ocean, the abstracted and vacant air that so often usurped the place of animation and intelligence in his countenance, would give place to the anxious and intelligent look of a seaman gifted with an experience beyond his years. His weather-beaten and hardy crew, having made their dispositions for of-fence, sat in profound silence, with their hands thrust into the bosoms of their jackets, but with their eyes earnestly regarding every cloud that was gathering in the threatening atmosphere, and exchanging looks of deep care, whenever the boat rose higher than usual on one of those long, heavy ground-swells that were heaving in from the ocean with increasing rapidity and magnitude.

Chapter II.

— "A horseman's coat shall hide
Thy taper shape and comeliness of side;
And with a bolder stride and looser air,
Mingled with men, a man thou must appear."
Prior, "Henry and Emma," ll. 437-438, 441-442.

WHEN the whale-boat obtained the position we have described, the young lieutenant, who, in consequence of commanding a schooner, was usually addressed by the title of captain, stepped on the rocks, followed by the youthful midshipman, who had quitted the barge, to aid in the hazardous duty of their expedition.

"This is, at best, but a Jacob's ladder we have to climb," said Barnstable, casting his eyes upwards at the difficult ascent, "and it's by no means certain that we shall be well received, when we get up, even though we should reach the top."

"We are under the guns of the frigate," returned the boy; "and you remember, sir, three oar blades and a pistol, repeated from the barge, will draw her fire."

"Yes, on our own heads. Boy, never be so foolish as to trust a long shot. It makes a great smoke and some noise, but it's a terrible uncertain manner of throwing old iron about. In such a business as this, I would sooner trust Tom Coffin and his harpoon to back me, than the best broadside that ever rattled out of the three decks of a ninety-gun ship. Come, gather your limbs together, and try if you can walk on terra firma, Master Coffin."

The seaman who was addressed by this dire appellation, arose slowly from the place where he was stationed as cockswain of the boat, and seemed to ascend high in air by the gradual evolution of numberless folds in his body. When erect, he stood nearly six feet and as many inches in his shoes, though, when elevated in his most perpendicular attitude, there was a forward inclination about his head and shoulders, that appeared to be the consequence of habitual confinement in limited lodgings. His whole frame was destitute of the rounded outlines of a well-formed man, though his enormous hands furnished a display of bones and sinews which gave indication of gigantic strength. On his head he wore a little, low, brown hat of wool, with an arched top, that threw an expression of peculiar solemnity and hardness over his harsh visage, the sharp prominent features of which were completely encircled by a set of black whiskers, that began to be grizzled a little with age. One of his hands grasped, with a sort of instinct, the staff of a bright harpoon, the lower end of which he placed firmly on the rock, as, in obedience to the order of his commander, he left the place, where, considering his vast dimentions, he had been established in an incredibly small space.

As soon as Captain Barnstable received this addition to his strength, he gave a few precautionary orders to the men in the boat, and proceeded to the difficult task of ascending the rocks. Notwithstanding the great daring and personal agility of Barnstable, he would have been completely baffled in this attempt, but for the assistance he occasionally received from his cockswain, whose prodigious strength, and great length of limbs, enabled him to make exertions which it would have been useless for most men to attempt. When within a few feet of the summit, they availed themselves of a projecting rock, to pause for consultation and breath; both of which seemed necessary for their further movements.

"This will be but a bad place for a retreat, if we should happen to fall in with enemies," said Barnstable. "Where are we to look for this pilot, Mr. Merry, or how are we to know him; and what certainty have you that he will not betray us?"

"The question you are to put to him is written on this bit of paper," returned the boy, as he handed the other the word of recognition; "we made the signal on the point of the rock at yon headland, but as he must have seen our boat, he will follow us to this place. As to his betraying us, he seems to have the confidence of Captain Munson, who has kept a bright look-out for him ever since we made the land."

"Ay," muttered the lieutenant, "and I shall have a bright look-out kept on him, now we are *on* the land. I like not this business of hugging the shore so closely, nor have I much faith in any traitor. What think you of it, Master Coffin?"

The hardy old seaman, thus addressed, turned his grave visage on his commander, and replied with a becoming gravity—

"Give me a plenty of sea-room, and good canvass, where there is no 'casion for pilots at all, sir. For my part, I was born on board a chebacco-man, and never could see the use of more land than now and then a small island, to raise a few vegetables, and to dry your fish—I'm sure the sight of it always makes me feel oncomfortable, unless we have the wind dead off shore."

"Ah! Tom, you are a sensible fellow," said Barnstable, with an air half comic, half serious. "But we must be moving; the sun is just touching those clouds to sea-ward, and God keep us from riding out this night at anchor in such a place as this."

Laying his hand on a projection of the rock above him, Barnstable swung himself forward, and following this movement with a desperate leap or two, he stood at once on the brow of the cliff. His cockswain very deliberately raised the midshipman after his officer, and proceeding with more caution, but less exertion, he soon placed himself by his side.

When they reached the level land, that lay above the cliffs, and began to inquire, with curious and wary eyes, into the surrounding scenery, the adventurers discovered a cultivated country, divided, in the usual manner, by hedges and walls. Only one habitation for man, however, and that a small dilapidated cottage, stood within a mile of them, most of the dwellings being placed as far as convenience would permit, from the fogs and damps of the ocean.

"Here seems to be neither any thing to apprehend, nor the object of our search," said Barnstable, when he had taken the whole view in his survey; "I fear we have landed to no purpose, Mr. Merry. What say you, long Tom; see you what we want?"

"I see no pilot, sir," returned the cockswain; "but it's an ill wind that blows luck to nobody; there is a mouthful of fresh meat stowed away under that row of bushes, that would make a double ration to all hands in the Ariel."

The midshipman laughed, as he pointed out to Barnstable the object of the cockswain's solicitude, which proved to be a fat ox, quietly ruminating under a hedge near them.

"There's many a hungry fellow aboard of us," said the boy

merrily, "who would be glad to second long Tom's motion, if the time and business would permit us to slay the animal."

"It is but a lubber's blow, Mr. Merry," returned the cockswain, without a muscle of his hard face yielding, as he struck the end of his harpoon violently against the earth, and then made a motion towards poising the weapon; "let Captain Barnstable but say the word, and I'll drive the iron through him to the quick; I've sent it to the seizing in many a whale, that hadn't a jacket of such blubber as that fellow wears."

"Pshaw! you are not on a whaling voyage, where every thing that offers is game," said Barnstable, turning himself pettishly away from the beast, as if he distrusted his own forbearance; "but stand fast! I see some one approaching behind the hedge. Look to your arms, Mr. Merry — the first thing we hear may be a shot."

"Not from that cruiser," cried the thoughtless lad; "he is a younker, like myself, and would hardly dare run down upon such a formidable force as we muster."

"You say true, boy," returned Barnstable, relinquishing the grasp he held on his pistol. "He comes on with caution, as if afraid. He is small, and is in drab, though I should hardly call it a pea-jacket — and yet he may be our man. Stand you both here, while I go and hail him."

As Barnstable walked rapidly towards the hedge, that in part concealed the stranger, the latter stopped suddenly, and seemed to be in doubt whether to advance or to retreat. Before he had decided on either, the active sailor was within a few feet of him.

"Pray, sir," said Barnstable, "what water have we in this bay?"

The slight form of the stranger started, with an extraordinary emotion, at this question, and he shrunk aside involuntarily, as if to conceal his features, before he answered, in a voice that was barely audible —

"I should think it would be the water of the German ocean."

"Indeed! you must have passed no small part of your short life in the study of geography, to be so well informed," returned the lieutenant; "perhaps, sir, your cunning is also equal to telling me how long we shall sojourn together, if I make you a prisoner, in order to enjoy the benefit of your wit?"

To this alarming intimation, the youth who was addressed made no reply; but, as he averted his face, and concealed it with both his hands, the offended seaman, believing that a salutary impression had been made upon the fears of his auditor, was about to proceed with his interrogatories. The singular agitation of the stranger's frame, however, caused the lieutenant to continue silent a few moments longer, when, to his utter amazement, he discovered that what he had mistaken for alarm, was produced by an endeavour, on the part of the youth, to suppress a violent fit of laughter.

"Now, by all the whales in the sea," cried Barnstable, "but you are merry out of season, young gentleman. It's quite bad enough to be ordered to anchor in such a bay as this, with a storm brewing before my eyes, without landing to be laughed at, by a stripling who has not strength to carry a beard if he had one, when I ought to be getting an offing for the safety of both body and soul. But I'll know more of you and your jokes, if I take you into my own mess, and am giggled out of my sleep for the rest of the cruise."

As the commander of the schooner concluded, he approached the stranger, with an air of offering some violence, but the other shrunk back from his extended arm, and exclaimed, with a voice in which real terror had gotten the better of mirth—

"Barnstable! dear Barnstable! would you harm me?"

The sailor recoiled several feet, at this unexpected appeal, and rubbing his eyes, he threw the cap from his head, before he cried—

"What do I hear! and what do I see! There lies the Ariel—and yonder is the frigate. Can this be Katherine Plowden!"

His doubts, if any doubts remained, were soon removed, for the stranger sunk on the bank at her side, in an attitude in which female bashfulness was beautifully contrasted to her attire, and gave vent to her mirth in an uncontrollable burst of merriment.

From that moment, all thought of his duty, and the pilot, or even of the Ariel, appeared to be banished from the mind of the seaman, who sprang to her side, and joined in her mirth, though he hardly knew why or wherefore.

When the diverted girl had in some degree recovered her

composure, she turned to her companion, who had sat good-naturedly by her side, content to be laughed at, and said —

"But this is not only silly, but cruel to others. I owe you an explanation of my unexpected appearance, and perhaps, also, of my extraordinary attire."

"I can anticipate every thing," cried Barnstable; "you heard that we were on the coast, and have flown to redeem the promises you made me in America. But I ask no more; the chaplain of the frigate —"

"May preach as usual, and to as little purpose," interrupted the disguised female; "but no nuptial benediction shall be pronounced over me, until I have effected the object of this hazardous experiment. You are not usually selfish, Barnstable; would you have me forgetful of the happiness of others?"

"Of whom do you speak?"

"My poor, my devoted cousin. I heard that two vessels, answering the description of the frigate and the Ariel, were seen hovering on the coast, and I determined at once to have a communication with you. I have followed your movements for a week, in this dress, but have been unsuccessful till now. To-day I observed you to approach nearer to the shore than usual, and happily, by being adventurous, I have been successful."

"Ay, God knows we are near enough to the land! But does Captain Munson know of your wish to get on board his ship?"

"Certainly not — none know of it but yourself. I thought that if Griffith and you could learn our situation, you might be tempted to hazard a little to redeem us from our thraldom. In this paper I have prepared such an account as will, I trust, excite all your chivalry, and by which you may govern your movements."

"Our movements!" interrupted Barnstable, "you will pilot us in person."

"Then there's two of them," said a hoarse voice near them.

The alarmed female shrieked as she recovered her feet, but she still adhered, with instinctive dependence, to the side of her lover. Barnstable, who recognised the tones of his cockswain, bent an angry brow on the sober visage that was peering at them above the hedge, and demanded the meaning of the interruption.

"Seeing you were hull-down, sir, and not knowing but the

chase might lead you ashore, Mr. Merry thought it best to have a look-out kept. I told him that you were overhauling the mail bags of the messenger for the news, but as he was an officer, sir, and I nothing but a common hand, I did as he ordered."

"Return, sir, where I commanded you to remain," said Barnstable, "and desire Mr. Merry to wait my pleasure."

The cockswain gave the usual reply of an obedient seaman, but before he left the hedge, he stretched out one of his brawny arms towards the ocean, and said, in tones of solemnity suited to his apprehensions and character—

"I showed you how to knot a reef-point, and pass a gasket, Captain Barnstable, nor do I believe you could even take two half hitches when you first came aboard of the Spalmacitty. These be things that a man is soon expart in, but it takes the time of his nat'ral life to larn to know the weather. There be streaked wind-galls in the offing, that speak as plainly, to all that see them, and know God's language in the clouds, as ever you spoke through a trumpet, to shorten sail; besides, sir, don't you hear the sea moaning, as if it knew the hour was at hand when it was to wake up from its sleep!"

"Ay, Tom," returned his officer, walking to the edge of the cliffs, and throwing a seaman's glance at the gloomy ocean, "'tis a threatening night indeed: but this pilot must be had—and—"

"Is that the man?" interrupted the cockswain, pointing towards a man who was standing not far from them, an attentive observer of their proceedings, at the same time that he was narrowly watched himself by the young midshipman. "God send that he knows his trade well, for the bottom of a ship will need eyes to find its road out of this wild anchorage."

"That must indeed be the man!" exclaimed Barnstable, at once recalled to his duty. He then held a short dialogue with his female companion, whom he left concealed by the hedge, and proceeded to address the stranger. When near enough to be heard, the commander of the schooner demanded—

"What water have you in this bay?"

The stranger, who seemed to expect this question, answered, without the least hesitation—

"Enough to take all out in safety, who have entered with confidence."

"You are the man I seek," cried Barnstable; "are you ready to go off?"

"Both ready and willing," returned the pilot, "and there is need of haste. I would give the best hundred guineas that ever were coined for two hours more use of that sun which has left us, or for even half the time of this fading twilight."

"Think you our situation so bad?" said the lieutenant. "Follow this gentleman to the boat then; I will join you by the time you can descend the cliffs. I believe I can prevail on another hand to go off with us."

"Time is more precious now than any number of hands," said the pilot, throwing a glance of impatience from under his lowering brows, "and the consequences of delay must be visited on those who occasion it."

"And, sir, I will meet the consequences with those who have a right to inquire into my conduct," said Barnstable, haughtily.

With this warning and retort, they separated; the young officer retracing his steps impatiently towards his mistress, muttering his indignation in suppressed execrations, and the pilot, drawing the leathern belt of his pea-jacket mechanically around his body, as he followed the midshipman and cockswain to their boat, in moody silence.

Barnstable found the disguised female who had announced herself as Katherine Plowden, awaiting his return, with intense anxiety depicted on every feature of her intelligent countenance. As he felt all the responsibility of his situation, notwithstanding his cool reply to the pilot, the young man hastily drew an arm of the apparent boy, forgetful of her disguise, through his own, and led her forward.

"Come, Katherine," he said, "the time urges to be prompt."

"What pressing necessity is there for immediate departure?" she inquired, checking his movements by withdrawing herself from his side.

"You heard the ominous prognostic of my cockswain, on the weather, and I am forced to add my own testimony to his opinion. 'Tis a crazy night that threatens us, though I cannot repent of coming into the bay, since it has led to this interview."

"God forbid that we should either of us have cause to repent of it," said Katherine, the paleness of anxiety chasing away the rich bloom that had mantled the animated face of the brunette. "But you have the paper—follow its directions, and come to our rescue; you will find us willing captives, if Griffith and yourself are our conquerors."

"What mean you, Katherine!" exclaimed her lover; "you at least are now in safety—'twould be madness to tempt your fate again. My vessel can and shall protect you, until your cousin is redeemed; and then, remember, I have a claim on you for life."

"And how would you dispose of me in the interval," said the young maiden, retreating slowly from his advances.

"In the Ariel—by heaven, you shall be her commander; I will bear that rank only in name."

"I thank you, thank you, Barnstable, but distrust my abilities to fill such a station," she said, laughing, though the colour that again crossed her youthful features was like the glow of a summer's sunset, and even her mirthful eyes seemed to reflect their tints. "Do not mistake me, saucy-one. If I have done more than my sex will warrant, remember it was through a holy motive, and if I have more than a woman's enterprise, it must be—"

"To lift you above the weakness of your sex," he cried, "and to enable you to show your noble confidence in me."

"To fit me for, and to keep me worthy of being one day your wife." As she uttered these words, she turned, and disappeared, with a rapidity that eluded his attempt to detain her, behind an angle of the hedge, that was near them. For a moment, Barnstable remained motionless through surprise, and when he sprang forward in pursuit, he was able only to catch a glimpse of her light form, in the gloom of the evening, as she again vanished in a little thicket at some distance.

Barnstable was about to pursue, when the air lighted with a sudden flash, and the bellowing report of a cannon rolled along the cliffs, and was echoed among the hills far inland.

"Ay, grumble away, old dotard!" the disappointed young sailor muttered to himself, while he reluctantly obeyed the signal; "you are in as a great a hurry to get out of your danger as you were to run into it."

The quick reports of three muskets from the barge beneath

where he stood, urged him to quicken his pace, and as he threw himself carelessly down the rugged and dangerous passes of the cliffs, his experienced eye beheld the well-known lights displayed from the frigate, which commanded the recall of all her boats.

Chapter III.

"In such a time as this it is not meet
That every nice offence should bear its comment."
Julius Caesar, IV.iii.7–8.

T HE CLIFFS threw their dark shadows wide on the waters, and the gloom of the evening had so far advanced, as to conceal the discontent that brooded over the ordinarily open brow of Barnstable, as he sprang from the rocks into the boat, and took his seat by the side of the silent pilot.

"Shove off," cried the lieutenant, in tones that his men knew must be obeyed. "A seaman's curse light on the folly that exposes planks and lives to such navigation, and all to burn some old timber-man, or catch a Norway trader asleep! give way, men, give way."

Notwithstanding the heavy and dangerous surf that was beginning to tumble in upon the rocks, in an alarming manner, the startled seamen succeeded in urging their light boat over the waves, and in a few seconds were without the point where danger was most to be apprehended. Barnstable had seemingly disregarded the breakers as they passed, but sat sternly eyeing the foam that rolled by them in successive surges, until the boat rose regularly on the long seas, when he turned his looks around the bay, in quest of the barge.

"Ay, Griffith has tired of rocking in his pillowed cradle," he muttered, "and will give us a pull to the frigate, when we ought to be getting the schooner out of this hard-featured landscape. This is just a place as one of your sighing lovers would doat on: a little land, a little water, and a good deal of rock. Damme, long Tom, but I am more than half of your mind, that an island, now and then, is all the terra firma that a seaman needs."

"It's reason and philosophy, sir," returned the sedate coxswain; "and what land there is, should always be a soft mud, or a sandy ooze, in order that an anchor might hold, and to make soundings sartin. I have lost many a deep-sea, besides hand-leads by the dozens, on rocky bottoms; but give me the roadsted where a lead comes up light, and an anchor heavy. There's a boat pulling athwart our fore-foot, Captain Barnstable; shall I run her aboard, or give her a birth, sir?"

"'Tis the barge!" cried the officer; "Ned has not deserted me after all!"

A loud hail from the approaching boat confirmed this opinion, and, in a few seconds, the barge and whale-boat were again rolling by each other's side. Griffith was no longer reclining on the cushions of his seats, but spoke earnestly, and with a slight tone of reproach in his manner.

"Why have you wasted so many precious moments, when every minute threatens us with new dangers? I was obeying the signal, but I heard your oars, and pulled back, to take out the pilot. Have you been successful?"

"There he is, and if he finds his way out, through the shoals, he will earn a right to his name. This bids fair to be a night when a man will need a spy-glass to find the moon. But when you hear what I have seen on those rascally cliffs, you will be more ready to excuse my delay, Mr. Griffith."

"You have seen the true man, I trust, or we incur this hazard to an evil purpose."

"Ay, I have seen him that is a true man, and him that is not," replied Barnstable, bitterly; "you have the boy with you, Griffith—ask him what his young eyes have seen."

"Shall I!" cried the young midshipman, laughing; "then I have seen a little clipper, in disguise, outsail an old man-of-war's-man in a hard chase, and I have seen a straggling rover in long-togs as much like my cousin—"

"Peace, gabbler!" exclaimed Barnstable, in a voice of thunder; "would you detain the boats with your silly nonsense, at a time like this? Away into the barge, sir, and if you find him willing to hear, tell Mr. Griffith what your foolish conjectures amount to, at your leisure."

The boy stepped lightly from the whale-boat to the barge, whither the pilot had already preceded him, and as he sunk, with a mortified air, by the side of Griffith, he said, in a low voice—

"And that won't be long, I know, if Mr. Griffith thinks and feels on the coast of England as he thought and felt at home."

A silent pressure of his hand, was the only reply that the young lieutenant made, before he paid the parting compliments to Barnstable, and directed his men to pull for their ship.

The boats were separating, and the plash of the oars was already heard, when the voice of the pilot was for the first time raised in earnest.

"Hold!" he cried; "hold water, I bid ye!"

The men ceased their efforts, at the commanding tones of his voice, and turning towards the whale-boat, he continued—

"You will get your schooner under-way immediately, Captain Barnstable, and sweep into the offing, with as little delay as possible. Keep the ship well open from the northern headland, and as you pass us, come within hail."

"This is a clean chart and plain sailing, Mr. Pilot," returned Barnstable; "but who is to justify my moving without orders, to Captain Munson? I have it in black and white, to run the Ariel into this feather-bed sort of a place, and I must at least have it by signal or word of mouth from my betters, before my cut-water curls another wave. The road may be as hard to find going out as it was coming in—and then I had daylight, as well as your written directions to steer by."

"Would you lie there to perish on such a night!" said the pilot, sternly. "Two hours hence, this heavy swell will break where your vessel now rides so quietly."

"There we think exactly alike; but if I get drowned now, I am drowned according to orders; whereas, if I knock a plank out of the schooner's bottom, by following your directions, 'twill be a hole to let in mutiny, as well as sea-water. How do I know but the old man wants another pilot or two?"

"That's philosophy," muttered the cockswain of the whale-boat, in a voice that was audible: "but it's a hard strain on a man's conscience to hold on in such an anchorage."

"Then keep your anchor down, and follow it to the bottom," said the pilot to himself; "it's worse to contend with a fool than a gale of wind; but if—"

"No, no, sir—no fool neither," interrupted Griffith. "Barnstable does not deserve that epithet, though he certainly carries the point of duty to the extreme. Heave up at once, Mr. Barnstable, and get out of this bay as fast as possible."

"Ah! you don't give the order with half the pleasure with which I shall execute it; pull away, boys — the Ariel shall never lay her bones in such a hard bed, if I can help it."

As the commander of the schooner uttered these words with a cheering voice, his men spontaneously shouted, and the whale-boat darted away from her companion, and was soon lost in the gloomy shadows cast from the cliffs.

In the mean time, the oarsmen of the barge were not idle, but by strenuous efforts they forced the heavy boat rapidly through the water, and in a few minutes she ran alongside of the frigate. During this period the pilot, in a voice which had lost all the startling fierceness and authority it had manifested in his short dialogue with Barnstable, requested Griffith to repeat to him, slowly, the names of the officers that belonged to his ship. When the young lieutenant had complied with this request, he observed to his companion —

"All good men and true, Mr. Pilot; and though this business in which you are just now engaged may be hazardous to an Englishman, there are none with us who will betray you. We need your services, and as we expect good faith from you, so shall we offer it to you in exchange."

"And how know you that I need its exercise?" asked the pilot, in a manner that denoted a cold indifference to the subject.

"Why, though you talk pretty good English, for a native," returned Griffith, "yet you have a small bur-r-r in your mouth that would prick the tongue of a man who was born on the other side of the Atlantic."

"It is but of little moment where a man is born, or how he speaks," returned the pilot, coldly, "so that he does his duty bravely, and in good faith."

It was perhaps fortunate for the harmony of this dialogue, that the gloom, which had now increased to positive darkness, completely concealed the look of scornful irony that crossed the handsome features of the young sailor, as he replied —

"True, true, so that he does his duty, as you say, in good faith. But, as Barnstable observed, you must know your road well to travel among these shoals on such a night as this. Know you what water we draw?"

"'Tis a frigate's draught, and I shall endeavour to keep you in four fathoms; less than that would be dangerous."

"She's a sweet boat!" said Griffith; "and minds her helm as a marine watches the eye of his sergeant at a drill; but you must give her room in stays, for she fore-reaches, as if she would put out the wind's eye."

The pilot attended, with a practised ear, to this description of the qualities of the ship that he was about to attempt extricating from an extremely dangerous situation. Not a syllable was lost on him; and when Griffith had ended, he remarked, with the singular coldness that pervaded his manner—

"That is both a good and a bad quality in a narrow channel. I fear it will be the latter, to-night, when we shall require to have the ship in leading strings."

"I suppose we must feel our way with the lead?" said Griffith.

"We shall need both eyes and leads," returned the pilot, recurring insensibly to his soliloquizing tone of voice. "I have been both in and out in darker nights than this, though never with a heavier draught than a half-two."

"Then, by heaven, you are not fit to handle that ship, among these rocks and breakers!" exclaimed Griffith; "your men of a light draught never know their water; 'tis the deep keel only, that finds a channel—pilot! pilot! beware how you trifle with us ignorantly; for 'tis a dangerous experiment to play at hazards with an enemy."

"Young man, you know not what you threaten, nor whom," said the pilot, sternly, though his quiet manner still remained undisturbed; "you forget that you have a superior here, and that I have none."

"That shall be as you discharge your duty," cried Griffith; "for if—"

"Peace," interrupted the pilot, "we approach the ship; let us enter in harmony."

He threw himself back on the cushions, when he had said this, and Griffith, though filled with the apprehensions of suffering, either by great ignorance, or treachery, on the part of his companion, smothered his feelings so far as to be silent, and they ascended the side of the vessel in apparent cordiality.

The frigate was already riding on lengthened seas, that rolled in from the ocean, at each successive moment, with increasing violence, though her topsails still hung supinely from her yards; the air, which continued to breathe, occasionally, from the land, being unable to shake the heavy canvass of which they were composed.

The only sounds that were audible, when Griffith and the pilot had ascended to the gangway of the frigate, were produced by the sullen dashing of the sea against the massive bows of the ship, and the shrill whistle of the boatswain's mate, as he recalled the side-boys, who were placed on either side of the gangway, to do honour to the entrance of the first lieutenant and his companion.

But though such a profound silence reigned among the hundreds who inhabited the huge fabric, the light produced by a dozen battle lanterns, that were arranged in different parts of the decks, served not only to exhibit, faintly, the persons of the crew, but the mingled feeling of curiosity and care that dwelt on most of their countenances.

Large groups of men were collected in the gangways, around the mainmast, and on the booms of the vessel, whose faces were distinctly visible, while numerous figures, lying along the lower yards, or bending out of the tops, might be dimly traced in the back ground, all of whom expressed, by their attitudes, the interest they took in the arrival of the boat.

Though such crowds were collected in other parts of the vessel, the quarter deck was occupied only by the officers, who were disposed according to their several ranks, and were equally silent and attentive as the remainder of the crew. In front stood a small collection of young men, who, by their similarity of dress, were the equals and companions of Griffith, though his juniors in rank. On the opposite side of the vessel was a larger assemblage of youths, who claimed Mr. Merry as their fellow. Around the capstern, three or four figures were standing, one of whom wore a coat of blue, with the scarlet facings of a soldier, and another the black vestments of the ship's chaplain. Behind these, and nearer the passage to the cabin, from which he had just ascended, stood the tall, erect form of the commander of the vessel.

After a brief salutation between Griffith and the junior officers, the former advanced, followed slowly by the pilot, to the place where he was expected by his veteran commander. The young man removed his hat entirely, as he bowed with a little more than his usual ceremony, and said—

"We have succeeded, sir, though not without more difficulty and delay than were anticipated."

"But you have not brought off the pilot," said the captain, "and without him, all our risk and trouble have been in vain."

"He is here," said Griffith, stepping aside, and extending his arm towards the man that stood behind him, wrapped to the chin in his coarse pea-jacket, and with his face shadowed by the falling rims of a large hat, that had seen much and hard service.

"This!" exclaimed the captain; "then there is a sad mistake—this is not the man I would have seen, nor can another supply his place."

"I know not whom you expected, Captain Munson," said the stranger, in a low, quiet voice; "but if you have not forgotten the day when a very different flag from that emblem of tyranny that now hangs over yon tafferel was first spread to the wind, you may remember the hand that raised it."

"Bring here the light!" exclaimed the commander, hastily.

When the lantern was extended towards the pilot, and the glare fell strong on his features, Captain Munson started, as he beheld the calm blue eye that met his gaze, and the composed, but pallid countenance of the other. Involuntarily raising his hat, and baring his silver locks, the veteran cried—

"It is he! though so changed—"

"That his enemies did not know him," interrupted the pilot, quickly; then touching the other by the arm as he led him aside, he continued, in a lower tone, "neither must his friends, until the proper hour shall arrive."

Griffith had fallen back, to answer the eager questions of his messmates, and no part of this short dialogue was overheard by the officers, though it was soon perceived that their commander had discovered his error, and was satisfied that the proper man had been brought on board his vessel. For many minutes the two continued to pace a part of the quarter-deck, by themselves, engaged in deep and earnest discourse.

As Griffith had but little to communicate, the curiosity of his listeners was soon appeased, and all eyes were directed towards that mysterious guide, who was to conduct them from a situation already surrounded by perils, which each moment not only magnified in appearance, but increased in reality.

Chapter IV.

— "behold the threaden sails,
Borne with the invisible and creeping winds,
Draw the huge bottoms through the furrowed sea,
Breasting the lofty surge."

Henry V, III. i.10–13.

IT HAS BEEN already explained to the reader, that there were threatening symptoms in the appearance of the weather to create serious forebodings of evil in the breast of a seaman. When removed from the shadows of the cliffs, the night was not so dark but objects could be discerned at some little distance, and in the eastern horizon there was a streak of fearful light impending over the gloomy waters, in which the swelling outline formed by the rising waves, was becoming each moment more distinct, and consequently more alarming. Several dark clouds overhung the vessel, whose towering masts apparently propped the black vapour, while a few stars were seen twinkling, with a sickly flame, in the streak of clear sky that skirted the ocean. Still, light currents of air, occasionally, swept across the bay, bringing with them the fresh odour from the shore, but their flitting irregularity too surely foretold them to be the expiring breath of the land breeze. The roaring of the surf, as it rolled on the margin of the bay, produced a dull, monotonous sound, that was only interrupted, at times, by a hollow bellowing, as a larger wave than usual broke violently against some cavity in the rocks. Every thing, in short, united to render the scene gloomy and portentous, without creating instant terror, for the ship rose easily on the long billows, without even straightening the heavy cable that held her to her anchor.

The higher officers were collected around the capstern, engaged in earnest discourse about their situation and prospects, while some of the oldest and most favoured seamen would extend their short walk to the hallowed precincts of the quarter-deck, to catch, with greedy ears, the opinions that fell from their superiors. Numberless were the uneasy glances that were thrown from both officers and men at their commander and the pilot, who still continued their secret communion in a distant part of the vessel. Once, an ungovernable curiosity, or the heedlessness of his years, led one of the youthful midshipmen near them, but a stern rebuke from his captain sent the boy, abashed and cowering, to hide his mortification among his fellows. This reprimand was received by the elder officers as an intimation that the consultation which they beheld, was to be strictly inviolate; and, though it by no means suppressed the repeated expressions of their impatience, it effectually prevented an interruption to the communications, which all, however, thought were unreasonably protracted for the occasion.

"This is no time to be talking over bearings and distances," observed the officer next in rank to Griffith. "But we should call the hands up, and try to kedge her off while the sea will suffer a boat to live."

"'Twould be a tedious and bootless job to attempt warping a ship for miles against a head-beating sea," returned the first lieutenant; "but the land-breeze yet flutters aloft, and if our light sails would draw, with the aid of this ebb tide we might be able to shove her from the shore."

"Hail the tops, Griffith," said the other, "and ask if they feel the air above; 'twill be a hint at least to set the old man and that lubberly pilot in motion."

Griffith laughed, as he complied with the request, and when he received the customary reply to his call, he demanded, in a loud voice —

"Which way have you the wind, aloft?"

"We feel a light cat's-paw, now and then, from the land, sir," returned the sturdy captain of the top; "but our topsail hangs in the clewlines, sir, without winking."

Captain Munson and his companion suspended their discourse, while this question and answer were exchanged, and then resumed their dialogue as earnestly as if it had received no interruption.

"If it did wink, the hint would be lost on our betters," said the officer of the marines, whose ignorance of seamanship added greatly to his perception of the danger, but who, from pure idleness, made more jokes than any other man in the ship.

"That pilot would not receive a delicate intimation through his ears, Mr. Griffith; suppose you try him by the nose."

"Faith, there was a flash of gunpowder between us in the barge," returned the first lieutenant, "and he does not seem a man to stomach such hints as you advise. Although he looks so meek and quiet, I doubt whether he has paid much attention to the book of Job."

"Why should he!" exclaimed the chaplain, whose apprehensions at least equalled those of the marine, and with a much more disheartening effect; "I'm sure it would have been a great waste of time; there are so many charts of the coast, and books on the navigation of these seas, for him to study, that I sincerely hope he has been much better employed."

A loud laugh was created at this speech, among the listeners, and it apparently produced the effect that was so long anxiously desired, by putting an end to the mysterious conference between their captain and the pilot. As the former came forward towards his expecting crew, he said, in the composed, steady manner, that formed the principal trait in his character—

"Get the anchor, Mr. Griffith, and make sail on the ship; the hour has arrived when we must be moving."

The cheerful "ay! ay! sir!" of the young lieutenant was hardly uttered, before the cries of half a dozen midshipmen were heard summoning the boatswain and his mates to their duty.

There was a general movement in the living masses that clustered around the mainmast, on the booms, and in the gangways, though their habits of discipline held the crew a moment longer in suspense. The silence was first broken by the sounds of the boatswain's whistle, followed by the hoarse cry of "all hands, up anchor, ahoy!"—the former rising on the night air, from its first low, mellow notes, to a piercing shrillness, that gradually died away on the waters; and the latter, bellowing through every cranny of the ship, like the hollow murmurs of distant thunder.

The change produced by this customary summons was magical. Human beings sprung out from between the guns, rushed up the hatches, threw themselves with careless activity from the booms, and gathered from every quarter so rapidly, that, in an instant, the deck of the frigate was alive with men.

The profound silence, that had hitherto been only interrupted by the low dialogue of the officers, was now exchanged for the stern orders of the lieutenants, mingled with the shriller cries of the midshipmen, and the hoarse bawling of the boatswain's crew, rising above the tumult of preparation and general bustle.

The captain and the pilot alone remained passive, in this scene of general exertion; for apprehension had even stimulated that class of officers which is called "idlers," to unusual activity, though frequently reminded by their more experienced messmates, that instead of aiding, they retarded, the duty of the vessel. The bustle, however, gradually ceased, and in a few minutes the same silence pervaded the ship as before.

"We are brought-to, sir," said Griffith, who stood overlooking the scene, holding in one hand a short speaking trumpet, and grasping, with the other, one of the shrouds of the ship, to steady himself in the position he had taken on a gun.

"Heave round, sir," was the calm reply.

"Heave round!" repeated Griffith, aloud.

"Heave round!" echoed a dozen eager voices at once, and the lively strains of a fife struck up a brisk air, to enliven the labour. The capstern was instantly set in motion, and the measured tread of the seamen was heard, as they stamped the deck in the circle of their march. For a few minutes, no other sounds were heard, if we except the voice of an officer, occasionally, cheering the sailors, when it was announced that they "were short," or, in other words, that the ship was nearly over her anchor.

"Heave and pall," cried Griffith; when the quivering notes of the whistle were again succeeded by a general stillness in the vessel.

"What is to be done now, sir?" continued the lieutenant; "shall we trip the anchor? There seems not a breath of air, and as the tide runs slack, I doubt whether the sea do not heave the ship ashore."

There was so much obvious truth in this conjecture, that all eyes turned from the light and animation afforded by the decks of the frigate, to look abroad on the waters, in a vain desire to pierce the darkness, as if to read the fate of their apparently devoted ship, from the aspect of nature.

"I leave all to the pilot," said the captain, after he had stood a short time by the side of Griffith, anxiously studying the heavens and the ocean. "What say you, Mr. Gray?"

The man who was, thus, first addressed by name, was leaning over the bulwarks, with his eyes bent in the same direction as the others; but as he answered, he turned his face towards the speaker, and the light from the deck fell full upon his quiet features, which exhibited a calmness bordering on the supernatural, considering his station and responsibility.

"There is much to fear from this heavy ground-swell," he said, in the same unmoved tones as before; "but there is certain destruction to us, if the gale that is brewing in the east, finds us waiting its fury in this wild anchorage. All the hemp that was ever spun into cordage would not hold a ship an hour, chafing on these rocks, with a north-easter pouring its fury on her. If the powers of man can compass it, gentlemen, we must get an offing, and that speedily."

"You say no more, sir, than the youngest boy in the ship can see for himself," said Griffith—"ha! here comes the schooner!"

The dashing of the long sweeps in the water, was now plainly audible, and the little Ariel was seen through the gloom, moving heavily under their feeble impulse. As she passed slowly under the stern of the frigate, the cheerful voice of Barnstable was first heard, opening the communications between them.

"Here's a night for spectacles, Captain Munson!" he cried; "but I thought I heard your fife, sir; I trust in God, you do not mean to ride it out here till morning?"

"I like the birth as little as yourself, Mr. Barnstable," returned the veteran seaman, in his calm manner, in which anxiety was however beginning to grow evident. "We are short, but are afraid to let go our hold of the bottom, lest the sea cast us ashore. How make you out the wind?"

"Wind!" echoed the other; "there is not enough to blow a lady's curl aside. If you wait, sir, till the land breeze fills your sails, you will wait another moon, I believe. I've got my eggshell out of that nest of gray-caps, but how it has been done in the dark, a better man than myself must explain."

"Take your directions from the pilot, Mr. Barnstable," returned his commanding officer, "and follow them strictly and to the letter."

A death-like silence, in both vessels, succeeded this order, for all seemed to listen eagerly to catch the words that fell from the man, on whom, even the boys now felt, depended their only hopes for safety. A short time was suffered to elapse, before his voice was heard, in the same low, but distinct tones as before—

"Your sweeps will soon be of no service to you," he said, "against the sea that begins to heave in; but your light sails will help them to get you out. So long as you can head east-and-by-north, you are doing well, and you can stand on till you open the light from that northern headland, when you can heave to, and fire a gun; but if, as I dread, you are struck aback, before you open the light, you may trust to your lead on the larboard tack, but beware, with your head to the southward, for no lead will serve you there."

"I can walk over the same ground on one tack as on the other," said Barnstable, "and make both legs of a length."

"It will not do," returned the pilot. "If you fall off a point to starboard from east-and-by-north, in going large, you will find both rocks and points of shoals to bring you up; and beware, as I tell you, of the starboard tack."

"And how shall I find my way; you will let me trust to neither time, lead, nor log."

"You must trust to a quick eye and a ready hand. The breakers only will show you the dangers, when you are not able to make out the bearings of the land. Tack in season, sir, and don't spare the lead, when you head to port."

"Ay, ay," returned Barnstable, in a low, muttering voice. "This is a sort of blind navigation with a vengeance, and all for no purpose that I can see—see! damme, eyesight is of about as much use now, as a man's nose would be in reading the bible."

"Softly, softly, Mr. Barnstable," interrupted his commander, for such was the anxious stillness in both vessels, that even the rattling of the schooner's rigging was heard, as she rolled in the trough of the sea—"the duty on which Congress has sent us must be performed at the hazard of our lives."

"I don't mind my life, Captain Munson," said Barnstable; "but there is a great want of conscience in trusting a vessel in such a place as this. However, it is a time to do, and not to talk. But if there be such danger to an easy draught of water, what will become of the frigate? had I not better play jackall, and try and feel the way for you."

"I thank you," said the pilot; "the offer is generous, but would avail us nothing. I have the advantage of knowing the ground well, and must trust to my memory and God's good favour. Make sail, make sail, sir, and if you succeed, we will venture to break ground."

The order was promptly obeyed, and in a very short time, the Ariel was covered with canvass. Though no air was perceptible on the decks of the frigate, the little schooner was so light, that she succeeded in stemming her way over the rising waves, aided a little by the tide, and in a few minutes, her low hull was just discernible in the streak of light along the horizon, with the dark outline of her sails rising above the sea, until their fanciful summits were lost in the shadows of the clouds.

Griffith had listened to the foregoing dialogue, like the rest of the junior officers, in profound silence; but when the Ariel began to grow indistinct to the eye, he jumped lightly from the gun to the deck, and cried —

"She slips off, like a vessel from the stocks! shall I trip the anchor, sir, and follow?"

"We have no choice," replied his captain. "You hear the question, Mr. Gray? shall we let go the bottom?"

"It must be done, Captain Munson; we may want more drift than the rest of this tide to get us to a place of safety," said the pilot; "I would give five years from a life, that I know will be short, if the ship lay one mile further seaward."

This remark was unheard by all, except the commander of the frigate, who again walked aside with the pilot, where they resumed their mysterious communications. The words of assent were no sooner uttered, however, than Griffith gave forth from his trumpet the command to "heave away!" Again the strains of the fife were followed by the tread of the men at the capstern. At the same time that the anchor was heaving up, the sails were loosened from the yards, and opened to invite the breeze. In effecting this duty, orders were thundered through the trumpet of the first lieutenant, and executed with the rapidity of thought. Men were to be seen, like spots in the dim light from the heavens, lying on every yard, or hanging as in air, while strange cries were heard issuing from every part of the rigging, and each spar of the vessel. "Ready the fore-royal," cried a shrill voice, as if from the clouds; "ready the fore yard," uttered the hoarser tones of a seaman beneath him; "all ready aft, sir," cried a third, from another quarter; and in a few moments, the order was given to "let fall."

The little light which fell from the sky, was now excluded by the falling canvass, and a deeper gloom was cast athwart the decks of the ship, that served to render the brilliancy of the lanterns even vivid, while it gave to objects outboard a more appalling and dreary appearance than before.

Every individual, excepting the commander and his associate, was now earnestly engaged in getting the ship under way. The sounds of "we're away," were repeated by a burst from fifty voices, and the rapid evolutions of the capstern announced that nothing but the weight of the anchor was to be lifted. The hauling of cordage, the rattling of blocks, blended with the shrill calls of the boatswain and his mates, succeeded; and though to a landsman all would have appeared confusion and hurry, long practice and strict discipline enabled the crew to exhibit their ship under a cloud of canvass, from her deck to the trucks, in less time than we have consumed in relating it.

For a few minutes, the officers were not disappointed by the result, for though the heavy sails flapped lazily against the masts, the light duck on the loftier spars swelled outwardly, and the ship began sensibly to yield to their influence.

"She travels! she travels!" exclaimed Griffith, joyously; "ah! the hussy! she has as much antipathy to the land as any fish that swims! it blows a little gale aloft, yet!"

"We feel its dying breath," said the pilot, in low, soothing tones, but in a manner so sudden as to startle Griffith, at whose elbow they were unexpectedly uttered. "Let us forget, young man, every thing but the number of lives that depend, this night, on your exertions and my knowledge."

"If you be but half as able to exhibit the one, as I am willing to make the other, we shall do well," returned the lieutenant, in the same tone. "Remember, whatever may be your feelings, that *we* are on an enemy's coast, and love it not enough to wish to lay our bones there."

With this brief explanation, they separated, the vessel requiring the constant and close attention of the officer to her movements.

The exultation produced in the crew by the progress of their ship through the water, was of short duration; for the breeze that had seemed to await their motions, after forcing the vessel for a quarter of a mile, fluttered for a few minutes amid their light canvass, and then left them entirely. The quarter-master, whose duty it was to superintend the helm, soon announced that he was losing the command of the vessel, as she was no longer obedient to her rudder. This ungrateful intelligence was promptly communicated to his commander, by Griffith, who suggested the propriety of again dropping an anchor.

"I refer you to Mr. Gray," returned the captain; "he is the pilot, sir, and with him rests the safety of the vessel."

"Pilots sometimes lose ships, as well as save them," said Griffith; "know you the man well, Captain Munson, who holds all our lives in his keeping, and so coolly as if he cared but little for the venture?"

"Mr. Griffith, I do know him; he is, in my opinion, both competent and faithful. Thus much I tell you, to relieve your anxiety; more you must not ask; — but is there not a shift of wind?"

"God forbid!" exclaimed his lieutenant; "if that north-easter catches us within the shoals, our case will be desperate indeed!"

The heavy rolling of the vessel caused an occasional expansion, and as sudden a re-action, in their sails, which left the oldest seamen in the ship in doubt which way the currents of air were passing, or whether there existed any that were not created by the flapping of their own canvass. The head of the ship, however, began to fall off from the sea, and notwithstanding the darkness, it soon became apparent that she was driving in, bodily, towards the shore.

During these few minutes of gloomy doubt, Griffith, by one of those sudden revulsions of the mind, that connect the opposite extremes of feeling, lost his animated anxiety, and relapsed into the listless apathy that so often came over him, even in the most critical moments of trial and danger. He was standing, with one elbow resting on the capstern, shading his eyes from the light of the battle-lantern that stood near him, with one hand, when he felt a gentle pressure of the other, that recalled his recollection. Looking affectionately, though still recklessly, at the boy who stood at his side, he said—

"Dull music, Mr. Merry."

"So dull, sir, that I can't dance to it," returned the midshipman. "Nor do I believe there is a man in the ship who would not rather hear 'The girl I left behind me,' than those execrable sounds."

"What sounds, boy! The ship is as quiet as the quaker meeting in the Jerseys, before your good old grandfather used to break the charm of silence with his sonorous voice."

"Ah! laugh at my peaceable blood, if thou wilt, Mr. Griffith," said the arch youngster; "but remember, there is a mixture of it in all sorts of veins. I wish I could hear one of the old gentleman's chants now, sir; I could always sleep to them, like a gull in a surf. But he that sleeps to-night, with that lullaby, will make a nap of it."

"Sounds! I hear no sounds, boy, but the flapping aloft; even that pilot, who struts the quarter-deck like an admiral, has nothing to say."

"Is not that a sound to open a seaman's ear?"

"It is in truth a heavy roll of the surf, lad, but the night air carries it heavily to our ears. Know you not the sounds of the surf yet, younker?"

"I know it too well, Mr. Griffith, and do not wish to know it better. How fast are we tumbling in towards that surf, sir?"

"I think we hold our own," said Griffith, rousing again; "though we had better anchor. Luff, fellow, luff, you are broadside to the sea!"

The man at the wheel repeated his former intelligence, adding a suggestion that he thought the ship "was gathering stern-way."

"Haul up your courses, Mr. Griffith," said Captain Munson, "and let us feel the wind."

The rattling of the blocks was soon heard, and the enormous sheets of canvass that hung from the lower yards were instantly suspended "in the brails." When this change was effected, all on board stood silent and breathless, as if expecting to learn their fate by the result. Several contradictory opinions were, at length, hazarded among the officers, when Griffith seized the candle from the lantern, and springing on one of the guns, held it on high, exposed to the action of the air. The little flame waved, with uncertain glimmering, for a moment, and then burned steadily, in a line with the masts. Griffith was about to lower his extended arm, when, feeling a slight sensation of coolness on his hand, he paused, and the light turned slowly towards the land, flared, flickered, and finally deserted the wick.

"Lose not a moment, Mr. Griffith," cried the pilot, aloud; "clew up and furl every thing but your three topsails, and let them be double-reefed. Now is the time to fulfil your promise."

The young man paused one moment, in astonishment, as the clear, distinct tones of the stranger struck his ears so unexpectedly; but turning his eyes to seaward, he sprang on the deck, and proceeded to obey the order, as if life and death depended on his despatch.

Chapter V.

"She rights, she rights, boys! ware off shore!"

G. A. Stevens, "The Storm." l. 64.

THE EXTRAORDINARY activity of Griffith, which communicated itself with promptitude to the crew, was produced by a sudden alteration in the weather. In place of the well-defined streak along the horizon, that has been already described, an immense body of misty light appeared to be moving in, with rapidity, from the ocean, while a distinct but distant roaring announced the sure approach of the tempest, that had so long troubled the waters. Even Griffith, while thundering his orders through the trumpet, and urging the men, by his cries, to expedition, would pause, for instants, to cast anxious glances in the direction of the coming storm, and the faces of the sailors who lay on the yards were turned, instinctively, towards the same quarter of the heavens, while they knotted the reef-points, or passed the gaskets, that were to confine the unruly canvass to the prescribed limits.

The pilot alone, in that confused and busy throng, where voice rose above voice, and cry echoed cry, in quick succession, appeared as if he held no interest in the important stake. With his eyes steadily fixed on the approaching mist, and his arms folded together, in composure, he stood calmly waiting the result.

The ship had fallen off, with her broadside to the sea, and was become unmanageable, and the sails were already brought into the folds necessary to her security, when the quick and heavy fluttering of canvass was thrown across the water, with all the gloomy and chilling sensations that such sounds produce, where darkness and danger unite to appal the seaman.

"The schooner has it!" cried Griffith; "Barnstable has held

on, like himself, to the last moment — God send that the squall leave him cloth enough to keep him from the shore!"

"His sails are easily handled," the commander observed, "and she must be over the principal danger. We are falling off before it, Mr. Gray; shall we try a cast of the lead?"

The pilot turned from his contemplative posture, and moved slowly across the deck, before he returned any reply to this question — like a man who not only felt that every thing depended on himself, but that he was equal to the emergency.

"'Tis unnecessary," he at length said; "'twould be certain destruction to be taken aback, and it is difficult to say, within several points, how the wind may strike us."

"'Tis difficult no longer," cried Griffith; "for here it comes, and in right earnest!"

The rushing sounds of the wind were now, indeed, heard at hand, and the words were hardly past the lips of the young lieutenant, before the vessel bowed down heavily to one side, and then, as she began to move through the water, rose again majestically to her upright position, as if saluting, like a courteous champion, the powerful antagonist with which she was about to contend. Not another minute elapsed, before the ship was throwing the waters aside, with a lively progress, and, obedient to her helm, was brought as near to the desired course, as the direction of the wind would allow. The hurry and bustle on the yards gradually subsided, and the men slowly descended to the deck, all straining their eyes to pierce the gloom in which they were enveloped, and some shaking their heads, in melancholy doubt, afraid to express the apprehensions they really entertained. All on board anxiously waited for the fury of the gale; for there were none so ignorant or inexperienced in that gallant frigate, as not to know, that as yet, they only felt the infant efforts of the wind. Each moment, however, it increased in power, though so gradual was the alteration, that the relieved mariners began to believe that all their gloomy forebodings were not to be realized. During this short interval of uncertainty, no other sounds were heard than the whistling of the breeze, as it passed quickly through the mass of rigging that belonged to the vessel, and the dashing of the spray, that began to fly from her bows, like the foam of a cataract.

"It blows fresh," cried Griffith, who was the first to speak in that moment of doubt and anxiety; "but it is no more than a cap-full of wind, after all. Give us elbow-room, and the right canvass, Mr. Pilot, and I'll handle the ship like a gentleman's yacht, in this breeze."

"Will she stay, think ye, under this sail?" said the low voice of the stranger.

"She will do all that man, in reason, can ask of wood and iron," returned the lieutenant; "but the vessel don't float the ocean that will tack under double-reefed topsails alone, against a heavy sea. Help her with the courses, pilot, and you shall see her come round like a dancing-master."

"Let us feel the strength of the gale first," returned the man who was called Mr. Gray, moving from the side of Griffith to the weather gangway of the vessel, where he stood in silence, looking ahead of the ship, with an air of singular coolness and abstraction.

All the lanterns had been extinguished on the deck of the frigate, when her anchor was secured, and as the first mist of the gale had passed over, it was succeeded by a faint light that was a good deal aided by the glittering foam of the waters, which now broke in white curls around the vessel, in every direction. The land could be faintly discerned, rising like a heavy bank of black fog, above the margin of the waters, and was only distinguishable from the heavens, by its deeper gloom and obscurity. The last rope was coiled, and deposited in its proper place, by the seamen, and for several minutes the stillness of death pervaded the crowded decks. It was evident to every one, that their ship was dashing at a prodigious rate through the waves; and as she was approaching, with such velocity, the quarter of the bay where the shoals and dangers were known to be situated, nothing but the habits of the most exact discipline could suppress the uneasiness of the officers and men within their own bosoms. At length the voice of Captain Munson was heard, calling to the pilot.

"Shall I send a hand into the chains, Mr. Gray," he said, "and try our water?"

Although this question was asked aloud, and the interest it excited drew many of the officers and men around him, in eager impatience for his answer, it was unheeded by the man to whom it was addressed. His head rested on his hand, as he leaned over the hammock-cloths of the vessel, and his whole air was that of one whose thoughts wandered from the pressing necessity of their situation. Griffith was among those who had approached the pilot, and after waiting a moment, from respect, to hear the answer to his commander's question, he presumed on his own rank, and leaving the circle that stood at a little distance, stepped to the side of the mysterious guardian of their lives.

"Captain Munson desires to know whether you wish a cast of the lead?" said the young officer, with a little impatience of manner. No immediate answer was made to this repetition of the question, and Griffith laid his hand, unceremoniously, on the shoulder of the other, with an intent to rouse him, before he made another application for a reply, but the convulsive start of the pilot held him silent in amazement.

"Fall back there," said the lieutenant, sternly, to the men who were closing around them in a compact circle; "away with you to your stations, and see all clear for stays." The dense mass of heads dissolved, at this order, like the water of one of the waves commingling with the ocean, and the lieutenant and his companion were left by themselves.

"This is not a time for musing, Mr. Gray," continued Griffith; "remember our compact, and look to your charge — is it not time to put the vessel in stays? of what are you dreaming?"

The pilot laid his hand on the extended arm of the lieutenant, and grasped it with a convulsive pressure, as he answered —

"'Tis a dream of reality. You are young, Mr. Griffith, nor am I past the noon of life; but should you live fifty years longer, you never can see and experience what I have encountered in my little period of three-and-thirty years!"

A good deal astonished at this burst of feeling, so singular at such a moment, the young sailor was at a loss for a reply; but as his duty was uppermost in his thoughts, he still dwelt on the theme that most interested him.

"I hope much of your experience has been on this coast, for the ship travels lively," he said, "and the daylight showed us so much to dread, that we do not feel over-valiant in the dark. How much longer shall we stand on, upon this tack?"

The pilot turned slowly from the side of the vessel, and walked towards the commander of the frigate, as he replied, in a tone that seemed deeply agitated by his melancholy reflections —

"You have your wish, then; much, very much of my early life was passed on this dreaded coast. What to you is all darkness and gloom, to me is as light as if a noon-day sun shone upon it. But tack your ship, sir, tack your ship; I would see how she works, before we reach the point, where she *must* behave well, or we perish."

Griffith gazed after him in wonder, while the pilot slowly paced the quarter-deck, and then, rousing from his trance, gave forth the cheering order that called each man to his station, to perform the desired evolution. The confident assurances which the young officer had given to the pilot, respecting the qualities of his vessel, and his own ability to manage her, were fully realized by the result. The helm was no sooner put a-lee, than the huge ship bore up gallantly against the wind, and dashing directly through the waves, threw the foam high into the air, as she looked boldly into the very eye of the wind, and then, yielding gracefully to its power, she fell off on the other tack, with her head pointed from those dangerous shoals that she had so recently approached with such terrifying velocity. The heavy yards swung round, as if they had been vanes to indicate the currents of the air, and in a few moments the frigate again moved, with stately progress, through the water, leaving the rocks and shoals behind her on one side of the bay, but advancing towards those that offered equal danger on the other.

During this time, the sea was becoming more agitated, and the violence of the wind was gradually increasing. The latter no longer whistled amid the cordage of the vessel, but it seemed to howl, surlily, as it passed the complicated machinery that the frigate obtruded on its path. An endless succession of white surges rose above the heavy billows, and the very air was glittering with the light that was disengaged from the ocean. The ship yielded, each moment, more and more before the storm, and in less than half an hour from the time that she had lifted her anchor, she was driven along, with tremendous fury, by the full power of a gale of wind. Still, the hardy and experienced mariners who directed her movements, held her to the course that was necessary to their preservation, and still Griffith gave forth, when directed by their unknown pilot, those orders that turned her in the narrow channel where alone safety was to be found.

So far, the performance of his duty appeared easy to the stranger, and he gave the required directions in those still, calm tones, that formed so remarkable a contrast to the responsibility of his situation. But when the land was becoming dim, in distance as well as darkness, and the agitated sea alone was to be discovered as it swept by them in foam, he broke in upon the monotonous roaring of the tempest, with the sounds of his voice, seeming to shake off his apathy, and rouse himself to the occasion.

"Now is the time to watch her closely, Mr. Griffith," he cried; "here we get the true tide and the real danger. Place the best quarter-master of your ship in those chains, and let an officer stand by him, and see that he gives us the right water."

"I will take that office on myself," said the captain; "pass a light into the weather mainchains."

"Stand by your braces!" exclaimed the pilot, with startling quickness. "Heave away that lead!"

These preparations taught the crew to expect the crisis, and every officer and man stood in fearful silence, at his assigned station, awaiting the issue of the trial. Even the quarter-master at the cun gave out his orders to the men at the wheel, in deeper and hoarser tones than usual, as if anxious not to disturb the quiet and order of the vessel.

While this deep expectation pervaded the frigate, the piercing cry of the leadsman, as he called, "by the mark seven," rose above the tempest, crossed over the decks, and appeared to pass away to leeward, borne on the blast, like the warnings of some water spirit.

"'Tis well," returned the pilot, calmly; "try it again."

The short pause was succeeded by another cry, "and a half-five!"

"She shoals! she shoals!" exclaimed Griffith; "keep her a good full."

"Ay! you must hold the vessel in command, now," said the pilot, with those cool tones that are most appalling in critical moments, because they seem to denote most preparation and care.

The third call "by the deep four!" was followed by a prompt direction from the stranger to tack.

Griffith seemed to emulate the coolness of the pilot, in issuing the necessary orders to execute this manœuvre.

The vessel rose slowly from the inclined position into which she had been forced by the tempest, and the sails were shaking violently, as if to release themselves from their confinement, while the ship stemmed the billows, when the well-known voice of the sailing-master was heard shouting from the forecastle—

"Breakers! breakers, dead ahead!"

This appalling sound seemed yet to be lingering about the ship, when a second voice cried—

"Breakers on our lee-bow!"

"We are in a bight of the shoals, Mr. Gray," cried the commander. "She loses her way; perhaps an anchor might hold her."

"Clear away that best-bower," shouted Griffith through his trumpet.

"Hold on!" cried the pilot, in a voice that reached the very hearts of all who heard him; "hold on every thing."

The young man turned fiercely to the daring stranger, who thus defied the discipline of his vessel, and at once demanded—

"Who is it that dares to countermand my orders?—is it not enough that you run the ship into danger, but you must interfere to keep her there! If another word—"

"Peace, Mr. Griffith," interrupted the captain, bending from the rigging, his gray locks blowing about in the wind, and adding a look of wildness to the haggard care that he exhibited by the light of his lantern; "yield the trumpet to Mr. Gray; he alone can save us."

Griffith threw his speaking trumpet on the deck, and as he walked proudly away, muttered, in bitterness of feeling—

"Then all is lost, indeed, and among the rest, the foolish hopes with which I visited this coast."

There was, however, no time for reply; the ship had been rapidly running into the wind, and as the efforts of the crew were paralyzed by the contradictory orders they had heard, she gradually lost her way, and in a few seconds, all her sails were taken aback.

Before the crew understood their situation, the pilot had applied the trumpet to his mouth and in a voice that rose above the tempest, he thundered forth his orders. Each command was given distinctly, and with a precision that showed him to be master of his profession. The helm was kept fast, the head yards swung up heavily against the wind, and the vessel was soon whirling round on her heel, with a retrograde movement.

Griffith was too much of a seaman, not to perceive that the pilot had seized, with a perception almost intuitive, the only method that promised to extricate the vessel from her situation. He was young, impetuous, and proud—but he was also generous. Forgetting his resentment and his mortification, he rushed forward among the men, and, by his presence and example, added certainty to the experiment. The ship fell off slowly before the gale, and bowed her yards nearly to the water, as she felt the blast pouring its fury on her broadside, while the surly waves beat violently against her stern, as if in reproach at departing from her usual manner of moving.

The voice of the pilot, however, was still heard, steady and calm, and yet so clear and high as to reach every ear; and the obedient seamen whirled the yards at his bidding, in despite of the tempest, as if they handled the toys of their childhood. When the ship had fallen off dead before the wind, her head sails were shaken, her after yards trimmed, and her helm shifted, before she had time to run upon the danger that had threatened, as well to leeward as to windward. The beautiful fabric, obedient to her government, threw her bows up gracefully towards the wind again, and as her sails were trimmed, moved out from amongst the dangerous shoals, in which she had been embayed, as steadily and swiftly as she had approached them.

A moment of breathless astonishment succeeded the accomplishment of this nice manœuvre, but there was no time for the usual expressions of surprise. The stranger still held the trumpet, and continued to lift his voice amid the howlings of the blast, whenever prudence or skill required any change in the management of the ship. For an hour longer, there was a fearful struggle for their preservation, the channel becoming, at each step, more complicated, and the shoals thickening around the mariners, on every side. The lead was cast rapidly, and the quick eye of the pilot seemed to pierce the darkness, with a keenness of vision that exceeded human power. It was apparent to all in the vessel, that they were under the guidance of one who understood the navigation thoroughly, and their exertions kept pace with their reviving confidence. Again and again, the frigate appeared to be rushing blindly on shoals, where the sea was covered with foam, and where destruction would have been as sudden as it was certain, when the clear voice of the stranger was heard warning them of the danger, and inciting them to their duty. The vessel was implicitly yielded to his government, and during those anxious moments when she was dashing the waters aside, throwing the spray over her enormous yards, each ear would listen eagerly for those sounds that had obtained a command over the crew, that can only be acquired, under such circumstances, by great steadiness and consummate skill. The ship was recovering from the inaction of changing her course, in one of those critical tacks that she had made so often, when the pilot, for the first time, addressed the commander of the frigate, who still continued to superintend the all-important duty of the leadsman.

"Now is the pinch," he said, "and if the ship behaves well, we are safe—but if otherwise, all we have yet done will be useless."

The veteran seaman whom he addressed left the chains, at this portentous notice, and calling to his first lieutenant, required of the stranger an explanation of his warning.

"See you yon light on the southern headland?" returned the pilot; "you may know it from the star near it—by its sinking, at times, in the ocean. Now observe the hom-moc, a little north of it, looking like a shadow in the horizon—'tis a hill far inland. If we keep that light open from the hill, we shall do well—but if not, we surely go to pieces."

"Let us tack again!" exclaimed the lieutenant.

The pilot shook his head, as he replied—

"There is no more tacking or box-hauling to be done to-night. We have barely room to pass out of the shoals on this course, and if we can weather the 'Devil's-Grip,' we clear their outermost point—but if not, as I said before, there is but an alternative."

"If we had beaten out the way we entered!" exclaimed Griffith, "we should have done well."

"Say, also, if the tide would have let us do so," returned the pilot, calmly. "Gentlemen, we must be prompt; we have but a mile to go, and the ship appears to fly. That topsail is not enough to keep her up to the wind; we want both jib and main-sail."

"'Tis a perilous thing, to loosen canvass in such a tempest!" observed the doubtful captain.

"It must be done," returned the collected stranger; "we perish, without it—see! the light already touches the edge of the hom-moc; the sea casts us to leeward!"

"It shall be done!" cried Griffith, seizing the trumpet from the hand of the pilot.

The orders of the lieutenant were executed almost as soon as issued, and every thing being ready, the enormous folds of the mainsail were trusted, loose, to the blast. There was an instant when the result was doubtful; the tremendous threshing of the heavy sail, seeming to bid defiance to all restraint, shaking the ship to her centre; but art and strength prevailed, and gradually the canvass was distended, and bellying as it filled, was drawn down to its usual place, by the power of a hundred men. The vessel yielded to this immense addition of force, and bowed before it, like a reed bending to a breeze. But the success of the measure was announced by a joyful cry from the stranger, that seemed to burst from his inmost soul.

"She feels it! she springs her luff! observe," he said, "the light opens from the hom-moc already; if she will only bear her can-vass, we shall go clear!"

A report, like that of a cannon, interrupted his exclamation, and something resembling a white cloud was seen drifting before the wind from the head of the ship, till it was driven into the gloom far to leeward.

"'Tis the jib, blown from the bolt-ropes," said the commander of the frigate. "This is no time to spread light duck—but the mainsail may stand it yet."

"The sail would laugh at a tornado," returned the lieutenant; "but that mast springs like a piece of steel."

"Silence all!" cried the pilot. "Now, gentlemen, we shall soon know our fate. Let her luff—luff you can!"

This warning effectually closed all discourse, and the hardy mariners, knowing that they had already done all in the power of man, to ensure their safety, stood in breathless anxiety, awaiting the result. At a short distance ahead of them, the whole ocean was white with foam, and the waves, instead of rolling on, in regular succession, appeared to be tossing about in mad gambols. A single streak of dark billows, not half a cable's length in width, could be discerned running into this chaos of water; but it was soon lost to the eye, amid the confusion of the disturbed element. Along this narrow path the vessel moved more heavily than before, being brought so near the wind as to keep her sails touching. The pilot, silently, proceeded to the wheel, and, with his own hands, he undertook the steerage of the ship. No noise proceeded from the frigate to interrupt the horrid tumult of the ocean, and she entered the channel among the breakers, with the silence of a desperate calmness. Twenty times, as the foam rolled away to leeward, the crew were on the eve of uttering their joy, as they supposed the vessel past the danger; but breaker after breaker would still heave up before them, following each other into the general mass, to check their exultation. Occasionally, the fluttering of the sails would be heard; and when the looks of the startled seamen were turned to the wheel, they beheld the stranger grasping its spokes, with his quick eye glancing from the water to the canvass. At length the ship reached a point, where she appeared to be rushing directly into the jaws of destruction, when, suddenly, her course was changed, and her head receded rapidly from the wind. At the same instant, the voice of the pilot was heard, shouting—

"Square away the yards!—in mainsail!"

A general burst from the crew echoed, "square away the yards!" and, quick as thought, the frigate was seen gliding along the channel, before the wind. The eye had hardly time to dwell on the foam, which seemed like clouds driving in the heavens, and directly the gallant vessel issued from her perils, and rose and fell on the heavy waves of the sea.

The seamen were yet drawing long breaths, and gazing about them like men recovered from a trance, when Griffith approached the man who had so successfully conducted them through their perils. The lieutenant grasped the hand of the other, as he said—

"You have this night proved yourself a faithful pilot, and such a seaman as the world cannot equal."

The pressure of the hand was warmly returned by the unknown mariner, who replied—

"I am no stranger to the seas, and I may yet find my grave in them. But you, too, have deceived me; you have acted nobly, young man, and Congress—"

"What of Congress?" asked Griffith, observing him to pause.

"Why, Congress is fortunate, if it has many such ships as this," said the stranger, coldly, walking away towards the commander.

Griffith gazed after him, a moment, in surprise; but as his duty required his attention, other thoughts soon engaged his mind.

The vessel was pronounced to be in safety. The gale was heavy and increasing, but there was a clear sea before them, and, as she slowly stretched out into the bosom of the ocean, preparations were made for her security during its continuance. Before midnight, every thing was in order. A gun from the Ariel soon announced the safety of the schooner also, which had gone out by another and an easier channel, that the frigate had not dared to attempt; when the commander directed the usual watch to be set, and the remainder of the crew to seek their necessary repose.

The captain withdrew with the mysterious pilot to his own cabin. Griffith gave his last order, and renewing his charge to the officer intrusted with the care of the vessel, he wished him a pleasant watch, and sought the refreshment of his own cot. For an hour, the young lieutenant lay musing on the events of the day. The remark of Barnstable would occur to him, in connexion with the singular comment of the boy; and then his thoughts would recur to the pilot, who, taken from the hostile shores of Britain, and with her accent on his tongue, had served them so faithfully and so well. He remembered the anxiety of Captain Munson to procure this stranger, at the very hazard from which they had just been relieved, and puzzled himself with conjecturing why a pilot was to be sought at such a risk. His more private feelings would then resume their sway, and the recollection of America, his mistress, and his home, mingled with the confused images of the drowsy youth. The dashing of the billows against the side of the ship, the creaking of guns and bulk-heads, with the roaring of the tempest, however, became gradually less and less distinct, until nature yielded to necessity, and the young man forgot even the romantic images of his love, in the deep sleep of a seaman.

I. John Paul Jones depicted as a privateer, shoots a, mythical Lt. Grub for attempting to strike the colors. By an unidentified artist (c. 1803).

II. John Paul Jones, "Commodore au Service des Etats-Unis de l'Amerique," in the battle between *Le bon Homme Richard* and the *Serapis*, 23 July 1779. Drawn by C. J. Notté and engraved by Carl Guttenberg.

III. John Paul Jones (in 1779-1780) by Richard Brookshaw.

John Paul Jones

Tels hommes rarement se peuvent présenter,
Et quand le Ciel les donne, il faut en profiter.

IV. John Paul Jones, "Dessiné d'après nature au mois de May 1780 par J. M. Moreau le Jeune." Engraved by J. B. Fosseyeux.

Chapter VI.

"The letter! ay! the letter!
'Tis there a woman loves to speak her wishes;
It spares the blushes of the love-sick maiden,
And every word's a smile, each line a tongue."

Duo.

THE SLUMBERS of Griffith continued till late on the following morning, when he was awakened by the report of a cannon, issuing from the deck above him. He threw himself, listlessly, from his cot, and perceiving the officer of marines near him, as his servant opened the door of his state-room, he inquired, with some little interest in his manner, if "the ship was in chase of any thing, that a gun was fired?"

"'Tis no more than a hint to the Ariel," the soldier replied, "that there is bunting abroad for them to read. It seems as if all hands were asleep on board her, for we have shown her signal, these ten minutes, and she takes us for a collier, I believe, by the respect she pays it."

"Say, rather, that she takes us for an enemy, and is wary," returned Griffith. "Brown Dick has played the English so many tricks himself, that he is tender of his faith."

"Why, they have shown him a yellow flag over a blue one, with a cornet, and that spells Ariel, in every signal-book we have; surely he can't suspect the English of knowing how to read Yankee."

"I have known Yankees read more difficult English," said Griffith, smiling; "but, in truth, I suppose that Barnstable has been, like myself, keeping a dead reckoning of his time, and his men have profited by the occasion. She is lying-to, I trust."

"Ay! like a cork in a mill-pond, and I dare say you are right. Give Barnstable plenty of sea-room, a heavy wind, and but little sail, and he will send his men below, put that fellow he calls long Tom at the tiller, and follow himself, and sleep as quietly as I ever could at church."

"Ah! yours is a somniferous orthodoxy, Captain Manual," said the young sailor, laughing, while he slipped his arms into the sleeves of a morning round-about, covered with the gilded trappings of his profession; "sleep appears to come most naturally to all you idlers. But give me a passage, and I will go up, and call the schooner down to us, in the turning of an hour-glass."

The indolent soldier raised himself from the leaning posture he had taken against the door of the state-room, and Griffith proceeded through the dark ward-room, up the narrow stairs, that led him to the principal battery of the ship, and thence, by another and broader flight of steps, to the open deck.

The gale still blew strong, but steadily; the blue water of the ocean was rising in mimic mountains, that were crowned with white foam, which the wind, at times, lifted from its kindred element, to propel, in mist, through the air, from summit to summit. But the ship rode on these agitated billows, with an easy and regular movement, that denoted the skill with which her mechanical powers were directed. The day was bright and clear, and the lazy sun, who seemed unwilling to meet the toil of ascending to the meridian, was crossing the heavens with a southern inclination, that hardly allowed him to temper the moist air of the ocean with his genial heat. At the distance of a mile, directly in the wind's eye, the Ariel was seen, obeying the signal, which had caused the dialogue we have related. Her low, black hull was barely discernible, at moments, when she rose to the crest of a larger wave than common; but the spot of canvass that she exposed to the wind, was to be seen, seeming to touch the water on either hand, as the little vessel rolled amid the seas. At times, she was entirely hid from view, when the faint lines of her raking masts would be again discovered, issuing, as it were, from the ocean, and continuing to ascend, until the hull itself would appear, thrusting its bows into the air, surrounded by foam, and apparently ready to take its flight into another element.

After dwelling a moment on the beautiful sight we have attempted to describe, Griffith cast his eyes upward, to examine, with the keenness of a seaman, the disposition of things aloft, and then turned his attention to those who were on the deck of the frigate.

His commander stood, in his composed manner, patiently awaiting the execution of his order by the Ariel, and at his side was placed the stranger, who had so recently acted such a conspicuous part in the management of the ship. Griffith availed himself of daylight and his situation, to examine the appearance of this singular being more closely than the darkness and confusion of the preceding night had allowed. He was a trifle below the middle size in stature, but his form was muscular and athletic, exhibiting the finest proportions of manly beauty. His face appeared rather characterized by melancholy and thought, than by that determined decision which he had so powerfully displayed in the moments of their most extreme danger; but Griffith well knew, that it could also exhibit looks of the fiercest impatience. At present, it appeared, to the curious youth, when compared to the glimpses he had caught by the lights of their lanterns, like the ocean at rest, contrasted with the waters around him. The eyes of the pilot rested on the deck, or when they did wander, it was with uneasy and rapid glances. The large pea-jacket, that concealed most of his other attire, was as roughly made, and of materials as coarse, as that worn by the meanest seaman in the vessel; and yet, it did not escape the inquisitive gaze of the young lieutenant, that it was worn with an air of neatness and care, that was altogether unusual in men of his profession. The examination of Griffith ended here, for the near approach of the Ariel attracted the attention of all on the deck of the frigate, to the conversation that was about to pass between their respective commanders.

As the little schooner rolled along under their stern, Captain Munson directed his subordinate to leave his vessel, and repair on board the ship. As soon as the order was received, the Ariel rounded-to, and drawing ahead into the smooth water occasioned by the huge fabric that protected her from the gale, the whale-boat was again launched from her decks, and manned by the same crew that had landed on those shores which were now faintly discerned far to leeward, looking like blue clouds on the skirts of the ocean.

When Barnstable had entered his boat, a few strokes of the oars sent it, dancing over the waves, to the side of the ship. The little vessel was then veered off, to a distance, where it rode in safety, under the care of a boat-keeper, and the officer and his men ascended the side of the lofty frigate.

The usual ceremonials of reception were rigidly observed by Griffith and his juniors, when Barnstable touched the deck; and though every hand was ready to be extended towards the reckless seaman, none presumed to exceed the salutations of official decorum, until a short and private dialogue had taken place between him and their captain.

In the mean time, the crew of the whale-boat passed forward, and mingled with the seamen of the frigate, with the exception of the cockswain, who established himself in one of the gangways, where he stood in the utmost composure, fixing his eyes aloft, and shaking his head, in evident dissatisfaction, as he studied the complicated mass of rigging above him. This spectacle soon attracted to his side some half-dozen youths, with Mr. Merry at their head, who endeavoured to entertain their guest in a manner that should most conduce to the indulgence of their own waggish propensities.

The conversation between Barnstable and his superior soon ended; when the former, beckoning to Griffith, passed the wondering group who had collected around the capstern, awaiting his leisure to greet him more cordially, and led the way to the ward-room, with the freedom of one who felt himself no stranger. As this unsocial manner formed no part of the natural temper or ordinary deportment of the man, the remainder of the officers suffered their first lieutenant to follow him alone, believing that duty required that their interview should be private. Barnstable was determined that it should be so, at all events; for he seized the lamp from the mess-table, and entered the state-room of his friend, closing the door behind them, and turning the key. When they were both within its narrow limits—pointing to the only chair the little apartment contained, with a sort of instinctive deference to his companion's rank—the commander of the schooner threw himself carelessly on a sea-chest, and, placing the lamp on the table, he opened the discourse as follows:

"What a night we had of it! twenty times I thought I could see the sea breaking over you, and I had given you over as drowned men, or, what is worse, as men driven ashore, to be led to the prison-ships of these islanders, when I saw your lights in answer to my gun. Had you hoisted the conscience out of a murderer, you wouldn't have relieved him more than you did me, by showing that bit of tallow and cotton, tip'd with flint and steel. — But, Griffith, I have a tale to tell of a different kind — "

"Of how you slept, when you found yourself in deep water, and how your crew strove to outdo their commander, and how all succeeded so well, that there was a gray-head on board here, that began to shake with displeasure," interrupted Griffith; "truly, Dick, you will get into lubberly habits on board that bubble in which you float about, where all hands go to sleep as regularly as the inhabitants of a poultry yard go to roost."

"Not so bad, not half so bad, Ned," returned the other, laughing; "I keep as sharp a discipline as if we wore a flag. To be sure, forty men can't make as much parade as three or four hundred; but as for making or taking in sail, I am your better, any day."

"Ay, because a pocket handkerchief is sooner opened and shut than a table-cloth. But I hold it to be unseamanlike, to leave any vessel without human eyes, and those open, to watch whether she goes east or west, north or south."

"And who is guilty of such a dead-man's watch?"

"Why, they say on board here, that when it blows hard, you seat the man you call long Tom by the side of the tiller, tell him to keep her head-to-sea, and then pipe all hands to their night-caps, where you all remain, comfortably stowed in your hammocks, until you are awakened by the snoring of your helmsman."

"'Tis a damned scandalous insinuation," cried Barnstable, with an indignation that he in vain attempted to conceal. "Who gives currency to such a libel, Mr. Griffith?"

"I had it of the marine," said his friend, losing the archness that had instigated him to worry his companion, in the vacant air of one who was careless of every thing; "but I don't believe half of it myself — I have no doubt you all had your eyes open, last night, whatever you might have been about this morning."

"Ah! this morning! there was an oversight, indeed! But I was studying a new signal-book, Griffith, that has a thousand times more interest for me, than all the bunting you can show, from the head to the heel of your masts."

"What! have you found out the Englishman's private talk?"

"No, no," said the other, stretching forth his hand, and grasping the arm of his friend. "I met, last night, one, on those cliffs, who has proved herself what I always believed her to be and loved her for, a girl of quick thought and bold spirit."

"Of whom do you speak?"

"Of Katherine—"

Griffith started from his chair involuntarily, at the sound of this name, and the blood passed quickly through the shades of his countenance, leaving it now pale as death, and then burning as if oppressed by a torrent from his heart. Struggling to overcome an emotion, which he appeared ashamed to betray even to the friend he most loved, the young man soon recovered himself so far as to resume his seat, when he asked, gloomily—

"Was she alone?"

"She was; but she left with me this paper, and this invaluable book, which is worth a library of all other works."

The eye of Griffith rested vacantly on the treasure that the other valued so highly, but his hand seized, eagerly, the open letter which was laid on the table for his perusal. The reader will at once understand, that it was in the handwriting of a female, and that it was the communication Barnstable had received from his betrothed, on the cliffs. Its contents were as follows:

"Believing that Providence may conduct me where we shall meet, or whence I may be able to transmit to you this account, I have prepared a short statement of the situation of Cecilia Howard and myself; not, however, to urge you and Griffith to any rash or foolish hazards, but that you may both sit down, and, after due consultation, determine what is proper for our relief.

"By this time, you must understand the character of Colonel Howard too well to expect he will ever consent to give his niece to a rebel. He has already sacrificed to his loyalty, as he calls it, (but I whisper to Cecilia, 'tis his treason,) not only his native country, but no small part of his fortune also. In the frankness of my disposition, (you know my frankness, Barnstable, but too well!) I confessed to him, after the defeat of the mad attempt Griffith made to carry off Cecilia, in Carolina, that I had been foolish enough to enter into some weak promise to the brother officer who had accompanied the young sailor in his traitorous visits to the plantation. Heigho! I sometimes think it would have been better for us all, if your ship had never been chased into the river, or after she was there, if Griffith had made no attempt to renew his acquaintance with my cousin. The colonel received the intelligence as such a guardian would hear that his ward was about to throw away thirty thousand dollars and herself on a traitor to his king and country. I defended you stoutly; said that you had no king, as the tie was dissolved; that America was your country, and that your profession was honourable; but it would not all do. He called you rebel; that I was used to. He said you were a traitor; that, in his vocabulary, amounts to the same thing. He even hinted that you were a coward; and that I knew to be false, and did not hesitate to tell him so. He used fifty opprobrious terms that I cannot remember, but among others were the beautiful epithets of 'disorganizer,' 'leveller,' 'democrat,' and 'jacobin.' (I hope he did not mean a monk!) In short, he acted Colonel Howard in a rage. But as his dominion does not, like that of his favourite kings, continue from generation to generation, and one short year will release me from his power, and leave me mistress of my own actions, that is, if your fine promises are to be believed, I bore it all very well, being resolved to suffer any thing but martyrdom, rather than abandon Cecilia. She, dear girl, has much more to distress her than I can have; she is not only the ward of Colonel Howard, but his niece, and his sole heir. I am persuaded this last circumstance makes no difference in either her conduct or her feelings, but he appears to think it gives him a right to tyrannize over her on all occasions. After all, Colonel Howard is a gentleman when you do not put him in a passion, and, I believe, a thoroughly honest man, and Cecilia even loves him. But a man who is driven from his country, in his sixtieth year, with the loss of near half his fortune, is not apt to canonize those who compel the change.

"It seems that when the Howards lived on this island, a hundred years ago, they dwelt in the county of Northumberland. Hither, then, he brought us, when political events, and his dread of becoming the uncle to a rebel, induced him to abandon America, as he says, for ever. We have been here now three months, and for two thirds of that time we lived in tolerable comfort; but latterly, the papers have announced the arrival of the ship and your schooner in France, and from that moment as strict a watch has been kept over us, as if we had meditated a renewal of the Carolina flight. The colonel, on his arrival here, hired an old building, that is part house, part abbey, part castle, and all prison, because it is said to have once belonged to an ancestor of his. In this delightful dwelling there are many cages, that will secure more uneasy birds than we are. About a fortnight ago an alarm was given in a neighbouring village, which is situated on the shore, that two American vessels, answering your description, had been seen hovering along the coast; and, as people in this quarter dream of nothing but that terrible fellow, Paul Jones, it was said that he was on board one of them. But I believe that Colonel Howard suspects who you really are. He was very minute in his inquiries, I hear; and since then, has established a sort of garrison in the house, under the pretence of defending it against marauders, like those who are said to have laid my Lady Selkirk under contribution.

"Now, understand me, Barnstable; on no account would I have you risk yourself on shore; neither must there be blood spilt, if you love me; but that you may know what sort of a place we are confined in, and by whom surrounded, I will describe both our prison and the garrison. The whole building is of stone, and not to be attempted with slight means. It has windings and turnings, both internally and externally, that would require more skill than I possess to make intelligible; but the rooms we inhabit are in the upper or third floor of a wing, that you may call a tower, if you are in a romantic mood, but which, in truth, is nothing but a wing. Would to God I could fly with it! If any accident should bring you in sight of the dwelling, you will know our rooms, by the three smoky vanes that whiffle about its pointed roof, and, also, by the windows in that story being occasionally open. Opposite to our windows, at the distance of half a mile, is a retired, unfrequented ruin, concealed, in a great measure, from observation by a wood, and affording none of the best accommodations, it is true, but shelter in some of its vaults or apartments. I have prepared, according to the explanations you once gave me on this subject, a set of small signals, of differently coloured silks, and a little dictionary of all the phrases that I could imagine as useful, to refer to, properly numbered to correspond with the key and the flags, all of which I shall send you with this letter. You must prepare your own flags, and of course I retain mine, as well as a copy of the key and book. If opportunity should ever offer, we can have, at least, a pleasant discourse together; you from the top of the old tower in the ruins, and I from the east window of my dressing-room! But now for the garrison. In addition to the commandant, Colonel Howard, who retains all the fierceness of his former military profession, there is, as his second in authority, that bane of Cecilia's happiness, Kit Dillon, with his long Savannah face, scornful eyes of black, and skin of the same colour. This gentleman, you know, is a distant relative of the Howards, and wishes to be more nearly allied. He is poor, it is true, but then, as the colonel daily remarks, he is a good and loyal subject, and no rebel. When I asked why he was not in arms in these stirring times, contending for the prince he loves so much, the colonel answers, that it is not his profession, that he has been educated for the law, and was destined to fill one of the highest judicial stations in the colonies, and that he hoped he should yet live to see him sentence certain nameless gentlemen to condign punishment. This was consoling, to be sure, but I bore it. However, he left Carolina with us, and here he is, and here he is likely to continue, unless you can catch him, and anticipate his judgment on himself. The colonel has long desired to see this gentleman the husband of Cecilia, and since the news of your being on the coast, the siege has nearly amounted to a storm. The consequences are, that my cousin at first kept her room, and then the colonel kept her there, and even now she is precluded from leaving the wing we inhabit. In addition to these two principal gaolers, we have four men servants, two black and two white; and an officer and twenty soldiers from the neighbouring town are billeted on us, by particular desire, until the coast is declared free from pirates! yes, that is the musical name they give you — and when their own people land, and plunder, and rob, and murder the men and insult the women, they are called heroes! It's a fine thing to be able to invent names and make dictionaries — and it must be your fault, if mine has been framed for no purpose. I declare, when I recollect all the insulting and cruel things I hear in this country, of my own and her people, it makes me lose my temper, and forget my sex; but do not let my ill humour urge you to any thing rash; remember your life, remember their prisons, remember your reputation, but do not, do not forget your

KATHERINE PLOWDEN.

"P. S. I had almost forgotten to tell you, that in the signal-book you will find a more particular description of our prison, where it stands, and a drawing of the grounds, &c."

When Griffith concluded this epistle, he returned it to the man to whom it was addressed, and fell back in his chair, in an attitude that denoted deep reflection.

"I knew she was here, or I should have accepted the command offered to me by our commissioners in Paris," he at length uttered; "and I thought that some lucky chance might throw her in my way; but this is bringing us close, indeed! This intelligence must be acted on, and that promptly. Poor girl, what does she not suffer, in such a situation!"

"What a beautiful hand she writes!" exclaimed Barnstable; "'tis as clear, and as pretty, and as small, as her own delicate fingers. Griff. what a log-book she would keep!"

"Cecilia Howard touch the coarse leaves of a log-book!" cried the other, in amazement; but perceiving Barnstable to be poring over the contents of his mistress's letter, he smiled at their mutual folly, and continued silent. After a short time spent in cool reflection, Griffith inquired of his friend the nature and circumstances of his interview with Katherine Plowden. Barnstable related it, briefly, as it occurred, in the manner already known to the reader.

"Then," said Griffith, "Merry is the only one, besides ourselves, who knows of this meeting, and he will be too chary of the reputation of his kinswoman to mention it."

"Her reputation needs no shield, Mr. Griffith," cried her lover; "'tis as spotless as the canvass above your head, and—"

"Peace, dear Richard; I entreat your pardon; my words may have conveyed more than I intended; but it is important that our measures should be secret, as well as prudently concerted."

"We must get them both off," returned Barnstable, forgetting his displeasure the moment it was exhibited, "and that too before the old man takes it into his wise head to leave the coast. Did you ever get a sight of his instructions, or does he keep silent?"

"As the grave. This is the first time we have left port, that he has not conversed freely with me on the nature of the cruise; but not a syllable has been exchanged between us on the subject, since we sailed from Brest."

"Ah! that is your Jersey bashfulness," said Barnstable; "wait till I come alongside him, with my eastern curiosity, and I pledge myself to get it out of him in an hour."

"'Twill be diamond cut diamond, I doubt," said Griffith, laughing; "you will find him as acute at evasion, as you can possibly be at a cross-examination."

"At any rate, he gives me a chance to-day; you know, I suppose, that he sent for me to attend a consultation of his officers, on important matters."

"I did not," returned Griffith, fixing his eyes intently on the speaker; "what has he to offer?"

"Nay, that you must ask your pilot; for while talking to me, the old man would turn and look at the stranger, every minute, as if watching for signals how to steer."

"There is a mystery about that man, and our connexion with him, that I cannot fathom," said Griffith. "But I hear the voice of Manual, calling for me; we are wanted in the cabin. Remember, you do not leave the ship without seeing me again."

"No, no, my dear fellow, from the public, we must retire to another private consultation."

The young men arose, and Griffith, throwing off the roundabout in which he had appeared on deck, drew on a coat of more formal appearance, and taking a sword carelessly in his hand, they proceeded together, along the passage already described, to the gun-deck, where they entered, with the proper ceremonials, into the principal cabin of the frigate.

Chapter VII.

"Sempronius, speak."

Addison, Cato, II.i.23.

T HE ARRANGEMENTS for the consultation were brief and simple. The veteran commander of the frigate received his officers with punctilious respect, and pointing to the chairs that were placed around the table, which was a fixture in the centre of his cabin, he silently seated himself, and his example was followed by all, without further ceremony. In taking their stations, however, a quiet, but rigid observance was paid to the rights of seniority and rank. On the right of the captain was placed Griffith, as next in authority; and opposite to him, was seated the commander of the schooner. The officer of marines, who was included in the number, held the next situation in point of precedence, the same order being observed to the bottom of the table, which was occupied by a hard-featured, square-built, athletic man, who held the office of sailing-master. When order was restored, after the short interruption of taking their places, the officer who had required the advice of his inferiors, opened the business on which he demanded their opinions.

"My instructions direct me, gentlemen," he said, "after making the coast of England, to run the land down—"

The hand of Griffith was elevated respectfully for silence, and the veteran paused, with a look that inquired the reason of his interruption.

"We are not alone," said the lieutenant, glancing his eye towards the part of the cabin where the pilot stood, leaning on one of the guns, in an attitude of easy indulgence.

The stranger moved not at this direct hint; neither did his eye change from its close survey of a chart that lay near him on the deck. The captain dropped his voice to tones of cautious respect, as he replied—

"'Tis only Mr. Gray. His services will be necessary on the occasion, and, therefore, nothing need be concealed from him."

Glances of surprise were exchanged among the young men, but Griffith bowing his silent acquiescence in the decision of his superior, the latter proceeded —

"I was ordered to watch for certain signals from the headlands that we made, and was furnished with the best of charts, and such directions as enabled us to stand into the bay we entered last night. We have now obtained a pilot, and one who has proved himself a skilful man; such a one, gentlemen, as no officer need hesitate to rely on, in any emergency, either on account of his integrity or his knowledge."

The veteran paused, and turned his looks on the countenances of the listeners, as if to collect their sentiments on this important point. Receiving no other reply than the one conveyed by the silent inclinations of the heads of his hearers, the commander resumed his explanations, referring to an open paper in his hand —

"It is known to you all, gentlemen, that the unfortunate question of retaliation has been much agitated between the two governments, our own and that of the enemy. For this reason, and for certain political purposes, it has become an object of solicitude with our commissioners in Paris, to obtain a few individuals of character from the enemy, who may be held as a check on their proceedings, while at the same time it brings the evils of war, from our own shores, home to those who have caused it. An opportunity now offers to put this plan in execution, and I have collected you, in order to consult on the means."

A profound silence succeeded this unexpected communication of the object of their cruise. After a short pause, their captain added, addressing himself to the sailing-master —

"What course would you advise me to pursue, Mr. Boltrope?"

The weather-beaten seaman who was thus called on to break through the difficulties of a knotty point, with his opinion, laid one of his short, bony hands on the table, and began to twirl an inkstand with great industry, while with the other he conveyed a pen to his mouth, which was apparently masticated with all the relish that he could possibly have felt had it been a leaf from the famous Virginian weed. But perceiving that he was expected to answer, after looking first to his right hand, and then to his left, he spoke as follows, in a hoarse, thick voice, in which the fogs of the ocean seemed to have united with sea-damps and colds, to destroy every thing like melody—

"If this matter is ordered, it is to be done, I suppose," he said; "for the old rule runs, 'obey orders, if you break owners;' though the maxim, which says, 'one hand for the owner, and t'other for yourself,' is quite as good, and has saved many a hearty fellow from a fall that would have balanced the purser's books. Not that I mean a purser's books are not as good as any other man's, but that when a man is dead, his account must be closed, or there will be a false muster. Well, if the thing is to be done, the next question is, how is it to be done? There is many a man that knows there is too much canvass on a ship, who can't tell how to shorten sail. Well, then, if the thing is really to be done, we must either land a gang to seize them or we must show false lights, and sham colours, to lead them off to the ship. As for landing, Captain Munson, I can only speak for one man, and that is myself, which is to say, that if you run the ship with her jib-boom into the king of England's parlour windows, why, I'm consenting, nor do I care how much of his crockery is cracked in so doing; but as to putting the print of my foot on one of his sandy beaches, if I do, that is always speaking for only one man, and saving your presence, may I hope to be d——d."

The young men smiled as the tough old seaman uttered his sentiments so frankly, rising with his subject, to that which with him was the climax of all discussion; but his commander, who was but a more improved scholar from the same rough school, appeared to understand his arguments entirely, and without altering a muscle of his rigid countenance, he required the opinion of the junior lieutenant.

The young man spoke firmly, but modestly, though the amount of what he said was not much more distinct than that uttered by the master, and was very much to the same purpose, with the exception, that he appeared to entertain no personal reluctance to trusting himself on dry ground.

The opinions of the others grew gradually more explicit and clear, as they ascended in the scale of rank, until it came to the turn of the captain of marines to speak. There was a trifling exhibition of professional pride about the soldier, in delivering his sentiments on a subject that embraced a good deal more of his peculiar sort of duty than ordinarily occurred in the usual operations of the frigate.

"It appears to me, sir, that the success of this expedition depends altogether upon the manner in which it is conducted." After this lucid opening, the soldier hesitated a moment, as if to collect his ideas for a charge that should look down all opposition, and proceeded. "The landing, of course, will be effected on a fair beach, under cover of the frigate's guns, and could it be possibly done, the schooner should be anchored in such a manner as to throw in a flanking fire on the point of debarkation. The arrangements for the order of march must a good deal depend on the distance to go over; though I should think, sir, an advanced party of seamen, to act as pioneers for the column of marines, should be pushed a short distance in front, while the baggage and baggage-guard might rest upon the frigate, until the enemy was driven into the interior, when it could advance without danger. There should be flank-guards, under the orders of two of the oldest midshipmen; and a light corps might be formed of the top-men, to co-operate with the marines. Of course, sir, Mr. Griffith will lead, in person, the musket-men and boarders, armed with their long pikes, whom I presume he will hold in reserve, as I trust my military claims and experience entitle me to the command of the main body."

"Well done, field marshal!" cried Barnstable, with a glee that seldom regarded time or place; "you should never let salt-water mould your buttons, but in Washington's camp, ay! and in Washington's tent, you should swing your hammock in future. Why, sir, do you think we are about to invade England?"

"I know that every military movement should be executed with precision, Captain Barnstable," returned the marine. "I am too much accustomed to hear the sneers of the sea-officers, to regard what I know proceeds from ignorance. If Captain Munson is disposed to employ me and my command in this expedition, I trust he will discover that marines are good for something more than to mount guard and pay salutes." Then, turning haughtily from his antagonist, he continued to address himself to their common superior, as if disdaining further intercourse with one who, from the nature of the case, must be unable to comprehend the force of what he said. "It will be prudent, Captain Munson, to send out a party to reconnoitre, before we march; and as it may be necessary to defend ourselves, in case of a repulse, I would beg leave to recommend that a corps be provided with entrenching tools, to accompany the expedition. They would be extremely useful, sir, in assisting to throw up field-works; though, I doubt not, tools might be found in abundance in this country, and labourers impressed for the service, on an emergency. — "

This was too much for the risibility of Barnstable, who broke forth in a fit of scornful laughter, which no one saw proper to interrupt; though Griffith, on turning his head, to conceal the smile that was gathering on his own face, perceived the fierce glance which the pilot threw at the merry seaman, and wondered at its significance and impatience. When Captain Munson thought that the mirth of the lieutenant was concluded, he mildly desired his reasons for amusing himself so exceedingly with the plans of the marine.

"'Tis a chart for a campaign!" cried Barnstable, "and should be sent off express to Congress, before the Frenchmen are brought into the field!"

"Have you any better plan to propose, Mr. Barnstable?" inquired the patient commander.

"Better! ay, one that will take no time, and cause no trouble, to execute it," cried the other; "'tis a seaman's job, sir, and must be done with a seaman's means."

"Pardon me, Captain Barnstable," interrupted the marine, whose jocular vein was entirely absorbed in his military pride; "if there be service to be done on shore, I claim it as my right to be employed."

"Claim what you will, soldier, but how will you carry on the war, with a parcel of fellows who don't know one end of a boat from the other," returned the reckless sailor. "Do you think, that a barge or a cutter is to be beached in the same manner you ground firelock, by word of command? No, no, Captain

Manual—I honour your courage, for I have seen it tried, but d——e if—"

"You forget we wait for your project, Mr. Barnstable," said the veteran.

"I crave your patience, sir; but no project is necessary. Point out the bearings and distance of the place where the men you want are to be found, and I will take the heel of the gale, and run into the land, always speaking for good water and no rocks. Mr. Pilot, you will accompany me, for you carry as true a map of the bottom of these seas, in your head, as ever was made of dry ground. I will look out for good anchorage, or, if the wind should blow off shore, let the schooner stand off and on, till we should be ready to take the broad sea again. I would land, out of my whale-boat, with long Tom and a boat's crew, and finding out the place you will describe, we shall go up, and take the men you want, and bring them aboard. It's all plain-sailing; though, as it is a well-peopled country, it may be necessary to do our shore work in the dark."

"Mr. Griffith, we only wait for your sentiments," proceeded the captain, "when, by comparing opinions, we may decide on the most prudent course."

The first lieutenant had been much absorbed in thought, during the discussion of the subject, and might have been, on that account, better prepared to give his opinion with effect. Pointing to the man who yet stood behind him, leaning on a gun, he commenced by asking—

"Is it your intention that man shall accompany the party?"

"It is."

"And from him you expect the necessary information, sir, to guide our movements?"

"You are altogether right."

"If, sir, he has but a moiety of the skill on the land that he possesses on the water, I will answer for his success," returned the lieutenant, bowing slightly to the stranger, who received the compliment by a cold inclination of his head. "I must desire the indulgence of both Mr. Barnstable and Captain Manual," he continued, "and claim the command as of right belonging to my rank."

"It belongs naturally to the schooner," exclaimed the impatient Barnstable.

"There may be enough for us all to do," said Griffith, elevating a finger to the other, in a manner, and with an impressive look, that was instantly comprehended. "I neither agree wholly with the one nor the other of these gentlemen. 'Tis said, that since our appearance on the coast, the dwellings of many of the gentry are guarded by small detachments of soldiers from the neighbouring towns."

"Who says it?" asked the pilot, advancing among them, with a suddenness that caused a general silence.

"I say it, sir," returned the lieutenant, when the momentary surprise had passed away.

"Can you vouch for it?"

"I can."

"Name a house, or an individual, that is thus protected."

Griffith gazed at the man who thus forgot himself in the midst of a consultation like the present, and yielding to his native pride, hesitated to reply. But mindful of the declarations of his captain, and the recent services of the pilot, he at length said, with a little embarrassment of manner—

"I know it to be the fact, in the dwelling of a Colonel Howard, who resides but a few leagues to the north of us."

The stranger started at the name, and then raising his eye keenly to the face of the young man, appeared to study his thoughts in his varying countenance. But the action, and the pause that followed, were of short continuance. His lip slightly curled, whether in scorn or with a concealed smile, would have been difficult to say, so closely did it resemble both, and as he dropped quietly back to his place at the gun, he said—

"'Tis more than probable you are right, sir; and if I might presume to advise Captain Munson, it would be to lay great weight on your opinion."

Griffith turned, to see if he could comprehend more meaning in the manner of the stranger than his words expressed, but his face was again shaded by his hand, and his eyes were once more fixed on the chart with the same vacant abstraction as before.

"I have said, sir, that I agree wholly neither with Mr. Barnstable nor Captain Manual," continued the lieutenant, after a short pause. "The command of this party is mine, as the senior officer, and I must beg leave to claim it. I certainly do not think the preparation that Captain Manual advises necessary; neither would I undertake the duty with as little caution as Mr. Barnstable proposes. If there are soldiers to be encountered, we should have soldiers to oppose to them; but as it must be sudden boat-work, and regular evolutions must give place to a seaman's bustle, a sea-officer should command. Is my request granted, Captain Munson?"

The veteran replied, without hesitation —

"It is, sir; it was my intention to offer you the service, and I rejoice to see you accept it so cheerfully."

Griffith with difficulty concealed the satisfaction with which he listened to his commander, and a radiant smile illumined his pale features, when he observed —

"With me, then, sir, let the responsibility rest. I request that Captain Manual, with twenty men, may be put under my orders, if that gentleman does not dislike the duty." The marine bowed, and cast a glance of triumph at Barnstable. "I will take my own cutter, with her tried crew, go on board the schooner, and when the wind lulls, we will run in to the land, and then be governed by circumstances."

The commander of the schooner threw back the triumphant look of the marine, and exclaimed, in his joyous manner —

"'Tis a good plan, and done like a seaman, Mr. Griffith. Ay, ay, let the schooner be employed, and if it be necessary, you shall see her anchored in one of their duck-ponds, with her broadside to bear on the parlour-windows of the best house in the island! But twenty marines! they will cause a jam in my little craft."

"Not a man less than twenty would be prudent," returned Griffith. "More service may offer than that we seek."

Barnstable well understood his allusion, but still he replied —

"Make it all seamen, and I will give you room for thirty. But these soldiers never know how to stow away their arms and legs, unless at a drill. One will take the room of two sailors; they swing their hammocks athwart-ships, heads to leeward, and then turn-out wrong end uppermost at the call. Why, damn it, sir, the chalk and rotten-stone of twenty soldiers will chock my hatches!"

"Give me the launch, Captain Munson!" exclaimed the indignant marine, "and we will follow Mr. Griffith in an open boat, rather than put Captain Barnstable to so much inconvenience."

"No, no, Manual," cried the other, extending his muscular arm across the table, with an open palm, to the soldier; "you would all become so many Jonahs in uniform, and I doubt whether the fish could digest your cartridge-boxes and bayonet-belts. You shall go with me, and learn, with your own eyes, whether we keep the cat's-watch aboard the Ariel, that you joke about."

The laugh was general, at the expense of the soldier, if we except the pilot and the commander of the frigate. The former was a silent, and apparently an abstracted, but in reality a deeply interested listener to the discourse; and there were moments when he bent his looks on the speakers, as if he sought more in their characters than was exhibited by the gay trifling of the moment. Captain Munson seldom allowed a muscle of his wrinkled features to disturb their repose; and if he had not the real dignity to repress the untimely mirth of his officers, he had too much good nature to wish to disturb their harmless enjoyments. He expressed himself satisfied with the proposed arrangements, and beckoned to his steward, to place before them the usual beverage, with which all their consultations concluded.

The sailing-master appeared to think that the same order was to be observed in their potations as in council, and helping himself to an allowance which retained its hue even in its diluted state, he first raised it to the light, and then observed—

"This ship's-water is nearly the colour of rum itself; if it only had its flavour, what a set of hearty dogs we should be. Mr. Griffith, I find you are willing to haul your land-tacks aboard. Well, it's natural for youth to love the earth; but there is one man, and he is sailing-master of this ship, who saw land enough, last night, to last him a twelve-month. But if you will go, here's a good land-fall and a better offing to you. Captain Munson, my respects to you. I say, sir, if we should keep the ship more to the south'ard, it's my opinion, and that's but one man's, we should fall in with some of the enemy's homeward-bound West-Indiamen, and find wherewithal to keep the life in us when we see fit to go ashore ourselves."

As the tough old sailor made frequent application of the glass to his mouth, with one hand, and kept a firm hold of the decanter with the other, during this speech, his companions were compelled to listen to his eloquence, or depart with their thirst unassuaged. Barnstable, however, quite coolly dispossessed the tar of the bottle, and mixing for himself a more equal potation, observed, in the act —

"That is the most remarkable glass of grog you have, Boltrope, that I ever sailed with; it draws as little water as the Ariel, and is as hard to find the bottom. If your spirit-room enjoys the same sort of engine to replenish it, as you pump out your rum, Congress will sail this frigate cheaply."

The other officers helped themselves with still greater moderation, Griffith barely moistening his lips, and the pilot rejecting the offered glass altogether. Captain Munson continued standing, and his officers, perceiving that their presence was no longer necessary, bowed, and took their leave. As Griffith was retiring last, he felt a hand laid lightly on his shoulder, and turning, perceived that he was detained by the pilot.

"Mr. Griffith," he said, when they were quite alone with the commander of the frigate, "the occurrences of the last night should teach us confidence in each other; without it, we go on a dangerous and fruitless errand."

"Is the hazard equal?" returned the youth. "I am known to all to be the man I seem — am in the service of my country — belong to a family, and enjoy a name, that is a pledge for my loyalty to the cause of America — and yet I trust myself on hostile ground, in the midst of enemies, with a weak arm, and under circumstances where treachery would prove my ruin. Who and what is the man who thus enjoys your confidence, Captain Munson? I ask the question less for myself than for the gallant men who will fearlessly follow wherever I lead."

A shade of dark displeasure crossed the features of the stranger, at one part of this speech, and at its close he sunk into deep thought. The commander, however, replied —

"There is a show of reason in your question, Mr. Griffith — and yet you are not the man to be told that implicit obedience is what I have a right to expect. I have not your pretensions, sir, by birth or education, and yet Congress have not seen proper to overlook my years and services. I command this frigate—"

"Say no more," interrupted the pilot. "There is reason in his doubts, and they shall be appeased. I like the proud and fearless eye of the young man, and while he dreads a gibbet from my hands, I will show him how to repose a noble confidence. Read this, sir, and tell me if you distrust me now?"

While the stranger spoke, he thrust his hand into the bosom of his dress, and drew forth a parchment, decorated with ribbands and bearing a massive seal, which he opened, and laid on the table before the youth. As he pointed with his finger, impressively, to different parts of the writing, his eye kindled with a look of unusual fire, and there was a faint tinge discernible on his pallid features, when he spoke.

"See!" he said. "Royalty itself does not hesitate to bear witness in my favour, and that is not a name to occasion dread to an American."

Griffith gazed with wonder at the fair signature of the unfortunate Louis, which graced the bottom of the parchment; but when his eye obeyed the signal of the stranger, and rested on the body of the instrument, he started back from the table, and fixing his animated eyes on the pilot, he cried, while a glow of fiery courage flitted across his countenance—

"Lead on! I'll follow you to death!"

A smile of gratified exultation struggled around the lips of the stranger, who took the arm of the young man, and led him into a state-room, leaving the commander of the frigate, standing in his unmoved and quiet manner, a spectator of, but hardly an actor in the scene.

Chapter VIII.

"Fierce bounding, forward sprung the ship,
Like grayhound starting from the slip,
To seize his flying prey."
Scott, *The Lord of the Isles*, Canto First, XXI.4–6.

ALTHOUGH the subject of the consultation remained a secret with those whose opinions were required, yet enough of the result leaked out among the subordinate officers, to throw the whole crew into a state of eager excitement. The rumour spread itself along the decks of the frigate, with the rapidity of an alarm, that an expedition was to attempt the shore on some hidden service, dictated by the Congress itself; and conjectures were made respecting its force and destination, with all that interest which might be imagined would exist among the men whose lives or liberties were to abide the issue. A gallant and reckless daring, mingled with the desire of novelty, however, was the prevailing sentiment among the crew, who would have received with cheers the intelligence that their vessel was commanded to force the passage of the united British fleet. A few of the older and more prudent of the sailors were exceptions to this thoughtless hardihood, and one or two, among whom the cockswain of the whale-boat was the most conspicuous, ventured to speak doubtingly of all sorts of land service, as being of a nature never to be attempted by seamen.

Captain Manual had his men paraded in the weather-gangway, and after a short address, calculated to inflame their military ardour and patriotism, acquainted them, that he required twenty volunteers, which was in truth half their number, for a dangerous service. After a short pause, the company stepped forward, like one man, and announced themselves as ready to follow him to the end of the world. The marine cast a look over his shoulder, at this gratifying declaration, in quest of Barnstable; but observing that the sailor was occupied with some papers, on a distant part of the quarter-deck, he proceeded to make a most impartial division among the candidates for glory; taking care, at the same time, to cull his company in such a manner as to give himself the flower of his men, and, consequently, to leave the ship the refuse.

While this arrangement was taking place, and the crew of the frigate was in this state of excitement, Griffith ascended to the deck, his countenance flushed with unusual enthusiasm, and his eyes beaming with a look of animation and gayety that had long been strangers to the face of the young man. He was giving forth the few necessary orders to the seamen he was to take with him from the ship, when Barnstable again motioned him to follow, and led the way once more to the state-room.

"Let the wind blow its pipe out," said the commander of the Ariel, when they were seated; "there will be no landing on the eastern coast of England, till the sea goes down. But this Kate was made for a sailor's wife! see, Griffith, what a set of signals she has formed, out of her own cunning head."

"I hope your opinion may prove true, and that you may be the happy sailor who is to wed her," returned the other. "The girl has indeed discovered surprising art in this business! where could she have learnt the method and system so well?"

"Where! why, where she learnt better things; how to prize a whole-hearted seaman, for instance. Do you think that my tongue was jammed in my mouth, all the time we used to sit by the side of the river in Carolina, and that we found nothing to talk about!"

"Did you amuse your mistress with treatises on the art of navigation, and the science of signals?" said Griffith, smiling.

"I answered her questions, Mr. Griffith, as any civil man would to a woman he loved. The girl has as much curiosity as one of my own townswomen who has weathered cape forty without a husband, and her tongue goes like a dog-vane in a calm, first one way and then another. But here is her dictionary. Now own, Griff., in spite of your college learning and sentimentals, that a woman of ingenuity and cleverness is a very good sort of a helpmate."

"I never doubted the merits of Miss Plowden," said the other, with a droll gravity that often mingled with his deeper feelings, the result of a sailor's habits, blended with native character. "But this indeed surpasses all my expectations! Why, she has, in truth, made a most judicious selection of

phrases. 'No. 168. **** indelible;' '169. **** end only with life;'
'170. **** I fear yours misleads me;' '171. —'"

"Pshaw!" exclaimed Barnstable, snatching the book from
before the laughing eyes of Griffith; "what folly, to throw away
our time now on such nonsense. What think you of this expedition to the land?"

"That it may be the means of rescuing the ladies, though it
fail in making the prisoners we anticipate."

"But this pilot! you remember that he holds us by our necks,
and can run us all up to the yard-arm of some English ship,
whenever he chooses to open his throat, at their threats or
bribes."

"It would have been better that he should have cast the ship
ashore, when he had her entangled in the shoals; it would have
been our last thought to suspect him of treachery then,"
returned Griffith. "I follow him with confidence, and must
believe that we are safer with him than we should be without
him."

"Let him lead to the dwelling of his fox-hunting ministers of
state," cried Barnstable, thrusting his book of signals into his
bosom; "but here is a chart that will show us the way to the
port we wish to find. Let my foot once more touch terra firma,
and you may write craven against my name, if that laughing
vixen slips her cable before my eyes, and shoots into the wind's
eye again, like a flying-fish chased by a dolphin. Mr. Griffith,
we must have the chaplain with us to the shore."

"The madness of love is driving you into the errors of the
soldier. Would you lie-by to hear sermons, with a flying party
like ours?"

"Nay, nay, we must lay-to for nothing that is not
unavoidable; but there are so many tacks in such a chase,
when one has time to breathe, that we might as well spend our
leisure in getting that fellow to splice us together. He has a
handy way with a prayer-book, and could do the job as well as
a bishop, and I should like to be able to say, that this is the last
time these two saucy names, which are written at the bottom of
this letter, should ever be seen sailing in the company of each
other."

"It will not do," said his friend, shaking his head, and
endeavouring to force a smile which his feelings suppressed; "it

will not do, Richard; we must yield our own inclinations to the service of our country; nor is this pilot a man who will consent to be led from his purpose."

"Then let him follow his purpose alone," cried Barnstable. "There is no human power, always saving my superior officer, that shall keep me from throwing abroad these tiny signals, and having a private talk with my dark-eyed Kate. But for a paltry pilot! he may luff and bear away as he pleases, while I shall steer as true as a magnet for that old ruin, where I can bring my eyes to bear on that romantic wing and three smoky vanes. Not that I'll forget my duty; no, I'll help you catch the Englishmen, but when that is done, hey! for Katherine Plowden and my true love!"

"Hush, madcap! the ward-room holds long ears, and our bulkheads grow thin by wear. I must keep you and myself to our duty. This is no children's game that we play; it seems the commissioners at Paris have thought proper to employ a frigate in the sport."

Barnstable's gayety was a little repressed by the grave manner of his companion; but after reflecting a moment, he started on his feet, and made the usual movements for departure.

"Whither?" asked Griffith, gently detaining his impatient friend.

"To old Moderate; I have a proposal to make, that may remove every difficulty."

"Name it to me, then; I am in his council, and may save you the trouble and mortification of a refusal."

"How many of those gentry does he wish to line his cabin with?"

"The pilot has named no less than six, all men of rank and consideration with the enemy. Two of them are peers, two more belong to the commons' house of parliament, one is a general, and the sixth, like ourselves, is a sailor, and holds the rank of captain. They muster at a hunting seat, near the coast, and believe me, the scheme is not without its plausibility."

"Well, then, there are two a-piece for us. You follow the pilot, if you will; but let me sheer off for this dwelling of Colonel Howard, with my cockswain and boat's-crew. I will surprise his house, release the ladies, and on my way back, lay my hands on two of the first lords I fall in with. I suppose, for our business, one is as good as another."

Griffith could not repress a faint laugh, while he replied —

"Though they are said to be each other's peers, there is, I believe some difference even in the quality of lords. England might thank us for ridding her of some among them. Neither are they to be found, like beggars, under every hedge. No, no, the men we seek must have something better than their nobility to recommend them to our favour. But let us examine more closely into this plan and map of Miss Plowden; something may occur, that shall yet bring the place within our circuit, like a contingent duty of the cruise."

Barnstable reluctantly relinquished his own wild plan, to the more sober judgment of his friend, and they passed an hour together, inquiring into the practicability, and consulting on the means, of making their public duty subserve the purposes of their private feelings.

The gale continued to blow heavily, during the whole of that morning; but towards noon, the usual indications of better weather became apparent. During these few hours of inaction in the frigate, the marines, who were drafted for service on the land, moved through the vessel with a busy and stirring air, as if they were about to participate in the glory and danger of the campaign their officer had planned, while the few seamen who were to accompany the expedition steadily paced the deck, with their hands thrust into the bosoms of their neat blue jackets, or, occasionally, stretched towards the horizon, as their fingers traced, for their less experienced shipmates, the signs of an abatement in the gale among the driving clouds. The last lagger among the soldiers had appeared with his knapsack on his back in the lee-gangway, where his comrades were collected, armed and accoutred for the strife, when Captain Munson ascended to the quarter-deck, accompanied by the stranger and his first lieutenant. A word was spoken by the latter in a low voice to a midshipman, who skipped gayly along the deck, and presently the shrill call of the boatswain was heard, preceding the hoarse cry of —

"Away there, you Tigers, away!"

A smart roll of the drum followed, and the marines paraded,

while the six seamen who belonged to the cutter that owned so
fierce a name, made their preparations for lowering their little
bark from the quarter of the frigate into the troubled sea.
Every thing was conducted in the most exact order, and with a
coolness and skill that bade defiance to the turbulence of the
angry elements. The marines were safely transported from the
ship to the schooner, under the favouring shelter of the former,
though the boat appeared, at times, to be seeking the cavities
of the ocean, and again, to be riding in the clouds, as she passed
from one vessel to the other.

At length, it was announced that the cutter was ready to
receive the officers of the party. The pilot walked aside, and
held private discourse, for a few moments, with the commander, who listened to his sentences with marked and
singular attention. When their conference was ended, the
veteran bared his gray head to the blasts, and offered his hand
to the other, with a seaman's frankness, mingled with the
deference of an inferior. The compliment was courteously
returned by the stranger, who turned quickly on his heel, and
directed the attention of those who awaited his movements, by
a significant gesture, to the gangway.

"Come gentlemen, let us go," said Griffith, starting from a
reverie, and bowing his hasty compliments to his brethren in
arms.

When it appeared that his superiors were ready to enter the
boat, the boy, who, by nautical courtesy, was styled Mr.
Merry, and who had been ordered to be in readiness, sprang
over the side of the frigate, and glided into the cutter, with
the activity of a squirrel. But the captain of marines paused,
and cast a meaning glance at the pilot, whose place it was to
precede him. The stranger, as he lingered on the deck, was examining the aspect of the heavens, and seemed unconscious of
the expectations of the soldier, who gave vent to his impatience, after a moment's detention, by saying—

"We wait for you, Mr. Gray."

Aroused by the sound of his name, the pilot glanced his
quick eye on the speaker, but instead of advancing, he gently
bent his body, as he again signed towards the gangway with
his hand. To the astonishment not only of the soldier, but of all
who witnessed this breach of naval etiquette, Griffith bowed

low, and entered the boat with the same promptitude as if he were preceding an admiral. Whether the stranger became conscious of his want of courtesy, or was too indifferent to surrounding objects to note occurrences, he immediately followed himself, leaving to the marine the post of honour. The latter, who was distinguished for his skill in all matters of naval or military etiquette, thought proper to apologize, at a fitting time, to the first lieutenant, for suffering his senior officer to precede him into a boat, but never failed to show a becoming exultation, when he recounted the circumstance, by dwelling on the manner in which he had brought down the pride of the haughty pilot.

Barnstable had been several hours on board his little vessel, which was every way prepared for their reception; and as soon as the heavy cutter of the frigate was hoisted on her deck, he announced that the schooner was ready to sail. It has been already intimated, that the Ariel belonged to the smallest class of sea-vessels, and as the symmetry of her construction reduced even that size in appearance, she was peculiarly well adapted to the sort of service in which she was about to be employed. Notwithstanding her lightness rendered her nearly as buoyant as a cork, and at times she actually seemed to ride on the foam, her low decks were perpetually washed by the heavy seas that dashed against her frail sides, and she tossed and rolled in the hollows of the waves, in a manner that compelled even the practised seamen who trod her decks to move with guarded steps. Still she was trimmed and cleared with an air of nautical neatness and attention that afforded the utmost possible room for her dimensions; and though in miniature, she wore the trappings of war as proudly as if the metal she bore was of a more fatal and dangerous character. The murderous gun which, since the period of which we are writing, has been universally adopted in all vessels of inferior size, was then in the infancy of its invention, and was known to the American mariner only by reputation, under the appalling name of a "smasher." Of a vast caliber, though short, and easily managed, its advantages were even in that early day beginning to be appreciated, and the largest ships were thought to be unusually well provided with the means of offence, when they carried two or three cannon of this formidable invention among their armament. At a later day this weapon has been improved and altered, until its use has become general in vessels of a certain size, taking its appellation from the Carron, on the banks of which river it was first moulded. In place of these carronades, six light brass cannon were firmly lashed to the bulwarks of the Ariel, their brazen throats blackened by the sea-water, which so often broke harmlessly over these engines of destruction. In the center of the vessel, between her two masts, a gun of the same metal, but of nearly twice the length of the others, was mounted on a carriage of a new and singular construction, which admitted of its being turned in any direction, so as to be of service in most of the emergencies that occur in naval warfare.

The eye of the pilot examined this armament closely, and then turned to the well-ordered decks, the neat and compact rigging, and the hardy faces of the fine young crew, with manifest satisfaction. Contrary to what had been his practice during the short time he had been with them, he uttered his gratification freely and aloud.

"You have a tight boat, Mr. Barnstable," he said, "and a gallant looking crew. You promise good service, sir, in time of need, and that hour may not be far distant."

"The sooner the better," returned the reckless sailor; "I have not had an opportunity of scaling my guns since we quitted Brest, though we passed several of the enemy's cutters coming up channel, with whom our bull-dogs longed for a conversation. Mr. Griffith will tell you, pilot, that my little sixes can speak, on occasion, with a voice nearly as loud as the frigate's eighteens."

"But not to as much purpose," observed Griffith; "'vox et preterea nihil,' as we said at the school."

"I know nothing of your Greek and Latin, Mr. Griffith," retorted the commander of the Ariel; "but if you mean that those seven brass playthings won't throw a round shot as far as any gun of their size and height above the water, or won't scatter grape and cannister with any blunderbuss in your ship, you may possibly find an opportunity that will convince you to the contrary, before we part company."

"They promise well," said the pilot, who was evidently ignorant of the good understanding that existed between the two officers, and wished to conciliate all under his directions, "and I doubt not they will argue the leading points of a combat with good discretion. I see that you have christened them—I suppose for their respective merits. They are indeed expressive names!"

"'Tis the freak of an idle moment," said Barnstable, laughing, as he glanced his eyes to the cannon, above which were painted the several quaint names of "boxer," "plumper," "grinder," "scatterer," "exterminator," and "nail-driver."

"Why have you thrown the midship-gun without the pale of your baptism?" asked the pilot; "or do you know it by the usual title of the 'old woman?'"

"No, no, I have no such petticoat terms on board me," cried the other; "but move more to starboard, and you will see its style painted on the cheeks of the carriage; it's a name that need not cause them to blush either."

"'Tis a singular epithet, though not without some meaning!"

"It has more than you, perhaps, dream of, sir. That worthy seaman whom you see leaning against the foremast, and who would serve, on occasion, for a spare spar himself, is the captain of that gun, and more than once has decided some warm disputes with John Bull, by the manner in which he has wielded it. No marine can trail his musket more easily than my cockswain can train his nine-pounder on an object; and thus from their connexion, and some resemblance there is between them in length, it has got the name which you perceive it carries; that of 'long Tom.'"

The pilot smiled as he listened, but turning away from the speaker, the deep reflection that crossed his brow but too plainly showed that he trifled only from momentary indulgence; and Griffith intimated to Barnstable, that as the gale was sensibly abating, they would pursue the object of their destination.

Thus recalled to his duty, the commander of the schooner forgot the delightful theme of expatiating on the merits of his vessel, and issued the necessary orders to direct their movements. The little schooner slowly obeyed the impulse of her helm, and fell off before the wind, when the folds of her squaresail, though limited by a prudent reef, were opened to the blasts, and she shot away from her consort, like a meteor dancing across the waves. The black mass of the frigate's hull soon sunk in distance, and long before the sun had fallen below the hills of England, her tall masts were barely distinguishable by the small cloud of sail that held the vessel to her station. As the ship disappeared, the land seemed to issue out of the bosom of the deep, and so rapid was their progress, that the dwellings of the gentry, the humbler cottages, and even the dim lines of the hedges, became gradually more distinct to the eyes of the bold mariners, until they were beset with the gloom of the evening, when the whole scene faded from their view in the darkness of the hour, leaving only the faint outline of the land visible in the tract before them, and the sullen billows of the ocean raging with appalling violence in their rear.

Still the little Ariel held on her way, skimming the ocean like a water-fowl seeking its place of nightly rest, and shooting in towards the land as fearlessly as if the dangers of the preceding night were already forgotten. No shoals or rocks appeared to arrest her course, and we must leave her gliding into the dark streak that was thrown from the high and rocky cliffs, that lined a basin of bold entrance, where the mariners often sought and found a refuge from the dangers of the German ocean.

Chapter IX.

"Sirrah! how dare you leave your barley broth,
To come in armour thus, against your king!"

Drama.

THE LARGE, irregular building, inhabited by Colonel Howard, well deserved the name it had received from the pen of Katherine Plowden. Notwithstanding the confusion in its orders, owing to the different ages in which its several parts had been erected, the interior was not wanting in that appearance of comfort which forms the great characteristic of English domestic life. Its dark and intricate mazes of halls, galleries, and apartments, were all well provided with good and substantial furniture, and whatever might have been the purposes of their original construction, they were now peacefully appropriated to the service of a quiet and well-ordered family.

There were divers portentous traditions, of cruel separations and blighted loves, which always linger, like cobwebs, around the walls of old houses, to be heard here also, and which, doubtless, in abler hands, might easily have been wrought up into scenes of high interest and delectable pathos. But our humbler efforts must be limited by an attempt to describe man as God has made him, vulgar and unseemly as he may appear to sublimated faculties, to the possessors of which enviable qualifications we desire to say, at once, that we are determined to eschew all things supernaturally refined, as we would the devil. To all those, then, who are tired of the company of their species, we would bluntly insinuate, that the sooner they throw aside our pages, and seize upon those of some more highly gifted bard, the sooner will they be in the way of quitting earth, if not of attaining heaven. Our business is solely to treat of man, and this fair scene on which he acts, and that not in his subtleties and metaphysical contradictions, but in his palpable nature, that all may understand our meaning as well as ourselves — whereby we manifestly reject the prodigious advantage of being thought a genius, by perhaps foolishly refusing the mighty aid of incomprehensibility to establish such a character.

Leaving the gloomy shadows of the cliffs, under which the little Ariel has been seen to steer, and the sullen roaring of the surf along the margin of the ocean, we shall endeavour to transport the reader to the dining parlour of St. Ruth's Abbey, taking the evening of the same day as the time for introducing another collection of those personages, whose acts and characters it has become our duty to describe.

The room was not of very large dimensions, and every part was glittering with the collected light of half a dozen candles, aided by the fierce rays that glanced from the grate, which held a most cheerful fire of seacoal. The mouldings of the dark oak wainscoting threw back upon the massive table of mahogany, streaks of strong light, which played among the rich fluids, that were sparkling on the board, in mimic haloes. The outline of this picture of comfort was formed by damask curtains of a deep red, and enormous oak chairs with leathern backs and cushioned seats, as if the apartment were hermetically sealed against the world and its chilling cares.

Around the table, which still stood in the center of the floor, were seated three gentlemen, in the easy enjoyment of their daily repast. The cloth had been drawn, and the bottle was slowly passing among them, as if those who partook of its bounty well knew that neither the time nor the opportunity would be wanting for their deliberate indulgence in its pleasures.

At one end of the table an elderly man was seated, who performed whatever little acts of courtesy the duties of a host would appear to render necessary, in a company where all seemed to be equally at their ease and at home. This gentleman was in the decline of life, though his erect carriage, quick movements, and steady hand, equally denoted that it was an old age free from the usual infirmities. In his dress, he belonged to that class whose members always follow the fashions of the age anterior to the one in which they live, whether from disinclination to sudden changes of any kind, or from the recollections of a period which, with them, has been hallowed by scenes and feelings that the chilling evening of life can neither revive nor equal. Age might possibly have thrown its blighting frosts on his thin locks, but art had laboured to conceal the ravages with the nicest care. An accurate outline of powder covered not only the parts where the hair actually remained, but wherever nature had prescribed that hair should grow. His countenance was strongly marked in features, if not in expression, exhibiting, on the whole, a look of noble integrity and high honour, which was a good deal aided in its effect, by the lofty receding forehead, that rose like a monument, above the whole, to record the character of the aged veteran. A few streaks of branching red mingled with a swarthiness of complexion that was rendered more conspicuous by the outline of unsullied white which nearly surrounded his prominent features.

Opposite to the host, who it will at once be understood was Colonel Howard, was the thin, yellow visage of Mr. Christopher Dillon, that bane to the happiness of her cousin, already mentioned by Miss Plowden.

Between these two gentlemen was a middle-aged, hard-featured man, attired in the livery of King George, whose countenance emulated the scarlet of his coat, and whose principal employment, at the moment, appeared to consist in doing honour to the cheer of his entertainer.

Occasionally, a servant entered or left the room in silence, giving admission, however, through the opened door, to the rushing sounds of the gale, as the wind murmured amid the angles and high chimneys of the edifice.

A man, in the dress of a rustic, was standing near the chair of Colonel Howard, between whom and the master of the mansion a dialogue had been maintained, which closed as follows. The colonel was the first to speak, after the curtain is drawn from between the eyes of the reader and the scene.

"Said you, farmer, that the Scotchman beheld the vessels with his own eyes?"

The answer was a simple negative.

"Well, well," continued the colonel, "you can withdraw."

The man made a rude attempt at a bow, which being returned by the old soldier with formal grace, he left the room. The host, turning to his companions, resumed the subject.

"If those rash boys have really persuaded the silly dotard who commands the frigate, to trust himself within the shoals, on the eve of such a gale as this, their case must have been hopeless indeed! Thus may rebellion and disaffection ever meet with the just indignation of Providence! It would not surprise me, gentlemen, to hear that my native land has been engulphed by earthquakes, or swallowed by the ocean, so awful and inexcusable has been the weight of her transgressions! And yet it was a proud and daring boy who held the second station in that ship! I knew his father well, and a gallant gentleman he was, who, like my own brother, the parent of Cecilia, preferred to serve his master on the ocean rather than on the land. His son inherited the bravery of his high spirit, without its loyalty. One would not wish to have such a youth drowned either."

This speech, which partook much of the nature of a soliloquy, especially towards its close, called for no immediate reply; but the soldier, having held his glass to the candle, to admire the rosy hue of its contents, and then sipped of the fluid so often that nothing but a clear light remained to gaze at, quietly replaced the empty vessel on the table, and, as he extended an arm towards the blushing bottle, he spoke, in the careless tones of one whose thoughts were dwelling on another theme—

"Ay, true enough, sir; good men are scarce, and, as you say, one cannot but mourn his fate, though his death be glorious; quite a loss to his majesty's service, I dare say, it will prove."

"A loss to the service of his majesty!" echoed the host—"his death glorious! no, Captain Borroughcliffe, the death of no rebel can be glorious; and how he can be a loss to his majesty's service, I am myself quite at a loss to understand."

The soldier, whose ideas were in that happy state of confusion that renders it difficult to command the one most needed, but who still, from long discipline, had them under a wonderful control for the disorder of his brain, answered, with great promptitude—

"I mean the loss of his example, sir. It would have been so appalling to others, to have seen the young man executed instead of shot in battle."

"He is drowned, sir."

"Ah! that is the next thing to being hanged; that circumstance had escaped me."

"It is by no means certain, sir, that the ship and schooner that the drover saw are the vessels you take them to have been," said Mr. Dillon, in a harsh, drawling tone of voice. "I should doubt their daring to venture so openly on the coast, and in the direct track of our vessels of war."

"These people are our countrymen, Christopher, though they are rebels," exclaimed the colonel. "They are a hardy and brave nation. When I had the honour to serve his majesty, some twenty years since, it was my fortune to face the enemies of my king in a few small affairs, Captain Borroughcliffe; such as the siege of Quebec, and the battle before its gates, a trifling occasion at Ticonderoga, and that unfortunate catastrophe of General Braddock — with a few others. I must say, sir, in favour of the colonists, that they played a manful game on the latter day; and this gentleman who now heads the rebels sustained a gallant name among us for his conduct in that disastrous business. He was a discreet, well-behaved young man, and quite a gentleman. I have never denied that Mr. Washington was very much of a gentleman."

"Yes," said the soldier, yawning, "he was educated among his majesty's troops, and he could hardly be otherwise. But I am quite melancholy about this unfortunate drowning, Colonel Howard. Here will be an end of my vocation, I suppose, and I am far from denying that your hospitality has made these quarters most agreeable to me."

"Then, sir, the obligation is only mutual," returned the host, with a polite inclination of his head; "but gentlemen, who, like ourselves, have been made free of the camp, need not bandy idle compliments about such trifles. If it were my kinsman Dillon, now, whose thoughts run more on Coke upon Littleton than on the gayeties of a mess-table, and a soldier's life, he might think such formalities as necessary as his hard words are to a deed. Come, Borroughcliffe, my dear fellow, I believe we have given an honest glass to each of the royal family, (God bless them all!) let us swallow a bumper to the memory of the immortal Wolfe."

"An honest proposal, my gallant host, and such a one as a soldier will never decline," returned the captain, who roused himself with the occasion. "God bless them all, say I, in echo, and if this gracious queen of ours ends as famously as she has begun, 'twill be such a family of princes as no other army in Europe can brag of around a mess-table."

"Ay, ay, there is some consolation in that thought, in the midst of this dire rebellion of my countrymen. But I'll vex myself no more with the unpleasant recollections; the arms of my sovereign will soon purge that wicked land of the foul stain."

"Of that there can be no doubt," said Borroughcliffe, whose thoughts still continued a little obscured by the sparkling Madeira that had long lain ripening under a Carolinian sun; "these Yankees fly before his majesty's regulars, like so many dirty clowns in a London mob before a charge of the horse-guards."

"Pardon me, Captain Borroughcliffe," said his host, elevating his person to more than its usually erect attitude; "they may be misguided, deluded, and betrayed, but the comparison is unjust. Give them arms and give them discipline, and he who gets an inch of their land from them, plentiful as it is, will find a bloody day on which to take possession."

"The veriest coward in Christendom would fight in a country where wine brews itself into such a cordial as this," returned the cool soldier; "I am a living proof that you mistook my meaning; for had not those loose-flapped gentlemen they call Vermontese and Hampshire-granters (God grant them his blessing for the deed!) finished two thirds of my company, I should not have been at this day under your roof, a recruiting instead of a marching officer; neither should I have been bound up in a covenant, like the law of Moses, could Burgoyne have made head against their long-legged marchings and counter-marchings. Sir, I drink their healths, with all my heart; and, with such a bottle of golden sunshine before me, rather than displease so good a friend, I will go through Gates's whole army, regiment by regiment, company by company, or, if you insist on the same, even man by man, in a bumper."

"On no account would I tax your politeness so far," returned the Colonel, abundantly mollified by this ample concession; "I stand too much your debtor, Captain Borroughcliffe, for so freely volunteering to defend my house against the attacks of my piratical, rebellious, and misguided countrymen, to think of requiring such a concession."

"Harder duty might be performed, and no favours asked, my respectable host," returned the soldier. "Country quarters are apt to be dull, and the liquor is commonly execrable; but in such a dwelling as this a man can rock himself in the very cradle of contentment. And yet there is one subject of complaint, that I should disgrace my regiment did I not speak of, for it is incumbent on me, both as a man and a soldier, to be no longer silent."

"Name it, sir, freely, and its cause shall be as freely redressed," said the host, in some amazement.

"Here we three sit, from morning to night," continued the soldier, "bachelors all, well provisioned and better liquored, I grant you, but like so many well fed anchorites, while two of the loveliest damsels in the island pine in solitude within a hundred feet of us, without tasting the homage of our sighs. This I will maintain is a reproach both to your character, Colonel Howard, as an old soldier, and to mine as a young one. As to our friend Coke on top of Littleton here, I leave him to the quiddities of the law to plead his own cause."

The brow of the host contracted for a moment, and the sallow cheek of Dillon, who had sat during the dialogue in a sullen silence, appeared to grow even livid; but gradually the open brow of the veteran resumed its frank expression, and the lips of the other relaxed into a jesuitical sort of a smile, that was totally disregarded by the captain, who amused himself with sipping his wine, while he waited for an answer, as if he analyzed each drop that crossed his palate.

After an embarrassing pause of a moment, Colonel Howard broke the silence.

"There is reason in Borroughcliffe's hint, for such I take it to be—"

"I meant it for a plain, matter-of-fact complaint," interrupted the soldier.

"And you have cause for it," continued the colonel. "It is unreasonable, Christopher, that the ladies should allow their dread of these piratical countrymen of ours to exclude us from their society, though prudence may require that they remain secluded in their apartments. We owe the respect to Captain Borroughcliffe, that at least we admit him to the sight of the coffee-urn in an evening."

"That is precisely my meaning," said the captain; "as for dining with them, why, I am well provided for here, but there is no one knows how to set hot water a hissing in so professional a manner as a woman. So forward, my dear and honoured colonel, and lay your injunctions on them, that they command your humble servant and Mr. Coke unto Littleton to advance and give the countersign of gallantry."

Dillon contracted his disagreeable features into something that was intended for a satirical smile, before he spoke as follows:

"Both the veteran Colonel Howard and the gallant Captain Borroughcliffe may find it easier to overcome the enemies of his majesty in the field than to shake a woman's caprice. Not a day has passed, these three weeks, that I have not sent my inquiries to the door of Miss Howard, as became her father's kinsman, with a wish to appease her apprehensions of the pirates; but little has she deigned me in reply, more than such thanks as her sex and breeding could not well dispense with."

"Well, you have been as fortunate as myself, and why you should be more so, I see no reason," cried the soldier, throwing a glance of cool contempt at the other; "fear whitens the cheek, and ladies best love to be seen when the roses flourish rather than the lilies."

"A woman is never so interesting, Captain Borroughcliffe," said the gallant host, "as when she appears to lean on man for support; and he who does not feel himself honoured by the trust is a disgrace to his species."

"Bravo! my honoured sir, a worthy sentiment, and spoken like a true soldier; but I have heard much of the loveliness of the ladies of the Abbey, since I have been in my present quarters, and I feel a strong desire to witness beauty encircled by such loyalty as could induce them to flee their native country, rather than to devote their charms to the rude keeping of the rebels."

The colonel looked grave, and for a moment fierce; but the expression of his displeasure soon passed away in a smile of forced gayety, and, as he cheerfully rose from his seat, he cried—

"You shall be admitted this very night, and this instant, Captain Borroughcliffe. We owe it, sir, to your services here, as well as in the field, and those froward girls shall be humoured no longer. Nay, it is nearly two weeks since I have seen my ward myself, nor have I laid my eyes on my niece but twice in all that time. Christopher, I leave the captain under your good care, while I go seek admission into the cloisters; we call that part of the building the cloisters, because it holds our nuns, sir! You will pardon my early absence from the table, Captain Borroughcliffe."

"I beg it may not be mentioned; you leave an excellent representative behind you, sir," cried the soldier, taking in the lank figure of Mr. Dillon in a sweeping glance, that terminated with a settled gaze on his decanter. "Make my devoirs to the recluses, and say all that your own excellent wit shall suggest as an apology for my impatience. Mr. Dillon, I meet you in a bumper to their healths and in their honour."

The challenge was coldly accepted, and while these gentlemen still held their glasses to their lips, Colonel Howard left the apartment, bowing low, and uttering a thousand excuses to his guest, as he proceeded, and even offering a very unnecessary apology of the same effect to his habitual inmate, Mr. Dillon.

"Is fear so very powerful within these old walls," said the soldier, when the door closed behind their host, "that your ladies deem it necessary to conceal themselves before even an enemy is known to have landed?"

Dillon coldly replied—

"The name of Paul Jones is terrific to all on this coast, I believe, nor are the ladies of St. Ruth singular in their apprehensions."

"Ah! the pirate has bought himself a desperate name, since the affair of Flamborough Head. But let him look to't, if he trusts himself in another Whitehaven expedition, while there is a detachment of the ——th in the neighbourhood, though the men should be nothing better than recruits."

"Our last accounts leave him safe in the court of Louis,"

returned his companion; "but there are men as desperate as himself, who sail the ocean under the rebel flag, and from one or two of them we have had much reason to apprehend the vengeance of disappointed men. It is they that we hope are lost in this gale."

"Hum! I hope they were dastards, then, or your hopes are a little unchristian, and —"

He would have proceeded, but the door opened, and his orderly entered, and announced, that a sentinel had detained three men, who were passing along the highway, near the Abbey, and who, by their dress, appeared to be seamen.

"Well, let them pass," cried the captain; "what, have we nothing to do better than to stop passengers, like footpads, on the king's highway! give them of your canteens, and let the rascals pass. Your orders were to give the alarm, if any hostile party landed on the coast, not to detain peaceable subjects on their lawful business."

"I beg your honour's pardon," returned the sergeant; "but these men seemed lurking about the grounds for no good, and as they kept carefully aloof from the place where our sentinel was posted, until to-night, Downing thought it looked suspiciously, and detained them."

"Downing is a fool, and it may go hard with him for his officiousness. What have you done with the men?"

"I took them to the guard-room in the east wing, your honour."

"Then feed them; and harkye, sirrah! liquor them well, that we hear no complaints, and let them go."

"Yes, sir, yes, your honour shall be obeyed; but there is a straight, soldierly looking fellow among them, that I think might be persuaded to enlist, if he were detained till morning. I doubt, sir, by his walk, but he has served already."

"Ha! what say you!" cried the captain, pricking up his ears, like a hound who hears a well-known cry, "served, think ye, already?"

"There are signs about him, your honour, to that effect. An old soldier is seldom deceived in such a thing, and considering his disguise, for it can be no other, and the place where we took him, there is no danger of a have-us corpses, until he is tied to us by the laws of the kingdom."

"Peace, you knave!" said Borroughcliffe, rising, and making a devious route towards the door; "you speak in the presence of my lord chief justice that is to be, and should not talk lightly of the laws. But still you say reason; give me your arm, sergeant, and lead the way to the east wing; my eyesight is good for nothing in such a dark night. A soldier should always visit his guard before the tattoo beats."

After emulating the courtesy of their host, Captain Borroughcliffe retired on this patriotic errand, leaning on his subordinate in a style of most familiar condescension. Dillon continued at the table, endeavouring to express the rancorous feelings of his breast by a satirical smile of contempt, that was necessarily lost on all but himself, as a large mirror threw back the image of his morose and unpleasant features.

But we must precede the veteran colonel in his visit to the "cloisters."

Chapter X.

"—And kindness like their own
Inspired those eyes affectionate and glad,
That seemed to love whate'er they looked upon;
Whether with Hebe's mirth her features shone,
Or if a shade more pleasing them o'ercast—
Yet so becomingly th' expression past,
That each succeeding look was lovelier than the last."
Campbell, *Gertrude of Wyoming*, II.iv.2–6, 8–9.

THE WESTERN WING of St. Ruth house, or abbey, as the building was indiscriminately called, retained but few vestiges of the uses to which it had been originally devoted. The upper apartments were small and numerous, extending on either side of a long, low, and dark gallery, and might have been the dormitories of the sisterhood who were said to have once inhabited that portion of the edifice; but the ground-floor had been modernized, as it was then called, about a century before, and retained just enough of its ancient character to blend the venerable with what was thought comfortable in the commencement of the reign of the third George. As this wing had been appropriated to the mistress of the mansion, ever since the building had changed its spiritual character for one of a more carnal nature, Colonel Howard continued the arrangement, when he became the temporary possessor of St. Ruth's, until, in the course of events, the apartments which had been appropriated for the accommodation and convenience of his niece, were eventually converted into her prison. But as the severity of the old veteran was as often marked by an exhibition of his virtues as of his foibles, the confinement and his displeasure constituted the sole subjects of complaint that were given to the young lady. That our readers may be better qualified to judge of the nature of their imprisonment, we shall transport them, without further circumlocution, into the presence of the two females, whom they must be already prepared to receive.

The withdrawing-room of St. Ruth's was an apartment which, tradition said, had formerly been the refectory of the little bevy of fair sinners who sought a refuge within its walls from the temptations of the world. Their number was not large, nor their entertainments very splendid, or this limited space could not have contained them. The room, however, was of fair dimensions, and an air of peculiar comfort, mingled with chastened luxury, was thrown around it, by the voluminous folds of the blue damask curtains that nearly concealed the sides where the deep windows were placed, and by the dark leathern hangings, richly stamped with cunning devices in gold, that ornamented the two others. Massive couches in carved mahogany, with chairs of a similar material and fashion, all covered by the same rich fabric that composed the curtains, together with a Turkey carpet, over the shaggy surface of which all the colours of the rainbow were scattered in bright confusion, united to relieve the gloomy splendour of the enormous mantel, deep, heavy cornices, and the complicated carvings of the massive wood-work which cumbered the walls. A brisk fire of wood was burning on the hearth, in compliment to the wilful prejudice of Miss Plowden, who had maintained, in her most vivacious manner, that seacoal was "only tolerable for blacksmiths and Englishmen." In addition to the cheerful blaze from the hearth, two waxen lights, in candlesticks of massive silver, were lending their aid to enliven the apartment. One of these was casting its rays brightly along the confused colours of the carpet on which it stood, flickering before the active movements of the form that played around it with light and animated inflexions. The posture of this young lady was infantile in grace, and, with one ignorant of her motives, her employment would have been obnoxious to the same construction. Divers small, square pieces of silk, strongly contrasted to each other in colour, lay on every side of her, and were changed, as she kneeled on the floor, by her nimble hands, into as many different combinations, as if she were humouring the fancies of her sex, or consulting the shades of her own dark, but rich complexion, in the shop of a mercer. The close satin dress of this young female served to display her small figure in its true proportions, while her dancing eyes of jet-black shamed the dies of the Italian manufacturer by their superior radiancy. A few ribands of pink, disposed about her person with an air partly studied, and yet carelessly coquettish, seemed rather to reflect than lend the rich bloom that mantled around her laughing countenance, leaving to the eye no cause to regret that she was not fairer.

Another female figure, clad in virgin white, was reclining on the end of a distant couch. The seclusion in which they lived might have rendered this female a little careless of her appearance, or, what was more probable, the comb had been found unequal to its burthen, for her tresses, which rivalled the hue and gloss of the raven, had burst from their confinement, and, dropping over her shoulders, fell along her dress in rich profusion, finally resting on the damask of the couch, in dark folds, like glittering silk. A small hand, which seemed to blush at its own naked beauties, supported her head, imbedded in the volumes of her hair, like the fairest alabaster set in the deepest ebony. Beneath the dark profusion of her curls, which, notwithstanding the sweeping train that fell about her person, covered the summit of her head, lay a low, spotless forehead of dazzling whiteness, that was relieved by two arches so slightly and truly drawn that they appeared to have been produced by the nicest touches of art. The fallen lids and long silken lashes concealed the eyes, that rested on the floor, as if their mistress mused in melancholy. The remainder of the features of this maiden were of a kind that is most difficult to describe, being neither regular nor perfect in their several parts, yet harmonizing and composing a whole, that formed an exquisite picture of female delicacy and loveliness. There might or there might not have been a tinge of slight red in her cheeks, but it varied with each emotion of her bosom, even as she mused in quiet, now seeming to steal insidiously over her glowing temples, and then leaving on her face an almost startling paleness. Her stature, as she reclined, seemed above the medium height of womanhood, and her figure was rather delicate than full, though the little foot that rested on the damask cushion before her, displayed a rounded outline that any of her sex might envy.

"Oh! I'm as expert as if I were signal officer to the lord high admiral of this realm!" exclaimed the laughing female on the floor, clapping her hands together in girlish exultation. "I do long, Cecilia, for an opportunity to exhibit my skill."

While her cousin was speaking, Miss Howard raised her head, with a faint smile, and as she turned her eyes towards the other, a spectator might have been disappointed, but could not have been displeased, by the unexpected change the action produced in the expression of her countenance. Instead of the piercing black eyes that the deep colour of her tresses would lead him to expect, he would have beheld two large, mild, blue orbs, that seemed to float in a liquid so pure as to be nearly invisible, and which were more remarkable for their tenderness and persuasion, than for the vivid flashes that darted from the quick glances of her companion.

"The success of your mad excursion to the seaside, my cousin, has bewildered your brain," returned Cecilia; "but I know not how to conquer your disease, unless we prescribe salt-water for the remedy, as in some other cases of madness."

"Ah! I am afraid your nostrum would be useless," cried Katherine; "it has failed to wash out the disorder from the sedate Mr. Richard Barnstable, who has had the regimen administered to him through many a hard gale, but who continues as fair a candidate for bedlam as ever. Would you think it, Cicely, the crazy-one urged me, in the ten minutes' conversation we held together on the cliffs, to accept of his schooner as a shower-bath!"

"I can think that your hardihood might encourage him to expect much, but surely he could not have been serious in such a proposal!"

"Oh! to do the wretch justice, he did say something of a chaplain to consecrate the measure, but there was boundless impudence in the thought. I have not, nor shall I forget it, or forgive him for it, these six and twenty years. What a fine time he must have had of it, in his little Ariel, among the monstrous waves we saw tumbling in upon the shore to-day, coz! I hope they will wash his impudence out of him! I do think the man cannot have had a dry thread about him, from sun to sun. I must believe it is a punishment for his boldness, and, be certain, I shall tell him of it. I will form half a dozen signals, this instant, to joke at his moist condition, in very revenge."

Pleased with her own thoughts, and buoyant with the secret hope that her adventurous undertaking would be finally crowned with complete success, the gay girl shook her black locks, in infinite mirth, and tossed the mimic flags gayly around her person, as she was busied in forming new combinations, in order to amuse herself with her lover's disastrous situation. But the features of her cousin clouded with the thoughts that were excited by her remarks, and she replied, in a tone that bore some little of the accents of reproach—

"Katherine! Katherine! can you jest when there is so much to apprehend! Forget you what Alice Dunscombe told us of the gale, this morning! and that she spoke of two vessels, a ship and a schooner, that had been seen venturing with fearful temerity within the shoals, only six miles from the Abbey, and that unless God in his gracious providence had been kind to them, there was but little doubt that their fate would be a sad one! Can you, that know so well who and what these daring mariners are, be merry about the selfsame winds that cause their danger?"

The thoughtless, laughing girl, was recalled to her recollection by this remonstrance, and every trace of mirth vanished from her countenance, leaving a momentary death-like paleness crossing her face, as she clasped her hands before her, and fastened her keen eyes vacantly on the splendid pieces of silk that now lay unheeded around her. At this critical moment the door of the room slowly opened, and Colonel Howard entered the apartment with an air that displayed a droll mixture of stern indignation, with a chivalric and habitual respect to the sex.

"I solicit your pardon, young ladies, for the interruption," he said; "I trust, however, that an old man's presence can never be entirely unexpected in the drawing-room of his wards."

As he bowed, the colonel seated himself on the end of the couch, opposite to the place where his niece had been reclining, for Miss Howard had risen at his entrance, and continued standing until her uncle had comfortably disposed of himself. Throwing a glance, which was not entirely free from self-commendation, around the comfortable apartment, the veteran proceeded, in the same tone as before—

"You are not without the means of making any guest

welcome, nor do I see the necessity of such constant seclusion from the eyes of the world as you thus rigidly practise."

Cecilia looked timidly at her uncle, with surprise, before she returned an answer to his remark.

"We certainly owe much to your kind attention, dear sir," she at length uttered; "but is our retirement altogether voluntary?"

"How can it be otherwise! are you not mistress of this mansion, madam! In selecting the residence where your, and, permit me to add, my ancestors, so long dwelt, in credit and honour, I have surely been less governed by any natural pride that I might have entertained on such a subject, than by a desire to consult your comfort and happiness. Every thing appears to my aged eyes as if we ought not to be ashamed to receive our friends within these walls. The cloisters of St. Ruth, Miss Howard, are not entirely bare, neither are their tenants wholly unworthy to be seen."

"Open, then, the portals of the Abbey, sir, and your niece will endeavour to do proper credit to the hospitality of its master."

"That was spoken like Harry Howard's daughter, frankly and generously!" cried the old soldier, insensibly edging himself nearer to his niece. "If my brother had devoted himself to the camp, instead of the sea, Cecilia, he would have made one of the bravest and ablest generals in his majesty's service — poor Harry! he might have been living at this very day, and at this moment leading the victorious troops of his sovereign through the revolted colonies in triumph. But he is gone, Cicely, and has left you behind him, as his dear representative, to perpetuate our family, and to possess what little has been left to us from the ravages of the times."

"Surely, dear sir," said Cecilia, taking his hand, which had unconsciously approached her person, and pressing it to her lips, "we have no cause to complain of our lot in respect to fortune, though it may cause us bitter regret that so few of us are left to enjoy it."

"No, no, no," said Katherine, in a low, hurried voice; "Alice Dunscombe is and must be wrong; providence would never abandon brave men to so cruel a fate!"

"Alice Dunscombe is here to atone for her error, if she has

fallen into one," said a quiet, subdued voice, in which the accents of a provincial dialect, however, were slightly perceptible, and which, in its low tones, wanted that silvery clearness that gave so much feminine sweetness to the words of Miss Howard, and which even rung melodiously in the ordinarily vivacious strains of her cousin.

The surprise created by these sudden interruptions caused a total suspension of the discourse. Katherine Plowden, who had continued kneeling, in the attitude before described, arose, and as she looked about her in momentary confusion, the blood again mantled her face with the fresh and joyous springs of life. The other speaker advanced steadily into the middle of the room, and after returning, with studied civility, the low bow of Colonel Howard, seated herself in silence on the opposite couch. The manner of her entrance, her reception, and her attire, sufficiently denoted that the presence of this female was neither unusual nor unwelcome. She was dressed with marked simplicity, though with a studied neatness, that more than compensated for the absence of ornaments. Her age might not have much exceeded thirty, but there was an adoption of customs in her attire that indicated she was not unwilling to be thought older. Her fair flaxen hair was closely confined by a dark bandeau, such as was worn in a nation further north by virgins only, over which a few curls strayed, in a manner that showed the will of their mistress alone restrained their luxuriance. Her light complexion had lost much of its brilliancy, but enough still remained to assert its original beauty and clearness. To this description might be added, fine, mellow blue eyes, beautifully white, though large teeth, a regular set of features, and a person that was clad in a dark lead-coloured silk, which fitted her full, but gracefully moulded form, with the closest exactness.

Colonel Howard paused a moment, after this lady was seated, and then turning himself to Katherine with an air that became stiff and constrained by attempting to seem extremely easy, he said—

"You no sooner summon Miss Alice, but she appears, Miss Plowden—ready and (I am bold to say, Miss Alice) able to defend herself against all charges that her worst enemies can allege against her."

"I have no charges to make against Miss Dunscombe," said Katherine, pettishly, "nor do I wish to have dissensions created between me and my friends, even by Colonel Howard."

"Colonel Howard will studiously avoid such offences in future," said the veteran, bowing; and turning stiffly to the others, he continued — "I was just conversing with my niece, as you entered, Miss Alice, on the subject of her immuring herself like one of veriest nuns who ever inhabited these cloisters. I tell her, madam, that neither her years, nor my fortune, nor, indeed, her own, for the child of Harry Howard was not left pennyless, require that we should live as if the doors of the world were closed against us, or there was no other entrance to St. Ruth's but through those antiquated windows. Miss Plowden, I feel it to be my duty to inquire why those pieces of silk are provided in such an unusual abundance, and in so extraordinary a shape?"

"To make a gala dress for the ball you are about to give, sir," said Katherine, with a saucy smile, that was only checked by the reproachful glance of her cousin. "You have taste in a lady's attire, Colonel Howard; will not this bright yellow form a charming relief to my brown face, while this white and black relieve one another, and this pink contrasts so sweetly with black eyes. Will not the whole form a turban fit for an empress to wear?"

As the arch maiden prattled on in this unmeaning manner, her rapid fingers entwined the flags in a confused maze, which she threw over her head in a form not unlike the ornament for which she intimated it was intended. The veteran was by far too polite to dispute a lady's taste, and he renewed the dialogue, with his slightly awakened suspicions completely quieted by her dexterity and artifice. But although it was not difficult to deceive Colonel Howard in matters of female dress, the case was very different with Alice Dunscombe. This lady gazed, with a steady eye and reproving countenance, on the fantastical turban, until Katherine threw herself by her side, and endeavoured to lead her attention to other subjects, by her playful motions and whispered questions.

"I was observing, Miss Alice," continued the colonel, "that although the times had certainly inflicted some loss on my estate, yet we were not so much reduced, as to be unable to receive our friends in a manner that would not disgrace the descendants of the ancient possessors of St. Ruth. Cecilia, here, my brother Harry's daughter, is a young lady that any uncle might be proud to exhibit, and I would have her, madam, show your English dames, that we rear no unworthy specimens of the parent stock on the other side of the Atlantic."

"You have only to declare your pleasure, my good uncle," said Miss Howard, "and it shall be executed."

"Tell us how we can oblige you, sir," continued Katherine, "and if it be in any manner that will relieve the tedium of this dull residence, I promise you at least one cheerful assistant to your scheme."

"You speak fair," cried the colonel, "and like two discreet and worthy girls! Well, then, our first step shall be to send a message to Dillon and the captain, and invite them to attend your coffee. I see the hour approaches."

Cecilia made no reply, but looked distressed, and dropped her mild eyes to the carpet; but Miss Plowden took it upon herself to answer.

"Nay, sir, that would be for them to proceed in the matter; as your proposal was that the first step should be ours, suppose we all adjourn to your part of the house, and do the honours of the tea-table in your drawing-room, instead of our own. I understand, sir, that you have had an apartment fitted up for that purpose, in some style; a woman's taste might aid your designs, however."

"Miss Plowden, I believe I intimated to you, some time since," said the displeased colonel, "that so long as certain suspicious vessels were known to hover on this coast, I should desire that you and Miss Howard would confine yourselves to this wing."

"Do not say that we confine ourselves," said Katherine, "but let it be spoken in plain English, that you confine us here."

"Am I a gaoler, madam, that you apply such epithets to my conduct! Miss Alice must form strange conclusions of our manners, if she receive her impressions from your very singular remarks. I—"

"All measures adopted from a dread of the ship and schooner that ran within the Devil's Grip, yester-eve, may be dispensed with now," interrupted Miss Dunscombe, in a melancholy, reflecting tone. "There are few living, who know the dangerous paths that can conduct even the smallest craft in safety from the land, with daylight and fair winds; but when darkness and adverse gales oppose them, the chance for safety lies wholly in God's kindness."

"There is truly much reason to believe they are lost," returned the veteran, in a voice in which no exultation was apparent.

"They are not lost!" exclaimed Katherine, with startling energy, leaving her seat, and walking across the room to join Cecilia, with an air that seemed to elevate her little figure to the height of her cousin. "They are skilful and they are brave, and what gallant sailors can do, will they do, and successfully; besides, in whose behalf would a just Providence sooner exercise its merciful power, than to protect the daring children of an oppressed country, while contending against tyranny and countless wrongs?"

The conciliating disposition of the colonel deserted him, as he listened. His own black eyes sparkled with a vividness unusual for his years, and his courtesy barely permitted the lady to conclude, ere he broke forth.

"What sin, madam, what damning crime, would sooner call down the just wrath of Heaven on the transgressors, than the act of foul rebellion? It was this crime, madam, that deluged England in blood in the reign of the first Charles; it is this crime that has dyed more fields red than all the rest of man's offences united; it has been visited on our race, as a condign punishment, from the days of the deservedly devoted Absalom, down to the present time; in short, it lost heaven for ever to some of the most glorious of its angels, and there is much reason to believe that it is the one unpardonable sin, named in the holy gospels."

"I know not that you have authority for believing it to be the heavy enormity that you mention, Colonel Howard," said Miss Dunscombe, anticipating the spirited reply of Katherine, and willing to avert it; she hesitated an instant, and then drawing a heavy, shivering sigh, she continued, in a voice that grew softer as she spoke—"'tis indeed a crime of magnitude, and one that throws the common backslidings of our lives, speaking by comparison, into the sunshine of his favour. Many there are, who sever the dearest ties of this life, by madly rushing into its sinful vortex, for I fain think the heart grows hard with the sight of human calamity, and becomes callous to the miseries its owner inflicts; especially where we act the wrongs on our own kith and kin, regardless who or how many that are dear to us suffer by our evil deeds. It is, besides, Colonel Howard, a dangerous temptation, to one little practised in the great world, to find himself suddenly elevated into the seat of power; and if it do not lead to the commission of great crimes, it surely prepares the way to it, by hardening the heart."

"I hear you patiently, Miss Alice," said Katherine, dancing her little foot, in affected coolness, "for you neither know of whom nor to whom you speak. But Colonel Howard has not that apology. Peace, Cecilia, for I must speak! Believe them not, dear girl; there is not a wet hair on their heads. For you, Colonel Howard, who must recollect that the sister's son of the mothers of both your niece and myself is on board that frigate, there is an appearance of cruelty in using such language."

"I pity the boy! from my soul I pity him!" exclaimed the veteran; "he is a child, and has followed the current that is sweeping our unhappy colonies down the tide of destruction. But there are others in that vessel, who have no excuse of ignorance to offer. There is a son of my old acquaintance, and the bosom friend of my brother Harry, Cecilia's father, dashing Hugh Griffith, as we called him. The urchins left home together, and were rated on board one of his majesty's vessels on the same day. Poor Harry lived to carry a broad pennant in the service, and Hugh died in command of a frigate. This boy, too! he was nurtured on board his father's vessel, and learned, from his majesty's discipline, how to turn his arms against his king. There is something shockingly unnatural in that circumstance, Miss Alice; 'tis like the child inflicting a blow on the parent. 'Tis such men as these, with Washington at their head, who maintain the bold front this rebellion wears."

"There are men, who have never worn the servile livery of Britain, sir, whose names are as fondly cherished in America as any that she boasts of," said Katherine, proudly; "ay, sir, and those who would gladly oppose the bravest officers in the British fleet."

"I contend not against your misguided reason," said Colonel Howard, rising with cool respect. "A young lady who ventures to compare rebels with gallant gentlemen engaged in their duty to their prince, cannot escape the imputation of possessing a misguided reason. No man—I speak not of women, who cannot be supposed so well versed in human nature—but no man, who has reached the time of life that entitles him to be called by that name, can consort with these disorganizers, who would destroy every thing that is sacred—these levellers, who would pull down the great, to exalt the little—these jacobins, who—who—"

"Nay, sir, if you are at a loss for opprobrious epithets," said Katherine, with provoking coolness, "call on Mr. Christopher Dillon for assistance; he waits your pleasure at the door."

Colonel Howard turned in amazement, forgetting his angry declamations at this unexpected intelligence, and beheld in reality the sombre visage of his kinsman, who stood holding the door in his hand, apparently as much surprised at finding himself in the presence of the ladies, as they themselves could be at his unusual visit.

Chapter XI.

"Prithee, Kate, let's stand aside, and see the end of this controversy."

The Taming of the Shrew, V.i.61-62.

DURING the warm discussions of the preceding chapter, Miss Howard had bowed her pale face to the arm of the couch, and sate an unwilling and distressed listener to the controversy; but now that another, and one whom she thought an unauthorized intruder on her privacy, was announced, she asserted the dignity of her sex as proudly, though with something more of discretion, than her cousin could possibly have done. Rising from her seat, she inquired—

"To what are we indebted for so unexpected a visit from Mr. Dillon? Surely he must know that we are prohibited going to the part of the dwelling where he resides, and I trust Colonel Howard will tell him that common justice requires we should be permitted to be private."

The gentleman replied, in a manner in which malignant anger was sufficiently mingled with calculating humility—

"Miss Howard will think better of my intrusion, when she knows that I come on business of importance to her uncle."

"Ah! that may alter the case, Kit; but the ladies must have the respect that is due to their sex. I forgot, somehow, to have myself announced; but that Borroughcliffe leads me deeper into my Madeira than I have been accustomed to go, since the time when my poor brother Harry, with his worthy friend, Hugh Griffith—the devil seize Hugh Griffith, and all his race—your pardon, Miss Alice—what is your business with me, Mr. Dillon?"

"I bear a message from Captain Borroughcliffe. You may remember that, according to your suggestions, the sentinels were to be changed every night, sir."

"Ay! ay! we practised that in our campaign against Montcalm; 'twas necessary to avoid the murders of their Indians, who were sure, Miss Alice, to shoot down a man at his post, if he were placed two nights running in the same place."

"Well, sir, your prudent precautions have not been thrown away," continued Dillon, moving farther into the apartment, as if he felt himself becoming a more welcome guest as he proceeded; "the consequences are, that we have already made three prisoners."

"Truly it has been a most politic scheme!" exclaimed Katherine Plowden, with infinite contempt. "I suppose, as Mr. Christopher Dillon applauds it so highly, that it has some communion with the law! and that the redoubtable garrison of St. Ruth are about to reap the high glory of being most successful thief-takers!"

The sallow face of Dillon actually became livid as he replied, and his whole frame shook with the rage that he vainly endeavoured to suppress.

"There may be a closer communion with the law, and its ministers, perhaps, than Miss Plowden can desire," he said; "for rebellion seldom finds favour in any Christian code."

"Rebellion!" exclaimed the colonel; "and what has this detention of three vagabonds to do with rebellion, Kit? Has the damnable poison found its way across the Atlantic? — your pardon, Miss Alice — but this is a subject on which you can feel with me; I know your sentiments on the allegiance that is due to our anointed sovereign. Speak, Mr. Dillon, are we surrounded by another set of demons! if so, we must give ourselves to the work, and rally round our prince; for this island is the main pillar of his throne."

"I cannot say that there is any appearance, at present, of an intention to rise in this island," said Dillon, with demure gravity; "though the riots in London warrant any precautionary measures on the part of his majesty's ministers, even to a suspension of the habeas corpus. But you have had your suspicions concerning two certain vessels that have been threatening the coast, for several days past, in a most piratical manner?"

The little foot of Katherine played rapidly on the splendid carpet, but she contented herself with bestowing a glance of the most sovereign contempt on the speaker, as if she disdained any further reply. With the colonel, however, this was touching a theme that lay nearest his heart, and he answered, in a manner worthy of the importance of the subject—

"You speak like a sensible man, and a loyal subject, Mr. Dillon. The habeas corpus, Miss Alice, was obtained in the reign of King John, along with magna charta, for the security of the throne, by his majesty's barons; some of my own blood were of the number, which alone would be a pledge that the dignity of the crown was properly consulted. As to our piratical countrymen, Christopher, there is much reason to think that the vengeance of an offended Providence has already reached them. Those who know the coast well, tell me that without a better pilot than an enemy would be likely to procure, it would be impossible for any vessel to escape the shoals among which they entered, on a dark night, and with an adverse gale; the morning has arrived, and they are not to be seen!"

"But be they friends or be they enemies, sir," continued Dillon, respectfully, "there is much reason to think that we have now in the Abbey those who can tell us something of their true character; for the men we have detained carry with them the appearance of having just landed, and wear not only the dress but the air of seamen."

"Of seamen!" echoed Katherine, a deadly paleness chasing from her cheeks the bloom which indignation had heightened.

"Of seamen, Miss Plowden," repeated Dillon, with malignant satisfaction, but concealing it under an air of submissive respect.

"I thank you, sir, for so gentle a term," replied the young lady, recollecting herself, and recovering her presence of mind in the same instant; "the imagination of Mr. Dillon is so apt to conjure the worst, that he is entitled to our praise for so far humouring our weakness, as not to alarm us with the apprehensions of their being pirates."

"Nay, madam, they may yet deserve that name," returned the other, coolly; "but my education has instructed me to hear the testimony before I pronounce sentence."

"Ah! that the boy has found in his Coke upon Littleton," cried the colonel; "the law is a salutary corrective to human infirmities, Miss Alice, and, among other things, it teaches patience to a hasty temperament. But for this cursed, unnatural rebellion, madam, the young man would, at this moment, have been diffusing its blessings from a judicial chair, in one of the colonies, ay! and I pledge myself, to all alike, black and white, red and yellow, with such proper distinctions as nature has made between the officer and the private. Keep a good heart, kinsman; we shall yet find a time! the royal arms have many hands, and things look better at the last advices. But, come, we will proceed to the guard-room, and put these stragglers to the question; runaways, I'll venture to predict, from one of his majesty's cruisers, or, perhaps, honest subjects engaged in supplying the service with men. Come, Kit, come, let us go, and—"

"Are we, then, to lose the company of Colonel Howard so soon?" said Katherine, advancing to her guardian, with an air of blandishment and pleasantry. "I know that he too soon forgets the hasty language of our little disputes, to part in anger, if, indeed, he will even quit us till he has tasted of our coffee."

The veteran turned to the speaker of this unexpected address, and listened with profound attention. When she had done, he replied, with a good deal of softness in his tones—

"Ah! provoking one! you know me too well to doubt my forgiveness; but duty must be attended to, though even a young lady's smiles tempt me to remain. Yes, yes, child, you, too, are the daughter of a very brave and worthy seaman; but you carry your attachment to that profession too far, Miss Plowden—you do, indeed you do."

Katherine might have faintly blushed, but the slight smile which mingled with the expression of her shame gave to her countenance a look of additional archness, and she laid her hand lightly on the sleeve of her guardian, to detain him, as she replied—

"Yet why leave us, Colonel Howard? It is long since we have seen you in the cloisters, and you know you come as a father; tarry, and you may yet add confessor to the title."

"I know thy sins already, girl," said the worthy colonel, unconsciously yielding to her gentle efforts to lead him back to his seat; "they are, deadly rebellion in your heart to your prince, a most inveterate propensity to salt-water, and a great disrespect to the advice and wishes of an old fellow whom your father's will and the laws of the realm have made the guardian of your person and fortune."

"Nay, say not the last, dear sir," cried Katherine; "for there is not a syllable you have ever said to me, on that foolish subject, that I have forgotten. Will you resume your seat again? Cecilia, Colonel Howard consents to take his coffee with us."

"But you forget the three men, honest Kit, there, and our respectable guest, Captain Borroughcliffe."

"Let honest Kit stay there, if he please; you may send a request to Captain Borroughcliffe to join our party; I have a woman's curiosity to see the soldier; and as for the three men—" she paused, and affected to muse a moment, when she continued, as if struck by an obvious thought—"Yes, and the men can be brought in, and examined here; who knows but they may have been wrecked in the gale, and need our pity and assistance, rather than deserve your suspicions."

"There is a solemn warning in Miss Plowden's conjecture, that should come home to the breasts of all who live on this wild coast," said Alice Dunscombe; "I have known many a sad wreck among the hidden shoals, and when the wind has blown but a gentle gale, compared to last night's tempest. The wars, and the uncertainties of the times, together with man's own wicked passions, have made great havoc with those who knew well the windings of the channels among the "Ripples." Some there were who could pass, as I have often heard, within a fearful distance of the "Devil's-Grip," the darkest night that ever shadowed England; but all are now gone, of that daring set, either by the hand of death, or, what is even as mournful, by unnatural banishment from the land of their fathers."

"This war has then probably drawn off most of them, for your recollections must be quite recent, Miss Alice," said the veteran; "as many of them were engaged in the business of robbing his majesty's revenue, the country is in some measure requited for their former depredations, by their present services, and at the same time it is happily rid of their presence. Ah! madam, ours is a glorious constitution, where things are so nicely balanced, that, as in the physical organization of a healthy, vigorous man, the baser parts are purified in the course of things, by its own wholesome struggles."

The pale features of Alice Dunscombe became slightly tinged with red, as the colonel proceeded, nor did the faint glow entirely leave her pallid face, until she had said—

"There might have been some who knew not how to respect the laws of the land, for such are never wanting; but there were others, who, however guilty they might be in many respects, need not charge themselves, with that mean crime, and yet who could find the passages that lie hid from common eyes, beneath the rude waves, as well as you could find the way through the halls and galleries of the Abbey, with a noonday sun shining upon its vanes and high chimneys."

"It is your pleasure, Colonel Howard, that we examine the three men, and ascertain whether they belong to the number of these gifted pilots?" said Christopher Dillon, who was growing uneasy at his awkward situation, and who hardly deemed it necessary to conceal the look of contempt which he cast at the mild Alice, while he spoke; "perhaps we may gather information enough from them, to draw a chart of the coast, that may gain us credit with my lords of the Admiralty."

This unprovoked attack on their unresisting and unoffending guest, brought the rich blood to the very temples of Miss Howard, who rose, and addressed herself to her kinsman, with a manner that could not easily be mistaken, any more than it could be condemned—

"If Mr. Dillon will comply with the wishes of Colonel Howard, as my cousin has expressed them, we shall not, at least, have to accuse ourselves of unnecessarily detaining men who probably are more unfortunate than guilty."

When she concluded, Cecilia walked across the apartment, and took a seat by the side of Alice Dunscombe, with whom she began to converse, in a low, soothing tone of voice. Mr. Dillon bowed with a deprecating humility, and having ascertained that Colonel Howard chose to give an audience, where he sate, to the prisoners, he withdrew to execute his mission, secretly exulting at any change that promised to lead to a renewal of an intercourse that might terminate more to his advantage, than the lofty beauty whose favour he courted, was, at present, disposed to concede.

"Christopher is a worthy, serviceable, good fellow," said the colonel, when the door closed, "and I hope to live, yet, to see him clad in ermine; I would not be understood literally, but figuratively, for furs would but ill comport with the climate of the Carolinas. I trust I am to be consulted by his majesty's ministers when the new appointments shall be made for the subdued colonies, and he may safely rely on my good word being spoken in his favour. Would he not make an excellent and independent ornament of the bench, Miss Plowden?"

Katherine compressed her lips a little, as she replied—

"I must profit by his own discreet rules, and see testimony to that effect, before I decide, sir. But listen!" The young lady's colour changed rapidly, and her eyes became fixed in a sort of feverish gaze on the door. "He has at least been active; I hear the heavy tread of men already approaching."

"Ah! it is he certainly; justice ought always to be prompt as well as certain, to make it perfect; like a drum-head court-martial, which, by the way, is as summary a sort of government as heart could wish to live under. If his majesty's ministers could be persuaded to introduce into the revolted colonies—"

"Listen!" interrupted Katherine, in a voice which bespoke her deep anxiety; "they draw near!"

The sound of footsteps was in fact now so audible as to induce the colonel to suspend the delivery of his plan for governing the recovered provinces. The long, low gallery, which was paved with a stone flagging, soon brought the footsteps of the approaching party more distinctly to their ears, and presently a low tap at the door announced their arrival. Colonel Howard arose, with the air of one who was to sustain the principal character in the ensuing interview, and bade them enter. Cecilia and Alice Dunscombe merely cast careless looks at the opening door, indifferent to the scene; but the quick eye of Katherine embraced, at a glance, every figure in the group. Drawing a long, quivering breath, she fell back on the couch, and her eyes again lighted with their playful expression, as she hummed a low, rapid air, with a voice in which even the suppressed tones were liquid melody.

Dillon entered, preceding the soldier, whose gait had become more steady, and in whose rigid eye a thoughtful expression had taken the place of its former vacant gaze. In short, something had manifestly restored to him a more complete command of his mental powers, although he might not have been absolutely sobered. The rest of the party continued in the gallery, while Mr. Dillon presented the renovated captain to the colonel, when the latter did him the same kind office with the ladies.

"Miss Plowden," said the veteran, for she offered first in the circle, "this is my friend, Captain Borroughcliffe; he has long been ambitious of this honour, and I have no doubt his reception will be such as to leave him no cause to repent he has been at last successful."

Katherine smiled, and answered, with ambiguous emphasis—

"I know not how to thank him, sufficiently, for the care he has bestowed on our poor persons."

The soldier looked steadily at her, for a moment, with an eye that seemed to threaten a retaliation in kind, ere he replied—

"One of those smiles, madam, would be an ample compensation for services that are more real than such as exist only in intention."

Katherine bowed with more complacency than she usually bestowed on those who wore the British uniform, and they proceeded to the next.

"This is Miss Alice Dunscombe, Captain Borroughcliffe, daughter of a very worthy clergyman who was formerly the curate of this parish, and a lady who does us the pleasure of giving us a good deal of her society, though far less than we all wish for."

The captain returned the civil inclination of Alice, and the colonel proceeded.

"Miss Howard, allow me to present Captain Borroughcliffe, a gentleman who, having volunteered to defend St. Ruth in these critical times, merits all the favour of its mistress."

Cecilia gracefully rose, and received her guest with sweet complacency. The soldier made no reply to the customary compliments that she uttered, but stood an instant gazing at her speaking countenance, and then, laying his hand involuntarily on his breast, bowed nearly to his sword-hilt.

These formalities duly observed, the colonel declared his

readiness to receive the prisoners. As the door was opened by Dillon, Katherine cast a cool and steady look at the strangers, and beheld the light glancing along the arms of the soldiers who guarded them. But the seamen entered alone; while the rattling of arms, and the heavy dash of the muskets on the stone pavement, announced that it was thought prudent to retain a force at hand, to watch these secret intruders on the grounds of the abbey.

Chapter XII.

"Food for powder; they'll fill a pit as well as better."
I Henry IV, IV.ii.66–67.

T HE THREE MEN, who now entered the apartment, appeared to be nothing daunted by the presence into which they were ushered, though clad in the coarse and weather-beaten vestments of seamen who had been exposed to recent and severe duty. They silently obeyed the direction of the soldier's finger, and took their stations in a distant corner of the room, like men who knew the deference due to rank, at the same time that the habits of their lives had long accustomed them to encounter the vicissitudes of the world. With this slight preparation, Colonel Howard began the business of examination.

"I trust ye are all good and loyal subjects," the veteran commenced, with a considerate respect for innocence, "but the times are such that even the most worthy characters become liable to suspicion; and, consequently, if our apprehensions should prove erroneous, you must overlook the mistake, and attribute it to the awful condition into which rebellion has plunged this empire. We have much reason to fear that some project is about to be undertaken on the coast by the enemy, who has appeared, we know, with a frigate and schooner; and the audacity of the rebels is only equalled by their shameless and wicked disrespect for the rights of the sovereign."

While Colonel Howard was uttering his apologetic preamble, the prisoners fastened their eyes on him with much interest; but when he alluded to the apprehended attack, the gaze of two of them became more keenly attentive, and, before he concluded, they exchanged furtive glances of deep meaning. No reply was made, however, and after a short pause, as if to allow time for his words to make a proper impression, the veteran continued —

"We have no evidence, I understand, that you are in the smallest degree connected with the enemies of this country; but as you have been found out of the king's highway, or, rather, on a by-path, which I must confess is frequently used by the people of the neighbourhood, but which is nevertheless nothing but a by-path, it becomes no more than what self-preservation requires of us, to ask you a few such questions as I trust will be satisfactorily answered. To use your own nautical phrases, 'from whence came ye, pray?' and 'whither are ye bound?'"

A low, deep voice·replied—"From Sunderland, last, and bound, over-land, to Whitehaven."

This simple and direct answer was hardly given, before the attention of the listeners was called to Alice Dunscombe, who uttered a faint shriek, and rose from her seat involuntarily, while her eyes seemed to roll fearfully, and perhaps a little wildly, round the room.

"Are you ill, Miss Alice?" said the sweet, soothing tones of Cecilia Howard; "you are, indeed you are; lean on me, that I may lead you to your apartment."

"Did you hear it, or was it only fancy!" she answered, her cheek blanched to the whiteness of death, and her whole frame shuddering as if in convulsions; "say, did you hear it too?"

"I have heard nothing but the voice of my uncle, who is standing near you, anxious, as we all are, for your recovery from this dreadful agitation."

Alice still gazed wildly from face to face. Her eye did not rest satisfied with dwelling on those who surrounded her, but surveyed, with a sort of frantic eagerness, the figures and appearance of the three men, who stood in humble patience, the silent and unmoved witnesses of this extraordinary scene. At length she veiled her eyes with both her hands, as if to shut out some horrid vision, and then removing them, she smiled languidly, as she signed for Cecilia to assist her from the room. To the polite and assiduous offers of the gentlemen, she returned no other thanks than those conveyed in her looks and gestures; but when the sentinels who paced the gallery were passed, and the ladies were alone, she breathed a long, shivering sigh, and found an utterance.

"'Twas like a voice from the silent grave!" she said, "but it could be no more than mockery. No, no, 'tis a just punishment for letting the image of the creature fill the place that should be occupied only with the Creator. Ah! Miss Howard, Miss Plowden, ye are both young—in the pride of your beauty and loveliness—but little do ye know, and less do ye dread, the temptations and errors of a sinful world."

"Her thoughts wander!" whispered Katherine, with anxious tenderness; "some awful calamity has affected her intellects!"

"Yes, it must be; my sinful thoughts have wandered, and conjured sounds that it would have been dreadful to have heard in truth, and within these walls," said Alice, more composedly, smiling with a ghastly expression, as she gazed on the two beautiful solicitous maidens who supported her yielding person. "But the moment of weakness is passed, and I am better; aid me to my room, and return, that you may not interrupt the reviving harmony between yourselves and Colonel Howard. I am now better, nay, I am quite restored."

"Say not so, dear Miss Alice," returned Cecilia; "your face denies what your kindness to us induces you to utter; ill, very ill, you are, nor shall even your own commands induce me to leave you."

"Remain, then," said Miss Dunscombe, bestowing a look of grateful affection on her lovely supporter; "and while our Katherine returns to the drawing-room, to give the gentlemen their coffee, you shall continue with me, as my gentle nurse."

By this time they had gained the apartment, and Katherine, after assisting her cousin to place Alice on her bed, returned to do the honours of the drawing-room.

Colonel Howard ceased his examination of the prisoners at her entrance, to inquire, with courtly solicitude, after the invalid; and, when his questions were answered, he again proceeded, as follows—

"This is what the lads would call plain-sailing, Borroughcliffe; they are out of employment in Sunderland, and have acquaintances and relatives in Whitehaven, to whom they are going for assistance and labour. All very probable, and perfectly harmless."

"Nothing more so, my respectable host," returned the jocund soldier; "but it seemeth a grievous misfortune that a trio of such flesh and blood should need work wherewithal to exercise their thews and sinews, while so many of the vessels of his majesty's fleet navigate the ocean in quest of the enemies of old England."

"There is truth in that; much truth in your remark," cried the colonel. "What say you, my lads, will you fight the Frenchman and the Don, ay! and even my own rebellious and infatuated countrymen? Nay, by heaven, it is not a trifle that shall prevent his majesty from possessing the services of three such heroes. Here are five guineas a-piece for you the moment that you put foot on board the Alacrity cutter; and that can easily be done, as she lies at anchor this very night, only two short leagues to the south of this, in a small port, where she is riding out the gale as snugly as if she were in a corner of this room."

One of the men affected to gaze at the money with longing eyes, while he asked, as if weighing the terms of the engagement—

"Whether the Alacrity was called a good sea-boat, and was thought to give a comfortable birth to her crew?"

"Comfortable!" echoed Borroughcliffe; "for that matter, she is called the bravest cutter in the navy. You have seen much of the world, I dare say; did you ever see such a place as the marine arsenal at Carthagena, in old Spain?"

"Indeed I have, sir," returned the seaman, in a cool, collected tone.

"Ah! you have! well, did you ever meet with a house in Paris that they call the Thuilleries? because it's a dog-kennel to the Alacrity."

"I have even fallen in with the place you mention, sir," returned the sailor; "and must own the birth quite good enough for such as I am, if it tallies with your description."

"The deuce take these blue-jackets," muttered Borroughcliffe, addressing himself unconsciously to Miss Plowden, near whom he happened to be at the time; "they run their tarry countenances into all the corners of the earth, and abridge a man most lamentably in his comparisons. Now, who the devil would have thought that fellow had ever put his sea-green eyes on the palace of King Louis!"

Katherine heeded not his speech, but sat eyeing the prisoners with a confused and wavering expression of countenance, while Colonel Howard renewed the discourse, by exclaiming—

"Come, come, Borroughcliffe, let us give the lads no tales for a recruit, but good, plain, honest English—God bless the language, and the land for which it was first made, too. There is no necessity to tell these men, if they are, what they seem to be, practical seamen, that a cutter of ten guns contains all the room and accommodation of a palace."

"Do you allow nothing for English oak and English comfort, mine host," said the immovable captain; "do you think, good sir, that I measure fitness and propriety by square and compass, as if I were planning Solomon's temple anew! All I mean to say is, that the Alacrity is a vessel of singular compactness and magical arrangement of room. Like the tent of that handsome brother of the fairy, in the Arabian Nights, she is big or she is little, as occasion needeth; and now, hang me, if I don't think I have uttered more in her favour than her commander would say to help me to a recruit, though no lad in the three kingdoms should appear willing to try how a scarlet coat would suit his boorish figure."

"That time has not yet arrived, and God forbid that it ever should, while the monarch needs a soldier in the field to protect his rights. But what say ye, my men? you have heard the recommendation that Captain Borroughcliffe has given of the Alacrity, which is altogether true—after making some allowances for language. Will ye serve? shall I order you a cheering glass a man, and lay by the gold, till I hear from the cutter that you are enrolled under the banners of the best of kings?"

Katherine Plowden, who hardly seemed to breathe, so close and intent was the interest with which she regarded the seamen, fancied she observed lurking smiles on their faces; but if her conjectures were true, their disposition to be merry went no farther, and the one who had spoken hitherto, replied, in the same calm manner as before—

"You will excuse us, if we decline shipping in the cutter, sir; we are used to distant voyages and large vessels, whereas the Alacrity is kept at coast duty, and is not of a size to lay herself alongside of a Don or a Frenchman with a double row of teeth."

"If you prefer that sort of sport, you must to the right-about for Yarmouth; there you will find ships that will meet any thing that swims," said the colonel.

"Perhaps the gentlemen would prefer abandoning the cares and dangers of the ocean for a life of ease and gayety," said the captain. "The hand that has long dallied with a marlinspike may be easily made to feel a trigger, as gracefully as a lady touches the keys of her piano. In short, there is and there is not a great resemblance between the life of a sailor and that of a soldier. There are no gales of wind, nor short-allowances, nor reefing topsails, nor shipwrecks, among soldiers — and at the same time, there is just as much, or even more grog-drinking, jollifying, care-killing fun around a canteen and an open knapsack, than there is on the end of a mess-chest, with a full can and a Saturday night's breeze. I have crossed the ocean several times, and I must own that a ship, in good weather, is very much the same as a camp or comfortable barracks; mind, I say only in very good weather."

"We have no doubt that all you say is true, sir," observed the spokesman of the three; "but what to you may seem a hardship, to us is pleasure. We have faced too many a gale to mind a cap-full of wind, and should think ourselves always in the calm latitudes, in one of your barracks, where there is nothing to do but to eat our grub, and to march a little fore and aft a small piece of green earth. We hardly know one end of a musket from the other."

"No!" said Borroughcliffe, musing; and then advancing with a quick step towards them, he cried, in a spirited manner — "attention! right dress!"

The speaker, and the seaman next him, gazed at the captain in silent wonder; but the third individual of the party, who had drawn himself a little aside, as if willing to be unnoticed, or perhaps pondering on his condition, involuntarily started at this unexpected order, and erecting himself, threw his head to the right, as promptly as if he had been on a parade ground.

"Oho! ye are apt scholars, gentlemen, and ye can learn, I see," continued Borroughcliffe. "I feel it to be proper that I detain these men till to-morrow morning, Colonel Howard, and yet I would give them better quarters than the hard benches of the guard-room."

"Act your pleasure, Captain Borroughcliffe," returned the host, "so you do but your duty to our royal master. They shall not want for cheer, and they can have a room over the servants' offices in the south side of the Abbey."

"Three rooms, my colonel, three rooms must be provided, though I give up my own."

"There are several small empty apartments there, where blankets might be taken, and the men placed for safe keeping, if you deem it necessary; though, to me, they seem like good, loyal tars, whose greatest glory it would be to serve their prince, and whose chief pleasure would consist in getting alongside of a Don or a Monsieur."

"We shall discuss these matters anon," said Borroughcliffe, dryly. "I see Miss Plowden begins to look grave at our abusing her patience so long, and I know that cold coffee is, like withered love, but a tasteless sort of a beverage. Come, gentlemen, en avant! you have seen the Thuilleries, and must have heard a little French. Mr. Christopher Dillon, know you where these three small apartments are 'situate, lying, and being,' as your parchments read?"

"I do, sir," said the complying lawyer, "and shall take much pleasure in guiding you to them. I think your decision that of a prudent and sagacious officer, and much doubt whether Durham Castle, or some other fortress, will be thought too big to hold them, ere long."

As this speech was uttered while the men were passing from the room, its effect on them was unnoticed; but Katherine Plowden, who was left for a few moments by herself, sat and pondered over what she had seen and heard, with a thoughtfulness of manner that was not usual to her gay and buoyant spirits. The sounds of the retiring footsteps, however, gradually grew fainter, and the return of her guardian alone, recalled the recollection of the young lady to the duties of her situation.

While engaged in the little offices of the tea-table, Katherine threw many furtive glances at the veteran; but, although he seemed to be musing, there was nothing austere or suspicious in his frank, open countenance.

"There is much useless trouble taken with these wandering seamen, sir," said Katherine, at length; "it seems to be the particular province of Mr. Christopher Dillon, to make all that come in contact with him excessively uncomfortable."

"And what has Kit to do with the detention of the men?"

"What! why, has he not undertaken to stand godfather to their prisons? — by a woman's patience, I think, Colonel Howard, this business will gain a pretty addition to the names of St. Ruth. It is already called a house, an abbey, a place, and by some a castle; let Mr. Dillon have his way for a month, and it will add gaol to the number."

"Kit is not so happy as to possess the favour of Miss Plowden; but still Kit is a worthy fellow, and a good fellow, and a sensible fellow, ay! and what is of more value than all these put together, Miss Katherine, Mr. Christopher Dillon is a faithful and loyal subject to his prince. His mother was my cousin-german, madam, and I cannot say how soon I may call him my nephew. The Dillons are of good Irish extraction, and I believe that even Miss Plowden will admit that the Howards have some pretensions to a name."

"Ah! it is those very things called names that I most allude to," said Katherine, quickly. "But an hour since, you were indignant, my dear guardian, because you suspected that I insinuated you ought to write gaoler behind the name of Howard, and even now you submit to have the office palmed upon you."

"You forget, Miss Katherine Plowden, that it is the pleasure of one of his majesty's officers to detain these men."

"But I thought that the glorious British constitution, which you so often mention," interrupted the young lady, spiritedly, "gives liberty to all who touch these blessed shores; you know, sir, that out of twenty blacks that you brought with you, how few remain; the rest having fled on the wings of the spirit of British liberty!"

This was touching a festering sore in the colonel's feelings, and his provoking ward well knew the effects her observation was likely to produce. Her guardian did not break forth in a violent burst of rage, or furnish those manifestations of his ire that he was wont to do on less important subjects, but he arose, with all his dignity concentred in a look, and, after making a violent effort to restrain his feelings within the bounds necessary to preserve the decorum of his exit, he ventured a reply.

"That the British constitution is glorious, madam, is most true. That this island is the sole refuge where liberty has been able to find a home, is also true. The tyranny and oppression of the Congress, which are grinding down the colonies to the powder of desolation and poverty, are not worthy of the sacred name. Rebellion pollutes all that it touches, madam. Although it often commences under the sanction of holy liberty, it ever terminates in despotism. The annals of the world, from the time of the Greeks and Romans down to the present day, abundantly prove it. There was that Julius Caesar — he was one of your people's men, and he ended a tyrant. Oliver Cromwell was another — a rebel, a demagogue, and a tyrant. The gradations, madam, are as inevitable as from childhood to youth, and from youth to age. As for the little affair that you have been pleased to mention, of the — of the — of my private concerns, I can only say that the affairs of nations are not to be judged of by domestic incidents, any more than domestic occurrences are to be judged of by national politics." The colonel, like many a better logician, mistook his antithesis for argument, and paused a moment to admire his own eloquence; but the current of his thoughts, which always flowed in torrents on this subject, swept him along in its course, and he continued — "Yes, madam, here, and here alone is true liberty to be found. With this solemn asseveration, which is not lightly made, but which is the result of sixty years' experience, I leave you, Miss Plowden; let it be a subject of deep reflection with you, for I too well understand your treacherous feelings not to know that your political errors encourage your personal foibles; reflect, for your own sake, if you love not only your own happiness, but your respectability and standing in the world. As for the black hounds that you spoke of, they are a set of rebellious, mutinous, ungrateful rascals; and if ever I meet one of the damned —"

The colonel had so far controlled his feelings, as to leave the presence of the lady before he broke out into the bitter invectives we have recorded, and Katherine stood a minute, pressing her forefinger on her lips, listening to his voice as it

grumbled along the gallery, until the sounds were finally excluded by the closing of a distant door. The wilful girl then
shook her dark locks, and a smile of arch mischief, blended
with an expression of regret, in her countenance, as she
spoke to herself, while with hurried hands she threw her tea-
equipage aside in a confused pile —

"It was perhaps a cruel experiment, but it has succeeded.
Though prisoners ourselves, we are at least left free for the
remainder of this night. These mysterious sailors must be examined more closely. If the proud eye of Edward Griffith
was not glaring under the black wig of one of them, I am no
judge of features; and where has Master Barnstable concealed
his charming visage! for neither of the others could be he.
But now for Cecilia."

Her light form glided from the room, while she was yet
speaking, and flitting along the dimly lighted passages, it
disappeared in one of those turnings that led to the more
secret apartments of the abbey.

Chapter XIII.

"How! Lucia, would'st thou have me sink away
In pleasing dreams, and lose myself in love—"

Addison, *Cato,* I. vi.447-448.

THE READER must not imagine that the world stood still during the occurrence of the scenes we have related. By the time the three seamen were placed in as many different rooms, and a sentinel was stationed in the gallery common to them all, in such a manner as to keep an eye on his whole charge at once, the hour had run deep into the night. Captain Borroughcliffe obeyed a summons from the colonel, who made him an evasive apology for the change in their evening's amusement, and challenged his guest to a renewal of the attack on the Madeira. This was too grateful a theme to be lightly discussed by the captain, and the abbey clock had given forth as many of its mournful remonstrances as the division of the hours would permit, before they separated. In the mean time, Mr. Dillon became invisible; though a servant, when questioned by the host on the subject, announced, that "he believed Mr. Christopher had chosen to ride over to ———, to be in readiness to join the hunt, on the morning, with the dawn." While the gentlemen were thus indulging themselves in the dining parlour, and laughing over the tales of other times and hard campaigns, two very different scenes occurred in other parts of the building.

When the quiet of the abbey was only interrupted by the howling of the wind, or by the loud and prolonged laughs which echoed through the passages from the joyous pair, who were thus comfortably established by the side of the bottle, a door was gently opened on one of the galleries of the "cloisters," and Katherine Plowden issued from it, wrapped in a close mantle, and holding in her hand a chamber lamp, which threw its dim light faintly along the gloomy walls in front, leaving all behind her obscured in darkness. She was, however, soon followed by two other female figures, clad in the same manner, and provided with similar lights. When all were in the gallery, Katherine drew the door softly to, and proceeded in front to lead the way.

"Hist!" said the low, tremulous voice of Cecilia, "they are yet up in the other parts of the house; and if it be as you suspect, our visit would betray them, and prove the means of their certain destruction."

"Is the laugh of Colonel Howard in his cups so singular and unknown to your ear, Cecilia, that you know it not?" said Katherine with a little spirit; "or do you forget that on such occasions he seldom leaves himself ears to hear, or eyes to see with. But follow me; it is as I suspect—it must be as I suspect; and unless we do something to rescue them, they are lost, without they have laid a deeper scheme than is apparent."

"It is a dangerous road ye both journey," added the placid tones of Alice Dunscombe; "but ye are young, and ye are credulous."

"If you disapprove of our visit," said Cecilia, "it cannot be right, and we had better return."

"No, no, I have said naught to disapprove of your present errand. If God has put the lives of those in your custody whom ye have taught yourselves to look up to with love and reverence, such as woman is bound to yield to one man, he has done it for no idle purpose. Lead us to their doors, Katherine; let us relieve our doubts, at least."

The ardent girl did not wait for a second bidding, but she led them, with light and quick steps, along the gallery, until they reached its termination, where they descended to the basement floor, by a flight of narrow steps, and carefully opening a small door, emerged into the open air. They now stood on a small plat of grass, which lay between the building and the ornamental garden, across which they moved rapidly, concealing their lights, and bending their shrinking forms before the shivering blasts that poured their fury upon them from the ocean. They soon reached a large but rough addition to the buildings, that concealed its plain architecture behind the more laboured and highly finished parts of the edifice, into which they entered through a massive door, that stood ajar, as if to admit them.

"Chloe has been true to my orders," whispered Katherine, as they passed out of the chilling air; "now, if all the servants are asleep, our chance to escape unnoticed amounts to certainty."

It became necessary to go through the servants' hall, which they effected unobserved, as it had but one occupant, an aged black man, who, being posted with his ear within two feet of a bell, in this attitude had committed himself to a deep sleep. Gliding through this hall, they entered divers long and intricate passages, all of which seemed as familiar to Katherine as they were unknown to her companions, until they reached another flight of steps, which they ascended. They were now near their goal, and stopped to examine whether any or what difficulties were likely to be opposed to their further progress.

"Now, indeed, our case seems hopeless," whispered Katherine, as they stood, concealed by the darkness, in one end of an extremely long, narrow passage; "here is the sentinel in the building, instead of being, as I had supposed, under the windows; what is to be done now?"

"Let us return," said Cecilia, in the same manner; "my influence with my uncle is great, even though he seems unkind to us at times. In the morning I will use it to persuade him to free them, on receiving their promise to abandon all such attempts in future."

"In the morning it will be too late," returned Katherine; "I saw that demon, Kit Dillon, mount his horse, under the pretence of riding to the great hunt of to-morrow, but I know his malicious eye too well to be deceived in his errand. He is silent that he may be sure, and if to-morrow comes, and finds Griffith within these walls, he will be condemned to a scaffold."

"Say no more," said Alice Dunscombe, with singular emotion; "some lucky circumstance may aid us with this sentinel."

As she spoke, she advanced; they had not proceeded far, before the stern voice of the soldier challenged the party.

"'Tis no time to hesitate," whispered Katherine; "we are

the ladies of the abbey, looking to our domestic affairs," she continued, aloud, "and think it a little remarkable that we are to encounter armed men, while going through our own dwelling."

The soldier respectfully presented his musket, and replied—

"My orders are to guard the doors of these three rooms, ladies; we have prisoners in them, and as for any thing else, my duty will be to serve you all in my power."

"Prisoners!" exclaimed Katherine, in affected surprise; "does Captain Borroughcliffe make St. Ruth's Abbey a gaol! Of what offences are the poor men guilty?"

"I know not, my lady; but as they are sailors, I suppose they have run from his majesty's service."

"This is singular, truly! and why are they not sent to the county prison?"

"This must be examined into," said Cecilia, dropping the mantle from before her face. "As mistress of this house, I claim a right to know whom its walls contain; you will oblige me by opening the doors, for I see you have the keys suspended from your belt."

The sentinel hesitated. He was greatly awed by the presence and beauty of the speakers, but a still voice reminded him of his duty. A lucky thought, however, interposed to relieve him from his dilemma, and at the same time to comply with the request, or, rather, order of the lady. As he handed her the keys, he said—

"Here they are, my lady; my orders are to keep the prisoners in, not to keep any one out. When you are done with them, you will please to return them to me, if it be only to save a poor fellow's eyes, for unless the door is kept locked, I shall not dare to look about me for a moment."

Cecilia promised to return the keys, and she had applied one of them to a lock, with a trembling hand, when Alice Dunscombe arrested her arm, and addressed the soldier.

"Say you there are three? are they men in years?"

"No, my lady, all good, serviceable lads, who couldn't do better than to serve his majesty, or, as it may prove, worse than to run from their colours."

"But are their years and appearance similar? I ask, for I

have a friend who has been guilty of some boyish tricks, and has tried the seas, I hear, among other foolish hazards.''

''There is no boy here. In the far room on the left is a smart, soldier-looking chap, of about thirty, who the captain thinks has carried a musket before now; on him I am charged to keep a particular eye. Next to him is as pretty a looking youth as eyes could wish to see, and it makes one feel mournful to think what he must come to, if he has really deserted his ship. In the room near you, is a smaller, quiet little body, who might make a better preacher than a sailor or a soldier either, he has such a gentle way with him.''

Alice covered her eyes with her hand a moment, and then recovering herself, proceeded—

''Gentleness may do more with the unfortunate men than fear; here is a guinea; withdraw to the far end of the passage, where you can watch them as well as here, while we enter, and endeavour to make them confess who and what they really are.''

The soldier took the money, and after looking about him in a little uncertainty, he at length complied, as it was obviously true they could only escape by passing him, near the flight of steps. When he was beyond hearing, Alice Dunscombe turned to her companions, and a slight glow appeared in feverish spots on her cheeks, as she addressed them.

''It would be idle to attempt to hide from you, that I expect to meet the individual whose voice I must have heard in reality to-night, instead of only imaginary sounds, as I vainly, if not wickedly supposed. I have many reasons for changing my opinion, the chief of which is that he is leagued with the rebellious Americans in this unnatural war. Nay, chide me not, Miss Plowden; you will remember that I found my being on this island. I come here on no vain or weak errand, Miss Howard, but to spare human blood.'' She paused, as if struggling to speak calmly. ''But no one can witness the interview except our God.''

''Go, then,'' said Katherine, secretly rejoicing at her determination, ''while we inquire into the characters of the others.''

Alice Dunscombe turned the key, and gently opening the

door, she desired her companions to tap for her, as they returned, and then instantly disappeared in the apartment.

Cecilia and her cousin proceeded to the next door, which they opened in silence, and entered cautiously into the room.

Katherine Plowden had so far examined into the arrangements of colonel Howard, as to know that at the same time he had ordered blankets to be provided for the prisoners, he had not thought it necessary to administer any further to the accommodations of men who had apparently made their beds and pillows of planks for the greater part of their lives.

The ladies accordingly found the youthful sailor whom they sought, with his body rolled in the shaggy covering, extended at his length along the naked boards, and buried in a deep sleep. So timid were the steps of his visiters, and so noiseless was their entrance, that they approached even to his side, without disturbing his slumbers. The head of the prisoner lay rudely pillowed on a billet of wood, one hand protecting his face from its rough surface, and the other thrust into his bosom, where it rested, with a relaxed grasp, on the handle of a dirk. Although he slept, and that heavily, yet his rest was unnatural and perturbed. His breathing was hard and quick, and something like the low, rapid murmurings of a confused utterance mingled with his respiration. The moment had now arrived when the character of Cecilia Howard appeared to undergo an entire change. Hitherto she had been led by her cousin, whose activity and enterprise seemed to qualify her so well for the office of guide; but now she advanced before Katherine, and, extending her lamp in such a manner as to throw the light across the face of the sleeper, she bent to examine his countenance, with keen and anxious eyes.

"Am I right?" whispered her cousin.

"May God, in his infinite compassion, pity and protect him!" murmured Cecilia, her whole frame involuntarily shuddering, as the conviction that she beheld Griffith flashed across her mind. "Yes, Katherine, it is he, and presumptuous madness has driven him here. But time presses; he must be awakened, and his escape effected at every hazard."

"Nay, then, delay no longer, but rouse him from his sleep."

"Griffith! Edward Griffith!" said the soft tones of Cecilia, "Griffith, awake!"

"Your call is useless, for they sleep nightly among tempests and boisterous sounds," said Katherine; "but I have heard it said that the smallest touch will generally cause one of them to stir."

"Griffith!" repeated Cecilia, laying her fair hand timidly on his own.

The flash of the lightning is not more nimble than the leap that the young man made to his feet, which he no sooner gained, than his dirk gleamed in the light of the lamps, as he brandished it fiercely with one hand, while with the other he extended a pistol, in a menacing attitude, towards his disturbers.

"Stand back!" he exclaimed; "I am your prisoner only as a corpse!"

The fierceness of his front, and the glaring eyeballs, that rolled wildly around him, appalled Cecilia, who shrunk back in fear, dropping her mantle from her person, but still keeping her mild eyes fastened on his countenance with a confiding gaze, that contradicted her shrinking attitude, as she replied —

"Edward, it is I; Cecilia Howard, come to save you from destruction; you are known even through your ingenious disguise."

The pistol and the dirk fell together on the blanket of the young sailor, whose looks instantly lost their disturbed expression in a glow of pleasure.

"Fortune at length favours me!" he cried. "This is kind, Cecilia; more than I deserve, and much more than I expected. But you are not alone."

"'Tis my cousin Kate; to her piercing eyes you owe your detection, and she has kindly consented to accompany me, that we might urge you to — nay, that we might, if necessary, assist you to fly. For 'tis cruel folly, Griffith, thus to tempt your fate."

"Have I tempted it, then, in vain! Miss Plowden, to you I

must appeal for an answer and a justification."

Katherine looked displeased, but after a moment's hesitation, she replied—

"Your servant, Mr. Griffith. I perceive that the erudite Captain Barnstable has not only succeeded in spelling through my scrawl, but he has also given it to all hands for perusal."

"Now you do both him and me injustice," said Griffith; "it surely was not treachery to show me a plan, in which I was to be a principal actor."

"Ah! doubtless your excuses are as obedient to your calls, as your men," returned the young lady; "but how comes it that the hero of the Ariel sends a deputy to perform a duty that is so peculiarly his own? is he wont to be second in rescues?"

"Heaven forbid that you should think so meanly of him, for a moment! We owe you much, Miss Plowden, but we may have other duties. You know that we serve our common country, and have a superior with us, whose beck is our law."

"Return, then, Mr. Griffith, while you may, to the service of our bleeding country," said Cecilia, "and, after the joint efforts of her brave children have expelled the intruders from her soil, let us hope there shall come a time when Katherine and myself may be restored to our native homes."

"Think you, Miss Howard, to how long a period the mighty arm of the British king may extend that time? We shall prevail; a nation fighting for its dearest rights must ever prevail; but 'tis not the work of a day, for a people, poor, scattered, and impoverished as we have been, to beat down a power like that of England; surely you forget that in bidding me to leave you with such expectations, Miss Howard, you doom me to an almost hopeless banishment!"

"We must trust to the will of God," said Cecilia; "if he ordain that America is to be free only after protracted sufferings, I can aid her but with my prayers; but you have an arm and an experience, Griffith, that might do her better service; waste not your usefulness, then, in visionary schemes for private happiness, but seize the moments as they offer, and return to your ship, if, indeed, it is yet in safety, and endeavour to forget this mad undertaking, and, for a time, the being who has led you to the adventure."

"This is a reception that I had not anticipated," returned Griffith; "for though accident, and not intention, has thrown me into your presence this evening, I did hope that when I again saw the frigate, it would be in your company, Cecilia."

"You cannot justly reproach me, Mr. Griffith, with your disappointment, for I have not uttered or authorized a syllable that could induce you or any one to believe that I would consent to quit my uncle."

"Miss Howard will not think me presumptuous, if I remind her that there was a time when she did not think me unworthy to be intrusted with her person and her happiness."

A rich bloom mantled on the face of Cecilia, as she replied—

"Nor do I now, Mr. Griffith; but you do well to remind me of my former weakness, for the recollection of its folly and imprudence only adds to my present strength."

"Nay," interrupted her eager lover, "if I intended a reproach, or harboured a boastful thought, spurn me from you for ever, as unworthy of your favour."

"I acquit you of both, much easier than I can acquit myself of the charge of weakness and folly," continued Cecilia; "but there are many things that have occurred, since we last met, to prevent a repetition of such inconsiderate rashness on my part. One of them is," she added, smiling sweetly, "that I have numbered twelve additional months to my age, and a hundred to my experience. Another, and perhaps a more important one, is, that my uncle then continued among the friends of his youth, surrounded by those whose blood mingles with his own; but here he lives a stranger, and, though he finds some consolation in dwelling in a building where his ancestors have dwelt before him, yet he walks as an alien through its gloomy passages, and would find the empty honour but a miserable compensation for the kindness and affection of one whom he has loved and cherished from her infancy."

"And yet he is opposed to you in your private wishes, Cecilia, unless my besotted vanity has led me to believe what it would now be madness to learn was false; and in your opinions of public things, you are quite as widely separated. I should think there could be but little happiness dependant on a connexion where there is no one feeling entertained in common."

"There is, and an all-important one," said Miss Howard; "'tis our love. He is my kind, my affectionate, and, unless thwarted by some evil cause, my indulgent uncle and guardian—and I am his brother Harry's child. This tie is not easily to be severed, Mr. Griffith, though, as I do not wish to see you crazed, I shall not add that your besotted vanity has played you false; but, surely, Edward, it is possible to feel a double tie, and so to act as to discharge our duties to both. I never, never can or will consent to desert my uncle, a stranger as he is in the land whose rule he upholds so blindly. You know not this England, Griffith; she receives her children from the colonies with cold and haughty distrust, like a jealous stepmother, who is wary of the favours that she bestows on her fictitious offspring."

"I know her in peace, and I know her in war," said the young sailor, proudly, "and can add, that she is a haughty friend, and a stubborn foe; but she grapples now with those who ask no more of her, than an open sea, and an enemy's favours. But this determination will be melancholy tidings for me to convey to Barnstable."

"Nay," said Cecilia, smiling, "I cannot vouch for others, who have no uncles, and who have an extra quantity of ill humour and spleen against this country, its people, and its laws, although profoundly ignorant of them all."

"Is Miss Howard tired of seeing me under the tiles of St. Ruth?" asked Katherine. "But hark! are there not footsteps approaching along the gallery?"

They listened, in breathless silence, and soon heard distinctly the approaching tread of more than one person. Voices were quite audible, and before they had time to consult on what was best to be done, the words of the speakers were distinctly heard at the door of their own apartment.

"Ay! he has a military air about him, Peters, that will make him a prize; come, open the door."

"This is not his room, your honour," said the alarmed soldier; "he quarters in the last room in the gallery."

"How know you that, fellow? come, produce the key, and open the way for me; I care not who sleeps here; there is no saying but I may enlist them all three."

A single moment of dreadful incertitude succeeded, when the sentinel was heard saying, in reply to this peremptory order—

"I thought your honour wanted to see the one with the black stock, and so left the rest of the keys at the other end of the passage; but—"

"But nothing, you loon; a sentinel should always carry his keys about him, like a goaler; follow, then, and let me see the lad who dresses so well to the right."

As the heart of Katherine began to beat less vehemently, she said—

"'Tis Borroughcliffe, and too drunk to see that we have left the key in the door; but what is to be done? we have but a moment for consultation."

"As the day dawns," said Cecilia, quickly, "I shall send here, under the pretence of conveying you food, my own woman—"

"There is no need of risking any thing for my safety," interrupted Griffith; "I hardly think we shall be detained, and if we are, Barnstable is at hand, with a force that would scatter these recruits to the four winds of heaven."

"Ah! that would lead to bloodshed, and scenes of horror!" exclaimed Cecilia.

"Listen!" cried Katherine, "they approach again!"

A man now stopped, once more, at their door, which was opened softly, and the face of the sentinel was thrust into the apartment.

"Captain Borroughcliffe is on his rounds, and for fifty of your guineas, I would not leave you here another minute."

"But one word more," said Cecilia.

"Not a syllable, my lady, for my life," returned the man; "the lady from the next room waits for you, and, in mercy to a poor fellow, go back where you came from."

The appeal was unanswerable, and they complied, Cecilia saying, as they left the room—

"I shall send you food in the morning, young man, and

directions how to take the remedy necessary to your safety."

In the passage they found Alice Dunscombe, with her face concealed in her mantle, and it would seem by the heavy sighs that escaped from her, deeply agitated by the interview which she had, just encountered.

But as the reader may have some curiosity to know what occurred to distress this unoffending lady so sensibly, we shall detain the narrative, to relate the substance of that which passed between her and the individual whom she sought.

Chapter XIV.

"As when a lion in his den
Hath heard the hunters' cries,
And rushes forth to meet his foes,
So did the Douglass rise —"
    Percy, "The Hermit of Warkworth," Canto II, ll. 209–212.

ALICE Dunscombe did not find the second of the prisoners buried, like Griffith, in sleep, but he was seated on one of the old chairs that were in the apartment, with his back to the door, and apparently looking through the small window, on the dark and dreary scenery, over which the tempest was yet sweeping in its fury. Her approach was unheeded, until the light from her lamp glared across his eyes, when he started from his musing posture, and advanced to meet her. He was the first to speak.

"I expected this visit," he said, "when I found that you recognised my voice, and I felt a deep assurance in my breast, that Alice Dunscombe would never betray me."

His listener, though expecting this confirmation of her conjectures, was unable to make an immediate reply, but she sunk into the seat he had abandoned, and waited a few moments, as if to recover her powers.

"It was, then, no mysterious warning! no airy voice that mocked my ear; but a dread reality!" she at length said. "Why have you thus braved the indignation of the laws of your country? on what errand of fell mischief has your ruthless temper again urged you to embark?"

"This is strong and cruel language, coming from you to me, Alice Dunscombe," returned the stranger, with cool asperity; "and the time has been, when I should have been greeted, after a shorter absence, with milder terms."

"I deny it not; I cannot, if I would, conceal my infirmity from myself or you; I hardly wish it to continue unknown to the world. If I have once esteemed you — if I have plighted to you my troth, and, in my confiding folly, forgot my higher duties, God has amply punished me for the weakness, in your own evil deeds."

"Nay, let not our meeting be embittered with useless and provoking recriminations," said the other; "for we have much to say before you communicate the errand of mercy on which you have come hither. I know you too well, Alice, not to see that you perceive the peril in which I am placed, and are willing to venture something for my safety. Your mother—does she yet live?"

"She is gone in quest of my blessed father," said Alice, covering her pale face with her hands; "they have left me alone, truly, for he who was to have been all to me, was first false to his faith, and has since become unworthy of my confidence."

The stranger became singularly agitated, his usually quiet eye glancing hastily from the floor to the countenance of his companion, as he paced the room with hurried steps; at length he replied—

"There is much, perhaps, to be said in explanation, that you do not know. I left the country, because I found in it nothing but oppression and injustice, and I could not invite you to become the bride of a wanderer, without either name or fortune. But I have now the opportunity of proving my truth. You say you are alone; be so no longer, and try how far you were mistaken in believing that I should one day supply the place to you of both father and mother."

There is something soothing to a female ear in the offer of even protracted justice, and Alice spoke with less of acrimony in her tones, during the remainder of their conference, if not with less of severity in her language.

"You talk not like a man whose very life hangs but on a thread that the next minute may snap asunder. Whither would you lead me? is it to the tower at London?"

"Think not I have weakly exposed my person without a sufficient protection," returned the stranger, with cool indifference; "there are many gallant men who only wait my signal, to crush the paltry force of this officer like a worm beneath my feet."

"Then has the conjecture of Colonel Howard been true! and the manner in which the enemy's vessels have passed the shoals, is no longer a mystery! you have been their pilot!"

"I have."

"What! would ye pervert the knowledge gained in the spring-time of your guileless youth to the foul purpose of bringing desolation to the doors of those you once knew and respected! John! John! is the image of the maiden whom in her morning of beauty and simplicity I believe you did love, so faintly impressed, that it cannot soften your hard heart to the misery of those among whom she has been born, and who compose her little world."

"Not a hair of theirs shall be touched, not a thatch shall blaze, nor shall a sleepless night befall the vilest among them — and all for your sake, Alice! England comes to this contest with a seared conscience, and bloody hands, but all shall be forgotten for the present, when both opportunity and power offer, to make her feel our vengeance, even in her vitals. I came on no such errand."

"What, then, has led you blindly into snares, where all your boasted aid would avail you nothing; for, should I call aloud your name, even here, in the dark and dreary passages of this obscure edifice, the cry would echo through the country, ere the morning, and a whole people would be found in arms to punish your audacity."

"My name has been sounded, and that in no gentle strains," returned the pilot, scornfully, "when a whole people have quailed at it; the craven, cowardly wretches, flying before the man they had wronged. I have lived to bear the banners of the new republic, proudly, in sight of the three kingdoms, when practised skill and equal arms have in vain struggled to pluck it down. Ay! Alice, the echoes of my guns are still roaring among your eastern hills, and would render my name more appalling than inviting to your sleeping yeomen."

"Boast not of the momentary success that the arm of God has yielded to your unhallowed efforts," said Alice; "for a day of severe and heavy retribution must follow; nor flatter yourself with the idle hope, that your name, terrible as ye have rendered it to the virtuous, is sufficient, of itself, to drive the thoughts of home, and country, and kin, from all who hear it. Nay, I know not that even now, in listening to you, I am not forgetting a solemn duty, which would teach me to proclaim your presence, that the land might know that her unnatural son is a dangerous burthen in her bosom."

The pilot turned quickly in his short walk; and, after reading her countenance, with the expression of one who felt his security, he said, in gentler tones—

"Would that be Alice Dunscombe! would that be like the mild, generous girl whom I knew in my youth? But, I repeat, the threat would fail to intimidate, even if you were capable of executing it. I have said that it is only to make the signal, to draw around me a force sufficient to scatter these dogs of soldiers to the four winds of heaven."

"Have you calculated your power justly, John?" said Alice, unconsciously betraying her deep interest in his safety. "Have you reckoned the probability of Mr. Dillon's arriving, accompanied by an armed band of horsemen, with the morning's sun? for it's no secret in the Abbey, that he is gone in quest of such assistance."

"Dillon!" exclaimed the pilot, starting; "who is he! and on what suspicion does he seek this addition to your guard?"

"Nay, John, look not at me, as if you would know the secrets of my heart. It was not I who prompted him to such a step; you cannot, for a moment, think that I would betray you! But too surely he has gone, and, as the night wears rapidly away, you should be using the hour of grace to effect your own security."

"Fear not for me, Alice," returned the pilot, proudly, while a faint smile struggled around his compressed lip; "and yet, I like not this movement, either. How call you his name? Dillon! is he a minion of King George?"

"He is, John, what you are not, a loyal subject of his sovereign lord the King, and, though a native of the revolted colonies, he has preserved his virtue uncontaminated amid the corruptions and temptations of the times."

"An American! and disloyal to the liberties of the human race! By Heaven, he had better not cross me; for if my arm reach him, it shall hold him forth as a spectacle of treason to the world."

"And has not the world enough of such a spectacle in yourself? Are ye not, even now, breathing your native air, though lurking through the mists of the island, with desperate intent against its peace and happiness?"

A dark and fierce expression of angry resentment flashed

from the eyes of the pilot, and even his iron frame seemed to shake with emotion, as he answered—

"Call you his dastardly and selfish treason, aiming, as it does, to aggrandize a few, at the expense of millions, a parallel case to the generous ardour that impels a man to fight in the defence of sacred liberty? I might tell you that I am armed in the common cause of my fellow subjects and countrymen; that though an ocean divided us in distance, yet are we a people of the same blood, and children of the same parents, and that the hand which oppresses one, inflicts an injury on the other. But I disdain all such narrow apologies. I was born on this orb, and I claim to be a citizen of it. A man with a soul, not to be limited by the arbitrary boundaries of tyrants and hirelings, but one who has the right as well as the inclination to grapple with oppression, in whose name soever it is exercised, or in whatever hollow and specious shape it founds its claim to abuse our race."

"Ah! John, John, though this may sound like reason to rebellious ears, to mine it seemeth only as the ravings of insanity. It is in vain ye build up your new and disorganizing systems of rule, or rather misrule, which are opposed to all that the world has ever yet done, or ever will see done in peace and happiness. What avail your subtleties and false reasonings against the heart! It is the heart which tells us where our home is, and how to love it."

"You talk like a weak and prejudiced woman, Alice," said the pilot, more composedly; "and one who would shackle nations with the ties that bind the young and feeble of your own sex together."

"And by what holier or better bond can they be united!" said Alice. "Are not the relations of domestic life of God's establishing, and have not the nations grown from families, as branches spread from the stem, till the tree overshadows the land! 'Tis an ancient and sacred tie that binds man to his nation, neither can it be severed without infamy."

The pilot smiled disdainfully, and throwing open the rough exterior of his dress, he drew forth, in succession, several articles, while a glowing pride lighted his countenance, as he offered them singly to her notice.

"See, Alice!" he said, "call you this infamy! This broad sheet
of parchment is stamped with a seal of no mean importance,
and it bears the royal name of the princely Louis also! And
view this cross! decorated as it is with jewels, the gift of the
same illustrious hand; it is not apt to be given to the children of
infamy, neither is it wise or decorous to stigmatize a man who
has not been thought unworthy to consort with princes and
nobles, by the opprobrious name of the 'Scotch pirate.'"

"And have ye not earned the title, John, by ruthless deeds
and bitter animosity! I could kiss the baubles ye show me, if
they were a thousand times less splendid, had they been laid
upon your breast by the hands of your lawful prince; but now
they appear to my eyes as indelible blots upon your attainted
name. As for your associates, I have heard of them! and it
seemeth that a queen might be better employed than encouraging by her smiles the disloyal subjects of other monarchs,
though even her enemies. God only knows when his pleasure
may suffer a spirit of disaffection to rise up among the people
of her own nation, and then the thought that she has encouraged
rebellion may prove both bitter and unwelcome."

"That the royal and lovely Antoinette has deigned to repay
my services with a small portion of her gracious approbation,
is not among the least of my boasts," returned the pilot, in affected humility, while secret pride was manifested even in his
lofty attitude. "But venture not a syllable in her dispraise, for
you know not whom you censure. She is less distinguished by
her illustrious birth and elevated station, than by her virtues
and loveliness. She lives the first of her sex in Europe — the
daughter of an emperor, the consort of the most powerful king,
and the smiling and beloved patroness of a nation who worship
at her feet. Her life is above all reproach, as it is above all earthly
punishment, were she so lost as to merit it, and it has been
the will of Providence to place her far beyond the reach of all
human misfortunes."

"Has it placed her above human errors, John! punishment is
the natural and inevitable consequence of sin, and unless she
can say more than has ever fallen to the lot of humanity to say
truly, she may yet be made to feel the chastening arm of One,
to whose eyes all her pageantry and power are as vacant as the
air she breathes — so insignificant must it seem when compared

to his own just rule! But if you vaunt that you have been permitted to kiss the hem of the robes of the French queen, and have been the companion of high-born and flaunting ladies, clad in their richest array, can ye yet say to yourself, that amid them all ye have found one whose tongue has been bold to tell you the truth, or whose heart has sincerely joined in her false professions!"

"Certainly none have met me with the reproaches that I have this night received from Alice Dunscombe, after a separation of six long years," returned the Pilot.

"If I have spoken to you the words of holy truth, John, let them not be the less welcome, because they are strangers to your ears. Oh! think that she who has thus dared to use the language of reproach to one whose name is terrible to all who live on the border of this island, is led to the rash act by no other motive than interest in your eternal welfare."

"Alice! Alice, you madden me with these foolish speeches! Am I a monster to frighten unprotected women and helpless children? What mean these epithets, as coupled with my name? Have you too lent a credulous ear to the vile calumnies with which the policy of your rulers has ever attempted to destroy the fair fame of those who oppose them, and those chiefly who oppose them with success. My name may be terrible to the officers of the royal fleet, but where and how have I earned a claim to be considered formidable to the helpless and unoffending?"

Alice Dunscombe cast a furtive and timid glance at the pilot, which spoke even stronger than her words, as she replied—

"I know not that all which is said of you and your deeds is true. I have often prayed, in bitterness and sorrow, that a tenth part of that which is laid to your charge may not be heaped on your devoted head at the great and final account. But, John, I have known you long and well, and Heaven forbid, that, on this solemn occasion, which may be the last of our earthly interviews, I should be found wanting in christian duty, through a woman's weakness. I have often thought, when I have heard the gall of bitter reproach and envenomed language hurled against your name, that they who spoke so rashly, little understood the man they vituperated. But, though ye are at times, and I may say almost always, as mild and even as the smoothest sea over which ye have ever sailed, yet God has mingled in your nature a fearful mixture of fierce passions, which, roused, are more like the southern waters when troubled with the tornado. It is difficult for me to say, how far this evil spirit may lead a man, who has been goaded by fancied wrongs, to forget his country and home, and who is suddenly clothed with power to show his resentments."

The pilot listened with rooted attention, and his piercing eye seemed to reach the seat of those thoughts which she but half expressed; still, he retained the entire command of himself, and answered more in sorrow than in anger—

"If any thing could convert me to your own peaceful and unresisting opinions, Alice, it would be the reflections that offer themselves at this conviction, that even you have been led, by the base tongues of my dastardly enemies, to doubt my honour and conduct. What is fame, when a man can be thus traduced to his nearest friends! But no more of these childish reflections! They are unworthy of myself, my office, and the sacred cause in which I have enlisted!"

"Nay, John, shake them not off," said Alice, unconsciously laying her hand on his arm; "they are as the dew to the parched herbage, and may freshen the feelings of your youth, and soften the heart that has grown hard, if hard it be, more by unnatural indulgence, than its own base inclinations."

"Alice Dunscombe," said the pilot, approaching her with solemn earnestness, "I have learnt much this night, though I came not in quest of such knowledge. You have taught me how powerful is the breath of the slanderer, and how frail is the tenure by which we hold our good names. Full twenty times have I met the hirelings of your prince in open battle, fighting ever manfully under that flag which was first raised to the breeze by my own hands, and which, I thank my God, I have never yet seen lowered an inch; but with no one act of cowardice or private wrong, in all that service, can I reproach myself; and yet, how am I rewarded! The tongue of the vile calumniator is keener than the sword of the warrior, and leaves a more indelible scar!"

"Never have ye uttered a truer sentiment, John, and God send that ye may encourage such thoughts to your own eternal advantage," said Alice, with engaging interest. "You say that you have risked your precious life in twenty combats, and observe how little of Heaven's favour is bestowed on the abettors of rebellion! They tell me that the world has never witnessed a more desperate and bloody struggle than this last, for which your name has been made to sound to the furthermost ends of the isle."

"'Twill be known wherever naval combats are spoken of," interrupted the pilot, the melancholy which had begun to lower in his countenance, giving place to a look of proud exultation.

"And yet, its fancied glory cannot shield your name from wrong, nor are the rewards of the victor equal, in a temporal sense, to those which the vanquished has received. Know you that our gracious monarch, deeming your adversary's cause so sacred, has extended to him his royal favour?"

"Ay! he has dubbed him knight!" exclaimed the pilot, with a scornful and bitter laugh; "let him be again furnished with a ship, and me with another opportunity, and I promise him an earldom, if being again vanquished can constitute a claim!"

"Speak not so rashly, nor vaunt yourself of possessing a protecting power, that may desert you, John, when you most need it, and least expect the change," returned his companion; "the battle is not always to the strong, neither is the race to the swift."

"Forget you, my good Alice, that your words will admit of a double meaning? Has the battle been to the strong! Though you say not well in denying the race to the swift. Yes, yes, often and again have the dastards escaped me by their prudent speed! Alice Dunscombe, you know not a thousandth part of the torture that I have been made to feel, by high born miscreants, who envy the merit they cannot equal, and detract from the glory of deeds that they dare not attempt to emulate. How have I been cast upon the ocean like some unworthy vessel that is commissioned to do a desperate deed, and then to bury itself in the ruin it has made! How many malignant hearts have triumphed, as they beheld my canvass open, thinking that it was spread to hasten me to a gibbet, or to a tomb in the bosom of the ocean; but I have disappointed them!"

The eyes of the pilot no longer gazed with their piercing and settled meaning, but they flashed with a fierce and wild pleasure, as he continued, in a louder voice—

"Yes, bitterly have I disappointed them! Oh! the triumph over my fallen enemies has been tame, to this heartfelt exultation which places me immeasurably above those false and craven hypocrites! I begged, I implored, the Frenchmen, for the meanest of their craft, which possessed but the common qualities of a ship of war; I urged the policy and necessity of giving me such a force, for even then I promised to be found in harm's way; but, envy and jealousy robbed me of my just dues, and of more than half my glory. They call me pirate! If I have a claim to the name, it was furnished more by the paltry outfit of my friends, than by any act towards my enemies!"

"And do not these recollections prompt you to return to your allegiance to your prince and native land, John?" said Alice, in a subdued voice.

"Away with the silly thought," interrupted the pilot, recalled to himself as if by a sudden conviction of the weakness he had betrayed; "it is ever thus where men are made conspicuous by their works—but to your visit—I have the power to rescue myself and companions from this paltry confinement, and yet I would not have it done with violence, for your sake. — Bring you the means of doing it in quiet?"

"When the morning arrives, you will all be conducted to the apartment where we first met. This will be done at the solicitation of Miss Howard, under the plea of compassion and justice, and with the professed object of inquiring into your situations. Her request will not be refused, and while your guard is stationed at the door, you will be shown, by another entrance through the private apartments of the wing, to a window, whence you can easily leap to the ground, where a thicket is at hand; afterwards we shall trust your safety to your own discretion."

"And if this Dillon, of whom you have spoken, should suspect the truth, how will you answer to the law for aiding our escape?"

"I believe he little dreams who is among the prisoners," said Alice, musing, "though he may have detected the character of one of your companions. But it is private feeling, rather than public spirit, that urges him on."

"I have suspected something of this," returned the pilot, with a smile, that crossed those features where ungovernable passions had so lately been exhibited, with an effect, that might be likened to the last glimmering of an expiring conflagration, serving to render the surrounding ruin more obvious. "This young Griffith has led me from my direct path, with his idle imprudence, and it is right that his mistress should incur some risk. But with you, Alice, the case is different; here you are only a guest, and it is unnecessary that you should be known in the unfortunate affair. Should my name get abroad, this recreant American, this Col. Howard, will find all the favour he has purchased by advocating the cause of tyranny, necessary to protect him from the displeasure of the ministry."

"I fear to trust so delicate a measure to the young discretion of my amiable friend," said Alice, shaking her head.

"Remember, that she has her attachment to plead in her excuse; but dare you say to the world that you still remember, with gentle feelings, the man whom you stigmatize with such opprobrious epithets!"

A slight colour gleamed over the brow of Alice Dunscombe, as she uttered in a voice that was barely audible—

"There is no longer a reason why the world should know of such a weakness, though it did exist." And, as the faint glow passed away, leaving her face pale, nearly as the hue of death, her eyes kindled with unusual fire, and she added, "They can but take my life, John, and that I am ready to lay down in your service!"

"Alice!" exclaimed the softened pilot, "my kind, my gentle Alice!"—

The knock of the sentinel at the door, was heard at this critical moment. Without waiting for a reply to his summons, the man entered the apartment, and, in hurried language, declared the urgent necessity that existed for the lady to retire. A few brief remonstrances were uttered by both Alice and the pilot, who wished to comprehend more clearly each other's intentions relative to the intended escape; but the fear of personal punishment rendered the soldier obdurate, and a dread of exposure at length induced the lady to comply. She arose, and was leaving the apartment with lingering steps, when the pilot, touching her hand, whispered to her impressively —

"Alice, we meet again before I leave this island for ever."

"We meet in the morning, John," she returned, in the same tone of voice, "in the apartments of Miss Howard."

He dropped her hand, and she glided from the room, when the impatient sentinel closed the door, and silently turned the key on his prisoner. The pilot remained in a listening attitude, until the light footsteps of the retiring pair were no longer audible, when he paced his confined apartment with perturbed steps, occasionally pausing to look out at the driving clouds, and the groaning oaks that were trembling and rocking their broad arms in the fitful gusts of the gale. In a few minutes the tempest in his own passions had gradually subsided to the desperate and still calmness that made him the man he was; when he again seated himself where Alice had found him, and began to muse on the events of the times, from which, the transition to projecting schemes of daring enterprise and mighty consequences, was but the usual employment of his active and restless mind.

Chapter XV.

"*Sir And.* I have no exquisite reason for't, but I've reason good
enough."

Twelfth Night, II.iii.145-146.

THE COUNTENANCE of Captain Borroughcliffe, when the
sentinel admitted him to the apartment he had selected, was in
that state of doubtful illumination, when looks of peculiar cunning blend so nicely with the stare of vacancy, that the human
face is rendered not unlike an April day, now smiling and inviting, and at the next moment clouded and dreary. It was
quite apparent that the soldier had an object for his unexpected visit, by the importance of his air, and the solemnity of
the manner with which he entered on the business. He waved
his hand for the sentinel to retire, with lofty dignity, and continued balancing his body, during the closing of the door, and
while a sound continued audible to his confused faculties, with
his eyes fixed in the direction of the noise, with that certain
sort of wise look, that in many men supplies the place of
something better. When the captain felt himself secure from
interruption, he moved round with quick military precision, in
order to face the man of whom he was in quest. Griffith had
been sleeping, though uneasily, and with watchfulness; and the
pilot had been calmly awaiting the visit which it seemed he had
anticipated; but their associate, who was no other than Captain Manual, of the marines, was discovered in a very different
condition from either. Though the weather was cool, and the
night tempestuous, he had thrown aside his pea-jacket, with
most of his disguise, and was sitting ruefully on his blanket,
wiping, with one hand, the large drops of sweat from his
forehead, and occasionally grasping his throat with the other,
with a kind of convulsed, mechanical movement. He stared
wildly at his visiter, though his entrance produced no other
alteration in these pursuits, than a more diligent application of
his handkerchief, and a more frequent grasping of his naked

neck, as if he were willing to ascertain by actual experiment, what degree of pressure the part was able to sustain, without exceeding a given quantity of inconvenience.

"Comrade, I greet ye!" said Borroughcliffe, staggering to the side of his prisoner, where he seated himself with an entire absence of ceremony; "Comrade, I greet ye! Is the kingdom in danger, that gentlemen traverse the island in the uniform of the regiment of incognitus, incognitii, 'torum—dammee, how I forget my Latin! Say, my fine fellow, are you one of these 'torums?"

Manual breathed a little hard, which, considering the manner he had been using his throat, was a thing to be expected; but, swallowing his apprehensions, he answered with more spirit than his situation rendered prudent, or the occasion demanded.

"Say what you will of me, and treat me as you please, I defy any man to call me tory with truth."

"You are no 'torum! Well, then, the war office has got up a new dress! Your regiment must have earned their facings in storming some water battery, or perhaps it has done duty as marines. Am I right?"

"I'll not deny it," said Manual, more stoutly; "I have served as a marine for two years, though taken from the line of"—

"The army," said Borroughcliffe, interrupting a most damning confession of which "state line" the other had belonged to. "I kept a dog watch myself, once, on board the fleet of my Lord Howe; but it is a service that I do not envy any man. Our afternoon parades were dreadfully unsteady, for it's a time, you know, when a man wants solid ground to stand on. However, I purchased my company with some prize money that fell in my way, and I always remember the marine service with gratitude. But this is dry work. I have put a bottle of sparkling Madeira in my pocket, with a couple of glasses, which we will discuss, while we talk over more important matters. Thrust your hand into my right pocket; I have been used to dress to the front so long, that it comes mighty awkward to me to make this backward motion, as if it were into a cartridge box."

Manual, who had been at a loss how to construe the manner of the other, perceived at once a good deal of plain English in this request, and he dislodged one of Colonel Howard's dusty bottles, with a dexterity that denoted the earnestness of his purpose. Borroughcliffe had made a suitable provision of glasses, and extracting the cork in a certain scientific manner, he tendered to his companion a bumper of the liquor, before another syllable was uttered by either of the expectants. The gentlemen concluded their draughts with a couple of smacks, that sounded not unlike the pistols of two practised duellists, though certainly a much less alarming noise; when the entertainer renewed the discourse.

"I like one of your musty-looking bottles, that is covered with dust and cobwebs, with a good southern tan on it," he said. "Such liquor does not abide in the stomach, but it gets into the heart at once, and becomes blood in the beating of a pulse. But how soon I knew you! That sort of knowledge is the freemasonry of our craft. I knew you to be the man you are, the moment I laid eyes on you in what we call our guard-room; but I thought I would humour the old soldier who lives here, by letting him have the formula of an examination, as a sort of deference to his age and former rank. But I knew you the instant I saw you. I have seen you before!"

The theory of Borroughcliffe, in relation to the incorporation of wine with the blood, might have been true in the case of the marine, whose whole frame appeared to undergo a kind of magical change by the experiment of drinking, which, the reader will understand, was diligently persevered in, while a drop remained in the bottle. The perspiration no longer rolled from his brow, neither did his throat manifest that uneasiness which had rendered such constant external applications necessary; but he settled down into an air of cool, but curious interest, which, in some measure, was the necessary concomitant of his situation.

"We may have met before, as I have been much in service, and yet I know not where you could have seen me," said Manual. "Were you ever a prisoner of war?"

"Hum! not exactly such an unfortunate devil; but a sort of conventional non-combatant. I shared the hardships, the glory, the equivocal victories, (where we killed and drove countless numbers of rebels—who were not,) and, wo is me! the capitulation of Burgoyne. But let that pass—which was more than the Yankees would allow us to do. You know not where I could have seen you? I have seen you on parade, in the field, in battle and out of battle, in camp, in barracks, in short, every where but in a drawing-room. No, no; I have never seen you before this night in a drawing-room!"

Manual stared in a good deal of wonder, and some uneasiness, at these confident assertions, which promised to put his life in no little jeopardy; and it is to be supposed that the peculiar sensation about the throat was revived, as he made a heavy draught before he said—

"You will swear to this—Can you call me by name?"

"I will swear to it in any court in Christendom," said the dogmatical soldier; "and your name is—is—Fugleman."

"If it is, I'll be damn'd!" exclaimed the other, with exulting precipitation.

"Swear not!" said Borroughcliffe, with a solemn air; "for what mattereth an empty name! Call thyself by what appellation thou wilt, I know thee. Soldier is written on thy martial front; thy knee bendeth not; nay, I even doubt if the rebellious member bow in prayer."—

"Come, sir," interrupted Manual, a little sternly; "no more of this trifling, but declare your will at once. Rebellious member, indeed! These fellows will call the skies of America rebellious heavens shortly!"

"I like thy spirit, lad," returned the undisturbed Borroughcliffe; "it sits as gracefully on a soldier, as his sash and gorget; but it is lost on an old campaigner. I marvel, however, that thou takest such umbrage at my slight attack on thy orthodoxy. I fear the fortress must be weak, where the outworks are defended with such a waste of unnecessary courage."

"I know not why or wherefore you have paid me this visit, Captain Borroughcliffe," said Manual, with a laudable discretion, which prompted him to reconnoitre the other's views a little, before he laid himself more open; "if captain be your rank, and Borroughcliffe be your name. But this I do know, that if it be only to mock me in my present situation, it is neither soldier-like nor manly; and it is what, in other circumstances, might be attended by some hazard."

"Hum!" said the other, with his immovable coolness; "I see

you set the wine down as nothing, though the king drinks not as good; for the plain reason that the sun of England cannot find its way through the walls of Windsor Castle, as easily as the sun of Carolina can warm a garret covered with cedar shingles. But I like your spirit more and more. So draw yourself up in battle array, and let us have another charge at this black bottle, when I shall lay before your military eyes a plan of the whole campaign."

Manual first bestowed an inquiring glance on his companion, when, discovering no other expression than foolish cunning, which was fast yielding before the encroaching footsteps of stupid inebriety, he quietly placed himself in the desired position. The wine was drunk, when Borroughcliffe proceeded to open his communications more unreservedly.

"You are a soldier, and I am a soldier. That you are a soldier, my orderly could tell; for the dog has both seen a campaign, and smelt villanous salt-petre, when compounded according to a wicked invention; but it required the officer to detect the officer. Privates do not wear such linen as this, which seemeth to me an unreasonably cool attire for the season; nor velvet stocks, with silver buckles; nor is there often the odorous flavour of sweet-scented pomatum to be discovered around their greasy locks. In short, thou art both soldier and officer."

"I confess it," said Manual; "I hold the rank of captain, and shall expect the treatment of one."

"I think I have furnished you with wine fit for a general," returned Borroughcliffe; "but have your own way. Now, it would be apparent to men, whose faculties had not been rendered clear by such cordials as this dwelling aboundeth with, that when you officers journey through the island, clad in the uniform incognitorum, which, in your case, means the marine corps, that something is in the wind of more than usual moment. Soldiers owe their allegiance to their prince, and next to him, to war, women, and wine. Of war, there is none in the realm; of women, plenty; but wine, I regret to say, that is, good wine, grows both scarce and dear. Do I speak to the purpose, comrade?"

"Proceed," said Manual, whose eyes were not less attentive

than his ears, in a hope to discover whether his true character were understood.

"En avant! in plain English, forward march! Well then, the difficulty lies between women and wine; which, when the former are pretty, and the latter rich, is a very agreeable sort of an alternative. That it is not wine of which you are in quest, I must believe, my comrade captain, or you would not go on the adventure in such shabby attire. You will excuse me, but who would think of putting any thing better than their port before a man in a pair of tarred trowsers. No! no! Hollands, green-and-yellow Hollands, is a potation good enough to set before one of thy present bearing."

"And yet I have met with him who has treated me to the choicest of the south-side Madeira?"

"Know you the very side from which the precious fluid comes! That looks more in favour of the wine. But, after all, woman, dear, capricious woman, who one moment fancies she sees a hero in regimentals, and the next, a saint in a cassock; and who always sees something admirable in a suitor, whether he be clad in tow or velvet—woman is at the bottom of this mysterious masquerading. Am I right, comrade?"

By this time, Manual had discovered that he was safe, and he returned to the conversation with a revival of all his ready wits, which had been strangely paralyzed by his previous disorder in the region of the throat. First bestowing a wicked wink on his companion, and a look that would have outdone the wisest aspect of Solomon, he replied—

"Ah! woman has much to answer for!"

"I knew it," exclaimed Borroughcliffe; "and this confession only confirms me in the good opinion I have always entertained of myself. If his majesty has any particular wish to close this American business, let him have a certain convention burnt, and a nameless person promoted, and we shall see! But, answer as you love truth; is it a business of holy matrimony, or a mere dalliance with the sweets of Cupid?"

"Of honest wedlock," said Manual, with an air as serious as if Hymen already held him in his fetters.

"'Tis honest! Is there money?"

"Is there money?" repeated Manual, with a sort of contemptuous echo. "Would a soldier part with his liberty, but with his life, unless the chains were made of gold?"

"That's the true military doctrine!" cried the other; "faith, you have some discretion in your amphibious corps, I find! But why this disguise, are the 'seniors grave,' as well as 'potent and reverend?' Why this disguise, I again ask?"

"Why this disguise!" repeated Manual, coolly; "Is there any such thing as love in your regiment without disguise? With us it is a regular symptom of the disease."

"A most just and discreet description of the passion, my amphibious comrade!" said the English officer; "and yet the symptoms in your case are attended by some very malignant tokens. Does your mistress love tar?"

"No; but she loveth me; and, of course, whatever attire I choose to appear in."

"Still discreet and sagacious! and yet only a most palpable feint to avoid my direct attack. You have heard of such a place as Gretna Green, a little to the north of this, I dare say, my aquatic comrade. Am I right?"

"Gretna Green!" said Manual, a little embarrassed by his ignorance; "some parade ground, I suppose?"

"Ay, for those who suffer under the fire of Master Cupid. A parade ground! well, there is some artful simplicity in that! But all will not do with an old campaigner. It is a difficult thing to impose on an old soldier, my water battery. Now listen and answer; and you shall see what it is to possess a discernment—therefore deny nothing. You are in love?"

"I deny nothing," said Manual, comprehending at once that this was his safest course.

"Your mistress is willing, and the money is ready, but the old people say, halt!"

"I am still mute."

"'Tis prudent. You say march—Gretna Green is the object; and your flight is to be by water?"

"Unless I can make my escape by water, I shall never make it," said Manual, with another sympathetic movement with his hand to his throat.

"Keep mute; you need tell me nothing. I can see into a mystery that is as deep as a well, to-night. Your companions are hirelings; perhaps your shipmates; or men to pilot you on this expedition?"

"One is my shipmate, and the other is our pilot," said Manual, with more truth than usual.

"You are well provided. One thing more, and I shall become mute in my turn. Does she whom you seek lie in this house?"

"She does not; she lies but a short distance from this place; and I should be a happy fellow, could I but once more put foot—"

"Eyes on her. Now listen, and you shall have your wish. You possess the ability to march yet, which, considering the lateness of the hour, is no trifling privilege; open that window—is it possible to descend from it?"

Manual eagerly complied, but he turned from the place in disappointment.

"It would be certain death to attempt the leap. The devil only could escape from it."

"So I should think," returned Borroughcliffe dryly. "You must be content to pass for that respectable gentleman for the rest of your days, in St. Ruth's Abbey. For through that identical hole must you wing your flight on the pinions of love."

"But how! The thing is impossible."

"In imagination only. There is some stir; a good deal of foolish apprehension; and a great excess of idle curiosity, among certain of the tenants of this house on your account. They fear the rebels, who, we all know, have not soldiers enough to do their work neatly at home, and who of course would never think of sending any here. You wish to be snug—I wish to serve a brother in distress. Through that window you must be supposed to fly—no matter how; while by following me you can pass the sentinel, and retire peaceably, like any other mortal, on your own two stout legs."

This was a result that exceeded all that Manual had anticipated from their amicable but droll dialogue; and the hint was hardly given, before he threw on the garments that agitation had before rendered such encumbrances, and in less time than we have taken to relate it, the marine was completely equipped for his departure. In the mean time, Captain Borroughcliffe raised himself to an extremely erect posture, which he maintained, with the inflexibility of a rigid martinet. When he found himself established on his feet, the soldier intimated to his prisoner that he was ready to proceed. The door was instantly opened by Manual, and together they entered the gallery.

"Who comes there?" cried the sentinel, with a vigilance and vigour that he intended should compensate for his previous neglect of duty.

"Walk straight, that he may see you," said Borroughcliffe, with much philosophy.

"Who goes there!" repeated the sentinel, throwing his musket to a poise, with a rattling sound that echoed along the naked walls.

"Walk crooked," added Borroughcliffe, "that if he fire he may miss."

"We shall be shot at, with this folly," muttered Manual. "We are friends, and your officer is one of us."

"Stand friends—advance officer and give the countersign," cried the sentinel.

"That is much easier said than done," returned his captain; "forward! Mr. Amphibious, you can walk like a postman—move to the front, and proclaim the magical word, 'loyalty;' 'tis a standing countersign, ready furnished to my hands by mine host, the colonel; your road is then clear before you—but hark—"

Manual made an eager step forward, when, recollecting himself, he turned, and added—

"My assistants, the seamen! I can do nothing without them."

"Lo! the keys are in the doors, ready for my admission," said the Englishman; "turn them and bring out your forces."

Quick as thought, Manual was in the room of Griffith, to whom he briefly communicated the situation of things, when he re-appeared in the passage, and then proceeded on a similar errand to the room of the pilot.

"Follow, and behave as usual," he whispered; "say not a word, but trust all to me."

The pilot arose, and obeyed these instructions without asking a question, with the most admirable coolness.

"I am now ready to proceed," said Manual, when they had joined Borroughcliffe.

During the short time occupied in these arrangements, the

sentinel and his captain had stood looking at each other, with great military exactitude. The former ambitious of manifesting his watchfulness; the latter awaiting the return of the marine. The captain now beckoned to Manual to advance and give the countersign.

"Loyalty," whispered Manual, when he approached the sentinel. But the soldier had been allowed time to reflect; and as he well understood the situation of his officer, he hesitated to allow the prisoner to pass. After a moment's pause, he said—

"Advance friends." At this summons, the whole party moved to the point of his bayonet; when the man continued, "The prisoners have the countersign, Captain Borroughcliffe, but I dare not let them pass."

"Why not?" asked the captain; "am I not here, sirrah; do you not know me?"

"Yes, sir, I know your honour, and respect your honour; but I was posted here by my sergeant, and ordered not to let these men pass out on any account."

"That's what I call good discipline," said Borroughcliffe, with an exulting laugh; "I knew the lad would not mind me any more than that he would obey the orders of that lamp. Here are no slaves of the lamp, my amphibious comrade; drill ye your marines in this consummate style to niceties?"

"What means this trifling?" said the pilot, sternly.

"Ah! I thought I should turn the laugh on you," cried Manual, affecting to join in the mirth; "we know all these things well, and we practise them in our corps; but though the sentinel cannot know you, the sergeant will; so let him be called, and orders be given through him to the man on post, that we may pass out."

"Your throat grows uneasy, I see," said Borroughcliffe; "you crave another bottle of the generous fluid. Well, it shall be done. Sentinel, you can throw up yon window, and give a call to the sergeant."

"The outcry will ruin us," said the pilot, in a whisper to Griffith.

"Follow me," said the young sailor. The sentinel was turning to execute the orders of his captain, as Griffith spoke; when springing forward, in an instant he wrenched the musket from his hands; a heavy blow with its butt, felled the astonished soldier to the floor; then, poising his weapon, Griffith exclaimed—

"Forward! we can clear our own way now!"

"On!" said the pilot, leaping lightly over the prostrate soldier, a dagger gleaming in one hand, and a pistol presented in the other.

Manual was by his side in an instant, armed in a similar manner; and the three rushed together from the building, without meeting any one to oppose their flight.

Borroughcliffe was utterly unable to follow; and so astounded was he by this sudden violence, that several minutes passed before he was restored to the use of his speech, a faculty which seldom deserted him. The man had recovered his senses and his feet, however; and the two stood gazing at each other in mute condolence. At length the sentinel broke the silence—

"Shall I give the alarm, your honour?"

"I rather think not, Peters. I wonder if there be any such thing as gratitude or good breeding in the marine corps!"

"I hope your honour will remember that I did my duty, and that I was disarmed while executing your orders."

"I can remember nothing about it, Peters, except that it is rascally treatment, and such as I shall yet make this amphibious, aquatic gentleman answer for. But, lock the door—look as if nothing had happened, and—"

"Ah! your honour, that is not so easily done as your honour may please to think. I have not any doubt but there is the print of the breech of a musket stamped on my back and shoulders, as plainly to be seen as that light."

"Then look as you please; but hold your peace, sirrah. Here is a crown to buy a plaster. I heard the dog throw away your musket on the stairs—go seek it, and return to your post; and when you are relieved, act as if nothing had happened. I take the responsibility on myself."

The man obeyed, and when he was once more armed, Borroughcliffe, a good deal sobered by the surprise, made the best of his way to his own apartment, muttering threats and execrations against the "corps of marines, and the whole race," as he called them, "of aquatic amphibii."

Chapter XVI.

"Away! away! the covey's fled the cover;
Put forth the dogs, and let the falcon fly —
I'll spend some leisure in the keen pursuit,
Nor longer waste my hours in sluggish quiet."

T HE SOLDIER passed the remainder of the night in the heavy sleep of a bacchanalian, and awoke late on the following morning, only when aroused by the entrance of his servant. When the customary summons had induced the captain to unclose his eye-lids, he arose in his bed, and after performing the usual operation of a diligent friction on his organs of vision, he turned sternly to his man, and remarked, with an ill-humour that seemed to implicate the innocent servant in the fault which his master condemned —

"I thought, sirrah, that I ordered Sergeant Drill not to let a drum-stick touch a sheep-skin while we quartered in the dwelling of this hospitable old colonel! Does the fellow despise my commands; or does he think the roll of a drum, echoing through the crooked passages of St. Ruth, a melody that is fit to disturb the slumbers of its inmates!"

"I believe, sir," returned the man, "it was the wish of Colonel Howard himself, that on this occasion the sergeant should turn out the guard by the roll of the drum."

"The devil it was! I see the old fellow loves to tickle the drum of his own ear now and then, with familiar sounds; but have you had a muster of the cattle from the farm-yard too, as well as a parade of the guard? I hear the trampling of feet, as if the old abbey were a second ark, and all the beasts of the field were coming aboard of us!"

"'Tis nothing but the party of dragoons from —— who are wheeling into the court-yard, sir, where the colonel has gone out to receive them."

"Court-yard! light dragoons!" repeated Borroughcliffe, in amazement; "and has it come to this, that twenty stout fellows of the ——th are not enough to guard such a rookery as this old abbey, against the ghosts and north-east storms, but we must have horse to reinforce us. Hum! I suppose some of these booted gentlemen have heard of this South-Carolina Madeira."

"Oh, no, Sir!" cried his man, "it is only the party that Mr. Dillon went to seek last evening, after you saw fit, sir, to put the three pirates in irons."

"Pirates in irons!" said Borroughcliffe, again passing his hands over his eyes, though in a more reflecting manner than before; "ha! oh! I remember to have put three suspicious looking rascals in the black-hole, or some such place; but what can Mr. Dillon, or the light dragoons, have to do with these fellows?"

"That we do not know, sir; but it is said below, sir, as some suspicions had fallen on their being conspirators and rebels from the colonies, and that they were great officers and tories in disguise; some said that one was General Washington, and others, that it was only three members of the Yankee parliament, come over to get our good old English fashions, to set themselves up with."

"Washington! Members of Congress! Go — go, simpleton, and learn how many these troopers muster, and what halt they make; but stay, place my clothes near me. Now, do as I bid you; and if the dragoon officer inquire for me, make my respects, and tell him I shall be with him soon. Go, fellow; go."

When the man left the room, the captain, while he proceeded with the business of the toilet, occasionally gave utterance to the thoughts that crowded on his recollection, after the manner of a soliloquy.

"Ay! my commission to a half-pay ensigncy, that some of these lazy fellows, who must have a four-legged beast to carry them to the wars, have heard of the 'south side.' South side! I believe I must put an advertisement in the London Gazette, calling that amphibious soldier to an account. If he be a true man, he will not hide himself under his incognito, but will give me a meeting. If that should fail, damme, I'll ride across to Yarmouth, and call out the first of the mongrel breed that I fall in with. 'Sdeath! was ever such an insult practised on a gentleman, and a soldier, before! Would that I only knew his name! Why, if the tale should get abroad, I shall be the standing joke of the mess-table, until some greater fool than myself can be found. It would cost me at least six duels to get rid of it. No, no; not a trigger will I pull in my own regiment about the silly affair; but I'll have a crack at some marine in very revenge; for that is no more than reasonable. That Peters! if the scoundrel should dare whisper any thing of the manner in which he was stamped with the breech of the musket! I can't flog him for it, but if I don't make it up to him, the first time he gives me a chance, I am ignorant of the true art of balancing regimental accounts."

By the time the recruiting officer had concluded this soliloquy, which affords a very fair exposition of the current of his thoughts, he was prepared to meet the new comers, and he accordingly descended to the court-yard, as in duty bound, to receive them in his proper person. Borroughcliffe encountered his host, in earnest conversation with a young man in a cavalry uniform, in the principal entrance of the abbey, and was greeted by the former with ——th.

"A good morning to you, my worthy guard and protector! here is rare news for your loyal ears. It seems that our prisoners are enemies to the king in disguise; and Cornet Fitzgerald—Captain Borroughcliffe, of the ——th, permit me to make you acqainted with Mr. Fitzgerald, of the ——th Light Dragoons." While the soldiers exchanged their salutations, the old man continued—"The cornet has been kind enough to lead down a detachment of his troop, to escort the rogues up to London, or some other place, where they will find enough good and loyal officers to form a court martial, that can authorize their execution as spies. Christopher Dillon, my worthy kinsman, Kit, saw into their real characters, at a glance, while you and I, like two unsuspecting boys, thought the rascals would have made fit men to serve the king. But Kit has an eye and a head that few enjoy like him, and I would that he might receive his dues at the English bar."

"It is to be desired, sir," said Borroughcliffe, with a grave aspect, that was produced chiefly by his effort to give effect to his sarcasm, but a little, also, by the recollection of the occurrences that were yet to be explained; "but what reason has Mr. Christopher Dillon to believe that the three seamen are more or less than they seem?"

"I know not what; but a good and sufficient reason, I will venture my life," cried the colonel; "Kit is a lad for reasons, which you know is the foundation of his profession, and knows how to deliver them manfully in the proper place; but you know, gentlemen, that the members of the bar cannot assume the open and bold front that becomes a soldier, without often endangering the cause in which they are concerned. No, no, trust me, Kit has his reasons, and in good time will he deliver them."

"I hope, then," said the captain, carelessly, "that it may be found that we have had a proper watch on our charge, Colonel Howard; I think you told me the windows were too high for an escape in that direction, for I had no sentinel outside of the building."

"Fear nothing, my worthy friend," cried his host; "unless your men have slept, instead of watching, we have them safe; but, as it will be necessary to convey them away before any of the civil authority can lay hands on them, let us proceed to the rear, and unkennel the dogs. A party of the horse might proceed at once with them to —— , while we are breaking our fasts. It would be no very wise thing to allow the civilians to deal with them, for they seldom have a true idea of the nature of the crime."

"Pardon me, sir," said the young officer of horse; "I was led to believe, by Mr. Dillon, that we might meet with a party of the enemy in some little force, and that I should find a pleasanter duty than that of a constable; besides, sir, the laws of the realm guaranty to the subject a trial by his peers, and it is more than I dare do to carry the men to the barracks, without first taking them before a magistrate."

"Ay! you speak of loyal and dutiful subjects," said the colonel; "and, as respects them, doubtless, you are right; but such privileges are withheld from enemies and traitors."

"It must be first proved that they are such, before they can receive the treatment or the punishment that they merit," returned the young man, a little positively, who felt the more confidence, because he had only left the Temple the year before. "If I take charge of the men at all, it will be only to transfer them safely to the civil authority."

"Let us go, and see the prisoners," cried Borroughcliffe, with a view to terminate a discussion that was likely to wax warm, and which he knew to be useless; "perhaps they may quietly enrol themselves under the banners of our sovereign, when all other interference, save that of wholesome discipline, will become unnecessary."

"Nay, if they are of a rank in life to render such a step probable," returned the cornet, "I am well content that the matter should be thus settled. I trust, however, that Captain Borroughcliffe will consider that the ——th light dragoons has some merit in this affair, and that we are far short of our numbers in the second squadron."

"We shall not be difficult at a compromise," returned the captain; "there is one a piece for us, and a toss of a guinea shall determine who has the third man. Sergeant! follow, to deliver over your prisoners, and relieve your sentry."

As they proceeded, in compliance with this arrangement, to the building in the rear, Colonel Howard, who made one of the party, observed—

"I dispute not the penetration of Captain Borroughcliffe, but I understand Mr. Christopher Dillon that there is reason to believe one of these men, at least, to be of a class altogether above that of a common soldier, in which case your plans may fall to the ground."

"And who does he deem the gentleman to be?" asked Borroughcliffe—"A Bourbon in disguise, or a secret representative of the rebel congress?"

"Nay, nay; he said nothing more; my kinsman Kit keeps a close mouth, whenever Dame Justice is about to balance her scales. There are men who may be said to have been born to be soldiers; of which number I should call the Earl Cornwallis, who makes such head against the rebels in the two Carolinas; others seem to be intended by nature for divines, and saints on earth, such as their Graces of York and Canterbury; while another class appear as if it were impossible for them to behold things, unless with discriminating, impartial, and disinterested eyes; to which, I should say, belong my Lord Chief Justice Mansfield, and my kinsman, Mr. Christopher Dillon. I trust, gentlemen, that when the royal arms have crushed this rebellion, that his majesty's ministers will see the propriety of extending the dignity of the peerage to the colonies, as a means of reward to the loyal, and a measure of policy, to prevent future disaffection; in which case, I hoipe to see my kinsman decorated with the ermine of justice, bordering the mantle of a peer."

"Your expectations, my excellent sir, are right reasonable, as I doubt not your kinsman will become, at some future day, that which he is not at present, unhappily for his deserts, right honourable," said Borroughcliffe. "But be of good heart, sir, from what I have seen of his merits, I doubt not that the law will yet have its revenge in due season, and that we shall be properly edified and instructed how to attain elevation in life, by the future exaltation of Mr. Christopher Dillon; though by what title he is to be then known, I am at a loss to say."

Colonel Howard was too much occupied with his own ex parte views of the war and things in general, to observe the shrewd looks that were exchanged between the soldiers; but he answered with perfect simplicity —

"I have reflected much on that point, and have come to the opinion, that as he has a small estate on that river, he should cause his first barony to be known by the title of 'Pedee.'"

"Barony!" echoed Borroughcliffe; "I trust the new nobles of a new world will disdain the old worn out distinctions of a hackneyed universe — eschew all baronies, mine host, and cast earldoms and dukedoms to the shades. The immortal Locke has unlocked his fertile mind to furnish you with appellations suited to the originality of your condition, and the nature of your country. Ah! here comes the Cacique of Pedee, in his proper person!"

As Borroughcliffe spoke, they were ascending the flight of stone steps which led to the upper apartments, where the prisoners were still supposed to be confined; and, at the same moment, the sullen, gloomy features of Dillon were seen as he advanced along the lower passage, with an expression of malicious exultation hovering above his dark brow, that denoted his secret satisfaction. As the hours had passed away, the period had come round when the man who had been present at the escape of Griffith and his friends, was again posted to perform the duty of sentinel. As this soldier well knew the situation of his trust, he was very coolly adjusted, with his back against the wall, endeavouring to compensate himself for his disturbed slumbers during the night, when the sounds of the approaching footsteps warned him to assume the appearance of watchfulness.

"How now, fellow!" cried Borroughcliffe; "what have you to say of your charge?"

"I believe the men sleep, your honour; for I have heard no noises from the rooms since I relieved the last sentinel."

"The lads are weary, and are right to catch what sleep they can in their comfortable quarters," returned the captain. "Stand to your arms, sirrah! and throw back your shoulders; and do not move like a crab, or a train-band corporal; do you not see an officer of horse coming up? Would you disgrace your regiment!"

"Ah! your honour, Heaven only knows whether I shall ever get my shoulders even again."

"Buy another plaster," said Borroughcliffe, slipping a shilling into his hand; "observe, you know nothing but your duty."

"Which is, your honour—"

"To mind me and be silent. But here comes the sergeant with his guard, he will relieve you."

The rest of the party had stopped at the other end of the gallery, to allow the few files of soldiers, who were led by the orderly, to pass them, when they all moved toward the prisons in a body. The sentinel was relieved in due military style; when Dillon placed his hand on one of the doors, and said, with a malicious sneer,

"Open here first, Mr. Sergeant; this cage holds the man we most want."

"Softly, softly, my Lord Chief Justice, and most puissant Cacique," said the captain; "the hour has not yet come to empannel a jury of fat yeomen, and no man must interfere with my boys but myself."

"The rebuke is harsh, I must observe, Captain Borroughcliffe," said the colonel; "but I pardon it because it is military. No, no, Kit; these nice points must be left to martial usages. Be not impatient, my cousin; I doubt not the hour will come, when you shall hold the scales of justice, and satisfy your loyal longings on many a traitor. Zounds! I could almost turn executioner myself in such a cause!"

"I can curb my impatience, sir," returned Dillon, with

hypocritical meekness, and great self-command, though his eyes were gleaming with savage exultation. "I beg pardon of Captain Borroughcliffe, if, in my desire to render the civil authority superior to the military, I have trespassed on your customs."

"You see, Borroughcliffe!" exclaimed the colonel, exultingly, "the lad is ruled by an instinct in all matters of law and justice. I hold it to be impossible that a man thus endowed can ever become a disloyal subject. But our breakfast waits, and Mr. Fitzgerald has breathed his horse this cool morning; let us proceed at once to the examination."

Borroughcliffe motioned to the sergeant to open the door, when the whole party entered the vacant room.

"Your prisoner has escaped!" cried the cornet, after a single moment employed in making sure of the fact.

"Never! it must not, shall not be," cried Dillon, quivering with rage, as he glanced his eyes furiously around the apartment; "here has been treachery! and foul treason to the king!"

"By whom committed, Mr. Christopher Dillon?" said Borroughcliffe, knitting his brow, and speaking in a suppressed tone; "dare you, or any man living, charge treason to the ——th?"

A very different feeling from rage appeared now to increase the shivering propensities of the future judge, who at once perceived it was necessary to moderate his passion, and he returned, as it were by magic, to his former plausible and insinuating manner, as he replied—

"Colonel Howard will understand the cause of my warm feelings, when I tell him, that this very room contained, last night, that disgrace to his name and country, as well as traitor to his king, Edward Griffith, of the rebel navy."

"What!" exclaimed the colonel, starting, "has that recreant youth dared to pollute the threshold of St. Ruth with his footstep! but you dream, Kit; there would be too much hardihood in the act."

"It appears not, sir," returned the other; "for though in this very apartment he most certainly was, he is here no longer. And yet from this window, though open, escape would seem to be impossible, even with much assistance."

"If I thought that the contumelious boy had dared to be guilty of such an act of gross impudence," cried the colonel, "I should be tempted to resume my arms, in my old age, to punish his effrontery. What! it is not enough that he entered my dwelling in the colony, availing himself of the distraction of the times, with an intent to rob me of my choicest jewel, ay! gentlemen, even of my brother Harry's daughter—but that he must also invade this hallowed island, with a like purpose, thus thrusting his treason, as it were, into the presence of his abused prince! No, no, Kit, thy loyalty misleads thee; he has never dared to do the deed!"

"Listen, sir, and you shall be convinced," returned the pliant Christopher. "I do not wonder at your unbelief; but as good testimony is the soul of justice, I cannot resist its influence. You know, that two vessels, corresponding in appearance to the two rebel cruisers that annoyed us so much in the Carolinas, have been seen on the coast for several days, which induced us to beg the protection of Captain Borroughcliffe. Three men are found, the day succeeding that on which we hear that these vessels came within the shoals, stealing through the grounds of St. Ruth, in sailors' attire. They are arrested, and in the voice of one of them, sir, I immediately detected that of the traitor Griffith. He was disguised, it is true, and cunningly so; but when a man has devoted his whole life to the business of investigating truth," he added, with an air of much modesty, "it is difficult to palm any disguise on his senses."

Colonel Howard was strongly impressed with the probability of these conjectures, and the closing appeal confirmed him immediately in his kinsman's opinion, while Borroughcliffe listened, with deep interest, to the speakers, and more than once bit his lip with vexation. When Dillon concluded, the soldier exclaimed—

"I'll swear there was a man among them, who has been used to the drill."

"Nothing more probable, my worthy friend," said Dillon; "for as the landing was never made without some evil purpose, rely on it, he came not unguarded or unprotected. I dare say, the three were all officers, and one of them might have been of the marines. That they had assistance is certain, and it was because I felt assured they had a force secreted at hand, that I went in quest of the reinforcement."

There was so much plausibility, and, in fact, so much truth, in all this, that conviction was unwillingly admitted by Borroughcliffe, who walked aside, a moment, to conceal the confusion which, in spite of his ordinary inflexibility of countenance, he felt was manifesting itself in his rubric visage, while he muttered—

"The amphibious dog! he was a soldier, but a traitor and an enemy. No doubt he will have a marvellous satisfaction in delighting the rebellious ears of his messmates, by rehearsing the manner in which he poured cold water down the back of one Borroughcliffe, of the ——th, who was amusing him, at the same time, by pouring good, rich south-side Madeira down his own rebellious throat. I have a good mind to exchange my scarlet coat for a blue jacket, on purpose to meet the sly rascal on the other element, where we can discuss the matter over again. Well, sergeant, do you find the other two?"

"They are gone together, your honour," returned the orderly, who just then re-entered from an examination of the other apartments; "and unless the evil one helped them off, it's a mysterious business to me."

"Colonel Howard," said Borroughcliffe, gravely, "your precious south-side cordial must be banished from the board, regularly with the cloth, until I have my revenge; for satisfaction of this insult is mine to claim, and I seek it this instant. Go, Drill; detail a guard for the protection of the house, and feed the rest of your command, then beat the general, and we will take the field. Ay! my worthy veteran host, for the first time since the days of the unlucky Charles Stuart, there shall be a campaign in the heart of England."

"Ah! rebellion, rebellion! accursed, unnatural, unholy rebellion, caused the calamity then and now!" exclaimed the colonel.

"Had I not better take a hasty refreshment for my men and their horses?" asked the cornet; "and then make a sweep for a few miles along the coast? It may be my luck to encounter the fugitives, or some part of their force."

"You have anticipated my very thoughts," returned Borroughcliffe. "The Cacique of Pedee may close the gates of St. Ruth, and, by barring the windows, and arming the servants, he can make a very good defence against an attack, should they think proper to assail our fortress; after he has repulsed them, leave it to me to cut off their retreat."

Dillon but little relished this proposal; for he thought an attempt to storm the abbey would be the most probable course adopted by Griffith, in order to rescue his mistress; and the jurist had none of the spirit of a soldier in his composition. In truth, it was this deficiency that had induced him to depart in person, the preceding night, in quest of the reinforcement, instead of sending an express on the errand. But the necessity of devising an excuse for a change in this dangerous arrangement, was obviated by Colonel Howard, who exclaimed, as soon as Borroughcliffe concluded his plan—

"To me, Captain Borroughcliffe, belongs of right, the duty of defending St. Ruth, and it shall be no boy's play to force my works; but Kit would rather try his chance in the open field, I know. Come, let us to our breakfast, and then he shall mount, and act as a guide to the horse, along the difficult passes of the seashore."

"To breakfast then let it be," cried the captain; "I distrust not my new commander of the fortress; and in the field the Cacique for ever! We follow you, my worthy host."

This arrangement was hastily executed in all its parts. The gentlemen swallowed their meal in the manner of men who ate only to sustain nature, and as a duty; after which the whole house became a scene of bustling activity. The troops were mustered and paraded; Borroughcliffe, setting apart a guard for the building, placed himself at the head of the remainder of his little party, and they moved out of the court-yard in open order, and at quick time. Dillon joyfully beheld himself mounted on one of the best of Colonel Howard's hunters, where he knew that he had the control, in a great measure, of his own destiny; his bosom throbbing with a powerful desire to destroy Griffith, while he entertained a lively wish to effect his object without incurring any personal risk. At his side was the young cornet, seated with practised grace in his saddle, who, after giving time for the party of foot soldiers to clear the premises, glanced his eye along the few files he led, and then gave the word to move. The little division of horse wheeled briskly into open column, and, the officer touching his cap to Colonel Howard, they dashed through the gateway together, and pursued their route towards the seaside, at a hand gallop.

The veteran lingered a few minutes, while the clattering of hoofs was to be heard, or the gleam of arms was visible, to hear and gaze at sounds and sights that he still loved; after which, he proceeded, in person, and not without a secret enjoyment of the excitement, to barricade the doors and windows, with an undaunted determination of making, in case of need, a stout defence.

St. Ruth lay but a short two miles from the ocean; to which numerous roads led, through the grounds of the abbey, which extended to the shore. Along one of these paths, Dillon conducted his party, until, after a few minutes of hard riding, they approached the cliffs, when, posting his troopers under cover of a little copse, the cornet rode in advance, with his guide, to the verge of the perpendicular rocks, whose bases were washed by the foam that still whitened the waters from the surges of the subsiding sea.

The gale had broken, before the escape of the prisoners, and as the power of the eastern tempest had gradually diminished, a light current from the south, that blew directly along the land, prevailed; and, though the ocean still rolled in fearful billows, their surfaces were smooth, and they were becoming, at each moment, less precipitous, and more regular. The eyes of the horsemen were cast in vain over the immense expanse of water, that was glistening brightly under the rays of the sun, which had just risen from its bosom, in quest of some object or distant sail, that might confirm their suspicions, or relieve their doubts. But every thing of that description appeared to have avoided the dangerous navigation, during the violence of the late tempest, and Dillon was withdrawing his eyes in disappointment, from the vacant view, when, as they fell towards the shore, he beheld that which caused him to exclaim —

"There they go! and, by Heaven, they will escape!"

The cornet looked in the direction of the other's finger, when he beheld, at a short distance from the land, and apparently immediately under his feet, a little boat, that looked like a dark shell upon the water, rising and sinking amid the waves, as if the men it obviously contained, were resting on their oars in idle expectation.

"'Tis they!" continued Dillon; "or, what is more probable, it is their boat waiting to convey them to their vessel; no common business would induce seamen to lie in this careless manner, within such a narrow distance of the surf."

"And what is to be done? They cannot be made to feel horse where they are; nor would the muskets of the foot be of any use. A light three pounder would do its work handsomely on them!"

The strong desire which Dillon entertained to intercept, or rather to destroy the party, rendered him prompt at expedients. After a moment of musing, he replied—

"The runaways must yet be on the land; and by scouring the coast, and posting men at proper intervals, their retreat can easily be prevented; in the mean time I will ride under the spur to —— bay, where one of his majesty's cutters now lies at anchor—It is but half an hour of hard riding, and I can be on board of her. The wind blows directly in her favour, and if we can once bring her down behind that headland, we shall infallibly cut off or sink these midnight depredators."

"Off, then!" cried the cornet, whose young blood was boiling for a skirmish; "you will at least drive them to the shore, where I can deal with them."

The words were hardly uttered, before Dillon, after galloping furiously along the cliffs, and turning short into a thick wood, that lay in his route, was out of sight. The loyalty of this gentleman was altogether of a calculating nature, and was intimately connected with what he considered his fealty to himself. He believed that the possession of Miss Howard's person and fortune were advantages that would much more than counterbalance any elevation that he was likely to obtain by the revolution of affairs in his native colony. He considered Griffith as the only natural obstacle to his success, and he urged his horse forward with a desperate determination to work the ruin of the young sailor, before another sun had set. When a man labours in an evil cause, with such feelings, and with such incentives, he seldom slights or neglects his work; and Mr. Dillon, accordingly, was on board the Alacrity, several minutes short of the time in which he had promised to perform the distance.

The plain old seaman, who commanded the cutter, listened to his tale with cautious ears; and examined into the state of the weather, and other matters, connected with his duty, with the slow and deliberate decision of one who had never done much to acquire a confidence in himself, and who had been but niggardly rewarded for the little he had actually performed.

As Dillon was urgent, however, and the day seemed propitious, he at length decided to act as he was desired, and the cutter was accordingly gotten under way.

A crew of something less than fifty men, moved with no little of their commander's deliberation; but as the little vessel rounded the point behind which she had been anchored, her guns were cleared, and the usual preparations were completed for immediate and actual service.

Dillon, sorely against his will, was compelled to continue on board, in order to point out the place where the unsuspecting boatmen were expected to be entrapped. Every thing being ready, when they had gained a safe distance from the land, the Alacrity was kept away before the wind, and glided along the shore, with a swift and easy progress, that promised a speedy execution of the business in which her commander had embarked.

Chapter XVII.

"*Pol.* Very like a whale."

Hamlet, III.ii.382.

NOTWITHSTANDING the object of their expedition was of a public nature, the feelings which had induced both Griffith and Barnstable to accompany the pilot, with so much willingness, it will easily be seen, were entirely personal. The short intercourse that he had maintained with his associates, enabled the mysterious leader of their party to understand the characters of his two principal officers so thoroughly, as to induce him, when he landed, with the purpose of reconnoitring to ascertain whether the objects of his pursuit still held their determination to assemble at the appointed hour, to choose Griffith and Manual as his only associates, leaving Barnstable in command of his own vessel, to await their return, and to cover their retreat. A good deal of argument, and some little of the authority of his superior officer, was necessary to make Barnstable quietly acquiesce in this arrangement; but as his good sense told him that nothing should be unnecessarily hazarded, until the moment to strike the final blow had arrived, he became gradually more resigned, taking care, however, to caution Griffith to reconnoitre the abbey while his companion was reconnoitring —— house. It was the strong desire of Griffith to comply with this injunction, which carried them a little out of their proper path, and led to the consequences that we have partly related. The evening of that day was the time when the pilot intended to complete his enterprise, thinking to entrap his game while enjoying the festivities that usually succeeded their sports, and an early hour in the morning was appointed when Barnstable should appear at the nearest point to the abbey, to take off his countrymen, in order that they might be as little as possible subjected to the gaze of their enemies, by daylight. If they failed to arrive at the appointed time, his instructions were, to return to his schooner, which lay snugly embayed in a secret and retired haven, that but few ever approached, either by land or water.

While the young cornet still continued gazing at the whaleboat (for it was the party from the schooner that he saw,) the hour expired for the appearance of Griffith and his companions, and Barnstable reluctantly determined to comply with the letter of his instructions, and leave them to their own sagacity and skill to regain the Ariel. The boat had been suffered to ride in the edge of the surf, since the appearance of the sun, and the eyes of her crew were kept anxiously fixed on the cliffs, though in vain, to discover the signal that was to call them to the place of landing. After looking at his watch for the twentieth time, and as often casting glances of uneasy dissatisfaction towards the shore, the lieutenant exclaimed—

"A charming prospect, this, Master Coffin, but rather too much poetry in it for your taste; I believe you relish no land that is of a harder consistency than mud!"

"I was born on the waters, sir," returned the cockswain, from his snug abode, where he was bestowed with his usual economy of room, "and it's according to all things for a man to love his natyve soil. I'll not deny, Captain Barnstable, but I would rather drop my anchor on a bottom that won't broom a keel, though at the same time, I harbour no great malice against dry land."

"I shall never forgive it, myself, if any accident has befallen Griffith, in this excursion," rejoined the lieutenant; "his pilot may be a better man on the water than on terra firma, long Tom."

The cockswain turned his solemn visage, with an extraordinary meaning, towards his commander, before he replied—

"For as long a time as I have followed the waters, sir, and that has been ever since I've drawn my rations, seeing that I was born while the boat was crossing Nantucket shoals, I've never known a pilot come off in greater need, than the one we fell in with, when we made that stretch or two on the land, in the dog-watch of yesterday."

"Ay! the fellow has played his part like a man; the occasion was great, and it seems that he was quite equal to his work."

"The frigate's people tell me, sir, that he handled the ship like a top," continued the cockswain; "but she is a ship that is a natural inimy of the bottom!"

"Can you say as much for this boat, Master Coffin?" cried Barnstable; "keep her out of the surf, or you'll have us rolling in upon the beach, presently, like an empty water-cask; you must remember that we cannot all wade, like yourself, in two-fathom-water."

The cockswain cast a cool glance at the crests of foam that were breaking over the tops of the billows, within a few yards of where their boat was riding, and called aloud to his men —

"Pull a stroke or two; away with her into dark water."

The drop of the oars resembled the movements of a nice machine, and the light boat skimmed along the water like a duck, that approaches to the very brink of some imminent danger, and then avoids it, at the most critical moment, apparently without an effort. While this necessary movement was making, Barnstable arose, and surveyed the cliffs, with keen eyes, and then turning once more in disappointment from his search, he said —

"Pull more from the land, and let her run down, at an easy stroke, to the schooner. Keep a look-out at the cliffs, boys; it is possible that they are stowed in some of the holes in the rocks, for it's no daylight business they are on."

The order was promptly obeyed, and they had glided along for nearly a mile, in this manner, in the most profound silence, when suddenly the stillness was broken by a heavy rush of air, and a dash of the water, seemingly at no great distance from them.

"By heaven, Tom," cried Barnstable, starting, "there is the blow of a whale."

"Ay, ay, sir," returned the cockswain, with undisturbed composure; "here is his spout, not half a mile to seaward; the easterly gale has driven the creater to leeward, and he begins to find himself in shoal water. He's been sleeping, while he should have been working to windward!"

"The fellow takes it coolly, too! he's in no hurry to get an offing!"

"I rather conclude, sir," said the cockswain rolling over his tobacco in his mouth, very composedly, while his little sunken eyes began to twinkle with pleasure at the sight, "the gentleman has lost his reckoning, and don't know which way to head, to take himself back into blue water."

"'Tis a fin-back!" exclaimed the lieutenant; "he will soon make head-way, and be off."

"No, sir, 'tis a right whale," answered Tom; "I saw his spout; he threw up a pair of as pretty rainbows as a Christian would wish to look at. He's a raal oil-butt, that fellow!"

Barnstable laughed, turned himself away from the tempting sight, and tried to look at the cliffs; and then unconsciously bent his longing eyes again on the sluggish animal, who was throwing his huge carcass, at times, for many feet from the water, in idle gambols. The temptation for sport, and the recollection of his early habits, at length prevailed over his anxiety in behalf of his friends, and the young officer inquired of his cockswain—

"Is there any whale-line in the boat, to make fast to that harpoon which you bear about with you in fair weather or foul?"

"I never trust the boat from the schooner without part of a shot, sir," returned the cockswain; "there is something nateral in the sight of a tub to my old eyes."

Barnstable looked at his watch, and again at the cliffs, when he exclaimed, in joyous tones—

"Give strong way, my hearties! There seems nothing better to be done; let us have a stroke of a harpoon at that impudent rascal."

The men shouted spontaneously, and the old cockswain suffered his solemn visage to relax into a small laugh, while the whale-boat sprung forward like a courser for the goal. During the few minutes they were pulling towards their game, long Tom arose from his crouching attitude in the stern-sheets, and transferred his huge frame to the bows of the boat, where he made such preparations to strike the whale as the occasion required. The tub, containing about half of a whale-line, was placed at the feet of Barnstable, who had been preparing an oar to steer with, in place of the rudder, which was unshipped, in order that, if necessary, the boat might be whirled round, when not advancing.

Their approach was utterly unnoticed by the monster of the deep, who continued to amuse himself with throwing the water, in two circular spouts, high into the air, occasionally

flourishing the broad flukes of his tail with a graceful but terrific force, until the hardy seamen were within a few hundred
feet of him, when he suddenly cast his head downward, and,
without an apparent effort, reared his immense body for many
feet above the water, waving his tail violently, and producing a
whizzing noise, that sounded like the rushing of winds.

The cockswain stood erect, poising his harpoon, ready for
the blow; but when he beheld the creature assume this formidable attitude, he waved his hand to his commander, who
instantly signed to his men to cease rowing. In this situation
the sportsmen rested a few moments, while the whale struck
several blows on the water, in rapid succession, the noise of
which re-echoed along the cliffs, like the hollow reports of so
many cannon. After this wanton exhibition of his terrible
strength, the monster sunk again into his native element, and
slowly disappeared from the eyes of his pursuers.

"Which way did he head, Tom?" cried Barnstable, the moment the whale was out of sight.

"Pretty much up and down, sir," returned the cockswain,
whose eye was gradually brightening with the excitement of
the sport; "he'll soon run his nose against the bottom, if he
stands long on that course, and will be glad to get another
snuff of pure air; send her a few fathoms to starboard, sir, and
I promise we shall not be out of his track."

The conjecture of the experienced old seaman proved true,
for, in a few minutes, the water broke near them, and another
spout was cast into the air, when the huge animal rushed, for
half his length, in the same direction, and fell on the sea, with
a turbulence and foam equal to that which is produced by the
launching of a vessel, for the first time, into its proper element.
After this evolution, the whale rolled heavily, and seemed to
rest from further efforts.

His slightest movements were closely watched by Barnstable
and his cockswain, and when he was in a state of comparative
rest, the former gave a signal to his crew, to ply their oars once
more. A few long and vigorous strokes sent the boat directly
up to the broadside of the whale, with its bows pointing
towards one of the fins, which was, at times, as the animal
yielded sluggishly to the action of the waves, exposed to view.
The cockswain poised his harpoon, with much precision, and

then darted it from him with a violence that buried the iron in the blubber of their foe. The instant the blow was made, long Tom shouted, with singular earnestness—

"Starn all!"

"Stern all!" echoed Barnstable; when the obedient seamen, by united efforts, forced the boat in a backward direction, beyond the reach of any blow from their formidable antagonist. The alarmed animal, however, meditated no such resistance; ignorant of his own power, and of the insignificance of his enemies, he sought refuge in flight. One moment of stupid surprise succeeded the entrance of the iron, when he cast his huge tail into the air, with a violence that threw the sea around him into increased commotion, and then disappeared, with the quickness of lightning, amid a cloud of foam.

"Snub him!" shouted Barnstable; "hold on, Tom; he rises already."

"Ay, ay, sir," replied the composed cockswain, seizing the line, which was running out of the boat with a velocity that rendered such a manœuvre rather hazardous, and causing it to yield more gradually round the large loggerhead that was placed in the bows of the boat for that purpose. Presently the line stretched forward, and, rising to the surface, with tremulous vibrations, it indicated the direction in which the animal might be expected to re-appear. Barnstable had cast the bows of the boat towards that point, before the terrified and wounded victim rose once more to the surface, whose time was, however, no longer wasted in his sports, but who cast the waters aside, as he forced his way, with prodigious velocity, along their surface. The boat was dragged violently in his wake, and cut through the billows with a terrific rapidity, that, at moments, appeared to bury the slight fabric in the ocean. When long Tom beheld his victim throwing his spouts on high again, he pointed with exultation to the jetting fluid, which was streaked with the deep red of blood, and cried—

"Ay! I've touched the fellow's life! it must be more than two foot of blubber that stops my iron from reaching the life of any whale that ever sculled the ocean!"

"I believe you have saved yourself the trouble of using the bayonet you have rigged for a lance," said his commander, who entered into the sport with all the ardour of one whose youth had been chiefly passed in such pursuits; "feel your line, Master Coffin; can we haul alongside of our enemy? I like not the course he is steering, as he tows us from the schooner."

"'Tis the creater's way, sir," said the cockswain; "you know they need the air in their nostrils, when they run, the same as a man; but lay hold, boys, and let's haul up to him."

The seamen now seized the whale-line, and slowly drew their boat to within a few feet of the tail of the fish, whose progress became sensibly less rapid, as he grew weak with the loss of blood. In a few minutes he stopped running, and appeared to roll uneasily on the water, as if suffering the agony of death.

"Shall we pull in, and finish him, Tom?" cried Barnstable; "a few sets from your bayonet would do it."

The cockswain stood examining his game, with cool discretion, and replied to this interrogatory—

"No, sir, no—he's going into his flurry; there's no occasion for disgracing ourselves by using a soldier's weapon in taking a whale. Starn off, sir, starn off! the creater's in his flurry!"

The warning of the prudent cockswain was promptly obeyed, and the boat cautiously drew off to a distance, leaving to the animal a clear space, while under its dying agonies. From a state of perfect rest, the terrible monster threw its tail on high, as when in sport, but its blows were trebled in rapidity and violence, till all was hid from view by a pyramid of foam, that was deeply died with blood. The roarings of the fish were like the bellowings of a herd of bulls, and to one who was ignorant of the fact, it would have appeared as if a thousand monsters were engaged in deadly combat, behind the bloody mist that obstructed the view. Gradually, these effects subsided, and when the discoloured water again settled down to the long and regular swell of the ocean, the fish was seen, exhausted, and yielding passively to its fate. As life departed, the enormous black mass rolled to one side, and when the white and glistening skin of the belly became apparent, the seamen well knew that their victory was achieved.

"What's to be done now," said Barnstable, as he stood and gazed with a diminished excitement at their victim; "he will yield no food, and his carcass will probably drift to land, and furnish our enemies with the oil."

"If I had but that creater in Boston Bay," said the cockswain, "it would prove the making of me; but such is my luck for ever! Pull up, at any rate, and let me get my harpoon and line — the English shall never get them while old Tom Coffin can blow."

"Don't speak too fast," said the strokesman of the boat; "whether he gets your iron or not, here he comes in chase!"

"What mean you, fellow?" cried Barnstable.

"Captain Barnstable can look for himself," returned the seaman, "and tell whether I speak truth."

The young sailor turned, and saw the Alacrity, bearing down before the wind, with all her sails set, as she rounded a headland, but a short half league to windward of the place where the boat lay.

"Pass that glass to me," said the captain with steady composure. "This promises us work in one of two ways; if she be armed, it has become our turn to run; if not, we are strong enough to carry her."

A very brief survey made the experienced officer acquainted with the true character of the vessel in sight; and, replacing the glass with much coolness, he said,

"That fellow shows long arms, and ten teeth, beside King George's pennant from his top-mast-head. Now, my lads, you are to pull for your lives; for whatever may be the notions of Master Coffin on the subject of his harpoon, I have no inclination to have my arms pinioned by John Bull, though his majesty himself put on the irons."

The men well understood the manner and meaning of their commander; and, throwing aside their coats, they applied themselves in earnest to their task. For half an hour a profound silence reigned in the boat, which made an amazing progress. But many circumstances conspired to aid the cutter; she had a fine breeze, with smooth water, and a strong tide in her favour; and, at the expiration of the time we have mentioned, it was but too apparent that the distance between the pursued and pursuers was lessened nearly half. Barnstable preserved his steady countenance, but there was an expression of care gathering around his dark brow, which indicated that he saw the increasing danger of their situation.

"That fellow has long legs, Master Coffin," he said, in a cheerful tone; "your whale-line must go overboard, and the fifth oar must be handled by your delicate hands."

Tom arose from his seat, and proceeding forward, he cast the tub and its contents together into the sea, when he seated himself at the bow oar, and bent his athletic frame with amazing vigour to the task.

"Ah! there is much of your philosophy in that stroke, long Tom," cried his commander; "keep it up, boys, and if we gain nothing else, we shall at least gain time for deliberation. Come, Master Coffin, what think you; we have three resources before us, let us hear which is your choice: first, we can turn and fight and be sunk; secondly, we can pull to the land, and endeavour to make good our retreat to the schooner in that manner; and, thirdly, we can head to the shore, and possibly by running under the guns of that fellow, get the wind of him, and keep the air in our nostrils, after the manner of the whale. Damn the whale! but for the tow the black rascal gave us, we should have been out of sight of this rover!"

"If we fight," said Tom, with quite as much composure as his commander manifested, "we shall be taken or sunk; if we land, sir, I shall be taken for one man, as I never could make any headway on dry ground; and if we try to get the wind of him by pulling under the cliffs, we shall be cut off by a parcel of lubbers that I can see running along their edges, hoping, I dare say, that they shall be able to get a skulking shot at a boat's crew of honest seafaring men."

"You speak with as much truth as philosophy, Tom," said Barnstable, who saw his slender hopes of success curtailed, by the open appearance of the horse and foot on the cliffs. "These Englishmen have not slept the last night, and I fear Griffith and Manual will fare but badly. That fellow brings a cap full of wind down with him—'tis just his play, and he walks like a race-horse. Ha! he begins to be in earnest!"

While Barnstable was speaking, a column of white smoke was seen issuing from the bows of the cutter, and as the report of a cannon was wafted to their ears, the shot was seen skipping from wave to wave, tossing the water in spray, and flying to a considerable distance beyond them. The seamen cast cursory glances in the direction of the passing ball, but it produced no manifest effect in either their conduct or appearance. The cockswain, who scanned its range with an eye of more practice than the rest, observed, "That's a lively piece for its metal, and it speaks with a good clear voice; but if they hear it aboard the Ariel, the man who fired it will be sorry it wasn't born dumb."

"You are the prince of philosophers, Master Coffin!" cried Barnstable; "there is some hope in that; let the Englishman talk away, and my life on it, the Ariels don't believe it is thunder; hand me a musket—I'll draw another shot."

The piece was given to Barnstable, who discharged it several times, as if to taunt their enemies, and the scheme was completely successful. Goaded by the insults, the cutter discharged gun after gun at the little boat, throwing the shot frequently so near as to wet her crew with the spray, but without injuring them in the least. The failure of these attempts of the enemy, excited the mirth of the reckless seamen, instead of creating any alarm; and whenever a shot came nearer than common, the cockswain would utter some such expression as—

"A ground swell, a long shot, and a small object, make a clean target;" or, "A man must squint straight to hit a boat."

As, notwithstanding their unsuccessful gunnery, the cutter was constantly gaining on the whale-boat, there was a prospect of a speedy termination of the chase, when the report of a cannon was thrown back like an echo from one of the Englishman's discharges, and Barnstable and his companions had the pleasure of seeing the Ariel stretching slowly out of the little bay where she had passed the night, with the smoke of the gun of defiance curling above her taper masts.

A loud and simultaneous shout of rapture was given by the lieutenant and all his boat's-crew, at this cheering sight, while the cutter took in all her light sails, and, as she hauled up on a wind, she fired a whole broadside at the successful fugitives. Many stands of grape, with several round shot, flew by the boat, and fell upon the water, near them, raising a cloud of foam, but without doing any injury.

"She dies in a flurry," said Tom, casting his eyes at the little vortex into which the boat was then entering.

"If her commander be a true man," cried Barnstable, "he'll not leave us on so short an acquaintance. Give way, my souls! give way! I would see more of this loquacious cruiser."

The temptation for exertion was great, and it was not

disregarded by the men; in a few minutes the whale-boat reached the schooner, when the crew of the latter received their commander and his companions with shouts and cheers that rung across the waters, and reached the ears of the disappointed spectators on the verge of the cliffs.

Chapter XVIII.

"Thus guided, on their course they bore,
Until they near'd the mainland shore;
When frequent on the hollow blast
Wild shouts of merriment were cast."
                    Scott, *The Lord of the Isles*, Canto First, XXIII.1-4.

T HE JOYFUL shouts and hearty cheers of the Ariel's crew
continued for some time after her commander had reached her
deck. Barnstable answered the congratulations of his officers
by cordial shakes of the hand, and after waiting for the ebullition of delight among the seamen to subside a little, he beckoned
with an air of authority for silence.

"I thank you, my lads, for your good will," he said, when all
were gathered around him in deep attention: "they have given
us a tough chase, and if you had left us another mile to go, we
had been lost. That fellow is a King's cutter, and though his
disposition to run to leeward is a good deal mollified, yet he
shows signs of fight. At any rate, he is stripping off some of his
clothes, which looks as if he were game. Luckily for us, Captain Manual has taken all the marines ashore with him,
(though what he has done with them or himself, is a mystery,)
or we should have had our decks lumbered with live cattle;
but, as it is, we have a good working breeze, tolerably smooth
water, and a dead match! There is a sort of national obligation
on us to whip that fellow, and, therefore, without more words
about the matter, let us turn to and do it, that we may get our
breakfasts."

To this specimen of marine eloquence, the crew cheered as
usual; the young men burning for the combat, and the few old
sailors who belonged to the schooner, shaking their heads with
infinite satisfaction, and swearing by sundry strange oaths,
that their captain "could talk, when there was need of such
thing, like the best Dictionary that ever was launched."

During this short harangue, and the subsequent comments,
the Ariel had been kept, under a cloud of canvass, as near to
the wind as she could lie, and as this was her best sailing, she

had stretched swiftly out from the land, to a distance whence the cliffs, and the soldiers who were spread along their summits, became plainly visible. Barnstable turned his glass repeatedly, from the cutter to the shore, as different feelings predominated in his breast, before he again spoke.

"If Mr. Griffith is stowed away among those rocks," he at length said, "he shall see as pretty an argument discussed, in as few words, as he ever listened to, provided the gentlemen in yonder cutter have not changed their minds as to the road they intend to journey — what think you, Mr. Merry?"

"I wish with all my heart and soul, sir," returned the fearless boy, "that Mr. Griffith was safe aboard us; it seems the country is alarmed, and God knows what will happen if he is taken! As to the fellow to windward, he'll find it easier to deal with the Ariel's boat, than with her mother; but he carries a broad sail; I question if he means to show play."

"Never doubt him, boy," said Barnstable, "he is working off the shore, like a man of sense, and besides, he has his spectacles on, trying to make out what tribe of Yankee Indians we belong to. You'll see him come to the wind presently, and send a few pieces of iron down this way, by way of letting us know where to find him. Much as I like your first lieutenant, Mr. Merry, I would rather leave him on the land this day, than see him on my decks. I want no fighting captain to work this boat for me! but tell the drummer, sir, to beat to quarters."

The boy, who was staggering under the weight of his melodious instrument, had been expecting this command, and, without waiting for the midshipman to communicate the order, he commenced that short rub-a-dub air, that will at any time rouse a thousand men from the deepest sleep, and cause them to fly to their means of offence, with a common soul. The crew of the Ariel had been collected in groups, studying the appearance of the enemy, cracking their jokes, and waiting only for this usual order to repair to the guns; and at the first tap of the drum, they spread with steadiness to the different parts of the little vessel, where their various duties called them. The cannon were surrounded by small parties of vigorous and athletic young men; the few marines were drawn up in array with muskets; the officers appeared in their boarding caps, with pistols stuck in their belts and naked sabres in their hands. Barnstable paced his little quarter-deck with a firm tread, dangling a speaking trumpet, by its lanyard, on his fore-finger, or occasionally applying the glass to his eye, which, when not in use, was placed under one arm, while his sword was resting against the foot of the mainmast; a pair of heavy ship's pistols were thrust in his belt also; and piles of muskets, boarding-pikes, and naked sabres, were placed on different parts of the deck. The laugh of the seamen was heard no longer; and those who spoke, uttered their thoughts only in low and indistinct whispers.

The English cutter held her way from the land, until she got an offing of more than two miles, when she reduced her sails to a yet smaller number, and heaving into the wind, she fired a gun in a direction opposite to that which pointed to the Ariel.

"Now I would wager a quintal of codfish, Master Coffin," said Barnstable, "against the best cask of porter that was ever brewed in England, that fellow believes a Yankee schooner can fly in the wind's eye! If he wishes to speak to us, why don't he give his cutter a little sheet, and come down."

The cockswain had made his arrangements for the combat, with much more method and philosophy than any other man in the vessel. When the drum beat to quarters, he threw aside his jacket, vest, and shirt, with as little hesitation as if he stood under an American sun, and with all the discretion of a man who had engaged in an undertaking that required the free use of his utmost powers. As he was known to be a privileged in-dividual in the Ariel, and one whose opinions, in all matters of seamanship, were regarded as oracles by the crew, and were listened to by his commander with no little demonstration of respect, the question excited no surprise. He was standing at the breech of his long gun, with his brawny arms folded on a breast that had been turned to the colour of blood by long ex-posure, his grizzled locks fluttering in the breeze, and his tall form towering far above the heads of all near him.

"He hugs the wind, sir, as if it was his sweetheart," was his answer; "but he'll let go his hold, soon; and if he don't, we can find a way to make him fall to leeward."

"Keep a good full!" cried the commander, in a stern voice, "and let the vessel go through the water. That fellow walks well, long Tom; but we are too much for him on a bowline;

though, if he continue to draw ahead in this manner, it will be night before we can get alongside him."

"Ay, ay, sir," returned the cockswain; "them cutters carries a press of canvass, when they seem to have but little; their gaffs are all the same as young booms, and spread a broad head to their mainsails. But it's no hard matter to knock a few cloths out of their bolt-ropes, when she will both drop astern and to leeward."

"I believe there is good sense in your scheme, this time," said Barnstable; "for I am anxious about the frigate's people — though I hate a noisy chase; speak to him, Tom, and let us see if he will answer."

"Ay, ay, sir," cried the cockswain, sinking his body in such a manner as to let his head fall to a level with the cannon that he controlled, when, after divers orders, and sundry movements, to govern the direction of the piece, he applied a match, with a rapid motion, to the priming. An immense body of white smoke rushed from the muzzle of the cannon, followed by a sheet of vivid fire, until, losing its power, it yielded to the wind, and, as it rose from the water, spread like a cloud, and, passing through the masts of the schooner, was driven far to leeward, and soon blended in the mists which were swiftly scudding before the fresh breezes of the ocean.

Although many curious eyes were watching this beautiful sight from the cliffs, there was too little of novelty in the exhibition to attract a single look, of the crew of the schooner, from the more important examination of the effect of the shot on their enemy. Barnstable sprang lightly on a gun, and watched the instant when the ball would strike, with keen interest, while long Tom threw himself aside from the line of the smoke, with a similar intention; holding one of his long arms extended towards his namesake, with a finger on the vent, and supporting his frame by placing the hand of the other on the deck, as his eyes glanced through an opposite port-hole, in an attitude that most men might have despaired of imitating with success.

"There go the chips!" cried Barnstable. "Bravo! Master Coffin, you never planted iron in the ribs of an Englishman with more judgment; let him have another piece of it, and if he like the sport, we'll play a game of long bowls with him!"

"Ay, ay, sir," returned the cockswain, who, the instant he witnessed the effects of his shot, had returned to superintend the reloading of his guns; "if he holds on half an hour longer, I'll dub him down to our own size, when we can close, and make an even fight of it."

The drum of the Englishman was now, for the first time, heard, rattling across the waters, and echoing the call to quarters, that had already proceeded from the Ariel.

"Ah! you have sent him to his guns!" said Barnstable; "we shall now hear more of it; wake him up, Tom—wake him up."

"We shall start him an end, or put him to sleep altogether, shortly," said the deliberate cockswain, who never allowed himself to be at all hurried, even by his commander. "My shot are pretty much like a shoal of porpoises, and commonly sail in each others' wake. Stand by—heave her breech forward—so; get out of that, you damned young reprobate, and let my harpoon alone."

"What are you at, there, Master Coffin?" cried Barnstable; "are you tongue-tied?"

"Here's one of the boys skylarking with my harpoon in the lee scuppers, and by-and-by, when I shall want it most, there'll be a no-man's-land to hunt for it in."

"Never mind the boy, Tom; send him aft here, to me, and I'll polish his behaviour; give the Englishman some more iron."

"I want the little villain to pass up my cartridges," returned the angry old seaman; "but if you'll be so good, sir, as to hit him a crack or two, now and then, as he goes by you to the magazine, the monkey will learn his manners, and the schooner's work will be all the better done for it. A young herring-faced monkey! to meddle with a tool ye don't know the use of. If your parents had spent more of their money on your edication, and less on your outfit, you'd ha' been a gentleman to what ye are now."

"Hurrah! Tom, hurrah!" cried Barnstable, a little impatiently; "is your namesake never to open his throat again!"

"Ay, ay, sir; all ready," grumbled the cockswain, "depress a little; so—so; a damn'd young baboon-behav'd curmudgeon; overhaul that forward fall more; stand by with your match

—but I'll pay him! fire." This was the actual commencement of the fight; for as the shot of Tom Coffin travelled, as he had intimated, very much in the same direction, their enemy found the sport becoming too hot to be endured in silence; and the report of the second gun from the Ariel, was instantly followed by that of the whole broadside of the Alacrity. The shot of the cutter flew in a very good direction, but her guns were too light to give them efficiency at that distance, and as one or two were heard to strike against the bends of the schooner, and fall back, innocuously, into the water, the cockswain, whose good humour became gradually restored, as the combat thickened, remarked, with his customary apathy—

"Them count for no more than love taps—does the Englishman think that we are firing salutes!"

"Stir him up, Tom! every blow you give him will help to open his eyes," cried Barnstable, rubbing his hands with glee, as he witnessed the success of his efforts to close.

Thus far the cockswain and his crew had the fight, on the part of the Ariel, altogether to themselves, the men who were stationed at the smaller and shorter guns, standing in perfect idleness by their sides; but in ten or fifteen minutes the commander of the Alacrity, who had been staggered by the weight of the shot that had struck him, found that it was no longer in his power to retreat, if he wished it; when he decided on the only course that was left for a brave man to pursue, and steered, boldly, in such a direction as would soonest bring him in contact with his enemy, without exposing his vessel to be raked by his fire. Barnstable watched each movement of his foe with eagle eyes, and when the vessels had got within a lessened distance, he gave the order for a general fire to be opened. The action now grew warm and spirited on both sides. The power of the wind was counteracted by the constant explosion of the cannon; and instead of driving rapidly to leeward, a white canopy of curling smoke hung above the Ariel, or rested on the water, lingering in her wake, so as to mark the path by which she was approaching to a closer and still deadlier struggle. The shouts of the young sailors, as they handled their instruments of death, became more animated and fierce, while the cockswain pursued his occupation with the silence and skill of one who laboured in a regular vocation. Barnstable was unusually composed and quiet, maintaining the grave deportment of a commander on whom rested the fortunes of the contest, at the same time that his dark eyes were dancing with the fire of suppressed animation.

"Give it them!" he occasionally cried, in a voice that might be heard amid the bellowing of the cannon; "never mind their cordage, my lads; drive home their bolts, and make your marks below their ridge ropes."

In the mean time, the Englishman played a manful game. He had suffered a heavy loss by the distant cannonade, which no metal he possessed could retort upon his enemy; but he struggled nobly to repair the error in judgment with which he had begun the contest. The two vessels gradually drew nigher to each other, until they both entered into the common cloud, created by their fire, which thickened and spread around them in such a manner as to conceal their dark hulls from the gaze of the curious and interested spectators on the cliffs. The heavy reports of the cannon were now mingled with the rattling of muskets and pistols, and, streaks of fire might be seen, glancing like flashes of lightning through the white cloud, which enshrouded the combatants, and many minutes of painful uncertainty followed, before the deeply interested soldiers, who were gazing at the scene, discovered on whose banners victory had alighted.

We shall follow the combatants into their misty wreath, and display to the reader the events as they occurred.

The fire of the Ariel was much the most quick and deadly, both because she had suffered less, and her men were less exhausted; and the cutter stood desperately on to decide the combat, after grappling, hand to hand. Barnstable anticipated her intention, and well understood her commander's reason for adopting this course, but he was not a man to calculate coolly his advantages, when pride and daring invited him to a more severe trial. Accordingly, he met the enemy half-way, and, as the vessels rushed together, the stern of the schooner was secured to the bows of the cutter, by the joint efforts of both parties. The voice of the English commander was now plainly to be heard, in the uproar, calling to his men to follow him.

"Away there, boarders! repel boarders on the starboard quarter!" shouted Barnstable through his trumpet.

This was the last order that the gallant young sailor gave with this instrument, for, as he spoke, he cast it from him, and seizing his sabre, flew to the spot where the enemy was about to make his most desperate effort. The shouts, execrations, and tauntings of the combatants, now succeeded to the roar of the cannon, which could be used no longer with effect, though the fight was still maintained with spirited discharges of the small arms.

"Sweep him from his decks!" cried the English commander, as he appeared on his own bulwarks, surrounded by a dozen of his bravest men; "drive the rebellious dogs into the sea!"

"Away there, marines!" retorted Barnstable, firing his pistol at the advancing enemy; "leave not a man of them to sup his grog again."

The tremendous and close volley that succeeded this order, nearly accomplished the command of Barnstable to the letter, and the commander of the Alacrity, perceiving that he stood alone, reluctantly fell back on the deck of his own vessel, in order to bring on his men once more.

"Board her! gray beards and boys, idlers and all!" shouted Barnstable, springing in advance of his crew — a powerful arm arrested the movement of the dauntless seaman, and before he had time to recover himself, he was drawn violently back to his own vessel, by the irresistible grasp of his cockswain.

"The fellow's in his flurry," said Tom, "and it wouldn't be wise to go within reach of his flukes; but I'll just step ahead and give him a set with my harpoon."

Without waiting for a reply, the cockswain reared his tall frame on the bulwarks, and was in the attitude of stepping on board of his enemy, when a sea separated the vessels, and he fell with a heavy dash of the waters into the ocean. As twenty muskets and pistols were discharged at the instant he appeared, the crew of the Ariel supposed his fall to be occasioned by his wounds, and were rendered doubly fierce by the sight, and the cry of their commander to —

"Revenge long Tom! board her; long Tom or death!"

They threw themselves forward in irresistible numbers, and forced a passage, with much bloodshed, to the forecastle of the Alacrity. The Englishman was overpowered, but still remained undaunted — he rallied his crew, and bore up most gallantly to the fray. Thrusts of pikes, and blows of sabres were becoming close and deadly, while muskets and pistols were constantly discharged by those who were kept at a distance by the pressure of the throng of closer combatants.

Barnstable led his men, in advance, and became a mark of peculiar vengeance to his enemies, as they slowly yielded before his vigorous assaults. Chance had placed the two commanders on opposite sides of the cutter's deck, and the victory seemed to incline towards either party, wherever these daring officers directed the struggle in person. But the Englishman, perceiving that the ground he maintained in person was lost elsewhere, made an effort to restore the battle by changing his position, followed by one or two of his best men. A marine, who preceded him, levelled his musket within a few feet of the head of the American commander, and was about to fire, when Merry glided among the combatants, and passed his dirk into the body of the man, who fell at the blow; shaking his piece, with horrid imprecations, the wounded soldier prepared to deal his vengeance on his youthful assailant, when the fearless boy leaped within its muzzle, and buried his own keen weapon in his heart.

"Hurrah!" shouted the unconscious Barnstable, from the edge of the quarter-deck, where, attended by a few men, he was driving all before him. "Revenge — long Tom and victory!"

"We have them!" exclaimed the Englishman; "handle your pikes! we have them between two fires."

The battle would probably have terminated very differently from what previous circumstances had indicated, had not a wild-looking figure appeared in the cutter's channels at that moment, issuing from the sea, and gaining the deck at the same instant. It was long Tom, with his iron visage rendered fierce by his previous discomfiture, and his grizzled locks drenched with the briny element, from which he had risen, looking like Neptune with his trident. Without speaking, he poised his harpoon, and with a powerful effort, pinned the unfortunate Englishman to the mast of his own vessel.

"Starn all!" cried Tom, by a sort of instinct, when the blow was struck; and catching up the musket of the fallen marine, he dealt out terrible and fatal blows with its butt, on all who approached him, utterly disregarding the use of the bayonet on its muzzle. The unfortunate commander of the Alacrity brandished his sword with frantic gestures, while his eyes rolled in horrid wildness, when he writhed for an instant in his passing agonies, and then, as his head dropped lifeless upon his gored breast, he hung against the spar, a spectacle of dismay to his crew. A few of the Englishmen stood, chained to the spot in silent horror at the sight, but most of them fled to their lower deck, or hastened to conceal themselves in the secret parts of the vessel, leaving to the Americans the undisputed possession of the Alacrity.

Two thirds of the cutter's crew suffered either in life or limbs, by this short struggle; nor was the victory obtained by Barnstable without paying the price of several valuable lives. The first burst of conquest was not, however, the moment to appreciate the sacrifice, and loud and reiterated shouts, proclaimed the exultation of the conquerors. As the flush of victory subsided, however, recollection returned, and Barnstable issued such orders as humanity and his duty rendered necessary. While the vessels were separating, and the bodies of the dead and wounded were removing, the conqueror paced the deck of his prize, as if lost in deep reflection. He passed his hand, frequently, across his blackened and blood-stained brow, while his eyes would rise to examine the vast canopy of smoke that was hovering above the vessels, like a dense fog exhaling from the ocean. The result of his deliberations was soon announced to the crew.

"Haul down all your flags," he cried; "set the Englishman's colours again, and show the enemy's jack above our ensign in the Ariel."

The appearance of the whole channel-fleet within half gun shot, would not have occasioned more astonishment among the victors, than this extraordinary mandate. The wondering seamen suspended their several employments, to gaze at the singular change that was making in the flags, those symbols that were viewed with a sort of reverence, but none presumed to comment openly on the procedure, except long Tom, who stood on the quarter-deck of the prize, straightening the pliable iron of the harpoon which he had recovered, with as much care and diligence as if it were necessary to the maintenance of their conquest. Like the others, however, he suspended his employment, when he heard this order, and manifested no reluctance to express his dissatisfaction at the measure.

"If the Englishmen grumble at the fight, and think it not fair play," muttered the old cockswain, "let us try it over again, sir; as they are somewhat short of hands, they can send a boat to the land, and get off a gang of them lazy riptyles, the soldiers, who stand looking at us, like so many red lizards crawling on a beach, and we'll give them another chance; but damme, if I see the use of whipping them, if this is to be the better-end of the matter."

"What's that you're grumbling there, like a dead north-easter, you horse mackerel!" said Barnstable; "where are our friends and countrymen who are on the land! are we to leave them to swing on gibbets or rot in dungeons!"

The cockswain listened with great earnestness, and when his commander had spoken, he struck the palm of his broad hand against his brawny thigh, with a report like a pistol, and answered,

"I see how it is, sir; you reckon the red coats have Mr. Griffith in tow. Just run the schooner into shoal water, Captain Barnstable, and drop an anchor, where we can get the long gun to bear on them, and give me the whale-boat and five or six men to back me — they must have long legs if they get an offing before I run them aboard!"

"Fool! do you think a boat's crew could contend with fifty armed soldiers!"

"Soldiers!" echoed Tom, whose spirits had been strongly excited by the conflict, snapping his fingers with ineffable disdain, "that for all the soldiers that were ever rigged: one whale could kill a thousand of them! and here stands the man that has kill'd his round hundred of whales!"

"Pshaw, you grampus, do you turn braggart in your old age!"

"It's no bragging, sir, to speak a log-book truth! but if Captain Barnstable thinks that old Tom Coffin carries a speaking trumpet for a figure head, let him pass the word forrard to man the boats."

"No, no, my old master at the marlingspike," said Barnstable, kindly, "I know thee too well, thou brother of Neptune!

but, shall we not throw the bread-room dust in those Englishmen's eyes, by wearing their bunting awhile, till something
may offer to help our captured countrymen."

The cockswain shook his head, and cogitated a moment, as
if struck with sundry new ideas, when he answered—

"Ay, ay, sir; that's blue-water-philosophy: as deep as the
sea! Let the riptyles clew up the corners of their mouths to
their eye-brows, now! when they come to hear the ra'al yankee
truth of the matter, they will sheet them down to their leather
neckcloths!"

With this reflection the cockswain was much consoled, and
the business of repairing damages and securing the prize, proceeded without further interruption on his part. The few
prisoners who were unhurt, were rapidly transferred to the
Ariel. While Barnstable was attending to this duty, an unusual
bustle drew his eyes to one of the hatchways, where he beheld a
couple of his marines dragging forward a gentleman, whose
demeanour and appearance indicated the most abject terror.
After examining the extraordinary appearance of this individual, for a moment, in silent amazement, the lieutenant
exclaimed—

"Who have we here! some amateur in fights! an inquisitive,
wonder-seeking non-combatant, who has volunteered to serve
his king, and perhaps draw a picture, or write a book, to serve
himself! Pray, sir, in what capacity did you serve in this
vessel?"

The captive ventured a sidelong glance at his interrogator,
in whom he expected to encounter Griffith, but perceiving that
it was a face he did not know, he felt a revival of confidence
that enabled him to reply—

"I came here by accident; being on board the cutter at the
time her late commander determined to engage you. It was not
in his power to land me, as I trust you will not hesitate to do;
your conjecture of my being a non-combatant—"

"Is perfectly true," interrupted Barnstable; "it requires no
spy-glass to read that name written on you from stem to stern;
but for certain weighty reasons—"

He paused to turn at a signal given him by young Merry,
who whispered eagerly in his ear—

"'Tis Mr. Dillon, kinsman of Colonel Howard; I've seen him often, sailing in the wake of my cousin Cicily."

"Dillon!" exclaimed Barnstable, rubbing his hands with pleasure; "what, Kit of that name! he with 'the Savannah face, eyes of black, and skin of the same colour;' he's grown a little whiter with fear; but he's a prize, at this moment, worth twenty Alacritys!"

These exclamations were made in a low voice, and at some little distance from the prisoner, whom he now approached, and addressed —

"Policy, and consequently duty, require that I should detain you for a short time, sir; but you shall have a sailor's welcome to whatever we possess, to lessen the weight of captivity."

Barnstable precluded any reply, by bowing to his captive, and turning away, to superintend the management of his vessels. In a short time it was announced that they were ready to make sail, when the Ariel and her prize were brought close to the wind, and commenced beating slowly along the land, as if intending to return to the bay whence the latter had sailed that morning. As they stretched into the shore, on the first tack, the soldiers on the cliffs rent the air with their shouts and acclamations, to which Barnstable, pointing to the assumed symbols that were fluttering in the breeze from his masts, directed his crew to respond in the most cordial manner. As the distance, and the want of boats, prevented any further communication, the soldiers, after gazing at the receding vessels for a time, disappeared from the cliffs, and were soon lost from the sight of the adventurous mariners. Hour after hour was consumed in the tedious navigation, against an adverse tide, and the short day was drawing to a close, before they approached the mouth of their destined haven. While making one of their numerous stretches, to and from the land, the cutter, in which Barnstable continued, passed the victim of their morning's sport, riding on the water, the waves curling over his huge carcass as on some rounded rock, and already surrounded by the sharks, who were preying on his defenceless body.

"See! Master Coffin," cried the lieutenant, pointing out the object to his cockswain, as they glided by it, "the shovel-nosed gentlemen are regaling daintily; you have neglected the christian's duty of burying your dead."

The old seaman cast a melancholy look at the dead whale, and replied,

"If I had the creatur in Boston Bay, or on the Sandy Point of Munny-Moy, 'twould be the making of me! But riches and honour are for the great and the larned, and there's nothing left for poor Tom Coffin to do, but to veer and haul on his own rolling-tackle, that he may ride out the rest of the gale of life, without springing any of his old spars."

"How now, long Tom!" cried his officer, "these rocks and cliffs will shipwreck you on the shoals of poetry yet; you grow sentimental!"

"Them rocks might wrack any vessel that struck them," said the literal cockswain; "and as for poetry, I wants none better than the good old song of Captain Kidd; but it's enough to raise solemn thoughts in a Cape Poge Indian, to see an eighty barrel whale devoured by shirks—'tis an awful waste of property! I've seen the death of two hundred of the creaturs, though it seems to keep the rations of poor old long Tom as short as ever."

The cockswain walked aft, while the vessel was passing the whale, and seating himself on the taffrail, with his face resting gloomily on his bony hand, he fastened his eyes on the object of his solicitude, and continued to gaze at it with melancholy regret, while it was to be seen glistening in the sunbeams, as it rolled its glittering side of white into the air, or the rays fell unreflected on the black and rougher coat of the back of the monster. In the mean time, the navigators diligently pursued their way for the haven we have mentioned, into which they steered with every appearance of the fearlessness of friends, and the exultation of conquerors.

A few eager and gratified spectators lined the edges of the small bay, and Barnstable concluded his arrangement for deceiving the enemy, by admonishing his crew, that they were now about to enter on a service that would require their utmost intrepidity and sagacity.

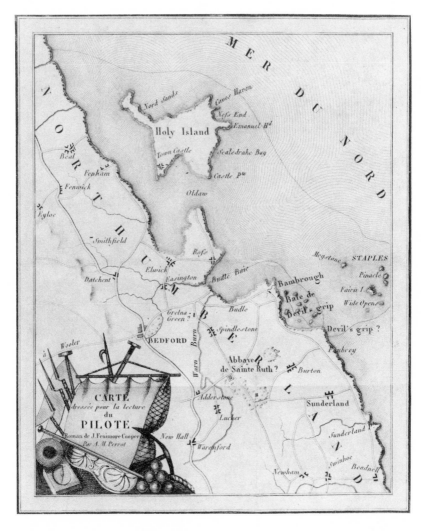

V. Map showing the setting for *The Pilot* as drawn by A. M. Perrot for Volume IX of *Oeuvres Complètes de J. Fenimore Cooper.*

Wainwright delt. fcalp.

VI. Cecilia and Katherine discover Griffith, drawn by Thomas Griffith Wainwright.

VII. Thomas Sully's painting (1841) of the scene shown on the opposite page.

LE PILOTE.

Tom Coffin cloua le malheureux capitaine contre son grand mat.

T. II. Ch. XVIII.

VIII. Long Tom pins the unfortunate English captain to his own mainmast. Drawn and engraved by Alfred Johannot.

Chapter XIX.

"Our trumpet called you to this gentle parle."
King John, II.i.205.

As GRIFFITH and his companions rushed from the offices of St. Ruth, into the open air, they encountered no one to intercept their flight, or communicate the alarm. Warned by the experience of the earlier part of the same night, they avoided the points where they knew the sentinels were posted, though fully prepared to bear down all resistance, and were soon beyond the probability of immediate detection. They proceeded, for the distance of half a mile, with rapid strides, and with the stern and sullen silence of men who, expecting to encounter immediate danger, were resolved to breast it with desperate resolution; but, as they plunged into a copse, that clustered around the ruin which has been already mentioned, they lessened their exertions to a more deliberate pace, and a short but guarded dialogue ensued.

"We have had a timely escape," said Griffith; "I would much rather have endured captivity, than have been the cause of introducing confusion and bloodshed into the peaceful residence of Colonel Howard."

"I would, sir, that you had been of this opinion some hours earlier," returned the pilot, with a severity in his tones that even conveyed more meaning than his words.

"I may have forgotten my duty, sir, in my anxiety to inquire into the condition of a family in whom I feel a particular interest," returned Griffith, in a manner in which pride evidently struggled with respect; "but this is not a time for regrets; I apprehend that we follow you on an errand of some moment, where actions would be more acceptable than any words of apology. What is your pleasure now?"

"I much fear that our project will be defeated," said the pilot, gloomily; "the alarm will spread with the morning fogs, and there will be musterings of the yeomen, and consultations of the gentry, that will drive all thoughts of amusement from their minds. The rumour of a descent will, at any time, force sleep from the shores of this island, to at least ten leagues inland."

"Ay, you have probably passed some pleasant nights, with your eyes open, among them, yourself, Master Pilot," said Manual; "they may thank the Frenchman, Thurot, in the old business of '56, and our own dare-devil, the bloody Scotchman, as the causes of their quarters being so often beaten up. After all, Thurot, with his fleet, did no more than bully them a little, and the poor fellow was finally extinguished by a few small cruisers, like a drummer's boy under a grenadier's cap; but honest Paul sung a different tune for his countrymen to dance to, and—"

"I believe you will shortly dance yourself, Manual," interrupted Griffith, quickly, "and in very pleasure that you have escaped an English prison."

"Say, rather, an English gibbet," continued the elated marine; "for had a court-martial or a court-civil discussed the manner of our entrance into this island, I doubt whether we should have fared better than the dare-devil himself, honest—"

"Pshaw!" exclaimed the impatient Griffith, "enough of this nonsense, Captain Manual; we have other matters to discuss now;—what course have you determined to pursue, Mr. Gray?"

The pilot started, like a man aroused from a deep musing at this question, and after a pause of a moment, he spoke in a low tone of voice, as if still under the influence of deep and melancholy feeling—

"The night has already run into the morning watch, but the sun is backward to show himself in this latitude in the heart of winter—I must depart, my friends, to rejoin you some ten hours hence; it will be necessary to look deeper into our scheme before we hazard any thing, and no one can do the service but myself—where shall we meet again?"

"I have reason to think that there is an unfrequented ruin, at no great distance from us," said Griffith; "perhaps we might find both shelter and privacy among its deserted walls."

"The thought is good," returned the pilot, "and 'twill answer a double purpose. Could you find the place where you put the marines in ambush, Captain Manual?"

"Has a dog a nose! and can he follow a clean scent!" exclaimed the marine; "do you think, Signior Pilota, that a general ever puts his forces in an ambuscade where he can't find them himself? 'Fore God! I knew well enough where the rascals lay snoring on their knapsacks, some half-an-hour ago, and I would have given the oldest majority in Washington's army to have had them where a small intimation from myself could have brought them in line ready dressed for a charge. I know not how you fared, gentlemen, but with me, the sight of twenty such vagabonds would have been a joyous spectacle; we would have tossed that Captain Borroughcliffe and his recruits on the points of our bayonets, as the devil would pitch —"

"Come, come, Manual," said Griffith, a little angrily, "you constantly forget our situation and our errand; can you lead your men hither without discovery, before the day dawns?"

"I want but the shortest half-hour that a bad watch ever travelled over to do it in."

"Then follow, and I will appoint a place of secret rendez-vous," rejoined Griffith; "Mr. Gray can learn our situation at the same time."

The pilot was seen to beckon, through the gloom of the night, for his companions to move forward, when they proceeded, with cautious steps, in quest of the desired shelter. A short search brought them in contact with a part of the ruinous walls that spread over a large surface, and which, in places, reared their black fragments against the sky, casting a deeper obscurity across the secret recesses of the wood.

"This will do," said Griffith, when they had skirted for some distance the outline of the crumbling fabric; "bring up your men to this point, where I will meet you, and conduct them to some more secret place, for which I shall search during your absence."

"A perfect paradise, after the cable-tiers of the Ariel!" exclaimed Manual; "I doubt not but a good spot might be selected among these trees for a steady drill; a thing my soul has pined after for six long months."

"Away, away!" cried Griffith; "here is no place for idle parades; if we find shelter from discovery and capture until you shall be needed in a deadly struggle, 'twill be well."

Manual was slowly retracing his steps to the skirts of the wood, when he suddenly turned, and asked—

"Shall I post a small picquet, a mere corporal's guard, in the open ground in front, and make a chain of sentinels to our works?"

"We have no works—we want no sentinels," returned his impatient commander; "our security is only to be found in secrecy. Lead up your men under the cover of the trees, and let those three bright stars be your landmarks—bring them in a range with the northern corner of the wood—"

"Enough, Mr. Griffith," interrupted Manual; "a column of troops is not to be steered like a ship, by compass, and bearings, and distances;—trust me, sir, the march shall be conducted with proper discretion, though in a military manner."

Any reply or expostulation was prevented by the sudden disappearance of the marine, whose retreating footsteps were heard, for several moments, as he moved at a deliberate pace through the underwood. During this short interval, the pilot stood reclining against a corner of the ruins in profound silence, but when the sounds of Manual's march were no longer audible, he advanced from under the deeper shadows of the wall, and approached his youthful companion.

"We are indebted to the marine for our escape," he said; "I hope we are not to suffer by his folly."

"He is what Barnstable calls a rectangular man," returned Griffith; "and will have his way in matters of his profession, though a daring companion in a hazardous expedition. If we can keep him from exposing us by his silly parade, we shall find him a man who will do his work like a soldier, sir, when need happens."

"'Tis all I ask; until the last moment he and his command must be torpid; for if we are discovered, any attempt of ours, with some twenty bayonets and a half-pike or two, would be useless against the force that would be brought to crush us."

"The truth of your opinion is too obvious," returned Griffith; "these fellows will sleep a week at a time in a gale at sea, but the smell of the land wakes them up, and I fear 'twill be hard to keep them close during the day."

"It must be done, sir, by the strong hand of force," said the pilot sternly, "if it cannot be done by admonition; if we had no more than the recruits of that drunken martinet to cope with, it would be no hard task to drive them into the sea; but I learned in my prison that horse are expected on the shore with the dawn; there is one they call Dillon who is on the alert to do us mischief."

"The miscreant!" muttered Griffith; "then you also have had communion, sir, with some of the inmates of St. Ruth?"

"It behooves a man who is embarked in a perilous enterprise to seize all opportunities to learn his hazard," said the pilot, evasively; "if the report be true, I fear we have but little hopes of succeeding in our plans."

"Nay, then, let us take the advantage of the darkness to regain the schooner; the coasts of England swarm with hostile cruisers, and a rich trade is flowing into the bosom of this island from the four quarters of the world; we shall not seek long for a foe worthy to contend with, nor for the opportunities to cut up the Englishman in his sinews of war—his wealth."

"Griffith," returned the pilot in his still, low tones, that seemed to belong to a man who never knew ambition, nor felt human passion, "I grow sick of this struggle between merit and privileged rank. It is in vain that I scour the waters which the King of England boastingly calls his own, and capture his vessels in the very mouths of his harbours, if my reward is to consist only of violated promises, and hollow professions;— but your proposition is useless to me; I have at length obtained a ship of a size sufficient to convey my person to the shores of honest, plain-dealing America, and I would enter the hall of congress, on my return, attended by a few of the legislators of this learned isle, who think they possess the exclusive privilege to be wise, and virtuous, and great."

"Such a retinue might doubtless be grateful both to your own feelings and those who would receive you," said Griffith, modestly; "but would it affect the great purposes of our struggle, or is it an exploit, when achieved, worth the hazard you incur?"

Griffith felt the hand of the pilot on his own, pressing it with a convulsive grasp, as he replied, in a voice, if possible, even more desperately calm than his former tones —

"There is glory in it, young man; if it be purchased with danger, it shall be rewarded by fame! It is true, I wear your republican livery, and call the Americans my brothers, but it is because you combat in behalf of human nature. Were your cause less holy, I would not shed the meanest drop that flows in English veins to serve it; but now, it hallows every exploit that is undertaken in its favour, and the names of all who contend for it shall belong to posterity. Is there no merit in teaching these proud islanders that the arm of liberty can pluck them from the very empire of their corruption and oppression?"

"Then let me go and ascertain what we most wish to know; you have been seen there, and might attract — "

"You little know me," interrupted the pilot; "the deed is my own. If I succeed, I shall claim the honour, and it is proper that I incur the hazard; if I fail, it will be buried in oblivion, like fifty others of my schemes, which, had I power to back me, would have thrown this kingdom in consternation, from the look-outs on the boldest of its head-lands, to those on the turrets of Windsor-Castle. But I was born without the nobility of twenty generations to corrupt my blood and deaden my soul, and am not trusted by the degenerate wretches who rule the French marine."

"'Tis said that ships of two decks are building from our own oak," said Griffith; "and you have only to present yourself in America, to be employed most honourably."

"Ay! the republics cannot doubt the man who has supported their flag, without lowering it an inch, in so many bloody conflicts! I do go there, Griffith, but my way lies on this path; my pretended friends have bound my hands often, but my enemies, never — neither shall they now. Ten hours will determine all I wish to know, and with you I trust the safety of the party till my return; be vigilant, but be prudent."

"If you should not appear at the appointed hour," exclaimed Griffith, as he beheld the pilot turning to depart, "where am I to seek, and how serve you?"

"Seek me not, but return to your vessel; my earliest years were passed on this coast, and I can leave the island, should it be necessary, as I entered it, aided by this disguise and my own knowledge; in such an event, look to your charge, and forget me entirely."

Griffith could distinguish the silent wave of his hand when the pilot concluded, and the next instant he was left alone. For several minutes the young man continued where he had been standing, musing on the singular endowments and restless enterprise of the being with whom chance had thus unexpectedly brought him in contact, and with whose fate and fortune his own prospects had, by the intervention of unlooked-for circumstances, become intimately connected. When the reflections excited by recent occurrences had passed away, he entered within the sweeping circle of the ruinous walls, and after a very cursory survey of the state of the dilapidated building, he was satisfied that it contained enough secret places to conceal his men, until the return of the pilot should warn them that the hour had come when they must attempt the seizure of the devoted sportsmen, or darkness should again facilitate their return to the Ariel. It was now about the commencement of that period of deep night which seamen distinguish as the morning watch, and Griffith ventured to the edge of the little wood, to listen if any sounds or tumult indicated that they were pursued. On reaching a point where his eye could faintly distinguish distant objects, the young man paused, and bestowed a close and wary investigation on the surrounding scene.

The fury of the gale had sensibly abated, but a steady current of sea air was rushing through the naked branches of the oaks, lending a dreary and mournful sound to the gloom of the dim prospect. At the distance of a short half mile, the confused outline of the pile of St. Ruth rose proudly against the streak of light which was gradually increasing above the ocean, and there were moments when the young seaman even fancied he could discern the bright caps that topped the waves of his own disturbed element. The long, dull roar of the surf, as it tumbled heavily on the beach, or dashed with unbroken violence against the hard boundary of rocks, was borne along by the blasts distinctly to his ears. It was a time and a situation to cause the young seaman to ponder deeply on the changes and chances of his hazardous profession. Only a few short hours had passed since he was striving with his utmost skill, and with all his collected energy, to guide the enormous fabric, in which so many of his comrades were now quietly sleeping on the broad ocean, from that very shore on which he now stood in cool indifference to the danger. The recollection of home, America, his youthful and enduring passion, and the character and charms of his mistress, blended in a sort of wild and feverish confusion, which was not, however, without its pleasures, in the ardent fancy of the young man, and he was slowly approaching, step by step, towards the abbey, when the sound of footsteps, proceeding evidently from the measured tread of disciplined men, reached his ears. He was instantly recalled to his recollection by this noise, which increased as the party deliberately approached, and in a few moments he was able to distinguish a line of men, marching in order towards the edge of the wood from which he had himself so recently issued. Retiring rapidly under the deeper shadow of the trees, he waited until it was apparent the party intended also to enter under its cover, when he ventured to speak —

"Who comes, and on what errand?" he cried.

"A skulker, and to burrow like a rabbit, or jump from hole to hole, like a wharf-rat!" said Manual, sulkily; "here have I been marching, within half-musket shot of the enemy, without daring to pull a trigger even, on their out-posts, because our muzzles are plugged with that universal extinguisher of gun-powder, called prudence. 'Fore God! Mr. Griffith, I hope you may never feel the temptation to do an evil deed which I felt just now to throw a volley of small shot into that dog-kennel of a place, if it were only to break its windows and let in the night air upon the sleeping sot who is dozing away the fumes of some as good, old, south-side — harkye, Mr. Griffith, one word in your ear."

A short conference took place between the two officers, apart from the men, at the close of which, as they rejoined the party, Manual might be heard urging his plans on the reluctant ears of Griffith, in the following words: —

"I could carry the old dungeon without waking one of the snorers; and, consider, sir, we might get a stock of as rich cordial from its cellars as ever oiled the throat of a gentleman!"

"'Tis idle, 'tis idle," said Griffith, impatiently; "we are not robbers of hen-roosts, nor wine-gaugers, to be prying into the vaults of the English gentry, Captain Manual, but honourable men, employed in the sacred cause of liberty and our country. Lead your party into the ruin, and let them seek their rest; we may have work for them with the dawn."

"Evil was the hour when I quitted the line of the army, to place a soldier under the orders of an awkward squad of tarry jackets!" muttered Manual, as he proceeded to execute an order that was delivered with an air of authority that he knew must be obeyed. "As pretty an opportunity for a surprise and a forage thrown away, as ever crossed the path of a partisan! but, by all the rights of man! I'll have an encampment in some order. Here, you sergeant, detail a corporal and three men for a picket, and station them in the skirts of this wood. We shall have a sentinel in advance of our position, and things shall be conducted with some air of discipline."

Griffith heard this order with great inward disgust; but as he anticipated the return of the pilot before the light could arrive to render this weak exposure of their situation apparent, he forbore exercising his power to alter the arrangement. Manual had, therefore, the satisfaction of seeing his little party quartered as he thought in a military manner, before he retired with Griffith and his men into one of the vaulted apartments of the ruin, which, by its open and broken doors invited their entrance. Here the marines disposed themselves to rest, while the two officers succeeded in passing the tedious hours, without losing their characters for watchfulness, by conversing with each other, or, at whiles, suffering their thoughts to roam in the very different fields which fancy would exhibit to men of such differing characters. In this manner, hour after hour passed, in listless quiet, or sullen expectation, until the day had gradually advanced, and it became dangerous to keep the sentinels and picket in a situation, where they were liable to be seen by any straggler who might be passing near the wood. Manual remonstrated against any alteration, as being entirely unmilitary, for he was apt to carry his notions of tactics to extremes whenever he came in collision with a sea-officer, but in this instance his superior was firm, and the only concession the captain could obtain was the permission to place a solitary sentinel within a few feet of the vault, though under the cover of the crumbling walls of the building itself. With this slight deviation in their arrangements, the uneasy party remained for several hours longer, impatiently awaiting the period when they should be required to move.

The guns first fired from the Alacrity had been distinctly audible, and were pronounced by Griffith, whose practised ear detected the metal of the piece that was used, as not proceeding from the schooner. When the rapid though distant rumbling of the spirited cannonade became audible, it was with difficulty that Griffith could restrain either his own feelings or the conduct of his companions within those bounds that prudence and their situation required. The last gun was, however, fired, and not a man had left the vault, and conjectures as to the result of the fight, succeeded to those which had been made on the character of the combatants during the action. Some of the marines would raise their heads from the fragments which served them as the pillows on which they were seeking disturbed and stolen slumbers, and after listening to the cannon, would again compose themselves to sleep, like men who felt no concern in a contest in which they did not participate. Others, more alive to events, and less drowsy, lavishly expended their rude jokes on those who were engaged in the struggle, or listened with a curious interest to mark the progress of the battle, by the uncertain index of its noise. When the fight had been some time concluded, Manual indulged his ill-humour more at length—

"There has been a party of pleasure, within a league of us, Mr. Griffith," he said, "at which, but for our present subterraneous quarters, we might have been guests, and thus laid some claim to the honour of sharing in the victory. But it is not too late to push the party on as far as the cliffs, where we shall be in sight of the vessels, and we may possibly establish a claim to our share of the prize-money."

"There is but little wealth to be gleaned from the capture of a king's cutter," returned Griffith, "and there would be less honour were Barnstable encumbered with our additional and useless numbers."

"Useless!" repeated Manual; "there is much good service to be got out of twenty-three well-drilled and well-chosen marines; look at those fellows, Mr. Griffith, and then tell me if you would think them an encumbrance in the hour of need?"

Griffith smiled, and glanced his eye over the sleeping group, for when the firing had ceased the whole party had again sought their repose, and he could not help admiring the athletic and sinewy limbs that lay scattered around the gloomy vault, in every posture that ease or whim dictated. From the stout frames of the men, his glance was directed to the stack of fire-arms, along whose glittering tubes and polished bayonets, strong rays of light were dancing, even in that dark apartment. Manual followed the direction of his eyes, and watched the expression of his countenance, with inward exultation, but he had the forbearance to await his reply before he manifested his feelings more openly.

"I know them to be true men," said Griffith, "when needed, but—hark! what says he?"

"Who goes there? what noise is that?" repeated the sentinel who was placed at the entrance of the vault.

Manual and Griffith sprang at the same instant from their places of rest, and stood, unwilling to create the slightest sounds, listening with the most intense anxiety to catch the next indications of the cause of their watchman's alarm. A short stillness, like that of death, succeeded, during which Griffith whispered—

"'Tis the pilot; his hour has been long passed."

The words were hardly spoken, when the clashing of steel in fierce and sudden contact was heard, and at the next instant the body of the sentinel fell heavily along the stone steps that led to the open air, and rolled lifelessly to their feet, with the bayonet that had caused his death projecting from a deep wound in his breast.

"Away, away! sleepers away!" shouted Griffith.

"To arms!" cried Manual, in a voice of thunder.

The alarmed marines, suddenly aroused from their slumbers at these thrilling cries, sprang on their feet in a confused cluster, and at that fatal moment a body of living fire darted into the vault, which re-echoed with the reports of twenty muskets. The uproar, the smoke, and the groans which escaped from many of his party, could not restrain Griffith another instant; his pistol was fired through the cloud which concealed the entrance of the vault, and he followed the leaden messenger, trailing a half-pike, and shouting to his men—

"Come on! follow, my lads; they are nothing but soldiers."

Even while he spoke, the ardent young seaman was rushing up the narrow passage, but as he gained the open space, his foot struck the writhing body of the victim of his shot, and he was precipitated headlong into a group of armed men.

"Fire! Manual, fire!" shouted the infuriated prisoner; "fire, while you have them in a cluster."

"Ay, fire, Mr. Manual," said Borroughcliffe, with great coolness, "and shoot your own officer; hold him up, boys! hold him up in front; the safest place is nighest to him."

"Fire!" repeated Griffith, making desperate efforts to release himself from the grasp of five or six men; "fire, and disregard me."

"If he do, he deserves to be hung," said Borroughcliffe; "such fine fellows are not sufficiently plenty to be shot at like wild beasts in chains. Take him from before the mouth of the vault, boys, and spread yourselves to your duty."

At the time Griffith issued from the cover, Manual was mechanically employed in placing his men in order, and the marines, accustomed to do every thing in concert and array, lost the moment to advance. The soldiers of Borroughcliffe reloaded their muskets, and fell back behind different portions of the wall, where they could command the entrance to the vault with their fire, without much exposure to themselves. This disposition was very coolly reconnoitred by Manual in person, through some of the crevices in the wall, and he hesitated to advance against the force he beheld, while so advantageously posted. In this situation several shots were fired by either party, without effect, until Borroughcliffe, perceiving the inefficacy of that mode of attack, summoned the garrison of the vault to a parly.

"Surrender to the forces of his majesty, King George the Third," he cried, "and I promise you quarter."

"Will you release your prisoner, and give us free passage to our vessels?" asked Manual; "the garrison to march out with all the honours of war, and officers to retain their side-arms?"

"Inadmissible," returned Borroughcliffe, with great gravity; "the honour of his majesty's arms, and the welfare of the realm, forbid such a treaty; but I offer you safe quarter, and honourable treatment."

"Officers to retain their side-arms, your prisoner to be released, and the whole party to return to America, on parole, not to serve until exchanged?"

"Not granted," said Borroughcliffe. "The most that I can yield, is a good potation of the generous south-side, and if you are the man I take you for, you will know how to prize such an offer."

"In what capacity do you summon us to yield? as men entitled to the benefit of the laws of arms, or as rebels to your king?"

"Ye are rebels all, gentlemen," returned the deliberate Borroughcliffe, "and as such ye must yield; though so far as good treatment and good fare goes, you are sure of it while in my power; in all other respects you lie at the mercy of his most gracious majesty."

"Then let his majesty show his gracious face, and come and take us, for I'll be—"

The asseveration of the marine was interrupted by Griffith, whose blood had sensibly cooled, and whose generous feelings were awakened in behalf of his comrades, now that his own fate seemed decided.

"Hold, Manual," he cried, "make no rash oaths; Captain Borroughcliffe, I am Edward Griffith, a lieutenant in the navy of the United American States, and I pledge you my honour, to a parole—"

"Release him," said Borroughcliffe.

Griffith advanced between the two parties, and spoke so loud as to be heard by both—

"I propose to descend to the vault and ascertain the loss and present strength of Captain Manual's party; if the latter be not greater than I apprehend, I shall advise him to a surrender on the usual conditions of civilized nations."

"Go," said the soldier; "but stay; is he a half-and-half—an amphibious—pshaw! I mean a marine?"

"He is, sir, a captain in that corps—"

"The very man," interrupted Borroughcliffe; "I thought I recollected the liquid sounds of his voice. It will be well to speak to him of the good fare of St. Ruth; and you may add, that I know my man; I shall besiege instead of storming him, with the certainty of a surrender when his canteen is empty. The vault he is in holds no such beverage as the cellars of the abbey."

Griffith smiled, in spite of the occasion and his vexation, and making a slight inclination of his head, he passed into the vault, giving notice to his friends, by his voice, in order to apprize them who approached.

He found six of the marines, including the sentinel, lying dead on the ragged pavement, and four others wounded, but stifling their groans, by the order of their commander, that they might not inform the enemy of his weakness. With the remainder of his command Manual had intrenched himself behind the fragment of a wall that intersected the vault, and regardless of the dismaying objects before him, maintained as bold a front, and as momentous an air, as if the fate of a walled town depended on his resolution and ingenuity.

"You see, Mr. Griffith," he cried, when the young sailor approached this gloomy but really formidable arrangement, "that nothing short of artillery can dislodge me; as for that drinking Englishman above, let him send down his men by platoons of eight or ten, and I'll pile them up on those steps, four and five deep."

"But artillery can and will be brought, if it should be necessary," said Griffith, "and there is not the least chance of your eventual escape; it may be possible for you to destroy a few of the enemy, but you are too humane to wish to do it unnecessarily."

"No doubt," returned Manual, with a grim smile; "and yet methinks I could find present pleasure in shooting seven of them—yes, just seven, which is one more than they have struck off my roster."

"Remember your own wounded," added Griffith; "they suffer for want of aid, while you protract a useless defence."

A few smothered groans, from the sufferers, seconded this appeal, and Manual yielded, though with a very ill grace, to the necessity of the case.

"Go, then, and tell him that we will surrender as prisoners of war," he said, "on the conditions that he grants me my side-arms, and that suitable care shall be taken of the sick — be particular to call them sick — for some lucky accident may yet occur before the compact is ratified, and I would not have him learn our loss."

Griffith, without waiting for a second bidding, hastened to Borroughcliffe with his intelligence.

"His side-arms!" repeated the soldier, when the other had done; "what are they, I pray thee, a marlingspike! for if his equipments be no better than thine own, my worthy prisoner, there is little need to quarrel about their ownership."

"Had I but ten of my meanest men, armed with such half-pikes, and Captain Borroughcliffe with his party were put at deadly strife with us," retorted Griffith, "he might find occasion to value our weapons more highly."

"Four such fiery gentlemen as yourself would have routed my command," returned Borroughcliffe, with undisturbed composure; "I trembled for my ranks when I saw you coming out of the smoke like a blazing comet from behind a cloud, and I shall never think of somersets without returning inward thanks to their inventor. But our treaty is made; let your comrades come forth and pile their arms."

Griffith communicated the result to the captain of marines, when the latter led the remnant of his party out of his sunken fortress into the open air.

The men, who had manifested throughout the whole business that cool subordination and unyielding front, mixed with the dauntless spirit that to this day distinguishes the corps of which they were members, followed their commander in sullen silence, and stacked their arms, with as much regularity and precision as if they had been ordered to relieve themselves after a march. When this necessary preliminary had been observed, Borroughcliffe unmasked his forces, and our adventurers found themselves once more in the power of the enemy, and under circumstances which rendered the prospects of a speedy release from their captivity nearly hopeless.

Chapter XX.

"If your Father will do me any honour, so;
If not, let him kill the next Percy himself;
I look to be either Earl or Duke, I can assure you."
1 Henry IV, V.iv.138–140.

MANUAL cast sundry discontented and sullen looks from his captors to the remnant of his own command, while the process of pinioning the latter was conducted, with much discretion, under the directions of Sergeant Drill, but meeting, in one of his dissatisfied glances, with the pale and disturbed features of Griffith, he gave vent to his ill-humour, as follows:

"This results from neglecting the precautions of military discipline. Had the command been with me, who, I may say, without boasting, have been accustomed to the duties of the field, proper picquets would have been posted, and instead of being caught like so many rabbits in a burrow, to be smoked out with brimstone, we should have had an open field for the struggle, or we might have possessed ourselves of these walls, which I could have made good for two hours at least, against the best regiment that ever wore King George's facings."

"Defend the outworks before retreating to the citadel!" cried Borroughcliffe; "'tis the game of war, and shows science; but had you kept closer to your burrow, the rabbits might now have all been frisking about in that pleasant abode. The eyes of a timid hind were greeted this morning, while journeying near this wood, with a passing sight of armed men, in strange attire, and as he fled, with an intent of casting himself into the sea, as fear will sometimes urge one of his kind to do, he luckily encountered me on the cliffs, who humanely saved his life, by compelling him to conduct us hither. There is often wisdom in science, my worthy contemporary in arms, but there is sometimes safety in ignorance."

"You have succeeded, sir, and have a right to be pleasant," said Manual, seating himself gloomily on a fragment of the ruin, and fastening his looks on the melancholy spectacle of the lifeless bodies, as they were successively brought from the vault and placed at his feet; "but these men have been my own children, and you will excuse me if I cannot retort your pleasantries. Ah! Captain Borroughcliffe, you are a soldier, and know how to value merit. I took those very fellows, who sleep on these stones so quietly, from the hands of nature, and made them the pride of our art. They were no longer men, but brave lads, who ate and drank, wheeled and marched, loaded and fired, laughed or were sorrowful, spoke or were silent, only at my will. As for soul, there was but one among them all, and that was in my keeping! Groan, my children, groan freely now; there is no longer a reason to be silent. I have known a single musket-bullet cut the buttons from the coats of five of them in a row, without raising the skin of a man. I could ever calculate, with certainty, how many it would be necessary to expend in all regular service, but this accursed banditti business has robbed me of the choicest of my treasures. You 'stand at ease' now, my children; groan, it will soften your anguish."

Borroughcliffe appeared to participate, in some degree, in the feelings of his captive, and he made a few appropriate remarks in the way of condolence, while he watched the preparations that were making by his own men to move. At length his orderly announced that substitutes for barrows were provided to sustain the wounded, and inquired if it were his pleasure to return to their quarters.

"Who has seen the horse?" demanded the captain; "which way did they march? Have they gained any tidings of the discovery of this party of the enemy?"

"Not from us, your honour," returned the sergeant; "they had ridden along the coast before we left the cliffs, and it was said their officer intended to scour the shore for several miles, and spread the alarm."

"Let him; it is all such gay gallants are good for. Drill, honour is almost as scarce an article with our arms just now, as promotion. We seem but the degenerate children of the heroes of Poictiers; — you understand me, sergeant?"

"Some battle fou't by his majesty's troops against the French, your honour," returned the orderly, a little at a loss to comprehend the expression of his officer's eye.

"Fellow, you grow dull on victory," exclaimed Borroughcliffe; "come hither, I would give you orders. Do you think, Mister Drill, there is more honour, or likely to be more profit, in this little morning's amusement than you and I can stand under?"

"I should not, your honour; we have both pretty broad shoulders—"

"That are not weakened by undue burthens of this nature," interrupted his captain, significantly; "if we let the news of this affair reach the ears of those hungry dragoons, they would charge upon us, open mouthed, like a pack of famished beagles, and claim at least half the credit, and certainly all the profit."

"But, your honour, there was not a man of them even—"

"No matter, Drill; I've known troops that have been engaged, and have suffered, cheated out of their share of victory by a well-worded despatch. You know, fellow, that in the smoke and confusion of a battle, a man can only see what passes near him, and common prudence requires that he only mention in his official letters what he knows can't be easily contradicted. Thus your Indians, and, indeed, all allies, are not entitled to the right of a general order, any more than to the right of a parade. Now, I dare say, you have heard of a certain battle of Blenheim?"

"Lord! your honour, 'tis the pride of the British army, that and the Culloden! 'Twas when the great Corporal John beat the French king, and all his lords and nobility, with half his nation in arms to back him!"

"Ay! there is a little of the barrack readings in the account, but it is substantially true; know you how many French were in the field, that day, Mister Drill?"

"I have never seen the totals of their muster, sir, in print, but judging by the difference betwixt the nations, I should suppose some hundreds of thousands."

"And yet, to oppose this vast army, the duke had only some ten or twelve thousand well-fed Englishmen! You look astounded, sergeant!"

"Why, your honour, that does seem rather an over-match for an old soldier to swallow; the random shot would sweep away so small a force."

"And yet the battle was fought, and the victory won! but the Duke of Marlborough had a certain Mr. Eugene, with some fifty or sixty thousand High-Dutchers, to back him. You never heard of Mr. Eugene?"

"Not a syllable, your honour; I always thought that Corporal John—"

"Was a gallant and great general; you thought right, Mister Drill. So would a certain nameless gentleman be also, if his majesty would sign a commission to that effect. However, a majority is on the high road to a regiment, and with even a regiment a man is comfortable! In plain English, Mister Drill, we must get our prisoners into the abbey with as little noise as possible, in order that the horse may continue their gambols along the coast, without coming to devour our meal. All the fuss must be made at the war-office. For that trifle you may trust me; I think I know who holds a quill that is as good in its way as the sword he wears. Drill is a short name, and can easily be written within the folds of a letter."

"Lord, your honour!" said the gratified halberdier, "I'm sure such an honour is more—but your honour can ever command me."

"I do; and it is, to be close, and to make your men keep close, until it shall be time to speak, when, I pledge myself, there shall be noise enough." Borroughcliffe shook his head, with a grave air, as he continued—"It has been a devil of a bloody fight, sergeant! look at the dead and wounded; a wood on each flank—supported by a ruin in the centre. Oh! ink! ink! can be spilt on the details with great effect. Go, fellow, and prepare to march."

Thus enlightened on the subject of his commander's ulterior views, the non-commissioned agent of the captain's wishes proceeded to give suitable instructions to the rest of the party, and to make the more immediate preparations for a march. The arrangements were soon completed. The bodies of the slain were left unsheltered, the seclusion of the ruin being deemed a sufficient security against the danger of any discovery, until darkness should favour their removal, in conformity with Borroughcliffe's plan, to monopolize the glory. The wounded were placed on rude litters, composed of the muskets and blankets of the prisoners, when the conquerors and vanquished moved together in a compact body from the ruin, in such a manner as to make the former serve as a mask to conceal the latter from the curious gaze of any casual passenger. There was but little, however, to apprehend on this head, for the alarm and the terror consequent on the exaggerated reports that flew through the country, effectually prevented any intruders on the usually quiet and retired domains of St. Ruth.

The party was emerging from the wood, when the cracking of branches, and rustling of dried leaves, announced, however, that an interruption of some sort was about to occur.

"If it should be one of their rascally patroles!" exclaimed Borroughcliffe, with very obvious displeasure; "they trample like a regiment of cavalry! but, gentlemen, you will acknowledge yourselves, that we were retiring from the field of battle when we met the reinforcement, if it should prove to be such."

"We are not disposed, sir, to deny you the glory of having achieved your victory single handed," said Griffith, glancing his eyes uneasily in the direction of the approaching sounds, expecting to see the pilot issue from the thicket in which he seemed to be entangled, instead of any detachment of his enemies.

"Clear the way, Caesar!" cried a voice at no great distance from them; "break through the accursed vines, on my right, Pompey! —press forward, my fine fellows, or we may be too late to smell even the smoke of the fight."

"Hum!" ejaculated the captain with his philosophic indifference of manner entirely re-established, "this must be a Roman legion just awoke from a trance of some seventeen centuries, and that the voice of a Centurion. We will halt, Mister Drill, and view the manner of an ancient march!"

While the captain was yet speaking, a violent effort disengaged the advancing party from the thicket of brambles in which they had been entangled, when two blacks, each bending under a load of fire-arms, preceded Colonel Howard into the clear space where Borroughcliffe had halted his detachment. Some little time was necessary to enable the veteran to arrange his disordered dress, and to remove the perspiring effects of the unusual toil from his features, before he could observe the addition to the captain's numbers.

"We heard you fire," cried the old soldier, making, at the same time, the most diligent application of his bandanna, "and I determined to aid you with a sortie, which, when judiciously timed, has been the means of raising many a siege; though, had Montcalm rested quietly within his walls, the plains of Abr'am might never have drunk his blood."

"Oh! his decision was soldierly, and according to all rules of war," exclaimed Manual, "and had I followed his example, this day might have produced a different tale!"

"Why, who have we here!" cried the colonel in astonishment; "who is it that pretends to criticise battles and sieges, dressed in such a garb!"

"'Tis a dux incognitorum, my worthy host," said Borroughcliffe, "which means, in our English language, a captain of marines in the service of the American Congress."

"What! have you then met the enemy! ay! and by the fame of the immortal Wolfe you have captured them!" cried the delighted veteran; "I was pressing on with a part of my garrison to your assistance, for I had seen that you were marching in this direction, and even the report of a few muskets was heard."

"A few!" interrupted the conqueror; "I know not what you call a few, my gallant and ancient friend; you may possibly have shot at each other by the week in the days of Wolfe, and Abercrombie, and Braddock, but I too have seen smart firing, and can hazard an opinion in such matters. There was as pretty a roll made by fire-arms at the battles on the Hudson, as ever rattled from a drum; it is all over, and many live to talk of it; but this has been the most desperate affair, for the numbers, I ever was engaged in! I speak always with a reference to the numbers. The wood is pretty well sprinkled with dead, and we have contrived to bring off a few of the desperately wounded with us, as you may perceive."

"Bless me!" exclaimed the surprised veteran, "that such an engagement should happen within musket shot of the Abbey, and I know so little of it! My faculties are on the wane, I fear, for the time has been when a single discharge would rouse me from the deepest sleep."

"The bayonet is a silent weapon," returned the composed captain, with a significant wave of his hand; "'tis the Englishman's pride, and every experienced officer knows, that one thrust from it is worth the fire of a whole platoon."

"What, did ye come to the charge!" cried the Colonel; "by the Lord, Borroughcliffe, my gallant young friend, I would have given twenty tierces of rice, and two able-bodied negroes, to have seen the fray!"

"It would have been a pleasant spectacle to witness sans disputation," returned the captain; "but victory is ours without the presence of Achilles, this time. I have them, all that survive the affair; at least, all that have put foot on English soil."

"Ay! and the king's cutter has brought in the schooner!" added Colonel Howard. — "Thus perish all rebellion for evermore! Where's Kit? my kinsman Mr. Christopher Dillon? I would ask him what the laws of the realm next prescribe to loyal subjects. Here will be work for the jurors of Middlesex, Captain Borroughcliffe, if not for a secretary of state's warrant. Where is Kit, my kinsman; the ductile, the sagacious, the loyal Christopher?"

"The Cacique 'non est,' as more than one bailiff has said of sundry clever fellows in our regiment, when there has been a pressing occasion for their appearance," said the soldier; "but the cornet of horse has given me reason to believe that his provincial lordship, who repaired on board the cutter to give intelligence of the position of the enemy, continued there to share the dangers and honours of naval combat."

"Ay, 'tis like him!" cried the colonel, rubbing his hands with glee; "'tis like him! he has forgotten the law and his peaceful occupations, at the sounds of military preparation, and has carried the head of a statesman into the fight, with the ardour and thoughtlessness of a boy."

"The Cacique is a man of discretion," observed the captain, with all his usual dryness of manner, "and will doubtless recollect his obligations to posterity and himself, though he be found entangled in the mazes of a combat. But I marvel that he does not return, for some time has now elapsed since the schooner struck her flag, as my own eyes have witnessed."

"You will pardon me, gentlemen," said Griffith, advancing towards them with uncontrollable interest; "but I have unavoidably heard part of your discourse, and cannot think you will find it necessary to withhold the whole truth from a disarmed captive; say you that a schooner has been captured this morning?"

"It is assuredly true," said Borroughcliffe, with a display of nature and delicacy in his manner that did his heart infinite credit; "but I forbore to tell you, because I thought your own misfortunes would be enough for one time. Mr. Griffith, this gentleman is Colonel Howard, to whose hospitality you will be indebted for some favours before we separate."

"Griffith!" echoed the colonel, in quick reply, "Griffith! what a sight for my old eyes to witness! — the child of worthy, gallant, loyal Hugh Griffith a captive, and taken in arms against his prince! Young man, young man, what would thy honest father, what would his bosom friend, my own poor brother Harry, have said, had it pleased God that they had survived to witness this burning shame and lasting stigma on thy respectable name?"

"Had my father lived, he would now have been upholding the independence of his native land," said the young man, proudly; "I wish to respect even the prejudices of Colonel Howard, and beg he will forbear urging a subject on which I fear we never shall agree."

"Never, while thou art to be found in the ranks of rebellion!" cried the Colonel. "Oh! boy, boy! how I could have loved and cherished thee, if the skill and knowledge obtained in the service of thy Prince, were now devoted to the maintenance of his unalienable rights! I loved thy father, worthy Hugh, even as I loved my own brother Harry."

"And his son should still be dear to you," interrupted Griffith, taking the reluctant hand of the Colonel into both his own.

"Ah! Edward, Edward!" continued the softened veteran, "how many of my day-dreams have been destroyed by thy perversity! nay, I know not that Kit, discreet and loyal as he is, could have found such favour in my eyes as thyself; there is a cast of thy father, in that face and smile, Ned, that might have won me to any thing short of treason—and then Cicily, provoking, tender, mutinous, kind, affectionate, good Cicily, would have been a link to unite us for ever."

The youth cast a hasty glance at the deliberate Borroughcliffe, who, if he had obeyed the impatient expression of his eye, would have followed the party that was slowly bearing the wounded towards the Abbey, before he yielded to his feelings, and answered—

"Nay, sir; let this then be the termination of our misunderstanding—your lovely niece shall be that link, and you shall be to me as your friend Hugh would have been had he lived, and to Cecilia twice a parent."

"Boy, boy," said the veteran, averting his face to conceal the working of his muscles, "you talk idly; my word is now plighted to my kinsman, Kit, and thy scheme is impracticable."

"Nothing is impracticable, sir, to youth and enterprise, when aided by age and experience like yours," returned Griffith; "this war must soon terminate."

"This war!" echoed the Colonel, shaking loose the grasp which Griffith held on his arm; "ay! what of this war, young man? Is it not an accursed attempt to deny the rights of our gracious sovereign, and to place tyrants, reared in kennels, on the throne of princes! a scheme to elevate the wicked at the expense of the good! a project to aid unrighteous ambition, under the mask of sacred liberty and the popular cry of equality! as if there could be liberty without order! or equality of rights, where the privileges of the sovereign are not as sacred as those of the people!"

"You judge us harshly, Colonel Howard," said Griffith—

"I judge you!" interrupted the old soldier, who, by this time, thought the youth resembled any one rather than his friend Hugh; "it is not my province to judge you at all; if it were! but the time will come, the time will come. I am a patient man, and can wait the course of things; yes, yes, age cools the blood, and we learn to suppress the passions and impatience of youth; but if the ministry would issue a commission of justice for the colonies, and put the name of old George Howard in it, I am a dog, if there should be a rebel alive in twelve months. Sir," turning sternly to Borroughcliffe, "in such a cause, I could prove a Roman, and hang—hang! yes, I do think, sir, I could hang my kinsman, Mister Christopher Dillon!"

"Spare the Cacique such an unnatural elevation, before his time," returned the captain, with a grave wave of the hand; "behold," pointing towards the wood, "there is a more befitting subject for the gallows! Mr. Griffith, yonder man calls himself your comrade?"

The eyes of Colonel Howard and Griffith followed the direction of his finger, and the latter instantly recognized the Pilot, standing in the skirts of the wood, with his arms folded, apparently surveying the condition of his friends.

"That man," said Griffith, in confusion, and hesitating to utter even the equivocal truth that suggested itself, "that man does not belong to our ship's company."

"And yet he has been seen in *your* company," returned the incredulous Borroughcliffe; "he was the spokesman in last night's examination, Col. Howard, and, doubtless, commands the rear guard of the rebels."

"You say true," cried the veteran; "Pompey! Caesar! present! fire!"

The blacks started at the sudden orders of their master, of whom they stood in the deepest awe, and, presenting their muskets, they averted their faces, and shutting their eyes, obeyed the bloody mandate.

"Charge!" shouted the Colonel, flourishing the ancient sword, with which he had armed himself, and pressing forward with all the activity that a recent fit of the gout would allow; "charge, and exterminate the dogs with the bayonet! push on, Pompey—dress, boys, dress."

"If your friend stand this charge," said Borroughcliffe to Griffith, with unmoved composure, "his nerves are made of iron; such a charge would break the Coldstreams, with Pompey in the ranks!"

"I trust in God," cried Griffith, "he will have forbearance enough to respect the weakness of Colonel Howard!—he presents a pistol!"

"But he will not fire; the Romans deem it prudent to halt; nay, by heaven, they counter-march to the rear. Holla! Colonel Howard, my worthy host, fall back on your reinforcements; the wood is full of armed men; they cannot escape us; I only wait for the horse to cut off the retreat."

The veteran, who had advanced within a short distance of the single man, who thus deliberately awaited the attack, halted at this summons, and, by a glance of his eye, ascertained that he stood alone. Believing the words of Borroughcliffe to be true, he slowly retired, keeping his face manfully towards his enemy, until he gained the support of the captain.

"Recall the troops, Borroughcliffe!" he cried, "and let us charge into the wood; they will fly before his majesty's arms like guilty scoundrels, as they are. As for the negroes, I'll teach the black rascals to desert their master at such a moment. They say Fear is pale, but d——e, Borroughcliffe, if I do not believe his skin is black."

"I have seen him of all colours; blue, white, black, and party-coloured," said the captain; "I must take the command of matters on myself, however, my excellent host; let us retire into the Abbey, and trust me to cut off the remainder of the rebels."

In this arrangement, the colonel reluctantly acquiesced, and the three followed the soldier to the dwelling, at a pace that was adapted to the infirmities of its master. The excitement of the onset, and the current of his ideas, had united, however, to banish every amicable thought from the breast of the Colonel, and he entered the Abbey with a resolute determination of seeing justice dealt to Griffith and his companions, even though it should push them to the foot of the gallows.

As the gentlemen disappeared from his view, among the shrubbery of the grounds, the Pilot replaced the weapon that was hanging from his hand, in his bosom, and, turning with a saddened and thoughtful brow, he slowly re-entered the wood.

Chapter XXI.

—"When these prodigies
Do so conjointly meet, let not men say,
These are their reasons, — They are natural;
For, I believe they are portentous things
Unto the climate that they point upon."
Julius Caesar, I.iii.28–32.

THE reader will discover, by referring to the time consumed in the foregoing events, that the Ariel, with her prize, did not anchor in the bay, already mentioned, until Griffith and his party, had been for several hours in the custody of their enemies. The supposed capture of the rebel schooner, was an incident that excited but little interest, and no surprise, among a people who were accustomed to consider their seamen as invincible; and Barnstable had not found it a difficult task to practise his deception on the few rustics whom curiosity induced to venture alongside the vessels during the short continuance of daylight. When, however, the fogs of evening began to rise along the narrow basin, and the curvatures of its margin were lost in the single outline of its dark and gloomy border, the young seaman thought it time to apply himself in earnest to his duty. The Alacrity, containing all his own crew, together with the Ariel's wounded, was gotten silently under way, and driving easily before the heavy air that swept from the land, she drifted from the harbour, until the open sea lay before her, when her sails were spread, and she continued to make the best of her way in quest of the frigate. Barnstable had watched this movement with breathless anxiety, for on an eminence that completely commanded the waters to some distance, a small but rude battery had been erected for the purpose of protecting the harbour against the depredations and insults of the smaller vessels of the enemy; and a guard of sufficient force to manage the two heavy guns it contained, was maintained in the work, at all times. He was ignorant how far his stratagem had been successful, and it was only when he heard the fluttering of the Alacrity's canvass, as she opened it to the breeze, that he felt he was, yet, secure.

"'Twill reach the Englishmen's ears," said the boy Merry, who stood on the forecastle of the schooner, by the side of his commander, listening with breathless interest to the sounds; "they set a sentinel on the point, as the sun went down, and if he is a trifle better than a dead man, or a marine asleep, he will suspect something is wrong."

"Never!" returned Barnstable, with a long breath, that announced all his apprehensions were removed; "he will be more likely to believe it a mermaid, fanning herself this cool evening, than to suspect the real fact. What say you, Master Coffin? will the soldier smell the truth?"

"They're a dumb race," said the cockswain, casting his eyes over his shoulders, to ascertain that none of their own marine guard was near him; "now, there was our sargeant, who ought to know something, seeing that he has been afloat these four years, maintained, dead in the face and eyes of what every man, who has ever doubled Good Hope, knows to be true, that there was no such vessel to be fallen in with in them seas, as the Flying Dutchman! and then, again, when I told him that he was a 'know-nothing,' and asked him if the Dutchman was a more unlikely thing, than that there should be places where the inhabitants split the year into two watches, and had day for six months, and night the rest of the time, the greenhorn laughed in my face, and I do believe he would have told me I lied, but for one thing."

"And what might that be?" asked Barnstable, gravely.

"Why, sir," returned Tom, stretching his bony fingers, as he surveyed his broad palm, by the little light that remained, "though I am a peaceable man, I can be roused."

"And you have seen the Flying Dutchman?"

"I never doubled the east cape; though I can find my way through Le Maire in the darkest night that ever fell from the heavens; but I have seen them that have seen her, and spoken her too."

"Well, be it so; you must turn flying Yankee, yourself, tonight, Master Coffin. Man your boat at once, sir, and arm your crew."

The cockswain paused a moment, before he proceeded to obey this unexpected order, and, pointing towards the battery, he inquired, with infinite phlegm—

"For shore-work, sir? Shall we take the cutlashes and pistols? or shall we want the pikes?"

"There may be soldiers in our way, with their bayonets," said Barnstable, musing; "arm as usual, but throw a few long pikes into the boat, and harkye, Master Coffin, out with your tub and whale-line; for I see you have rigged yourself anew in that way."

The cockswain, who was moving from the forecastle, turned short at this new mandate, and, with an air of remonstrance, ventured to say—

"Trust an old whaler, Captain Barnstable, who has been used to these craft all his life. A whale-boat is made to pull with a tub and line in it, as naturally as a ship is made to sail with ballast, and—"

"Out with it, out with it," interrupted the other, with an impatient gesture, that his cockswain knew signified a positive determination. Heaving a sigh at what he deemed his commander's prejudice, Tom applied himself, without farther delay, to the execution of the orders. Barnstable laid his hand familiarly on the shoulder of the boy, and led him to the stern of his little vessel, in profound silence. The canvass hood that covered the entrance to the cabin was thrown partly aside; and by the light of the lamp that was burning in the small apartment, it was easy to overlook, from the deck, what was passing beneath them. Dillon sat supporting his head with his two hands, in a manner that shaded his face, but in an attitude that denoted deep and abstracted musing.

"I would that I could see the face of my prisoner," said Barnstable, in an under tone, that was audible only to his companion. "The eye of a man is a sort of light-house, to tell one how to steer into the haven of his confidence, boy."

"And sometimes a beacon, sir, to warn you, there is no safe anchorage near him," returned the ready boy.

"Rogue!" muttered Barnstable, "your cousin Kate spoke there."

"If my cousin Plowden were here, Mr. Barnstable, I know

that her opinion of yon gentleman would not be at all more favourable."

"And yet, I have determined to trust him! Listen, boy, and tell me if I am wrong; you have a quick wit, like some others of your family, and may suggest something advantageous." The gratified midshipman swelled with the conscious pleasure of possessing his commander's confidence, and followed to the taffrail, over which Barnstable leaned, while he delivered the remainder of his communication. "I have gathered from the 'long-shore-men who have come off, this evening, to stare at the vessel which the rebels have been able to build, that a party of seamen and marines have been captured in an old ruin near the Abbey of St. Ruth, this very day."

"'Tis Mr. Griffith!" exclaimed the boy.

"Ay! the wit of your cousin Katherine was not necessary to discover that. Now, I have proposed to this gentleman with the Savannah face, that he should go into the Abbey, and negotiate an exchange. I will give him for Griffith, and the crew of the Alacrity for Manual's command and the Tigers."

"The Tigers!" cried the lad, with emotion; "have they got my Tigers, too! would to God that Mr. Griffith had permitted me to land!"

"It was no boy's work they were about, and room was scarcer in their boat than live-lumber. But this Mr. Dillon has accepted my proposition, and has pledged himself that Griffith shall return within an hour after he is permitted to enter the Abbey: will he redeem his honour from the pledge?"

"He may," said Merry, musing a moment, "for I believe he thinks the presence of Mr. Griffith under the same roof with Miss Howard, a thing to be prevented, if possible; he may be true in this instance, though he has a hollow look."

"He has bad-looking light-houses, I will own," said Barnstable; "and yet he is a gentleman, and promises fair; 'tis unmanly to suspect him in such a matter, and I will have faith! Now listen, sir. The absence of older heads must throw great responsibility on your young shoulders; watch that battery as closely as if you were at the mast-head of your frigate, on the look-out for an enemy; the instant you see lights moving in it, cut, and run into the offing; you will find me somewhere under the cliffs, and you will stand off and on, keeping the Abbey in sight, until you fall in with us."

Merry gave an attentive ear to these and divers other solemn injunctions that he received from his commander, who, having sent the officer next to himself in authority in charge of the prize, (the third in command being included in the list of the wounded,) was compelled to intrust his beloved schooner to the vigilance of a lad whose years gave no promise of the experience and skill that he actually possessed.

When his admonitory instructions were ended, Barnstable stepped again to the opening in the cabin-hood, and for a single moment before he spoke, once more examined the countenance of his prisoner, with a keen eye. Dillon had removed his hands from before his sallow features, and, as if conscious of the scrutiny his looks were to undergo, had concentrated the whole expression of his forbidding aspect in a settled gaze of hopeless submission to his fate. At least, so thought his captor, and the idea touched some of the finer feelings in the bosom of the generous young seaman. Discarding, instantly, every suspicion of his prisoner's honour, as alike unworthy of them both, Barnstable summoned him, in a cheerful voice, to the boat. There was a flashing of the features of Dillon, at this call, which gave an indefinable expression to his countenance, that again startled the sailor; but it was so very transient, and could so easily be mistaken for a smile of pleasure at his promised liberation, that the doubts it engendered passed away almost as speedily as the equivocal expression itself. Barnstable was in the act of following his companion into the boat, when he felt himself detained by a slight hold of his arm.

"What would you have?" he asked of the midshipman, who had given him the signal.

"Do not trust too much to that Dillon, sir," returned the anxious boy, in a whisper; "if you had seen his face, as I did, when the binnacle light fell upon it, as he came up the cabin ladder, you would put no faith in him."

"I should have seen no beauty," said the generous lieutenant, laughing; "but, there is long-Tom, as hard-featured a youth of two score and ten as ever washed in brine, who has a heart as big, ay, bigger than that of a kraaken. A bright watch to you, boy, and remember, a keen eye on the battery." As he was yet speaking, Barnstable crossed the gunwale of his little vessel, and it was not until he was seated by the side of his prisoner, that he continued, aloud—"Cast the stops off your sails, Mr. Merry, and see all clear, to make a run of every thing; recollect, you are short-handed, sir. God bless ye! and d'ye hear? if there is a man among you who shuts more than one eye at a time, I'll make him, when I get back, open both wider than if Tom Coffin's friend, the Flying Dutchman, was booming down upon him. God bless ye, Merry, my boy; give 'em the square-sail, if this breeze off-shore holds on till morning; shove off."

As Barnstable gave the last order, he fell back on his seat, and, drawing his boat-cloak around him, maintained a profound silence, until they had passed the two small headlands that formed the mouth of the harbour. The men pulled, with muffled oars, their long, vigorous strokes, and the boat glided, with amazing rapidity, past the objects that could be yet indistinctly seen along the dim shore. When, however, they had gained the open ocean, and the direction of their little bark was changed to one that led them in a line with the coast, and within the shadows of the cliffs, the cockswain, deeming that the silence was no longer necessary to their safety, ventured to break it, as follows—

"A square-sail is a good sail to carry on a craft, dead afore it, and in a heavy sea; but if fifty years can teach a man to know the weather, it's my judgment that should the Ariel break ground after the night turns at eight bells, she'll need her main-sail to hold her up to her course."

The lieutenant started at this sudden interruption, and casting his cloak from his shoulders, he looked abroad on the waters, as if seeking those portentous omens which disturbed the imagination of his cockswain.

"How now, Tom," he said, sharply, "have ye turned croaker in your old age? what see you, to cause such an old woman's ditty!"

"'Tis no song of an old woman," returned the cockswain, with solemn earnestness, "but the warning of an old man; and one who has spent his days where there were no hills to prevent the winds of heaven from blowing on him, unless they were hills of salt water and foam. I judge, sir, there'll be a heavy north-easter setting in upon us afore the morning watch is called."

Barnstable knew the experience of his old messmate too well, not to feel uneasiness at such an opinion, delivered in so confident a manner; but after again surveying the horizon, the heavens, and the ocean, he said, with a continued severity of manner—

"Your prophecy is idle, this time, Master Coffin; every thing looks like a dead calm. This swell is what is left from the last blow; the mist over-head is nothing but the nightly fog, and you can see, with your own eyes, that it is driving seaward; even this land-breeze is nothing but the air of the ground mixing with that of the ocean; it is heavy with dew and fog, but it's as sluggish as a Dutch galliot."

"Ay, sir, it is damp, and there is little of it," rejoined Tom; "but as it comes only from the shore, so it never goes far on the water. It is hard to learn the true signs of the weather, Captain Barnstable, and none get to know them well, but such as study little else, or feel but little else. There is only One who can see the winds of heaven, or who can tell when a hurricane is to begin, or where it will end. Still, a man isn't like a whale or a porpoise, that takes the air in his nostrils, but never knows whether it is a south-easter or a north-wester that he feeds upon. Look, broad-off to leeward, sir; see the streak of clear sky shining under the mists; take an old sea-faring man's word for it, Captain Barnstable, that whenever the light shines out of the heavens in that fashion, 'tis never done for nothing; besides, the sun set in a dark bank of clouds, and the little moon we had was dry and windy."

Barnstable listened attentively, and with increasing concern, for he well knew that his cockswain possessed a quick and almost unerring judgment of the weather, notwithstanding the confused medley of superstitious omens and signs with which it was blended; but, again throwing himself back in his boat, he muttered—

"Then let it blow; Griffith is worth a heavier risk, and if the battery can't be cheated, it can be carried."

Nothing further passed on the state of the weather. Dillon

had not ventured a single remark since he entered the boat, and the cockswain had the discretion to understand that his officer was willing to be left to his own thoughts. For near an hour they pursued their way with diligence, the sinewy seamen, who wielded the oars, urging their light boat along the edge of the surf with unabated velocity, and, apparently, with untired exertions. Occasionally, Barnstable would cast an inquiring glance at the little inlets that they passed, or would note, with a seaman's eye, the small portions of sandy beach that were scattered here and there along the rocky boundaries of the coast. One, in particular, a deeper inlet than common, where a run of fresh water was heard gurgling as it met the tide, he pointed out to his cockswain, by significant, but silent gestures, as a place to be especially noted. Tom, who understood the signal as intended for his own eye alone, made his observations on the spot, with equal taciturnity, but with all the minuteness that would distinguish one long accustomed to find his way, whether by land or water, by land-marks, and the bearings of different objects. Soon after this silent communication between the lieutenant and his cockswain, the boat was suddenly turned, and was in the act of dashing upon the spit of sand before it, when Barnstable checked the movement by his voice—

"Hold water!" he said; "'tis the sound of oars!"

The seamen held their boat at rest, while a deep attention was given to the noise that had alarmed the ears of their commander.

"See, sir," said the cockswain, pointing towards the eastern horizon; "it is just rising into the streak of light to seaward of us—now it settles in the trough—ah! here you have it again!"

"By heavens!" cried Barnstable, "'tis a man-of-war's stroke it pulls; I saw the oar-blades as they fell! and, listen to the sound! neither your fisherman nor your smuggler pulls such a regular oar."

Tom had bowed his head nearly to the water, in the act of listening, and now, raising himself, he spoke with confidence—

"That is the Tiger; I know the stroke of her crew as well as I do of my own. Mr. Merry has made them learn the new-fashioned jerk, as they dip their blades, and they feather with such a roll in their rullocks! I could swear to the stroke."

"Hand me the night-glass," said his commander, impatiently; "I can catch them, as they are lifted into the streak. You are right, by every star in our flag, Tom! — but there is only one man in her stern-sheets. By my good eyes, I believe it is that accursed Pilot, sneaking from the land, and leaving Griffith and Manual to die in English prisons. To shore with you — beach her at once."

The order was no sooner given, than it was obeyed, and in less than two minutes, the impatient Barnstable, Dillon, and the cockswain, were standing together on the sands.

The impression he had received, that his friends were abandoned to their fate by the Pilot, urged the generous young seaman to hasten the departure of his prisoner, as he was fearful every moment might interpose some new obstacle to the success of his plans.

"Mr. Dillon," he said, the instant they were landed, "I exact no new promise — your honour is already plighted" —

"If oaths can make it stronger," interrupted Dillon, "I will take them."

"Oaths cannot — the honour of a gentleman is, at all times, enough. I shall send my cockswain with you to the Abbey, and you will either return with him, in person, within two hours, or give Mr. Griffith and Captain Manual to his guidance. Proceed, sir; you are conditionally free; there is an easy opening by which to ascend the cliffs."

Dillon, once more, thanked his generous captor, and then proceeded to force his way up the rough eminence.

"Follow, and obey his instructions," said Barnstable to his cockswain, aloud.

Tom, long accustomed to implicit obedience, handled his harpoon, and was quietly following in the footsteps of his new leader, when he felt the hand of the lieutenant on his shoulder.

"You saw where the brook emptied over the hillock of sand?" said Barnstable, in an under tone.

Tom nodded assent.

"You will find us there, riding without the surf — 'twill not do to trust too much to an enemy."

The cockswain made a gesture of great significance with his weapon, that was intended to indicate the danger their prisoner would incur, should he prove false; when, applying the wooden end of the harpoon to the rocks, he ascended the ravine at a rate that soon brought him to the side of his companion.

Chapter XXII.

"Ay, marry, let me have him to sit under
He's like to be a cold soldier."

2 Henry IV, III.ii.122–123.

BARNSTABLE lingered on the sands for a few minutes, until the footsteps of Dillon and the cockswain were no longer audible, when he ordered his men to launch their boat once more into the surf. While the seamen pulled leisurely towards the place he had designated, as the point where he would await the return of Tom, the lieutenant first began to entertain serious apprehensions concerning the good faith of his prisoner. Now, that Dillon was beyond his control, his imagination presented, in very vivid colours, several little circumstances in the other's conduct, which might readily excuse some doubts of his good faith, and, by the time they had reached the place of rendezvous, and had cast a light grapnel into the sea, his fears had rendered him excessively uncomfortable. Leaving the lieutenant to his reflections, on this unpleasant subject, we shall follow Dillon and his fearless and unsuspecting companion, in their progress towards St. Ruth.

The mists, to which Tom had alluded, in his discussion with his commander, on the state of the weather, appeared to be settling nearer to the earth, and assuming, more decidedly, the appearance of a fog, hanging above them, in sluggish volumes, but little agitated by the air. The consequent obscurity added deeply to the gloom of the night, and it would have been difficult for one, less acquainted than Dillon with the surrounding localities, to find the path which led to the dwelling of Colonel Howard. After some little search, this desirable object was effected, and the civilian led the way, with rapid strides, towards the Abbey.

"Ay, ay!" said Tom, who followed his steps, and equalled his paces, without any apparent effort, "you shore-people have an easy way to find your course and distance, when you get into the track. I was once left by the craft I belonged to, in Boston, to find my way to Plymouth, which is a matter of fifteen leagues, or thereaway; and, so finding nothing was bound up the bay, after lying-by for a week, I concluded to haul aboard my land-tacks. I spent the better part of another week in a search for some hooker, on board which I might work my passage across the country, for money was as scarce then with old Tom Coffin as it is now, and is likely to be, unless the fisheries get a good luff soon; but it seems that nothing but your horse-flesh, and horned cattle, and jack-asses, are privileged to do the pulling and hauling in your shore-hookers; and I was forced to pay a week's wages for a birth, besides keeping a banyan on a mouthful of bread and cheese, from the time we hove-up in Boston, 'till we came-to in Plymouth town."

"It was certainly an unreasonable exaction, on the part of the waggoners, from a man in your situation," said Dillon, in a friendly, soothing tone of voice, that denoted a willingness to pursue the conversation.

"My situation was that of a cabin passenger," returned the cockswain; "for there was but one hand forward, beside the cattle I mentioned—that was he who steered—and an easy birth he had of it; for there his course lay a-tween walls of stone, and fences; and, as for his reckoning, why, they had stuck up bits of stone on-end, with his day's work footed up, ready to his hand, every half league or so. Besides, the land-marks were so plenty, that a man, with half-an-eye, might steer her, and no fear of getting to leeward."

"You must have found yourself, as it were, in a new world," observed Dillon.

"Why, to me, it was pretty much the same as if I had been set afloat in a strange country, though I may be said to be a native of those parts, being born on the coast. I had often heard shore-men say, that there was as much 'arth as water in the world, which I always set down as a rank lie, for I've sailed with a flowing sheet months an-end, without falling in with as much land or rock as would answer a gull to lay its eggs on; but I will own, that a-tween Boston and Plymouth, we were out-of-sight of water for as much as two full watches."

Dillon pursued this interesting subject with great diligence, and, by the time they reached the wall, which enclosed the large paddock that surrounded the Abbey, the cockswain was deeply involved in a discussion of the comparative magnitude of the Atlantic Ocean and the Continent of America.

Avoiding the principal entrance to the building, through the great gates which communicated with the court in front, Dillon followed the windings of the wall until it led them to a wicket, which he knew was seldom closed for the night, until the hour for general rest had arrived. Their way now lay in the rear of the principal edifice, and soon conducted them to the confused pile which contained the offices. The cockswain followed his companion, with a confiding reliance on his knowledge and good faith, that was somewhat increased by the freedom of communication that had been maintained during their walk from the cliffs. He did not perceive any thing extraordinary in the other's stopping at the room, which had been provided as a sort of barracks for the soldiers of Captain Borroughcliffe. A conference which took place between Dillon and the sergeant, was soon ended, when the former beckoned to the cockswain to follow, and, taking a circuit round the whole of the offices, they entered the Abbey together, by the door through which the ladies had issued, when in quest of the three prisoners, as has been already related. After a turn or two among the narrow passages of that part of the edifice, Tom, whose faith in the facilities of land navigation began to be a little shaken, found himself following his guide through a long, dark gallery, that was terminated at the end toward which they were approaching, by a half-open door, that admitted a glimpse into a well-lighted and comfortable apartment. To this door, Dillon hastily advanced, and, throwing it open, the cockswain enjoyed a full view of the very scene that we described, in introducing Col. Howard to the acquaintance of the reader, and under circumstances of great similitude. The cheerful fire of coal, the strong and glaring lights, the tables of polished mahogany, and the blushing fluids, were still the same in appearance, while the only perceptible change was in the number of those, who partook of the cheer. The master of the mansion, and Borroughcliffe, were seated opposite to each other, employed in discussing the events of the day, and diligently pushing to and fro the glittering vessel, that contained a portion of the generous liquor they both loved so well; a task which each moment rendered lighter.

"If Kit would but return," exclaimed the veteran, whose back was to the opening door, "bringing with him his honest brows encircled, as they will be, or ought to be, with laurel, I should be the happiest old fool, Borroughcliffe, in his majesty's realm of Great Britain!"

The captain, who felt the necessity for the unnatural restraint he had imposed on his thirst, to be removed by the capture of his enemies, pointed towards the door with one hand, while he grasped the sparkling reservoir of the "south side" with the other, and answered —

"Lo! the Cacique himself! his brow inviting the diadem — ha! who have we in his highness' train? By the Lord, sir Cacique, if you travel with a body guard of such grenadiers, old Frederic of Prussia himself will have occasion to envy you the corps! a clear six-footer in nature's stockings! and the arms as unique as the armed!"

The colonel did not, however, attend to half of his companion's exclamations, but turning, he beheld the individual he had so much desired, and received him with a delight proportioned to the unexpectedness of the pleasure. For several minutes, Dillon was compelled to listen to the rapid questions of his venerable relative, to all of which he answered with a prudent reserve, that might, in some measure, have been governed by the presence of the cockswain. Tom stood with infinite composure, leaning on his harpoon, and surveying, with a countenance where wonder was singularly blended with contempt, the furniture and arrangements of an apartment that was far more splendid than any he had before seen. In the mean time, Borroughcliffe entirely disregarded the private communications that passed between his host and Dillon, which gradually became more deeply interesting, and finally drew them to a distant corner of the apartment, but taking a most undue advantage of the absence of the gentleman, who had so lately been his boon companion, he swallowed one potation after another, as if a double duty had devolved on him, in consequence of the desertion of the veteran. Whenever his eye did wander from the ruby tints of his glass, it was to survey, with unrepressed admiration, the inches of the cockswain, about whose stature and frame there were numberless excellent points to attract the gaze of a recruiting officer. From this double pleasure, the captain was, however, at last summoned, to participate in the councils of his friends.

Dillon was spared the disgreeable duty of repeating the artful tale he had found it necessary to palm on the colonel, by the ardour of the veteran himself, who executed the task in a manner that gave to the treachery of his kinsman every appearance of a justifiable artifice and of unshaken zeal in the cause of his prince. In substance, Tom was to be detained as a prisoner, and the party of Barnstable were to be entrapped, and of course to share a similar fate. The sunken eye of Dillon cowered before the steady gaze which Borroughcliffe fastened on him, as the latter listened to the plaudits the colonel lavished on his cousin's ingenuity; but the hesitation that lingered in the soldier's manner vanished, when he turned to examine their unsuspecting prisoner, who was continuing his survey of the apartment, while he innocently imagined the consultations he witnessed were merely the proper and preparatory steps to his admission into the presence of Mr. Griffith.

"Drill," said Borroughcliffe, aloud, "advance and receive your orders." The cockswain turned quickly, at this sudden mandate, and, for the first time, perceived that he had been followed into the gallery by the orderly, and two files of the recruits, armed. "Take this man to the guard-room, and feed him; and see that he dies not of thirst."

There was nothing alarming in this order, and Tom was following the soldiers, in obedience to a gesture from the captain, when their steps were arrested in the gallery, by the cry of "Halt."

"On recollection, Drill," said Borroughcliffe, in a tone from which all dictatorial sounds were banished, "show the gentleman into my own room, and see him properly supplied."

The orderly gave such an intimation of his comprehending the meaning of his officer, as the latter was accustomed to receive, when Borroughcliffe returned to his bottle, and the cockswain followed his guide, with an alacrity and good will that were not a little increased by the repeated mention of the cheer that awaited him.

Luckily for the impatience of Tom, the quarters of the captain were at hand, and the promised entertainment by no means slow in making its appearance. The former was an apartment that opened from a lesser gallery, which communicated with the principal passage already mentioned; and the latter was a bountiful but ungarnished supply of that staple of the British isles, called roast beef; of which the kitchen of Colonel Howard was never without a due and loyal provision. The sergeant, who certainly understood one of the signs of his captain to imply an attack on the citadel of the cockswain's brain, mingled, with his own hands, a potation, that he styled a rummer of grog, and which he thought would have felled the animal itself that Tom was so diligently masticating, had it been alive, and in its vigour. Every calculation that was made on the infirmity of the cockswain's intellect, under the stimulus of Jamaica, was, however, futile. He swallowed glass after glass, with prodigious relish, but, at the same time, with immoveable steadiness; and the eyes of the sergeant, who felt it incumbent to do honour to his own cheer, were already glistening in his head, when, happily for the credit of his art, a tap at the door announced the presence of his captain, and relieved him from the impending disgrace of being drunk blind by a recruit.

As Borroughcliffe entered the apartment, he commanded his orderly to retire, adding—

"Mr. Dillon will give you instructions, which you are implicitly to obey."

Drill, who had sense enough remaining to apprehend the displeasure of his officer, should the latter discover his condition, quickened his departure, and the cockswain soon found himself alone with the captain. The vigour of Tom's attacks on the remnant of the sirloin was now much abated, leaving in its stead that placid quiet which is apt to linger about the palate, long after the cravings of the appetite have been appeased. He had seated himself on one of the trunks of Borroughcliffe, utterly disdaining the use of a chair, and, with the trencher in his lap, was using his own jack-knife on the dilapidated fragment of the ox, with something of that nicety with which the female goule, of the Arabian Tales, might be supposed to pick her rice with the point of her bodkin. The captain drew a seat nigh the cockswain, and, with a familiarity and kindness infinitely condescending, when the difference in their several conditions is considered, he commenced the following dialogue:

"I hope you have found your entertainment to your liking, Mr. a—a—I must own my ignorance of your name."

"Tom," said the cockswain, keeping his eyes roaming over the contents of the trencher; "commonly called long-Tom, by my shipmates."

"You have sailed with discreet men, and able navigators, it would seem, as they understand longitude so well," rejoined the captain; "but you have a patronymick—I would say, another name?"

"Coffin," returned the cockswain; "I'm called Tom, when there is any hurry, such as letting go the haulyards, or a sheet; long-Tom, when they want to get to windward of an old seaman, by fair weather; and long-Tom Coffin, when they wish to hail me, so that none of my cousins of the same name, about the islands, shall answer; for I believe the best man among them can't measure much over a fathom, taking him from his head-works to his heel."

"You are a most deserving fellow," cried Borroughcliffe, "and it is painful to think to what a fate the treachery of Mr. Dillon has consigned you."

The suspicions of Tom, if he ever entertained any, were lulled to rest too effectually by the kindness he had received, to be awakened by this equivocal lament; he, therefore, after renewing his intimacy with the rummer, contented himself by saying, with a satisfied simplicity—

"I am consigned to no one, carrying no cargo but this Mr. Dillon, who is to give me Mr. Griffith in exchange, or go back to the Ariel himself, as my prisoner."

"Ah! my good friend, I fear you will find, when the time comes to make this exchange, that he will refuse to do either."

"But I'll be d——d if he don't do one of them; my orders are to see it done, and back he goes; or Mr. Griffith, who is as good a seaman, for his years, as ever trod a deck, slips his cable from this here anchorage."

Borroughcliffe affected to eye his companion with great commiseration; an exhibition of compassion that was, however, completely lost on the cockswain, whose nerves were strung to their happiest tension, by his repeated libations, while his wit was, if any thing, quickened by the same cause, though his own want of guile rendered him slow to comprehend its existence in others. Perceiving it necessary to speak plainly, the captain renewed the attack in a more direct manner—

"I am sorry to say that you will not be permitted to return to the Ariel, and that your commander, Mr. Barnstable, will be a prisoner within the hour; and in fact, that your schooner will be taken, before the morning breaks."

"Who'll take her?" asked the cockswain, with a grim smile, on whose feelings, however, this combination of threatened calamities was beginning to make some impression.

"You must remember, that she lies immediately under the heavy guns of a battery that can sink her in a few minutes; an express has already been sent to acquaint the commander of the work with the Ariel's true character; and as the wind has already begun to blow from the ocean, her escape is impossible."

The truth, together with its portentous consequences, now began to glare across the faculties of the cockswain. He remembered his own prognostics on the weather, and the helpless situation of the schooner, deprived of more than half her crew, and left to the keeping of a boy, while her commander himself was on the eve of captivity. The trencher fell from his lap to the floor, his head sunk on his knees, his face was concealed between his broad palms, and in spite of every effort the old seaman could make to conceal his emotion, he fairly groaned aloud.

For a moment, the better feelings of Borroughcliffe prevailed, and he paused, as he witnessed this exhibition of suffering in one whose head was already sprinkled with the marks of time; but his habits, and the impressions left by many years passed in collecting victims for the wars, soon resumed their ascendancy, and the recruiting officer diligently addressed himself to an improvement of his advantage.

"I pity, from my heart, the poor lads whom artifice or mistaken notions of duty may have led astray, and who will thus be taken in arms against their sovereign; but, as they are

found in the very island of Britain, they must be made examples to deter others. I fear, that unless they can make their
peace with government, they will all be condemned to death."

"Let them make their peace with God, then; your government can do but little to clear the log-account of a man whose
watch is up for this world."

"But, by making their peace with those who have the power,
their lives may be spared," said the captain, watching, with
keen eyes, the effect his words produced on the cockswain.

"It matters but little when a man hears the messenger pipe
his hammock down for the last time; he keeps his watch in
another world, though he goes below in this. But to see wood
and iron, that has been put together after such moulds as the
Ariel's, go into strange hands, is a blow that a man may
remember long after the purser's books have been squared
against his name for ever. I would rather that twenty shot
should strike my old carcass, than one should hull the schooner
that didn't pass out above her water-line."

Borroughcliffe replied, somewhat carelessly, "I may be
mistaken, after all; and, instead of putting any of you to death,
they may place you all on board the prison-ships, where you
may yet have a merry time of it, these ten or fifteen years to
come."

"How's that, shipmate!" cried the cockswain, with a start; "a
prison-ship, d'ye say? you may tell them they can save the expense of one man's rations, by hanging him, if they please, and
that is old Tom Coffin."

"There is no answering for their caprice; to-day, they may
order a dozen of you shot for rebels; to-morrow they may
choose to consider you as prisoners of war, and send you to the
hulks for a dozen years."

"Tell them, brother, that I'm a rebel, will ye? and ye'll tell
'em no lie—one that has fou't them since Manly's time, in
Boston bay, to this hour. I hope the boy will blow her up! it
would be the death of poor Richard Barnstable, to see her in
the hands of the English!"

"I know of one way," said Borroughcliffe, affecting to muse,
"and but one, that will certainly avert the prison-ship; for, on
second thoughts, they will hardly put you to death."

"Name it, friend," cried the cockswain, rising from his seat in evident perturbation, "and if it lies in the power of man, it shall be done."

"Nay," said the captain, dropping his hand familiarly on the shoulder of the other, who listened with the most eager attention, "'tis easily done, and no dreadful thing in itself; you are used to gun-powder, and know its smell from otto of roses?"

"Ay, ay," cried the impatient old seaman; "I have had it flashing under my nose by the hour; what then?"

"Why, then, what I have to propose will be nothing to a man like you—you found the beef wholesome, and the grog mellow?"

"Ay, ay, all well enough; but what is that to an old sailor?" asked the cockswain, unconsciously grasping the collar of Borroughcliffe's coat, in his agitation; "what then?"

The captain manifested no displeasure at this unexpected familiarity, but smiled, with suavity, as he unmasked the battery, from behind which he had hitherto carried on his attacks.

"Why, then, you have only to serve your King, as you have before served the Congress—and let me be the man to show you your colours."

The cockswain stared at the speaker intently, but it was evident he did not clearly comprehend the nature of the proposition, and the captain pursued the subject—

"In plain English, enlist in my company, my fine fellow, and your life and liberty are both safe."

Tom did not laugh aloud, for that was a burst of feeling in which he was seldom known to indulge, but every feature of his weather-beaten visage contracted into an expression of bitter, ironical contempt. Borroughcliffe felt the iron fingers, that still grasped his collar, gradually tightening about his throat, like a vice, and, as the arm slowly contracted, his body was drawn, by a power that it was in vain to resist, close to that of the cockswain, who, when their faces were within a foot of each other, gave vent to his emotions in words:—

"A messmate, before a shipmate; a shipmate, before a stranger; a stranger, before a dog; but a dog before a soldier!"

As Tom concluded, his nervous arm was suddenly extended

to the utmost, the fingers relinquishing their grasp at the same time, and, when Borroughcliffe recovered his disordered faculties, he found himself in a distant corner of the apartment, prostrate among a confused pile of chairs, tables, and wearing apparel. In endeavouring to rise from this humble posture, the hand of the captain fell on the hilt of his sword, which had been included in the confused assemblage of articles produced by his overthrow.

"How now, scoundrel!" he cried, baring the glittering weapon, and springing on his feet; "you must be taught your distance, I perceive."

The cockswain seized the harpoon which leaned against the wall, and dropped its barbed extremity within a foot of the breast of his assailant, with an expression of the eye that denoted the danger of a nearer approach. The captain, however, wanted not for courage, and, stung to the quick by the insult he had received, he made a desperate parry, and attempted to pass within the point of the novel weapon of his adversary. The slight shock was followed by a sweeping whirl of the harpoon, and Borroughcliffe found himself without arms, completely at the mercy of his foe. The bloody intentions of Tom vanished with his success; for, laying aside his weapon, he advanced upon his antagonist, and seized him with an open palm. One more struggle, in which the captain discovered his incompetency to make any defence against the strength of a man who managed him as if he had been a child, decided the matter. When the captain was passive in the hands of his foe, the cockswain produced sundry pieces of sennit, marline, and ratlin-stuff, from his pockets, which appeared to contain as great a variety of small cordage as a boatswain's store-room, and proceeded to lash the arms of the conquered soldier to the posts of his bed, with a coolness that had not been disturbed since the commencement of hostilities, a silence that seemed inflexible, and a dexterity that none but a seaman could equal. When this part of his plan was executed, Tom paused a moment, and gazed around him as if in quest of something. The naked sword caught his eye, and, with this weapon in his hand, he deliberately approached his captive, whose alarm prevented his observing, that the cockswain had snapped the blade asunder from the handle, and that he had already encircled the latter with marline.

"For God's sake," exclaimed Borroughcliffe, "murder me not in cold blood!"

The silver hilt entered his mouth as the words issued from it, and the captain found, while the line was passed and repassed, in repeated involutions across the back of his neck, that he was in a condition to which he often subjected his own men, when unruly, and which is universally called, being 'gagged.' The cockswain now appeared to think himself entitled to all the privileges of a conqueror; for, taking the light in his hand, he commenced a scrutiny into the nature and quality of the worldly effects that lay at his mercy. Sundry articles, that belonged to the equipments of a soldier, were examined, and cast aside, with great contempt, and divers garments of plainer exterior, were rejected as unsuited to the frame of the victor. He, however, soon encountered two articles, of a metal that is universally understood. But uncertainty as to their use appeared greatly to embarrass him. The circular prongs of these curiosities were applied to either hand, to the wrists, and even to the nose, and the little wheels, at their opposite extremity, were turned and examined with as much curiosity and care, as a savage would expend on a watch, until the idea seemed to cross the mind of the honest seaman, that they formed part of the useless trappings of a military man, and he cast them aside, also, as utterly worthless. Borroughcliffe, who watched every movement of his conqueror, with a good humour that would have restored perfect harmony between them, could he but have expressed half what he felt, witnessed the safety of a favourite pair of spurs, with much pleasure, though nearly suffocated, by the mirth that was unnaturally repressed. At length, the cockswain found a pair of handsomely mounted pistols, a sort of weapon, with which he seemed quite familiar. They were loaded, and the knowledge of that fact appeared to remind Tom of the necessity of departing, by bringing to his recollection the danger of his commander and the Ariel. He thrust the weapons into the canvass belt that encircled his body, and, grasping his harpoon, approached the bed, where Borroughcliffe was seated in duresse.

"Harkye, friend," said the cockswain, "may the Lord forgive you, as I do, for wishing to make a soldier of a sea-faring man, and one who has followed the waters since he was an hour old, and one who hopes to die off soundings, and to be buried in brine. I wish you no harm, friend, but you'll have to keep a stopper on your conversation 'till such time as some of your messmates call in this way, which I hope will be as soon after I get an offing as may be."

With these amicable wishes, the cockswain departed, leaving Borroughcliffe the light, and the undisturbed possession of his apartment, though not in the most easy or the most enviable situation imaginable. The captain heard the bolt of his lock turn, and the key rattle as the cockswain withdrew it from the door—two precautionary steps, which clearly indicated that the vanquisher deemed it prudent to secure his retreat, by insuring the detention of the vanquished, for at least a time.

Chapter XXIII.

"Whilst Vengeance, in the lurid air,
Lifts her red arm, expos'd and bare: —
Who, Fear, this ghastly train can see,
And look not madly wild, like thee?"
                    Collins, "Ode to Fear," ll. 20-21, 24-25.

I T IS certain that Tom Coffin had devised no settled plan of operations, when he issued from the apartment of Borroughcliffe, if we except a most resolute determination to make the best of his way to the Ariel, and to share her fate, let it be either to sink or swim. But this was a resolution much easier formed by the honest seaman, than executed, in his present situation. He would have found it less difficult to extricate a vessel from the dangerous shoals of the "Devil's-Grip," than to thread the mazes of the labyrinth of passages, galleries, and apartments, in which he found himself involved. He remembered, as he expressed it to himself, in a low soliloquy, "to have run into a narrow passage from the main channel, but whether he had sheered to the starboard or larboard hand," was a material fact, that had entirely escaped his memory. Tom was in that part of the building that Colonel Howard had designated as the "cloisters," and in which, luckily for him, he was but little liable to encounter any foe; the room occupied by Borroughcliffe being the only one in the entire wing, that was not exclusively devoted to the service of the ladies. The circumstance of the soldier's being permitted to invade this sanctuary, was owing to the necessity, on the part of Colonel Howard, of placing either Griffith, Manual, or the recruiting officer, in the vicinity of his wards, or of subjecting his prisoners to a treatment that the veteran would have thought unworthy of his name and character. This recent change in the quarters of Borroughcliffe operated doubly to the advantage of Tom, by lessening the chance of the speedy release of his uneasy captive, as well as by diminishing his own danger. Of the former circumstance he was, however, not aware, and the consideration of the latter was a sort of reflection to which the cockswain was, in no degree, addicted.

Following, necessarily, the line of the wall, he soon emerged from the dark and narrow passage in which he had first found himself, and entered the principal gallery, that communicated with all the lower apartments of that wing, as well as with the main body of the edifice. An open door, through which a strong light was glaring, at a distant end of this gallery, instantly caught his eye, and the old seaman had not advanced many steps towards it, before he discovered that he was approaching the very room which had so much excited his curiosity, and by the identical passage through which he had entered the Abbey. To turn, and retrace his steps, was the most obvious course, for any man to take, who felt anxious to escape; but the sounds of high conviviality, bursting from the cheerful apartment, among which the cockswain thought he distinguished the name of Griffith, determined Tom to advance and reconnoitre the scene more closely. The reader will anticipate that when he paused in the shadow, the doubting old seaman stood once more near the threshold which he had so lately crossed, when conducted to the room of Borroughcliffe. The seat of that gentleman was now occupied by Dillon, and Colonel Howard had resumed his wonted station at the foot of the table. The noise was chiefly made by the latter, who had evidently been enjoying a more minute relation of the means by which his kinsman had entrapped his unwary enemy.

"A noble ruse!" cried the veteran, as Tom assumed his post, in ambush; "a most noble and ingenious ruse, and such a one as would have baffled Caesar! he must have been a cunning dog, that Caesar; but I do think, Kit, you would have been too much for him; hang me, if I don't think you would have puzzled Wolfe himself, had you held Quebec, instead of Montcalm! Ah! boy, we want you in the colonies, with the ermine over your shoulders; such men as you, cousin Christopher, are sadly, sadly wanted there to defend his majesty's rights."

"Indeed, dear sir, your partiality gives me credit for qualities I do not possess," said Dillon, dropping his eyes, perhaps with a feeling of conscious unworthiness, but with an air of much humility; "the little justifiable artifice —"

"Ay! there lies the beauty of the transaction," interrupted the colonel, shoving the bottle from him, with the free, open air of a man who never harboured disguise; "you told no lie; no mean deception, that any dog, however base and unworthy, might invent; but you practised a neat, a military, a — a — yes, a classical deception on your enemy; a classical deception, that is the very term for it! such a deception as Pompey, or Mark Antony, or — or — you know those old fellows' names better than I do, Kit; but name the cleverest fellow that ever lived in Greece or Rome, and I shall say he is a dunce, compared to you. 'Twas a real Spartan trick, both simple and honest."

It was extremely fortunate for Dillon, that the animation of his aged kinsman kept his head and body in such constant motion, during this apostrophe, as to intercept the aim that the cockswain was deliberately taking at his head, with one of Borroughcliffe's pistols; and perhaps the sense of shame, which induced him to sink his face on his hands, was another means of saving his life, by giving the indignant old seaman time for reflection.

"But you have not spoken of the ladies," said Dillon, after a moment's pause; "I should hope, they have borne the alarm of the day like kinswomen of the family of Howard."

The colonel glanced his eyes around him, as if to assure himself they were alone, and dropped his voice, as he answered —

"Ah! Kit, they have come to, since this rebel scoundrel, Griffith, has been brought into the Abbey; we were favoured with the company of even Miss Howard, in the dining-room, to-day. There was a good deal of 'dear uncleing,' and 'fears that my life might be exposed by the quarrels and skirmishes of these desperadoes who have landed;' as if an old fellow, who served through the whole war, from '56 to '63, was afraid to let his nose smell gunpowder, any more than if it were snuff! But it will be a hard matter to wheedle an old soldier out of his allegiance! This Griffith goes to the Tower, at least, Mr. Dillon."

"It would be advisable to commit his person to the civil authority, without delay."

"To the constable of the Tower, the Earl Cornwallis, a good and loyal nobleman, who is, at this moment, fighting the rebels in my own native province, Christopher," interrupted the colonel; "that will be what I call retributive justice; but," continued the veteran, rising with an air of gentlemanly dignity, "it will not do to permit even the constable of the Tower of London, to surpass the master of St. Ruth, in hospitality and kindness to his prisoners. I have ordered suitable refreshments to their apartments, and it is incumbent on me to see that my commands have been properly obeyed. Arrangements must also be made for the reception of this Captain Barnstable, who will, doubtless, soon be here."

"Within the hour, at farthest," said Dillon, looking uneasily at his watch.

"We must be stirring, boy," continued the colonel, moving towards the door that led to the apartments of his prisoners; "but there is a courtesy due to the ladies, as well as to those unfortunate violators of the laws—go, Christopher, convey my kindest wishes to Cecilia; she don't deserve them, the obstinate vixen, but then she is my brother Harry's child! and while there, you arch dog, plead your own cause. Mark Antony was a fool to you at a 'ruse,' and yet Mark was one of your successful suitors, too; there was that Queen of the Pyramids—"

The door closed on the excited veteran, at these words, and Dillon was left standing by himself, at the side of the table, musing, as if in doubt, whether to venture on the step that his kinsman had proposed, or not.

The greater part of the preceding discourse was unintelligible to the cockswain, who had waited its termination with extraordinary patience, in hopes he might obtain some information that he could render of service to the captives. Before he had time to decide on what was now best for him to do, Dillon, suddenly, determined to venture himself in the cloisters; and, swallowing a couple of glasses of wine in a breath, he passed the hesitating cockswain, who was concealed by the opening door, so closely as to brush his person, and moved down the gallery with those rapid strides, which men, who act under the impulse of forced resolutions, are very apt to assume, as if to conceal their weakness from themselves. Tom hesitated no longer, but, aiding the impulse given to the door by Dillon as he passed, so as to darken the passage, he followed the sounds of the other's footsteps, while he trod, in the manner already described, the stone pavement of the gallery. Dillon paused an instant at the turning that led to the room of Borroughcliffe, but whether irresolute which way to urge his steps, or listening to the incautious and heavy tread of the cockswain, is not known; if the latter, he mistook them for the echoes of his own footsteps, and moved forward again, without making any discovery.

The light tap which Dillon gave on the door of the withdrawing-room of the cloisters, was answered by the soft voice of Cecilia Howard herself, who bid the applicant enter. There was a slight confusion evident in the manner of the gentleman as he complied with the bidding, and in its hesitancy, the door was, for an instant, neglected.

"I come, Miss Howard," said Dillon, "by the commands of your uncle, and, permit me to add, by my own—"

"May heaven shield us!" exclaimed Cecilia, clasping her hands in affright, and rising involuntarily from her couch; "are we, too, to be imprisoned and murdered?"

"Surely Miss Howard will not impute to me"—Dillon paused, observing that the wild looks, not only of Cecilia, but of Katherine and Alice Dunscombe, also, were directed at some other object, and turning, to his manifest terror, he beheld the gigantic frame of the cockswain, surmounted by an iron visage fixed in settled hostility, in possession of the only passage from the apartment.

"If there's murder to be done," said Tom, after surveying the astonished group with a stern eye, "it's as likely this here liar will be the one to do it, as another; but you have nothing to fear from a man who has followed the seas too long, and has grappled with too many monsters, both fish and flesh, not to know how to treat a helpless woman. None, who know him, will say, that Thomas Coffin ever used uncivil language, or unseaman-like conduct, to any of his mother's kind."

"Coffin!" exclaimed Katherine, advancing with a more confident air, from the corner, into which terror had driven her with her companions.

"Ay, Coffin," continued the old sailor, his grim features gradually relaxing, as he gazed on her bright looks; "'tis a solemn word, but it's a name that passes over the shoals, among the islands, and along the cape, oftener than any other.

My father was a Coffin, and my mother was a Joy; and the two names can count more flukes than all the rest in the island together; though the Worths, and the Gar'ners, and the Swaines, dart better harpoons, and set truer lances, than any men who come from the weather-side of the Atlantic."

Katherine listened to this digression in honour of the whalers of Nantucket, with marked complacency, and, when he concluded, she repeated, slowly—

"Coffin! this, then, is long-Tom!"

"Ay, ay, long-Tom, and no sham in the name either," returned the cockswain, suffering the stern indignation that had lowered around his hard visage, to relax into a low laugh, as he gazed on her animated features; "the Lord bless your smiling face and bright black eyes, young madam; you have heard of old long-Tom, then? most likely, 'twas something about the blow he strikes at the fish—ah! I'm old and I'm stiff, now, young madam, but, afore I was nineteen, I stood at the head of the dance, at a ball on the cape, and that with a part-ner almost as handsome as yourself—ay! and this was after I had three broad flukes logg'd against my name."

"No," said Katherine, advancing in her eagerness a step or two nigher to the old tar, her cheeks flushing while she spoke, "I had heard of you as an instructer in a seaman's duty, as the faithful cockswain, nay, I may say, as the devoted companion and friend of Mr. Richard Barnstable—but, perhaps, you come now as the bearer of some message or letter from that gentleman."

The sound of his commander's name suddenly revived the recollection of Coffin, and with it, all the fierce sternness of his manner returned. Bending his eyes keenly on the cowering form of Dillon, he said, in those deep, harsh tones, that seem peculiar to men, who have braved the elements, until they ap-pear to have imbibed some of their roughest qualities—

"Liar! how now? what brought old Tom Coffin into these shoals and narrow channels? was it a letter? ha! but by the Lord that maketh the winds to blow, and teacheth the lost mariner how to steer over the wide waters, you shall sleep this night, villain, on the planks of the Ariel; and if it be the will of God, that beautiful piece of handicraft is to sink at her moor-ings, like a worthless hulk, ye shall still sleep in her; ay, and a sleep that shall not end, 'till they call all hands, to foot up the days'-work of this life, at the close of man's longest voyage."

The extraordinary vehemence, the language, the attitude of the old seaman, commanding in its energy, and the honest indignation that shone in every look of his keen eyes, together with the nature of the address, and its paralyzing effect on Dillon, who quailed before it like the stricken deer, united to keep the female listeners, for many moments, silent, through amazement. During this brief period, Tom advanced upon his nerveless victim, and lashing his arms together behind his back, he fastened him, by a strong cord, to the broad canvass belt that he constantly wore around his own body, leaving to himself, by this arrangement, the free use of his arms and weapons of offence, while he secured his captive.

"Surely," said Cecilia, recovering her recollection the first of the astonished group, "Mr. Barnstable has not commissioned you to offer this violence to my uncle's kinsman, under the roof of Colonel Howard? — Miss Plowden, your friend has strangely forgotten himself, in this transaction, if this man acts in obedience to his orders!"

"My friend, my cousin Howard," returned Katherine, "would never commission his cockswain, or any one, to do an unworthy deed. Speak, honest sailor; why do you commit this outrage on the worthy Mr. Dillon, Colonel Howard's kinsman, and a cupboard cousin of St. Ruth's Abbey?"

"Nay, Katherine —"

"Nay, Cecilia, be patient, and let the stranger have utterance; he may solve the difficulty altogether."

The cockswain, understanding that an explanation was expected from his lips, addressed himself to the task, with an energy suitable both to the subject and to his own feelings. In a very few words, though a little obscured by his peculiar diction, he made his listeners understand the confidence that Barnstable had reposed in Dillon, and the treachery of the latter. They heard him with increased astonishment, and Cecilia hardly allowed him time to conclude, before she exclaimed —

"And did Colonel Howard, could Colonel Howard listen to this treacherous project?"

"Ay, they spliced it together among them," returned Tom; "though one part of this cruise will turn out but badly."

"Even Borroughcliffe, cold and hardened as he appears to be by habit, would spurn at such dishonour," added Miss Howard.

"But, Mr. Barnstable?" at length Katherine succeeded in saying, when her feelings permitted her utterance, "said you not, that soldiers were in quest of him?"

"Ay, ay, young madam," the cockswain replied, smiling with grim ferocity, "they are in chase, but he has shifted his anchorage; and even if they should find him, his long pikes would make short work of a dozen red-coats. The Lord of tempests and calms have mercy though, on the schooner! Ah! young madam, she is as lovely to the eyes of an old sea-faring man, as any of your kind can be to human nature."

"But why this delay? — away then, honest Tom, and reveal the treachery to your commander; you may not yet be too late — why delay a moment?"

"The ship tarries for want of a pilot — I could carry three fathom over the shoals of Nantucket, the darkest night that ever shut the windows of heaven, but I should be likely to run upon breakers in this navigation. As it was, I was near getting into company that I should have had to fight my way out of."

"If that be all, follow me," cried the ardent Katherine; "I will conduct you to a path that leads to the ocean, without approaching the sentinels."

Until this moment, Dillon had entertained a secret expectation of a rescue, but when he heard this proposal, he felt his blood retreating to his heart, from every part of his agitated frame, and his last hope seemed wrested from him. Raising himself from the abject, shrinking attitude, in which both shame and dread had conspired to keep him, as though he had been fettered to the spot, he approached Cecilia, and cried, in tones of horror —

"Do not, do not consent, Miss Howard, to abandon me to the fury of this man! your uncle, your honourable uncle, even now, applauded and united with me in my enterprise, which is no more than a common artifice in war."

"My uncle would unite, Mr. Dillon, in no project of deliberate treachery, like this," said Cecilia, coldly.

"He did, I swear by—"

"Liar!" interrupted the deep tones of the cockswain.

Dillon shivered with agony and terror, while the sounds of this appalling voice sunk into his inmost soul; but as the gloom of the night, the secret ravines of the cliffs, and the turbulence of the ocean, flashed across his imagination, he again yielded to a dread of the horrors to which he should be exposed, in encountering them at the mercy of his powerful enemy, and he continued his solicitations—

"Hear me, once more hear me—Miss Howard, I beseech you, hear me; am I not of your own blood and country! will you see me abandoned to the wild, merciless, malignant fury of this man, who will transfix me with that—oh! God! if you had but seen the sight I beheld in the Alacrity!—hear me, Miss Howard, for the love you bear your Maker, intercede for me. Mr. Griffith shall be released—"

"Liar!" again interrupted the cockswain.

"What promises he?" asked Cecilia, turning her averted face once more at the miserable captive.

"Nothing at all that will be fulfilled," said Katherine; "follow, honest Tom, and I, at least, will conduct you in good faith."

"Cruel, obdurate Miss Plowden; gentle, kind Miss Alice, you will not refuse to raise your voice in my favour; your heart is not hardened by any imaginary dangers to those you love."

"Nay, address not me," said Alice, bending her meek eyes to the floor; "I trust your life is in no danger, and I pray that he who has the power, will have the mercy, to see you unharmed."

"Away," said Tom, grasping the collar of the helpless Dillon, and rather carrying than leading him into the gallery; "if a sound, one quarter as loud as a young porpoise makes, when he draws his first breath, comes from you, villain, you shall see the sight of the Alacrity over again. My harpoon keeps its edge well, and the old arm can yet drive it to the seizing."

This menace effectually silenced even the hard, perturbed breathings of the captive, who, with his conductor, followed the light steps of Katherine, through some of the secret mazes of the building, until, in a few minutes, they issued through a small door, into the open air. Without pausing to deliberate, Miss Plowden led the cockswain through the grounds, to a different wicket from the one by which he had entered the paddock, and pointing to the path, which might be dimly traced along the faded herbage, she bad God bless him, in a voice that discovered her interest in his safety, and vanished from his sight, like an aerial being.

Tom needed no incentive to his speed, now that his course lay so plainly before him, but, loosening his pistols in his belt, and poising his harpoon, he crossed the fields at a gait that compelled his companion to exert his utmost powers, in the way of walking, to equal. Once or twice, Dillon ventured to utter a word or two, but a stern "silence," from the cockswain, warned him to cease, until, perceiving that they were approaching the cliffs, he made a final effort to obtain his liberty, by hurriedly promising a large bribe. The cockswain made no reply, and the captive was secretly hoping that his scheme was producing its wonted effects, when he unexpectedly felt the keen, cold edge of the barbed iron of the harpoon pressing against his breast, through the opening of his ruffles, and even rasing the skin.

"Liar," said Tom, "another word, and I'll drive it through your heart."

From that moment, Dillon was as silent as the grave. They reached the edge of the cliffs, without encountering the party that had been sent in quest of Barnstable, and at a point near where they had landed. The old seaman paused an instant on the verge of the precipice, and cast his experienced eyes along the wide expanse of water that lay before him. The sea was no longer sleeping, but already in heavy motion, and rolling its surly waves against the base of the rocks on which he stood, scattering their white crests high in foam. The cockswain, after bending his looks along the whole line of the eastern horizon, gave utterance to a low and stifled groan, and then striking the staff of his harpoon violently against the earth, he pursued his way along the very edge of the cliffs, muttering certain dreadful denunciations, which the conscience of his appalled listener did not fail to apply to himself. It appeared to the latter, that his angry and excited leader sought the giddy verge of the precipice with a sort of wanton recklessness, so daring were the steps that he took along its brow, notwithstanding the darkness of the hour, and the violence of the blasts that occasionally rushed by them, leaving behind a kind of reaction, that more than once brought the life of the manacled captive in imminent jeopardy. But it would seem, the wary cockswain had a motive for this, apparently, inconsiderate desperation. When they had made good quite half the distance between the point where Barnstable had landed, and that where he had appointed to meet his cockswain, the sounds of voices were brought indistinctly to their ears, in one of the momentary pauses of the rushing winds, and caused the cockswain to make a dead stand in his progress. He listened intently, for a single minute, when his resolution appeared to be taken. He turned to Dillon, and spoke; though his voice was suppressed and low, it was deep and resolute.

"One word, and you die; over the cliffs. You must take a seaman's ladder; there is footing on the rocks, and crags for your hands. Over the cliff, I bid ye, or I'll cast ye into the sea, as I would a dead enemy."

"Mercy, mercy," implored Dillon; "I could not do it in the day; by this light I shall surely perish."

"Over with ye," said Tom, "or—"

Dillon waited for no more, but descended, with trembling steps, the dangerous precipice that lay before him. He was followed by the cockswain, with a haste that unavoidably dislodged his captive from the trembling stand he had taken on the shelf of a rock, who, to his increased horror, found himself dangling in the air, his body impending over the sullen surf, that was tumbling in, with violence, upon the rocks beneath him. An involuntary shriek burst from Dillon, as he felt his person thrust from the narrow shelf, and his cry sounded amidst the tempest, like the screechings of the spirit of the storm.

"Another such call, and I cut your tow-line, villain," said the determined seaman, "when nothing short of eternity will bring you up."

The sounds of footsteps and voices were now distinctly audible, and presently a party of armed men appeared on the edges of the rocks, directly above them.

"It was a human voice," said one of them, "and like a man in distress."

"It cannot be the men we are sent in search of," returned

Sergeant Drill; "for no watch-word that I ever heard sounded like that cry."

"They say, that such cries are often heard, in storms, along this coast," said a voice, that was uttered with less of military confidence than the two others; "and they are thought to come from drowned seamen."

A feeble laugh arose among the listeners, and one or two forced jokes were made, at the expense of their superstitious comrade; but the scene did not fail to produce its effect on even the most sturdy among the unbelievers in the marvellous; for, after a few more similar remarks, the whole party retired from the cliffs, at a pace that might have been accelerated by the nature of their discourse. The cockswain, who had stood, all this time, firm as the rock which supported him, bearing up not only his own weight, but the person of Dillon also, raised his head above the brow of the precipice, as they withdrew, to reconnoitre, and then drawing up the nearly insensible captive, and placing him in safety on the bank, he followed himself. Not a moment was wasted in unnecessary explanations, but Dillon found himself again urged forward, with the same velocity as before. In a few minutes they gained the desired ravine, down which Tom plunged, with a seaman's nerve, dragging his prisoner after him, and directly they stood where the waves rose to their feet, as they flowed far and foaming across the sands. The cockswain stooped so low as to bring the crests of the billows in a line with the horizon, when he discovered the dark boat playing in the outer edge of the surf.

"What hoa! Ariels there!" shouted Tom, in a voice that the growing tempest carried to the ears of the retreating soldiers, who quickened their footsteps, as they listened to sounds which their fears taught them to believe supernatural.

"Who hails?" cried the well-known voice of Barnstable.

"Once your master, now your servant," answered the cockswain, with a watch-word of his own invention.

"'Tis he," returned the lieutenant; "veer away, boys, veer away. You must wade into the surf."

Tom caught Dillon in his arms, and throwing him, like a cork, across his shoulder, he dashed into the streak of foam that was bearing the boat on its crest, and before his companion had time for remonstrance or entreaty, he found himself once more by the side of Barnstable.

"Who have we here?" asked the lieutenant; "this is not Griffith!"

"Haul out, and weigh your grapnel," said the excited cockswain; "and then, boys, if you love the Ariel, pull while the life and the will is left in you."

Barnstable knew his man, and not another question was asked, until the boat was without the breakers; now skimming the rounded summits of the waves, or settling into the hollows of the seas, but always cutting the waters asunder, as she urged her course, with amazing velocity, towards the haven where the schooner had been left at anchor. Then, in a few, but bitter sentences, the cockswain explained to his commander the treachery of Dillon, and the danger of the schooner.

"The soldiers are slow at a night muster," Tom concluded, "and from what I overheard, the express will have to make a crooked course, to double the head of the bay; so, that but for this north-easter, we might weather upon them yet; but it's a matter that lies altogether in the will of Providence. Pull, my hearties, pull—every thing depends on your oars to-night."

Barnstable listened, in deep silence, to this unexpected narration, which sounded in the ears of Dillon like his funeral knell. At length, the suppressed voice of the lieutenant was heard, also, uttering—

"Wretch! if I should cast you into the sea, as food for the fishes, who could blame me? But if my schooner goes to the bottom, she shall prove your coffin."

Chapter XXIV.

"Had I been any God of power, I would
Have sunk the sea within the earth, ere
It should the good ship so have swallowed."

The Tempest, I.i.10–12.

THE ARMS of Dillon were released from their confinement, by the cockswain, as a measure of humane caution against accidents, when they entered the surf, and the captive now availed himself of the circumstance, to bury his features in the folds of his attire, where he brooded over the events of the last few hours with that mixture of malignant passion and pusillanimous dread of the future, that formed the chief ingredients in his character. From this state of apparent quietude, neither Barnstable nor Tom seemed disposed to rouse him by their remarks, for both were too much engaged with their own gloomy forebodings, to indulge in any unnecessary words. An occasional ejaculation from the former, as if to propitiate the spirit of the storm, as he gazed on the troubled appearance of the elements, or a cheering cry from the latter, to animate his crew, were alone heard amid the sullen roaring of the waters, and the mournful whistling of the winds, that swept heavily across the broad waste of the German ocean. There might have been an hour consumed thus, in a vigorous struggle between the seamen and the growing billows, when the boat doubled the northern headland of the desired haven, and shot, at once, from its boisterous passage along the margin of the breakers, into the placid waters of the sequestered bay. The passing blasts were still heard rushing above the high-lands that surrounded, and, in fact, formed the estuary, but the profound stillness of deep night, pervaded the secret recesses, along the unruffled surface of its waters. The shadows of the hills seemed to have accumulated, like a mass of gloom, in the centre of the basin, and though every eye involuntarily turned to search, it was in vain that the anxious seamen endeavoured to discover their little vessel, through its density. While the boat glided into this quiet scene, Barnstable anxiously observed —

"Every thing is as still as death."

"God send it is not the stillness of death!" ejaculated the cockswain; "here, here," he continued, speaking in a lower tone, as if fearful of being overheard, "here she lies, sir, more to-port; look into the streak of clear sky above the marsh, on the starboard hand of the wood, there; that long black line is her main-top-mast; I know it by the rake; and there is her night-pennant fluttering about that bright star; ay, ay, sir, there go our own stars aloft yet, dancing among the stars in the heavens! God bless her! God bless her! she rides as easy and as quiet as a gull asleep!"

"I believe all in her sleep too," returned his commander; "ha! by heaven, we have arrived in good time; the soldiers are moving!"

The quick eye of Barnstable had detected the glimmering of passing lanterns, as they flitted across the embrasures of the battery, and, at the next moment, the guarded but distinct sounds of an active bustle, on the decks of the schooner, were plainly audible. The lieutenant was rubbing his hands together, with a sort of ecstacy, that probably will not be understood by the great majority of our readers, while long-Tom was actually indulging in a paroxysm of his low, spiritless laughter, as these certain intimations of the safety of the Ariel, and of the vigilance of her crew, were conveyed to their ears; when the whole hull and taper spars of their floating home, became unexpectedly visible, and the sky, the placid basin, and the adjacent hills, were illuminated by a flash as sudden and as vivid as the keenest lightning. Both Barnstable and his cockswain, seemed instinctively to strain their eyes towards the schooner, with an effort to surpass human vision, but ere the rolling reverberations of the report of a heavy piece of ordnance, from the heights, had commenced, the dull, whistling rush of the shot swept over their heads, like the moaning of a hurricane, and was succeeded by the plash of the waters, which was followed, in a breath, by the rattling of the mass of iron, as it bounded with violent fury from rock to rock, shivering and tearing the fragments that lined the margin of the bay.

"A bad aim with the first gun, generally leaves your enemy clean decks," said the cockswain, with his deliberate sort of philosophy; "smoke makes but dim spectacles; besides, the night always grows darkest, as you call off the morning watch."

"That boy is a miracle for his years!" rejoined the delighted lieutenant; "see, Tom, the younker has shifted his birth in the dark, and the Englishmen have fired by the day-range they must have taken, for we left him in a direct line between the battery and yon hommoc! what would have become of us, if that heavy fellow had plunged upon our decks, and gone out below the water-line!"

"We should have sunk into English mud, for eternity, as sure as our metal and kentledge would have taken us down," responded Tom; "such a point-blanker would have torn off a streak of our wales, outboard, and not even left the marines time to say a prayer! tend bow there!"

It is not to be supposed that the crew of the whale-boat continued idle, during this interchange of opinions between the lieutenant and his cockswain; on the contrary, the sight of their vessel acted on them like a charm, and, believing that all necessity for caution was now over, they had expended their utmost strength in efforts, that had already brought them, as the last words of Tom indicated, to the side of the Ariel. Though every nerve of Barnstable was thrilling with the excitement produced, by his feelings passing from a state of the most doubtful apprehension, to that of a revived and almost confident hope of effecting his escape, he assumed the command of his vessel, with all that stern but calm authority, that seamen find it most necessary to exert, in the moments of extremest danger. Any one of the heavy shot that their enemies continued to hurl from their heights into the darkness of the haven, he well knew must prove fatal to them, as it would, unavoidably, pass through the slight fabric of the Ariel, and open a passage to the water, that no means he possessed could remedy. His mandates were, therefore, issued, with a full perception of the critical nature of the emergency, but with that collectedness of manner, and intonation of voice, that were best adapted to enforce a ready and animated obedience.

Under this impulse, the crew of the schooner soon got their anchor freed from the bottom, and, seizing their sweeps, they forced her, by their united efforts, directly in the face of the battery, under that shore, whose summit was now crowned with a canopy of smoke, that every discharge of the ordnance tinged with dim colours, like the faintest tints that are reflected from the clouds toward a setting sun. So long as the seamen were enabled to keep their little bark under the cover of the hill, they were, of course, safe; but Barnstable perceived, as they emerged from its shadow, and were drawing nigh the passage which led into the ocean, that the action of his sweeps would no longer avail them, against the currents of air they encountered, neither would the darkness conceal their movements from his enemy, who had already employed men on the shore to discern the position of the schooner. Throwing off at once, therefore, all appearance of disguise, he gave forth the word to spread the canvass of his vessel, in his ordinary cheerful manner.

"Let them do their worst now, Merry," he added; "we have brought them to a distance that I think will keep their iron above water, and we have no dodge about us, younker!"

"It must be keener marksmen than the militia, or volunteers, or fencibles, or whatever they call themselves, behind yon grass-bank, to frighten the saucy Ariel from the wind," returned the reckless boy; "but why have you brought Jonah aboard us again, sir? look at him, by the light of the cabin lamp; he winks at every gun, as if he expected the shot would hull his own ugly, yellow physiognomy. And what tidings have we, sir, from Mr. Griffith, and the marine?"

"Name him not," said Barnstable, pressing the shoulder on which he lightly leaned, with a convulsive grasp, that caused the boy to yield with pain; "name him not, Merry; I want my temper and my faculties at this moment undisturbed, and thinking of the wretch unfits me for my duty. But, there will come a time! go forward, sir; we feel the wind, and have a narrow passage to work through."

The boy obeyed a mandate which was given in the usual prompt manner of their profession, and which, he well understood, was intended to intimate, that the distance which years and rank had created between them, but which Barnstable often chose to forget while communing with Merry, was now to be resumed. The sails had been loosened and set; and, as the vessel approached the throat of the passage, the gale, which was blowing with increasing violence, began to make a very sensible impression on the light bark. The cockswain, who, in the absence of most of the inferior officers, had been acting, on the forecastle, the part of one who felt, from his years and experience, that he had some right to advise, if not to command, at such a juncture, now walked to the station which his commander had taken, near the helmsman, as if willing to place himself in the way of being seen.

"Well, Master Coffin," said Barnstable, who well understood the propensity his old shipmate had to commune with him, on all important occasions, "what think you of the cruise, now? Those gentlemen on the hill make a great noise, but I have lost even the whistling of their shot; one would think they could see our sails against the broad band of light which is opening to seaward."

"Ay, ay, sir, they see us, and mean to hit us, too, but we are running across their fire, and that with a ten-knot breeze; but when we heave in stays, and get in a line with their guns, we shall see, and, it may be, feel, more of their work than we do now; a thirty-two an't trained as easily as a fowling-piece or a ducking gun."

Barnstable was struck with the truth of this observation, but as there existed an immediate necessity for placing the schooner in the very situation to which the other alluded, he gave his orders at once, and the vessel came about, and ran with her head pointing towards the sea, in as short a time as we have taken to record it.

"There, they have us now, or never," cried the lieutenant, when the evolution was completed; "if we fetch to windward of the northern point, we shall lay out into the offing, and in ten minutes we might laugh at Queen Anne's pocket-piece; which, you know, old boy, sent a ball from Dover to Calais."

"Ay, sir, I've heard of the gun," returned the grave seaman, "and a lively piece it must have been, if the streights were always of the same width they are now. But I see that, Captain Barnstable, which is more dangerous than a dozen of the heaviest cannon that were ever cast, can be at half a league's distance. The water is bubbling through our lee-scuppers, already, sir."

"And what of that? haven't I buried her guns often, and yet kept every spar in her without crack or splinter?"

"Ay, ay, sir, you have done it, and can do it again, where there is sea-room, which is all that a man wants for comfort in this life. But when we are out of these chops, we shall be embayed, with a heavy north-easter setting dead into the bight; it is that which I fear, Captain Barnstable, more than all the powder and ball in the whole island."

"And yet, Tom, the balls are not to be despised, either; those fellows have found out their range, and send their iron within hail, again; we walk pretty fast, Master Coffin, but a thirty-two can out-travel us, with the best wind that ever blew."

Tom threw a cursory glance towards the battery, which had renewed its fire with a spirit that denoted they saw their object, as he answered—

"It is never worth a man's while to strive to dodge a shot, for they are all commissioned to do their work, the same as a ship is commissioned to cruise in certain latitudes; but for the winds and the weather, they are given for a seafaring man to guard against, by making or shortening sail, as the case may be. Now, the headland to the southward stretches full three leagues to windward, and the shoals lie to the north; among which God keep us from ever running this craft again!"

"We will beat her out of the bight, old fellow," cried the lieutenant; "we shall have a leg of three leagues in length to do it in."

"I have known longer legs too short," returned the cockswain, shaking his head; "a tumbling sea, with a lee-tide, on a lee-shore, make a sad lee-way."

The lieutenant was in the act of replying to this saying, with a cheerful laugh, when the whistling of a passing shot was instantly succeeded by the crash of splintered wood, and at the next moment the head of the main-mast, after tottering for an instant in the gale, fell toward the deck, bringing with it the main-sail, and the long line of top-mast, that had been bearing the emblems of America, as the cockswain had expressed it, among the stars of the heavens.

"That was a most unlucky hit!" Barnstable suffered to escape him, in the concern of the moment; but, instantly resuming all his collectedness of manner and voice, he gave his orders to clear the wreck, and secure the fluttering canvass.

The mournful forebodings of Tom seemed to vanish with the appearance of a necessity for his exertions, and he was foremost among the crew in executing the orders of their commander. The loss of all the sail on the main-mast forced the Ariel so much from her course, as to render it difficult to weather the point, that jutted, under her lee, for some distance into the ocean. This desirable object was, however, effected, by the skill of Barnstable, aided by the excellent properties of his vessel; and the schooner, borne down by the power of the gale, from whose fury she had now no protection, passed heavily along the land, heading, as far as possible, from the breakers, while the seamen were engaged in making their preparations to display as much of their main-sail, as the stump of the mast would allow them to spread. The firing from the battery ceased, as the Ariel rounded the little promontory; but Barnstable, whose gaze was now bent intently on the ocean, soon perceived that, as his cockswain had predicted, he had a much more threatening danger to encounter, in the elements. When their damages were repaired, so far as circumstances would permit, the cockswain returned to his wonted station near the lieutenant, and after a momentary pause, during which his eyes roved over the rigging, with a seaman's scrutiny, he resumed the discourse.

"It would have been better for us that the best man in the schooner should have been dubb'd of a limb, by that shot, than that the Ariel should have lost her best leg; a main-sail, close-reefed, may be prudent canvass, as the wind blows, but it holds a poor luff to keep a craft to windward."

"What would you have, Tom Coffin!" retorted his commander; "you see she draws ahead, and off-shore; do you expect a vessel to fly in the very teeth of the gale, or would you have me ware and beach her, at once?"

"I would have nothing, nothing, Captain Barnstable," returned the old seaman, sensibly touched at his commander's displeasure; "you are as able as any man who ever trod a plank to work her into an offing; but, sir, when that soldier-officer told me of the scheme to sink the Ariel at her anchor, there were such feelings come athwart my philosophy as never crossed it afore. I thought I saw her a wrack, as plainly, ay, as plainly as you may see the stump of that mast; and, I will own it, for it's as natural to love the craft you sail in, as it is to love one's self, I will own that my manhood fetched a heavy lee-lurch at the sight."

"Away with ye, ye old sea-croaker! forward with ye, and see that the head-sheets are trimmed flat. But hold! come hither, Tom; if you have sights of wrecks, and sharks, and other beautiful objects, keep them stowed in your own silly brain; don't make a ghost-parlour of my forecastle. The lads begin to look to leeward, now, oftener than I would have them. Go, sirrah, go, and take example from Mr. Merry, who is seated on your namesake there, and is singing as if he were a chorister in his father's church."

"Ah! Captain Barnstable, Mr. Merry is a boy, and knows nothing, so fears nothing. But I shall obey your orders, sir; and if the men fall astern, this gale, it shan't be for any thing they'll hear from old Tom Coffin."

The cockswain lingered a moment, notwithstanding his promised obedience, and then ventured to request, that—

"Captain Barnstable would please to call Mr. Merry from the gun; for I know, from having followed the seas my natural life, that singing in a gale is sure to bring the wind down upon a vessel the heavier; for He who rules the tempests is displeased that man's voice shall be heard, when He chooses to send His own breath on the water."

Barnstable was at a loss, whether to laugh at his cockswain's infirmity, or to yield to the impression which his earnest and solemn manner had a powerful tendency to produce, amid such a scene. But, making an effort to shake off the superstitious awe that he felt creeping around his own heart, the lieutenant relieved the mind of the worthy old seaman so far as to call the careless boy from his perch, to his own side; where respect for the sacred character of the quarter-deck, instantly put an end to the lively air he had been humming. Tom walked slowly forward, apparently much relieved by the reflection that he had effected so important an object.

The Ariel continued to struggle against the winds and ocean for several hours longer, before the day broke on the tempestuous scene, and the anxious mariners were enabled to form a more accurate estimate of their real danger. As the violence of the gale increased, the canvass of the schooner had been gradually reduced, until she was unable to show more than was absolutely necessary to prevent her driving, helplessly, on the land. Barnstable watched the appearance of the weather, as the light slowly opened upon them, with an intense anxiety, which denoted, that the presentiments of the cockswain were no longer deemed idle. On looking to windward, he beheld the green masses of water that were rolling in towards the land, with a violence that seemed irresistible, crowned with ridges of foam; and there were moments when the air appeared filled with sparking gems, as the rays of the rising sun fell upon the spray that was swept from wave to wave. Towards the land, the view was still more appalling. The cliffs, but a short half-league under the lee of the schooner, were, at times, nearly hid from the eye by the pyramids of water, which the furious element, so suddenly restrained in its violence, cast high into the air, as if seeking to overleap the boundaries that nature had fixed to its dominion. The whole coast, from the distant headland at the south, to the well-known shoals that stretched far beyond their course, in the opposite direction, displayed a broad belt of foam, into which, it would have been certain destruction, for the proudest ship that ever swam, to have entered. Still the Ariel floated on the billows, lightly and in safety, though yielding to the impulses of the waters, and, at times, appearing to be engulphed in the yawning chasms, which, apparently, opened beneath her to receive the little fabric. The low rumour of acknowledged danger, had found its way through the schooner, and the seamen, after fastening their hopeless looks on the small spot of canvass that they were still able to show to the tempest, would turn to view the dreary line of coast, that seemed to offer so gloomy an alternative. Even Dillon, to whom the report of their danger had found its way, crept from his place of concealment in the cabin, and moved about the decks, unheeded, devouring, with greedy ears, such opinions as fell from the lips of the sullen mariners.

At this moment of appalling apprehension, the cockswain exhibited the calmest resignation. He knew all had been done, that lay in the power of man, to urge their little vessel from the land, and it was now too evident to his experienced eyes, that it had been done in vain; but, considering himself as a sort of fixture in the schooner, he was quite prepared to abide her fate, be it for better or for worse. The settled look of gloom that gathered around the frank brow of Barnstable, was, in no degree, connected with any considerations of himself, but proceeded from that sort of parental responsibility, from which the sea-commander is never exempt. The discipline of the crew, however, still continued perfect and unyielding. There had, it is true, been a slight movement made by one or two of the older seamen, which indicated an intention to drown the apprehensions of death in ebriety; but Barnstable had called for his pistols, in a tone that checked the procedure instantly, and, although the fatal weapons were, untouched by him, left to lie exposed on the capstern, where they had been placed by his servant, not another symptom of insubordination appeared among the devoted crew. There was even, what to a landsman might seem an appalling affectation of attention to the most trifling duties of the vessel; and the men, who, it should seem, ought to be devoting the brief moments of their existence to the mighty business of the hour, were constantly called to attend to the most trivial details of their profession. Ropes were coiled, and the slightest damages occasioned by the waves, which at short intervals, swept across the low decks of the Ariel, were repaired, with the same precision and order, as if she yet lay embayed in the haven from which she had just been driven. In this manner, the arm of authority was kept extended over the silent crew, not with the vain desire to preserve a lingering, though useless exercise of power, but with a view to maintain that unity of action, that now could alone afford them even a ray of hope.

"She can make no head against this sea, under that rag of canvass," said Barnstable, gloomily; addressing the cockswain, who, with folded arms, and an air of cool resignation, was balancing his body on the verge of the quarter-deck, while the schooner was plunging madly into waves that nearly buried her in their bosom; "the poor little thing trembles like a frightened child, as she meets the water."

Tom sighed heavily, and shook his head, before he answered —

"If we could have kept the head of the main-mast an hour longer, we might have got an offing, and fetched to windward of the shoals; but, as it is, sir, mortal man can't drive a craft to windward — she sets bodily in to land, and will be in the breakers in less than an hour, unless God wills that the wind shall cease to blow."

"We have no hope left us, but to anchor; our ground tackle may yet bring her up."

Tom turned to his commander, and replied, solemnly, and with that assurance of manner, that long experience only can give a man in moments of great danger —

"If our sheet-cable was bent to our heaviest anchor, this sea would bring it home, though nothing but her launch was riding by it. A north-easter in the German ocean must and will blow itself out; nor shall we get the crown of the gale until the sun falls over the land. Then, indeed, it may lull; for the winds do often seem to reverence the glory of the heavens, too much to blow their might in its very face!"

"We must do our duty to ourselves and the country," returned Barnstable; "go, get the two bowers spliced, and have a kedge bent to a hawser; we'll back our two anchors together, and veer to the better end of two hundred and forty fathoms; it may yet bring her up. See all clear there for anchoring, and cutting away the masts — we'll leave the wind nothing but a naked hull to whistle over."

"Ay, if there was nothing but the wind, we might yet live to see the sun sink behind them hills," said the cockswain; "but what hemp can stand the strain of a craft that is buried, half the time, to her foremast in the water!"

The order was, however, executed by the crew, with a sort of desperate submission to the will of their commander; and when the preparations were completed, the anchors and kedge were dropped to the bottom, and the instant that the Ariel tended to the wind, the axe was applied to the little that was left of her long, raking masts. The crash of the falling spars, as they came, in succession, across the decks of the vessel, appeared to produce no sensation amid that scene of complicated danger, but the seamen proceeded in silence to their hopeless duty, of clearing the wrecks. Every eye followed the floating timbers, as the waves swept them away from the vessel, with a sort of feverish curiosity, to witness the effect produced by their collision with those rocks that lay so fearfully near them; but long before the spars entered the wide border of foam, they were hid from view by the furious element in which they floated. It was, now, felt by the whole crew of the Ariel, that their last means of safety had been adopted, and, at each desperate and headlong plunge the vessel took, into the bosom of the seas that rolled upon her forecastle, the anxious seamen thought they could perceive the yielding of the iron that yet clung to the bottom, or could hear the violent surge of the parting strands of the cable, that still held them to their anchors. While the minds of the sailors were agitated with the faint hopes that had been excited, by the movements of their schooner, Dillon had been permitted to wander about the deck unnoticed; his rolling eyes, hard breathing, and clenched hands, excited no observation among the men, whose thoughts were yet dwelling on the means of safety. But, now, when, with a sort of frenzied desperation, he would follow the retiring waters along the decks, and venture his person nigh the group that had collected around and on the gun of the cockswain, glances of fierce or of sullen vengeance were cast at him, that conveyed threats of a nature that he was too much agitated to understand.

"If ye are tired of this world, though your time, like my own, is probably but short in it," said Tom to him, as he passed the cockswain in one of his turns, "you can go forward among the men; but if ye have need of the moments to foot up the reck'ning of your doings among men, afore ye're brought to face your maker, and hear the log-book of heaven, I would advise you to keep as nigh as possible to Captain Barnstable or myself."

"Will you promise to save me, if the vessel is wrecked!" exclaimed Dillon, catching at the first sounds of friendly interest that had reached his ears, since he had been recaptured; "Oh!

if you will, I can secure you future ease; yes, wealth, for the remainder of your days!"

"Your promises have been too ill kept, afore this, for the peace of your soul," returned the cockswain, without bitterness, though sternly; "but it is not in me to strike even a whale, that is already spouting blood."

The intercessions of Dillon were interrupted by a dreadful cry, that arose among the men forward, and which sounded with increased horror, amid the roarings of the tempest. The schooner rose on the breast of a wave at the same instant, and, falling off with her broadside to the sea, she drove in towards the cliffs, like a bubble on the rapids of a cataract.

"Our ground tackle has parted," said Tom, with his resigned patience of manner undisturbed; "she shall die as easy as man can make her!" While he yet spoke, he seized the tiller, and gave to the vessel such a direction, as would be most likely to cause her to strike the rocks with her bows foremost.

There was, for one moment, an expression of exquisite anguish, betrayed in the dark countenance of Barnstable; but at the next, it passed away, and he spoke cheerfully to his men —

"Be steady, my lads, be calm; there is yet a hope of life for *you* — our light draught will let us run in close to the cliffs, and it is still falling water — see your boats clear, and be steady."

The crew of the whale-boat, aroused, by this speech, from a sort of stupor, sprang into their light vessel, which was quickly lowered into the sea, and kept riding on the foam, free from the sides of the schooner, by the powerful exertions of the men. The cry for the cockswain was earnest and repeated, but Tom shook his head, without replying, still grasping the tiller, and keeping his eyes steadily bent on the chaos of waters, into which they were driving. The launch, the largest boat of the two, was cut loose from the "gripes," and the bustle and exertion of the moment rendered the crew insensible to the horror of the scene that surrounded them. But the loud, hoarse call of the cockswain, to "look out — secure yourselves!" suspended even their efforts, and at that instant the Ariel settled on a wave that melted from under her, heavily on the rocks. The shock was so violent, as to throw all who disregarded the warning cry, from their feet, and the universal quiver that pervaded the vessel was like the last shudder of animated nature. For a time long enough to breathe, the least experienced among the men supposed the danger to be past; but a wave of great height followed the one that had deserted them, and raising the vessel again, threw her roughly still further on her bed of rocks, and at the same time its crest broke over her quarter, sweeping the length of her decks, with a fury that was almost resistless. The shuddering seamen beheld their loosened boat, driven from their grasp, and dashed against the base of the cliffs, where no fragment of her wreck could be traced, at the receding of the waters. But the passing billow had thrown the vessel into a position which, in some measure, protected her decks from the violence of those that succeeded it.

"Go, my boys, go," said Barnstable, as the moment of dreadful uncertainty passed; "you have still the whale-boat, and she, at least, will take you nigh the shore; go into her, my boys; God bless you, God bless you all; you have been faithful and honest fellows, and I believe he will not yet desert you; go, my friends, while there is a lull."

The seamen threw themselves, in a mass, into the light vessel, which nearly sunk under the unusual burthen; but when they looked around them, Barnstable, and Merry, Dillon, and the cockswain, were yet to be seen on the decks of the Ariel. The former was pacing, in deep, and perhaps bitter melancholy, the wet planks of the schooner, while the boy hung, unheeded, on his arm, uttering disregarded petitions to his commander, to desert the wreck. Dillon approached the side where the boat lay, again and again, but the threatening countenances of the seamen as often drove him back in despair. Tom had seated himself on the heel of the bowsprit; where he continued, in an attitude of quiet resignation, returning no other answers to the loud and repeated calls of his shipmates, than by waving his hand toward the shore.

"Now hear me," said the boy, urging his request to tears; "if not for my sake, or for your own sake, Mr. Barnstable, or for the hopes of God's mercy; go into the boat, for the love of my cousin Katherine."

The young lieutenant paused in his troubled walk, and for a moment, he cast a glance of hesitation at the cliffs; but, at the next instant, his eyes fell on the ruin of his vessel, and he answered —

"Never, boy, never; if my hour has come, I will not shrink from my fate."

"Listen to the men, dear sir; the boat will be swamped along-side the wreck, and their cry is, that without you they will not let her go."

Barnstable motioned to the boat, to bid the boy enter it, and turned away in silence.

"Well," said Merry, with firmness, "if it be right that a lieutenant shall stay by the wreck, it must also be right for a midshipman; shove off; neither Mr. Barnstable nor myself will quit the vessel."

"Boy, your life has been intrusted to my keeping, and at my hands will it be required," said his commander, lifting the struggling youth, and tossing him into the arms of the seamen. "Away with ye, and God be with you; there is more weight in you, now, than can go safe to land."

Still, the seamen hesitated, for they perceived the cockswain moving, with a steady tread, along the deck, and they hoped he had relented, and would yet persuade the lieutenant to join his crew. But Tom, imitating the example of his commander, seized the latter, suddenly, in his powerful grasp, and threw him over the bulwarks, with an irresistible force. At the same moment, he cast the fast of the boat from the pin that held it, and lifting his broad hands high into the air, his voice was heard in the tempest.

"God's will be done with me," he cried; "I saw the first timber of the Ariel laid, and shall live just long enough to see it torn out of her bottom; after which I wish to live no longer."

But his shipmates were swept far beyond the sounds of his voice, before half these words were uttered. All command of the boat was rendered impossible, by the numbers it contained, as well as the raging of the surf; and, as it rose on the white crest of a wave, Tom saw his beloved little craft for the last time; it fell into a trough of the sea, and in a few moments more its fragments were ground into splinters on the adjacent rocks. The cockswain still remained where he had cast off the rope, and beheld the numerous heads and arms that appeared rising, at short intervals, on the waves; some making powerful and well-directed efforts to gain the sands, that were becoming visible as the tide fell, and others wildly tossed, in the frantic movements of helpless despair. The honest old seaman gave a cry of joy, as he saw Barnstable issue from the surf, bearing the form of Merry in safety to the sands, where, one by one, several seamen soon appeared also, dripping and exhausted. Many others of the crew were carried, in a similar manner, to places of safety; though, as Tom returned to his seat on the bowsprit, he could not conceal, from his reluctant eyes, the lifeless forms that were, in other spots, driven against the rocks, with a fury that soon left them but few of the outward vestiges of humanity.

Dillon and the cockswain were now the sole occupants of their dreadful station. The former stood, in a kind of stupid despair, a witness of the scene we have related; but as his curdled blood began again to flow more warmly through his heart, he crept close to the side of Tom, with that sort of selfish feeling that makes even hopeless misery more tolerable, when endured in participation with another.

"When the tide falls," he said, in a voice that betrayed the agony of fear, though his words expressed the renewal of hope, "we shall be able to walk to land."

"There was One, and only One, to whose feet the waters were the same as a dry deck," returned the cockswain; "and none but such as have his power will ever be able to walk from these rocks to the sands." The old seaman paused, and turning his eyes, which exhibited a mingled expression of disgust and compassion, on his companion, he added, with reverence — "Had you thought more of him in fair weather, your case would be less to be pitied in this tempest."

"Do you still think there is much danger?" asked Dillon.

"To them that have reason to fear death; listen! do you hear that hollow noise beneath ye?"

"'Tis the wind, driving by the vessel!"

"'Tis the poor thing herself," said the affected cockswain, "giving her last groans. The water is breaking up her decks, and in a few minutes more, the handsomest model that ever cut a wave, will be like the chips that fell from her timbers in framing!"

"Why, then, did you remain here!" cried Dillon, wildly.

"To die in my coffin, if it should be the will of God," returned Tom; "these waves, to me, are what the land is to you; I was born on them, and I have always meant that they should be my grave."

"But I—I" shrieked Dillon, "I am not ready to die! —I cannot die! —I will not die!"

"Poor wretch!" muttered his companion; "you must go, like the rest of us; when the death-watch is called, none can skulk from the muster."

"I can swim," Dillon continued, rushing, with frantic eagerness, to the side of the wreck. "Is there no billet of wood, no rope, that I can take with me?"

"None; every thing has been cut away, or carried off by the sea. If ye are about to strive for your life, take with ye a stout heart and a clean conscience, and trust the rest to God!"

"God!" echoed Dillon, in the madness of his frenzy; "I know no God! there is no God that knows me!"

"Peace!" said the deep tones of the cockswain, in a voice that seemed to speak in the elements; "blasphemer, peace!"

The heavy groaning, produced by the water, in the timbers of the Ariel, at that moment, added its impulse to the raging feelings of Dillon, and he cast himself headlong into the sea.

The water, thrown by the rolling of the surf on the beach, was necessarily returned to the ocean, in eddies, in different places, favourable to such an action of the element. Into the edge of one of these counter-currents, that was produced by the very rocks on which the schooner lay, and which the watermen call the "under-tow," Dillon had, unknowingly, thrown his person, and when the waves had driven him a short distance from the wreck, he was met by a stream that his most desperate efforts could not overcome. He was a light and powerful swimmer, and the struggle was hard and protracted. With the shore immediately before his eyes, and at no great distance, he was led, as by a false phantom, to continue his efforts, although they did not advance him a foot. The old seaman, who, at first, had watched his motions with careless indifference, understood the danger of his situation at a glance, and, forgetful of his own fate, he shouted aloud, in a voice that was driven over the struggling victim, to the ears of his shipmates on the sands—

"Sheer to-port, and clear the under-tow! sheer to the southward!"

Dillon heard the sounds, but his faculties were too much obscured by terror, to distinguish their object; he, however, blindly yielded to the call, and gradually changed his direction, until his face was once more turned towards the vessel. The current swept him diagonally by the rocks, and he was forced into an eddy, where he had nothing to contend against but the waves, whose violence was much broken by the wreck. In this state, he continued still to struggle, but with a force that was too much weakened, to overcome the resistance he met. Tom looked around him for a rope, but all had gone over with the spars, or been swept away by the waves. At this moment of disappointment, his eyes met those of the desperate Dillon. Calm, and inured to horrors, as was the veteran seaman, he involuntarily passed his hand before his brow, to exclude the look of despair he encountered; and when, a moment afterwards, he removed the rigid member, he beheld the sinking form of the victim, as it gradually settled in the ocean, still struggling, with regular but impotent strokes of the arms and feet, to gain the wreck, and to preserve an existence that had been so much abused in its hour of allotted probation.

"He will soon know his God, and learn that his God knows him!" murmured the cockswain to himself. As he yet spoke, the wreck of the Ariel yielded to an overwhelming sea, and, after an universal shudder, her timbers and planks gave way, and were swept towards the cliffs, bearing the body of the simple-hearted cockswain among the ruins.

IX. Long Tom on the bowsprit of the wreck of the *Ariel*, drawn by F. O. C. Darley engraved by John Wrightman.

X. The wreck of the *Ariel*, drawn by Samuel Austin, engraved by W. Miller for pirated editions of *The Pilot* between 1831 and 1840.

XI. The wreck of the *Ariel* drawn by James Hamilton, engraved by J. McGoffin.

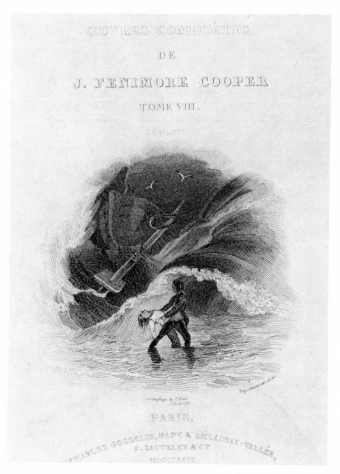

XII. The wreck of the *Ariel* and Barnstable's rescue of Merry, drawn and engraved by Tony Johannot.

Chapter XXV.

"Let us think of them that sleep,
Full many a fathom deep,
By thy wild and stormy steep,
Elsinore!"

> Campbell, "Battle of the Baltic," VII.6-9.

Long and dreary did the hours appear to Barnstable, before the falling tide had so far receded, as to leave the sands entirely exposed to his search for the bodies of his lost shipmates. Several had been rescued from the wild fury of the waves themselves, and one by one, as the melancholy conviction that life had ceased was forced on the survivors, they had been decently interred, in graves dug on the very margin of that element on which they had passed their lives. But still the form longest known and most beloved was missing, and the lieutenant paced the broad space that was now left between the foot of the cliffs and the raging ocean, with hurried strides and a feverish eye, watching and following those fragments of the wreck that the sea still continued to cast on the beach. Living and dead, he now found, that of those who had lately been in the Ariel, only two were missing. Of the former, he could muster but twelve, besides Merry and himself, and his men had already interred more than half that number of the latter, which, together, embraced all who had trusted their lives to the frail keeping of the whale-boat.

"Tell me not, boy, of the impossibility of his being safe," said Barnstable, in deep agitation, which he in vain struggled to conceal from the anxious youth, who thought it unnecessary to follow the uneasy motions of his commander, as he strode along the sands. "How often have men been found floating on pieces of wreck, days after the loss of their vessel? and you can see, with your own eyes, that the falling water has swept the planks this distance; ay, a good half league from where she struck. Does the look-out, from the top of the cliffs, make no signal of seeing him yet?"

"None, sir, none; we shall never see him again. The men say, that he always thought it sinful to desert a wreck, and that he did not even strike-out once for his life, though he has been known to swim an hour, when a whale has stove his boat. God knows, sir," added the boy, hastily dashing a tear from his eye, by a stolen movement of his hand, "I loved Tom Coffin better than any foremast-man in either vessel. You seldom came aboard the frigate but we had him in the steerage among us reefers, to hear his long-yarns, and share our cheer. We all loved him, Mr. Barnstable, but love cannot bring the dead to life again."

"I know it, I know it," said Barnstable, with a huskiness in his voice, that betrayed the depth of his emotion; "I am not so foolish as to believe in impossibilities; but while there is a hope of his living, I will never abandon poor Tom Coffin to such a dreadful fate. Think, boy, he may, at this moment, be looking at us, and praying to his Maker that he would turn our eyes upon him; ay, praying to his God, for Tom often prayed, though he did it in his watch, standing, and in silence."

"If he had clung to life so strongly," returned the midshipman, "he would have struggled harder to preserve it."

Barnstable stopped short in his hurried walk, and fastened a look of opening conviction on his companion; but, as he was about to speak in reply, the shouts of the seamen reached his ears, and, turning, they saw the whole party running along the beach, and motioning, with violent gestures, to an intermediate point in the ocean. The lieutenant and Merry hurried back, and, as they approached the men, they distinctly observed a human figure, borne along by the waves, at moments seeming to rise above them, and already floating in the last of the breakers. They had hardly ascertained so much, when a heavy swell carried the inanimate body far upon the sands, where it was left by the retiring waters.

"'Tis my cockswain!" cried Barnstable, rushing to the spot. He stopped suddenly, however, as he came within view of the features, and it was some little time before he appeared to have collected his faculties sufficiently to add, in tones of deep horror—"what wretch is this, boy! his form is unmutilated, and yet observe the eyes! they seem as if the sockets would not contain them, and they gaze as wildly as if their owner yet had life — the hands are open and spread, as though they would still buffet the waves!"

"The Jonah! the Jonah!" shouted the seamen, with savage exultation, as they successively approached the corpse; "away with his carrion into the sea again! give him to the sharks! let him tell his lies in the claws of the lobsters!"

Barnstable had turned away from the revolting sight, in disgust, but when he discovered these indications of impotent revenge, in the remnant of his crew, he said, in that voice, which all respected, and still obeyed —

"Stand back! back with ye, fellows! would you disgrace your manhood and seamanship, by wreaking your vengeance on him whom God has already in judgment!" A silent, but significant gesture towards the earth, succeeded his words, and he walked slowly away.

"Bury him in the sands, boys," said Merry, when his commander was at some little distance; "the next tide will unearth him."

The seamen obeyed his orders, while the midshipman rejoined his commander, who continued to pace along the beach, occasionally halting, to throw his uneasy glances over the water, and then hurrying onward, at a rate that caused his youthful companion to exert his greatest power to maintain the post he had taken at his side. Every effort to discover the lost cockswain was, however, after two hours' more search, abandoned as fruitless, and with reason; for the sea was never known to give up the body of the man who might be, emphatically, called its own dead.

"There goes the sun, already dropping behind the cliffs," said the lieutenant, throwing himself on a rock; "and the hour will soon arrive to set the dog-watches; but we have nothing left to watch over, boy; the surf and rocks have not even left us a whole plank, that we may lay our heads on for the night."

"The men have gathered many articles on yon beach, sir," returned the lad; "they have found arms to defend ourselves with, and food to give us strength to use them."

"And who shall be our enemy?" asked Barnstable, bitterly; "shall we shoulder our dozen pikes, and carry England by boarding?"

"We may not lay the whole island under contribution," continued the boy, anxiously watching the expression of his commander's eye; "but we may still keep ourselves in work, until the cutter returns from the frigate. I hope, sir, you do not think our case so desperate, as to intend yielding as prisoners."

"Prisoners!" exclaimed the lieutenant; "no, no, lad, it has not got to that, yet! England has been able to wreck my craft, I must concede, but she has, as yet, obtained no other advantage over us. She was a precious model, Merry! the cleanest run, and the neatest entrance, that art ever united on the stem and stern of the same vessel! Do you remember the time, younker, when I gave the frigate my topsails, in beating out of the Chesapeake? I could always do it, in smooth water, with a whole-sail-breeze. But she was a frail thing! a frail thing, boy, and could bear but little."

"A mortar-ketch would have thumped to pieces where she lay," returned the midshipman.

"Ay, it was asking too much of her, to expect she could hold together on a bed of rocks. Merry, I loved her; dearly did I love her; she was my first command, and I knew and loved every timber and bolt in her beautiful frame!"

"I believe it is as natural, sir, for a seaman to love the wood and iron in which he has floated over the depths of the ocean, for so many days and nights," rejoined the boy, "as it is for a father to love the members of his own family."

"Quite, quite, ay, more so," said Barnstable, speaking as if he were choked by emotion. Merry felt the heavy grasp of the lieutenant on his slight arm, while his commander continued, in a voice that gradually increased in power, as his feelings predominated; "and yet, boy, a human being cannot love the creature of his own formation as he does the works of God. A man can never regard his ship as he does his shipmates. I sailed with him, boy, when every thing seemed bright and happy, as at your age; when, as he often expressed it, I knew nothing and feared nothing. I was then a truant from an old father and a kind mother, and he did that for me, which no parents could have done in my situation — he was my father and mother on the deep! — hours, days, even months, has he passed in teaching me the art of our profession; and now, in my manhood, he has followed me from ship to ship, from sea to sea, and has only quitted me to die, where I should have died — as if he felt the disgrace of abandoning the poor Ariel to her fate, by herself!"

"No—no—no—'twas his superstitious pride!" interrupted Merry; but perceiving that the head of Barnstable had sunk between his hands, as if he would conceal his emotion, the boy added no more, but he sat respectfully watching the display of feeling that his officer, in vain, endeavoured to suppress. Merry felt his own form quiver with sympathy at the shuddering which passed through Barnstable's frame; and the relief experienced by the lieutenant himself, was not greater than that which the midshipman felt, as the latter beheld large tears forcing their way through the other's fingers, and falling on the sands at his feet. They were followed by a violent burst of emotion, such as is seldom exhibited in the meridian of life, but which, when it conquers the nature of one who has buffeted the chances of the world with the loftiness of his sex and character, breaks down every barrier, and seems to sweep before it, like a rushing torrent, all the factitious defences which habit and education have created to protect the pride of manhood. Merry had often beheld the commanding severity of the lieutenant's manner, in moments of danger, with deep respect; he had been drawn towards him by kindness and affection, in times of gayety and recklessness; but he now sate, for many minutes, profoundly silent, regarding his officer with sensations that were nearly allied to awe. The struggle with himself was long and severe in the bosom of Barnstable; but, at length, the calm of relieved passions succeeded to his emotion. When he arose from the rock, and removed his hands from his features, his eye was hard and proud, his brow slightly contracted, and he spoke in a voice so harsh, that it startled his companion—

"Come, sir; why are we here and idle! are not yon poor fellows looking up to us for advice, and orders how to proceed in this exigency? Away, away, Mr. Merry; it is not a time to be drawing figures in the sand with your dirk; the flood-tide will soon be in, and we may be glad to hide our heads in some cavern among these rocks. Let us be stirring, sir, while we have the sun, and muster enough food and arms to keep life in us, and our enemies off us, until we can once more get afloat."

The wondering boy, whose experience had not yet taught

him to appreciate the reaction of the passions, started at this unexpected summons to his duty, and followed Barnstable towards the group of distant seamen. The lieutenant, who was instantly conscious how far pride had rendered him unjust, soon moderated his long strides, and continued in milder tones, which were quickly converted into his usual frank communications, though they still remained tinged with a melancholy, that time only could entirely remove—

"We have been unlucky, Mr. Merry, but we need not despair—these lads have gotten together abundance of supplies, I see; and, with our arms, we can easily make ourselves masters of some of the enemy's smaller craft, and find our way back to the frigate, when this gale has blown itself out. We must keep ourselves close, though, or we shall have the redcoats coming down upon us, like so many sharks around a wreck. Ah! God bless her, Merry! there is not such a sight to be seen on the whole beach as two of her planks holding together."

The midshipman, without adverting to this sudden allusion to their vessel, prudently pursued the train of ideas, in which his commander had started.

"There is an opening into the country, but a short distance south of us, where a brook empties into the sea," he said. "We might find a cover in it, or in the wood above, into which it leads, until we can have a survey of the coast, or can seize some vessel to carry us off."

"There would be a satisfaction in waiting 'till the morning watch, and then carrying that accursed battery, which took off the better leg of the poor Ariel!" said the lieutenant—"the thing might be done, boy; and we could hold the work too, until the Alacrity and the frigate draw in to land."

"If you prefer storming works to boarding vessels, there is a fortress of stone, Mr. Barnstable, which lies directly on our beam. I could see it through the haze, when I was on the cliffs, stationing the look-out—and—"

"And what, boy? speak without a fear; this is a time for free consultation."

"Why, sir, the garrison might not all be hostile—we should liberate Mr. Griffith and the marines; besides—"

"Besides what, sir?"

"I should have an opportunity, perhaps, of seeing my cousin Cecilia, and my cousin Katherine."

The countenance of Barnstable grew animated as he listened, and he answered, with something of his usual cheerful manner—

"Ay, that, indeed, would be a work worth carrying! and the rescuing of our shipmates, and the marines, would read like a thing of military discretion—ha! boy! all the rest would be incidental, younker; like the capture of the fleet, after you have whipped the convoy."

"I do suppose, sir, that if the Abbey be taken, Colonel Howard will own himself a prisoner of war."

"And Colonel Howard's wards! now, there is good sense in this scheme of thine, Master Merry, and I will give it proper reflection. But here are our poor fellows; speak cheeringly to them, sir, that we may hold them in temper for our enterprise."

Barnstable and the midshipman joined their shipwrecked companions, with that air of authority which is seldom wanting between the superior and the inferior, in nautical intercourse, but at the same time, with a kindness of speech and looks, that might have been a little increased by their critical situation. After partaking of the food which had been selected from among the fragments that still lay scattered, for more than a mile, along the beach, the lieutenant directed the seamen to arm themselves with such weapons as offered, and, also, to make a sufficient provision, from the schooner's stores, to last them for four-and-twenty hours longer. These orders were soon executed; and the whole party, led by Barnstable and Merry, proceeded along the foot of the cliffs, in quest of the opening in the rocks, through which the little rivulet found a passage to the ocean. The weather contributed, as much as the seclusion of the spot, to prevent any discovery of the small party, which pursued its object with a disregard of caution that might, under other circumstances, have proved fatal to its safety. Barnstable paused in his march when they had all entered the deep ravine, and ascended nearly to the brow of the precipice, that formed one of its sides, to take a last and more scrutinizing survey of the sea. His countenance exhibited the abandonment of all hope, as his eye moved slowly from the northern to the southern boundary of the horizon, and he prepared to pursue his march, by moving, reluctantly, up the stream, when the boy, who still clung to his side, exclaimed joyously —

"Sail ho! It must be the frigate in the offing!"

"A sail!" repeated his commander; "where-away do you see a sail in this tempest? Can there be another as hardy and unfortunate as ourselves!"

"Look to the starboard hand of the point of rock to windward!" cried the boy; "now you lose it — ah! now the sun falls upon it! 'tis a sail, sir, as sure as canvass can be spread in such a gale!"

"I see what you mean," returned the other, "but it seems a gull, skimming the sea! nay, now it rises, indeed, and shows itself like a bellying topsail; pass up that glass, lads; here is a fellow in the offing who may prove a friend."

Merry waited the result of the lieutenant's examination with youthful impatience, and did not fail to ask, immediately —

"Can you make it out, sir? is it the ship or the cutter?"

"Come, there seemeth yet some hope left for us, boy," returned Barnstable, closing the glass; "'tis a ship, lying-to under her main-topsail. If one might but dare to show himself on these heights, he would raise her hull, and make sure of her character! But I think I know her spars, though even her topsail dips, at times, when there is nothing to be seen but her bare poles, and they shortened by her top-gallant-masts."

"One would swear," said Merry, laughing, as much through the excitement produced by this intelligence, as at his conceit, "that Captain Munson would never carry wood aloft, when he can't carry canvass. I remember, one night, Mr. Griffith was a little vexed, and said, around the capstern, he believed the next order would be, to rig in the bowsprit, and house lower-masts!"

"Ay, ay, Griffith is a lazy dog, and sometimes gets lost in the fogs of his own thoughts," said Barnstable; "and I suppose old Moderate was in a breeze. However, this looks as if he were in earnest; he must have kept the ship away, or she would never have been where she is; I do verily believe the old gentleman remembers that he has a few of his officers and men on this accursed island. This is well, Merry, for should we take the Abbey, we have a place at hand in which to put our prisoners."

"We must have patience till the morning," added the boy, "for no boat would attempt to land in such a sea."

"No boat could land! The best boat that ever floated, boy, has sunk in these breakers! But the wind lessens, and before morning, the sea will fall. Let us on, and find a birth for our poor lads, where they can be made more comfortable."

The two officers now descended from their elevation, and led the way still further up the deep and narrow dell, until, as the ground rose gradually before them, they found themselves in a dense wood, on a level with the adjacent country.

"Here should be a ruin at hand, if I have kept a true reckoning, and know my courses and distances," said Barnstable; "I have a chart about me, that speaks of such a land-mark."

The lieutenant turned away from the laughing expression of the boy's eye, as the latter archly inquired—

"Was it made by one who knows the coast well, sir? or was it done by some school-boy, to learn his maps, as the girls work samplers?"

"Come, younker, no sampler of your impudence. But look ahead; can you see any habitation that has been deserted?"

"Ay, sir, here is a pile of stones before us, that looks as dirty and ragged, as if it was a soldier's barrack; can this be what you seek?"

"Faith, this has been a whole town in its day! we should call it a city in America, and furnish it with a Mayor, Aldermen, and Recorder—you might stow old Faneuil-Hall in one of its lockers."

With this sort of careless dialogue, which Barnstable engaged in, that his men might discover no alteration in his manner, they approached the mouldering walls that had proved so frail a protection to the party under Griffith.

A short time was passed in examining the premises, when the wearied seamen took possession of one of the dilapidated apartments, and disposed themselves to seek that rest of which they had been deprived by the momentous occurrences of the past night.

Barnstable waited until the loud breathing of the seamen

assured him that they slept, when he aroused the drowsy boy, who was fast losing his senses in the same sort of oblivion, and motioned to him to follow. Merry arose, and they stole together from the apartment, with guarded steps, and penetrated more deeply into the gloomy recesses of the place.

Chapter XXVI.

Mercury — "I permit thee to be Sosia again."
Dryden, *Amphitryon,* V.i.306.

WE MUST leave the two adventurers winding their way among the broken piles, and venturing boldly beneath the tottering arches of the ruin, to accompany the reader, at the same hour, within the more comfortable walls of the Abbey; where, it will be remembered, Borroughcliffe was left, in a condition of very equivocal ease. As the earth had, however, in the interval, nearly run its daily round, circumstances had intervened to release the soldier from his confinement — and no one, ignorant of the fact, would suppose, that the gentleman who was now seated at the hospitable board of Colonel Howard, directing, with so much discretion, the energies of his masticators to the delicacies of the feast, could read, in his careless air and smiling visage, that those foragers of nature had been so recently condemned, for four long hours, to the mortification of discussing the barren subject of his own sword-hilt. Borroughcliffe, however, maintained not only his usual post, but his well-earned reputation at the table, with his ordinary coolness of demeanour; though, at times, there were fleeting smiles, that crossed his military aspect, which sufficiently indicated, that he considered the matter of his reflection to be of a particularly ludicrous character. In the young man, who sat by his side, dressed in the deep blue jacket of a seaman, with the fine, white linen of his collar contrasting strongly with the black silk handkerchief, that was tied, with studied negligence, around his neck, and whose easy air and manner contrasted still more strongly with this attire, the reader will discover Griffith. The captive paid much less devotion to the viands than his neighbour, though he affected more attention to the business of the table than he actually bestowed, with a sort of consciousness that it would relieve the blushing maiden who presided. The laughing eyes of Katherine Plowden were glittering by the side of the mild countenance of Alice Dunscombe, and, at times, were fastened, in droll interest, on the rigid and upright exterior that Captain Manual maintained, directly opposite to where she was seated. A chair had, also, been placed for Dillon—of course, it was vacant.

"And so, Borroughcliffe," cried Colonel Howard, with a freedom of voice, and a vivacity in his air, that announced the increasing harmony of the repast, "the sea-dog left you nothing to chew but the cud of your resentment!"

"That and my sword-hilt!" returned the immoveable recruiting officer; "gentlemen, I know not how your Congress rewards military achievements; but if that worthy fellow were in my company, he should have a halbert within a week—spurs I would not offer him, for he affects to spurn their use."

Griffith smiled, and bowed in silence to the liberal compliment of Borroughcliffe; but Manual took on himself the task of replying—

"Considering the drilling the man has received, his conduct has been well enough, sir; though a well-trained soldier would not only have made prisoners, but he would have secured them."

"I perceive, my good comrade, that your thoughts are running on the exchange," said Borroughcliffe, good humouredly; "we will fill, sir, and, by permission of the ladies, drink to a speedy restoration of rights to both parties—the statu quo ante bellum."

"With all my heart," cried the colonel; "and Cicily and Miss Katherine will pledge the sentiment in a woman's sip; will ye not, my fair wards?—Mr. Griffith, I honour this proposition of yours, which will not only liberate yourself, but restore to us my kinsman, Mr. Christopher Dillon. Kit had imagined the thing well; ha! Borroughcliffe! 'twas ingeniously contrived, but the fortune of war interposed itself to his success; and yet, it is a deep and inexplicable mystery to me, how Kit should have been conveyed from the Abbey with so little noise, and without raising the alarm."

"Christopher is a man who understands the philosophy of silence, as well as that of rhetoric," returned Borroughcliffe, "and must have learned, in his legal studies, that it is, sometimes, necessary to conduct matters sub silentio. You smile at my Latin, Miss Plowden; but, really, since I have become an inhabitant of this Monkish abode, my little learning is stimulated to unwonted efforts—nay, you are pleased to be yet more merry! I used the language, because silence is a theme in which you ladies take but little pleasure."

Katherine, however, disregarded the slight pique that was apparent in the soldier's manner; but, after following the train of her own thoughts in silent enjoyment for a moment longer, she seemed to yield to their drollery, and laughed, until her dark eyes flashed with merriment. Cecilia did not assume the severe gravity with which she sometimes endeavoured to repress, what she thought, the unseasonable mirth of her cousin, and the wondering Griffith fancied, as he glanced his eye from one to the other, that he could discern a suppressed smile playing among the composed features of Alice Dunscombe. Katherine, however, soon succeeded in repressing the paroxysm, and, with an air of infinitely comic gravity, she replied to the remark of the soldier—

"I think I have heard of such a process in nautical affairs as towing; but I must appeal to Mr. Griffith for the correctness of the term?"

"You could not speak with more accuracy," returned the young sailor, with a look that sent the conscious blood to the temples of the lady, "though you had made marine terms your study."

"The profession requires less thought, perhaps, than you imagine, sir; but is this towing often done, as Captain Borroughcliffe—I beg his pardon—as the Monks have it, sub silentio?"

"Spare me, fair lady," cried the captain, "and we will establish a compact of mutual grace; you to forgive my learning, and I to suppress my suspicions."

"Suspicions, sir, is a word that a lady must defy."

"And defiance a challenge that a soldier can never receive; so, I must submit to talk English, though the fathers of the church were my companions. I suspect that Miss Plowden has it in her power to explain the manner of Mr. Christopher Dillon's departure."

The lady did not reply, but a second burst of merriment succeeded, of a liveliness and duration quite equal to the former.

"How's this!" exclaimed the colonel; "permit me to say, Miss Plowden, your mirth is very extraordinary! I trust no disrespect has been offered to my kinsman? Mr. Griffith, our terms are, that the exchange shall only be made on condition that equally good treatment has been extended to the parties!"

"If Mr. Dillon can complain of no greater evil than that of being laughed at by Miss Plowden, sir, he has reason to call himself a happy fellow."

"I know not, sir; God forbid that I should forget what is due to my guests, gentlemen—but ye have entered my dwelling as foes to my prince."

"But not to Colonel Howard, sir."

"I know no difference, Mr. Griffith. King George or Colonel Howard—Colonel Howard or King George. Our feelings, our fortunes, and our fate, are as one; with the mighty odds that Providence has established between the prince and his people! I wish no other fortune, than to share, at an humble distance, the weal or wo of my sovereign!"

"You are not called upon, dear sir, to do either, by the thoughtlessness of us ladies," said Cecilia, rising; "but here comes one who should turn our thoughts to a more important subject—our dress."

Politeness induced Colonel Howard, who both loved and respected his niece, to defer his remarks to another time; and Katherine, springing from her chair, with childish eagerness, flew to the side of her cousin, who was directing a servant that had announced the arrival of one of those erratic vendors of small articles, who supply, in remote districts of the country, the places of more regular traders, to show the lad into the dining-parlour. The repast was so far ended, as to render this interruption less objectionable, and as all felt the object of Cecilia to be the restoration of harmony, the boy was ushered into the room, without further delay. The contents of his small basket, consisting, chiefly, of essences, and the smaller articles of female economy, were playfully displayed on the table, by Katherine, who declared herself the patroness of the itinerant youth, and who laughingly appealed to the liberality of the gentlemen in behalf of her protégé.

"You perceive, my dear guardian, that the boy must be loyal; for he offers, here, perfume, that is patronized by no less than two royal dukes! do suffer me to place a box aside, for your especial use? you consent; I see it in your eye. And, Captain Borroughcliffe, as you appear to be forgetting the use of your own language, here is even a horn-book for you! How admirably provided he seems to be! You must have had St. Ruth in view, when you laid in your stock, child?"

"Yes, my lady," the boy replied, with a bow that was studiously awkward; "I have often heard of the grand ladies that dwell in the old Abbey, and I have journeyed a few miles beyond my rounds, to gain their custom."

"And surely they cannot disappoint you. Miss Howard, that is a palpable hint to your purse; and I know not that even Miss Alice can escape contribution, in these troublesome times. Come, aid me, child; what have you to recommend, in particular, to the favour of these ladies?"

The lad approached the basket, and rummaged its contents, for a moment, with the appearance of deep, mercenary interest; and then, without lifting his hand from the confusion he had caused, he said, while he exhibited something within the basket to the view of his smiling observer—

"This, my lady."

Katherine started, and glanced her eyes, with a piercing look, at the countenance of the boy, and then turned them, uneasily, from face to face, with conscious timidity. Cecilia had effected her object, and had resumed her seat, in silent abstraction—Alice was listening to the remarks of Captain Manual and the host, as they discussed the propriety of certain military usages—Griffith seemed to hold communion with his mistress, by imitating her silence; but Katherine, in her stolen glances, met the keen look of Borroughcliffe, fastened on her face, in a manner that did not fail instantly to suspend the scrutiny.

"Come, Cecilia," she cried, after a pause of a moment, "we trespass too long on the patience of the gentlemen; not only to keep possession of our seats, ten minutes after the cloth has been drawn! but even to introduce our essences, and tapes, and needles, among the Madeira, and—shall I add, segars, colonel?"

"Not while we are favoured with the company of Miss Plowden, certainly."

"Come, my coz; I perceive the colonel is growing particularly polite, which is a never-failing sign that he tires of our presence."

Cecilia rose, and was leading the way to the door, when Katherine turned to the lad, and added—

"You can follow us to the drawing-room, child, where we can make our purchases, without exposing the mystery of our toilets."

"Miss Plowden has forgotten my horn-book, I believe," said Borroughcliffe, advancing from the standing group who surrounded the table; "possibly I can find some work in the basket of the boy, better fitted for the improvement of a grown-up young gentleman, than this elementary treatise."

Cecilia, observing him to take the basket from the lad, resumed her seat, and her example was necessarily followed by Katherine; though not without some manifest indications of vexation.

"Come hither, boy, and explain the uses of your wares. This is soap, and this a penknife, I know; but what name do you affix to this?"

"That? that is tape," returned the lad, with an impatience that might very naturally be attributed to the interruption that was thus given to his trade.

"And this?"

"That?" repeated the stripling, pausing, with a hesitation between sulkiness and doubt; "that?—"

"Come, this is a little ungallant!" cried Katherine; "to keep three ladies dying with impatience to possess themselves of their finery, while you detain the boy, to ask the name of a tambouring-needle!"

"I should apologize for asking questions that are so easily answered; but perhaps he will find the next more difficult to solve," returned Borroughcliffe, placing the subject of his inquiries in the palm of his hand, in such a manner as to conceal it from all but the boy and himself. "This has a name, too; what is it?"

"That?—that—is sometimes called—white-line."

"Perhaps you mean a white lie?"

"How, sir!" exclaimed the lad, a little fiercely, "a lie!"

"Only a white one," returned the captain. "What do you call this, Miss Dunscombe?"

"We call it bobbin, sir, generally, in the north," said the placid Alice.

"Ay, bobbin, or white-line; they are the same thing," added the young trader.

"They are! I think, now, for a professional man, you know but little of the terms of your art," observed Borroughcliffe, with an affectation of irony; "I never have seen a youth of your years who knew less. What names, now, would you affix to this, and this, and this?"

While the captain was speaking, he drew from his pockets the several instruments that the cockswain had made use of, the preceding night, to secure his prisoner.

"That," exclaimed the lad, with the eagerness of one who would vindicate his reputation, "is ratlin-stuff; and this is marline; and that is sennit."

"Enough, enough," said Borroughcliffe; "you have exhibited sufficient knowledge, to convince me that you *do* know something of your *trade*, and nothing of these articles. Mr. Griffith, do you claim this boy?"

"I believe I must, sir," said the young sea-officer, who had been intently listening to the examination. "On whatever errand you have ventured here, Mr. Merry, it is useless to affect further concealment."

"Merry!" exclaimed Cecilia Howard; "is it you, then, my cousin? are you, too, fallen into the power of your enemies! was it not enough that—"

The young lady recovered her recollection in time to suppress the remainder of the sentence, though the grateful expression of Griffith's eye sufficiently indicated that he had, in his thoughts, filled the sentence with expressions abundantly flattering to his own feelings.

"How's this, again!" cried the colonel; "my two wards embracing and fondling a vagrant, vagabond pedler, before my eyes! is this treason, Mr. Griffith? or what means the extraordinary visit of this young gentleman?"

"Is it extraordinary, sir," said Merry himself, losing his assumed awkwardness, in the ease and confidence of one whose faculties had been early exercised, "that a boy, like myself, destitute of mother and sisters, should take a little risk on himself, to visit the only two female relatives he has in the world?"

"Why this disguise, then? surely, young gentleman, it was unnecessary to enter the dwelling of old George Howard, on such an errand, clandestinely, even though your tender years have been practised on, to lead you astray from your allegiance. Mr. Griffith and Captain Manual must pardon me, if I express sentiments, at my own table, that they may find unpleasant; but this business requires us to be explicit."

"The hospitality of Colonel Howard is unquestionable," returned the boy; "but he has a great reputation for his loyalty to the crown."

"Ay, young gentleman; and, I trust, with some justice."

"Would it, then, be safe, to intrust my person in the hands of one who might think it his duty to detain me?"

"This is plausible enough, Captain Borroughcliffe, and I doubt not the boy speaks with candour. I would, now, that my kinsman, Mr. Christopher Dillon, were here, that I might learn if it would be misprision of treason, to permit this youth to depart, unmolested, and without exchange?"

"Inquire of the young gentleman, after the Cacique," returned the recruiting officer, who, apparently satisfied in producing the exposure of Merry, had resumed his seat at the table; "perhaps he is, in verity, an ambassador, empowered to treat on behalf of his highness."

"How say you, sir," demanded the colonel; "do you know any thing of my kinsman?"

The anxious eyes of the whole party were fastened on the boy, for many moments, witnessing the sudden change from careless freedom to deep horror, expressed in his countenance. At length he uttered, in an under tone, the secret of Dillon's fate.

"He is dead."

"Dead!" repeated every voice in the room.

"Yes, dead," said the boy, gazing at the pallid faces of those who surrounded him.

A long and fearful silence succeeded the announcement of

this intelligence, which was only interrupted by Griffith, who said—

"Explain the manner of his death, sir, and where his body lies."

"His body lies interred in the sands," returned Merry, with a deliberation that proceeded from an opening perception, that if he uttered too much, he might betray the loss of the Ariel, and, consequently, endanger the liberty of Barnstable.

"In the sands!" was echoed from every part of the room.

"Ay, in the sands; but how he died, I cannot explain."

"He has been murdered!" exclaimed Colonel Howard, whose command of utterance was now amply restored to him; "he has been treacherously, and dastardly, and basely murdered!"

"He has *not* been murdered," said the boy, firmly; "nor did he meet his death among those who deserve the name either of traitors or of dastards."

"Said you not that he was dead? that my kinsman was buried in the sands of the sea-shore?"

"Both are true, sir—"

"And you refuse to explain how he met his death, and why he has been thus ignominiously interred?"

"He received his interment by my orders, sir; and if there be ignominy about his grave, his own acts have heaped it on him. As to the manner of his death, I cannot, and will not speak."

"Be calm, my cousin," said Cecilia, in an imploring voice; "respect the age of my uncle, and remember his strong attachment to Mr. Dillon."

The veteran had, however, so far mastered his feelings, as to continue the dialogue with more recollection.

"Mr. Griffith," he said, "I shall not act hastily—you and your companion will be pleased to retire to your several apartments. I will so far respect the son of my brother Harry's friend, as to believe your parole will be sacred. Go, gentlemen; you are unguarded."

The two prisoners bowed low to the ladies and their host, and retired. Griffith, however, lingered a moment on the threshold, to say—

"Colonel Howard, I leave the boy to your kindness and consideration. I know you will not forget that his blood mingles with that of one who is most dear to you."

"Enough, enough, sir," said the veteran, waving his hand to him to retire; "and you, ladies; this is not a place for you, either."

"Never will I quit this child," said Katherine, "while such a horrid imputation lies on him. Colonel Howard, act your pleasure on us both, for I suppose you have the power; but his fate shall be my fate."

"There is, I trust, some misconception in this melancholy affair," said Borroughcliffe, advancing into the centre of the agitated group; "and I should hope, by calmness and moderation, all may yet be explained — young gentleman, you have borne arms, and must know, notwithstanding your youth, what it is to be in the power of your enemies."

"Never!" returned the proud boy; "I am a captive for the first time."

"I speak, sir, in reference to our power."

"You may order me to a dungeon; or, as I have entered the Abbey in disguise, possibly, to a gibbet."

"And is that a fate to be met so calmly, by one so young!"

"You dare not do it, Captain Borroughcliffe," cried Katherine, involuntarily throwing an arm around the boy, as if to shield him from harm; "you would blush to think of such a cold-blooded act of vengeance, Colonel Howard."

"If we could examine the young man, where the warmth of feeling, which these ladies exhibit, might not be excited," said the captain, apart to his host, "we should gain important intelligence."

"Miss Howard, and you, Miss Plowden," said the veteran, in a manner that long habit had taught his wards to respect, "your young kinsman is not in the keeping of savages, and you can safely confide him to my custody. I am sorry that we have so long kept Miss Alice standing, but she will find relief on the couches of your drawing-room, Cecilia."

Cecilia and Katherine permitted themselves to be conducted to the door, by their polite, but determined guardian, where he bowed to their retiring persons, with the exceeding courtesy that he never failed to use, when in the least excited.

"You appear to know your danger, Mr. Merry," said Borroughcliffe, after the door was closed; "I trust you also know what duty would dictate to one in my situation."

"Do it, sir," returned the boy; "you have a king to render an account to, and I have a country."

"I may have a country, also," said Borroughcliffe, with a calmness that was not in the least disturbed by the taunting air with which the youth delivered himself. "It is possible for me, however, to be lenient, even merciful, when the interests of that prince, to whom you allude, are served — you came not on this enterprise alone, sir?"

"Had I come better attended, Captain Borroughcliffe might have heard these questions, instead of putting them."

"I am happy, sir, that your retinue has been so small; and yet, even the rebel schooner called the Ariel might have furnished you with a more becoming attendance. I cannot but think, that you are not far distant from your friends."

"He is near his enemies, your honour," said Sergeant Drill, who had entered the room, unobserved; "for here is a boy who says he has been seized in the old ruin, and robbed of his goods and clothes; and, by his description, this lad should be the thief."

Borroughcliffe signed to the boy, who stood in the back ground, to advance, and he was instantly obeyed, with all that eagerness which a sense of injury on the part of the sufferer could excite. The tale of this unexpected intruder was soon told, and was briefly this:

He had been assaulted by a man and a boy, (the latter was in presence,) while arranging his effects, in the ruin, preparatory to exhibiting them to the ladies of the Abbey, and had been robbed of such part of his attire as the boy had found necessary for his disguise, together with his basket of valuables. He had been put into an apartment of an old tower, by the man, for safe keeping; but as the latter frequently ascended to its turret, to survey the country, he had availed himself of this remissness, to escape. And, to conclude, he demanded a restoration of his property, and vengeance for his wrongs.

Merry heard his loud and angry details with scornful composure, and before the offended pedler was through his narrative, had devested himself of the borrowed garments, which he threw to the other, with singular disdain.

"We are beleaguered, mine host! beset! besieged!" cried Borroughcliffe, when the other had ended. "Here is a rare plan to rob us of our laurels! ay, and of our rewards! but, harkye, Drill! they have old soldiers to deal with, and we shall look into the matter. One would wish to triumph on foot; you understand me? — there was no horse in the battle. Go, fellow, I see you grow wiser; take this young gentleman — and remember *he is* a young gentleman — put him in safe keeping, but see him supplied with all he wants."

Borroughcliffe bowed politely to the haughty bend of the body with which Merry, who now began to think himself a martyr to his country, followed the orderly from the room.

"There is metal in the lad!" exclaimed the captain; "and if he live to get a beard, 'twill be a hardy dog who ventures to pluck it. I am glad, mine host, that this 'wandering jew' has arrived, to save the poor fellow's feelings, for I detest tampering with such a noble spirit. I saw, by his eye, that he had squinted oftener over a gun, than through a needle!"

"But they have murdered my kinsman! — the loyal, the learned, the ingenious Mr. Christopher Dillon!"

"If they have done so, they shall be made to answer it," said Borroughcliffe, re-seating himself at the table, with a coolness that furnished an ample pledge of the impartiality of his judgment; "but let us learn the facts, before we do aught hastily."

Colonel Howard was fain to comply with so reasonable a proposition, and he resumed his chair, while his companion proceeded to institute a close examination of the pedler boy.

We shall defer, until the proper time may arrive, recording the result of his inquiries; but shall so far satisfy the curiosity of our readers, as to tell them, that the captain learned sufficient to convince him, a very serious attempt was meditated on the Abbey; and, as he thought, enough, also, to enable him to avert the danger.

Chapter XXVII.

— "I have not seen
So likely an embassador of love."
The Merchant of Venice, III.i.91–92.

CECILIA and Katherine separated from Alice Dunscombe in the lower gallery of the cloisters; and the cousins
ascended to the apartment which was assigned them as a
dressing-room. The intensity of feeling that was gradually ac-
cumulating in the breasts of the ladies, as circumstances
brought those in whom their deepest interests were centered,
into situations of extreme delicacy, if not of actual danger,
perhaps, in some measure, prevented them from experiencing
all that concern which the detection and arrest of Merry might
be supposed to excite. The boy, like themselves, was an only
child of one of those three sisters, who caused the close connexion of so many of our characters, and his tender years had led
his cousins to regard him with an affection that exceeded the
ordinary interest of such an affinity; but they knew, that in the
hands of Colonel Howard his person was safe, though his
liberty might be endangered. When the first emotions,
therefore, which were created by his sudden appearance, after
so long an absence, had subsided, their thoughts were rather
occupied by the consideration of what consequences, to others,
might proceed from his arrest, than by any reflections on the
midshipman's actual condition. Secluded from the observations of any strange eyes, the two maidens indulged their feelings, without restraint, according to their several
temperaments. Katherine moved to and fro, in the apartment,
with feverish anxiety, while Miss Howard, by concealing her
countenance under the ringlets of her luxuriant, dark hair,
and shading her eyes with a fair hand, seemed to be willing to
commune with her thoughts more quietly.

"Barnstable cannot be far distant," said the former, after a
few minutes had passed; "for he never would have sent that

child on such an errand, by himself!"

Cecilia raised her mild, blue eyes to the countenance of her cousin, as she answered—

"All thoughts of an exchange must now be abandoned; and perhaps the persons of the prisoners will be held as pledges, to answer for the life of Dillon."

"Can the wretch be dead! or is it merely a threat, or some device of that urchin? he is a forward child, and would not hesitate to speak and act boldly, on emergency."

"He is dead!" returned Cecilia, veiling her face again, in horror; "the eyes of the boy, his whole countenance, confirmed his words! I fear, Katherine, that Mr. Barnstable has suffered his resentment to overcome his discretion, when he learned the treachery of Dillon; surely, surely, though the hard usages of war may justify so dreadful a revenge on an enemy, it was unkind to forget the condition of his own friends!"

"Mr. Barnstable has done neither, Miss Howard," said Katherine, checking her uneasy footsteps, her light form swelling with pride; "Mr. Barnstable is equally incapable of murdering an enemy, or of deserting a friend!"

"But retaliation is neither deemed nor called murder, by men in arms."

"Think it what you will, call it what you will, Cecilia Howard, I will pledge my life, that Richard Barnstable has to answer for the blood of none but the open enemies of his country."

"The miserable man may have fallen a sacrifice to the anger of that terrific seaman, who led him hence as a captive!"

"That terrific seaman, Miss Howard, has a heart as tender as your own. He is—"

"Nay, Katherine," interrupted Cecilia, "you chide me unkindly; let us not add to our unavoidable misery, by such harsh contention."

"I do not contend with you, Cecilia! I merely defend the absent and the innocent from your unkind suspicions, my cousin."

"Say, rather, your sister," returned Miss Howard, their hands involuntarily closing upon each other, "for we are surely sisters! But let us strive to think of something less horrible. Poor, poor Dillon! now that he has met a fate so terrible, I can even fancy

him less artful and more upright than we had thought him!
You agree with me, Katherine, I see by your countenance,
and we will dwell no longer on the subject. — Katherine! my
cousin Kate, what see you?"

Miss Plowden, as she relinquished her pressure of the hand
of Cecilia, had renewed her walk with a more regulated step;
but she was yet making her first turn across the room, when
her eyes became keenly set on the opposite window, and her
whole frame was held in an attitude of absorbed attention. The
rays of the setting sun fell bright upon her dark glances, which
seemed fastened on some distant object, and gave an additional glow to the mantling colour that was slowly stealing,
across her cheeks, to her temples. Such a sudden alteration in
the manner and appearance of her companion, had not failed
to catch the attention of Cecilia, who, in consequence, interrupted herself by the agitated question we have related.
Katherine slowly beckoned her companion to her side, and,
pointing in the direction of the wood that lay in view, she
said —

"See yon tower, in the ruin! Do you observe those small
spots of pink and yellow that are fluttering above its walls?"

"I do. They are the lingering remnants of the foliage of some
tree; but they want the vivid tints which grace the autumn of
our own dear America!"

"One is the work of God, and the other has been produced
by the art of man. Cecilia, those are no leaves, but they are my
own childish signals, and without doubt Barnstable himself is
on that ruined tower. Merry, cannot, will not, betray him!"

"My life should be a pledge for the honour of our little
cousin," said Cecilia. "But you have the telescope of my uncle
at hand, ready for such an event! one look through it will
ascertain the truth — "

Katherine sprang to the spot where the instrument stood,
and with eager hands she prepared it for the necessary observation.

"It is he!" she cried the instant her eye was put to the glass. "I
even see his head above the stones. How unthinking to expose
himself so unnecessarily!"

"But what says he, Katherine!" exclaimed Cecilia; "you
alone can interpret his meaning."

The little book which contained the explanations of Miss Plowden's signals was now hastily produced, and its leaves rapidly run over in quest of the necessary number.

"'Tis only a question to gain my attention. I must let him know he is observed."

When Katherine, as much to indulge her secret propensities, as with any hope of its usefulness, had devised this plan for communicating with Barnstable, she had, luckily, not forgotten to arrange the necessary means to reply to his interrogatories. A very simple arrangement of some of the ornamental cords of the window-curtains, enabled her to effect this purpose; and her nimble fingers soon fastened the pieces of silk to the lines, which were now thrown into the air, when these signals in miniature were instantly displayed in the breeze.

"He sees them!" cried Cecilia, "and is preparing to change his flags."

"Keep then your eye on him, my cousin, and tell me the colours that he shows, with their order, and I will endeavour to read his meaning."

"He is as expert as yourself! There are two more of them fluttering above the stones again: the upper is white, and the lower black."

"White over black," repeated Katherine, rapidly, to herself, as she turned the leaves of her book. — "'*My messenger: has he been seen?*' — To that we must answer the unhappy truth. Here it is — yellow, white, and red — '*he is a prisoner.*' How fortunate that I should have prepared such a question and answer. What says he, Cecilia, to this news?"

"He is busy making his changes, dear. Nay, Katherine, you shake so violently as to move the glass! Now he is done; 'tis yellow over black, this time."

"'*Griffith, or who?*' He does not understand us; but I had thought of the poor boy, in making out the numbers — ah! here it is; yellow, green, and red — '*my cousin Merry.*' — He cannot fail to understand us now."

"He has already taken in his flags. The news seems to alarm him, for he is less expert than before. He shows them now — they are green, red and yellow."

"The question is, '*Am I safe?*' 'Tis that which made him tardy,

Miss Howard," continued Katherine. "Barnstable is ever slow to consult his safety. But how shall I answer him? should we mislead him now, how could we ever forgive ourselves!"

"Of Andrew Merry there is no fear," returned Cecilia; "and I think if Captain Borroughcliffe had any intimation of the proximity of his enemies, he would not continue at the table."

"He will stay there while wine will sparkle, and man can swallow," said Katherine; "but we know, by sad experience, that he is a soldier on an emergency; and yet, I'll trust to his ignorance this time—here, I have an answer: '*you are yet safe, but be wary.*'"

"He reads your meaning with a quick eye, Katherine; and he is ready with his answer too: he shows green over white this time. Well! do you not hear me? 'tis green over white. Why, you are dumb—what says he, dear?"

Still Katherine answered not, and her cousin raised her eyes from the glass, and beheld her companion gazing earnestly at the open page, while the glow which excitement had before brought to her cheek, was increased to a still deeper bloom.

"I hope your blushes and his signals are not ominous, Kate," added Cecilia; "can green imply his jealousy, as white does your purity? what says he, coz?"

"He talks, like yourself, much nonsense," said Katherine, turning to her flags, with a pettish air, that was singularly contradicted by her gratified countenance; "but the situation of things requires that I should talk to Barnstable more freely."

"I can retire," said Cecilia, rising from her chair with a grave manner.

"Nay, Cecilia, I do not deserve these looks—'tis you who exhibit levity now! But you can perceive, for yourself, that evening is closing in, and that some other medium for conversation, besides the eyes, may be adopted.—Here is a signal, which will answer: '*When the Abbey clock strikes nine, come with care to the wicket, which opens, at the east side of the Paddock, on the road: until then, keep secret.*' I had prepared this very signal, in case an interview should be necessary."

"Well, he sees it," returned Cecilia, who had resumed her place by the telescope, "and seems disposed to obey you, for I no longer discern his flags or his person."

Miss Howard now arose from before the glass, her observa-

tions being ended; but Katherine did not return the instrument to its corner, without fastening one long and anxious
look through it, on what now appeared to be the deserted
tower. The interest and anxiety produced by this short and imperfect communication between Miss Plowden and her lover,
did not fail to excite reflections in both the ladies, that furnished
materials to hold them in earnest discourse, until the entrance
of Alice Dunscombe announced that their presence was expected below. Even the unsuspecting Alice, on entering,
observed a change in the countenances and demeanor of the
two cousins, which betrayed that their secret conference had
not been entirely without contention. The features of Cecilia
were disturbed and anxious, and their expression was not
unlike melancholy; while the dark flashing eye, flushed
temples, and proud, determined step of Katherine, exhibited
in an equal, if not a greater degree, a very different emotion.
As no reference to the subject of their conversation was,
however, made by either of the young ladies, after the entrance of Alice, she led the way, in silence, to the drawing
room.

The ladies were received, by Col. Howard and Borroughcliffe, with marked attention. In the former there were
moments when a deep gloom would, in spite of his very obvious exertions to the contrary, steal over his open, generous
countenance; but the recruiting officer maintained an air of
immovable coolness and composure. Twenty times did he
detect the piercing looks of Katherine fastened on him, with an
intentness, that a less deliberative man might have had the
vanity to misinterpret; but even this flattering testimonial of
his power to attract, failed to disturb his self-possession. It was
in vain that Katherine endeavoured to read his countenance,
where every thing was fixed in military rigidity, though his
deportment appeared more than usually easy and natural.
Tired at length with her fruitless scrutiny, the excited girl
turned her gaze upon the clock; to her amazement, she
discovered that it was on the stroke of nine, and, disregarding a
deprecating glance from her cousin, she arose and quitted the
apartment. Borroughcliffe opened the door for her exit, and,
while the lady civilly bowed her head in acknowledgment of his
attention, their eyes once more met; but she glided quickly by

him, and found herself alone in the gallery. Katherine hesitated, more than a minute, to proceed, for she thought she had detected in that glance a lurking expression, that manifested conscious security mingled with secret design. It was not her nature, however, to hesitate, when circumstances required that she should be both prompt and alert; and, throwing over her slight person a large cloak, that was in readiness for the occasion, she stole warily from the building.

Although Katherine suspected, most painfully, that Borroughcliffe had received intelligence that might prove dangerous to her lover, she looked around her in vain, on gaining the open air, to discover any alteration in the arrangements for the defence of the Abbey, which might confirm her suspicions, or the knowledge of which might enable her to instruct Barnstable how to avoid the secret danger. Every disposition remained as it had been since the capture of Griffith and his companion. She heard the heavy, quick steps of the sentinel, who was posted beneath their windows, endeavouring to warm himself, on his confined post; and as she paused to listen, she also detected the rattling of arms from the soldier, who, as usual, guarded the approach to that part of the building where his comrades were quartered. The night had set in cloudy and dark, although the gale had greatly subsided towards the close of the day; still the wind swept heavily, and, at moments, with a rushing noise, among the irregular walls of the edifice; and it required the utmost nicety of ear, to distinguish even these well-known sounds, among such accompaniments. When Katherine, however, was satisfied that her organs had not deceived her, she turned an anxious eye in the direction of what Borroughcliffe called his "barracks." Every thing in that direction appeared so dark and still as to create a sensation of uneasiness, by its very quiet. It might be the silence of sleep that now pervaded the ordinarily gay and mirthful apartment! or it might be the stillness of a fearful preparation! There was no time, however, for further hesitation, and Katherine drew her cloak more closely about her form, and proceeded, with light and guarded steps, to the appointed spot. As she approached the wicket the clock struck the hour, and she again paused, while the mournful sounds were borne by her on the wind, as if expecting that each stroke on the bell, would prove a signal to unmask some secret design of Burroughcliffe. As the last vibration melted away, she opened the little gate, and issued on the highway. The figure of a man sprung forward from behind an angle of the wall, as she appeared; and, while her heart was still throbbing with the suddenness of the alarm, she found herself in the arms of Barnstable. After the first few words of recognition and pleasure which the young sailor uttered, he acquainted his mistress with the loss of his schooner, and the situation of the survivors.

"And now, Katherine," he concluded, "you have come, I trust, never to quit me; or, at most, to return no more to that old Abbey, unless it be to aid in liberating Griffith, and then to join me again for ever."

"Why, truly, there is so much to tempt a young woman to renounce her home and friends, in the description you have just given of your condition, that I hardly know how to refuse your request, Barnstable. You are very tolerably provided with a dwelling in the ruin; and I suppose certain predatory schemes are to be adopted to make it habitable! St. Ruth is certainly well supplied with the necessary articles, but whether we should not be shortly removed to the Castle at York, or the gaol at Newcastle, is a question that I put to your discretion."

"Why yield your thoughts to such silly subjects, lovely trifler!" said Barnstable, "when the time and the occasion both urge us to be in earnest?"

"It is a woman's province to be thrifty, and to look after the comforts of domestic life," returned his mistress; "and I would discharge my functions with credit. But I feel you are vexed, for, to see your dark countenance is out of the question, on such a night. When do you propose to commence housekeeping, if I should yield to your proposals?"

"I have not concluded relating my plans, and your provoking wit annoys me! The vessel I have taken, will, unquestionably, come into the land, as the gale dies; and I intend making my escape in her, after beating this Englishman, and securing the liberty of Miss Howard and yourself. I could see the Frigate in the offing, even before we left the cliffs."

"This certainly sounds better!" rejoined Katherine, in a manner that indicated she was musing on their prospects; "and yet there may exist some difficulties in the way that you little suspect."

"Difficulties! there are none — there can be none."

"Speak not irreverently of the mazes of love, Mr. Barnstable. When was it ever known to exist unfettered or unembarrassed? even I have an explanation to ask of you, that I would much rather let alone."

"Of me! ask what you will, or how you will; I am a careless, unthinking fellow, Miss Plowden; but to you I have little to answer for — unless a foolish sort of adoration be an offence against your merits."

Barnstable felt the little hand that was supported on his arm, pressing the limb, as Katherine replied, in a tone so changed from its former forced levity, that he started as the first sounds reached his ears. "Merry has brought in a horrid report!" she said; "I would I could believe it untrue! but the looks of the boy, and the absence of Dillon, both confirm it."

"Poor Merry! he too has fallen into the trap! but they shall yet find one who is too cunning for them. Is it to the fate of that wretched Dillon that you allude?"

"He *was* a wretch," continued Katherine, in the same voice, "and he deserved much punishment at your hands, Barnstable; but life is the gift of God, and is not to be taken whenever human vengeance would appear to require a victim."

"His life was taken by him who bestowed it," said the sailor. "Is it Katherine Plowden who would suspect me of the deed of a dastard!"

"I do not suspect you — I did not suspect you," cried Katherine; "I will never suspect any evil of you again. You are not, you cannot be angry with me, Barnstable? had you heard the cruel suspicions of my cousin Cecilia, and had your imagination been busy in portraying your wrongs and the temptations to forget mercy, like mine, even while my tongue denied your agency in the suspected deed, you would — you would at least have learned, how much easier it is to defend those we love against the open attacks of others, than against our own jealous feelings."

"Those words, love and jealousy, will obtain your acquittal," cried Barnstable, in his natural voice; and, after uttering a few more consoling assurances to Katherine, whose excited feelings found vent in tears, he briefly related the manner of Dillon's death.

"I had hoped I stood higher in the estimation of Miss Howard, than to be subjected to even her suspicions," he said, when he had ended his explanation. "Griffith has been but a sorry representative of our trade, if he has left such an opinion of its pursuits."

"I do not know that Mr. Griffith would altogether have escaped my conjectures, had he been the disappointed commander, and you the prisoner," returned Katherine; "you know not how much we have both studied the usages of war, and with what dreadful pictures of hostages, retaliations, and military executions, our minds are stored! but a mountain is raised off my spirits, and I could almost say, that I am now ready to descend the valley of life in your company."

"It is a discreet determination, my good Katherine, and God bless you for it; the companion may not be so good as you deserve, but you will find him ambitious of your praise. Now let us devise means to effect our object."

"Therein lies another of my difficulties. Griffith, I much fear, will not urge Cecilia to another flight, against her—her—what shall I call it, Barnstable—her caprice, or her judgment? Cecilia will never consent to desert her uncle, and I cannot muster the courage to abandon my poor cousin, in the face of the world, in order to take shelter with even Mr. Richard Barnstable!"

"Speak you from the heart now, Katherine?"

"Very nearly—if not exactly."

"Then have I been cruelly deceived! It is easier to find a path in the trackless ocean, without chart or compass, than to know the windings of a woman's heart!"

"Nay, nay, foolish man; you forget that I am but small, and how very near my head is to my heart; too nigh, I fear, for the discretion of their mistress! but is there no method of forcing Griffith and Cecilia to their own good, without undue violence?"

"It cannot be done; he is my senior in rank, and the instant I release him he will claim the command. A question might be raised, at a leisure moment, on the merits of such a claim—but even my own men are, as you know, nothing but a draft from the frigate, and they would not hesitate to obey the orders of the first lieutenant, who is not a man to trifle on matters of duty."

"'Tis vexatious, truly," said Katherine, "that all my well concerted schemes in behalf of this wayward pair, should be frustrated by their own wilful conduct! But, after all, have you justly estimated your strength, Barnstable? are you certain that you would be successful, and that without hazard, too, if you should make the attempt?"

"Morally, and what is better, physically certain. My men are closely hid, where no one suspects an enemy to lie; they are anxious for the enterprise, and the suddenness of the attack will not only make the victory sure, but it will be rendered bloodless. You will aid us in our entrance, Katherine: I shall first secure this recruiting officer, and his command will then surrender without striking a blow. Perhaps, after all, Griffith will hear reason; if he do not, I will not yield my authority to a released captive, without a struggle."

"God send that there shall be no fighting!" murmured his companion, a little appalled at the images his language had raised before her imagination; "and, Barnstable, I enjoin you, most solemnly, by all your affection for me, and by every thing you deem most sacred, to protect the person of Col. Howard at every hazard. There must be no excuse, no pretence, for even an insult to my passionate, good, obstinate, but kind old guardian. I believe I have given him already more trouble than I am entitled to give any one, and Heaven forbid, that I should cause him any serious misfortune!"

"He shall be safe, and not only he, but all that are with him; as you will perceive, Katherine, when you hear my plan. Three hours shall not pass over my head before you will see me master of that old Abbey. Griffith, ay, Griffith must be content to be my inferior, until we get afloat again."

"Attempt nothing unless you feel certain of being able to maintain your advantage, not only against your enemies, but also against your friends," said the anxious Katherine. "Rely on it, both Cecilia and Griffith are refining so much on their feelings, that neither will be your ally."

"This comes of passing the four best years of his life within walls of brick, poring over Latin Grammars and Syntaxes, and such other nonsense, when he should have been rolling them away in a good box of live oak, and studying, at most, how to sum up his day's work, and tell where his ship lies after a blow. Your college learning may answer well enough for a man who has to live by his wits, but it can be of little use to one who is never afraid to read human nature, by looking his fellow creatures full in the face, and whose hand is as ready as his tongue. I have generally found the eye that was good at Latin was dull at a compass, or in a night-squall: and yet, Grif is a seaman; though I have heard him even read the testament in Greek! Thank God, I had the wisdom to run away from school the second day they undertook to teach me a strange tongue, and I believe I am the more honest man, and the better seaman, for my ignorance!"

"There is no telling what you might have been, Barnstable, under other circumstances," retorted his mistress, with a playfulness of manner that she could not always repress, though it was indulged at the expense of him she most loved; "I doubt not but, under proper training, you would have made a reasonably good priest."

"If you talk of priests, Katherine, I shall remind you that we carry one in the ship. But listen to my plan; we may talk further of priestcraft when an opportunity may offer."

Barnstable then proceeded to lay before his mistress a project he had formed for surprising the Abbey that night, which was so feasible, that Katherine, notwithstanding her recent suspicions of Borroughcliffe's designs, came gradually to believe it would succeed. The young seaman answered her objections with the readiness of an ardent mind, bent on executing its purposes, and with a fertility of resources that proved he was no contemptible enemy, in matters that required spirited action. Of Merry's remaining firm and faithful he had no doubt, and, although he acknowledged the escape of the pedler boy, he urged that the lad had seen no other of his party besides himself, whom he mistook for a common marauder.

As the disclosure of these plans was frequently interrupted by little digressions, connected with the peculiar emotions of the lovers, more than an hour flew by, before they separated. But Katherine, at length, reminded him how swiftly the time was passing, and how much remained to be done, when he reluctantly consented to see her once more through the wicket, where they parted.

Miss Plowden adopted the same precaution in returning to the house, she had used on leaving it; and she was congratulating herself on its success, when her eye caught a glimpse of the figure of a man, who was apparently following at some little distance, in her footsteps, and dogging her motions. As the obscure form, however, paused also when she stopped to give it an alarmed, though inquiring look, and then slowly retired towards the boundary of the paddock, Katherine believing it to be Barnstable watching over her safety, entered the Abbey, with every idea of alarm entirely lost in the pleasing reflection of her lover's solicitude.

Chapter XXVIII.

"He looks abroad and soon appears,
O'er Horncliffe-hill, a plump of spears,
Beneath a pennon gay."

Scott, *Marmion,* Canto First, III.1–4.

THE SHARP sounds of the supper-bell were ringing along the gallery, as Miss Plowden gained the gloomy passage; and she quickened her steps to join the ladies, in order that no further suspicions might be excited by her absence. — Alice Dunscombe was already proceeding to the dining parlour, as Katherine passed through the door of the drawing room, but Miss Howard had loitered behind, and was met by her cousin alone.

"You have then been so daring as to venture, Katherine?" exclaimed Cecilia.

"I have," returned the other, throwing herself into a chair, to recover her agitation—"I have, Cecilia; and I have met Barnstable, who will soon be in the Abbey, and its master."

The blood, which had rushed to the face of Cecilia on first seeing her cousin, now retreated to her heart, leaving every part of her fine countenance of the whiteness of her polished temples, as she said—

"And we are to have a night of blood!"

"We are to have a night of freedom, Miss Howard; freedom to you, and to me; to Andrew Merry, to Griffith, and to his companion!"

"What freedom more than we now enjoy, Katherine, is needed by two young women? Think you I can remain silent, and see my uncle betrayed before my eyes? his life perhaps endangered?"

"Your own life and person will not be held more sacred, Cecilia Howard, than that of your uncle. If you will condemn Griffith to a prison, and perhaps to a gibbet, betray Barnstable, as you have threatened—an opportunity will not be wanting at the supper table, whither I shall lead the way, since the mistress of the house appears to forget her duty."

Katherine arose, and, with a firm step, and proud eye, she moved along the gallery, to the room where their presence was expected by the rest of the family. Cecilia followed, in silence, and the whole party immediately took their several places at the board.

The first few minutes were passed in the usual attentions of the gentlemen to the ladies, and the ordinary civilities of the table; during which, Katherine had so far regained the equanimity of her feelings, as to commence a watchful scrutiny of the manners and looks of her guardian and Borroughcliffe, in which she determined to persevere until the eventful hour when she was to expect Barnstable should arrive. Col. Howard had, however, so far got the command of himself, as no longer to betray his former abstraction. In its place Katherine fancied, at moments, that she could discover a settled look of conscious security, mingled a little with an expression of severe determination; such as, in her earlier days, she had learned to dread as sure indications of the indignant, but upright justice of an honourable mind. Borroughcliffe, on the other hand, was cool, polite, and as attentive to the viands as usual, with the alarming exception of discovering much less devotion to the Pride of the Vineyards, than he commonly manifested on such occasions. In this manner the meal passed by, and the cloth was removed, though the ladies appeared willing to retain their places longer than was customary. Col. Howard, filling up the glasses of Alice Dunscombe, and himself, passed the bottle to the recruiting officer, and, with a sort of effort that was intended to rouse the dormant cheerfulness of his guests, cried —

"Come, Borroughcliffe, the ruby lips of your neighbours would be still more beautiful, were they moistened with this rich cordial, and that too, accompanied by some loyal sentiment. Miss Alice is ever ready to express her fealty to her Sovereign; in her name, I can give the health of His Most Sacred Majesty, with defeat and death to all traitors!"

"If the prayers of an humble subject, and one of a sex that has but little need to mingle in the turmoil of the world, and that has less right to pretend to understand the subtilties of statesmen, can much avail a High and Mighty Prince, like him who sits on the throne, then will he never know temporal evil," returned Alice, meekly; "but I cannot wish death to any one, not even to my enemies, if any I have, and much less to a people who are the children of the same family with myself."

"Children of the same family!" the Colonel repeated, slowly, and with a bitterness of manner that did not fail to attract the painful interest of Katherine; "children of the same family! Ay! even as Absalom was the child of David, or as Judas was of the family of the holy Apostles! But let it pass unpledged—let it pass. The accursed spirit of rebellion has invaded my dwelling, and I no longer know where to find one of my household, that has not been assailed by its malign influence!"

"Assailed I may have been, among others," returned Alice; "but not corrupted, if purity, in this instance, consist in loyalty—"

"What sound is that?" interrupted the Colonel, with startling suddenness. "Was it not the crash of some violence, Captain Borroughcliffe?"

"It may have been one of my rascals who has met with a downfall in passing from the festive board, where you know I regale them to-night, in honour of our success!—to his blanket," returned the Captain, with admirable indifference; "or it may be the very spirit of whom you have spoken so freely, my host, that has taken umbrage at your remarks, and is passing from the hospitable walls of St. Ruth into the open air, without submitting to the small trouble of ascertaining the position of doors. In the latter case there may be some dozen perches or so of wall to replace in the morning."

The Colonel, who had risen, glanced his eyes, uneasily, from the speaker to the door, and was, evidently, but little disposed to enter into the pleasantry of his guest.

"There are unusual noises, Capt. Borroughcliffe,. in the grounds of the Abbey, if not in the building itself," he said, advancing, with a fine military air, from the table to the centre of the room, "and, as master of the mansion, I will inquire who it is that thus unseasonably disturbs these domains. If as friends, they shall have welcome, though their visit be unexpected; and if enemies, they shall also meet with such a reception as will become an old soldier!"

"No, no," cried Cecilia, entirely thrown off her guard by the manner and language of the veteran, and rushing into his arms. "Go not out, my uncle, go not into the terrible fray, my kind, my good uncle! you are old; you have already done more than your duty; why should you be exposed to danger?"

"The girl is mad with terror, Borroughcliffe," cried the Colonel, bending his glistening eyes fondly on his niece, "and you will have to furnish my good-for-nothing, gouty old person with a corporal's guard, to watch my night-cap, or the silly child will have an uneasy pillow, till the sun rises once more. But you do not stir, sir?"

"Why should I?" cried the captain; "Miss Plowden yet deigns to keep me company, and it is not in the nature of one of the ——th, to desert his bottle and his standard at the same moment. For, to a true soldier, the smiles of a lady are as imposing in the parlour, as the presence of his colours in the field."

"I continue undisturbed, Captain Borroughcliffe," said Katherine, "because I have not been an inhabitant, for so many months, of St. Ruth, and not learned to know the tunes which the wind can play among its chimneys and pointed roofs. The noise which has taken Col. Howard from his seat, and which has so unnecessarily alarmed my cousin Cicely, is nothing but the Æolian Harp of the Abbey sounding a double bass."

The captain fastened on her composed countenance, while she was speaking, a look of open admiration, that brought, though tardily, the colour more deeply to her cheeks; and he answered, with something extremely equivocal, both in his emphasis and his air—

"I have avowed my allegiance, and I will abide by it. So long as Miss Plowden will deign to bestow her company, so long will she find me among her most faithful and persevering attendants, come who may, or what will."

"You compel me to retire," returned Katherine, rising, "whatever may have been my gracious intentions in the matter; for even female vanity must crimson, at an adoration so profound as that which can chain Capt. Borroughcliffe to a supper-table! As your alarm has now dissipated, my cousin, will you lead the way? Miss Alice and myself attend you."

"But not into the paddock, surely, Miss Plowden," said the captain; "the door, the key of which you have just turned, communicates with the vestibule. This is the passage to the drawing room."

The lady faintly laughed, as if in derision of her own forgetfulness, while she bowed her acknowledgment, and moved towards the proper passage; she observed—

"The madness of fear has assailed some, I believe, who have been able to affect a better disguise than Miss Howard."

"Is it the fear of present danger, or of that which is in reserve?" asked the captain; "but, as you have stipulated so generously in behalf of my worthy host here, and of one, also, who shall be nameless, because he has not deserved such a favour at your hands, your safety shall be one of my especial duties in these times of peril."

"There is peril then!" exclaimed Cecilia; "your looks announce it, Capt. Borroughcliffe! The changing countenance of my cousin tells me that my fears are too true!"

The soldier had now risen also, and, casting aside the air of badinage, which he so much delighted in, he came forward into the centre of the apartment, with the manner of one who felt it was time to be serious.

"A soldier is ever in peril, when the enemies of his king are at hand, Miss Howard," he answered; "and that such is now the case, Miss Plowden can testify, if she will. But you are the allies of both parties—retire, then, to your own apartments, and await the result of the struggle which is at hand."

"You speak of danger and hidden perils," said Alice Dunscombe; "know ye aught that justifies your fears?"

"I know all," Borroughcliffe coolly replied.

"All!" exclaimed Katherine.

"All!" echoed Alice, in tones of horror. "If, then, you know all, you must know his desperate courage, and powerful hand, when opposed—yield in quiet, and he will not harm ye. Believe me, believe one who knows his very nature, that no lamb can be more gentle than he would be, with unresisting women; nor any lion more fierce, with his enemies!"

"As we happen not to be of the feminine gender," returned

Borroughcliffe, with an air somewhat splenetic, "we must abide the fury of the king of beasts. His paw is, even now, at the outer door; and, if my orders have been obeyed, his entrance will be yet easier than that of the wolf, to the respectable female ancestor of the little red-riding-hood."

"Stay your hand for one single moment!" said Katherine, breathless with interest; "you are the master of my secret, Capt. Borroughcliffe, and bloodshed may be the consequence. I can yet go forward, and, perhaps, save many inestimable lives. Pledge to me your honour, that they who come hither as your enemies, this night, shall depart in peace, and I will pledge to you my life for the safety of the Abbey."

"Oh! hear her, and shed not human blood!" cried Cecilia.

A loud crash interrupted further speech, and the sounds of heavy footsteps were heard in the adjoining room, as if many men were alighting on its floor, in quick succession. Borroughcliffe drew back, with great coolness, to the opposite side of the large apartment, and took a sheathed sword from the table where it had been placed; at the same moment the door was burst open, and Barnstable entered alone, but heavily armed.

"You are my prisoners, gentlemen," said the sailor, as he advanced; "resistance is useless, and without it you shall receive favour. Ha! Miss Plowden! my advice was, that you should not be present at this scene."

"Barnstable, we are betrayed!" cried the agitated Katherine. "But it is not yet too late. Blood has not yet been spilt, and you can retire, without that dreadful alternative, with honour. Go, then, delay not another moment; for, should the soldiers of Capt. Borroughcliffe come to the rescue of their commander, the Abbey would be a scene of horror!"

"Go you away; go, Katherine," said her lover, with impatience; "this is no place for such as you. But, Capt. Borroughcliffe, if such be your name, you must perceive that resistance is in vain. I have ten good pikes in this outer room, in twenty better hands, and it will be madness to fight against such odds."

"Show me your strength," said the captain, "that I may take counsel with mine honour."

"Your honour shall be appeased, my brave soldier, for such

is your bearing, though your livery is my aversion, and your cause most unholy! Heave-ahead, boys! but hold your hands for orders."

The party of fierce-looking sailors, whom Barnstable led, on receiving this order, rushed into the room in a medley; but, notwithstanding the surly glances, and savage characters of their dress and equipments, they struck no blow, nor committed any act of hostility. The ladies shrunk back appalled, as this terrific little band took possession of the hall; and even Borroughcliffe, was seen to fall back towards a door, which, in some measure, covered his retreat. The confusion of this sudden movement had not yet subsided, when sounds of strife were heard rapidly approaching from a distant part of the building, and presently one of the numerous doors of the apartment was violently opened, when two of the garrison of the Abbey rushed into the hall, vigorously pressed by twice their number of seamen, seconded by Griffith, Manual, and Merry, who were armed with such weapons of offence as had presented themselves to their hands, at their unexpected liberation. There was a movement on the part of the seamen, who were already in possession of the room, that threatened instant death to the fugitives; but Barnstable beat down their pikes with his sword, and sternly ordered them to fall back. Surprise produced the same pacific result among the combatants; and as the soldiers hastily sought a refuge behind their own officers, and the released captives, with their liberators, joined the body of their friends, the quiet of the hall, which had been so rudely interrupted, was soon restored.

"You see, sir," said Barnstable, after grasping the hands of Griffith and Manual, in a warm and cordial pressure, "that all my plans have succeeded. Your sleeping guard are closely watched in their barracks, by one party, our officers are released, and your sentinels cut off by another, while, with a third, I hold the centre of the Abbey, and am, substantially, in possession of your own person. In consideration, therefore, of what is due to humanity, and to the presence of these ladies, let there be no struggle! I shall impose no difficult terms, nor any long imprisonment."

The recruiting officer manifested a composure, throughout the whole scene, that would have excited some uneasiness in his invaders, had there been opportunity for minute observation; but his countenance now gradually assumed an appearance of anxiety, and his head was frequently turned, as if listening for further, and more important interruptions. He answered, however, to this appeal, with his ordinary deliberation.

"You speak of conquests, sir, before they are achieved. My venerable host and myself are not so defenceless as you may choose to imagine." While speaking, he threw aside the cloth of a side table, from beneath which, the colonel and himself were instantly armed with a brace of pistols each. "Here are the death warrants of four of your party, and these brave fellows at my back can account for two more. I believe, my transatlantic warrior, that we are now something in the condition of Cortes and the Mexicans, when the former overran part of your continent—I being Cortes, armed with artificial thunder and lightning, and you the Indians, with nothing but your pikes and slings, and such other antediluvian inventions. Shipwrecks and sea-water are fatal dampers of gun-powder!"

"That we are unprovided with fire-arms, I will not deny," said Barnstable; "but we are men who are used, from infancy, to depend on our good right arms for life and safety, and we know how to use them, though we should even grapple with death! As for the trifles in your hands, gentlemen, you are not to suppose that men who are trained to look in at one end of a thirty-two pounder, loaded with grape, while the match is put to the other, will so much as wink at their report, though you fired them by fifties. What say you, boys! is a pistol a weapon to repel boarders?"

The discordant and disdainful laughs that burst from the restrained seamen, were a sufficient pledge of their indifference to so trifling a danger. Borroughcliffe noted their hardened boldness, and taking the supper bell, which was lying near him, he rang it, for a minute, with great violence. The heavy tread of trained footsteps soon followed this extraordinary summons; and presently, the several doors of the apartment were opened, and filled with armed soldiers, wearing the livery of the English crown.

"If you hold these smaller weapons in such vast contempt," said the recruiting officer, when he perceived that his men had possessed themselves of all the avenues, "it is in my power to try the virtue of some more formidable. After this exhibition of my strength, gentlemen, I presume you cannot hesitate to submit as prisoners of war."

The seamen had been formed in something like military array, by the assiduity of Manual, during the preceding dialogue; and as the different doors had discovered fresh accessions to the strength of the enemy, the marine industriously offered new fronts, until the small party was completely arranged in a hollow square, that might have proved formidable in a charge, bristled as it was with the deadly pikes of the Ariel.

"Here has been some mistake," said Griffith, after glancing his eye at the formidable array of the soldiers; "I take precedence of Mr. Barnstable, and I shall propose to you, Capt. Borroughcliffe, terms that may remove this scene of strife from the dwelling of Col. Howard."

"The dwelling of Col. Howard," cried the veteran, "is the dwelling of his king, or of the meanest servant of the crown! so, Borroughcliffe, spare not the traitors on my behalf; accept no other terms, than such unconditional submission as is meet to exact from the rebellious subjects of the Anointed of the Lord."

While Griffith spoke, Barnstable folded his arms, in affected composure, and glanced his eyes expressively at the shivering Katherine, who, with her companions, still continued agitated spectators of all that passed, chained to the spot by their apprehensions; but to this formidable denunciation, of the master of the Abbey, he deemed proper to reply—

"Now, by every hope I have of sleeping again on salt water, old gentleman, if it were not for the presence of these three trembling females, I should feel tempted to dispute, at once, the title of his majesty—you may make such a covenant as you will with Mr. Griffith, but if it contain one syllable about submission to your king, or of any other allegiance, than that which I owe to the Continental Congress, and the state of Massachusetts, you may as well consider the terms violated at once; for not an article of such an agreement will I consider as binding on me, or on any that shall choose to follow me as leader."

"Here are but two leaders, Mr. Barnstable," interrupted the haughty Griffith; "the one of the enemy, and the other, of the arms of America. Capt. Borroughcliffe, to you, as the former, I address myself. The great objects of the contest, which now unhappily divides England from her ancient colonies, can be, in no degree, affected by the events of this night; while, on the other hand, by a rigid adherence to military notions, much private evil and deep domestic calamity, must follow any struggle in such a place. We have but to speak, sir, and these rude men, who already stand impatiently handling their instruments of death, will aim them at each other's lives; and who can say that he shall be able to stay their hands when and where he will! I know you to be a soldier, and that you are not yet to learn how much easier it is to stimulate to blood, than to glut vengeance."

Borroughcliffe, unused to the admission of violent emotions, and secure in the superiority of his own party, both in numbers and equipments, heard him with the coolest composure to the end, and then answered in his customary manner.

"I honour your logic, sir. Your premises are indisputable, and the conclusion most obvious. Commit, then, these worthy tars to the good keeping of honest Drill, who will see their famished natures revived by divers eatables, and a due proportion of suitable fluids; while we can discuss the manner in which you are to return to the colonies, around a bottle of liquor, which my friend Manual there, assures me has come from the sunny side of the island of Madeira, to be drunk in a bleak corner of that of Britain. By my palate! but the rascals brighten at the thought! They know by instinct, sir, that a shipwrecked mariner is a fitter companion to a ration of beef and a pot of porter, than to such unsightly things as bayonets and boarding-pikes!"

"Trifle not unseasonably!" exclaimed the impatient young sailor. "You have the odds in numbers, but whether it will avail you much in a deadly struggle of hand to hand, is a question you must put to your prudence: we stand not here to ask terms, but to grant them. You must be brief, sir, for the time is wasting while we delay."

"I have offered to you the means of obtaining in perfection the enjoyment of the three most ancient of the numerous family of the arts — eating, drinking, and sleeping! What more do you require?"

"That you order these men, who fill the pass to the outer door, to fall back and give us room. I would take, in peace, these armed men from before the eyes of those who are unused to such sights. Before you oppose this demand, think how easily these hardy fellows could make a way for themselves, against your divided force."

"Your companion, the experienced Capt. Manual, will tell you that such a manœuvre would be very unmilitary, with a superior body in your rear!"

"I have not leisure, sir, for this folly," cried the indignant Griffith. "Do you refuse us an unmolested retreat from the Abbey?"

"I do."

Griffith turned, with a look of extreme emotion, to the ladies, and beckoned to them to retire, unable to give utterance to his wishes in words. After a moment of deep silence, however, he once more addressed Borroughcliffe in the tones of conciliation.

"If Manual and myself will return to our prisons, and submit to the will of your government," he said, "can the rest of the party return to the frigate unmolested?"

"They cannot," replied the soldier, who, perceiving that the crisis approached, was gradually losing his artificial deportment in the interest of the moment. "You, and all others, who willingly invade the peace of these realms, must abide the issue."

"Then God protect the innocent and defend the right!"

"Amen."

"Give way, villains!" cried Griffith, facing the party that held the outer door; "give way, or you shall be riddled with our pikes!"

"Show them your muzzles, men!" shouted Borroughcliffe; "but pull no trigger till they advance."

There was an instant of bustle and preparation, in which the rattling of fire-arms, blended with the suppressed execrations and threats of the intended combatants; and Cecilia and Katherine had both covered their faces to veil the horrid sight that was momentarily expected, when Alice Dunscombe advanced, boldly, between the points of the threatening weapons, and spoke in a voice that stayed the hands that were already uplifted.

"Hear me, men! if men ye be, and not demons, thirsting for each other's blood; though ye walk abroad in the semblance of him who died that ye might be elevated to the rank of angels! call ye this war? Is this the glory that is made to warm the hearts of even silly and confiding women? Is the peace of families to be destroyed to gratify your wicked lust for conquest; and is life to be taken in vain, in order that ye may boast of the foul deed in your wicked revels! Fall back, then, ye British soldiers! if ye be worthy of that name, and give passage to a woman; and remember that the first shot that is fired, will be buried in her bosom!"

The men, thus enjoined, shrunk before her commanding mien, and a way was made for her exit through that very door which Griffith had, in vain, solicited might be cleared for himself and party. But Alice, instead of advancing, appeared to have suddenly lost the use of those faculties which had already effected so much. Her figure seemed rooted to the spot where she had spoken, and her eyes were fixed in a settled gaze as if dwelling on some horrid object. While she yet stood in this attitude of unconscious helplessness, the door-way became again darkened, and the figure of the Pilot was seen on its threshold, clad, as usual, in the humble vestments of his profession, but heavily armed with the weapons of naval war. For an instant, he stood a silent spectator of the scene; and then advanced calmly, but with searching eyes, into the centre of the apartment.

Chapter XXIX.

Don Pedro. "Welcome Signior: you are almost come to part, almost a fray."

Much Ado about Nothing, V.i.113-114.

"**D**OWN with your arms, you Englishmen!" said the daring intruder; "and you, who fight in the cause of sacred liberty, stay your hands, that no unnecessary blood may flow. Yield yourself, proud Britons, to the power of the Thirteen Republics!"

"Ha!" exclaimed Borroughcliffe, grasping a pistol, with an air of great resolution, "the work thickens — I had not included this man in my estimate of their numbers. Is he a Sampson, that his single arm can change the face of things so suddenly! Down with your own weapon, you masquerader, or, at the report of this pistol, your body shall become a target for twenty bullets."

"And thine for a hundred!" returned the pilot — "without there! wind your call, fellow, and bring in our numbers. We will let this confident gentleman feel his weakness."

He had not done speaking, before the shrill whistle of a boatswain rose gradually on the ears of the listeners, until the sense of hearing became painfully oppressed, by the piercing sounds that rung under the arched roof of the hall, and penetrated even to the most distant recesses of the Abbey. A tremendous rush of men followed, who drove in before them the terrified fragment of Borroughcliffe's command, that had held the vestibule; and the outer room became filled with a dark mass of human bodies.

"Let them hear ye, lads!" cried their leader; "the Abbey is your own!"

The roaring of a tempest was not louder than the shout that burst from his followers, who continued their cheers, peal on peal, until the very roof of the edifice appeared to tremble with their vibrations. Numerous dark and shaggy heads were seen moving around the passage; some cased in the iron-bound caps of the frigate's boarders, and others glittering with the brazen ornaments of her marine guard. The sight of the latter did not fail to attract the eye of Manual, who rushed among the throng, and soon re-appeared, followed by a trusty band of his own men, who took possession of the posts held by the soldiers of Borroughcliffe, while the dialogue was continued between the leaders of the adverse parties.

Thus far Col. Howard had yielded to his guest, with a deep reverence for the principles of military subordination, the functions of a commander, but, now that affairs appeared to change so materially, he took on himself the right to question these intruders into his dwelling.

"By what authority, sir," the colonel demanded, "is it that you dare thus to invade the castle of a subject of this realm? Do you come backed by the commission of the lord lieutenant of the county, or has your warrant the signature of His Majesty's Secretary for the Home Department?"

"I bear no commission from any quarter," returned the pilot; "I rank only an humble follower of the friends of America; and having led these gentlemen into danger, I have thought it my duty to see them extricated. They are now safe; and the right to command all that hear me, rests with Mr. Griffith, who is commissioned by the Continental Congress for such service."

When he had spoken he fell back from the position he occupied, in the centre of the room, to one of its sides, where, leaning his body against the wainscot, he stood a silent observer of what followed —

"It appears, then, that it is to you, degenerate son of a most worthy father, that I must repeat my demand," continued the veteran. "By what right is my dwelling thus rudely assailed? and why is my quiet, and the peace of those I protect, so daringly violated?"

"I might answer you, Col. Howard, by saying that it is according to the laws of arms, or rather in retaliation for the thousand evils that your English troops have inflicted, between Maine and Georgia; but I wish not to increase the unpleasant character of this scene, and I therefore will tell you, that our advantage shall be used with moderation. The instant that our men can be collected, and our prisoners properly secured, your dwelling shall be restored to your authority. We are no freebooters, sir, and you will find it so after our departure. Capt. Manual, draw off your guard into the grounds, and make your dispositions for a return march to our boats—let the boarders fall back, there! out with ye! out with ye—tumble out, you boarders!"

The amicable order of the young lieutenant, which was delivered after the stern, quick fashion of his profession, operated on the cluster of dark figures, that were grouped around the door, like a charm; and as the men whom Barnstable had led, followed their shipmates into the court-yard, the room was now left to such only, as might be termed the gentlemen of the invading party, and the family of Col. Howard.

Barnstable had continued silent since his senior officer had assumed the command, listening most attentively to each syllable that fell from either side; but now that so few remained, and the time pressed, he spoke again—

"If we are to take boat so soon, Mr. Griffith, it would be seemly that due preparations should be made to receive the ladies, who are to honour us with their presence; shall I take that duty on myself?"

The abrupt proposal produced a universal surprise in his hearers; though the abashed and conscious expression of Katherine Plowden's features, sufficiently indicated, that to her, at least, it was not altogether unexpected. The long silence that succeeded the question, was interrupted by Col. Howard.

"Ye are masters, gentlemen; help yourselves to whatever best suits your inclinations. My dwelling, my goods, and my wards, are alike at your disposal—or, perhaps Miss Alice, here, good and kind Miss Alice Dunscombe, may suit the taste of some among ye! Ah! Edward Griffith! Edward Griffith! little did I ever—"

"Breathe not that name in levity again, thou scoffer, or even your years may prove a feeble protection!" said a stern, startling voice from behind. All eyes turned involuntarily at the unexpected sounds, and the muscular form of the Pilot was seen resuming its attitude of repose against the wall, though every fibre in his frame was working with suppressed passion.

When the astonished looks of Griffith ceased to dwell on this extraordinary exhibition of interest in his companion, they were turned imploringly towards the fair cousins, who still occupied the distant corner, whither fear had impelled them.

"I have said, that we are not midnight marauders, Col. Howard," he replied; "but if any there be here, who will deign to commit themselves to our keeping, I trust it will not be necessary to say, at this hour, what will be their reception."

"We have not time for unnecessary compliments," cried the impatient Barnstable; "here is Merry, who, by years and blood, is a suitable assistant for them, in arranging their little baggage — what say you, urchin, can you play the ladies' maid on emergency?"

"Ay, sir, and better than I acted the pedler-boy," cried the gay youngster; "to have my merry cousin Kate, and my good cousin Cicely for shipmates, I could play our common grandmother! Come, coz, let us be moving; you will have to allow a little lee-way in time, for my awkwardness."

"Stand back, young man," said Miss Howard, repulsing his familiar attempt to take her arm; and then advancing, with a maidenly dignity, nigher to her guardian, she continued, "I cannot know what stipulations have been agreed to by my cousin Plowden, in the secret treaty she has made this night with Mr. Barnstable; this for myself, Col. Howard, I would have you credit your brother's child when she says, that, to her, the events of the hour have not been more unexpected than to yourself."

The veteran gazed at her, for a moment, with an expression of his eye that denoted reviving tenderness; but gloomy doubts appeared to cross his mind again, and he shook his head, as he walked proudly away.

"Nay, then," added Cecilia, her head dropping meekly on her bosom, "I may be discredited by my uncle, but I cannot be disgraced wtihout some act of my own."

She slowly raised her mild countenance again, and bending her eyes on her lover, she continued, while a rich rush of blood passed over her fine features —

"Edward Griffith, I will not, I cannot say how humiliating it is to think that you can, for an instant, believe I would again forget myself so much as to wish to desert him whom God has given me for a protector, for one chosen by my own erring passions. And you, Andrew Merry! learn to respect the child of your mother's sister, if not for her own sake, at least for that of her who watched your cradle!"

"Here appears to be some mistake," said Barnstable, who participated, however, in no trifling degree, in the embarrassment of the abashed boy; "but, like all other mistakes on such subjects, it can be explained away, I suppose. Mr. Griffith, it remains for you to speak: — damn it, man," he whispered, "you are as dumb as a cod-fish — I am sure so fine a woman is worth a little fair weather talk: — you are muter than a four-footed beast — even an ass can bray!"

"We will hasten our departure, Mr. Barnstable," said Griffith, sighing heavily, and rousing himself, as if from a trance. "These rude sights cannot but appal the ladies. You will please, sir, to direct the order of our march to the shore. Captain Manual has charge of our prisoners, who must all be secured, to answer for an equal number of our own countrymen."

"And our countrywomen!" said Barnstable, "are they to be forgotten, in the selfish recollection of our own security!"

"With them we have no right to interfere, unless at their request."

"By Heaven! Mr. Griffith, this may smack of learning," cried the other, "and it may plead bookish authority as its precedent; but, let me tell you, sir, it savours but a little of a sailor's love."

"Is it unworthy of a seaman, and a gentleman, to permit the woman he calls his mistress to be so, other than in name?"

"Well, then, Griff, I pity you, from my soul. I would rather have had a sharp struggle for the happiness that I shall now obtain so easily, than that you should be thus cruelly disappointed. But you cannot blame me, my friend, that I avail myself of fortune's favour. Miss Plowden, your fair hand. Colonel Howard, I return you a thousand thanks for the care you have taken, hitherto, of this precious charge, and believe me, sir, that I speak frankly, when I say, that next to myself, I should choose to intrust her with you in preference to any man on earth."

The Colonel turned to the speaker, and bowed low, while he answered with grave courtesy —

"Sir, you repay my slight services with too much gratitude. If Miss Katherine Plowden has not become under my guardianship, all that her good father, Capt. John Plowden, of the Royal Navy, could have wished a daughter of his to be, the fault, unquestionably, is to be attributed to my inability to instruct, and to no inherent quality in the young lady herself. I will not say, take her, sir, since you have her in your possession already, and it would be out of my power to alter the arrangement; therefore, I can only wish that you may find her as dutiful as a wife, as she has been, hitherto, as a ward and a subject."

Katherine had yielded her hand, passively, to her lover, and suffered him to lead her more into the circle than she had before been; but now she threw off his arm, and shaking aside the dark curls which she had rather invited to fall in disorder around her brow, she raised her face and looked proudly up, with an eye that sparkled with the spirit of its mistress, and a face that grew pale with emotion at each moment, as she proceeded —

"Gentlemen, the one may be as ready to receive as the other is to reject; but has the daughter of John Plowden no voice in this cool disposal of her person! If her guardian tires of her presence, other habitations may be found, without inflicting so severe a penalty on this gentleman, as to compel him to provide for her accommodation in a vessel which must be already straitened for room!"

She turned, and rejoined her cousin with such an air of maidenly resentment, as a young woman would be apt to discover, who found herself the subject of matrimonial arrangement, without her own feelings being at all consulted. Barnstable, who knew but little of the windings of the female heart, or how necessary to his mistress, notwithstanding her previous declarations, the countenance of Cecilia was, to any decided and open act in his favour, stood in stupid wonder at her declaration. He could not conceive that a woman who had already ventured so much in secret in his behalf, and who had so often avowed her weakness, should shrink to declare it again, at such a crisis, though the eyes of a universe were on her! He looked from one of the party to the other, and met in every face an expression of delicate reserve, except in those of the guardian of his mistress, and of Borroughcliffe.

The colonel had given a glance of returning favour at her, whom, he now conceived, to be his repentant ward, while the countenance of the entrapped captain exhibited a look of droll surprise, blended with the expression of bitter ferocity it had manifested since the discovery of his own mishap.

"Perhaps, sir," said Barnstable, addressing the latter, fiercely, "you see something amusing about the person of this lady, to divert you thus unseasonably. We tolerate no such treatment of our women in America!"

"Nor do we quarrel before ours in England," returned the soldier, throwing back the fierce glance of the sailor, with interest; "but I was thinking of the revolutions that time can produce! nothing more I do assure you. It is not half an hour since I thought myself a most happy fellow; secure in my plans for overreaching the scheme you had laid to surprise me; and now I am as miserable a dog as wears a single epaulette, and has no hope of seeing its fellow!"

"And in what manner, sir, can this sudden change apply to me?" asked Katherine, with all her spirit.

"Certainly not to your perseverance in the project to assist my enemies, madam," returned the soldier with affected humility; "nor to your zeal for their success, or your consummate coolness at the supper table! But I find it is time that I should be superannuated—I can no longer serve my king with credit, and should take to serving my God, like all other worn out men of the world! My hearing is surely defective, or a paddock wall has a most magical effect in determining sounds!"

Katherine waited not to hear the close of this sentence, but walked to a distant part of the room, to conceal the burning blushes that covered her countenance. The manner in which the plans of Barnstable had become known to his foe, was no longer a mystery. Her conscience also reproached her a little, with some unnecessary coquetry as she remembered, that quite one half of the dialogue between her lover and herself, under the shadow of that very wall to which Borroughcliffe alluded, had been on a subject altogether foreign to contention and tumults. As the feelings of Barnstable were by no means so sensitive as those of his mistress, and his thoughts much occupied with the means of attaining his object, he did not so readily comprehend the indirect allusion of the soldier, but turned abruptly away to Griffith, and observed, with a serious air—

"I feel it my duty, Mr. Griffith, to suggest, that we have standing instructions to secure all the enemies of America, wherever they may be found, and to remind you, that the States have not hesitated to make prisoners of females, in many instances."

"Bravo!" cried Borroughcliffe; "if the ladies will not go as your mistresses, take them as your captives!"

"'Tis well for you, sir, that you are a captive yourself, or you should be made to answer for this speech," retorted the irritated Barnstable. "It is a responsible command, Mr. Griffith, and must not be disregarded."

"To your duty, Mr. Barnstable," said Griffith, again arousing from deep abstraction; "you have your orders, sir; let them be executed promptly."

"I have also the orders of our common superior, Capt. Munson, Mr. Griffith; and I do assure you, sir, that in making out my instructions for the Ariel—poor thing! there are no two of her timbers hanging together!—but my instructions were decidedly particular on that head."

"And my orders now supersede them."

"But am I justifiable in obeying a verbal order from an inferior, in direct opposition to a written instruction?"

Griffith had hitherto manifested in his deportment nothing more than a cold determination to act, but the blood now flew to every vessel in his cheeks and forehead, and his dark eyes flashed fire, as he cried authoritatively—

"How, sir! do you hesitate to obey?"

"By heaven, sir, I would dispute the command of the Continental Congress itself, should they bid me so far to forget my duty to—to—"

"Add yourself, sir!—Mr. Barnstable, let this be the last of it. To your duty, sir."

"My duty calls me here, Mr. Griffith."

"I must act, then, or be bearded by my own officers. Mr.

Merry, direct Capt. Manual to send in a serjeant, and a file of marines."

"Bid him come on himself!" cried Barnstable, maddened to desperation by his disappointment; "'tis not his whole corps that can disarm me—let them come on! Hear, there, you Ariels! rally around your captain."

"The man among them, who dares to cross that threshold without my order, dies," cried Griffith, menacing, with a naked hanger, the seamen, who had promptly advanced at the call of their old commander. "Yield your sword, Mr. Barnstable, and spare yourself the disgrace of having it forced from you by a common soldier."

"Let me see the dog who dare attempt it!" exclaimed Barnstable, flourishing his weapon in fierce anger. Griffith had extended his own arm, in the earnestness of his feelings, and their hangers crossed each other. The clashing of the steel operated on both like the sound of the clarion on a war-horse, and there were sudden and rapid blows, and as rapid parries, exchanged between the flashing weapons.

"Barnstable! Barnstable!" cried Katherine, rushing into his arms, "I will go with you to the ends of the earth!"

Cecilia Howard did not speak; but when Griffith recovered his coolness, he beheld her beautiful form kneeling at his feet, with her pale face bent imploringly on his own disturbed countenance. The cry of Miss Plowden had separated the combatants, before an opportunity for shedding blood had been afforded, but the young men exchanged looks of keen resentment, notwithstanding the interference of their mistresses. At this moment Col. Howard advanced, and raising his niece from her humble posture, said—

"This is not a situation for a child of Harry Howard, though she knelt in the presence, and before the throne of her Sovereign. Behold, my dear Cecilia, the natural consequences of this rebellion! It scatters discord in their ranks; and, by its damnable levelling principles, destroys all distinction of rank among themselves; even these rash boys know not where obedience is due!"

"It is due to me," said the Pilot, who now stepped forward among the agitated group, "and it is time that I enforce it. Mr. Griffith, sheath your sword. And you, sir, who have defied the

authority of your senior officer, and have forgotten the obligation of your oath, submit, and return to your duty."

Griffith started at the sounds of his calm voice, as if with
sudden recollection; and then bowing low, he returned the
weapon to its scabbard. But Barnstable still encircled the waist
of his mistress with one arm, while, with the other, he brandished his hanger, and laughed with scorn at this extraordinary assumption of authority.

"And who is this!" he cried, "who dares give such an order to
me!"

The eyes of the Pilot flashed with a terrible fire, while a
fierce glow seemed to be creeping over his whole frame, which
actually quivered with passion. But, suppressing this exhibition of his feelings, by a sudden and powerful effort, he
answered, in an emphatic manner—

"One who has a right to order, and who *will* be obeyed!"

The extraordinary manner of the speaker, contributed as
much as his singular assertion, to induce Barnstable, in his
surprise, to lower the point of his weapon, with an air that
might easily have been mistaken for submission. The Pilot
fastened his glowing eyes on him, for an instant, and then
turning to the rest of the listeners, he continued, more
mildly—

"It is true that we came not here as marauders, and that our
wish is, to do no unnecessary acts of severity to the aged and
the helpless. But this officer of the Crown, and this truant
American, in particular, are fairly our prisoners; as such, they
must be conducted on board our ship."

"But the main object of our expedition?"—said Griffith.

"'Tis lost," returned the Pilot, hastily—"'tis sacrificed to
more private feelings; 'tis like a hundred others, ended in
disappointment, and is forgotten, sir, for ever. But the interests of the Republics must not be neglected., Mr.
Griffith.—Though we are not madly to endanger the lives of
those gallant fellows, to gain a love-smile from one young
beauty, neither are we to forget the advantages they may have
obtained for us, in order to procure one of approbation from
another. This Col. Howard will answer well, in a bargain with
the minions of the Crown, and may purchase the freedom of
some worthy patriot, who is deserving of his liberty. Nay, nay,

suppress that haughty look, and turn that proud eye on any, rather than me! he goes to the frigate, sir, and that immediately."

"Then," said Cecilia Howard, timidly approaching the spot where her uncle stood, a disdainful witness of the dissensions amongst his captors; "then, will I go with him! He shall never be a resident among his enemies alone!"

"It would be more ingenuous, and more worthy of my brother's daughter," said her uncle, coldly, "if she ascribed her willingness to depart to its proper motive." Disregarding the look of deep distress with which Cecilia received this mortifying rejection of her tender attention, the old man walked towards Borroughcliffe, who was gnawing the hilt of his sword, in very vexation at the downfall of his high-raised hopes, and placing himself by his side, with an air of infinitely dignified submission, he continued, "act your pleasure on us, gentlemen: you are the conquerors, and we must even submit. A brave man knows as well how to yield, with decorum, as to defend himself stoutly, when he is not surprised, as we have been. But if an opportunity should ever offer! — Act your pleasures, gentlemen; no two lambs were ever half so meek as Capt. Borroughcliffe and myself."

The smile of affected, but bitter resignation, that the colonel bestowed on his fellow prisoner, was returned by that officer, with an attempt at risibility that abundantly betokened the disturbed state of his feelings. The two, however, succeeded in so far maintaining appearances, as to contemplate the succeeding movements of the conquerors, with a sufficient degree of composure.

The colonel steadily, and coldly, rejected the advances of his niece, who bowed meekly to his will, and relinquished, for the present, the hope of bringing him to a sense of his injustice. She, however, employed herself in earnest, to give such directions as were necessary to enforce the resolution she had avowed, and in this unexpected employment she found both a ready and a willing assistant in her cousin. The latter, unknown to Miss Howard, had, in anticipation of some such event as the present, long since made, in secret, all those preparations which might become necessary to a sudden flight from the Abbey. In conjunction with her lover then, who, perceiving that the plan of the Pilot was furthering his own views, deemed it most wise to forget his quarrel with that mysterious individual, she flew to point out the means of securing those articles which were already in preparation. Barnstable and Merry accompanied her light steps among the narrow, dark passages of the Abbey, with the utmost delight; the former repeatedly apostrophizing her wit and beauty, and, indeed, all of her various merits, and the latter, laughing, and indulging those buoyant spirits, that a boy of his years and reflection might be supposed to feel even in such a scene. It was fortunate for her cousin, that Katherine had possessed so much forethought, for the attention of Cecilia Howard was directed much more to the comforts of her uncle, than to those which were necessary for herself. Attended by Alice Dunscombe, the young mistress of St. Ruth moved through the solitary apartments of the building, listening to the mild, religious consolation of her companion, in silence, at times yielding to those bursts of mortified feeling, that she could not repress, or again as calmly giving her orders to her maids, as if the intended movement was one of but ordinary interest. All this time, the party in the dining hall remained stationary. The Pilot, as if satisfied with what he had already done, sunk back to his reclining attitude against the wall, though his eyes keenly watched every movement of the preparations, in a manner which denoted that his was the master spirit that directed the whole. Griffith had, however, resumed, in appearance, the command, and the busy seamen addressed themselves for orders to him alone. In this manner an hour was consumed, when Cecilia and Katherine, appearing in succession, attired in a suitable manner for their departure, and the baggage of the whole party having been already entrusted to a petty officer, and a party of his men, Griffith gave forth the customary order to put the whole in motion. The shrill, piercing whistle of the boatswain once more rung among the galleries and ceilings of the Abbey, and was followed by the deep, hoarse cry of—

"Away, there! you shore-draft! away, there, you boarders! ahead, heave ahead, sea-dogs!"

This extraordinary summons was succeeded by the roll of a drum, and the strains of a fife, from without, when the whole party moved from the building in the order that had been previously prescribed by Capt. Manual, who acted as the marshal of the forces on the occasion.

The Pilot had conducted his surprise with so much skill and secrecy as to have secured every individual about the Abbey, whether male or female, soldier or civilian; and as it might be dangerous to leave any behind who could convey intelligence into the country, Griffith had ordered that every human being, found in the building, should be conducted to the cliffs; to be held in durance, at least, until the departure of the last boat to the cutter, which he was informed, lay close in to the land, awaiting their re-embarkation. The hurry of the departure had caused many lights to be kindled in the Abbey, and the contrast between the glare within, and the gloom without, attracted the wandering looks of the captives, as they issued into the paddock. One of those indefinable, and unaccountable feelings, which so often cross the human mind, induced Cecilia to pause at the great gate of the grounds, and look back at the Abbey, with a presentiment that she was to behold it for the last time. The dark and ragged outline of the edifice was clearly delineated against the northern sky, while the open windows, and neglected doors, permitted a view of the solitude within. Twenty tapers were shedding their useless light in the empty apartments, as if in mockery of the deserted walls, and Cecilia turned, shuddering, from the sight, to press nigher to the person of her indignant uncle, with a secret impression, that her presence would soon be more necessary than ever to his happiness.

The low hum of voices in front, with the occasional strains of the fife, and the stern mandates of the sea-officers, soon recalled her, however, from these visionary thoughts to the surrounding realities, while the whole party pursued their way with diligence to the margin of the ocean.

Chapter XXX.

"A chieftain to the Highlands bound,
Cries 'Boatman, do not tarry!
And I'll give thee a silver pound,
To row us o'er the ferry.'"

Campbell, "Lord Ullin's Daughter," ll. 1–4.

THE SKY had been without a cloud during the day, the gale having been dry and piercing, and thousands of stars were now shining through a chill atmosphere. As the eye, therefore, became accustomed to the change of light, it obtained a more distinct view of surrounding objects. At the head of the line, that was stretched along the narrow pathway, marched a platoon of the marines, who maintained the regular, and steady front of trained warriors. They were followed, at some little distance, by a large and confused body of seamen, heavily armed, whose disposition to disorder and rude merriment, which became more violent from their treading on solid ground, was with difficulty restrained by the presence and severe rebukes of their own officers. In the centre of this confused mass, the whole of the common prisoners were placed, but were no otherwise attended to by their nautical guard, than as they furnished the subjects of fun and numberless quaint jokes. At some distance in their rear, marched Col. Howard and Borroughcliffe, arm in arm, both maintaining the most rigid and dignified silence, though under the influence of very bitter feelings. Behind these again, and pressing as nigh as possible to her uncle, was Miss Howard, leaning on the arm of Alice Dunscombe, and surrounded by the female domestics of the establishment of St. Ruth. Katherine Plowden moved lightly by herself, in the shadow of this group, with elastic steps, but with a maiden coyness, that taught her to veil her satisfaction with the semblance of captivity. Barnstable watched her movements with delight, within six feet of her, but submitted to the air of caprice in his mistress, which seemed to require that he should come no nearer. Griffith, avoiding the direct line of the party, walked on its skirts in such a situation that his eye could command its whole extent, in order, if necessary, to direct the movements. Another body of the marines marched at the close of the procession, and Manual, in person, brought up the rear. The music had ceased by command, and nothing was now audible, but the regular tread of the soldiers, with the sighs of the dying gale, interrupted occasionally by the voice of an officer, or the hum of low dialogue.

"This has been a Scotch prize that we've taken," muttered a surly old seaman; "a ship without head-money or cargo! There was kitchen timber enough in the old jug of a place, to have given an outfit in crockery and knee-buckles, to every lad in the ship; but, no! let a man's mouth water ever so much for food and raiment, damme if the officers would give him leave to steal even so good a thing as a spare Bible."

"You may say all that, and then make but a short yarn of the truth," returned the messmate, who walked by his side; "if there had been such a thing as a ready-made prayer handy, they would have choused a poor fellow out of the use of it. — I say, Ben, I'll tell ye what; it's my opinion, that if a chap is to turn soldier and carry a musket, he should have soldiers' play, and leave to plunder a little — now the devil a thing have I laid my hands on to-night, except this firelock, and my cutlash — unless you can call this bit of a table-cloth something of a windfall."

"Ay! you have fallen in there with a fresh bolt of duck, I see!" said the other, in manifest admiration of the texture of his companion's prize — "why, it would spread as broad a clue as our mizen-royal, if it was loosened! well, your luck hasn't been every man's luck — for my part, I think this here hat was made for some fellow's great toe; I've rigged it on my head both fore-and-aft, and athwart ships; but curse the inch can I drive it down — I say, Sam! you'll give us a shirt off that table cloth?"

"Ay, ay, you can have one corner of it; or for that matter, ye can take the full half, Nick; but I don't see that we go off to the ship any richer than we landed, unless you may muster she-cattle among your prize money."

"No richer!" interrupted a waggish young sailor, who had been hitherto a silent listener to the conversation between his older, and more calculating shipmates; "I think we are set up for a cruise in them seas where the day watches last six months; don't you see we have caught a double allowance of midnight!"

While speaking he laid his hands on the bare and woolly heads of Col. Howard's two black slaves, who were moving near him, both occupied in mournful forebodings on the results that were to flow from this unexpected loss of their liberty. "Slue your faces this way, gentlemen," he added; "there; don't you think that a sight to put out the binnacle lamps? there's darkness visible for ye!"

"Let the niggars alone," grumbled one of the more aged speakers; "what are ye sky-larking with the like of them for? the next thing they'll sing out, and then you'll hear one of the officers in your wake. For my part, Nick, I can't see why it is that we keep dodging along shore here, with less than ten fathoms under us, when, by stretching into the broad Atlantic, we might fall in with a Jamaica-man every day or two, and have sugar hogsheads, and rum puncheons as plenty aboard us as hard fare is now."

"It is all owing to that Pilot," returned the other; "for d'ye see, if there was no bottom, there would be no Pilots. This is a dangerous cruising ground, where we stretch into five fathoms, and then drop our lead on a sand-spit, or a rock! Besides, they make night work of it too! If we had day-light for fourteen hours instead of seven, a man might trust to feeling his way for the other ten."

"Now, a'n't ye a couple of old horse-marines!" again interrupted the young sailor; "don't you see that Congress wants us to cut up Johnny Bull's coasters, and that old Blow-Hard has found the days too short for his business, and so he has landed a party to get hold of night. Here we have him! and when we get off to the ship, we shall put him under hatches, and then you'll see the face of the sun again! Come, my lilies! let these two old gentlemen look into your cabin windows — what? you won't! Then I must squeeze your woollen night-caps for ye!"

The negroes, who had been submitting to his humours with the abject humility of slavery, now gave certain low intimations that they were suffering pain, under the rough manipulation of their tormentor.

"What's that!" cried a stern voice, whose boyish tones seemed to mock the air of authority that was assumed by the speaker—"who's that, I say, raising that cry among ye?"

The wilful young man slowly removed his two hands from the woolly polls of the slaves, but as he suffered them to fall reluctantly along their sable temples, he gave the ear of one of the blacks a tweak that caused him to give vent to another cry, that was uttered with a much greater confidence of sympathy than before.

"Do ye hear, there!" repeated Merry—"who's sky-larking with those negroes?"

"'Tis no one, sir," the sailor answered with affected gravity; "one of the pale faces has hit his shin against a cob-web, and it has made his ear ache!"

"Harkye, you mister Jack Joker! how came you in the midst of the prisoners! did not I order you to handle your pike, sir, and to keep in the outer line!"

"Ay, ay, sir, you did; and I obeyed orders as long as I could; but these niggars have made the night so dark, that I lost my way!"

A low laugh passed through the confused crowd of seamen, and even the midshipman might have been indulging himself in a similar manner at this specimen of quaint humour, from the fellow, who was one of those licensed men that are to be found in every ship. At length—

"Well, sir," he said, "you have found out your false reckoning now; so get you back to the place where I bid you stay."

"Ay, ay, sir, I'm going. By all the blunders in the purser's book, Mr. Merry, but that cob-web has made one of these niggars shed tears! Do let me stay to catch a little ink, sir, to write a letter with to my poor old mother—devil the line has she had from me since we sailed from the Chesapeake!"

"If ye don't mind me at once, Mr. Jack Joker, I'll lay my cutlass over your head," returned Merry, his voice now betraying a much greater sympathy in the sufferings of that abject race, who are still in some measure, but who formerly were much more, the butts of the unthinking and licentious among our low countrymen; "then ye can write your letter in red ink if ye will!"

"I wouldn't do it for the world," said Joker, sneaking away, towards his proper station—"the old lady wouldn't forget the hand, and swear it was a forgery—I wonder, though, if the breakers on the coast of Guinea be black! as I've heard old seamen say who have cruised in them latitudes."

His idle levity was suddenly interrupted by a voice that spoke above the low hum of the march, with an air of authority, and a severity of tone, that could always quell, by a single word, the most violent ebullition of merriment in the crew.

The low buzzing sounds of "Ay, there goes Mr. Griffith!" and of "Jack has woke up the first lieutenant, he had better now go to sleep himself;" were heard passing among the men. But these suppressed communications soon ceased, and even Jack Joker himself pursued his way with diligence, on the skirts of the party, as mutely as if the power of speech did not belong to his organization.

The reader has too often accompanied us over the ground between the Abbey and the ocean, to require any description of the route pursued by the seamen during the preceding characteristic dialogue; and we shall at once pass to the incidents which occurred on the arrival of the party at the cliffs. As the man who had so unexpectedly assumed a momentary authority within St. Ruth, had unaccountably disappeared from among them, Griffith continued to exercise the right of command, without referring to any other for consultation. He never addressed himself to Barnstable, and it was apparent that both the haughty young men felt that the tie which had hitherto united them in such close intimacy, was, for the present at least, entirely severed. Indeed, Griffith was only restrained by the presence of Cecilia and Katherine, from arresting his refractory inferior on the spot; and Barnstable, who felt all the consciousness of error, without its proper humility, with difficulty so far repressed his feelings, as to forbear exhibiting in the presence of his mistress, such a manifestation of his spirit as his wounded vanity induced him to imagine was necessary to his honour. The two, however, acted in harmony on one subject, though it was without concert or communication. The first object with both the young men, was to secure the embarkation of the fair cousins; and Barnstable proceeded instantly to the boats, in order to hasten the preparations that were necessary before they could receive these unexpected captives: the descent of the Pilot having been made in such force as to require the use of all the frigate's boats, which were left riding in the outer edge of the surf, awaiting the return of the expedition. A loud call from Barnstable gave notice to the officer in command, and in a few moments the beach was crowded with the busy and active crews of the "cutters," "launches," "barges," "jolly-boats," "pinnaces," or by whatever names the custom of the times attached to the different attendants of vessels of war. Had the fears of the ladies themselves been consulted, the frigate's launch would have been selected for their use, on account of its size; but Barnstable, who would have thought such a choice on his part humiliating to his guests, ordered the long, low barge of Capt. Munson to be drawn upon the sand, it being peculiarly the boat of honour. The hands of fifty men were applied to the task, and it was soon announced to Col. Howard and his wards, that the little vessel was ready for their reception. Manual had halted on the summit of the cliffs with the whole body of the marines, where he was busily employed in posting picquets and sentinels, and giving the necessary instructions to his men to cover the embarkation of the seamen, in a style that he conceived to be altogether military. The mass of the common prisoners, including the inferior domestics of the Abbey, and the men of Borroughcliffe, were also held in the same place, under a suitable guard; but Col. Howard and his companion, attended by the ladies and their own maids, had descended the rugged path to the beach, and were standing passively on the sands, when the intelligence that the boat waited for them, was announced.

"Where is he?" asked Alice Dunscombe, turning her head, as if anxiously searching for some other than those around her.

"Where is who?" inquired Barnstable; "we are all here, and the boat waits."

"And will he tear me—even me, from the home of my infancy! the land of my birth and my affections!"

"I know not of whom you speak, madam, but if it be of Mr. Griffith, he stands there, just without that cluster of seamen."

Griffith, hearing himself thus named, approached the ladies, and, for the first time since leaving the Abbey, addressed them: — "I hope I am already understood," he said, "and that it is unnecessary for me to say, that no female here is a prisoner; though should any choose to trust themselves on board our ship, I pledge to them the honour of an officer, that they shall find themselves protected, and safe."

"Then will I not go," said Alice.

"It is not expected of you," said Cecilia; "you have no ties to bind you to any here." — (The eyes of Alice, were still wandering over the listeners.) "Go, then, Miss Alice, and be the mistress of St. Ruth, until my return; or," she added, timidly, "until Col. Howard may declare his pleasure."

"I obey you, dear child; but the agent of Col. Howard, at B— will undoubtedly be authorized to take charge of his effects."

While no one but his niece alluded to his will, the master of the Abbey had found, in his resentment, a sufficient apology for his rigid demeanor; but he was far too well bred to hear, in silence, such a modest appeal to his wishes, from so fair, and so loyal a subject as Alice Dunscombe.

"To relieve you, madam, and for no other reason, will I speak on this subject," he said; "otherwise, I should leave the doors and windows of St. Ruth open, as a melancholy monument of rebellion, and seek my future compensation from the Crown, when the confiscated estates of the leaders of this accursed innovation on the rights of Princes, shall come to the hammer. But you, Miss Alice, are entitled to every consideration that a lady can expect from a gentleman. Be pleased, therefore, to write to my agent, and request him to seal up my papers, and transmit them to the office of his Majesty's Secretary of State. They breathe no treason, madam, and are entitled to official protection. The house, and most of the furniture, as you know, are the property of my landlord, who, in due time, will doubtless take charge of his own interest. I kiss your hand, Miss Alice, and I hope we shall yet meet at St. James's — depend on it, madam, that the Royal Charlotte shall yet honour your merits; I know she cannot but estimate your loyalty."

"Here I was born, in humble obscurity—here I have lived, and here I hope to die in quiet," returned the meek Alice; "if I have known any pleasure, in late years, beyond that which every Christian can find in our daily duties, it has been, my sweet friends, in your accidental society.—Such companions, in this remote corner of the kingdom, has been a boon too precious to be enjoyed without alloy, it seems, and I have now to exchange the past pleasure for present pain. Adieu! my young friends; let your trust be in Him, to whose eyes both prince and peasant, the European and the American, are alike, and we shall meet again, though it be neither in the island of Britain, nor on your own wide continent."

"That," said Col. Howard, advancing and taking her hand with kindness, "that is the only disloyal sentiment I have ever heard fall from the lips of Miss Alice Dunscombe! Is it to be supposed that Heaven has established orders among men, and that it does not respect the works of its own formation! But adieu; no doubt if time was allowed us for suitable explanations, we should find but little or no difference of opinion on this subject."

Alice did not appear to consider the matter as worthy of further discussion at such a moment, for she gently returned the colonel's leave-taking, and then gave her undivided attention to her female friends. Cecilia wept bitterly on the shoulder of her respected companion, giving vent to her regret at parting, and her excited feelings, at the same moment; and Katherine pressed to the side of Alice, with the kindliness prompted by her warm, but truant heart. Their embraces were given and received in silence, and each of the young ladies moved towards the boat, as she withdrew herself from the arms of Miss Dunscombe. Col. Howard would not precede his wards, neither would he assist them into the barge. That attention they received from Barnstable, who, after seeing the ladies and their attendants seated, turned to the gentlemen, and observed—

"The boat waits."

"Well, Miss Alice," said Borroughcliffe, in bitter irony, "you are entrusted, by our excellent host, with a message to his agent; will you do a similar service to me, and write a report to the commander of the district, and just tell him what a dolt—ay, use the plainest terms, and say what an ass, one Capt. Borroughcliffe has proved himself in this affair. You may throw in, by way of episode, that he has been playing bo-peep with a rebellious young lady from the Colonies, and, like a great boy, has had his head broken for his pains! Come, my worthy host, or rather, fellow prisoner, I follow you, as in duty bound."

"Stay," cried Griffith; "Capt. Borroughcliffe does not embark in that boat."

"Ha! sir; am I to be herded with the common men? Forget you that I have the honour to bear the commission of his Britannic Majesty, and that—"

"I forget nothing that a gentleman is bound to remember, Capt. Borroughcliffe; among other things, I recollect the liberality of your treatment to myself, when a prisoner. The instant the safety of my command will justify such a step, not only you, but your men, shall be set at liberty."

Borroughcliffe started in surprise; but his feelings were too much soured by the destruction of those visions of glory, in which he had been luxuriously indulging for the last day or two, to admit of his answering as became a man. He swallowed his emotions, therefore, by a violent effort, and walked along the beach, affecting to whistle a low, but lively air.

"Well, then," cried Barnstable—"all our captives are seated. The boat waits only for its officers!"

In his turn, Griffith walked away, in haughty silence, as if disdaining to hold communion with his former friend. Barnstable paused a moment, from a deference that long habit had created for his superior officer, and which was not to be shaken off by every burst of angry passion; but perceiving that the other had no intention to return, he ordered the seamen to raise the boat from the sand and bear it bodily into the water. The command was instantly obeyed; and by the time the young lieutenant was in his seat the barge was floating in the still heavy, though no longer dangerous surf, and the crew sprang into their places.

"Bear her off, boys!" he cried; "never mind a wet jacket. I've seen many a worthy fellow tumbling on this beach in a worse time than this! Now you have her head to sea; give way, my souls, give way."

The seamen rose simultaneously at their oars, and, by an

united effort, obtained the command of their boat; which, after making a few sudden ascents and as many heavy pitches in the breakers, gained the smoother seas of the swelling ocean, and stemmed the waters, in a direction for the place where the Alacrity was supposed to be in waiting.

Chapter XXXI.

"His only plot was this—that much provoked,
He raised his vengeful arm against his country."
Thomson, Coriolanus, V.iv. 30-31.

ALICE Dunscombe remained on the sands, watching the dark spot that was soon hid amid the waves, in the obscurity of night, and listening, with melancholy interest, to the regulated sounds of the oars, which were audible long after the boat had been blended with the gloomy outline of the eastern horizon. When all traces of her departed friends were to be found only in her own recollections, she slowly turned from the sea, and hastening to quit the bustling throng, that were preparing for the embarkation of the rest of the party, she ascended the path that conducted her once more to the summit of those cliffs, along which she had so often roved, gazing at the boundless element that washed their base, with sensations that might have been peculiar to her own situation.

The soldiers of Borroughcliffe, who were stationed at the head of the pass, respectfully made way; nor did any of the sentinels of Manual heed her retiring figure, until she approached the rear guard of the marines, who were commanded by their vigilant captain in person.

"Who goes there!" cried Manual, advancing without the dusky group of soldiers, as she approached them.

"One who possesses neither the power nor the inclination to do ye harm," answered the solitary female; "'tis Alice Dunscombe, returning, by permission of your leader, to the place of her birth."

"Ay," muttered Manual, "this is one of Griffith's unmilitary exhibitions of his politeness! does the man think that there was ever a woman who had no tongue! Have you the countersign, madam, that I may know you bear a sufficient warrant to pass?"

"I have no other warrant besides my sex and weakness, unless Mr. Griffith's knowledge that I have left him, can be so considered."

"The two former are enough," said a voice, that proceeded from a figure which had hitherto stood unseen, shaded by the trunk of an oak, that spread its wide, but naked arms above the spot where the guard was paraded.

"Who have we here!" Manual again cried; "come in; yield or you will be fired at."

"What, will the gallant Capt. Manual fire on his own rescuer!" said the Pilot, with cool disdain, as he advanced from the shadow of the tree. "He had better reserve his bullets for his enemies, than waste them on his friends."

"You have done a dangerous deed, sir, in approaching, clandestinely, a guard of marines! I wonder that a man who has already discovered, to-night, that he has some knowledge of tactics, by so ably conducting a surprise, should betray so much ignorance in the forms of approaching a picquet!"

"'Tis now of no moment," returned the Pilot; "my knowledge and my ignorance are alike immaterial, as the command of the party is surrendered to other, and perhaps more proper hands. But I would talk to this lady alone, sir; she is an acquaintance of my youth, and I will see her on her way to the Abbey."

"The step would be unmilitary, Mr. Pilot, and you will excuse me if I do not consent to any of our expedition straggling without the sentries. If you choose to remain here to hold your discourse, I will march the picquet out of hearing; though I must acknowledge I see no ground so favourable as this we are on, to keep you within the range of our eyes. You perceive that I have a ravine to retreat into, in case of surprise, with this line of wall on my left flank, and the trunk of that tree to cover my right. A very pretty stand might be made here, on emergency; for even the oldest troops fight the best when their flanks are properly covered, and a way to make a regular retreat is open in their rear."

"Say no more, sir; I would not break up such a position on any account," returned the Pilot; "the lady will consent to retrace her path for a short distance."

Alice followed his steps, in compliance with this request, until he had led her to a place, at some little distance from the marines, where a tree had been prostrated by the late gale. She seated herself quietly on its trunk, and appeared to await with patience his own time for the explanation of his motives, in seeking the interview. The Pilot paced, for several minutes, back and forth, in front of the place where she was seated, in profound silence, as if communing with himself, when, suddenly throwing off his air of absence, he came to her side, and assumed a position similar to the one which she herself had taken.

"The hour is at hand, Alice, when we must part," he at length commenced; "it rests with yourself whether it shall be for ever."

"Let it then be for ever, John," she returned, with a slight tremor in her voice.

"That word would have been less appalling, had this accidental meeting never occurred. And yet your choice may have been determined by prudence—for what is there in my fate that can tempt a woman to wish that she might share it!"

"If ye mean your lot is that of one who can find but few, or even none, to partake of his joys, or to share in his sorrows, whose life is a continual scene of dangers and calamities, of disappointments and mishaps, then do ye know but little of the heart of woman, if ye doubt of either her ability or her willingness, to meet them with the man of her choice."

"Say you thus, Alice! then have I misunderstood your meaning, or misinterpreted your acts. My lot is not altogether that of a neglected man, unless the favour of princes, and the smiles of queens, are allowed to go for nothing. My life is, however, one of many and fearful dangers; and yet it is not filled altogether with calamities and mishaps; is it, Alice?" He paused a moment, but in vain, for her answer. "Nay, then, I have been deceived in the estimation that the world has affixed to my combats and enterprises! I am not, Alice, the man I would be, or even the man I had deemed myself."

"You have gained a name, John, among the warriors of the age," she answered, in a subdued voice; "and it is a name that may be said to be written in blood!"

"The blood of my enemies, Alice!"

"The blood of the subjects of your natural prince! The blood of those who breathe the air you first breathed, and who were taught the same holy lessons of instruction that you were first taught; but which, I fear, you have too soon forgotten!"

"The blood of the slaves of despotism!" he sternly interrupted her; "the blood of the enemies of freedom! you have dwelt so long in this dull retirement, and you have cherished so blindly the prejudices of your youth, that the promise of those noble sentiments I once thought I could see budding in Alice Dunscombe, has not been fulfilled."

"I have lived and thought only as a woman, as become my sex and station," Alice meekly replied; "and when it shall be necessary for me to live and think otherwise, I should wish to die."

"Ay, there lie the first seeds of slavery! A dependant woman is sure to make the mother of craven and abject wretches, who dishonour the name of man!"

"I shall never be the mother of children good or bad" — said Alice, with that resignation in her tones that showed she had abandoned the natural hopes of her sex. — "Singly and unsupported have I lived; alone and unlamented must I be carried to my grave."

The exquisite pathos of her voice, as she uttered this placid speech, blended as it was with the sweet and calm dignity of virgin pride, touched the heart of her listener, and he continued silent many moments, as if in reverence of her determination. Her sentiments awakened in his own breast those feelings of generosity and disinterestedness, which had nearly been smothered in restless ambition and the pride of success. He resumed the discourse, therefore, more mildly, and with a much greater exhibition of deep feeling, and less of passion, in his manner.

"I know not, Alice, that I ought, situated as I am, and contented, if not happy, as you are, even to attempt to revive in your bosom those sentiments which I was once led to think existed there. It cannot, after all, be a desirable fate, to share the lot of a rover like myself; one who may be termed a Quixote in the behalf of liberal principles, and who may be hourly called to seal the truth of those principles with his life."

"There never existed any sentiment in my breast, in which you are concerned, that does not exist there still, and unchanged," returned Alice, with her single-hearted sincerity.

"Do I hear you aright! or have I misconceived your resolution to abide in England! or have I not rather mistaken your early feelings?"

"You have fallen into no error now nor then. The weakness may still exist, John, but the strength to struggle with it, has, by the goodness of God, grown with my years. It is not, however, of myself, but of you, that I would speak. I have lived like one of our simple daisies, which in the budding may have caught your eye; and I shall also wilt like the humble flower, when the winter of my time arrives, without being missed from the fields that have known me for a season. But your fall, John, will be like that of the oak that now supports us, and men shall pronounce on the beauty and grandeur of the noble stem while standing, as well as of its usefulness when felled."

"Let them pronounce as they will!" returned the proud stranger. "The truth must be finally known, and when that hour shall come, they will say, he was a faithful and gallant warrior in his day; and a worthy lesson for all who are born in slavery, but would live in freedom, shall be found in his example!"

"Such may be the language of that distant people, whom ye have adopted in the place of those that once formed home and kin to ye," said Alice, glancing her eye timidly at his countenance, as if to discern how far she might venture, without awakening his resentment; "but what will the men of the land of your birth transmit to their children, who will be the children of those that are of your own blood?"

"They will say, Alice, whatever their crooked policy may suggest, or their disappointed vanity can urge. But the picture must be drawn by the friends of the hero as well as by his enemies! Think you that there are not pens as well as swords in America?"

"I have heard that America called a land, John, where God has lavished his favours with an unsparing hand; where he has bestowed many climes with their several fruits, and where his power is exhibited no less than his mercy. It is said her rivers are without any known end, and that lakes are found in her bosom, which would put our German ocean to shame! The plains, teeming with verdure, are spread over wide degrees, and yet those sweet valleys, which a single heart can hold, are not wanting. In short, John, I hear it is a broad land, that can furnish food for each passion, and contain objects for every affection."

"Ay, you have found those, Alice, in your solitude, who have been willing to do her justice! It is a country, that can form a world of itself; and why should they who inherit it, look to other nations for their laws?"

"I pretend not to reason on the right of the children of that soil, to do whatever they may deem most meet for their own welfare," returned Alice—"but can men be born in such a land, and not know the feeling which binds a human being to the place of his birth?"

"Can you doubt that they should be patriotic?" exclaimed the Pilot, in surprise. "Do not their efforts in this sacred cause—their patient sufferings—their long privations, speak loudly in their behalf?"

"And will they, who know so well how to love home, sing the praises of him, who has turned his ruthless hand against the land of his fathers?"

"Forever harping on that word, home!" said the Pilot, who now detected the timid approaches of Alice to her hidden meaning. "Is a man a stick or a stone, that he must be cast into the fire, or buried in a wall, wherever his fate may have doomed him to appear on the earth? The sound of home is said to feed the vanity of an Englishman, let him go where he will; but it would seem to have a still more powerful charm with English women!"

"It is the dearest of all terms to every woman, John, for it embraces the dearest of all ties! If your dames of America are ignorant of its charm, all the favours which God has lavished on their land, will avail their happiness but little."

"Alice," said the Pilot, rising in his agitation, "I see but too well the object of your allusions. But on this subject we can never agree; for not even your powerful influence can draw me from the path of glory in which I am now treading. But our time is growing brief; let us then talk of other things.—This may be the last time that I shall ever put foot on the island of Britain."

Alice paused to struggle with the feelings excited by this remark, before she pursued the discourse. But, soon shaking off the weakness, she added, with a rigid adherence to that course which she believed to be her duty —

"And now, John, that you have landed, is the breaking up of a peaceful family, and the violence ye have shown towards an aged man, a fit exploit for one whose object is the glory of which ye have spoken?"

"Think you that I have landed, and placed my life in the hands of my enemies, for so unworthy an object! No, Alice, my motive for this undertaking has been disappointed, and therefore will ever remain a secret from the world. But duty to my cause has prompted the step which you so unthinkingly condemn. This Col. Howard has some consideration with those in power, and will answer to exchange for a better man. As for his wards, you forget their home, their magical home, is in America; unless, indeed, they find them nearer at hand, under the proud flag of a frigate, that is now waiting for them in the offing."

"You talk of a frigate!" said Alice, with sudden interest in the subject — "Is she your only means of escaping from your enemies?"

"Alice Dunscombe has taken but little heed of passing events, to ask such a question of me!" returned the haughty Pilot. "The question would have sounded more discreetly, had it been, 'is she the only vessel with you that your enemies will have to escape from?'"

"Nay, I cannot measure my language at such a moment," continued Alice, with a still stronger exhibition of anxiety. "It was my fortune to overhear a part of a plan that was intended to destroy, by sudden means, those vessels of America that were in our seas."

"That might be a plan more suddenly adopted than easily executed, my good Alice. And who were these redoubtable schemers?"

"I know not but my duty to the king should cause me to suppress this information," said Alice, hesitating.

"Well, be it so," returned the Pilot, coolly; "it may prove the means of saving the persons of some of the royal officers from death or captivity. I have already said, this may be the last of my visits to this island, and consequently, Alice, the last of our interviews —"

"And yet," said Alice, still pursuing the train of her own thoughts, "there can be but little harm in sparing human blood; and least of all in serving those whom we have long known and regarded!"

"Ay, that is a simple doctrine, and one that is easily maintained," he added, with much apparent indifference; "and yet king George might well spare some of his servants — the list of his abject minions is so long!"

"There was a man named Dillon, who lately dwelt in the Abbey, but who has mysteriously disappeared," continued Alice; "or rather who was captured by your companions: know you aught of him, John?"

"I have heard there was a miscreant of that name, but we have never met. Alice, if it please heaven that this should be the last" —

"He was a captive in a schooner called the Ariel," she added, still unheeding his affected indifference to her communication, "and when permitted to return to St. Ruth, he lost sight of his solemn promise, and of his plighted honour, to wreak his malice. Instead of effecting the exchange that he had conditioned to see made, he plotted treason against his captors. Yes! it was most foul treason! for his treatment was generous and kind, and his liberation certain."

"He was a most unworthy scoundrel! But, Alice" —

"Nay, listen, John," she continued, urged to even a keener interest in his behalf, by his apparent inattention; "and yet I should speak tenderly of his failings, for he is already numbered with the dead! One part of his scheme must have been frustrated, for he intended to destroy that schooner which you call the Ariel, and to have taken the person of the young Barnstable."

"In both of which he has failed! The person of Barnstable I have rescued, and the Ariel has been stricken by a hand far mightier than any of this world! she is wrecked."

"Then is the frigate your only means of escape! Hasten, John, and seem not so proud and heedless, for the hour may come when all your daring will not profit ye against the machinations of secret enemies. This Dillon had also planned that expresses should journey to a sea-port at the south, with the intelligence that your vessels were in these seas, in order that ships might be despatched to intercept your retreat."

The Pilot lost his affected indifference as she proceeded, and before she ceased speaking, his eye was endeavouring to anticipate her words, by reading her countenance through the dusky medium of the star-light.

"How know you this, Alice?" he asked quickly—"and what vessel did he name?"

"Chance made me an unseen listener to their plan, and—I know not but I forget my duty to my prince!—but, John, 'tis asking too much of weak woman, to require that she shall see the man whom she once viewed with eyes of favour, sacrificed, when a word of caution, given in season, might enable him to avoid the danger!"

"Once viewed with an eye of favour! Is it then so!" said the Pilot, speaking in a vacant manner. "But, Alice, heard ye the force of the ships, or their names? Give me their names, and the first lord of your British admiralty shall not give so true an account of their force, as I will furnish from this list of my own."

"Their names were certainly mentioned," said Alice, with tender melancholy, "but the name of one far nearer to me was ringing in my ears, and has driven them from my mind."

"You are the same good Alice I once knew! And my name was mentioned? What said they of the Pirate? Had his arm stricken a blow that made them tremble in their Abbey? Did they call him coward, girl?"

"It was mentioned in terms that pained my heart as I listened. For, it is ever too easy a task to forget the lapse of years, nor are the feelings of youth to be easily eradicated."

"Ay, there is luxury in knowing, that with all their affected abuse, the slaves dread me in their secret holds!" exclaimed the Pilot, pacing in front of his listener, with quick steps. "This it is to be marked, among men, above all others in your calling! I hope yet to see the day when the third George shall start at the sound of that name, even within the walls of his palace."

Alice Dunscombe heard him in deep and mortified silence. It was too evident that a link in the chain of their sympathies was broken, and that the weakness in which she had been unconsciously indulging, was met by no correspondent emotions in him. After sinking her head for a moment on her bosom, she arose with a little more than her usual air of meekness, and recalled the Pilot to a sense of her presence, by saying, in a yet milder voice —

"I have now communicated all that it can profit you to know, and it is meet that we separate."

"What, thus soon!" he cried, starting and taking her hand. "This is but a short interview, Alice, to precede so long a separation."

"Be it short, or be it long, it must now end," she replied. "Your companions are on the eve of departure, and I trust you would be one of the last who would wish to be deserted. If ye do visit England again, I hope it may be with altered sentiments, so far as regards her interests. I wish ye peace, John, and the blessings of God, as ye may be found to deserve them."

"I ask no farther, unless it may be the aid of your gentle prayers! But the night is gloomy, and I will see you in safety to the Abbey."

"It is unnecessary," she returned, with womanly reserve. "The innocent can be as fearless on occasion, as the most valiant among you warriors. But here is no cause for fear. I shall take a path that will conduct me in a different way from that which is occupied by your soldiers, and where I shall find none but Him who is ever ready to protect the helpless. Once more, John, I bid ye adieu." Her voice faltered as she continued — "ye will share the lot of humanity, and have your hours of care and weakness; at such moments ye can remember those ye leave on this despised island, and perhaps among them ye may think of some whose interest in your welfare has been far removed from selfishness."

"God be with you, Alice!" he said, touched with her emotion, and losing all vain images in more worthy feelings — "but I cannot permit you to go alone."

"Here we part, John," she said firmly, "and for ever! 'Tis for the happiness of both, for I fear we have but little in common." She gently wrested her hand from his grasp, and once more bidding him adieu, in a voice that was nearly inaudible, she turned and slowly disappeared, moving, with lingering steps, in the direction of the Abbey.

The first impulse of the Pilot was, certainly, to follow, and insist on seeing her on the way; but the music of the guard on the cliffs, at that moment sent forth its martial strains, and the whistle of the boatswain was heard winding its shrill call among the rocks, in those notes that his practised ear well understood to be the last signal for embarking.

Obedient to the summons, this singular man, in whose breast the natural feelings, that were now on the eve of a violent eruption, had so long been smothered by the visionary expectations of a wild ambition, and perhaps of fierce resentments, pursued his course, in deep abstraction, towards the boats. He was soon met by the soldiers of Borroughcliffe, deprived of their arms, it is true, but unguarded, and returning peacefully to their quarters. The mind of the Pilot, happily for the liberty of these men, was too much absorbed in his peculiar reflections, to note this act of Griffith's generosity, nor did he arouse from his musing until his steps were arrested by suddenly encountering a human figure in the path-way. A light tap on his shoulder was the first mark of recognition he received, when Borroughcliffe, who stood before him, said—

"It is evident, sir, from what has passed this evening, that you are not what you seem. You may be some rebel admiral or general, for aught that I know, the right to command having been strangely contested among ye this night. But let who will own the chief authority, I take the liberty of whispering in your ear that I have been scurvily treated by you—I repeat, most scurvily treated by you all, generally, and by you in particular."

The Pilot started at this strange address, which was uttered with all the bitterness that could be imparted to it by a disappointed man, but he motioned with his hand for the captain to depart, and turned aside to pursue his own way.

"Perhaps I am not properly understood," continued the

obstinate soldier; "I say, sir, you have treated me scurvily, and I would not be thought to say this to any gentleman, without wishing to give him an opportunity to vent his anger."

The eye of the Pilot, as he moved forward, glanced at the pistols which Borroughcliffe held in his hands, the one by the handle, and the other by its barrel, and the soldier even fancied that his footsteps were quickened by the sight. After gazing at him until his form was lost in the darkness, the captain muttered to himself—

"He is no more than a common pilot after all! No true gentleman would have received so palpable a hint with such a start. Ah! here comes the party of my worthy friend whose palate knows a grape of the north side of Madeira, from one of the south. The dog has the throat of a gentleman! we will see how he can swallow a delicate allusion to his faults!"

Borroughcliffe stepped aside to allow the marines, who were also in motion for the boats, to pass, and watched with keen looks for the person of the commander. Manual, who had been previously apprized of the intention of Griffith to release the prisoners, had halted to see that none but those who had been liberated by authority, were marching into the country. This accidental circumstance gave Borroughcliffe an opportunity of meeting the other at some little distance from either of their respective parties.

"I greet you, sir," said Borroughcliffe, "with all affection. This has been a pleasant forage for you, Capt. Manual."

The marine was far from being disposed to wrangle, but there was that in the voice of the other which caused him to answer—

"It would have been far pleasanter, sir, if I had met an opportunity of returning to Capt. Borroughcliffe some of the favours that I have received at his hands."

"Nay, then, dear sir, you weigh my modesty to the earth! Surely you forget the manner in which my hospitality has already been requited—by some two hours' mouthing of my sword hilt; with a very unceremonious ricochet into a corner; together with a love-tap, received over the shoulders of one of my men, by so gentle an instrument as the butt of a musket! Damme, sir, but I think an ungrateful man only a better sort of beast!"

"Had the love tap been given to the officer instead of the man," returned Manual, with all commendable coolness, "it would have been better justice; and the ramrod might have answered as well as the butt, to floor a gentleman who carried the allowance of four thirsty fiddlers under one man's jacket."

"Now, that is rank ingratitude to your own cordial of the south side, and a most biting insult! I really see but one way of terminating this wordy war, which if not discreetly ended, may lead us far into the morning."

"Elect your own manner of determining the dispute, sir; I hope, however, it will not be by your innate knowledge of mankind, which has already mistaken a captain of marines in the service of Congress, for a runaway lover, bound to some green place or other."

"You might just as well tweak my nose, sir!" said Borroughcliffe. "Indeed, I think it would be the milder reproach of the two! will you make your selection of these, sir? They were loaded for a very different sort of service, but I doubt not will answer on occasion."

"I am provided with a pair, that are charged for any service," returned Manual, drawing a pistol from his own belt, and stepping backward a few paces.

"You are destined for America, I know," said Borroughcliffe, who stood his ground with consummate coolness; "but it would be more convenient for me, sir, if you could delay your march for a single moment."

"Fire and defend yourself!" exclaimed Manual furiously, retracing his steps towards his enemy.

The sounds of the two pistols were blended in one report, and the soldiers of Borroughcliffe and the marines all rushed to the place, on the sudden alarm. Had the former been provided with arms, it is probable a bloody fray would have been the consequence of the sight that both parties beheld on arriving at the spot, which they did simultaneously. Manual lay on his back, without any signs of life, and Borroughcliffe had changed his cool, haughty, upright attitude, for a recumbent posture, which was somewhat between lying and sitting.

"Is the poor fellow actually expended?" said the Englishman, in something like the tones of regret; "well, he had a soldier's metal in him, and was nearly as great a fool as myself!"

The marines had, luckily for the soldiers and their captain, by this time discovered the signs of life in their own commander, who had been only slightly stunned by the bullet which had grazed his crown, and who being assisted on his feet, stood a minute or two rubbing his head, as if awaking from a dream. As Manual came gradually to his senses he recollected the business in which he had just been engaged, and, in his turn, inquired after the fate of his antagonist.

"I am here, my worthy incognito," cried the other, with a voice of perfect good nature; "lying in the lap of mother Earth, and all the better for opening a vein or two in my right leg; — though I do think that the same effect might have been produced without treating the bone so roughly! — But I opine that I saw you also reclining on the bosom of our common ancestor."

"I was down for a few minutes, I do believe," returned Manual; "there is the path of a bullet across my scalp!"

"Humph! on the head!" said Borroughcliffe, dryly; "the hurt is not likely to be mortal, I see. — Well, I shall offer to raffle with the first poor devil I can find that has but one good leg, for who shall have both; and that will just set up a beggar and a gentleman! — Manual, give me your hand; we have drank together, and we have fought; surely there is nothing now to prevent our being sworn friends!"

"Why," returned Manual, continuing to rub his head, "I see no irremoveable objections — but you will want a surgeon? can I order any thing to be done? There go the signals again to embark — march the fellows down at quick time, sergeant: my own man may remain with me, or, I can do altogether without assistance."

"Ah! you are what I call a well made man, my dear friend!" exclaimed Borroughcliffe; "no weak points about your fortress! such a man is worthy to be the *head* of a whole corps, instead of a solitary company; — Gently, Drill, gently; handle me as if I were made of potter's clay; — I will not detain you longer, my friend Manual, for I hear signal after signal; they must be in want of some of your astonishing reasoning faculties to set them afloat."

Manual might have been offended at the palpable allusions that his new friend made to the firmness of his occiput, had not his perception of things been a little confused, by a humming sound that seemed to abide near the region of thought. As it was, he reciprocated the good wishes of the other, whom he shook most cordially by the hand, and once more renewed his offers of service, after exchanging sundry friendly speeches.

"I thank you quite as much as if I were not at all indebted to you for letting blood, thereby saving me a fit of apoplexy; but Drill has already despatched a messenger to B—— for a leech, and the lad may bring the whole dépôt down upon you. — Adieu, once more, and remember, that if you ever visit England again as a friend, you are to let me see you."

"I shall do it without fail; and I shall keep you to your promise, if you once more put foot in America."

"Trust me for that; I shall stand in need of your excellent head to guide me safely among those rude foresters! Adieu; cease not to bear me in your thoughts."

"I shall never cease to remember you, my good friend," returned Manual, again scratching the member, which was snapping in a manner that caused him to fancy he heard it. Once more these worthies shook each other by the hand, and again they renewed their promises of future intercourse; after which they separated like two reluctant lovers — parting in a manner that would have put to shame the friendship of Orestes and Pylades!

Chapter XXXII.

"Nay, answer me: stand, and unfold yourself."

Hamlet, I.i.2.

DURING the time occupied by the incidents that occurred after the Pilot had made his descent on the land, the Alacrity, now under the orders of Mr. Boltrope, the master of the frigate, lay off and on, in readiness to receive the successful mariners. The direction of the wind had been gradually changing from the north-east to the south, during the close of the day; and long before the middle watches of the night, the wary old seaman, who, it may be remembered, had expressed, in the council of war, such a determined reluctance to trust his person within the realm of Britain, ordered the man who steered the cutter to stand in boldly for the land. Whenever the lead told them that it was prudent to tack, the course of the vessel was changed; and in this manner the seamen continued to employ the hours in patient attendance on the adventurers. The sailing-master, who had spent the early years of his life as the commander of divers vessels employed in trading, was apt, like many men of his vocation and origin, to mistake the absence of refinement for the surest evidence of seamanship; and, consequently, he held the little courtesies and punctilios of a man-of-war in high disdain. His peculiar duties of superintending the expenditure of the ship's stores, in their several departments; of keeping the frigate's log-book; and of making his daily examinations into the state of her sails and rigging, brought him so little in collision with the gay, laughing, reckless young lieutenants, who superintended the ordinary management of the vessel, that he might be said to have formed a distinct species of the animal, though certainly of the same genus with his more polished messmates. Whenever circumstances, however, required that he should depart from the dull routine of his duty, he made it a rule, as far as possible, to associate himself with such of the crew as possessed habits and opinions the least at variance with his own.

By a singular fatality, the chaplain of the frigate was, as respects associates, in a condition, nearly assimilated to that of this veteran tar.

An earnest desire to ameliorate the situation of those who were doomed to meet death on the great deep, had induced an inexperienced and simple-hearted divine to accept this station, in the fond hope, that he might be made the favoured instrument of salvation to many, who were then existing in a state of the most abandoned self-forgetfulness. Neither our limits, nor our present object, will permit the relation of the many causes that led, not only to an entire frustration of all his visionary expectations, but to an issue which rendered the struggle of the good divine with himself both arduous and ominous, in order to maintain his own claims to the merited distinctions of his sacred office. The consciousness of his backsliding had so far lessened the earthly, if not the spiritual pride of the chaplain, as to induce him to relish the society of the rude master, whose years had brought him, at times, to take certain views of futurity, that were singularly affected by the peculiar character of the individual. It might have been that both found themselves out of their places — but it was owing to some such secret sympathy, let its origin be what it would, that the two came to be fond of each other's company. On the night in question, Mr. Boltrope had invited the chaplain to accompany him in the Alacrity; adding, in his broad, rough language, that as there was to be fighting on shore, "his hand might come in play with some poor fellow or other." This singular invitation had been accepted, as well from a desire to relieve the monotony of a sea life, by any change, as perhaps with a secret yearning in the breast of the troubled divine, to get as nigh to terra firma as possible. Accordingly, after the Pilot had landed with his boisterous party, the sailing-master and the chaplain, together with a boatswain's-mate and some ten or twelve seamen, were left in quiet possession of the cutter. The first few hours of this peaceable intercourse, had been spent by the worthy messmates, in the little cabin of the vessel, over a can of grog, the savoury relish of which was much increased by a characteristic disquisition on polemical subjects, which our readers have great reason to regret it is not our present humour to record. When, however, the winds invited the nearer approach to the hostile shores already mentioned, the prudent sailing-master adjourned the discussion to another and more suitable time, removing himself and the can, by the same operation, to the quarter-deck.

"There," cried the honest tar, placing the wooden vessel, with great self-contentment, by his side on the deck, "this is ship's comfort! There is a good deal of what I call a lubber's fuss, parson, kept up on board a ship that shall be nameless, but which bears, about three leagues distant, broad off in the ocean, and which is lying-to under a close-reefed maintopsail, a foretopmast-staysail and foresail — I call my hand a true one in mixing a can — take another pull at the halyards! 'twill make your eye twinkle like a light-house, this dark morning! You won't? well we must give no offence to the Englishman's rum." — After a potent draught had succeeded this considerate declaration, he added — "You are a little like our first lieutenant, parson, who drinks, as I call it, nothing but the elements — which is, water stiffened with air!"

"Mr. Griffith may indeed be said to set a wholesome example to the crew," returned the chaplain, perhaps with a slight consciousness that it had not altogether possessed its due weight with himself.

"Wholesome!" cried Boltrope; "let me tell you, my worthy leaf-turner, that if you call such a light diet wholesome, you know but little of salt water and sea-fogs! However, Mr. Griffith is a seaman; and if he gave his mind less to trifles and gimcracks, he would be, by the time he got to about our years, a very rational sort of a companion. — But you see, parson, just now, he thinks too much of small follies; such as man-of-war disciplyne. — Now there is rationality in giving a fresh nip to a rope, or in looking well at your mats, or even in crowning a cable; but damme, priest, if I see the use — luff, luff, ye lubber; don't ye see, sir, you are steering for Garmany! — if I see the use, as I was saying, of making a rumpus about the time when a man changes his shirt; whether it be this week, or next week, or for that matter, the week after, provided it be bad weather. I sometimes am mawkish about attending muster, (and I believe I have as little to fear on the score of behaviour as any man,) lest it should be found I carried my tobacco in the wrong cheek!"

"I have indeed thought it somewhat troublesome to myself, at times; and it is in a striking degree vexatious to the spirit, especially when the body has been suffering under sea-sickness."

"Why, yes, you were a little apt to bend your duds wrong for the first month, or so," said the master; "I remember you got the marine's scraper on your head, once, in your hurry to bury a dead man! Then you never looked as if you belonged to the ship, so long as those cursed black knee-breeches lasted! For my part, I never saw you come up the quarter-deck ladder, but I expected to see your shins give way across the combing of the hatch—a man does look like the devil, priest, scudding about a ship's decks in that fashion, under bare poles! But now the tailor has found out the articles ar'n't sea-worthy, and we have got your lower stanchions cased in a pair of purser's slops, I am puzzled often to tell your heels from those of a main-top-man!"

"I have good reason to be thankful for the change," said the humbled priest, "if the resemblance you mention existed, while I was clad in the usual garb of one of my calling."

"What signifies a calling?" returned Boltrope, catching his breath after a most persevering draught; "a man's shins are his shins, let his upper works belong to what sarvice they may. I took an early prejudyce against knee-breeches, perhaps from a trick I've always had of figuring the Devil as wearing them. You know, parson, we seldom hear much said of a man, without forming some sort of an idea concerning his rigging and fashion-pieces—and so as I had no particular reason to believe that Satan went naked—keep full ye lubber; now you are running into the wind's eye, and be d——d to ye!—but as I was saying, I always took a conceit that the devil wore knee-breeches and a cock'd hat. There's some of our young lieu-tenants, who come to muster on Sundays in cock'd hats, just like soldier-officers; but, d'ye see, I would sooner show my nose under a night cap, than under a scraper!"

"I hear the sound of oars!" exclaimed the chaplain, who find-ing this image more distinct than even his own vivid concep-tions of the great Father of evil, was quite willing to conceal his inferiority by changing the discourse—"Is not one of our boats returning?"

"Ay, ay, 'tis likely; if it had been me, I should have been land-sick before this—ware round, boys, and stand by to heave-to on the other tack."

The cutter, obedient to her helm, fell off before the wind, and rolling an instant in the trough of the sea, came up again easily to her oblique position, with her head towards the cliffs, and gradually losing her way, as her sails were brought to counteract each other, finally became stationary. During the performance of this evolution, a boat had hove up out of the gloom, in the direction of the land, and by the time the Alacrity was in a state of rest, it had approached so nigh as to admit of hailing.

"Boat ahoy!" murmured Boltrope, through a trumpet, which, aided by his lungs, produced sounds not unlike the roaring of a bull.

"Ay, ay," was thrown back from a clear voice, that swept across the water with a fulness that needed no factitious aid to render it audible.

"Ay, there comes one of the lieutenants, with his ay, ay," said Boltrope—"pipe the side, there, you boatswain's-mate! But here's another fellow more on our quarter! boat a-hoy!"

"Alacrity"—returned another voice, in a direction different from the other.

"Alacrity! There goes my commission of Captain of this craft, in a whiff," returned the sailing-master.—"That is as much as to say, here comes one, who will command when he gets on board. Well, well, it is Mr. Griffith, and I can't say, notwithstanding his love of knee-buckles, and small wares, but I'm glad he's out of the hands of the English! Ay, here they all come upon us at once! here is another fellow, that pulls like the jolly-boat, coming up on our lee-beam, within hail—let us see if he is asleep—boat a-hoy!"

"Flag," answered a third voice from a small, light-rowing boat which had approached very near the cutter, in a direct line from the cliffs, without being observed.

"Flag!" echoed Boltrope, dropping his trumpet in amazement—"that's a big word to come out of a jolly-boat! Jack Manly himself could not have spoke it with a fuller mouth—but I'll know who it is that carries such a weather helm, with a Yankee man-of-war's prize! Boat a-hoy! I say."

This last call was uttered in those short menacing tones, that are intended to be understood as intimating that the party hailing is in earnest; and it caused the men who were rowing, and who were now quite close to the cutter, to suspend their strokes, simultaneously, as if they dreaded that the cry would be instantly succeeded by some more efficient means of ascertaining their character. The figure that was seated by itself in the stern of the boat, started at this second summons, and then, as if with sudden recollection, a quiet voice replied—

"No—no."

"'No—no,' and 'flag,' are very different answers," grumbled Boltrope; "what know-nothing have we here!"

He was yet muttering his dissatisfaction at the ignorance of the individual that was approaching, whoever it might be, when the jolly-boat came slowly to their side, and the Pilot stepped from her stern-sheets on the decks of the prize.

"Is it you, Mr. Pilot?" exclaimed the sailing-master, raising a battle lantern within a foot of the other's face, and looking with a sort of stupid wonder at the proud and angry eye he encountered—"is it you! well, I should have rated you for a man of more experience than to come booming down upon a man-of-war in the dark, with such a big word in your mouth, when every boy in the two vessels knows that we carry no swallow-tailed bunting abroad! Flag! why you might have got a shot, had there been soldiers."

The Pilot threw him a still fiercer glance, and turning away with a look of disgust, he walked along the quarter-deck towards the stern of the vessel, with an air of haughty silence, as if disdaining to answer. Boltrope kept his eyes fastened on him for a moment longer, with some appearance of scorn, but the arrival of the boat first hailed, which proved to be the barge, immediately drew his attention to other matters. Barnstable had been rowing about in the ocean for a long time, unable to find the cutter, and as he had been compelled to suit his own demeanour to those with whom he was associated, he reached the Alacrity in no very good-humoured mood. Col. Howard and his niece had maintained, during the whole period, the most rigid silence, the former from pride, and the latter touched with her uncle's evident displeasure; and Katherine, though secretly elated with the success of all her projects, was content to emulate their demeanour for a short time, in order to save appearances. Barnstable had several times addressed himself to the latter, without receiving any other answer than such as was absolutely necessary to prevent the lover from taking direct offence, at the same time that she intimated by her manner her willingness to remain silent. Accordingly, the lieutenant, after aiding the ladies to enter the cutter, and offering to perform the same service to Col. Howard, which was coldly declined, turned, with that sort of irritation that is by no means less rare in vessels of war than with poor human nature generally, and gave vent to his spleen where he dared.

"How's this! Mr. Boltrope!" he cried, "here are boats coming alongside with ladies in them, and you keep your gaff swayed up till the leach of the sail is stretched like a fiddle-string — settle away your peak-halyards, sir, settle away!"

"Ay, ay, sir," grumbled the master; "settle away that peak there; though the craft wouldn't forge ahead a knot in a month, with all her gibs hauled over!" He walked sulkily forward among the men, followed by the meek divine; and added, "I should as soon have expected to see Mr. Barnstable come off with a live ox in his boat as a petticoat! The Lord only knows what the ship is coming to next, parson! what between cocked hats and epaulettes, and other knee-buckle matters, she was a sort of no-mans-land before, and now, what with the women, and their band-boxes, they'll make another Noah's Ark of her. I wonder they didn't all come aboard in a coach and six, or a one horse shay!"

It was a surprising relief to Barnstable to be able to give utterance to his humour, for a few moments, by ordering the men to make sundry alterations in every department of the vessel, in a quick, hurried voice, that abundantly denoted, not only the importance of his improvements, but the temper in which they were dictated. In his turn, however, he was soon compelled to give way by the arrival of Griffith, in the heavily rowing launch of the frigate, which was crowded with a larger body of the seamen who had been employed in the expedition. In this manner, boat after boat speedily arrived, and the whole party were once more happily embarked in safety, under their national flag.

The small cabin of the Alacrity was relinquished to Col. Howard and his wards, with their attendants. The boats were dropped astern, each protected by its own keeper; and Griffith gave forth the mandate, to fill the sails and steer broad off into the ocean. For more than an hour the cutter held her course in this direction, gliding gracefully through the glittering waters, rising and settling heavily on the long, smooth billows, as if conscious of the unusual burden that she was doomed to carry; but at the end of that period, her head was once more brought near the wind, and she was again held at rest; awaiting the appearance of the dawn, in order to discover the position of the prouder vessel, on which she was performing the humble duty of a tender. More than a hundred and fifty living men were crowded within her narrow limits; and her decks presented, in the gloom, as she moved along, the picture of a mass of human heads.

As the freedom of a successful expedition was unavoidably permitted, loud jokes, and louder merriment, broke on the silent waters, from the reckless seamen, while the exhilarating can passed from hand to hand, strange oaths, and dreadful denunciations breaking forth, at times, from some of the excited crew against their enemy. At length the bustle of re-embarking gradually subsided, and many of the crew descended to the hold of the cutter, in quest of room to stretch their limbs, when a clear, manly voice, was heard rising above the deep in those strains that a seaman most loves to hear. Air succeeded air, from different voices, until even the spirit of harmony grew dull with fatigue, and verses began to be heard where songs were expected, and fleeting lines succeeded stanzas. The decks were soon covered with prostrate men, seeking their natural rest, under the open heavens, and perhaps dreaming, as they yielded heavily to the rolling of the vessel, of scenes of other times in their own hemisphere. The dark glances of Katherine were concealed beneath her falling lids; and even Cecilia, with her head bowed on the shoulder of her cousin, slept sweetly in innocence and peace. Boltrope groped his way into the hold among the seamen, where, kicking one of the most fortunate of the men from his birth, he established himself in his place, with all that cool indifference to the other's comfort, that had grown with his experience, from the time when he was treated thus cavalierly in his own person, to the present moment. In this manner, head was dropped after head, on the planks, the guns, or on whatever first offered for a pillow, until Griffith and Barnstable, alone, were left pacing the different sides of the quarter-deck, in haughty silence.

Never did a morning watch appear so long to the two young sailors, who were thus deprived, by resentment and pride, of that frank and friendly communion, that had for so many years sweetened the tedious hours of their long, and at times, dreary service. To increase the embarrassment of their situation, Cecilia and Katherine, suffering from the confinement of the small and crowded cabin, sought the purer air of the deck, about the time when the deepest sleep had settled on the senses of the wearied mariners. They stood, leaning against the taffrail, discoursing with each other, in low and broken sentences; but a sort of instinctive knowledge of the embarrassment which existed between their lovers, caused a guarded control over every look or gesture which might be construed into an encouragement for one of the young men to advance at the expense of the other. Twenty times, however, did the impatient Barnstable feel tempted to throw off the awkward restraint, and approach his mistress; but in each instance was he checked by the secret consciousness of error, as well as by that habitual respect for superior rank that forms a part of the nature of a sea-officer. On the other hand, Griffith manifested no intention to profit by this silent concession in his favour, but continued to pace the short quarter-deck with strides more hurried than ever; and was seen to throw many an impatient glance towards that quarter of the heavens, where the first signs of the lingering day might be expected to appear. At length Katherine, with a ready ingenuity, and perhaps with some secret coquetry, removed the embarrassment, by speaking first, taking care to address the lover of her cousin—

"How long are we condemned to these limited lodgings, Mr. Griffith?" she asked; "truly, there is a freedom in your nautical customs, which, to say the least, is novel to us females, who have been accustomed to the division of space!"

"The instant that there is light to discover the frigate, Miss Plowden," he answered, "you shall be transferred from a vessel of an hundred, to one of twelve hundred tons. If your situation there be less comfortable, than when within the walls of St. Ruth, you will not forget that they who live on the ocean, claim it as a merit to despise the luxuries of the land."

"At least, sir," returned Katherine, with a sweet grace, which she well knew how to assume on occasion, "what we shall enjoy will be sweetened by liberty, and embellished by a sailor's hospitality. To me, Cicely, the air of this open sea is as fresh and invigorating, as if it were wafted from our own distant America!"

"If you have not the arm of a patriot, you at least possess a most loyal imagination, Miss Plowden," said Griffith, laughing; "this soft breeze blows in the direction of the fens of Holland, instead of the broad plains of America. — Thank God, there come the signs of day, at last! unless the currents have swept the ship far to the north, we shall surely see her with the light."

This cheering intelligence drew the eyes of the fair cousins towards the east, where their delighted looks were long fastened, while they watched the glories of the sun rising over the water. As the morning had advanced, a deeper gloom was spread across the ocean, and the stars were gleaming in the heavens, like balls of twinkling fire. But now, a streak of pale light showed itself along the horizon, growing brighter, and widening at each moment, until long, fleecy clouds became visible, where nothing had been seen before but the dim base of the arch that overhung the dark waters. This expanding light, which, in appearance, might be compared to a silvery opening in the heavens, was soon tinged with a pale flush, which quickened with sudden transitions into glows yet deeper, until a belt of broad flame bounded the water, diffusing itself more faintly towards the zenith, where it melted into the pearl-coloured sky, or played on the fantastic volumes of a few light clouds with inconstant glimmering. While these beautiful transitions were still before the eyes of the youthful admirers of their beauties, a voice was heard above them, crying as if from the heavens—

"Sail—ho! The frigate lies broad off to sea-ward, sir!"

"Ay, ay; you have been watching with one eye asleep, fellow," returned Griffith, "or we should have heard you before! Look a little north of the place where the glare of the sun is coming, Miss Plowden, and you will be able to see our gallant vessel."

An involuntary cry of pleasure burst from the lips of Katherine, as she followed his directions, and first beheld the frigate through the medium of the fluctuating colours of the morning. The undulating outline of the lazy ocean, which rose and fell heavily against the bright boundary of the heavens, was without any relief to distract the eye, as it fed eagerly on the beauties of the solitary ship. She was riding sluggishly on the long seas, with only two of her lower and smaller sails spread, to hold her in command; but her tall masts and heavy yards were painted against the fiery sky, in strong lines of deep black, while even the smallest cord in the mazes of her rigging, might be distinctly traced, stretching from spar to spar, with the beautiful accuracy of a picture. At moments, when her huge hull rose on a billow, and was lifted against the back ground of sky, its shape and dimensions were brought into view, but these transient glimpses were soon lost, as it settled into the trough, leaving the waving spars bowing gracefully towards the waters, as if about to follow the vessel into the bosom of the deep. As a clearer light gradually stole on the senses, the delusion of colours and distance vanished together, and when a flood of day preceded the immediate appearance of the sun, the ship became plainly visible, within a mile of the cutter, her black hull checkered with ports, and her high tapering masts exhibiting their proper proportions and hues.

At the first cry of "a sail," the crew of the Alacrity had been aroused from their slumbers, by the shrill whistle of the boatswain, and long before the admiring looks of the two cousins had ceased to dwell on the fascinating sight of morning chasing night from the hemisphere, the cutter was again in motion to join her consort. It seemed but a moment before their little vessel was in what the timid females thought, a dangerous proximity to the frigate, under whose lee she slowly passed, in order to admit of the following dialogue between Griffith and his aged commander:

"I rejoice to see you, Mr. Griffith!" cried the captain, who stood in the channel of his ship, waving his hat, in the way of cordial greeting. "You are welcome back, Capt. Manual; welcome, welcome, all of you, my boys! as welcome as a breeze in the calm latitudes." As his eye, however, passed along the deck of the Alacrity, it encountered the shrinking figures of Cecilia and Katherine, and a dark shade of displeasure crossed his decent features, while he added—"How's this, gentlemen! The frigate of Congress is neither a ball-room, nor a church, that it is to be thronged with women!"

"Ay, ay," muttered Boltrope to his friend the chaplain, "now the old man has hauled out his mizzen, you'll see him carry a weather helm! He wakes up about as often as the trades shift their points, and that's once in six months. But when there has been a neap-tide in his temper for any time, you're sure to find it followed by a flood with a vengeance. Let us hear what the first lieutenant can say in favour of his petticoat quality!"

The blushing sky had not exhibited a more fiery glow,than gleamed in the fine face of Griffith for a moment; but struggling with his disgust, he answered with bitter emphasis—

"'Twas the pleasure of Mr. Gray, sir, to bring off the prisoners."

"Of Mr. Gray!" repeated the captain, instantly losing every trace of displeasure, in an air of acquiescence. "Come-to, sir, on the same tack with the ship, and I will hasten to order the accommodation ladder rigged, to receive our guests!"

Boltrope listened to this sudden alteration in the language of his commander, with sufficient wonder; nor was it until he had shaken his head repeatedly, with the manner of one who saw deeper than his neighbours into a mystery, that he found leisure to observe—

"Now, parson, I suppose if you held an almanack in your fist, you'd think you could tell which way we shall have the wind to-morrow! but damn me, priest, if better calculators than you havn't failed! Because a lubberly—no, he's a thorough seaman, I'll say that for the fellow!—because a pilot chooses to say, 'bring me off these here women,' the ship is to be so cluttered with she-cattle, that a man will be obliged to spend half his time in making his manners! Now mind what I

tell you, priest, this very frolic will cost Congress the price of a
year's wages for an able-bodied seaman, in bunting and canvass for screens; besides the wear and tear of running-gear in
shortening sail, in order that the women need not be 'stericky
in squalls!'"

The presence of Mr. Boltrope being required, to take charge
of the cutter, the divine was denied an opportunity of dissen-
ting from the opinions of his rough companion; for the
loveliness of their novel shipmates, had not failed to plead
loudly in their favour, with every man in the cutter whose
habits and ideas had not become rigidly set in obstinacy.

By the time the Alacrity was hove-to, with her head towards
the frigate, the long line of boats that she had been towing during the latter part of the night, were brought to her side, and
filled with men. A wild scene of unbridled merriment and
gayety succeeded, while the seamen were exchanging the confinement of the prize for their accustomed lodgings in the ship,
during which the reins of discipline were slightly relaxed.
Loud laughter was echoed from boat to boat, as they glided by
each other; and rude jests, interlarded with quaint humours
and strange oaths, were freely bandied from mouth to mouth.
The noise, however, soon ceased, and the passage of Col.
Howard and his wards was then effected, with less precipitancy,
and due decorum. Capt. Munson, who had been holding a
secret dialogue with Griffith and the Pilot, received his unexpected guests with plain hospitality, but with an evident desire
to be civil. He politely yielded to their service his two convenient state-rooms, and invited them to partake, in common
with himself, of the comforts of the great cabin.

XIII. The dying Colonel Howard attended by Katherine, Cecilia, Griffith, and Barnstable, drawn and engraved by Alfred Johannot.

THE PILOT.

It is he! she cried, the instant her eye was put to the glass.

The little book which contained the explanations of Miss Plowden's signals was now hastily produced.

Page 306.

London, Published by Henry Colburn & Richard Bentley, 1831.

XIV. Cecilia and Katherine prepare to signal Barnstable, drawn by Sir William Boxall and engraved by Dean in 1831 as the frontispiece for Volume I of Colburn and Bentley's Standard Novels.

THE PILOT

BY

J. F. COOPER.

"Pyramids of fog! and wreathing clouds!
By heaven! he shouted "tis a tall ship! Royals,
skysails, and studding sails all abroad."

Page 542.

LONDON.

COLBURN AND BENTLEY,
NEW BURLINGTON STREET.

1831.

XV. "Pyramids of fog! and wreathing clouds! By Heaven!" he shouted, " 'tis a tall ship!" Title page illustration by an unknown artist for the 1831 Colburn and Bentley edition of *The pilot*.

ŒUVRES COMPLÈTES

DE

J. FENIMORE COOPER

TOME IX.

LE PILOTE.

PARIS,

CHARLES GOSSELIN, MAME & DELAUNAY-VALLÉE,
A. SAUTELET & Cⁱᵉ

MDCCCXXVII.

XVI. Departure of the Pilot, "For a long time the young man [Griffith] stood an abstracted gazer . . . watching the small boat as it glided towards the open ocean." Drawn and engraved by Tony Johannot.

Chapter XXXIII.

"Furious press the hostile squadron,
Furious he repels their rage,
Loss of blood at length enfeebles;
Who can war with thousands wage?"
                    Percy (tr.), "Gentle River, Gentle River," ll. 53-56.

WE CANNOT detain the narrative, to detail the scenes which busy wonder, aided by the relation of divers marvellous feats, produced among the curious seamen who remained in the ship, and their more fortunate fellows, who had returned in glory from an expedition to the land. For nearly an hour the turbulence of a general movement was heard, issuing from the deep recesses of the frigate, and the boisterous sounds of hoarse merriment were listened to by the officers in indulgent silence; but all these symptoms of unbridled humour ceased by the time the morning repast was ended, when the regular sea-watch was set, and the greater portion of those whose duty did not require their presence on the vessel's deck, availed themselves of the opportunity to repair the loss of sleep sustained in the preceding night. Still no preparations were made to put the ship in motion, though long and earnest consultations, which were supposed to relate to their future destiny, were observed by the younger officers, to be held between their captain, the first lieutenant, and the mysterious Pilot. The latter threw many an anxious glance along the eastern horizon, searching it minutely with his glass, and then would turn his impatient looks at the low, dense bank of fog, which, stretching across the ocean like a barrier of cloud, entirely intercepted the view towards the south. To the north and along the land, the air was clear, and the sea without spot of any kind; but in the east a small white sail had been discovered since the opening of day, which was gradually rising above the water, and assuming the appearance of a vessel of some size. Every officer on the quarter-deck in his turn, had examined this distant sail, and had ventured an opinion on its destination and character; and even Katherine, who with her cousin was enjoying, in the open air, the novel beauties of the ocean, had been tempted to place her sparkling eye to a glass, to gaze at the stranger.

"It is a collier," Griffith said, "who has hauled from the land in the late gale, and who is luffing up to his course again. If the wind holds here in the south, and he does not get into that fog bank, we can stand off for him and get a supply of fuel before eight bells are struck."

"I think his head is to the northward, and that he is steering off the wind," returned the Pilot, in a musing manner. "If that Dillon succeeded in getting his express far enough along the coast, the alarm has been spread, and we must be wary. The convoy of the Baltic trade is in the North Sea, and news of our presence could easily have been taken off to it by some of the cutters that line the coast — I could wish to get the ship as far south as the Helder!"

"Then we lose this weather tide!" exclaimed the impatient Griffith; "surely we have the cutter as a look-out! besides, by beating into the fog, we shall lose the enemy, if enemy it be, and it is thought meet for an American frigate to skulk from her foes!"

The scornful expression that kindled the eye of the Pilot, like a gleam of sunshine lighting for an instant some dark dell and laying bare its secrets, was soon lost in the usually quiet look of his glance, though he hesitated like one who was struggling with his passions, before he answered —

"If prudence and the service of the States require it, even this proud frigate must retreat and hide from the meanest of her enemies. My advice, Capt. Munson, is, that you make sail, and beat the ship to windward, as Mr. Griffith has suggested, and that you order the cutter to precede us, keeping more in with the land."

The aged seaman, who evidently suspended his orders, only to receive an intimation of the other's pleasure, immediately commanded his youthful assistant to issue the necessary mandates to put these measures in force. Accordingly, the Alacrity, which vessel had been left under the command of the junior lieutenant of the frigate, was quickly under way; and making short stretches to windward, she soon entered the bank of fog, and was lost to the eye. In the mean time the canvass of the ship was loosened, and spread leisurely in order not to disturb the portion of the crew who were sleeping, and following her little consort, she moved heavily through the water, bearing up against the dull breeze.

The quiet of regular duty had succeeded to the bustle of making sail, and as the rays of the sun fell less obliquely on the distant land, Katherine and Cecilia were amusing Griffith by vain attempts to point out the rounded eminences which they fancied lay in the vicinity of the deserted mansion of St. Ruth. Barnstable, who had resumed his former station in the frigate, as her second lieutenant, was pacing the opposite side of the quarter-deck, holding under his arm the speaking trumpet, which denoted that he held the temporary control of the motions of the ship, and inwardly cursing the restraint that kept him from the side of his mistress. At this moment of universal quiet, when nothing above low dialogues interrupted the dashing of the waves as they were thrown lazily aside by the bows of the vessel, the report of a light cannon burst out of the barrier of fog, and rolled by them on the breeze, apparently vibrating with the rising and sinking of the waters.

"There goes the cutter!" exclaimed Griffith, the instant the sound was heard.

"Surely," said the captain. "Somers is not so indiscreet as to scale his guns, after the caution he has received!"

"No idle scaling of guns is intended there," said the Pilot, straining his eyes to pierce the fog, but soon turning away in disappointment at his inability to succeed—"that gun is shotted, and has been fired in the hurry of a sudden signal!—can your look-outs see nothing, Mr. Barnstable?"

The lieutenant of the watch hailed the man aloft, and demanded if any thing were visible in the direction of the wind, and received for answer, that the fog intercepted the view in that quarter of the heavens, but that the sail in the east was a ship, running large or before the wind. The Pilot shook his head doubtingly at this information, but still he manifested a strong reluctance to relinquish the attempt of getting more to the southward. Again he communed with the commander of the frigate, apart from all other ears, and while they yet deliberated, a second report was heard, leaving no doubt that the Alacrity was firing signal guns for their particular attention.

"Perhaps," said Griffith, "he wishes to point out his position, or to ascertain ours; believing that we are lost like himself in the mist."

"We have our compasses!" returned the doubting captain; "Somers has a meaning in what he says!"

"See!" cried Katherine, with girlish delight, "see, my cousin! see, Barnstable! how beautifully that vapour is wreathing itself in clouds above the smoky line of fog! It stretches already into the very heavens like a lofty pyramid!"

Barnstable sprang lightly on a gun, as he repeated her words—

"Pyramids of fog! and wreathing clouds! By heaven!" he shouted, "'tis a tall ship! Royals, skysails, and studding-sails all abroad! She is within a mile of us, and comes down like a race horse, with a spanking breeze, dead before it! Now know we why Somers is speaking in the mist!"

"Ay," cried Griffith, "and there goes the Alacrity, just breaking out of the fog, hovering in for the land!"

"There is a mighty hull under all that cloud of canvass, Capt. Munson," said the observant but calm Pilot—"it is time, gentlemen, to edge away to leeward."

"What, before we know from whom we run!" cried Griffith; "my life on it, there is no single ship king George owns, but would tire of the sport before she had played a full game of bowls with"—

The haughty air of the young man was daunted by the severe look he encountered in the eye of the Pilot, and he suddenly ceased, though inwardly chafing with impatient pride.

"The same eye that detected the canvass above the fog, might have seen the flag of a vice-admiral fluttering still nearer the heavens," returned the collected stranger; "and England, faulty as she may be, is yet too generous to place a flag-officer in time of war, in command of a frigate, or a captain in command of a fleet. She knows the value of those who shed their blood in her behalf, and it is thus that she is so well served! believe me, Capt. Munson, there is nothing short of a ship of the line under that symbol of rank, and that broad show of canvass!"

"We shall see, sir, we shall see," returned the old officer, whose manner grew decided, as the danger appeared to thicken; "beat to quarters, Mr. Griffith, for we have none but enemies to expect on this coast."

The order was instantly issued, when Griffith remarked, with a more temperate zeal —

"If Mr. Gray be right, we shall have reason to thank God that we are so light of heel!"

The cry of "a strange vessel close aboard the frigate," having already flown down the hatches, the ship was in an uproar at the first tap of the drum. The seamen threw themselves from their hammocks and lashing them rapidly into long, hard bundles, they rushed to the decks, where they were dexterously stowed in the netting, to aid the defences of the upper part of the vessel. While this tumultuous scene was exhibiting, Griffith gave a secret order to Merry, who disappeared, leading his trembling cousins to a place of safety in the inmost depths of the ship.

The guns were cleared of their lumber, and loosened. The bulk-heads were knocked down, and the cabin relieved of its furniture, and the gun deck exhibited one unbroken line of formidable cannon, arranged in all the order of a naval battery ready to engage. Arm chests were thrown open, and the decks strewed with pikes, cutlasses, pistols, and all the various weapons for boarding. In short, the yards were slung, and every other arrangement was made with a readiness and dexterity that were actually wonderful, though all was performed amid an appearance of disorder and confusion that rendered the ship another Babel during the continuance of the preparations. In a very few minutes every thing was completed, and even the voices of the men ceased to be heard answering to their names, as they were mustered at their stations, by their respective officers. Gradually the ship became as quiet as the grave, and when even Griffith or his commander found it necessary to speak, their voices were calmer, and their tones more mild than usual. The course of the vessel was changed to an oblique line from that in which their enemy was approaching, though the appearance of flight was to be studiously avoided to the last moment. When nothing further remained to be done, every eye became fixed on the enormous pile of swelling canvass that was rising, in cloud over cloud, far above the fog, and which was manifestly moving, like driving vapour, swiftly to the north. Presently the dull, smoky boundary of the mist which rested on the water, was pushed aside in vast volumes, and the long taper spars that projected from the bowsprit of the strange ship, issued from the obscurity, and were quickly followed by the whole of the enormous fabric, to which they were merely light appendages. For a moment, streaks of reluctant vapour clung to the huge, floating pile, but they were soon taken off by the rapid vessel, and the whole of her black hull became distinct to the eye.

"One, two, three rows of teeth!" said Boltrope, deliberately counting the tiers of guns that bristled along the sides of the enemy; "a three decker! Jack Manly would show his stern to such a fellow! and even the bloody Scotchman would run!"

"Hard up with your helm, quarter-master!" cried Capt. Munson; "there is indeed no time to hesitate, with such an enemy within a quarter of a mile! Turn the hands up Mr. Griffith, and pack on the ship from her trucks to her lower studding-sail booms. Be stirring, sir, be stirring! Hard up with your helm! Hard up, and be damn'd to you!"

The unusual earnestness of their aged commander acted on the startled crew like a voice from the deep, and they waited not for the usual signals of the boatswain and drummer to be given, before they broke away from their guns, and rushed tumultuously to aid in spreading the desired canvass. There was one minute of ominous confusion, that, to an inexperienced eye would have foreboded the destruction of all order in the vessel, during which every hand, and each tongue, seemed in motion; but it ended in opening the immense folds of light duck which were displayed along the whole line of the masts, far beyond the ordinary sails, overshadowing the waters for a great distance, on either side of the vessel. During the moment of inaction that succeeded this sudden exertion, the breeze which had brought up the three decker, fell fresher on the sails of the frigate, and she started away from her dangerous enemy with a very perceptible advantage in point of sailing.

"The fog rises!" cried Griffith; "give us but the wind for an hour, and we shall run her out of gun-shot!"

"These ninety's are very fast off the wind;" returned the captain, in a low tone, that was intended only for the ears of his first lieutenant and the Pilot, "and we shall have a struggle for it."

The quick eye of the stranger was glancing over the movements of his enemy, while he answered—

"He finds we have the heels of him already! he is making ready, and we shall be fortunate to escape a broadside! Let her yaw a little, Mr. Griffith; touch her lightly with the helm; if we are raked, sir, we are lost!"

The captain sprang on the taffrail of his ship, with the activity of a younger man, and in an instant he perceived the truth of the other's conjecture.

Both vessels now ran for a few minutes, keenly watching each other's motions like two skilful combatants; the English ship making slight deviations from the line of her course, and then, as her movements were anticipated by the other, turning as cautiously in the opposite direction, until a sudden and wide sweep of her huge bows, told the Americans plainly on which tack to expect her. Capt. Munson made a silent, but impressive gesture with his arm, as if the crisis were too important for speech, which indicated to the watchful Griffith, the way he wished the frigate sheered, to avoid the weight of the impending danger. Both vessels whirled swiftly up to the wind, with their heads towards the land, and as the huge black side of the three-decker, checkered with its triple batteries, frowned full upon her foe, it belched forth a flood of fire and smoke, accompanied by a bellowing roar that mocked the surly moanings of the sleeping ocean. The nerves of the bravest man in the frigate contracted their fibres, as the hurricane of iron hurtled by them, and each eye appeared to gaze in stupid wonder, as if tracing the flight of the swift engines of destruction. But the voice of Capt. Munson was heard in the din, shouting, while he waved his hat earnestly in the required direction—

"Meet her! meet her with the helm, boy! meet her, Mr. Griffith, meet her!"

Griffith had so far anticipated this movement, as to have already ordered the head of the frigate to be turned in its former course when, struck by the unearthly cry of the last tones uttered by his commander, he bent his head, and beheld the venerable seaman driven through the air, his hat still waving, his gray hair floating in the wind, and his eye set in the wild look of death.

"Great God!" exclaimed the young man, rushing to the side of the ship, where he was just in time to see the lifeless body disappear in the waters that were dyed in his blood; "he has been struck by a shot! Lower-away the boat, lower-away the jolly-boat, the barge, the tiger, the—"

"'Tis useless," interrupted the calm, deep voice of the Pilot; "he has met a warrior's end, and he sleeps in a sailor's grave! The ship is getting before the wind again, and the enemy is keeping his vessel away."

The youthful lieutenant was recalled by these words to his duty, and reluctantly turned his eyes away from the bloody spot on the waters, which the busy frigate had already passed, to resume the command of the vessel with a forced composure.

"He has cut some of our running gear," said the master, whose eye had never ceased to dwell on the spars and rigging of the ship, "and there's a splinter out of the main-top-mast, that is big enough for a fid! He has let day-light through some of our canvass too, but taking it by-and-large, the squall has gone over and little harm done.—Didn't I hear something said of Capt. Munson getting jamm'd by a shot?"

"He is killed!"—said Griffith, speaking in a voice that was yet husky with horror—"he is dead, sir, and carried overboard; there is more need that we forget not ourselves, in this crisis."

"Dead!" said Boltrope, suspending the operation of his active jaws for a moment, in surprise; "and buried in a wet jacket! well, it is lucky 'tis no worse, for, damme if I did not think every stick in the ship would have been cut out of her!"

With this consolatory remark on his lips, the master walked slowly forward, continuing his orders to repair the damages with a singleness of purpose that rendered him, however uncouth as a friend, an invaluable man in his station.

Griffith had not yet brought his mind to the calmness that was so essential to discharge the duties which had thus suddenly and awfully devolved on him, when his elbow was lightly touched by the Pilot, who had drawn closer to his side—

"The enemy appear satisfied with the experiment," said the

stranger, "and as we work the quicker of the two, he loses too much ground to repeat it, if he be a true seaman."

"And yet, as he finds we leave him so fast," returned Griffith, "he must see that all his hopes rest, in cutting us up aloft. I dread that he will come by the wind again, and lay us under his broadside; we should need a quarter of an hour to run without his range, if he were anchored!"

"He plays a surer game—see you not that the vessel we made in the eastern board, shows the hull of a frigate? 'Tis past a doubt that they are of one squadron, and that the expresses have sent them in our wake. The English admiral has spread a broad clue, Mr. Griffith, and as he gathers in his ships, he sees that his game has been successful."

The faculties of Griffith had been too much occupied with the hurry of the chase to look at the ocean; but startled at the information of the Pilot, who spoke coolly, though like a man sensible of the existence of approaching danger, he took the glass from the other, and with his own eye examined the different vessels in sight. It is certain that the experienced officer, whose flag was flying above the light sails of the three-decker, saw the critical situation of his chase, and reasoned much in the same manner as the Pilot, or the fearful expedient apprehended by Griffith, would have been adopted. Prudence, however, dictated that he should prevent his enemy from escaping by pressing so closely on his rear, as to render it impossible for the American to haul across his bows and run into the open sea between his own vessel and the nearest frigate of his squadron. The unpractised reader will be able to comprehend the case better by accompanying the understanding eye of Griffith as it glanced from point to point, following the whole horizon. To the west lay the land, along which the Alacrity was urging her way industriously, with the double purpose of keeping her consort abeam, and of avoiding a dangerous proximity to their powerful enemy. To the east, bearing off the starboard bow of the American frigate, was the vessel first seen, and which now began to exhibit the hostile appearance of a ship of war, steering in a line converging towards themselves, and rapidly drawing nigher, while far in the north-east, was a vessel, as yet faintly discerned, whose evolutions could not be mistaken by one who understood the movements of nautical warfare.

"We are hemmed in, effectually," said Griffith, dropping the glass from his eye; "and I know not but our wisest course would be to haul in to the land, and cutting every thing light adrift, endeavour to pass the broadside of the flag-ship?"

"Provided she left a rag of canvass to do it with!" returned the Pilot. "Sir, 'tis an idle hope! She would strip your ship, in ten minutes, to her plank shears. Had it not been for a lucky wave on which so many of her shot struck and glanced upward, we should have nothing to boast of left from the fire she has already given; we must stand on, and drop the three decker as far as possible."

"But the frigates!" said Griffith, "what are we to do with the frigates?"

"Fight them!" returned the Pilot, in a low, determined voice, "fight them! Young man, I have borne the stars and stripes aloft in greater straits than this, and even with honour! Think not that my fortune will desert me now!"

"We shall have an hour of desperate battle!"

"On that we may calculate; but I have lived through whole days of bloodshed! you seem not one to quail at the sight of an enemy."

"Let me proclaim your name to the men!" said Griffith; "'twill quicken their blood, and at such a moment, be a host in itself."

"They want it not," returned the Pilot, checking the hasty zeal of the other with his hand. "I would be unnoticed, unless I am known as becomes me. I will share your danger, but would not rob you of a tittle of your glory. Should we come to a grapple," he continued, while a smile of conscious pride gleamed across his face, "I will give forth the word as a war-cry, and, believe me, these English will quail before it!"

Griffith submitted to the stranger's will, and after they had deliberated further on the nature of their evolutions, he gave his attention again to the management of the vessel. The first object which met his eye, on turning from the Pilot, was Col. Howard, pacing the quarter-deck, with a determined brow, and a haughty mien, as if already in the enjoyment of that triumph which now seemed certain.

"I fear, sir," said the young man, approaching him with respect, "that you will soon find the deck unpleasant and dangerous: your wards are — "

"Mention not the unworthy term!" interrupted the colonel. "What greater pleasure can there be than to inhale the odour of loyalty that is wafted from yonder floating tower of the king! — And danger! you know but little of old George Howard, young man, if you think he would for thousands miss seeing that symbol of rebellion levelled before the flag of his Majesty."

"If that be your wish, Col. Howard," returned Griffith, biting his lip as he looked around at the wondering seamen who were listeners, "you will wait in vain — but I pledge you my word, that when that time arrives, you shall be advised, and that your own hands shall do the ignoble deed."

"Edward Griffith, why not this moment? This is your moment of probation — submit to the clemency of the crown, and yield your crew to the royal mercy! In such a case I would remember the child of my brother Harry's friend; and believe me, my name is known to the ministry. And you, misguided and ignorant abettors of rebellion! cast aside your useless weapons, or prepare to meet the vengeance of yonder powerful and victorious servant of your prince."

"Fall back! back with ye, fellows!" cried Griffith, fiercely, to the men who were gathering around the colonel, with looks of sullen vengeance. "If a man of you dare approach him, he shall be cast into the sea."

The sailors retreated at the order of their commander; but the elated veteran had continued to pace the deck for many minutes before stronger interests diverted the angry glances of the seamen to other objects.

Notwithstanding the ship of the line was slowly sinking beneath the distant waves, and in less than an hour from the time she had fired the broadside, no more than one of her three tiers of guns was visible from the deck of the frigate, she yet presented an irresistible obstacle against retreat to the south. On the other hand the ship first seen, drew so nigh as to render the glass no longer necessary in watching her movements. She proved to be a frigate, though one so materially lighter than the American, as to have rendered her conquest easy, had not her two consorts continued to press on for the scene of battle with such rapidity. During the chase the scene had shifted from the point opposite to St. Ruth, to the verge of those shoals where our tale commenced. As they approached the latter, the smallest of the English ships drew so nigh as to render the combat unavoidable. Griffith and his crew had not been idle in the intermediate time, but all the usual preparations against the casualties of a sea-fight had been duly made, when the drum once more called the men to their quarters, and the ship was deliberately stripped of her unnecessary sails, like a prizefighter about to enter the arena, casting aside the incumbrances of dress; at the instant she gave this intimation of her intention to abandon flight, and trust the issue to the combat, the nearest English frigate also took in her light canvass in token of her acceptance of the challenge.

"He is but a little fellow," said Griffith to the Pilot, who hovered at his elbow with a sort of fatherly interest in the other's conduct of the battle, "though he carries a stout heart."

"We must crush him at a blow," returned the stranger; "not a shot must be delivered until our yards are locking."

"I see him training his twelves upon us already; we may soon expect his fire."

"After standing the brunt of a Ninety-gun-ship," observed the collected Pilot, "we shall not shrink from the broadside of a Two-and-thirty!"

"Stand to your guns, men!" cried Griffith, through his trumpet — "not a shot is to be fired without the order."

This caution, so necessary to check the ardour of the seamen, was hardly uttered, before their enemy became wrapped in sheets of fire and volumes of smoke, as gun after gun hurled its iron missiles at their vessel in quick succession. Ten minutes might have passed, the two vessels sheering closer to each other every foot they advanced, during which time the crew of the American were compelled, by their commander, to suffer the fire of their adversary, without returning a shot. This short period, which seemed an age to the seamen, was distinguished in their vessel by deep silence. Even the wounded and dying, who fell in every part of the ship, stifled their groans, under the influence of the severe discipline, which gave a character to every man and each movement of the vessel; and those officers who were required to speak, were heard only in the lowest tones of resolute preparation. At length the ship slowly entered the skirts of the smoke that enveloped their enemy, and Griffith heard the man who stood at his side whisper the word "now."

"Let them have it!" cried Griffith, in a voice that was heard in the remotest parts of the ship.

The shout that burst from the seamen, appeared to lift the decks of the vessel, and the affrighted frigate trembled like an aspen, with the recoil of her own massive artillery, that shot forth a single sheet of flame, the sailors having disregarded, in their impatience, the usual order of firing. The effect of the broadside on the enemy was still more dreadful, for a death-like silence succeeded to the roar of the guns, which was only broken by the shrieks and execrations that burst from her, like the moanings of the damned. During the few moments in which the Americans were again loading their cannon, and the English were recovering from their confusion, the vessel of the former moved slowly past her antagonist, and was already doubling across her bows, when the latter was suddenly, and, considering the inequality of their forces, it may be added desperately, headed into her enemy. The two frigates grappled. The sudden and furious charge made by the Englishman, as he threw his masses of daring seamen along his bowsprit, and out of his channels, had nearly taken Griffith by surprise; but Manual, who had delivered his first fire with the broadside, now did good service, by ordering his men to beat back the intruders, by a steady and continued discharge. Even the wary Pilot lost sight of their other foes, in the high daring of that moment, and smiles of stern pleasure were exchanged between him and Griffith, as both comprehended at a glance their advantages.

"Lash his bowsprit to our mizzen-mast," shouted the lieutenant, "and we will sweep his decks as he lies!"

Twenty men sprang eagerly forward to execute the order, among the foremost of whom were Boltrope and the stranger.

"Ay, now he's our own!" cried the busy master, "and we will take an owner's liberties with him, and break him up—for by the eternal—"

"Peace, rude man," said the Pilot, in a voice of solemn remonstrance; "at the next instant you may face your God; mock not his awful name!"

The master found time, before he threw himself from the spar on the deck of the frigate again, to cast a look of amazement at his companion, who, with a steady mien, but with an eye that lighted with a warrior's ardour, viewed the battle that raged around him, like one who marked its progress, to control the result.

The sight of the Englishmen, rushing onward with shouts, and bitter menaces, warmed the blood of Col. Howard, who pressed to the side of the frigate, and encouraged his friends, by his gestures and voice, to come on.

"Away with ye, old croaker!" cried the master, seizing him by the collar; "away with ye to the hold, or I'll order you fired from a gun."

"Down with your arms, rebellious dog!" shouted the colonel, carried beyond himself by the ardour of the fray; "down to the dust, and implore the mercy of your injured prince!"

Invigorated by a momentary glow, the veteran grappled with his brawny antagonist, but the issue of the short struggle was yet suspended, when the English, driven back by the fire of the marines, and the menacing front that Griffith, with his boarders presented, retreated to the forecastle of their own ship, and attempted to return the deadly blows they were receiving in their hull from the cannon that Barnstable directed. A solitary gun was all they could bring to bear on the Americans, but this, loaded with cannister, was fired so near as to send its glaring flame into the very faces of the enemies. The struggling colonel, who was already sinking beneath the arm of his foe, felt the rough grasp loosen from his throat, at the flash, and the two combatants sunk powerless on their knees, facing each other.

"How now, brother!" exclaimed Boltrope, with a smile of grim fierceness; "some of that grist has gone to your mill, ha!"

No answer could, however be given, before the yielding forms of both fell to the deck, where they lay helpless, amid the din of the battle and the wild confusion of the eager combatants.

Notwithstanding the furious struggle they witnessed, the elements did not cease their functions; and urged by the breeze, and lifted irresistibly on a wave, the American ship was forced through the water still further across the bows of her enemy. The idle fastenings of hemp and iron, were snapped asunder, like strings of tow, and Griffith saw his own ship borne away from the Englishman at the instant that the bowsprit of the latter was torn from its lashings, and tumbled into the sea, followed by spar after spar, until nothing of all her proud tackling was remaining, but the few parted and useless ropes that were left dangling along the stumps of her lower masts. As his own stately vessel moved from the confusion she had caused, and left the dense cloud of smoke in which her helpless antagonist lay, the eye of the young man glanced anxiously towards the horizon, where he now remembered he had more foes to contend against.

"We have shaken off the thirty-two most happily!" he said to the Pilot, who followed his motions with singular interest; "but here is another fellow sheering in for us, who shows as many ports as ourselves, and who appears inclined for a closer interview; besides the hull of the Ninety is rising again, and I fear she will be down but too soon!"

"We must keep the use of our braces and sails," returned the Pilot, "and on no account close with the other frigate — we must play a double game, sir, and fight this new adversary with our heels as well as with our guns."

"'Tis time then that we were busy, for he is shortening sail, and as he nears so fast we may expect to hear from him every minute; what do you propose, sir?"

"Let him gather in his canvass," returned the Pilot, "and when he thinks himself snug, we can throw out a hundred men at once upon our yards and spread every thing alow and aloft; we may then draw ahead of him by surprise; if we can once get him in our wake I have no fears of dropping them all."

"A stern chase is a long chase," cried Griffith, "and the thing may do! Clear up the decks, here, and carry down the wounded; and as we have our hands full, the poor fellows who have done with us, must go overboard at once."

This melancholy duty was instantly attended to, while the

young seaman who commanded the frigate returned to his duty, with the absorbed air of one who felt its high responsibility. These occupations, however, did not prevent his hearing the sounds of Barnstable's voice, calling eagerly to young Merry. Bending his head towards the sound, Griffith beheld his friend, looking anxously up the main hatch, with a face grimed with smoke, his coat off, and his shirt bespattered with human blood—"Tell me, boy," he said, "is Mr. Griffith untouched? They say that a shot came in upon the quarter deck that tripped up the heels of half a dozen."

Before Merry could answer, the eyes of Barnstable, which even while he spoke were scanning the state of the vessel's rigging, encountered the kind looks of Griffith, and from that moment perfect harmony was restored between the friends.

"Ah! you are there Griff. and with a whole skin, I see," cried Barnstable, smiling with pleasure; "they have passed poor Boltrope down into one of his own store-rooms! If that fellow's bowsprit had held on ten minutes longer, what a mark I should have made on his face and eyes!"

"'Tis perhaps best as it is," returned Griffith; "but what have you done with those whom we are most bound to protect?"

Barnstable made a significant gesture towards the depths of the vessel as he answered—

"On the cables; safe as wood, iron, and water can keep them—though Katherine has had her head up three times to—"

A summons from the Pilot drew Griffith away, and the young officers were compelled to forget their individual feelings, in the pressing duties of their stations.

The ship which the American frigate had now to oppose, was a vessel of near her own size and equipage, and when Griffith looked at her again, he perceived that she had made her preparations to assert her equality in manful fight.

Her sails had been gradually reduced to the usual quantity, and, by certain movements on her decks, the lieutenant and his constant attendant the Pilot, well understood that she only wanted to lessen her distance a few hundred yards to begin the action.

"Now spread every thing," whispered the stranger.

Griffith applied the trumpet to his mouth, and shouted in a voice that was carried even to his enemy—"Let fall—out with your booms—sheet home—hoist away of every thing!"

The inspiriting cry was answered by a universal bustle; fifty men flew out on the dizzy heights of the different spars, while broad sheets of canvass rose as suddenly along the masts, as if some mighty bird were spreading its wings. The Englishman instantly perceived his mistake, and he answered the artifice by a roar of artillery. Griffith watched the effects of the broadside with an absorbing interest, as the shot whistled above his head, but when he perceived his masts untouched and the few unimportant ropes only that were cut, he replied to the uproar with a burst of pleasure. A few men were however seen clinging with wild frenzy to the cordage, dropping from rope to rope like wounded birds fluttering through a tree, until they fell heavily into the ocean, the sullen ship sweeping by them, in cold indifference. At the next instant the spars and masts of their enemy exhibited a display of men similar to their own, when Griffith again placed the trumpet to his mouth, and shouted aloud:

"Give it to them; drive them from their yards, boys; scatter them with your grape—unreeve their rigging!"

The crew of the American wanted but little encouragement to enter on this experiment with hearty good will, and the close of his cheering words were uttered amid the deafening roar of his own cannon. The Pilot had, however, mistaken the skill and readiness of their foe, for notwithstanding the disadvantageous circumstances under which the Englishman increased his sail, the duty was steadily and dexterously performed.

The two ships were now running rapidly on parallel lines, hurling at each other their instruments of destruction, with furious industry, and with severe and certain loss to both, though with no manifest advantage in favour of either. Both Griffith and the Pilot witnessed with deep concern this unexpected defeat of their hopes, for they could not conceal from themselves, that each moment lessened their velocity through the water, as the shot of their enemy, stripped the canvass from the yards, or dashed aside the lighter spars in their terrible progress.

"We find our equal here!" said Griffith to the stranger. "The Ninety is heaving up again, like a mountain, and if we continue to shorten sail at this rate, she will soon be down upon us!"

"You say true, sir," returned the Pilot, musing; "the man shows judgment as well as spirit; but—"

He was interrupted by Merry, who rushed from the forward part of the vessel, his whole face betokening the eagerness of his spirit, and the importance of his intelligence—

"The breakers!" he cried, when nigh enough to be heard amid the din; "we are running dead on a ripple, and the sea is white not two hundred yards ahead!"

The Pilot jumped on a gun, and bending to catch a glimpse through the smoke, he shouted, in those clear, piercing tones, that could be even heard among the roaring of the cannon. "Port, port your helm! we are on the Devil's Grip! pass up the trumpet, sir; port your helm, fellow; give it them, boys—give it to the proud English dogs!" Griffith unhesitatingly relinquished the symbol of his rank, fastening his own firm look on the calm but quick eye of the Pilot, and gathering assurance from the high confidence he read in the countenance of the stranger. The seamen were too busy with their cannon and their rigging to regard the new danger, and the frigate entered one of the dangerous passes of the shoals, in the heat of a severely contested battle. The wondering looks of a few of the older sailors glanced at the sheets of foam that flew by them, in doubt whether the wild gambols of the waves were occasioned by the shot of the enemy, when suddenly the noise of cannon was succeeded by the sullen wash of the disturbed element, and presently the vessel glided out of her smoky shroud, and was boldly steering in the centre of the narrow passages. For ten breathless minutes longer the Pilot continued to hold an uninterrupted sway, during which the vessel ran swiftly by ripples and breakers, by streaks of foam and darker passages of deep water, when he threw down his trumpet and exclaimed—

"What threatened to be our destruction has proved our salvation!—keep yonder hill crowned with wood, one point open from the church tower at its base, and steer east and by north; you will run through these shoals on that course in an hour, and by so doing, you will gain five leagues of your enemy, who will have to double their tail."

The moment he stepped from the gun, the Pilot lost the air of authority that had so singularly distinguished his animated form, and even the close interest he had manifested in the incidents of the day, became lost in the cold, settled reserve he had affected during his intercourse with his present associates. Every officer in the ship, after the breathless suspense of uncertainty had passed, rushed to those places where a view might be taken of their enemies. The Ninety was still steering boldly onward, and had already approached the Two-and-thirty, which lay, a helpless wreck, rolling on the unruly seas, that were rudely tossing her on their wanton billows. The frigate last engaged was running along the edge of the ripple, with her torn sails flying loosely in the air, her ragged spars tottering in the breeze, and every thing above her hull exhibiting the confusion of a sudden and unlooked-for check to her progress. The exulting taunts and mirthful congratulations of the seamen, as they gazed at the English ships, were, however, soon forgotten in the attention that was required to their own vessel. The drums beat the retreat, the guns were lashed, the wounded again removed, and every individual, able to keep the deck, was required to lend his assistance in repairing the damages of the frigate and securing her masts.

The promised hour carried the ship safely through all the dangers, which were much lessened by daylight, and by the time the sun had begun to fall over the land, Griffith, who had not quitted the deck during the day, beheld his vessel once more cleared of the confusion of the chase and battle, and ready to meet another foe. At this period he was summoned to the cabin, at the request of the ship's chaplain. Delivering the charge of the frigate to Barnstable, who had been his active assistant, no less in their subsequent labours than in the combat, he hastily divested himself of the vestiges of the fight, and proceeded to obey the repeated and earnest call.

Chapter XXXIV.

"Whither, 'midst falling dew,
While glow the heavens with the last steps of day,
Far, through their rosy depths, dost thou pursue
Thy solitary way?"

Bryant, "To a Waterfowl," ll. 1–4.

WHEN THE young seaman, who now commanded the frigate, descended from the quarter-deck in compliance with the often repeated summons, he found the vessel restored to the same neatness as if nothing had occurred to disturb its order. The gun-deck had been cleansed of its horrid stains, and the smoke of the fight had long since ascended through the hatches, and mingled with the clouds that flitted above the ship. As he walked along the silent batteries, even the urgency of his visit could not prevent him from glancing his eyes towards the splintered sides, those terrible vestiges, by which the paths of the shot of their enemy might be traced; and by the time he tapped lightly at the door of the cabin, his quick look had embraced every material injury the vessel had sustained in her principal points of defence. The door was opened by the surgeon of the frigate, who, as he stepped aside to permit Griffith to enter, shook his head with that air of meaning, which, in one of his profession, is understood to imply the abandonment of all hopes, and then immediately quitted the apartment, in order to attend to those who might profit by his services.

The reader is not to imagine that Griffith had lost sight of Cecilia and her cousin during the occurrences of that eventful day; on the contrary, his troubled fancy had presented her terror and distress, even in the hottest moments of the fight, and the instant that the crew were called from their guns, he had issued an order to replace the bulk-heads of the cabin, and to arrange its furniture for their accommodation, though the higher and imperious duties of his station had precluded his attending to their comfort in person. He expected, therefore, to find the order of the rooms restored, but he was by no means prepared to encounter the scene he was now to witness.

Between two of the sullen cannon, which gave such an air of singular wildness to the real comfort of the cabin, was placed a large couch, on which the Colonel was lying, evidently near his end. Cecilia was weeping by his side, her dark ringlets falling in unheeded confusion around her pale features, and sweeping in their rich exuberance the deck on which she knelt. Katherine leaned tenderly over the form of the dying veteran, while her dark, tearful eyes seemed to express self-accusation blended with deep commiseration. A few attendants of both sexes surrounded the solemn scene, all of whom appeared to be under the influence of the hopeless intelligence which the medical officer had but that moment communicated. The servants of the ship had replaced the furniture with a care that mocked the dreadful struggle that so recently disfigured the warlike apartment, and the stout, square frame of Boltrope occupied the opposite settee, his head resting on the lap of the Captain's Steward, and his hand gently held in the grasp of his friend the Chaplain. Griffith had heard of the wound of the master, but his own eyes now conveyed the first intelligence of the situation of Colonel Howard. When the shock of this sudden discovery had a little subsided, the young man approached the couch of the latter, and attempted to express his regret and pity, in a voice that afforded an assurance of his sincerity.

"Say no more, Edward Griffith," interrupted the Colonel, waving his hand feebly for silence; "it seemeth to be the will of God that this rebellion should triumph, and it is not for vain man to impeach the acts of Omnipotence! To my erring faculties, it wears an appearance of mystery, but doubtless it is to answer the purpose of his own inscrutable providence! I have sent for you, Edward, on a business that I would fain see accomplished before I die, that it may not be said old George Howard neglected his duty, even in his last moments. You see this weeping child at my side; tell me, young man, do you love the maiden?"

"Am I to be asked such a question?" exclaimed Griffith.

"And will you cherish her — will you supply to her the places of father and mother, will you become the fond guardian of her innocence and weakness?"

Griffith could give no other answer than a fervent pressure of the hand he had clasped.

"I believe you," continued the dying man; "for however he may have forgotten to inculcate his own loyalty, worthy Hugh Griffith could never neglect to make his son a man of honour. I had weak, and perhaps evil wishes in behalf of my late unfortunate kinsman, Mr. Christopher Dillon; but they have told me that he was false to his faith. If this be true, I would refuse him the hand of the girl, though he claimed the fealty of the British realms! But he has passed away, and I am about to follow him into a world where we shall find but one Lord to serve, and it may have been better for us both had we more remembered our duty to Him, while serving the Princes of the the earth. One thing further—know you this officer of your congress well; this Mr. Barnstable?"

"I have sailed with him for years," returned Griffith, "and can answer for him as myself."

The veteran made an effort to rise, which in part succeeded, and he fastened on the youth a look of keen scrutiny that gave to his pallid features an expression of solemn meaning, as he continued—

"Speak not now, sir, as the companion of his idle pleasures, and as the unthinking associate commends his fellow, but remember that your opinion is given to a dying man who leans on your judgment for advice. The daughter of John Plowden is a trust not to be neglected, nor will my death prove easy, if a doubt of her being worthily bestowed shall remain!"

"He is a gentleman," returned Griffith, "and one whose heart is not less kind than gallant—he loves your ward, and great as may be her merit, he is deserving of it all—like myself, he has also loved the land that gave him birth, before the land of his ancestors, but—"

"That is now forgotten," interrupted the Colonel; "after what I have this day witnessed I am forced to believe that it is the pleasure of Heaven that you are to prevail! But, sir, a disobedient inferior will be apt to make an unreasonable commander. The recent contention between you—"

"Remember it not, dear sir," exclaimed Griffith with generous zeal—"'twas unkindly provoked, and it is already forgotten and pardoned. He has sustained me nobly throughout the day, and my life on it, that he knows how to treat a woman as a brave man should!"

"Then am I content!" said the veteran, sinking back on his couch; "let him be summoned."

The whispered message, which Griffith gave requesting Mr. Barnstable to enter the cabin, was quickly conveyed, and he had appeared before his friend deemed it discreet to disturb the reflections of the veteran by again addressing him. When the entrance of the young sailor was announced, the Colonel again roused himself, and addressed his wondering listener, though in a manner much less confiding and familiar, than that which he had adopted towards Griffith.

"The declarations you made last night, relative to my ward, the daughter of the late Captain John Plowden, sir, have left me nothing to learn on the subject of your wishes. Here, then, gentlemen, you both obtain the reward of your attentions! Let that reverend divine hear you pronounce the marriage vows, while I have strength to listen, that I may be a witness against ye, in heaven, should ye forget their tenor!"

"Not now, not now," murmured Cecilia; "Oh ask it not now, my uncle!"

Katherine spoke not, but deeply touched by the tender interest her guardian manifested in her welfare, she bowed her face to her bosom, in subdued feeling, and suffered the tears that had been suffusing her eyes to roll down her cheeks in large drops, till they bathed the deck.

"Yes, now, my love," continued the Colonel, "or I fail in my duty. I go shortly to stand face to face with your parents, my children; for the man, who dying, expects not to meet worthy Hugh Griffith and honest Jack Plowden in heaven, can have no clear view of the rewards that belong to lives of faithful service to the country, or of gallant loyalty to the King! I trust no one can justly say, that I ever forgot the delicacy due to your gentle sex; but it is no moment for idle ceremony when time is shortening into minutes, and heavy duties remain to be discharged. I could not die in peace, children, were I to leave you here in the wide ocean, I had almost said in the wide world, without that protection which becomes your tender years and still more tender characters. If it has pleased God to remove your guardian, let his place be supplied by those he wills to succeed him!"

Cecilia no longer hesitated, but she arose slowly from her knees, and offered her hand to Griffith with an air of forced resignation. Katherine submitted to be led by Barnstable to her side, and the chaplain who had been an affected listener to the dialogue, in obedience to an expressive signal from the eye of Griffith, opened the prayer book from which he had been gleaning consolation for the dying master, and commenced reading, in trembling tones, the marriage service. The vows were pronounced by the weeping brides in voices more distinct and audible than if they had been uttered amid the gay crowds that usually throng a bridal; for though they were the irreclaimable words that bound them forever to the men, whose power over their feelings they thus proclaimed to the world, the reserve of maiden diffidence was lost in one engrossing emotion of solemnity, created by the awful presence in which they stood. When the benediction was pronounced, the head of Cecilia dropped on the shoulder of her husband, where she wept violently, for a moment, and then resuming her place at the couch, she once more knelt at the side of her uncle. Katherine received the warm kiss of Barnstable, passively, and returned slowly to the spot whence she had been led.

Colonel Howard succeeded in raising his person, to witness the ceremony, and had answered to each prayer with a fervent "amen." He fell back with the last words, and a look of satisfaction shone in his aged and pallid features, that declared the interest he had taken in the scene.

"I thank you, my children," he at length uttered, "I thank you, for I know how much you have sacrificed to my wishes. You will find all my papers relative to the estates of my wards, gentlemen, in the hands of my banker in London, and you will also find there my will, Edward, by which you will learn that Cicely has not come to your arms an unportioned bride. What my wards are in persons and manners your eyes can witness, and I trust the vouchers in London will show that I have not been an unfaithful steward to their pecuniary affairs!"

"Name it not—say no more, or you will break my heart," cried Katherine, sobbing aloud, in the violence of her remorse at having ever pained so true a friend. "Oh! talk of yourself, think of yourself; we are unworthy — at least I am unworthy of another thought!"

The dying man extended a hand to her in kindness, and continued, though his voice grew feebler as he spoke —

"Then to return to myself — I would wish to lie, like my ancestors, in the bosom of the earth — and in consecrated ground."

"It shall be done," whispered Griffith; "I will see it done myself."

"I thank thee, my son," said the veteran; "for such thou art to me in being the husband of Cicely — you will find in my will, that I have liberated and provided for all my slaves — except those ungrateful scoundrels who deserted their master — they have seized their own freedom, and they need not be indebted to me for the same. There is, Edward, also an unworthy legacy to the King; his Majesty will deign to receive it — from an old and faithful servant, and you will not miss the trifling gift." A long pause followed, as if he had been summing up the account of his earthly duties, and found them duly balanced, when he added, "kiss me Cicely — and you, Katherine — I find you have the genuine feelings of honest Jack, your father. — My eyes grow dim — which is the hand of Griffith? Young gentleman, I have given you all that a fond old man had to bestow — deal tenderly with the precious child — we have not properly understood each other — I had mistaken both you and Mr. Christopher Dillon, I believe; perhaps I may have also mistaken my duty to America — but I was too old to change my politics or my religion — I — I — I lov'd the King — God bless him — "

His words became fainter and fainter as he proceeded, and the breath deserted his body with this benediction on his livid lips, which the proudest monarch might covet from so honest a man.

The body was instantly borne into a state-room by the attendants, and Griffith and Barnstable supported their brides into the after-cabin, where they left them seated on the sofa that lined the stern of the ship, weeping bitterly, in each other's arms.

No part of the preceding scene had been unobserved by

Boltrope, whose small, hard eyes, were observed by the young men to twinkle, when they returned into the state apartment, and they approached their wounded comrade to apologize for the seeming neglect that their conduct had displayed.

"I heard you were hurt, Boltrope," said Griffith, taking him kindly by the hand; "but as I know you are not unused to being marked by shot, I trust we shall soon see you again on deck."

"Ay, ay," returned the master, "you'll want no spy-glasses to see the old hulk as you launch it into the sea. I have had shot, as you say, before now to tear my running gear, and even to knock a splinter out of some of my timbers, but this fellow has found his way into my bread-room; and the cruise of life is up!"

"Surely the case is not so bad, honest David," said Barnstable; "you have kept afloat, to my knowledge, with a bigger hole in your skin than this unlucky hit has made!"

"Ay, ay," returned the master, "that was in my upper works, where the doctor could get at it with a plug; but this chap has knocked away the shifting-boards, and I feel as if the whole cargo was broken up. — You may say, that Tourniquet rates me all the same as a dead man, for after looking at the shot-hole, he has turned me over to the parson here, like a piece of old junk which is only fit to be worked up into something new. Captain Munson had a lucky time of it! I think you said, Mr. Griffith, that the old gentleman was launched overboard with every thing standing, and that Death made but one rap at his door, before he took his leave!"

"His end was indeed sudden!" returned Griffith; "but it is what we seamen must expect."

"And for which there is so much the more occasion to be prepared," the chaplain ventured to add, in a low, humble, and, perhaps, timid voice.

The sailing-master looked keenly from one to the other as they spoke, and, after a short pause, he continued with an air of great submission —

"'Twas his luck; and I suppose it is sinful to begrudge a man his lawful luck. As for being prepared, parson, that is your business and not mine; therefore, as there is but little time to spare, why, the sooner you set about it the better; and to save unnecessary trouble, I may as well tell you not to strive to make too much of me, for, I must own it to my shame, I never took learning kindly. If you can fit me for some middling birth in the other world, like the one I hold in this ship, it will suit me as well, and, perhaps, be easier to all hands of us."

If there was a shade of displeasure, blended with the surprise, that crossed the features of the divine at this extraordinary limitation of his duties, it entirely disappeared when he considered, more closely, the perfect expression of simplicity with which the dying master uttered his wishes. After a long and melancholy pause, which neither Griffith nor his friend felt any inclination to interrupt, the chaplain replied—

"It is not the province of man to determine on the degrees of the merciful dispensations of the Deity, and nothing that I can do, Mr. Boltrope, will have any weight in making up the mighty and irrevocable decree. What I said to you last night, in our conversation on this very subject, must still be fresh in your memory, and there is no good reason why I should hold a different language to you now."

"I can't say that I log'd all that pass'd," returned the master, "and that which I do recollect chiefly fell from myself, for the plain reason that a man remembers his own, better than his neighbor's ideas. And this puts me in mind, Mr. Griffith, to tell you, that one of the forty-two's from the three-decker, travelled across the forecastle, and cut the best bower within a fathom of the clinch, as handily as an old woman would clip her rotten yarn with a pair of tailor's shears!—If you will be so good as to order one of my mates to shift the cable end-for-end, and make a new bend of it, I'll do as much for you another time."

"Mention it not," said Griffith; "rest assured that every thing shall be done for the security of the ship in your department—I will superintend the whole duty in person; and I would have you release your mind from all anxiety on the subject, to attend to your more important interests elsewhere."

"Why," returned Boltrope, with a little show of pertinacity, "I have an opinion, that the cleaner a man takes his hands into the other world, of the matters of duty in this, the better he will be fitted to handle any thing new.—Now the parson, here, undertook to lay down the doctrine last night, that it was no matter how well or how ill a man behaved himself, so that he squared his conscience by the lifts and braces of faith, which I take to be a doctrine that is not to be preach'd on shipboard, for it would play the devil with the best ship's company that was ever mustered."

"Oh! no — no — dear Mr. Boltrope, you mistook me and my doctrine altogether!" exclaimed the chaplain; "at least you mistook —"

"Perhaps, sir," interrupted Griffith, gently, "our honest friend will not be more fortunate now. Is there nothing earthly that hangs upon your mind, Boltrope? no wish to be remembered to any one, nor any bequest to make of your property?"

"He has a mother, I know," said Barnstable in a low voice; "he often spoke of her to me in the night watches; I think she must still be living."

The master, who distinctly heard his young shipmates, continued for more than a minute rolling the tobacco, which he still retained, from one side of his mouth to the other, with an industry that denoted singular agitation for the man, and raising one of his broad hands, with the other he picked the worn skin from fingers, which were already losing their brownish yellow hue in the fading colour of death, before he answered —

"Why, yes, the old woman still keeps her grip upon life, which is more than can be said of her son David. The old man was lost the time the Susan and Dorothy was wrecked on the back of Cape Cod; you remember it, Mr. Barnstable? you were then a lad, sailing on whaling voyages from the island! well, ever since that gale, I've endeavoured to make smooth water for the old woman myself, though she has had but a rough passage of it, at the best; the voyage of life, with her, having been pretty much crossed by rugged weather and short stores."

"And you would have us carry some message to her?" said Griffith, kindly.

"Why, as to messages," continued the master, whose voice was rapidly growing more husky and broken, "there never has been many compliments — passed between us, for the reason — that she is not more used to receive them — than I am to make them. But if any one of you will overhaul — the purser's books, and see what there is standing there — to my side of the leaf — and take a little pains to get it to the old woman — you will find her moor'd in the lee side of a house — ay, here it is, No. 10 Cornhill, Boston. I took care — to get her a good warm birth, seeing that a woman of eighty, wants a snug anchorage — at her time of life, if ever."

"I will do it myself, David," cried Barnstable, struggling to conceal his emotion; "I will call on her the instant we let go our anchor in Boston harbor, and as your credit can't be large, I will divide my own purse with her!"

The sailing-master was powerfully affected by this kind offer, the muscles of his hard weather-beaten face working convulsively, and it was a moment before he could trust his voice in reply.

"I know you would, Dickey, I know you would," he at length uttered, grasping the hand of Barnstable with a portion of his former strength; "I know you would give the old woman one of your own limbs, if it would do a service — to the mother of a messmate — which it would not — seeing that I am not the son of a — cannibal; but you are out of your own father's books, and it's too often shoal water in your pockets to help any one — more especially since you have just been spliced to a pretty young body — that will want all your spare coppers."

"But I am master of my own fortune," said Griffith, "and am rich."

"Ay, ay, I have heard it said you could build a frigate and set her afloat all a-taunt-o without thrusting your hand — into any man's purse — but your own!"

"And I pledge you the honor of a naval officer," continued the young sailor, "that she shall want for nothing; not even the care and tenderness of a dutiful son."

Boltrope appeared to be choking; he made an attempt to raise his exhausted frame on the couch, but fell back exhausted and dying, perhaps a little prematurely, through the powerful and unusual emotions that were struggling for utterance. "God forgive me my misdeeds!" he, at length, said, "and chiefly for ever speaking a word against your disciplyne; remember the best bower — and look to the slings of the lower yards — and — and — he'll do it Dickey, he'll do it! I'm casting off — the fasts — of life — and so God bless ye all — and give ye good weather — going large — or on a bowline!"

The tongue of the master failed him, but a look of heart-felt satisfaction gleamed across his rough visage, as its muscles suddenly contracted, when the faded lineaments slowly settled into the appalling stiffness of death.

Griffith directed the body to be removed to the apartment of the Master, and proceeded with a heavy heart to the upper deck. The Alacrity had been unnoticed during the arduous chase of the frigate, and favored by day-light, and her light draught of water, she had easily effected her escape also among the mazes of the shoals. She was called down to her consort by signal, and received the necessary instructions how to steer during the approaching night. The British ships were now only to be faintly discovered, like small white specks on the dark sea, and as it was known that a broad barrier of shallow water lay between them, the Americans no longer regarded their presence as at all dangerous.

When the necessary orders had been given, and the vessels were fully prepared, they were once more brought up to the wind, and their heads pointed in the direction of the coast of Holland. The wind, which freshened towards the decline of day, hauled round with the sun, and when that luminary retreated from the eye, so rapid had been the progress of the mariners, it seemed to sink in the bosom of the ocean, the land having long before settled into its watery bed. All night the frigate continued to dash through the seas with a sort of sullen silence, that was soothing to the melancholy of Cecilia and Katherine, neither of whom closed an eye during that gloomy period. In addition to the scene they had witnessed, their feelings were harrowed by the knowledge that, in conformity to the necessary plans of Griffith, and in compliance with the new duties he had assumed, they were to separate in the morning for an indefinite period, and possibly forever.

With the appearance of light, the boatswain sent his rough summons through the vessel, and the crew were collected in solemn silence in her gang-ways, to "bury the dead." The bodies of Boltrope, of one or two of her inferior officers, and of several common men, who had died of their wounds in the night, were, with the usual formalities, committed to the deep; when the yards of the ship were again braced by the wind, and she glided along the trackless waste, leaving no memorial in the midst of the ever-rolling waters, to mark the place of their sepulture.

When the sun had gained the meridian the vessels were once more hove-to, and the preparations were made for a final separation. The body of Colonel Howard was transferred to the Alacrity, whither it was followed by Griffith and his cheerless bride, while Katherine hung fondly from a window of the ship, suffering her own scalding tears to mingle with the brine of the ocean. After every thing was arranged, Griffith waved his hand to Barnstable, who had now succeeded to the command of the frigate, and the yards of the latter were braced sharp to the wind, when she proceeded to the dangerous experiment of forcing her way to the shores of America, by attempting the pass of the streights of Dover, and running the gauntlet through the English ships that crowded their own channel; an undertaking, however, for which she had the successful example of the Alliance frigate, which had borne the stars of America along the same hazardous path but a few months previously.

In the meanwhile the Alacrity, steering more to the west, drew in swiftly towards the shores of Holland, and about an hour before the setting of the sun, had approached so nigh as to be once more hove into the wind, in obedience to the mandate of Griffith. A small light boat was lowered into the sea, when the young sailor, and the pilot, who had found his way into the cutter unheeded, and almost unseen, ascended from the small cabin together. The stranger glanced his eyes along the range of coast, as if he would ascertain the exact position of the vessel, and then turned them on the sea and the western horizon to scan the weather. Finding nothing in the appearance of the latter to induce him to change his determination, he offered his hand frankly to Griffith, and said—

"Here we part. As our acquaintance has not led to all we wished, let it be your task, sir, to forget we ever met."

Griffith bowed respectfully, but in silence, when the other continued, shaking his hand contemptuously towards the land—

"Had I but a moiety of the navy of that degenerate republic, the proudest among those haughty islanders should tremble in his castle, and be made to feel there is no security against a foe that trusts his own strength and knows the weakness of his enemy! But," he muttered in a lower and more hurried voice, "this has been like Liverpool, and — Whitehaven — and Edinburgh, and fifty more! it is past, sir; let it be forgotten."

Without heeding the wondering crew, who were collected as curious spectators of his departure, the stranger bowed hastily to Griffith, and springing into the boat, he spread her light sail with the readiness of one who had nothing to learn even in the smallest matters of his daring profession. Once more, as the boat moved briskly away from the cutter, he waved his hand in adieu, and Griffith fancied, that even through the distance, he could trace a smile of bitter resignation, lighting his calm features with a momentary gleam. For a long time the young man stood an abstracted gazer at his solitary progress, watching the small boat as it glided towards the open ocean, nor did he remember to order the head sheets of the Alacrity drawn, in order to put the vessel again in motion, until the dark speck was lost in the strong glare that fell, obliquely across the water, from the setting sun.

Many wild and extraordinary conjectures were uttered among the crew of the cutter, as she slowly drew in towards her friendly haven, on the appearance of the mysterious pilot, during their late hazardous visit to the coast of Britain, and on his still more extraordinary disappearance, as it were, amid the stormy wastes of the North sea. Griffith himself was not observed to smile, nor to manifest any other evidence of his being a listener to their rude discourse, until it was loudly announced that a small boat was seen pressing for their own harbor, across the fore foot of the cutter, under a single lug-sail. Then, indeed, the sudden and cheerful lighting of his troubled eye, might have betrayed to more accurate observers, the vast relief that was imparted to his feelings by the interesting discovery.

Chapter XXXV.

"Come all you kindred Chieftains of the deep!
In mighty phalanx, round your brother bend;
Hush every murmur that invades his sleep—
And guard the laurels that o'ershade your friend!"

Lines on Tripp.

HERE, perhaps it would be wise to suffer the curtain of our imperfect drama to fall before the reader, trusting that the imagination of every individual can readily supply the due proportions of health, wealth, and happiness, that the rigid rules of poetic justice would award to the different characters of the legend. But as we are not disposed to part so coldly from those with whom we have long held amicable intercourse, and as there is no portion of that in reservation which is not quite as true as all that has been already related, we see no unanswerable reason for dismissing the dramatis personae so abruptly. We shall therefore proceed to state briefly, the outlines of that which befel them in after-life, regretting, at the same time, that the legitimate limits of a modern tale will not admit of such a dilatation of many a merry or striking scene, as might create the pleasing hope of beholding hereafter, some more of our rude sketches quickened into life, by the spirited pencil of Dunlap.

Following the course of the frigate, then, towards those shores, from which, perhaps, we should never have suffered our truant pen to have wandered, we shall commence the brief task with Barnstable, and his laughing, weeping, gay, but affectionate, bride—the black-eyed Katherine. The ship fought her way, gallantly, through swarms of the enemy's cruisers, to the port of Boston, where Barnstable was rewarded for his services by promotion, and a more regular authority to command his vessel.

During the remainder of the war, he continued to fill that station with ability and zeal, nor did he return to the dwelling of his fathers, which he soon inherited, by regular descent, until after peace had established not only the independence of his country, but his own reputation, as a brave and successful sea-officer. When the Federal Government laid the foundation of its present navy, Captain Barnstable was once more tempted by the offer of a new commission to desert his home; and for many years he was employed among that band of gallant seamen who served their country so faithfully in times of trial and high daring. Happily, however, he was enabled to accomplish a great deal of the more peaceful part of his service accompanied by Katherine, who, having no children, eagerly profited by his consent, to share his privations and hardships on the ocean. In this manner they passed merrily, and we trust happily, down the vale of life together, Katherine entirely discrediting the ironical prediction of her former guardian, by making, every thing considered, a very obedient, and certainly, so far as attachment was concerned, a most devoted wife.

The boy, Merry, who in due time became a man, clung to Barnstable and Katherine, so long as it was necessary to hold him in leading strings; and when he received his regular promotion, his first command was under the shadow of his kinsman's broad pendant. He proved to be in his meridian, what his youth had so strongly indicated, a fearless, active, and reckless sailor, and his years might have extended to this hour, had he not fallen untimely, in a duel with a foreign officer.

The first act of Captain Manual, after landing once more on his native soil, was to make interest to be again restored to the line of the army. He encountered but little difficulty in this attempt, and was soon in possession of the complete enjoyment of that which his soul had so long pined after, "a steady drill." He was in time to share in all the splendid successes which terminated the war, and also to participate in his due proportion of the misery of the army. His merits were not forgotten, however, in the reorganization of the forces, and he followed both St. Clair and his more fortunate successor, Wayne, in the western campaigns. About the close of the century, when the British made their tardy relinquishment of the line of posts along the frontiers, Captain Manual was ordered to take charge, with his company, of a small stockade on our side of one of those mighty rivers, that sets bounds to the territories of the Republic in the north. The British flag was waving over the ramparts of a more regular fortress, that had been recently built, directly opposite, within the new lines of the Canadas. Manual was not a man to neglect the observances of military etiquette, and understanding that the neighbouring fort was commanded by a field officer, he did not fail to wait on that gentleman, in proper time, with a view to cultivate the sort of acquaintance that their mutual situations would render not only agreeable, but highly convenient. The American martinet, in ascertaining the rank of the other, had not deemed it at all necessary to ask his name, but when the red-faced, comical-looking officer with one leg, who met him, was introduced as Major Borroughcliffe, he had not the least difficulty in recalling to recollection his quondam acquaintance of St. Ruth. The intercourse between these worthies was renewed with remarkable gusto, and at length arrived to so regular a pass, that a log cabin was erected on one of the islands in the river, as a sort of neutral territory, where their feastings and revels might be held without any scandal to the discipline of their respective garrisons. Here the qualities of many a saddle of savory venison were discussed, together with those of sundry pleasant fowls, as well as of divers strange beasts that inhabit those western wilds, while, at the same time, the secret places of the broad river were vexed, that nothing might be wanting that could contribute to the pleasures of their banquets. A most equitable levy was regularly made on their respective pockets, to sustain the foreign expenses of this amicable warfare, and a suitable division of labour was also imposed on the two Commandants, in order to procure such articles of comfort as were only to be obtained from those portions of the globe, where the art of man had made a nearer approach to the bounties of nature, than in the vicinity of their fortifications. All liquids in which malt formed an ingredient, as well as the deep-coloured wines of Oporto, were suffered to enter the Gulf of St. Lawrence, and were made to find their way, under the superintendence of Borroughcliffe, to their destined goal; but Manual was, solely, entrusted with the more important duty of providing the generous liquor of Madeira, without any other restriction on his judgment, than an occasional injunction from his coadjutor, that it should not fail to be the product of the "South-side!"

It was not unusual for the younger officers of the two garrisons to allude to the battle in which Major Borroughcliffe had lost his limb — the English ensign invariably whispering to the American on such occasions, that it occurred during the late contest, in a desperate affair on the North Eastern coast of their island, in which the Major commanded, in behalf of his country, with great credit and signal success; and for which service he obtained his present rank "without purchase!" A sort of national courtesy prevented the two veterans, for by this time both had earned that honourable title, from participating at all in these delicate allusions; though whenever, by any accident, they occurred near the termination of the revels, Borroughcliffe would so far betray his consciousness of what was passing, as to favor his American friend with a leer of singular significance, which generally produced in the other that sort of dull recollection, which all actors and painters endeavour to represent by scratching the head. In this manner year after year rolled by, the most perfect harmony existing between the two posts, notwithstanding the angry passions that disturbed their respective countries, when an end was suddenly put to the intercourse by the unfortunate death of Manual. This rigid observer of discipline, never trusted his person on the neutral island without being accompanied by a party of his warriors, who were posted as a regular picquet, sustaining a suitable line of sentries; a practice which he also recommended to his friend, as being highly conducive to discipline, as well as a salutary caution against a surprise on the part of either garrison. The Major, however, dispensed with the formality in his own behalf, but was sufficiently good-natured to wink at the want of confidence it betrayed in his boon companion. On one unhappy occasion, when the discussions of a new importation had made a heavy inroad on the morning, Manual left the hut to make his way towards his picquet, in such a state of utter mental aberration, as to forget the countersign when challenged by a sentinel, when, unhappily, he met his death by a shot from a soldier, whom he had drilled to such an exquisite state of insensibility, that the man cared but little whether he killed friend or enemy, so long as he kept within military usage, and the hallowed limits established by the articles of war. He lived long enough, however, to commend the fellow for the deed, and died while delivering an eulogium to Borroughcliffe, on the high state of perfection to which he had brought his command!

About a year before this melancholy event, a quarter cask of wine had been duly ordered from the South side of the island of Madeira, which was, at the death of Manual, toiling its weary way up the rapids of the Mississippi and the Ohio; having been made to enter by the port of New-Orleans, with the intention of keeping it as long as possible under a genial sun! The untimely fate of his friend imposed on Borroughcliffe the necessity of attending to this precious relick of their mutual tastes; and he procured a leave of absence from his superior, with the laudable desire to proceed down the streams and superintend its farther advance in person. The result of his zeal was a high fever, that set in the day after he reached his treasure, and as the Doctor and the Major espoused different theories, in treating a disorder so dangerous in that climate, the one advising abstemiousness, and the other administering repeated draughts of the cordial that had drawn him so far from home, the disease was left to act its pleasure. Borroughcliffe died in three days; and was carried back and interred by the side of his friend, in the very hut which had so often resounded with their humours and festivities! We have been thus particular in relating the sequel of the lives of these rival chieftains, because, from their want of connexion with any kind heart of the other sex, no widows and orphans were left to lament their several ends, and furthermore, as they were both mortal, and might be expected to die at a suitable period, and yet did not terminate their career until each had attained the mature age of three-score, the reader can find no just grounds of dissatisfaction at being allowed this deep glance into the womb of fate.

The chaplain abandoned the seas in time to retrieve his character, a circumstance which gave no little satisfaction to Katherine, who occasionally annoyed her worthy husband on the subject of the informality of their marriage.

Griffith and his mourning bride conveyed the body of Colonel Howard in safety to one of the principal towns in Holland, where it was respectfully and sorrowfully interred; after which the young man removed to Paris, with a view of erasing the sad images, which the hurried and melancholy events of the few preceding days had left on the mind of his lovely companion. — From this place Cecilia held communion, by letter, with her friend Alice Dunscombe, and such suitable provision was made in the affairs of her late uncle as the times would permit. Afterwards, when Griffith obtained the command which had been offered him, before sailing on the cruise in the North Sea, they returned together to America. The young man continued a sailor until the close of the war, when he entirely withdrew from the ocean, and devoted the remainder of his life to the conjoint duties of a husband and a good citizen.

As it was easy to reclaim the estates of Colonel Howard, which, in fact, had been abandoned more from pride than necessity, and which had never been confiscated, their joint inheritances made the young couple extremely affluent, and we shall here take occasion to say, that Griffith remembered his promise to the dying master, and saw such a provision made for the childless mother, as her situation and his character required.

It might have been some twelve years after the short cruise, which it has been our task to record in these volumes, that Griffith, who was running his eyes carelessly over a file of newspapers, was observed by his wife to drop the bundle from before his face, and pass his hand slowly across his brow, like a man who had been suddenly struck with renewed impressions of some former event, or who was endeavouring to recall to his mind images that had long since faded.

"See you any thing in that paper, to disturb you Griffith?" said the still lovely Cecilia. "I hope that now we have our confederate government, the States will soon recover from their losses—but it is one of those plans to create a new navy, that has met your eye! Ah! truant! you sigh to become a wanderer again, and pine after your beloved ocean!"

"I have ceased sighing and pining since you have begun to smile," he returned, with a vacant manner, and without removing his hand from his brow.

"Is not the new order of things, then, likely to succeed? Does the Congress enter into contention with the President?"

"The wisdom and name of Washington will smooth the way for the experiment, until time shall mature the system.

Cecilia, do you remember the man who accompanied Manual and myself to St. Ruth, the night we became your uncle's prisoners, and who afterwards led the party which liberated us, and rescued Barnstable?"

"Surely I do; he was the pilot of your ship, it was then said; and I remember the shrewd soldier we entertained, even suspected that he was one greater than he seemed."

"The soldier surmised the truth; but you saw him not on that fearful night, when he carried us through the shoals! and you could not witness the calm courage with which he guided the ship into those very channels again, while the confusion of battle was among us!"

"I heard the dreadful din! And I can easily imagine the horrid scene," returned his wife, her recollections chasing the colour from her cheeks even at that distance of time; "but what of him? is his name mentioned in those papers? Ah! they are English prints! you called his name Gray, if I remember?"

"That was the name he bore with us! he was a man who had formed romantic notions of glory, and wished every thing concealed in which he acted a part that he thought would not contribute to his renown. It has been, therefore, in compliance with a solemn promise made at the time, that I have ever avoided mentioning his name — he is now dead!"

"Can there have been any connexion between him and Alice Dunscombe?" said Cecilia, dropping her work in her lap, in a thoughtful manner. — "She met him alone, at her own urgent request, the night Katherine and myself saw you in your confinement, and even then my cousin whispered that they were acquainted! The letter I received yesterday, from Alice, was sealed with black, and I was pained with the melancholy, though gentle manner, in which she wrote of passing from this world into another!"

Griffith glanced his eye at his wife, with a look of sudden intelligence, and then answered like one who began to see with the advantages of a clearer atmosphere.

"Cecilia, your conjecture is surely true! Fifty things rush to my mind at that one surmise — his acquaintance with that particular spot — his early life — his expedition — his knowledge of the abbey, all confirm it! He, altogether, was indeed a man of marked character!"

"Why has he not been among us," asked Cecilia; "he appeared devoted to our cause?"

"His devotion to America proceeded from desire of distinction, his ruling passion, and perhaps a little also from resentment at some injustice which he claimed to have suffered from his own countrymen. He was a man, and not therefore without foibles—among which may have been reckoned the estimation of his own acts; but they were most daring, and deserving of praise! neither did he at all merit the obloquy that he received from his enemies. His love of liberty may be more questionable; for if he commenced his deeds in the cause of these free States, they terminated in the service of a despot! He is now dead—but had he lived in times and under circumstances, when his consummate knowledge of his profession, his cool, deliberate, and even desperate courage, could have been exercised in a regular, and well-supported Navy, and had the habits of his youth better qualified him to have borne, meekly, the honors he acquired in his age, he would have left behind him no name in its lists that would have descended to the latest posterity of his adopted countrymen with greater renown!"

"Why, Griffith," exclaimed Cecilia, in a little surprise, "you are zealous in his cause! Who was he?"

"A man who held a promise of secrecy while living, which is not at all released by his death. It is enough to know, that he was greatly instrumental in procuring our sudden union, and that our happiness might have been wrecked in the voyage of life had we not met the unknown pilot of the German Ocean."

Perceiving her husband to rise, and carefully collect the papers in a bundle, before he left the room, Cecilia made no further remark at the time, nor was the subject ever revived between them!

Explanatory Notes

1.1–2 TO WILLIAM BRANFORD SHUBRICK: Shubrick and Cooper had
been midshipmen in the Navy together and Shubrick remained
Cooper's closest friend as well as his strongest tie to the Navy. Shubrick
acknowledged the dedication in the following letter, postmarked Boston
and dated "Sep^t 13th 1823." (MS:YCAL)

My Dear Cooper

I have just read with mingled feelings of pain & pleasure your letter of the 7th and the very flattering evidence of your friendship
which it [conveys?]. I assure you I participate as sincerely in your
domestic griefs as I rejoice in the well merited fame which the
literary world accords you — I certainly expected to have seen you
before this and have more than once taken my pen to ask you why
your promised visit was delayed, but I have each time been either
called off by some duty or a constitutional indolence has overcome
my good purpose. October is however our most pleasant month,
and unless something unforeseen happens I shall be quite at your
service, for as long a time as you can stay with me and I trust I can
with the assistance of my *horses* and waggon (not "chay"), show you
some as fine views as you have every [?] enjoyed — I had heard that
poor Hoffman was unshiped [?] and could in imagination see him
day by day taking in his waistcoat and drawing tighter the buckle of
his pantaloons; but I hope a residence at Oyster Bay will counteract
the effects of "starvation" in New York — if you see him do remind
him that he owes me a letter. — Our friend the serpent has I fear left
us for ever, for he has not been seen for some months — —

I have just at this time to ship [sleep?] "with one eye open" for
Mrs Shubrick is in daily expectation of giving me another tie to life.
I will apprise you of the event as soon as it takes place —

The dedication is all that I could wish and more than I had a
right to expect, but there is exactly one superfluous letter in it — my
middle name is Branford not Brandford, I hope it is not too late to
alter it, though I suppose none but my own family would detect the
error[.]

I hope soon to hear from you to learn that both Mrs Cooper &

yourself are quite restored, present my most respectful regards to her, kiss Sue for me & believe that I am sincerely & faithfully yours
WBShubrick

4.10–12 Milford . . . projects: The *Milford* and the *Solebay* were British frigates John Paul Jones, in the *Alfred*, successfully eluded; the *Drake* was a British sloop of war and the *Triumph* an English Letter-of Marque. Jones's "desperate projects" included his attempt to burn British ships at Whitehaven, his plan to kidnap Lord Selkirk, and his decision to seize ships in port at Edinburgh and demand payment from the Scottish capital. J. Fenimore Cooper, *Lives of Distinguished American Naval Officers* (Philadelphia: Carey & Hart, 1846), II, pp. 22, 21, 35, 95, 34, 36–8, 56.

4.18 last officers: While Cooper could have referred to Commodore John Barry, head of the navy at his death in 1803, "not long since" indicates that he probably meant Commodore Joshua Barney, who died in 1818. *Dictionary of American Biography* (New York: Charles Scribner's Sons, 1928), I, 654 and I, 632–35.

12.9 Nagurs: British propaganda indicated that the rebel colonials were black, according to a note on this word in the first Italian translation (1829) which says, "Così gl' Inglesi solevano significare gli Americani." (Thus the English were accustomed to identifying the Americans.) The British public's surprise on discovering that Americans were white is described in Fanning's *Narrative* (p. 22). Cooper's own footnote in Chapter IV of *Wing-and-Wing* says:

As recently as 1828, the author of this book was at Leghorn. The Delaware, 80, had just left there; and speaking of her appearance to a native of the place, who supposed the writer to be an Englishman, the latter observed — "of course, her people were all blacks." "I thought so, too, Signore, until I went on board the ship," was the answer; "but they are as white as you and I are."

See also the *Letters and Journals*, II.12 for the Coopers' similar experiences in Germany.

40.30 pall: This variant spelling for pawl means to prevent the capstan from recoiling by using short stout bars (pawls) to arrest it.

43.5 play jackall: The jackal was at one time believed to go before the lion and hunt up his prey for him.

49.12 wind may strike us: Nathaniel Fanning's description of a storm contained details Cooper used in the ensuing scenes and in his description of the wreck of the *Ariel*.

At 10 P. M. the wind shifted suddenly into the W. S. W and blew a heavy gale — took in top gallant sails, and close reefed our top sails — soon after took in our topsails and reefed our courses, and we carried them as long as the ship would bear them. The night was very dark, and we lost sight of the fleet. We were obliged to carry some sail in order to weather the *Pin Marks*, a long range of sunken rocks about a league from the land, and which we judged to be to leeward of us. At midnight we were obliged to hand our courses, as it blew so violent that we could not suffer a single yard of canvass. The ship at the same time lay in a very dangerous situation, nearly upon her beam ends, and in the trough of the sea, and leaked so bad that with both chain pumps constantly going we could not keep her free. Some French soldiers which we had on board, and who were stationed at the cranks of the pumps, let go of them, crossed themselves, and went to prayers. They were driven from this by the officers to the cranks again; and it became necessary to keep lifted naked hangers over their heads, and threaten them with instant death if they quit their duty, or if they did not work with all their strength; without this they would again leave off and go to prayers. Soon after, one of our chain pumps got choked in such a manner that it would deliver no water. Jones in all this time shewed a great deal of presence of mind, and kept, with his own hands, sounding with the deep sea lead; and at last finding that we were shoaling water very fast, and that we should in a short time be upon the Pin Marks, without something was soon done to prevent it. In this extremity a consultation of captain Jones and his principal officers was had upon the quarter-deck, and the result was, that orders were given for cutting away our fore-mast and letting go the sheet anchor; and the latter was executed without loss of time. We sounded now in thirty-five fathoms of water. The sheet cable was now paid out to the better end; but she did not look to her anchor; another cable was spliced to the first, and paid out to the better end; she did not yet bring up; the third cable was also spliced to the end of the second; when after paying out about seven eights of this last, and the fore-mast cut away at the same time, and when it had fell over board to the leeward, the ship brought to and rid head to the wind, and the sea now run mountains high. By the time of which I am now speaking we had not less than three hundred fathoms of cable paid out—in a few minutes after the ship brought to to her anchor. The ship laboured so hard, rolled so deep, and would bring up so sudden that it sprung our main-mast just below our gun-deck, and as this was now in the greatest danger of being ripped up, orders were given to cut away the main-mast above the quarter-deck, which was immediately carried into execution; and when this fell over the side to leeward it forced off the head of the mizzen-mast. By this time we had freed the ship of water, but when her masts were gone her motion was so quick and violent that the most expert seamen on board could not stand upon their legs, neither upon the quarter-deck nor fore-castle without holding on to something. The chain pump which had been choked was cleared, and notwithstanding the gale kept increasing, yet our anchor and cables held on so well, that some faint hopes were now entertained that our lives would be spared: however, the gale did not abate much until the morning of the 9th. At meridian of this day the wind had abated so much that we began to get up and rig our jury masts. At 4 P.M. we had them erected and rigged, and what spars and sails we could muster upon them; and there being at this time but a moderate breeze at about W. N. W, a fair wind for L'Orient, and the sea tolerable smooth, we hove in upon our cables till it was short apeak, and then exerted ourselves every way which we could think of in order to purchase our anchor, and after trying a long time without being able to weigh it, orders were given by captain Jones to save all we could of the cable and then cut it away, which was done and we made sail for L'Orient, where we soon after arrived and came to anchor. (Fanning, *Narrative*, pp. 89–91).

53.26 cun: American spelling variant for con, the post from which a ship is steered.

59.15 Congress—": John Paul Jones had good reason not to promise any reward from Congress which made two men, who had been his junior lieutenants in 1775, captains above him in 1776. Cooper, *Lives*, II, 17.

61.6 *Duo*: No one has located this source which Cooper also quoted from for three epigraphs in *The Pioneers*.

68.19–20 Lady Selkirk: On 23 April 1778, Jones landed on St. Mary's Isle intending to kidnap the fourth Earl of Selkirk. Learning that the Earl was not at home, Jones prepared to depart, but two officers and some of the crew demanded that they be allowed to carry off some of the Selkirks' silver. Jones later purchased the silver from these men and returned it to the Selkirks, and his letter of apology to Lady Selkirk gained wide circulation. Cooper, *Lives*, II, 38–9.

69.14 same colour: One of the meanings of "black" in Webster's 1828 dictionary was "that which is destitute of light or whiteness." Kit Dillon's complexion was swarthy.

80.31 land-tacks: In nautical usage, a tack was a wire, rope, or other kind of lashing, but the word acquired a transferred sense of general gear. Tom Coffin uses the same term at 246.6.

90.30–31 "vox et pretera nihil": "A voice, and beyond that nothing. Stated by Plutarch to be a Spartan saying in reference to the nightingale, on seeing one plucked of its feathers." W. G. Benham, *Putnam's Complete Book of Quotations* (New York: G. P. Putnam's Sons, 1926), p. 687.

93.4 *Drama*: The play has not been located.

95.36 negative: Unless this applies to what the peasant has said or not said, this is an error since the Scotch drover did see the ships. (See Dillon's statement at 97.4).

98.3 princes: Married to George III in 1761, Queen Charlotte Sophia had given birth, by 1765, to three sons, the first of whom would become George IV and the third William IV of England. Queen Charlotte had a total of fifteen children.

101.35 Flamborough Head: Site of the famous battle between the *Bon Homme Richard* and the *Serapis*, 23 September 1779. Cooper, *Lives*, II, 64–86.

165.5-6 "seniors grave" . . . "potent and reverent": "Most potent, grave, and reverend Signiors," *Othello*, I.iii.76.

170.5 quiet.": The source has not been located.

175.27 Cacique of Pedee: In drawing up the "Fundamental Constitutions" for the province of Carolina in 1669, John Locke and Lord Ashley used the West Indian word for chief, *Cacique*, as the lowest rank of the proposed nobility. Under their plan, each Cacique would get 24,000 acres of land. Edward McCrady, *The History of South Carolina under the Proprietary Government 1670-1719* (New York, 1897; reprint ed., New York: Paladin Press, 1969), pp. 94-7.

189.21-22 loggerhead . . . bows: The loggerhead, a post around which the whaleline is run to increase the drag, should be in the stern.

208.5-6 Sandy Point of Munny-Moy: Monomoy Island south of Cape Cod.

208.16 song of Captain Kidd: Don C. Seitz's edition of *The Tryal of Capt. William Kidd* (originally published in London in 1707) gives "Ye Lamentable Ballard of Captain Kidd" in twenty-five stanzas. (New York: Rufus Rockwell Wilson, Inc. 1936), pp. 227-30. In his introduction to *A Sailor's Garland* (New York: The Macmillan Co., 1928), John Masefield said that a "fragment" of a song about Captain Kidd "may still be heard at sea. It is sung to the very excellent tune of Samuel Hall." p. xviii.

208.17 Cape Poge Indian: Probably the Punkapoag or Ponkapog Indians living on Massachusetts Bay, according to the synonymy given in *New Handbook of North American Indians* (Washington: Smithsonian Institute, 1978), XV, 187.

210.8-9 Frenchman, Thurot, in the old business of '56: In 1756, François Thurot planned to enter Portsmouth harbor at night on a barque "stripped as flat as a raft" and burn Portsmouth and its dockyards. The plan was thwarted when spies working as clerks in the French ministry warned the English. Maurice Besson, *The Scourge of the Indies*, tr. Everard Thornton (New York: Random House, 1929), p. 256.

225.37 Poictiers: Variant spelling for Poitiers.

226.26 Corporal John: This was the common soldier's affectionate name for John Churchill, First Duke of Marlborough, during the Wars of the Spanish Succession. Winston S. Churchill, *Marlborough* (London: George G. Harrap & Co., Ltd. 1934), II, 565.

227.2 Mr. Eugene: During the battle of Blenheim, Prince Eugene of Savoy "was repulsed in three attacks, but carried the fourth, and broke in; and so he was master of their camp, cannon, and baggage," but historians, drawing on Marlborough's "copious account" of the battle, gave the glory of the victory to Marlborough and slighted the actions of Prince Eugene. Justin McCarthy, *The Reign of Queen Anne* (London: Chatto & Windus, 1902), I, 138-140.

236.34 Le Maire: This strait is in the South Atlantic between Tierra del Fuego and Staten Island off the southern end of Argentina.

246.14 banyan: Banyan or banian was a term applied to Hindoo traders; sailors extended the usage to apply to meatless diets.

253.33 Manly's time: After receiving his naval commission from General Washington 24 October 1775, John Manly "fired the first and last gun of the naval operations of the American patriots." *The National Cyclopaedia of American Biography* (New York: James T White & Co., 1907), V, 163.

260.32 from '56 to '63: Colonel Howard refers to the last years of the French and Indian wars.

275.34 Queen Anne's pocket-piece: OED gives under pocket-pistol "1784–5 *Chron.* in *Ann. Reg.* 323/2 At Dover . . . the large gun, well known by the name of Queen Anne's pocket pistol." Yvonne Noble of William and Mary reports the gun is now known as "Queen Elizabeth's pocket pistol." A guidebook says the gun was given to Henry VIII by Emperor Charles V, and that this couplet refers to the gun:

> Polish me well and keep me clean
> And I'll carry a ball to Calais green.

Walter Jerrold, *Folkstone and Dover* (Glasgow: Blackie and son, n.d. [1935?]), p. 57.

388.16 Helder: Den Helder, a city in the north-western part of the Netherlands, was long used as a naval base.

392.12 Jack Manly: See note at 253.33

417.17 Alliance frigate: The *Alliance* left the Texel and ran through the British channel with Jones managing to elude all British ships and return safely to France. Cooper, *Lives*, II, 88.

418.3 Liverpool: Lafayette, Franklin and Jones planned an amphibious assault on Liverpool in the spring of 1779, but the King of France had other plans. Samuel Eliot Morison, *John Paul Jones* (Boston: Little, Brown, & Co., 1959), p. 188.

426.12 despot: In April 1788, John Paul Jones became a Rear Admiral in the Imperial Russian Navy of Catherine II, Empress of Russia. Cooper, *Lives*, II. 103–5.

TEXTUAL APPARATUS

Textual Commentary

Charles Wiley published *The Pilot* in New York City in two volumes on 7 January 1824.[1] Using different stages of the sheets of this Wiley edition as his printer's copy, John Miller brought out the first British edition, in three volumes, in London near the end of the same month.[2] The second Wiley edition, which appeared on 11 February 1824, contains numerous authorial revisions, and was possibly prepared with assistance from Cooper's friend Captain William Branford Shubrick of the Navy, to whom the book was dedicated.[3] Cooper did not prepare a further revision until 1849, when he supplied a new preface and a few corrections of the text for Putnam's Author's Revised edition. Though *The Pilot* was the first and most popular title in Richard Bentley's famous Standard Novels series, its publication in this format, first issued by Colburn and Bentley in 1831, predated the arrangement by which Cooper was paid for extensive revisions, notes, and new prefaces for other early works.[4]

THE WILEY FIRST EDITION (1824)

No manuscript from the text of *The Pilot* is known to exist, save for a fragment, the upper-left corner of a sheet, in the Clifton Waller Barrett Collection at the Alderman Library of the University of Virginia.[5] In the absence of any other pre-publication form, the copy-text for the present edition of *The Pilot* is, except for that fragment, the Wiley first edition, presumably set from Cooper's manuscript and corrected in proof by him. In the copies examined, three gatherings from Volume II exist in two states, apparently the result of compositorial changes in the standing type.[6] In gathering 2 of two of the copies examined, letters in the end-line word "us" (22.1) seem to be working out of the line. The present editor conjectures that pressmen, confronted by a blank in the forme, inserted the letters backwards in attempting to replace the word, producing "su" in the second state. In the presumed first state of gathering 21, the word "breeze" (248.29) is not followed by a comma; and "ninety's" (248.36) is not capitalized. In gathering 22, the presumed first state has "durpose" for "purpose" at 251.17. Since no single copy examined contains all the presumed earlier readings, the gatherings were apparently bound in random sequence. The copy-text for the present edition is the text of the Wiley first edition, including its earliest readings.

THE MILLER OR ENGLISH FIRST EDITION (1824)

The Miller edition differs substantively from its printer's copy in approximately 100 instances.[7] On casual inspection, all these variants might appear to be compositorial restylings. Close examination of the variants and the circumstances of the transmission of the text suggest strongly, however, that the more striking of these variants are authorial and therefore eligible for consideration as emendations in the present text. The seeming disparity in the levels of authority of the different classes of variants can be resolved if, as external and internal evidence suggests, the Miller text is regarded as consisting of three segments, each requiring an editorial strategy appropriate to the status of its text at the point of its transmission.

In his letter of 28 June 1823, anticipating an arrangement with Cooper to publish *The Pilot*, John Miller urged the novelist "to favour me with the first Volume, as soon as it is printed, & also of [sic] the second—the last Volume should come in sheets by the different packetships, & towards the conclusion it would be advisable to send corrected proof sheets, without waiting for the [working*]."[8] Available evidence reveals that Cooper did transmit the text in three packets, approximately in the manner Miller had recommended.

Parcel 1: The first installment (consisting of Volume I bound, corresponding to Volumes I—II.1–162 of the Miller) was carried or sent to Cooper's friend, James De Peyster Ogden, who was in London on business. Misconstruing the author's "directions," Ogden gave the volume first to John Murray, who had published *The Pioneers* and wished to consider publishing *The Pilot*. On 6 September 1823 Ogden informed Cooper of his transaction with evident self-satisfaction, though he had been instructed "to hand . . . the 1st volume of the Pilot" to Miller if he found "Miller was in good credit."[9]

Parcel 2: In a further letter, dated exactly one week later, Ogden wrote Cooper: "Murray is to publish the 'Pilot' on the usual terms, therefore please send him the other volume as soon as it is ready—".[10] By this time, Ogden had met with John Miller. His reception had been "civil & polite," but he had become uneasily aware of Miller's dissatisfaction and of his own misunderstanding of Cooper's preference for Miller, a preference he now seemed to share though he remained convinced of the advantages of Murray's imprint. Much later Cooper stated that he "had a good deal of difficulty in getting the Pilot out of [Murray's] hands";[11] his tactic, though not now known, was possibly suggested by Ogden. In his letter of 13 September, Ogden advised Cooper to write Miller and explain "that it was [his] intention to have given him the first offer, but that Mr. Ogden construed [his] instructions (written in a hurry) differently, & thought himself at liberty to offer it elsewhere."[12] A letter to this effect, or a letter bluntly authorizing

---

*i.e., the corrections in the proof.

Miller to take over the publication, accompanied by a new installment of sheets from Wiley's Volume II (especially if corrected in Cooper's script as sheets for Murray's edition of *The Pioneers* had been corrected) would surely have effected Cooper's purpose. This tactic would also explain why unique authorial interventions should begin to appear precisely at the start of the second segment (parcel two) and be confined to this portion of the Miller text (II.163–220).

Parcel 3: Miller's letter to Cooper of 5 February 1824 reveals that the British publisher received his final installment (presumably uncorrected sheets for Wiley's Volume II) by the packet of 24 December, which "had a long passage," and that he printed Volume III "very hastily," fearing "the Columbia—(1st Jany) might arrive—& bring perfect Copies before I was ready to publish."[13] Apparently Cooper did not wait to correct the standing type before transmitting these last sheets, for the Miller variants seem to contain readings earlier than those of the Wiley copy-text.

PARCEL 1

Since copy for Wiley Volume I (corresponding to Volume I—Volume II.162 of Miller) was deposited for copyright in New York on 1 August 1823, one would expect that Cooper would not have had anything further to do with its text. As if in corroboration, all of the twenty-one Miller variants for this first half of the work are no more than minor restyling of awkwardnesses, changes typical of British compositorial adjustment of an American text. At I.4.26, for example, "bit craft" in the Wiley becomes "bit o'craft" in the Miller, whose compositor evidently responded to the apparently unidiomatic dialogue. The dialect form "oncomfortable" at I.14.1 in the Wiley becomes "uncomfortable" in the Miller; the battle "of Flamborough Head" becomes the battle "off Flamborough Head" at I.119.26. Since these variants seem to be sophistications by the Miller compositors, the Cooper Edition rejects them and the other Miller variants in this section, retaining the copy-text readings.

PARCEL 2

With the beginning of the Miller resetting of the Wiley Volume II material, the number and import of the Miller variants increase markedly, supporting the probability that they originate with Cooper's unique scribal corrections on at least the first thirty pages of this next shipment. Fifteen of the twenty-four substantive variants unique to this edition and occurring within these few pages are interconnected in a manner that is not characteristic of the previous Miller variants.

In the following examples, these variants are indicated by double bars.

WILEY FIRST EDITION:	MILLER EDITION:
They proceeded, for the distance of half a mile, with rapid strides, and with the stern and sullen silence of men who //expected// to encounter immediate danger, //resolved// to breast it with desperate resolution;	They proceeded, for the distance of half a mile, with rapid strides, and with the stern and sullen silence of men who, //expecting// to encounter immediate danger, //were resolved// to breast it with desperate resolution; (209.10–14)

The Miller reading is more idiomatic and graceful. While a compositor could have made two such closely allied changes, they point more persuasively toward authorial origin. Other Miller readings resolve odd phrasing ("of winter" for "of a winter" at 210.32–33), improve syntax ("also" is deleted from 216.22 and inserted at 216.21) and correct errors ("forbid" for "forbids" at 221.5)—again possible compositorial changes but more likely changes originating with Cooper. One further pair of changes is especially suggestive of authorial intervention:

WILEY FIRST EDITION:	MILLER EDITION:
From the stout frames of the men, his glance was directed to the stack of fire-arms, //from// whose glittering tubes and polished bayonets, strong rays of light were //reflected// . . .	From the stout frames of the men, his glance was directed to the stack of fire-arms, //along// whose glittering tubes and polished bayonets, strong rays of light were //dancing// . . . (219.11–14)

This Miller reading, not at all characteristic of compositorial restyling, resembles rather the increased specificity of Cooper's revisions for the second Wiley edition of *The Pilot*, and also for *The Pioneers, Lionel Lincoln*, and *The Last of the Mohicans*. Accordingly, the Cooper Edition accepts fifteen of these twenty-four variants as authorial.

The remaining nine Miller variants in this section are, however, here considered nonauthorial. While external and internal evidence does point to some authorial intervention in at least these thirty pages, the nature of some other variants indicate that the restyling of the text by the Miller compositors continued. The substitution of "that" for "which" at 220.4 seems compositorial, as does the omission of the phrase "some of" from "with some of the" at 213.11. These readings are therefore rejected in the Cooper Edition.

PARCEL 3

While apparent compositorial restyling continues beyond approximately page 30 of the Wiley Volume II, other Miller variants in this third segment seem too complex to be attributable to house-styling alone. Their provenance, unlike the authorial variants discussed above, seems attributable to a third situation: the transmission of penultimate Wiley proof to Miller, run off from formes that Cooper subsequently continued to improve. Perhaps he sent the proof to Miller before his final revisions were incorporated in the Wiley standing type; or perhaps he felt the revises he sent were perfected but then had second thoughts. Whichever the case, key Wiley readings are clearly superior, exhibiting greater economy and exactness and removing repetition — characteristics of Cooper's practices of revision throughout his career.

At 391.24, for example, the Miller has "preparation" where the Wiley has "arrangement." At lines 27–28, the Wiley and the Miller both have "preparations," presenting in the Miller the same word twice in close proximity. Cooper was always careful to avoid such repetition, usually changing one of the identical words to a synonym: evident in the Wiley reading ("arrangement . . . preparations") but not in the Miller. Similarly, at 418.26 Miller has "seen" both here and at line 28, while Wiley reads "observed" and "seen" respectively. Other Wiley readings in this section, when compared with their Miller variants, also seem to indicate authorial preference. At 418.15–17, the Miller reads, " . . . nor did he remember to order the head sheets of the Alacrity to be drawn, in order to put the vessel again in motion. . . ." The Wiley has the more economical, " . . . nor did he remember to order the head sheets of the Alacrity drawn, in order to put the vessel again in motion. . . ." Further, at 409.6, the context calls for a "message" (the Wiley reading) rather than an "order" (the Miller); at 408.37, "The recent contention between you — " (Wiley) is more precise than "after what I so lately witnessed" (Miller) and avoids repetition of "witnessed" which occurs four lines earlier. At 408.8 Miller has "after that" where Wiley has the more specific "If this be true." The Cooper Edition retains the copy-text readings at these points on the assumption that they reflect the author's final intentions for this portion of the text.

WILEY SECOND EDITION (1824)[14]

On 11 February Wiley published a second edition of *The Pilot*, incorporating many authorial revisions. In January, while Cooper was visiting Shubrick in Boston, they evidently discussed the Wiley first edition. Upon his return to New York, Cooper wrote to Shubrick that "Wiley had the book in the hands of five printers . . . for a reprint" and added, "so much for our *joint* efforts."[15] Captain Shubrick may have made a technical suggestion: at 344.9–345.7, Griffith and Barnstable threaten to fight with their *hangers* rather than with the first edition's *sabres*. Another significant revision perhaps generated by conversation with Shubrick is Griffith's increased respect for the pilot in the conclusion: in the first edition, John Paul Jones had not merited "one half the obloquy that he received from his enemies", whereas the Wiley second edition states that he did not "at all merit" it (426.9).

The substantive variants appearing in the Wiley second edition fall into five categories, all consonant with Cooper's practices when revising. In the absence of his printer's copy, and in conformity to practice in other volumes of this edition, variants are accepted as authorial 1) when they contribute to concision by eliminating superfluous words and phrases; 2) when they increase the precision and clarity of the text; 3) when they increase the incidence of dialect and nautical jargon; 4) when they increase *vraisemblance* and 5) when they fit the action or speech more appropriately to the character. Of the 454 variants appearing in the Wiley second edition, over four hundred fall into one of these categories and are thus accepted by the Cooper Edition.

i. *Deletion*

Many of these revisions achieve concision by dropping superfluous elements. In the following list of examples, the words in italics are deleted in the second edition.

11.19	readers, *in imagination*, selecting
11.29	toil *in husbandry*
93.12	apartments, *or by such other names as they were properly to be distinguished*, were
109.3	with *momentary* surprise
240.31	interruption *to his musing*
267.35	fail *to cause him*

ii. *Clarity*

In this type of variant, the diction of the second edition is syntactically more specific and clear. Many of these variants condense the phrasing as they clarify the meaning.

35.35	until the hour and season [in the first edition] *becomes* until the proper hour [in the second]
115.4	cannot but be subjected to *becomes* cannot escape
119.21	of courtesy, if not of softness *becomes* of softness
165.25	marine friend *becomes* water battery
256.19	well understood by all *becomes* universally understood
277.17	the canvass of their most important sail *becomes* their main-sail

iii. *Dialect and Nautical Jargon*

Evidently, Cooper also hoped to increase the color of his characters' speech. At 21.3, one of Long Tom's first appearances, the second edition has him desire "a plenty" of sea room instead of the first edition's "plenty." The British characters Alice Dunscombe and Colonel Howard are made to say "an" instead of "a" before a word like "humble" (e.g. 302.19). Whereas in the first edition the cockswain says, "he keeps his watch in another world, though he does not here," the second edition reads, "he keeps his watch in another world, though he goes below in this" (253.11–12). At 264.39, Long Tom's phrase "patched it up" is rendered in the second edition "spliced it together." Since all these variants seem linked in the sense that they achieve the same effect, they are presumed to be authorial and accepted by the Cooper Edition.

iv. *Vraisemblance*[16]

Closely associated with variants that increase the clarity of the text are those which substitute concrete expressions for abstract. For example, at 29.20, "crisis" becomes "breakers." At 123.23, the second edition puts Burroughcliffe in "the British uniform" instead of "dress" and at 140.4 has the girls enter Griffith's room "cautiously" instead of "slowly." Finally, the second edition deletes "looking" from the expression "dusty looking bottles" at 161.1.

v. *Appropriateness*

Some of the second edition variants refine the level and tone of speech. Griffith, for example, too well-mannered to interrupt another person, "returned" an answer at 32.29 rather than "interrupted." "Sir" is added to a seaman's reply to Griffith at 38.30 but cut from Dillon's remark to Burroughcliffe at 101.33, Dillon being a sycophant who would be courteous only to those he has designs on. Captain Munson's compliment is "courteously," not "carelessly" returned by the Pilot at 88.18; and the Pilot's manners are similarly improved when he protects Alice's anonymity ("Miss Dunscombe" becomes "the lady" at 360.39) as they withdraw for their farewell interview.

Second edition variants which introduce errors or anomalies and normalize dialect are rejected by the Cooper Edition. For example, "sand-spits" is printed as "sand-pits" twice (13.36; 17.1), and an "s" is dropped from "gets" at 191.6 that would have a seaman using the subjunctive. Fourteen obvious misprints (such as the wrong chapter number, "timed" for "timid" or "yon" for "you") are rejected as well.

NONAUTHORIAL EDITIONS (1827, 1831)

Two nonauthorial editions of *The Pilot* are included in the transmission of the text: the Carey, Lea & Carey stereotype edition published in 1827 and the Colburn and Bentley edition of 1831. The Carey edition, set from the Wiley second edition, was the first reprint of *The Pilot* to be stereotyped. It was authorized by Cooper, but he was in Europe at the time of publication and was not involved in the preparation of the text. Plates from this edition were used long after Cooper's death, and an impression of this edition served in turn as printer's copy for the first of the Bentley Standard Novels. Since this publication preceded Cooper's arrangement with Bentley to correct and add new introductions and notes to his early works, he did not participate in the preparation of this volume of the Standard Novels either.[17]

While without textual authority, these two editions do introduce a total of fifty-four substantive variants into the text of *The Pilot*. Except for changes necessary to correct errors or ambiguities in the earlier authorial editions, all those changes are rejected. Since neither edition is authorial, neither is cited in the Emendations or Rejected Readings lists, but since these editions' variants are perpetuated in the last of the revised editions, the Putnam edition of 1849, diacritical marks in the lists indicate which variants appeared for the first time in each nonauthorial edition. For example, the misreading "orders" for "officers" at 72.5–6, cited as appearing in the Putnam edition in Rejected Readings, actually first appeared in the Carey, Lea & Carey edition in 1827, as signified by the degree sign preceding the entry, and remained throughout all succeeding editions. Similarly, the reading "pull" for "pall" at 40.30, also cited in Rejected Readings as appearing in the Putnam edition, first appeared in the Colburn and Bentley in 1831, as the dagger indicates.

PUTNAM EDITION (1849)[18]

When G. P. Putnam undertook to publish a uniform revised edition of Cooper's works, *The Pilot* was one of the twelve books completed before the project was discontinued. Using the Bentley's Standard Novels editions as printer's copy, Cooper usually intervened sparingly in the texts and paid most of his attention to updating the introductions he had written for Bentley in the early 1830s. Only the original 1823 "Preface" of *The Pilot* had been reprinted in the Standard Novels, however, so Cooper wrote a completely new introduction in 1849. The manuscript of this "Preface," now at the Beinecke Library, Yale University, serves as copy-text for this portion of the present edition.[19]

Since he had not revised the text of *The Pilot* in a quarter of a century, Cooper seems to have re-read it carefully. Collation reveals more than 150 variants between the Bentley text and the Putnam edition. While these must be examined with uncommon suspicion because Cooper delegated much responsibility to his stereotyper, John Fagan, about two-thirds of the

Putnam variants survive such scrutiny and are accepted as authorial. The remainder are rejected as house-styling or as changes a stereotyper would have made.[20]

Many of the variants are clustered together as though Cooper were reworking passages he found unsatisfactory. The two interviews between Alice and the pilot seem to have drawn his attention, for instance, and changes in both scenes affect the content and cadence of their speeches. In the first interview, Alice complains of revolutions which threaten "all that the world has ever yet done, or will ever see done in peace and happiness." (151.21–23) The revision, reversing "will" and "ever," emphasizes her lack of faith in revolutions. Ten lines later, the addition of "the" before "nations" puts her argument by analogy into appropriate parallel structure. On the following page, "only" after "eyes" (which makes her seem unreasonable) is cut. In the second of their meetings (360ff), the addition of "a" before "man" in "Is man a stick or a stone, that he must be cast into the fire. . . ." (364.25–26) indicates that the pilot is thinking of himself not mankind. Twelve lines later, Alice's "power" is changed, in the pilot's speech, to "powerful influence." (This change, like the substitution of "agreed to" for "made" with regard to Kate at 339.23, may reflect Cooper's reaction to the women's rights movement, something he was concurrently writing about in *The Ways of the Hour*.[21]) In the following line, timing and tone are altered by the addition of "But" to the sentence that began, "Our time is growing brief. . . ." At 365.36, the substitution of "these" for "those" brings the threat of betrayal closer, and on the next page the suggestion that this may be the lovers' last meeting is strengthened by substituting "should" for "shall" at 366.19.

The Putnam variants include the usual changes to avoid repetition: "portentous" had appeared fourteen lines earlier and becomes "confident" at 241.7. Other substantive variants with an accompanying change in punctuation alter the speed and dramatic effect of sentences. Double bars indicate the segment thus affected at 393.36–394.2.

WILEY FIRST EDITION	PUTNAM
Griffith had so far anticipated this movement, as to//have, already, ordered the head of the frigate turned in its former course, when struck by the unearthly cry of the last tones uttered by his commander,//he bent his head, and beheld the venerable seaman driven through the air, his hat still waving, his gray hair floating in the wind, and his eye set in the wild look of death.	Griffith had so far anticipated this movement, as to//have already ordered the head of the frigate to be turned in its former course when, struck by the unearthly cry of the last tones uttered by his commander,//he bent his head, and beheld the venerable seaman driven through the air, his hat still waving, his gray hair floating in the wind, and his eye set in the wild look of death.

The present edition accepts even small and isolated changes that seem necessary for clarity. For example, the deletion of "of" at 54.3 corrects the copy-text's suggestion that the pilot has ignored two previous warnings of "by the deep four" water before ordering a change in the ship's course. When, in brief, Putnam variants increase accuracy and concision or eliminate repetition of words or similar sounds, they are considered authorial.

The remainder of the Putnam variants either introduce errors or resemble compositorial missettings. For example, "effects" for "efforts" at 49.32 "order" for "orders" at 264.20, and "your" for "you" at 368.27 do not increase accuracy or concision. They and other variants like them are rejected in the Cooper Edition.

CONCLUSION

The present edition of *The Pilot* contains no silent emendations. Except for the fragment of manuscript of the text and the manuscript of the 1849 Preface, the copy-text is the earliest state of the text of the first edition, published in 1824. Emendations of substantives derive from the three authorial editions (the Miller first edition 1824, Wiley second edition 1824 and Putnam 1849) that Cooper revised. Obvious errors in the copy-text that were corrected by subsequent nonauthorial editions (Carey and Lea 1827 and Colburn and Bentley 1831) are accepted on the authority of the Cooper Edition and identified in Textual Notes.

Epigraphs which have been identified are expanded to include the name of the author (unless obvious), title and location of the passage. Shakespearean epigraphs are keyed to *The Riverside Shakespeare*, ed. G. B. Evans, et al. (Boston: Houghton Mifflin, 1973). Other epigraphs are keyed to standard editions or to editions as nearly contemporary with the book as possible. All these expansions have been reported on the Emendations list.

Without attempting in any way to duplicate the visual appurtenances of the first edition, the Cooper Edition of *The Pilot* reprints the copy-text exactly, emending it with Cooper's revisions in 1823 and 1824 and Cooper's further revisions for Putnam a quarter of a century later.

NOTES TO TEXTUAL COMMENTARY

1. New-York *Statesman*, 7 January 1824.

2. London *Literary Gazette*, 31 January 1824.

3. *Boston Commercial Gazette*, 12 January 1824, announced Cooper's presence; second edition announced in New-York *Statesman*, 12 February 1824.

4. JFC to Richard Bentley [8? August 1831]; *The Letters and Journals of James Fenimore Cooper*, ed., James Franklin Beard. 6 vols. (Cambridge, Mass.: Belknap Press of Harvard University Press, 1960–68), II, 132 (hereafter referred to as *Letters and Journals*).

5. This fragment measures some 6.5 centimeters high and seven centimeters wide and contains parts of thirteen lines of writing in Cooper's hand on cream laid (unlined) paper with vertical chainlines 27 millimeters

The Pilot (1824–1860)

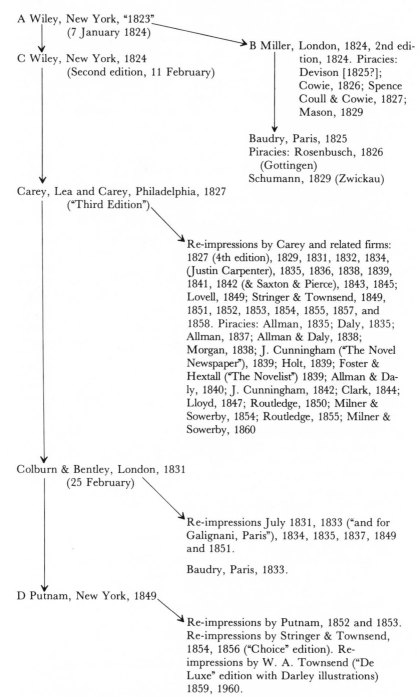

A Wiley, New York, "1823"
    (7 January 1824)

C Wiley, New York, 1824
    (Second edition, 11 February)

B Miller, London, 1824, 2nd edition, 1824. Piracies:
Devison [1825?];
Cowie, 1826; Spence
Coull & Cowie, 1827;
Mason, 1829

Baudry, Paris, 1825
Piracies: Rosenbusch, 1826
    (Gottingen)
Schumann, 1829 (Zwickau)

Carey, Lea and Carey, Philadelphia, 1827
    ("Third Edition")

Re-impressions by Carey and related firms:
1827 (4th edition), 1829, 1831, 1832, 1834,
(Justin Carpenter), 1835, 1836, 1838, 1839,
1841, 1842 (& Saxton & Pierce), 1843, 1845;
Lovell, 1849; Stringer & Townsend, 1849,
1851, 1852, 1853, 1854, 1855, 1857, and
1858. Piracies: Allman, 1835; Daly, 1835;
Allman, 1837; Allman & Daly, 1838;
Morgan, 1838; J. Cunningham ("The Novel
Newspaper"), 1839; Holt, 1839; Foster &
Hextall ("The Novelist") 1839; Allman & Daly, 1840; J. Cunningham, 1842; Clark, 1844;
Lloyd, 1847; Routledge, 1850; Milner &
Sowerby, 1854; Routledge, 1855; Milner &
Sowerby, 1860

Colburn & Bentley, London, 1831
    (25 February)

Re-impressions July 1831, 1833 ("and for
Galignani, Paris"), 1834, 1835, 1837, 1849
and 1851.

Baudry, Paris, 1833.

D Putnam, New York, 1849

Re-impressions by Putnam, 1852 and 1853.
Re-impressions by Stringer & Townsend,
1854, 1856 ("Choice" edition). Re-impressions by W. A. Townsend ("De
Luxe" edition with Darley illustrations)
1859, 1960.

apart and no visible watermark. The ink may have been black, but appears to be standard brown ink rusted to red-brown.

The only substantive difference between this piece of AMS and the copy-text is the correction of Cooper's "away" in the first line of the fragment to "way" (43.15). The AMS "discernable" is printed as "discernible" (43.17), and Cooper's capitalized Captain and Pilot are printed in lower case at 43.26 and 43.30 while the AMS "Capt." is printed out in full at 43.28. AMS has no punctuation at the end of the paragraph at 43.23 and the quotation marks precede a dash at the end of the paragraph at 43.31. Finally, AMS does not begin new paragraphs at 43.20 and 43.26.

Four deletions of from one to four words are clear and two words are inserted above the line in the manuscript. The most interesting revision is Cooper's insertion of "fanciful" for the canceled "lofty" to describe the "summits" of the ship's sails at 43.19.

6. Hinman collations of five copies of the first edition (the American Antiquarian Society First Edition, Beard 1, Beard 2, Madison 1 and House 1) disclose no substantive variations.

7. Hinman collations of three copies of the first edition (Beard 1, the American Antiquarian Society First Edition, and Yale University ZA-C235-106pb) reveal no significant textual variations among the three.

8. John Miller to JFC, 28 June 1823; MS: Yale Collection of American Literature, Beinecke Rare Book and Manuscript Library, Yale University (henceforth referred to as YCAL).

9. James De Peyster Ogden to JFC; MS: YCAL.

10. James De Peyster Ogden to JFC, 13 September 1823; MS: YCAL.

11. *Letters and Journals*, IV, 108.

12. Ogden to JFC, 13 September 1823.

13. John Miller to JFC, 5 February 1824; MS: YCAL

14. The following second editions were collated by machine: Beard 1, American Antiquarian Society 19th Century, Harvard AL 1077.332. The only substantive difference found was that the AAS copy contains unrevised pages (in signature 6) from the first edition at I.62–65. The AAS copy also has an erroneous page number (722 for 227) in the first volume. Otherwise, collation shows only poorly inked pages, shifting type, loss of type, and pages reset without change.

15. See Cooper to Shubrick [25–30? January – 5 February 1824], *Letters and Journals*, I, 110.

16. See Cooper's comments on *vraisemblance* as technique in Scott's *The Pirate* in his 1849 preface to *The Pilot*.

17. Sight collation substantiates the history of the transmission of the text as set forth in David Kaser, *The Cost Book of Carey & Lea,* p. 246, and in the *Letters and Journals*, II, 130 and VI, 11.

18. Five copies (Beard 1, Beard 2, Beard 3, Madison 1, and Trinity College 810 C777p) of the 1849 Putnam edition were collated on the Hinman machine. No substantive differences appeared. The 1849 Beard 2 was also collated against the 1852 Putnam (American Antiquarian Society G256.C777.P852), the 1854 Stringer and Townsend (American Anti-

quarian Society G256.C777.P854.pi.), and the 1856 Stringer and Townsend (Choice) owned by James F. Beard. While a number of pages were reset, particularly in the 1856 Stringer and Townsend, the only substantive difference was that the correct Putnam "eye" (98.33) was misprinted as "the" in the 1856 Choice edition. Differences in accidentals among these editions consist largely of lost punctuation and damaged or omitted page numbers.

19. Cooper wrote the preface for the Putnam edition of 1849 on three legal sized sheets of blue, lined stationery without watermarks or chain lines. He used black ink and the first page has "vii" written in the upper right-hand corner, while the second page has a "2" centered at the top and the third sheet is not numbered.

Cooper's manuscript changes include deletions of what he considered superfluous words: "as a peculiar property" originally followed "boast" at the end of the first sentence, for example. One contemplated addition, written in between lines 18 and 19 of the first page of the manuscript ("There were many subjects introduced in [illeg] [illeg] in an,") would presumably have added further comments about the lack of qualifications of most authors to write a sea novel, but this tentative addition was itself deleted and the already existing "It would have been hypercritical" statement allowed to stand without other preliminary remarks.

Other deletions improve the choice or arrangement of words. In the second sentence of the first paragraph, for instance, Cooper originally wrote "origin" of this book, which he canceled for "execution and conception"; he then deleted this pair of nouns and reversed their order so that "conception" precedes "execution."

Added words are often qualifiers, so that "were thought" becomes "were then very generally thought," "an instance" becomes "a very marked instance" and "this knowledge" becomes "this universal knowledge." Lengthier additions make the tone of the preface more frank and modest. Speaking of one prediction of success for the book, Cooper added "which it probably never attained" and another reader's "perfect assurance" that seamen would like it became "perfect and most gratifying assurance."

One long addition shows Cooper, in an afterthought, questioning the motives of some self-appointed reformers: "having, quite half of the time, some selfish, personal, end to answer." Two other lengthy additions are obviously intended to clarify the context. To the sentence that originally ended with "ships" (at 6.2-3) Cooper added "than any that are to be found in the Pirate." He also inserted "after he had made some progress in the work" after "undertaking" (at 6.7) in order to give the reader an accurate account of the book's composition.

20. The Putnam edition modernizes the spelling of words like *berth* for Cooper's *birth*. Cooper's use of what is now the past participle (*sprung*) for the preterite was backed by the authority of Webster's 1828 *Dictionary* which declared such forms as *sprang, shrank,* and *rang* "obsolete" or "almost obsolete." So rigid was Putnam's or Fagan's preference for the *a* form of such words that Sir Walter Scott's *sprung* was changed to *sprang* in the epigraph to Chapter VIII in the Putnam edition.

21. Cooper's letter (30 March 1849) instructing Fagan to change *and* to *or* in the introduction to the Putnam edition of *The Spy* goes on to mention both the revision of *The Pilot* and his work on what would be *The Ways of the Hour*. *Letters and Journals*, VI, 20.

Textual Notes

The following notes explain emendations and rejected readings requiring more specific information than the Textual Commentary could provide.

1.6 This revision is an example of exact coincident alteration in the Miller and the Putnam edition. The Miller is given as the source because it is historically the first edition to make the revision.

1.17 The first edition was printed in two volumes, the Putnam in one.

11.2–3 Cooper altered the words italicized below; the original lines read:

> Sullen waves incessant *flowing*
> Rudely dash against *its* sides;

Dibdin's Charms of Melody (Dublin: Brett Smith, 1797), p. 14.

19.6 The omitted lines read:

> The short Trunk-Hose shall show Thy Foot and Knee
> Licentious, and to common Eye-sight free:

H. Bunker Wright and Monroe K. Spears, eds., *The Literary Works of Mathew Prior* (Oxford: Clarendon Press, 1959), I:290–291.

29.2 Cooper preferred to have all epigraphs enclosed in quotation marks; here, and in the epigraph to Chapter XXIX, and on the title page the present edition corrects the omission.

29.3 Cooper has changed Cassius "his comment" to "its comment." *The Riverside Shakespeare*, p. 1125.

37.3 *The Riverside Shakespeare* gives line 11 as: "Borne with th' invisible and creeping wind," p. 947.

41.37 The Colburn and Bentley edition omitted a period at end-line after "believe," leading the Putnam to attempt this correction.

48.2 In Cooper's time, most reprintings of George Alexander Stevens' "The Storm" followed Charles Dibdin's nonsensical "we're" for the correct "ware." In the note to Volume II of his *History of the Navy* (Philadelphia: Lea and Blanchard, 1839), Cooper says, "To 'ware,' is a corruption of 'to veer,' and there is ancient authority for the spelling adopted; to 'wear,' being an unmeaning term." The same protest against misprinting "wear" for "ware" also appears in the second American edition of Cooper's *History*, in the 1839 Bentley, and in the 1839 Baudry. In the copy-text, "ware" is printed correctly at 277.36 and misprinted at 378.4.

48.23 This revision is an example of exact coincident alteration in the
Miller and Wiley second edition. Coincidental alterations in B and C
also occur at 151.39, 183.2, 205.29, 316.18–19, 319.17 and 396.13. B
is cited as the earlier edition.

68.13 "People" clearly means everyone, including Colonel Howard,
whereas the original "the people" might be misconstrued as referring
only to the peasants.

79.39 Webster's 1828 *Dictionary* gives "chock" as a noun used in marine
language and coming from "choke"; as verbs the two forms were in-
terchangeable.

83.2–4 The text given in *The Poetical Works* of Sir Walter Scott, Bart.,
(Edinburgh: A. & C. Block, 1851), p. 414 agrees with the copy-text
reading.

94.20 Colburn and Bentley's repair of syntax here, incorporated by the
Putnam edition, is necessary to resolve the ambiguity of the copy-
text.

104.9 Line 7 of this passage, deleted by Cooper, reads: "(As if for
heavenly musing meant alone)."

116.28 This change in punctuation seems substantive, as the words
enclosed by dashes become a hasty aside while the Colonel rushes
ahead with his speech.

148.7 The error in agreement was corrected by Colburn and Bentley and
is accepted by the present edition.

159.2 *The Riverside Shakespeare* gives "I have" for Cooper's "I've" (p. 418).

209.2 *The Riverside Shakespeare* gives "call'd" (p. 775).

224.2–4 *The Riverside Shakespeare* prints this passage as prose and does not
capitalize Father, Earl or Duke (p. 880).

245.2 In *The Riverside Shakespeare*, Falstaff's speech begins with "Yea"
(p. 905).

250.20 Manual refers to the military profession as an "art" at 225.7; the
meaning of "heart" is not clear.

258.6 The omitted lines read:
     On whom that ravening brood of Fate
     Who lap the blood of sorrow, wait;
William Collins, *The Poetical Works of William Collins* (London:
Pickering, 1853), p. 24.

271.3–4 *The Riverside Shakespeare* text ends the second line of this passage
with "earth or ere" and the third with "swallow'd, and" (p. 1612).

278.8 Though this variant may at first seem to be simply a change in
spelling, the Wiley second edition changes the meaning because
"croker" is a kind of bird.

289.4 The copy-text agrees with J. L. Robertson's edition of *The Complete
Poetical Works of Thomas Campbell* (London: Oxford University Press,
1907), p. 191.

294.31 This obvious error was first corrected by the Carey, Lea and Carey
edition, but is accepted on the authority of the present edition.

302.17 The grammatical correction here originated with the Colburn and Bentley edition, but is accepted by the present edition on its own authority.

335.13 Consistency in dialect here was imposed by the Carey, Lea and Carey edition, but is accepted as according with the preponderant use of "ye" in Alice's speech.

359.2 Cooper change Thomson's "blot" to "plot." James Thomson, *Coriolanus* (London: A. Miller, 1749), p. 61.

387.6 Percy's translation of "Rio verde, Rio verde" from the *Historia de las civiles guerras de Granada* (Madrid, 1694) was published in the first American edition of his *Reliques of Ancient English Poetry* (Philadelphia: Moore, 1823), I.363.

Emendations

The following list records all changes introduced into the copy-text of *The Pilot*. The reading of the Cooper Edition appears to the left of the square bracket. The source for that reading appears to the right of the bracket, followed by a semicolon, the copy-text reading, and the copy-text symbol. If not listed, the readings of texts which fall between the copy-text and the source cited for the reading of the Cooper Edition may be presumed to agree substantively with the copy-text reading. If an intervening reading does not agree substantively with the copy-text, that intervening reading and its symbol are recorded after the copy-text reading and symbol.

Within an entry, the curved dash ~ represents the exact word that appears before the square bracket and is used in recording punctuation and paragraphing variants. A caret ʌ to the right of the bracket signals the absence of a mark of punctuation of the left. An asterisk indicates that the reading is discussed in the Textual Notes. The abbreviation CE identifies emendations initiated by the Cooper Edition.

The following texts are referred to:

AMS   Author's Manuscript, "Preface" (1849)
A   New York: Charles Wiley, 1824 [Two Volumes]
B   London: John Miller, 1824 [Three Volumes]
C   New York: Charles Wiley, 1824 [Two Volumes], Second Edition
D   New York: G. P. Putnam, 1849

Title
  page 7   "List . . . me."]CE; ʌ~ . . . ~.ʌ A
Title
  page 8   G. A. Stevens, "The Storm," 1.2]CE; [*omitted*] A
1.2   Branford]C; Brandford A
1.3   Esq.] D; Esquire A
1.4   U. S. Navy] D; Mast. Com. U. S. Navy A
*1.6   brings] B; causes A
1.10–11   are those of] D; are A
1.16   has] D; have A
*1.17   this volume] D; these volumes A

3.28	Smollett] CE; Smollet A (*Also corrected at* 3.31 *and* 3.32.)
5.3	probable] D; probable that AMS
5.10	"The Pirate,"] D; ʌ the Pirate ʌ AMS
6.2	ships than] D; ~.~ AMS
6.7	undertaking,] D; ~ʌ AMS
6.29	Water-Fowl] D; water-Fowl AMS
6.32	Thanatopsis]CE; Thanitopsis AMS
6.33	plagiarism.] D; plagirism ʌ AMS
6.33–34	of this] D; This AMS
6.38–39	book which] D; ~.~ AMS
7.2	critic] D; purpose AMS
7.3	one now] D; and now AMS
7.4	chosen] D; chosen for this purpose AMS
7.13	it much] D; much it AMS
7.34	reformation by] D; ~,~ AMS
8.1	even,] D; ~ʌ AMS
8.1	benefited] D; benifitted AMS
8.5	that] D; than AMS
8.9	men] D; men, when far removed from the ordinary charities of life AMS
8.12	personal] D; ~, AMS
8.20	Church] D; church AMS
8.22	conceit] D; conciet AMS
8.35	the effort] D; this effort AMS
8.35	making] D; made AMS
8.38	manner, — by] D; ~, ʌ~ AMS
8.38–39	unnecessary. π Cooperstown, August 10, 1849] D; unnecessary AMS
11.4	"Fresh and Strong," *Dibdin's Charms of Melody*, 11.3-4] CE; *Song* A
11.19	readers] C; readers, in imagination, A
11.20	a peculiar interest] D; peculiar interests A
11.22	take the] D; take A
11.27	was] C; were A
11.29	toil] C; toil in husbandry A
12.36	rarely, or] C; rarely, with A
14.4	peasants] C; peasantry A
14.5	concerning] C; on A
14.6	contraband] C; a contraband A
14.22	hand] C; hands A
15.14	to the place where] C; to where A
*19.6	Prior, "Henry and Emma," 11.437–438, 441–442] CE; *Prior*, A
19.16	even though we should] D; though we should even A
20.2–3	indication] D; indications A
20.14	he gave] C; after giving A
20.15	and proceeded] C; he proceeded A

21.3	a plenty] C; plenty A
22.3	It is] C; It's A
22.6	towards poising the] C; toward poising his A
22.39	sojourn together] C; detain you A
24.13	experiment] C; experiment of mine A
25.6	commanded] C; ordered A
*29.2	"In] CE; ʌ~ A
*29.3	comment."] CE; ~.ʌ A
29.4	*Julius Caesar*, IV.iii.7–8] CE; *Shakspeare* A
29.12	planks] C; both planks A
29.20	breakers as they] C; crisis they had A
30.1	sartin] C; sartain A
30.15	but I] C; when I A
30.33	this?] C; ~. A
31.12	continued] C; continued, in the same manner A
31.39	no, sir] ~ʌ~ A
31.39	neither] C; either A
32.7–8	with a] C; with his A
32.15	all the] C; all that A
32.15	authority] C; authority that A
32.29	returned] C; interrupted A
32.32	but of] C; of but A
32.40	observed] C; said A
33.16	to-night] D; to/night A
33.25	these rocks] C; the rocks A
33.37	enter] C; enter her A
34.30	several ranks] C; ranks A
34.34	rank. On]C; rank; and on A
34.39	nearer] C; nearer to A
35.10	captain,] C; captain, doubtingly; A
35.35	proper hour] C; hour and season A
35.36	answer] C; reply to A
37.6	*Henry V*, III.i.10–13] CE; *Shakspeare* A
37.8	were threatening symptoms] C; was something threatening A
38.11–12	all, however,] C; all A
38.18	warping] C; to warp A
38.24	above] C; move A
38.30	land, sir] C; land A
39.1	would] D; will A
39.33	that] C; that again A
40.8	apprehension] C; their apprehensions A
40.10	unusual activity] C; attempt something A
40.11	instead of aiding, they retarded] C; they retarded, instead of forwarded A
40.23	labour] C; gloomy scene A
40.30	quivering] C; quavering A
41.24	feeble] C; inadequate A

41.36	fills] C; fill A
42.6	even the boys] C; all A
43.15	way] A; away AMS
43.17	discernible] A; discernable AMS
43.17	horizon, with] C; horizon; A
43.20	¶Griffith] A; ʌ~AMS
43.23	cried—] A; ~ʌAMS
43.26	¶"We] A; ʌ"~AMS
43.26	captain] A; Captain AMS
43.28	Captain] A; Capt. AMS
43.28	more drift] C; more A
43.30	pilot] A; Pilot AMS
43.31	seaward."] A; ~"—AMS
43.32	except] D; excepting A
44.8	hoarser] C; hoarse A
44.21	hauling] C; howling A
44.25	from her] C; from the A
46.20	to-night] D; to/night A
47.4–5	the candle] C; a candle A
*48.2	ware] D; wear A
48.3	G. A. Stevens, "The Storm," 1.64] CE; *Song* A
*48.23	waiting] B; awaiting A
49.31–32	as yet, they] C; they, as yet, A
50.11	you shall] C; you'll A
52.7	noon-day] C; noon day A
53.4	alone safety was] D; safety was, alone, A
53.11	alone was] C; was only A
54.3	call] D; call of A
54.17	cried] C; said A
55.40	required] D; directed A
57.1–2	to-night] C; to night A
57.24	sail] C; sails A
58.26	heave up] C; rise A
59.3	sea] D; open sea A
59.7	lieutenant] D; young lieutenant A
59.18	walking away] C; and walking A
59.28	soon] C; had A
59.30	when the] C; and the A
61.13	fired?"] C; fired?"
	¶The soldier replied—A
61.14–15	Ariel," the soldier replied, "that] C; Ariel, that A
61.29	lying-to] CE; lying/too A
63.1	so recently acted] C; acted so recently A
63.5–6	a trifle] C; rather A
66.30	what] D; on what A
67.27	last] D; latter A
*68.13	people] D; the people A

69.27	The colonel has long desired to see this gentleman] D; This gentleman the colonel has long desired to see A
69.39-40	invent names and make dictionaries] C; make dictionaries and invent names A
70.7	KATHERINE] C; "∼A
70.10	grounds, &c."] D; ∼, "&c. A
70.15-16	he at length] C; at length he A
70.27	inquired] D; required A
71.27-28	to another] C; to an A
72.3	Addison, *Cato*, II.i.23] CE; *Cato* A
73.23	and for] C; and A
73.26	while at] D; at A
74.13	man's] C; man's books A
76.2	guard and] D; guard or A
76.16	fit] C; burst A
77.34	received] C; recived A
79.33	it all] D; it A
80.29	itself] D; of itself A
81.1	application] C; applications A
81.11	as you] C; when you A
82.5	dreads] C; fears A
83.5	Scott, *The Lord of the Isles.* Canto First, XXI.4-6] CE; *Lord of the Isles* A
86.11	no] C; yes A
87.14	and they] C; aud together A
87.14-15	they passed an hour together] C; together they passed an hour A
87.38	Tigers] C; tigers A
88.5	bade] D; bid A
88.16	head] C; head again A
88.18	courteously] C; carelessly A
88.26-27	who, by nautical courtesy, was styled Mr. Merry] C; who was styled Mr. Merry, by nautical courtesy A
89.16	sail] D; proceed A
89.18	as the symmetry of] C; as A
90.4-5	of these] C; of A
90.32	Greek and] D; Greek or A
91.2	argue] C; argue all A
91.15	carriage;] C; carriage, and A
91.37	The little schooner slowly] C; Slowly the little schooner A
92.12	tract] C; track A
92.17	were already forgotten] C; were forgotten, like the warnings of an ill-remembered experience A
93.6	name] D; description A
93.12	apartments] C; apartments, or by such other names as they were properly to be distinguished A
*94.20	red, and] D; red, A
95.12-13	a swarthiness of complexion] C; the swarthiness A

97.1	hanged] C; hung A
97.9	they are] C; they be A
97.34	as his] C; as all his A
98.36–37	man, in a bumper] C; man A
100.19	appease] C; soften A
100.25	when] C; where A
101.17	recluses] D; recluses, my dear colonel A
101.26	walls,] D; ~ ? A
101.32–33	apprehensions] C; apprehensions, sir A
102.9	announced] C; announced, with military precision A
*104.9	Campbell, *Gertrude of Wyoming*, II.iv.2-6, 8-9] CE; *Gertrude of Wyoming* A
104.21	appropriated] C; set apart A
105.34	changed, as she kneeled on the floor] C; changed A
105.38	close] C; dark A
106.12	shoulders] C; shoulder A
108.20	thoughtless, laughing girl,] C; laughing maiden A
108.34	to the place] C; to A
109.3	with] C; with momentary A
109.4	returned an] C; returned any A
109.9	your] C; yours A
109.12	might] D; might well A
109.18	the portals of the Abbey] C; its portals A
110.34	turning] C; turned A
110.34	Katherine] C; ~; A
111.18	Katherine,] C; Katherine, promptly, and A
112.20	proceed] C; take steps A
113.10	Cecilia] C; her cousin A
113.11	height of her cousin] C; other's height A
113.12	successfully] C; do it successfully A
115.4	escape] C; but be subjected to A
115.10	jacobins] D; jacobites A
116.4	*The Taming of the Shrew*, V.i.61-62] CE; *Shakspeare* A
116.12	inquired] C; inquired, with cool but delicate reserve A
*116.28	Alice—what] C; Alice. What A
117.24	know] C; have heard A
117.24	allegiance that is] C; allegiance A
118.13	vessel] C; vessels A
118.32	weakness] C; weaknesses A
119.21	of softness] C; of courtesy, if not of softness A
120.1	laws of the realm] C; laws A
120.13	struck] C; stricken A
120.37	the physical organization] C; that A
122.27–28	presently a low tap at the door] C; a low tap at the door presently A
123.23	the British uniform]; his dress A
125.3	*1 Henry IV*, IV. ii.66-67] CE; *Falstaff* A

125.17	apprehensions] C; apprehensions of you A
125.22	who] C; as he A
125.28-29	before he] C; when A
127.10	be; my] C; be that my A
127.14	beautiful] C; beautifully A
127.17	yourselves] C; you A
129.2	prisoners] C; group of prisoners A
129.35	conjectures] C; conjecture A
130.12	nor short-allowances, nor] C; or short-allowances, or A
130.13	topsails, nor] C; topsails, or A
130.15-16	knapsack, than] C; knapsack, as A
130.19-20	barracks; mind, I say only in very good weather] C; barracks A
130.40	these men] C; this man A
131.13	chief] D; principal A
131.22	read?"] D; ~." A
132.7	by a] C; by my A
132.36	effects] C; effect A
133.31	encourage] C; encourage you in A
135.4	Addison, *Cato*, I.vi.447–448] CE; *Cato* A
136.33	door] C; door, they A
137.32-33	comes, and finds] C; come, and find A
140.1	desired] C; bade A
140.4	cautiously] C; slowly A
140.38	driven] C; driveu A
143.28	additional] C; more A
144.16-17	fictitious] C; factitious
147.6	Percy, "The Hermit of Warkworth," Canto II, 11.209–212] CE; *Percy* A
*148.7	are] D; am A
148.32	London?]; ~ ! A
149.15	on no such] C; not on such an A
150.5	youth?] C;~!A
151.15	whose name soever] C; whosoever's name A
151.22	ever will] D; will ever A
151.32	not the] D; not A
151.38	while] C; with A
151.38	lighted] C; lighting A
151.39	notice.] B; ~, A
152.13	eyes] D; eyes only A
152.14	As for] C; As to A
152.25	lofty] C; proud A
153.10	Pilot] C; pilot, reproachfully A
153.21	has] D; have A
154.9	reach] C; reach to A
154.20	Alice] C; Alice, with deep interest A
156.14	act] C; acts A
156.25	all be] D; be all A

156.34	discretion.] C; ∼ ? A
157.14	by] C; by his A
157.22	the brow] D; the pallid brow A
159.4	*Twelfth Night*, II.iii. 145–46] CE; *Twelfth Night* A
159.6	apartment] D; apartment that A
159.23	had been calmly awaiting the] C; was calmly waiting a A
159.23	seemed] C; seems A
159.26	condition from either] C; condition A
159.27–28	with most] C; and much A
160.39	had been at a loss] C; knew not A
160.39	manner] C; manner or language A
161.1	dusty] C; dusty looking A
161.30	cool, but curious] C; cool and collected curiosity and A
163.9	on his] D; at his A
163.14	communications] C; communication A
163.28	your own] C; your A
165.25	water battery] C; marine friend A
165.39	to-night] C; to/night A
166.8–9	put foot] C; put A
173.19–20	proceed at once] D; proceed A
173.21	no very] D; no A
173.21	allow the civilians to] D; let the civilians A
177.10–11	proceed at once] C; proceed A
179.15	discuss the] C; discuss this A
180.17	as a] C; as A
180.39	and, the officer] C; ∼∧∼∼, A
181.6	barricade] C; barricado A
181.16	still whitened the waters] C; was still capped in white sheets A
182.5–6	be of any use] C; touch them A
182.12	intervals] C; places A
182.22	Dillon] C; Dillon was out of sight A
182.24	route, was out of sight] C; route A
183.2	deliberate] B; deliberative A
184.3	*Hamlet*, III.ii.382] CE; *Shakspeare* A
184.22–23	while his companion was] C; at the same time they were A
184.23	Griffith] C; the latter A
185.6	hour] C; hour had A
185.8	and leave] C; and to leave A
185.20	bestowed] D; disposed A
185.24	keel, though] C; keel, but, A
185.32	I have] C; I've A
186.25	nearly] D; near A
190.7	let's] D; let us A
193.14	of the enemy] D; to injure them A
195.6	Scott, *The Lord of the Isles*, Canto First, XXIII.1–4] CE; *Lord of the Isles* A
195.20	all the] D; all his A

196.14	As to] D; as ~ A
196.15	sail;] C; ~, A
196.21	by way] D; by the way A
198.4	gaffs] CE; gafts A
203.29	wild-looking] C; wild looking A
204.26	to the] D; to his A
204.28	our] C; our own A
205.29	fingers] B; finger A
207.31–32	While making] C; As they made A
208.16	Kidd] D; Kid A
208.26	while it was] C; until it was no longer A
208.35	deceiving the] C; deceiving his A
209.1	Chapter XIX] D; Chapter I A
209.3	*King John*, II.i.205] CE; *King John* A
209.12	who, expecting] B; who expected A
209.13	were resolved] B; resolved A
210.32–33	of winter] B; of a winter A
210.33	depart] C; leave you A
215.4	in such an event, look to your charge] C; look to your charge, in such an event A
215.10–11	unexpectedly brought him] C; brought him, unexpectedly, A
215.11–12	fortune] C; fortunes A
215.13	become] C; become so A
215.17–18	enough secret places] C; secret places enough A
215.18	conceal] C; conceal all A
216.20	trees] C; wood A
216.21	intended also] B; intended A
216.22	cover] B; cover also A
216.27	even, on their out-posts] C; on their out-posts even A
217.2	consider, sir] C; consider A
217.37	a situation] C; open view A
217.37	were] C; would be A
218.4	the permission] C; liberty A
218.5	though under the] C; and under A
218.7	party] C; group A
218.12	metal of] C; weight of metal carried by A
218.20	been] C; been previously A
218.22	fragments which] C; fragments of the building, that A
218.22	as the] C; as A
218.30	some time concluded] C; concluded some time A
219.8	party had again]C; party A
219.13	along whose] B; from whose A
219.14	dancing] B; reflected A
219.23	Griffith sprang at the same instant] C; Griffith both sprang A
219.26	watchman's] B; guardian's A
219.33	lifelessly to] C; lifelessly at A
220.17	making] C; making several A

220.34	shots] B; shot A
221.5	forbid] B; forbids A
221.32–33	so loud] B; so A
222.3	Ruth;] C; Ruth's, A
222.5	a surrender] C; his surrendering A
224.1	Chapter XX] D; Chapter II A
224.5	*1 Henry IV*, V.iv.138–140] CE; *Falstaff* A
224.6	sundry] C; several A
224.9	but meeting] B; when meeting A
224.11	as follows:] B; by saying—A
225.38	fou't] C; fout A
228.4	however] B; indeed A
228.25	"break] C;" "~ A
229.9	Abr'am] C; Abram A
229.10	all] C; all the A
229.23	was] D; were A
230.10	able-bodied] C; able bodied A
230.17	perish all] C; perish A
230.22	Kit, my kinsman;] C; Kit? My kinsman, A
230.23	Christopher?]C; Christopher. A
230.26	appearance] C; presence A
230.30	of naval] D; of the naval A
230.37	with all] C; with A
233.7	behold] C; but, sir A
234.4	advanced] C; advanced to A
234.27	justice] C; that justice was A
235.1	Chapter XXI]D; Chapter III A
235.7	*Julius Caesar*, I.iii.28–32] CE; Casca A
236.24	year into] C; year in A
237.20	determination. Heaving] C; determination; and, heaving A
237.21	Tom] C; he A
237.27	overlook] C; survey A
238.15	was] C; is A
239.24	countenance] C; conntenance A
239.38	but, there] C; now, there A
240.19	past] D; by A
240.28	should the Ariel break] C; if the Ariel breaks A
240.31	interruption] C; interruption to his musing A
241.6	not to feel] D; to feel no A
241.7	confident] D; portentous A
241.29	fashion] C; way A
242.32	saw the] C; saw its A
244.3	false; when] C; false; and A
245.1	Chapter XXII] D; Chapter IV A
245.4	*2 Henry IV*, III.ii.122–23] CE; *Falstaff* A
245.21–22	with his commander, on the state of the weather] C; of the state of the weather with his commander A

245.28	find] D; have found A
246.6	land-tacks] C; land tacks A
246.18	waggoners] C; stage-owners A
247.14	somewhat] D; a good deal A
247.28	end toward] C; end to A
249.21	admission into] C; admission to A
250.5	passage] C; one A
250.32	remnant] D; remnants A
250.33	stead] D; place A
251.5	Mr. a—a—I] C; Mr.—I A
251.30	or] C; or to A
253.12	goes below in this] C; does not here A
253.25	them] C; them that A
253.26	hanging] C; shooting A
253.33	fou't] C; fout A
254.25	fellow,] C; fellow," he added," A
255.29	from his] C; from A
255.31-32	conquered soldier] C; conquered A
256.1	observing] C; discovering A
256.19	universally understood] C; well understood by all A
256.19	But uncertainty] C; But the uncertainty A
256.32	by the mirth] C; by mirth A
257.7	call in] C; call A
257.14	which] C; that A
258.1	Chapter XXIII] D; Chapter V A
*258.6	Collins, "Ode to Fear," 11.20-21, 24-25] CE; *Collins* A
259.20	near the] C; near that A
259.35	wanted] C; wanting A
260.17	hands] C; two hands A
261.15	those] C; these A
261.29	captives] C; captive officers A
262.4	tread] C; treads A
262.19	Dillon paused] C; but Dillon A
262.22	and turning] C; turned, and A
262.24	passage] C; passage to or A
262.32	will] C; will ever A
263.23	as an] C; as the A
264.39	spliced it together] C; patched it up A
266.18	Nothing at all] D; Nothing A
267.28	stood,] C; stood, and A
267.35	fail] C; fail to cause him A
268.3	this] C; his A
268.11	spoke;] D; spoke; but A
268.14	footing] C; ~, A
268.14	rocks, and crags] C; rocks and crags, A
268.18	by this light I shall surely perish] C; I shall surely perish by this light A

268.19	or] C; or I A
268.21	that] D; which A
268.29	amidst] C; amid A
268.35	party] C; group A
268.39	men] C; party A
269.11	more] C; more very A
269.17	drawing] C; drew A
269.18	placing] C; first placing A
269.25	stooped so low] C; stooped, so A
269.30	which] C; that A
269.31	supernatural] D; unnatural A
269.32	well-known] C; well known A
269.33-34	cockswain, with] C; cockswain, in A
270.5-6	excited cockswain] C; cockswain sternly A
270.15	schooner] C; Ariel A
270.23	sounded in] C; sounded to A
271.1	Chapter XXIV] D; Chapter VI A
271.5	*The Tempest* I.i.10-12] CE; *Tempest,* A
272.1-2	anxiously observed] C; observed A
274.10	nigh] C; nigh to A
275.40	can] C; could A
276.4	crack] C; a crack A
276.4	splinter] C; a splinter A
276.30	I have] C; I've A
276.31	shaking his head] C; with a deep sigh A
277.2	but, instantly] C; then, instantly A
277.5	vanish with] C; vanish, at A
277.17	their main-sail] C; the canvass of their most important sail A
277.18	the mast] C; their mast A
277.29	should have been dubb'd of] C; had lost A
277.32	holds] C; carries A
277.35	the gale] C; a gale A
278.2	my philosophy] C; me A
278.2-3	crossed it] C; crossed me A
278.19	astarn] D; astern A
278.34	worthy old] D; worthy A
279.9	intense] C; intensity of A
279.21	overleap] C; overstep A
279.22	fixed] D; affixed A
279.23	well-known] C; well known A
279.26	that ever] D; that A
279.34	still able] C; enabled A
280.2	calmest] C; most calm A
280.2	knew] C; knew that A
280.13	by one or] C; by A
280.14	older] C; oldest A
280.17	were,] C; ∼∧ A

280.17	left] C; but were left A
280.21	seem an appalling] C; seem, a dreadful A
280.27	which] C; that A
281.9	wind] C; winds A
282.3	silence to] C; silence, in A
282.19	deck] D; vessel A
282.21	excited] C; exciting A
283.9	roarings] C; roaring A
283.11	broadside] C; broad side A
284.12	billow] C; wave A
284.21	mass] C; mass of human bodies A
285.11	by the] C; by a A
285.12	shove] C; "∼ A
288.14	but all] C; but not one presented itself to his hands; all A
288.18	brow,] C; brow, as if A
289.1	Chapter XXV] D; Chapter VII A
289.6	Campbell, "Battle of the Baltic," VII.6–9] CE; *Campbell* A
289.28	unnecessary] C; necessary A
290.6	hand] C; hand, that was occasioned by the doubtful character of his years A
*294.31	in to] D; into A
294.36	without a] C; without A
294.38	all be] C; be all A
294.39	marines] D; marine A
296.3–4	exclaimed joyously] C; exclaimed A
296.22	might] C; did A
296.22	dare to] C; dare A
296.23	would] C; might A
299.1	Chapter XXVI] D; Chapter VIII A
299.3	Dryden, *Amphitryon*, V.i.306] CE; *Dryden* A
299.6	accompany] C; conduct A
299.21	fleeting] C; passing A
299.26	white] C; clean A
300.37	conveyed] C; conducted A
*302.17	are as] D; is as A
302.19–20	an humble] C; a humble A
302.29	announced] C; announced to her A
302.40	protégé] D; protegée A
303.21–22	something within the basket] C; something A
303.24	eyes] D; eye A
303.33	fail instantly] C; fail A
304.10	toilets] C; good looks A
304.13–14	work in the basket of the boy] C; work A
304.15	treatise] C; treatise, in the basket of the boy A
305.13	was] C; was yet A
307.16	the name either] C; either the name A
308.21	that a] C; that A

310.2	of the] C; of his A
310.26	an ample pledge] C; a pledge A
311.1	Chapter XXVII] D; Chapter IX A
311.4	*The Merchant of Venice*, III.i.91–92] CE; *Merchant of Venice* A
311.16	of so] D; between so A
312.24–25	has to answer for] C; has A
312.25–26	country] C; country to answer for A
312.37	their] D; as their A
312.38	closing] D; closed A
316.6	both] C; both of A
316.13	expression was] D; expression A
316.18–19	entrance] B; endance A
317.2–3	she had detected in that glance] C; in that glance she had detected A
317.27	well-known] C; well known A
318.32	concluded relating my plans] C; concluded A
319.11–12	merits." ¶Barnstable] C; ~."∧~ A
319.13	replied] C; continued A
319.17	confirm] B; confir A
319.21–22	voice, "and] C; ~," ~ A
320.9	pursuits."] D; ~.∧ A
320.24	Barnstable—] C; ~ ? A
321.15	Katherine: I] C; Katherine, and I A
321.37	the anxious Katherine. "Rely] C; Katherine, anxiously; "rely A
322.3	at most] D; at the most A
322.24	of priestcraft] C; of that A
322.39	by] C; by in the interview A
323.2	through] D; enter A
324.1	Chapter XXVIII] D; Chapter X A
324.2	"He] C; ∧~ A
324.5	Scott, *Marmion*, Canto First, III.1–4] CE; *Marmion* A
325.16	his former abstraction] C; the same abstraction as before A
325.38	of an] C; of a A
326.19–20	Captain Burroughcliffe] D; Burroughcliffe A
327.16	at the] C; in the A
328.8	while] C; as A
330.21	were already] D; already were A
331.1	for] D; for more A
332.31	females,] D; females, but A
333.22	these] D; those A
334.23	Manual] C; Mauual A
*335.13	ye] D; you A
336.1	Chapter XXIX] D; Chapter XI A
336.2	"Welcome] CE; ∧~ A
336.3	fray."] CE; ~.∧ A
336.4	*Much Ado about Nothing*, V.i.113–114] CE; *Much ado about nothing* A

337.20	only an] C; only a A
337.39	I therefore will] D; will A
338.33	Dunscombe] D; Dunscomb A
339.23	agreed to] D; made A
340.15	rousing himself] C; rousing A
340.16	appal] C; be appalling to A
340.26	of a] D; of A
341.11	therefore, I] C; I, therefore A
342.13	America!"] D; ~!ʌ A
342.35	Barnstable] D; Borroughcliffe A
342.36	mystery. Her conscience also] C; mystery, and her conscience A
342.36	little] C; little also A
342.37	coquetry as] C; coquetry; for A
344.9	hanger] C; sabre A
344.16	hangers] C; sabres A
345.7	hanger] C; sabre A
345.38	This] D; ~, A
345.38	Howard] D; ~, A
347.9–10	feel even in such a scene] D; feel, in such a scene, and under such circumstances A; feel, in such a horrid scene C
348.13–14	attracted the wandering looks of the captives] C; was most striking to the females A
349.1	Chapter XXX] D; Chapter XII A
349.2	"A chieftain] D; ʌ~~ A
349.5	ferry.'"] D; ~.'ʌ A
349.6	Campbell, "Lord Ullin's Daughter," 11.1–4] CE; *Lord Ullin's Daughter* A
349.35	come] D; approach A
351.21	is a] C; is A
354.2–3	captives: the] D; ~ — The A; ~. The C
359.1	Chapter XXXI] D; Chapter XIII A
359.2	"His] D; ʌ~ A
359.3	country."] D; ~.ʌ A
359.4	Thomson, *Coriolanus*, V.iv.30–31] CE; *Thomson* A
360.3	considered] C; construed A
360.6	above] C; nearly over A
360.16	already discovered] C; discovered already A
360.23	on her way] C; part of the way back A
360.38	the lady] C; Miss Dunscombe A
361.6	seeking the] C; seeking this A
361.10	the one] C; that A
361.13	"it] D; ʌ~ A
361.30	are allowed to go for nothing.] D; can be thus termed! A
362.38	Quixote] C; Quixotte A
364.1–2	The plains] C; That plains A
364.25	Is a] D; Is A
364.37	powerful influence] D; power A

364.38	But our] D; Our A
365.6	to be] C; to he A
365.35	easily] C; it can be A
365.36	these] D; those A
366.6	still] C; as if A
366.12-13	of his] C; of the A
366.19	should] D; shall A
366.22-23	communication, "and] C; ~—~ A
368.3-4	silence. It] C; silence; for it A
368.28	shall] C; will A
368.30	ready] D; present A
369.36	imparted] C; mparted A
370.10	pilot] D; Pilot A
370.34-35	has already] C; has A
372.37	afloat."] C; ~.ʌ A
374.1	Chapter XXXII] CE; Chapter XIV A; Chapter XXXI D
374.3	*Hamlet*, I.i.2] CE; *Hamlet* A
374.29	ordinary management] C; usual conduct A
376.17	won't] D; wont A
378.4	ware] D; wear A
378.31	he's] D; he is A
378.34	a-hoy!"] C; ~!ʌ A
378.37	observed.] C; ~." A
380.16	gaff] CE; gaft A
380.28	band-boxes] D; ban/boxes A
381.34	of scenes] C; of the scenes A
387.1	Chapter XXXIII] D; Chapter XV A
*387.6	Percy (tr.), "Gentle River, Gentle River," 11. 53-56] CE; *Spanish War Song* A
389.39	doubt that] D; doubt but A
390.7	see, Barnstable] D; ~ʌ~ A
392.28	ended in] D; ended with A
392.37	rises!"] D; ~!ʌ A
392.40	ears] D; ear A
393.36-37	have already] D; ~,~, A
393.37	to be turned] D; turned A
393.38	course when,] D; ~,~ʌ A
394.7	the—"] C; ~—ʌ A
394.14	waters] D; dark waters A
394.16	He has] C; He's A
394.33	purpose] A2; durpose A1
395.37	ship] C; vessel A
396.11	have] D; have had A
396.13	far] B; ar A
400.5	spar on] C; spar, to A
400.30	struggling] C; yielding A
400.31-32	throat, at the flash C; throat A

401.29	sir?"] C; ~?ʌ A
401.35	stern chase] C; stern chace A
401.35	Griffith, "and] C; ~,ʌ~A
402.2	its high] C; all its A
402.3	These] C; His A
402.16	pleasure;] C; ~;" A
402.21	are most] C; are A
402.21	protect?"C; ~?ʌ A
403.3	home—] C; home, and A
403.3	away of] C; away A
403.20	shouted] C; called A
404.3	be down] C; be A
404.13	The Pilot] D; "~~ A
406.1	Chapter XXXIV] D; Chapter XVI A
406.2	"Whither] D; ʌ~ A
406.5	way?"] D; ~]ʌ A
406.6	Bryant, "To a Waterfowl," 11.1-4] CE; *Bryant* A
409.20	tenor!"] D; ~!ʌ A
410.3	him!"] D; ~!ʌ A
410.23	warm] C; cold A
410.27	"amen."] D; '~.' A
412.7	deck."] D; ~.ʌ A
412.8	spy-glasses] C; spy-glasess A
412.29	expect."] D; ~.ʌ A
414.33	her?"] D; ~?ʌ A
415.5	ever."] D; ~.ʌ A
416.35	"bury the dead."] D; '~~~.' A
418.2	But,"] D; ~", A
419.1	Chapter XXXV] D; Chapter XVII A
419.2	"Come] D; ʌ~ A
419.5	friend!"] D; ~!ʌ A
422.35	when, unhappily] C; and, melancholy to relate A
424.38	President?"] D; ~?ʌ A
424.39	"The] D; ʌ~ A
425.25	Dunscombe] D; Dunscomb A
426.9	at all merit] C; merit one half A

Rejected Readings

The following list records all the substantive variant readings which appear in the texts subsequent to the accepted reading and which are rejected in the Cooper Edition. The reading accepted in the Cooper Edition appears to the left of the square bracket. The source for that reading appears to the right of the bracket, followed by a semicolon, the variant reading, and its source. All texts which contain the rejected reading are cited to the right of the bracket; texts which are subsequent to the accepted reading and not cited may be presumed to agree with the accepted reading. An asterisk indicates that the reading is discussed in Textual Notes.

Two sigla are also used in this list. The degree sign (°) indicates that the rejected reading actually first appeared in the non-authorial Carey and Lea stereotype edition of *The Pilot* in 1827 and was incorporated in subsequent editions. The dagger (†) preceding an entry means that the rejected reading actually first appeared in the non-authorial Colburn and Bentley edition in 1831 and was incorporated in subsequent editions.

Variant readings reported in this list include dialect spellings and obvious compositorial missettings. Variants in punctuation, preferred British spellings (color-colour), and other spellings which do not affect pronunciation are not cited on this list.

The following texts are referred to:

AMS Author's Manusacript, "Preface" (1849)
A   New York: Charles Wiley, 1824 [Two Volumes]
B   London: John Miller, 1824 [Three Volumes]
C   New York: Charles Wiley, 1824 [Two Volumes], Second Edition
D   New York: G. P. Putnam, 1849

1849 Preface
5.5   accidents] AMS; accident D
6.35–36   The Pilot] AMS; the Pilot D
8.23   was] AMS; was so D

Text
†11.3   dash] A; dash'd D
12.12   rason] A; reason C-D

13.28	bit craft] A; bit o'craft B
13.36	sand-spits] A; sand-pits C-D
14.15	this sentiment] A; his sentiment B
14.31	guid] A; good C-D
15.28	distinguish] A; distinguished B
17.1	sand-spits] A; sand-pits C-D
21.4	'casion] A; occasion C-D
21.8	oncomfortable] A; uncomfortable B-D
23.33	contrasted to] A; contrasted with D
33.30	know not] A; know no C
35.14	and with his] A; and his D
†37.26	rocks] A; rock D
39.36	by this] A; by the C-D
40.2	exchanged] A; changed D
†40.30	pall] A; pull D
41.16	was ever A]; ever was D
*41.37	moon, I believe.] A; moon. I believe ʌ D
†46.3	on the] A; on his D
†46.20	a surf] A; the surf D
49.32	efforts] A; effects D
51.22	companion] A; companions C-D
57.4–5	an alternative] A; one alternative B
†57.24	seeming] A; seemed D
62.18	who] A; which B
64.40	out of] A; of D
65.22	on board] A; aboard D
67.11	it would not all] A; all would not B
67.17	jacobin] A; jacobite C
°72.5–6	officers] A; orders D
79.4	oppose to] A; oppose D
*79.39	chock] A; choke B,D
81.2	mouth, with] A; mouth with the C
83.3	Like]A; Like a D
87.25	deck] A; decks B
90.10	others] A; other D
91.24	from] A; form C
96.6	has been] A; had been D
†98.3	army in] A; army of D
†99.21	our] A; our old D
101.35	of Flamborough] A; off Flamborough B
†103.15	visit] A; visits D
104.24	Ruth's] A; Ruth C,D
†105.35	were] A; was D
111.30	suspicions] A; suspicion D
112.36	receive] A; receives B
113.13	whose] A; what D
114.32	'tis like] A; 'tis D

114.34	front] A; front that D
117.15	rage that] A; rage D
†120.34	for their] A; for the D
127.9	intellects] A; intellect D
127.11–12	have heard] A; hear D
133.8	worthy of] A; worthy D
135.1	Chapter XIII] A; Chapter VIII C
136.16	without] A; unless D
138.30	please to] A; please D
†138.31	eyes] A; eye D
140.15	timid] A; timed C
141.11	of the] A; of D
141.25	come] A; comes B
143.14	and her] A; and D
149.17	you] A; yon C
151.8	are we] A; we are B
†153.34	last] A; last, the last D
156.1	piercing] A; pierced B
157.27	and she] A; she B
164.12	thy] A; the C-D
174.34	appear] A; appears D
†174.39	rebellion, that] A; rebellion, D
175.35	hours had] A; hours D
176.5	of your] A; to your C-D
176.21	party had] A; party D
†178.3	it is] A; is it D
178.12	as good] A; as a good D
185.22	natyve] A; native D
°186.2	natural] A; nateral D
187.31	frame] A; from C; form D
†189.29	along their] A; along the D
†190.27	bellowings] A; bellowing D
191.6	gets] A; get C-D
197.6	thrust in] A; thrust into D
199.11	him an] A; him on D
202.26	within] A; within the B
202.31	of the waters into] A; on the waters of B
†208.20	old long] A; old D
209.12	who, expecting] B; who expected C-D
209.13	were resolved] B; resolved C-D
210.17	very] A; very great B
211.15	points] A; point C-D
211.28	that] A; which were B; which C
213.3	force] A; fore C
213.11	with some of] A; with B
213.37	affect] A; effect B, D
215.22	seamen] A; seaman C

215.23	and Griffith] A; when Griffith B
216.21	intended also] B; intended C-D
216.22	cover] B; cover also C-D
219.13	along whose] B; from whose C-D
219.14	dancing] B; reflected C-D
219.26	watchman's]B; guardian's C-D
220.4–5	which concealed] A; that concealed B
220.5	the leaden] A; his leaden B
220.34	shots] B; shot C
221.32–33	so loud] B; so C-D
222.6	vault] A; vaults B
223.14	with his] A; and his D
223.15	us] A$_1$; su A$_2$
†223.36	prospects] A; prospect D
224.9	but meeting] B; when meeting C-D
224.11	as follows:] B; when meeting C-D
226.35	only some] A; only D
228.4	however] B; indeed C-D
231.20	that they] A; they B
237.21	farther] A; further B, D
†240.15	drawing] A; drawing back D
241.8	ocean] A; oceans B
242.3	near] A; nearly D
246.26	on-end] A; on an end D
*250.20	art] A; heart C-D
251.10	would] A; will C-D
251.10	understand] A; understood D
°253.29	you] A; you to be D
254.35	words] A; these words B
256.37	and the] A; and of the D
259.36	dear sir] A; sir B
262.39	name] A; word D
264.1	foot up] A; foot up at B
264.20	orders] A; order D
267.18	rasing] A; raising B-C
268.15	cast ye] A; cast you B
†268.31	such] A; such a D
°271.10	where] A; when D
271.20	were alone] A; alone were D
272.15	heaven] A; heavens B
272.27	spars] A; stars D
275.28	about] A; out B
†275.32	windward of] A; windward off D
°276.13	Master] A; Mr. C,D
276.32	make] A; makes D
276.35	the crash] A; a crash D
276.37	toward] A; towards B

277.20	intently] A; entirely B
277.39	man who] A; man that D
*278.8	sea-croaker] A; sea-croker C
278.23	please to] A; please D
†279.18	at times] A; at all times D
°281.28	masts] A; mast D
282.14	thought] A; thought that D
†283.1	you future] A; your future D
284.37	hopes] A; hope B, D
°285.30	torn] A; turn D
285.34	and, as] A; and, and as D
287.33	hard] A; heard C
288.28	after an] A; after a C
*289.4	By thy] A; By the C-D
295.8	boy] A; hoy C-D
†297.13	have kept] A; have D
298.3	motioned to] A; motioned D
299.26-27	the black] A; a black B
300.20	his conduct] A; the conduct D
302.21	You] A; Your C
†305.25	have] A; have now D
305.36	my eyes] A; mine eyes B
°306.2	little] A; like D
°306.28	you, sir,] A; you? D
317.21	approach to] A; approach of C-D
317.26	of ear] A; of the ear B
325.17	could] A; should C
336.8	Britons] A; Briton B, †D
339.13	ladies'] A; lady's C
344.32	she] A; he C-D
350.21	soldiers'] A; soldier's D
°351.34	two old] A; two D
355.19	hear] A; bear C-D
363.12	wilt] A; fade B
364.14	feeling] A; feelings C-D
°364.14	binds] A; bind D
†367.16	weak] A; a weak D
368.27	you] A; your D
371.32	probable] A; probable that D
375.9	inexperienced] A; experienced D
376.4	nearer] A; near D
376.35	ye] A; you C-D
381.7	an hour] A; half an hour B
383.3	an hundred] A; a hundred B
°385.10	that it is] A; that is D
385.27	rigged] A; to be rigged B
388.2	eye] A; eyes B

391.24	arrangement] A; preparation B
397.35	against] A; against a B
398.13	to the] A; to a B
398.31	closer] A; close D
399.13	more dreadful] A; more B
399.14	roar] A; dreadful roar B
403.4	inspiriting] A; inspiring D
403.12	ropes only] A; ropes B
404.31	boldly steering] A; steering boldly B
404.38	east and by] A; east by D
405.2	tail] A; Sail B
405.5	form] A; person B
406.3	glow] A; glows C
406.9	often repeated summons] A; summons he had received B
406.29	troubled] A; busy B
407.2	witness] A; witness within them B
407.17	warlike apartment] A; warlike cabin B
407.33	said] A; said that D
408.8	faith. If this be true] A; faith; after that B
408.12	may] A; would B
408.36–37	commander. The recent contention between you] A; commander; after what I so lately witnessed B
409.6	whispered] A; whispering D
409.6	message] A; order B
409.6	requesting] A; to request B
409.7	conveyed] A; executed B
409.13	adopted] A; used B
†410.24	returned slowly] A; returned D
411.6	Then to return] A; To return then B
411.16	is, Edward, also] A; is also, Edward B
411.27	have also] A; also have D
412.28	indeed sudden] A; sudden indeed B
413.12	degrees] A; decrees B, †D
413.20	chiefly fell] A; fell chiefly D
414.19	for] A; in B
414.21	fingers] A; his fingers B
416.38	were, with the usual formalities, committed to the deep] A; were committed to the deep with the usual formalities B
418.17	drawn] A; to be drawn B
418.26	observed] A; seen B
420.3	once more tempted] A; tempted B
420.9	eagerly] A; easily B
420.39	sets] A; set B
421.23	vexed] A; searched B
422.1	younger] A; young D

422.36	he had] A; he D
425.37	at] A; with B
425.39	He, altogether, was indeed a man] A; He was a man indeed B
426.5	claimed] A; is said B

Word Division

List A records compounds hyphenated at the end of the line in the copy-text and resolved as hyphenated or one word as listed below. If the compound or possible compound occurs elsewhere in the copy-text or if Cooper's manuscripts of this period fairly consistently followed one practice respecting it, the resolution was made on that basis. Otherwise first editions of his works of this period were used as guides. List B is a guide to transcription of compounds hyphenated at the end of the line in the Cooper Edition: compounds recorded here should be transcribed as given; words divided at the end of the line and not listed should be transcribed as one word.

LIST A

4.6	Bon-Homme
7.3	messmate
11.28	north-eastern
15.38	whale-boat
16.30	whale-boat
19.24	broadside
27.19	saucy-one
28.3	well-known
33.16	to-night
35.14	pea-jacket
38.19	head-beating
41.12	ground-swell
41.37	egg-shell
42.12–13	east-and-by-north
42.22	east-and-by-north
44.14	outboard
46.20	to-night
53.17	quarter-master
53.20	mainchains
54.10	well-known
61.29	lying-to
61.31	sea-room
62.5	hour-glass
65.24	head-to-sea

65.24	night-caps
66.21	handwriting
4.5	sea-damps
74.22	jib-boom
75.20	baggage-guard
75.22	flank-guards
77.16	plain-sailing
80.9	cat's-watch
80.38	homeward-bound
84.31	dog-vane
85.19	fox-hunting
95.4	outline
95.20	middle-aged
98.32	counter-marchings
98.33	sunshine
105.40	jet-black
106.20	forehead
108.37	self-commendation
123.39	sword-hilt
128.20	sea-boat
131.37	tea-table
159.27	pea-jacket
165.39	to-night
168.28	cannot
186.35	windward
191.22	top-mast-head
192.32	race-horse
202.38	bloodshed
204.22	blood-stained
216.14	footsteps
218.38	prize-money
219.4	well-drilled
229.30	fire-arms
233.40	counter-march
239.38	long-Tom
241.5	messmate
241.27	sea-faring
249.26	guard-room
253.5	log-account
253.28	to-day
255.29	ratlin-stuff
257.13	cockswain
261.40	footsteps
269.1	watch-word
271.28	high-lands
272.7	to-port
276.25	windward

278.36	quarter-deck
281.5	main-mast
281.18	north-easter
294.14	red-coats
296.6	where-away
304.4	never-failing
304.39	white-line
307.19	sea-shore
312.18	footsteps
326.13	household
338.3	freebooters
339.15	pedler-boy
347.11	forethought
350.32	fore-and-aft
352.29	cob-web
364.28	Englishman
379.19	sailing-master
380.28	band-boxes
384.1	sea-ward
389.12	quarter-deck
392.4	bowsprit
392.18	studding-sail
394.6	lower-away
407.28	rebellion
415.11	weather-beaten
423.8	New-Orleans

LIST B

4.6	Bon-Homme
18.19	weather-beaten
41.37	egg-shell
42.12	east-and-by-north
44.6	fore-royal
53.35	half-five
57.1	to-night
65.24	night-caps
70.8	signal-book
74.5	sea-damps
75.22	flank-guards
77.16	plain-sailing
80.38	homeward-bound
83.25	weather-gangway
83.34	quarter-deck
95.20	hard-featured
98.14	horse-guards
108.37	self-commendation

122.16	court-martial
126.6	self-preservation
128.39	sea-green
134.5	tea-equipage
186.6	two-fathom-water
197.2	fore-finger
215.12	unlooked-for
223.2	side-arms
223.13	half-pikes
236.25	green-horn
236.37	to-night
242.39	new-fashioned
246.27	land-marks
272.23	long-Tom
279.17	half-league
279.22	head-land
294.14	red-coats
302.31	dining-parlour
377.6	sea-sickness
377.33	knee-breeches
379.23	man-of-war
379.25	swallow-tailed
380.17	fiddle-string
381.24	re-embarking
387.16	sea-watch
399.13	death-like
405.11	Two-and-thirty
412.21	shot-hole
413.27	end-for-end
420.1	sea-officer